displacement

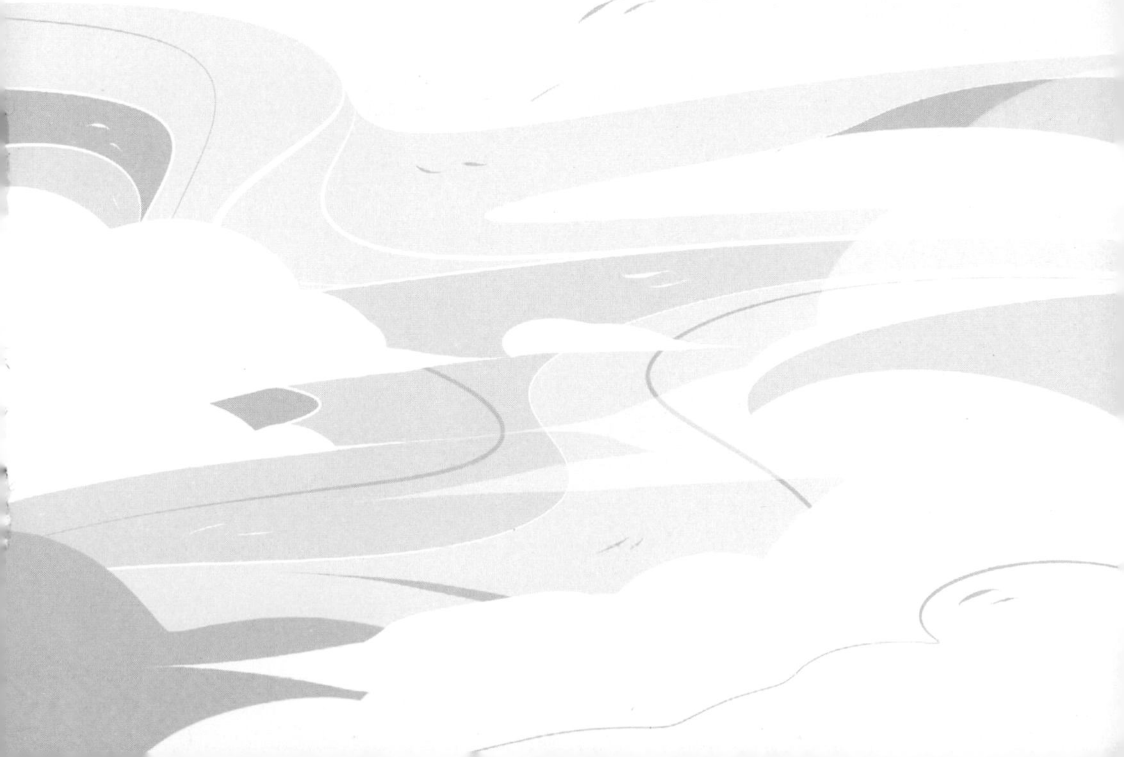

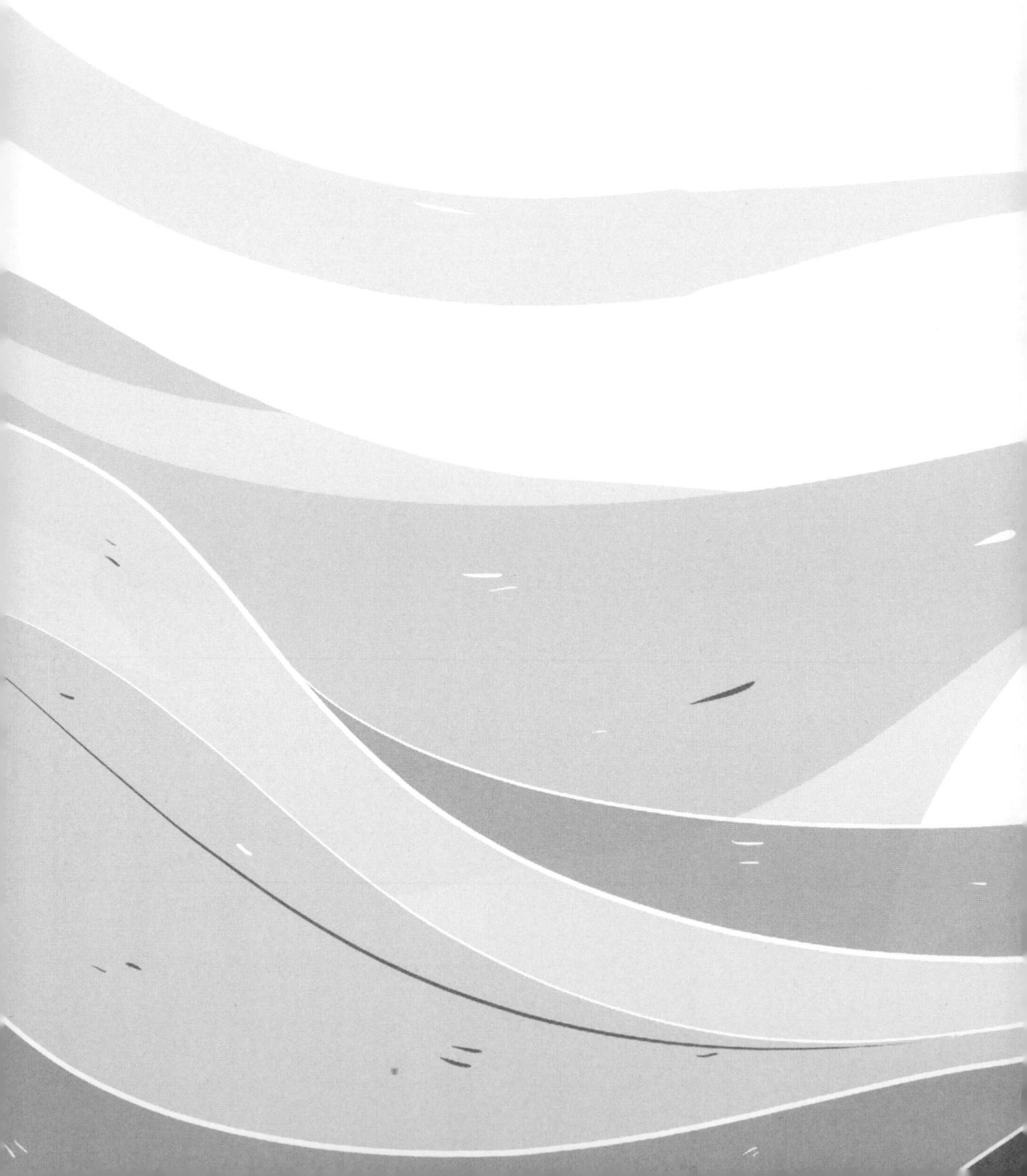

displacement

kiku hughes

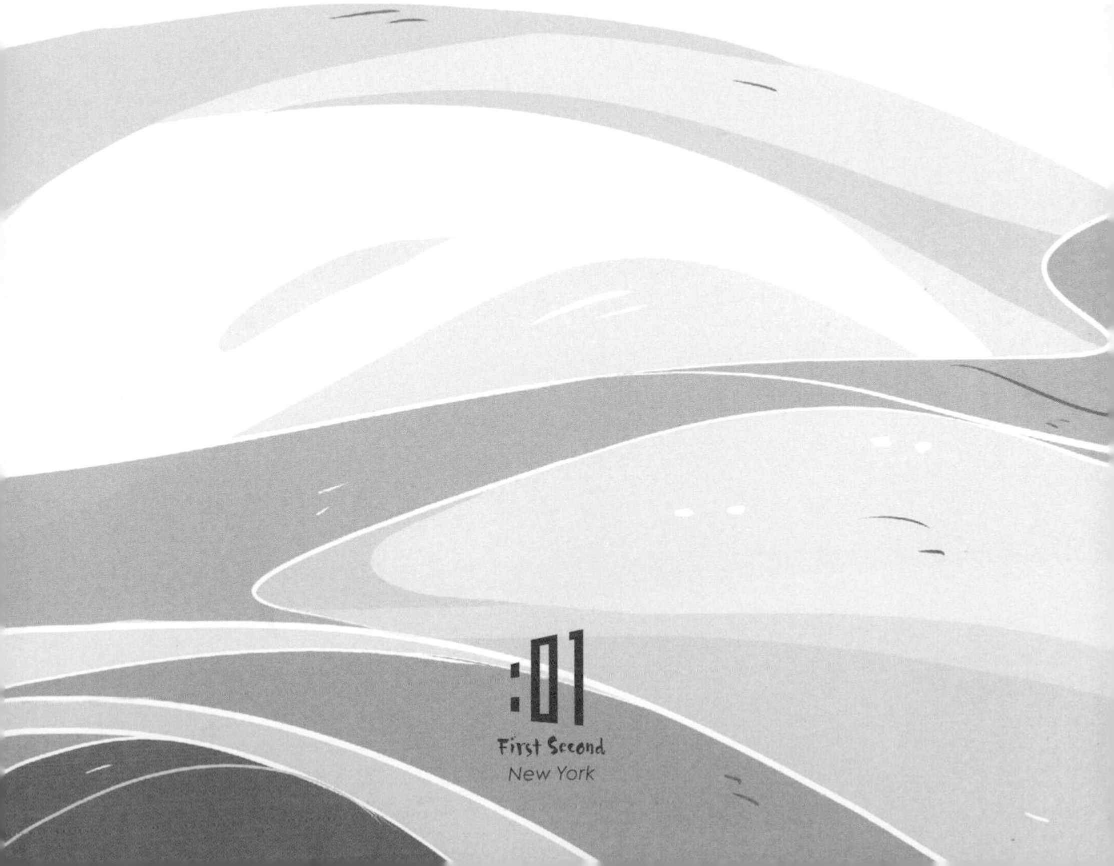

First Second
New York

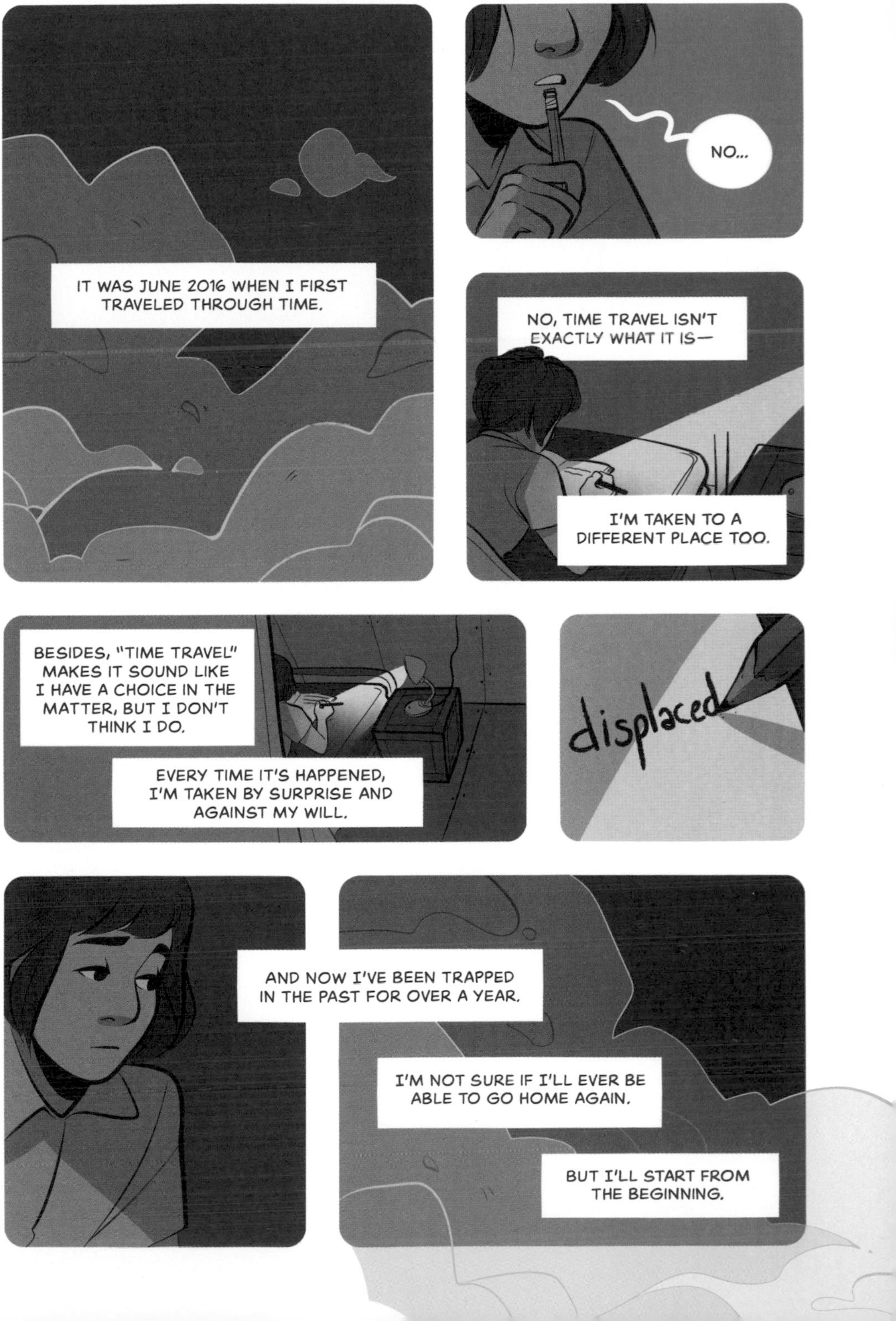
IT WAS JUNE 2016 WHEN I FIRST TRAVELED THROUGH TIME.
NO...
NO, TIME TRAVEL ISN'T EXACTLY WHAT IT IS—
I'M TAKEN TO A DIFFERENT PLACE TOO.
BESIDES, "TIME TRAVEL" MAKES IT SOUND LIKE I HAVE A CHOICE IN THE MATTER, BUT I DON'T THINK I DO.
EVERY TIME IT'S HAPPENED, I'M TAKEN BY SURPRISE AND AGAINST MY WILL.
displaced
AND NOW I'VE BEEN TRAPPED IN THE PAST FOR OVER A YEAR.
I'M NOT SURE IF I'LL EVER BE ABLE TO GO HOME AGAIN.
BUT I'LL START FROM THE BEGINNING.

part I:
the west

1

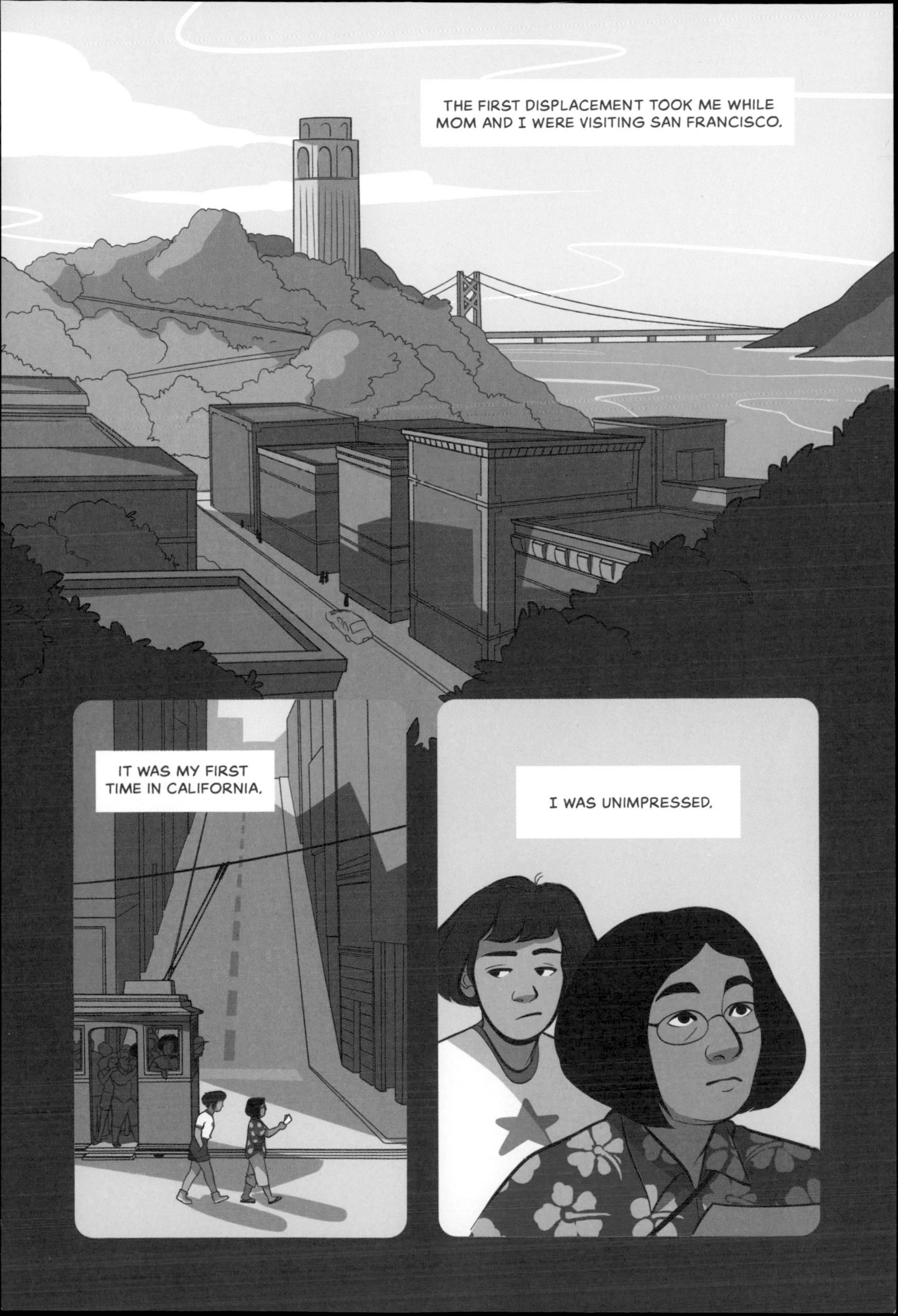
THE FIRST DISPLACEMENT TOOK ME WHILE MOM AND I WERE VISITING SAN FRANCISCO.
IT WAS MY FIRST TIME IN CALIFORNIA.
I WAS UNIMPRESSED.

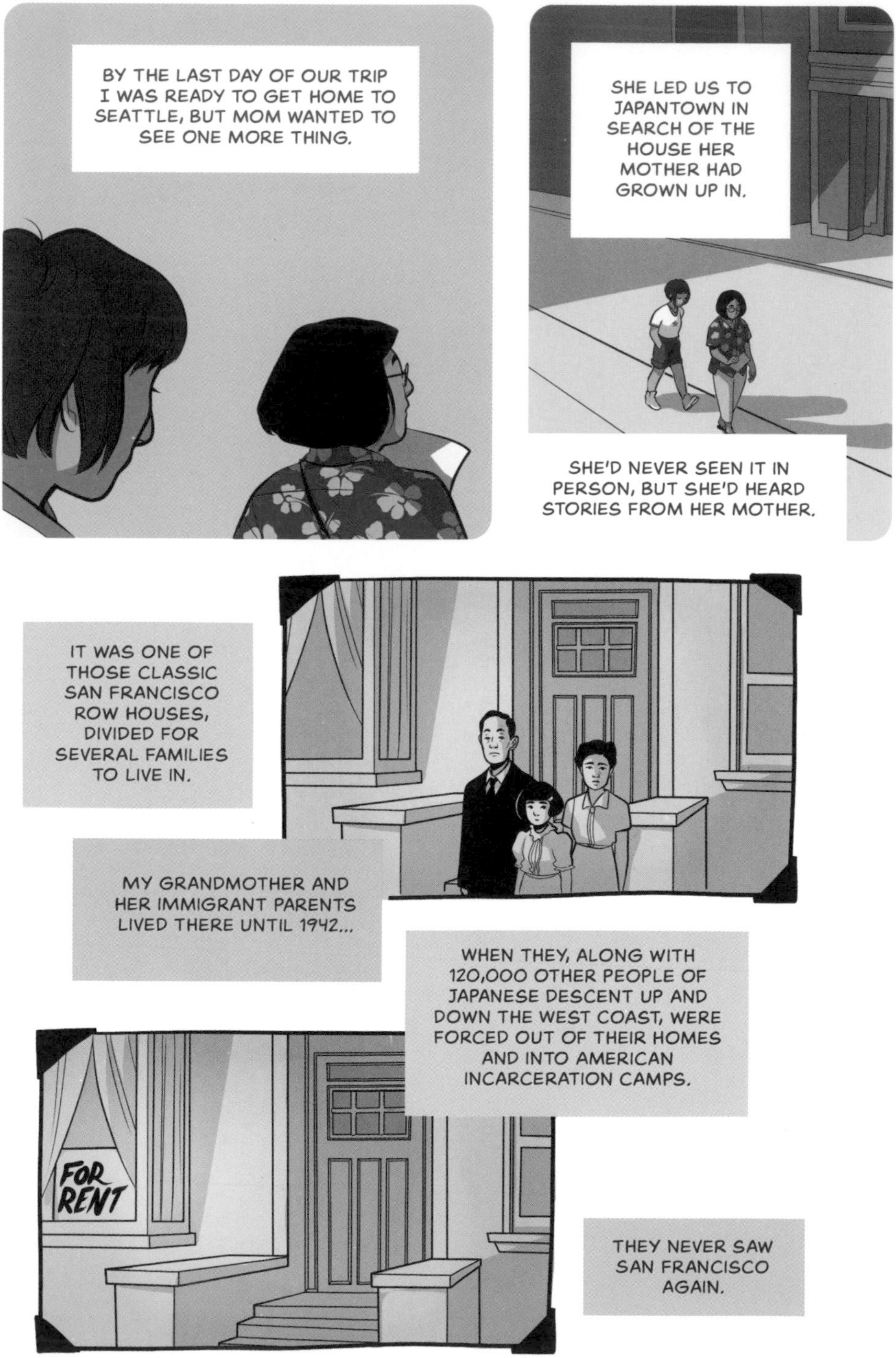
BY THE LAST DAY OF OUR TRIP I WAS READY TO GET HOME TO SEATTLE, BUT MOM WANTED TO SEE ONE MORE THING.
SHE LED US TO JAPANTOWN IN SEARCH OF THE HOUSE HER MOTHER HAD GROWN UP IN.
SHE'D NEVER SEEN IT IN PERSON, BUT SHE'D HEARD STORIES FROM HER MOTHER.
IT WAS ONE OF THOSE CLASSIC SAN FRANCISCO ROW HOUSES, DIVIDED FOR SEVERAL FAMILIES TO LIVE IN.
MY GRANDMOTHER AND HER IMMIGRANT PARENTS LIVED THERE UNTIL 1942...
WHEN THEY, ALONG WITH 120,000 OTHER PEOPLE OF JAPANESE DESCENT UP AND DOWN THE WEST COAST, WERE FORCED OUT OF THEIR HOMES AND INTO AMERICAN INCARCERATION CAMPS.
FOR RENT
THEY NEVER SAW SAN FRANCISCO AGAIN.

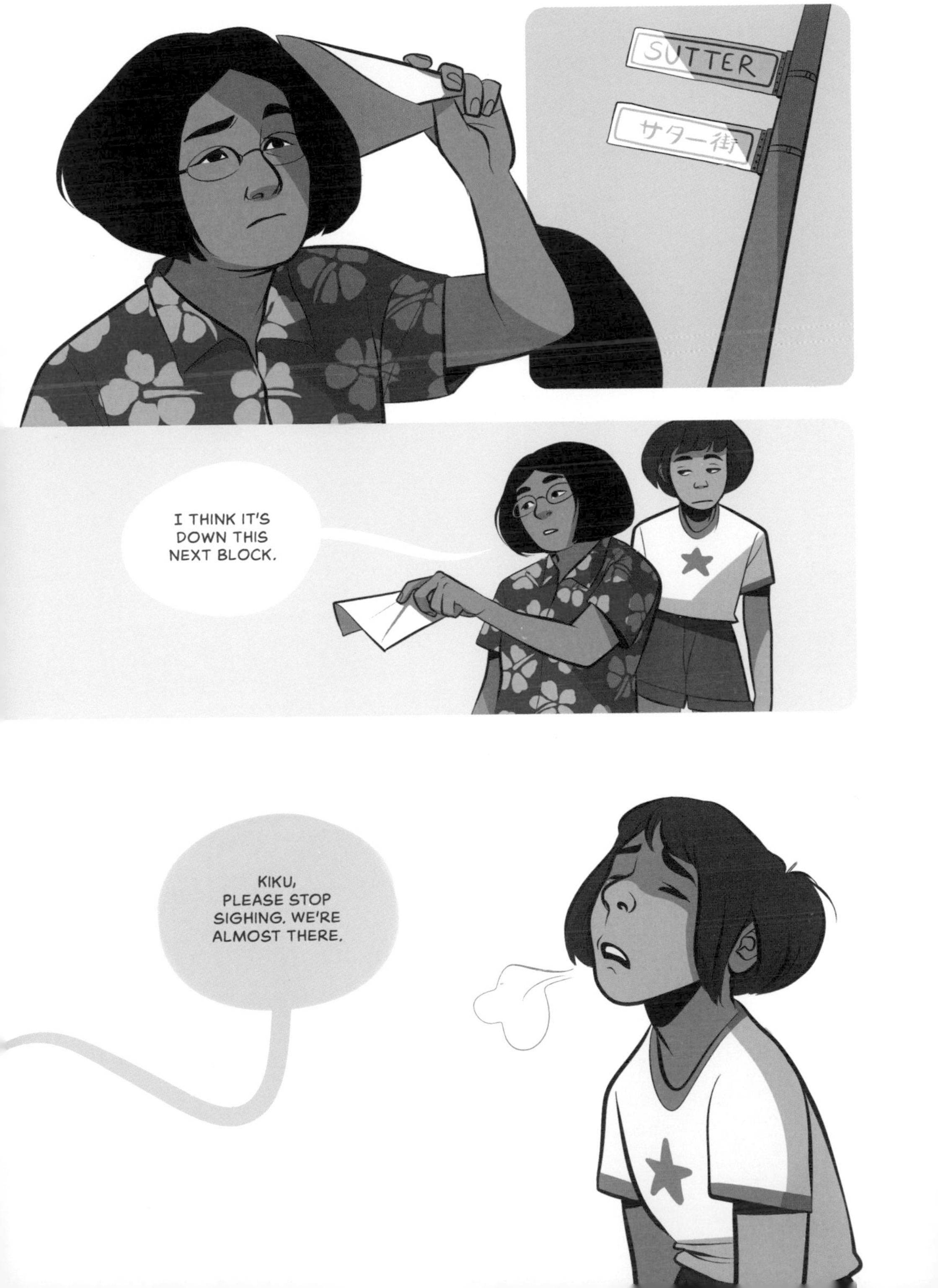
SUTTER
サター街
I THINK IT'S DOWN THIS NEXT BLOCK.
KIKU, PLEASE STOP SIGHING. WE'RE ALMOST THERE.

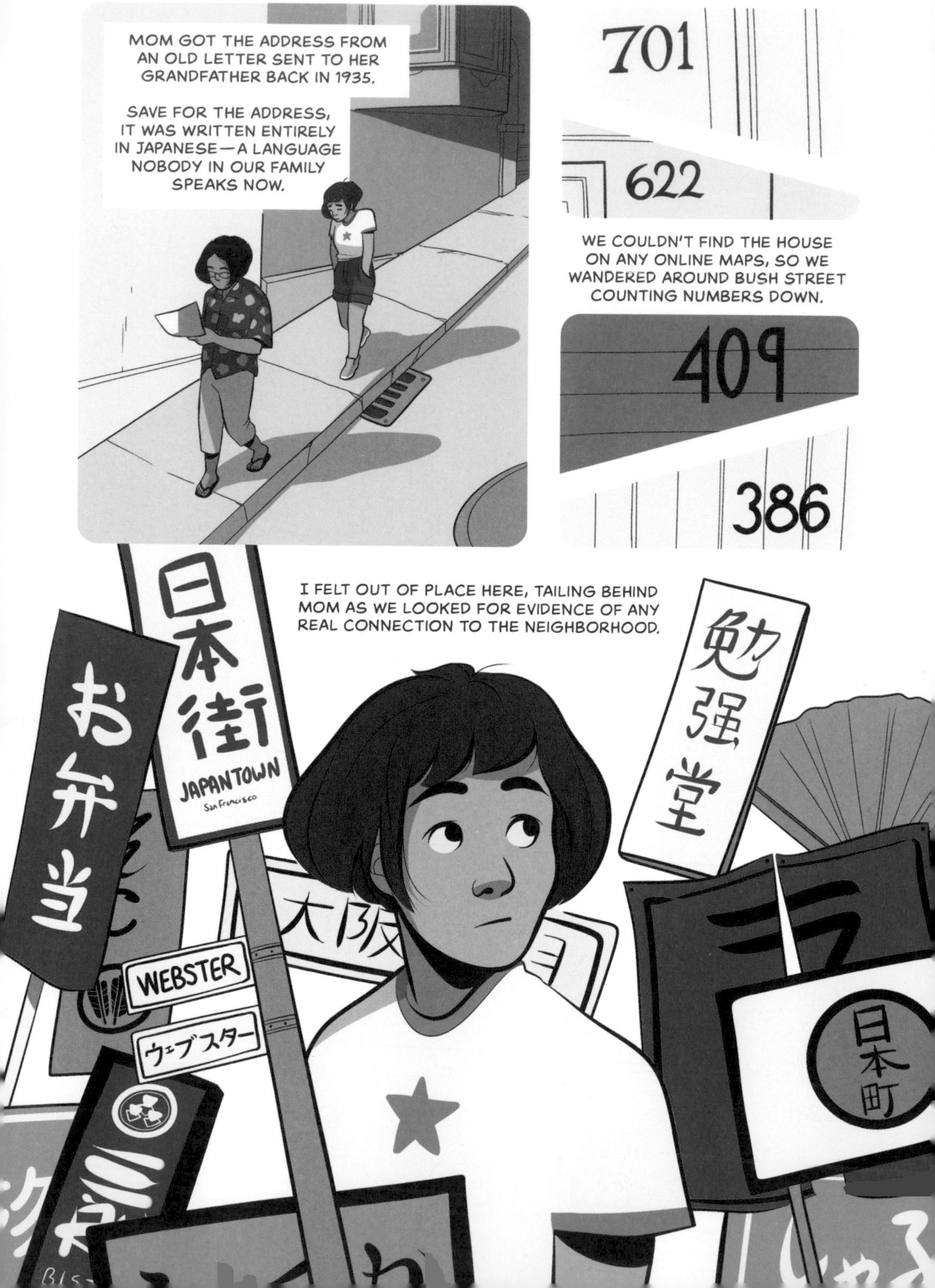
MOM GOT THE ADDRESS FROM AN OLD LETTER SENT TO HER GRANDFATHER BACK IN 1935.
SAVE FOR THE ADDRESS, IT WAS WRITTEN ENTIRELY IN JAPANESE—A LANGUAGE NOBODY IN OUR FAMILY SPEAKS NOW.
701
622
WE COULDN'T FIND THE HOUSE ON ANY ONLINE MAPS, SO WE WANDERED AROUND BUSH STREET COUNTING NUMBERS DOWN.
409
386
I FELT OUT OF PLACE HERE, TAILING BEHIND MOM AS WE LOOKED FOR EVIDENCE OF ANY REAL CONNECTION TO THE NEIGHBORHOOD.
日本街
JAPANTOWN
San Francisco
お弁当
勉强堂
大阪
WEBSTER
ウェブスター
日本町

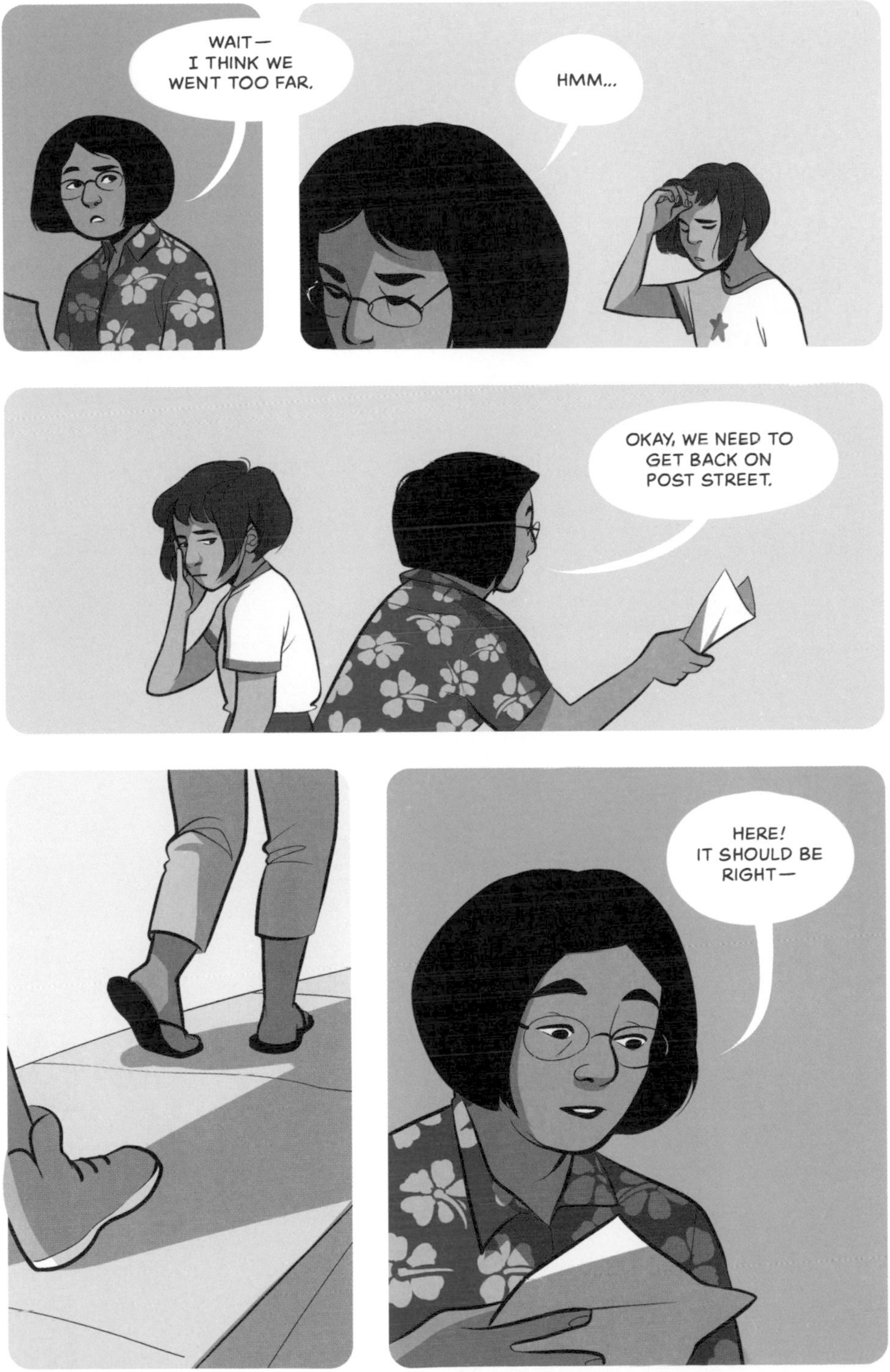
WAIT—
I THINK WE
WENT TOO FAR.
HMM...
OKAY, WE NEED TO
GET BACK ON
POST STREET.
HERE!
IT SHOULD BE
RIGHT—

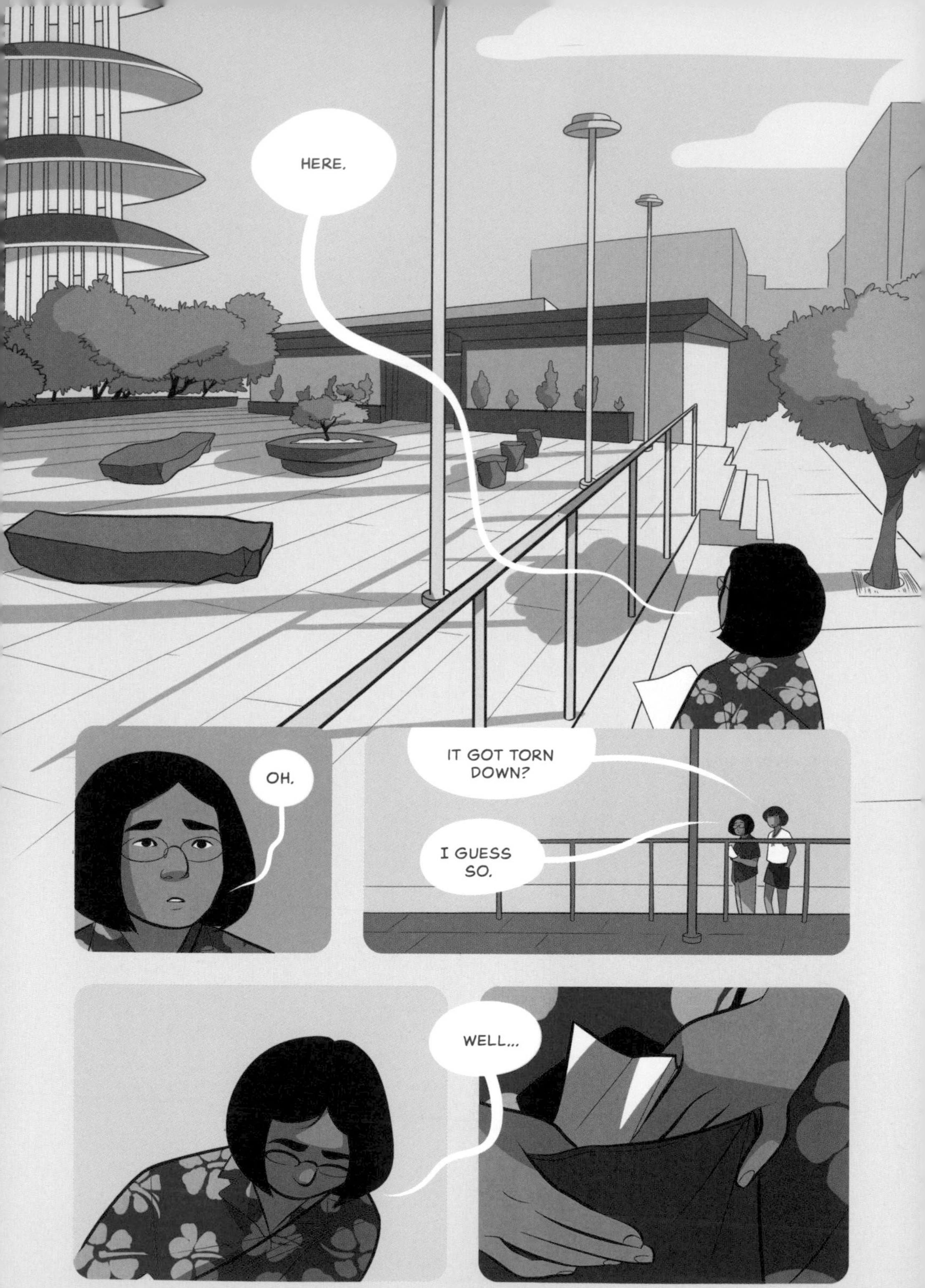
HERE.
OH.
IT GOT TORN DOWN?
I GUESS SO.
WELL...

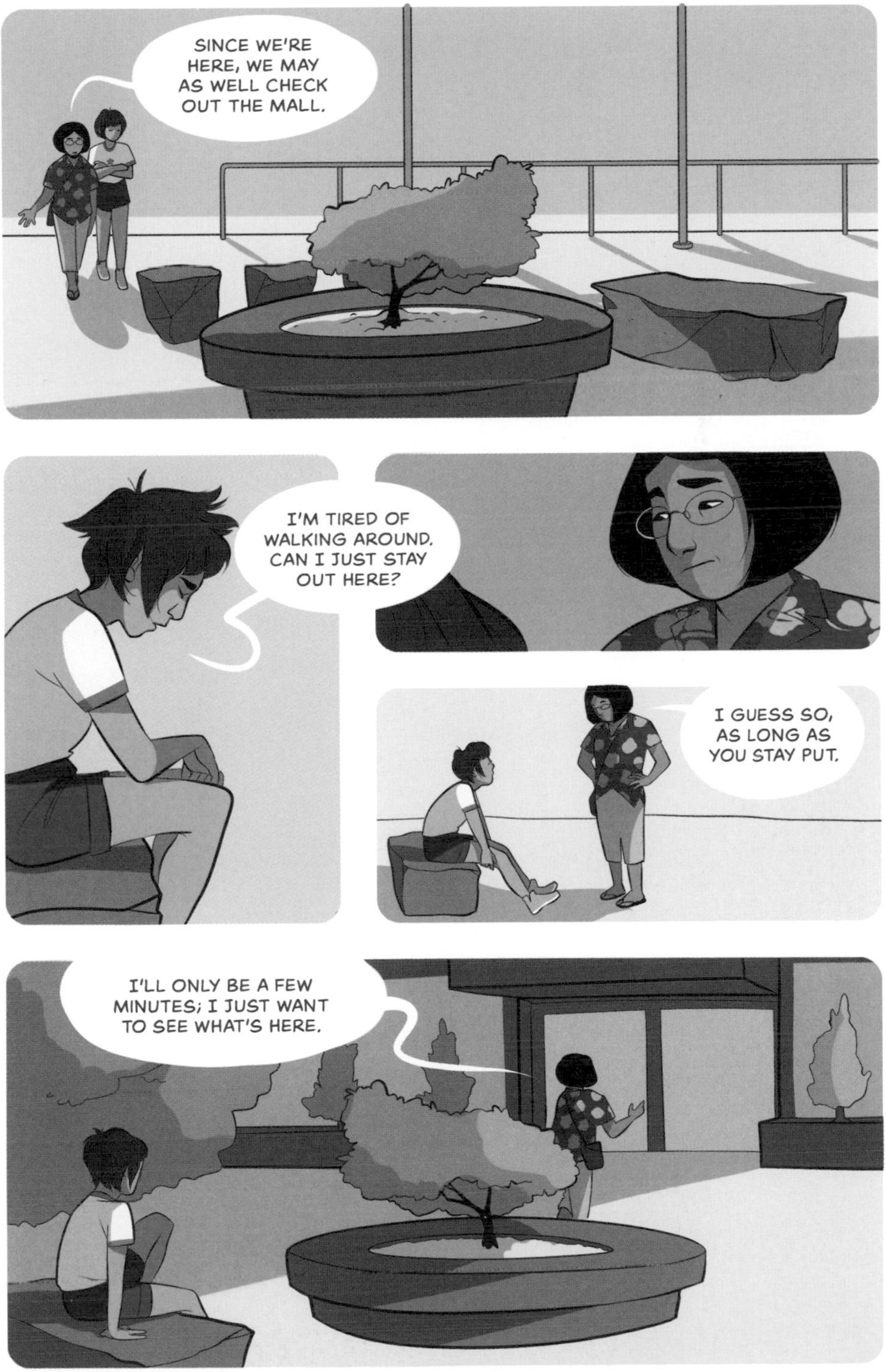
SINCE WE'RE HERE, WE MAY AS WELL CHECK OUT THE MALL.
I'M TIRED OF WALKING AROUND. CAN I JUST STAY OUT HERE?
I GUESS SO, AS LONG AS YOU STAY PUT.
I'LL ONLY BE A FEW MINUTES; I JUST WANT TO SEE WHAT'S HERE.

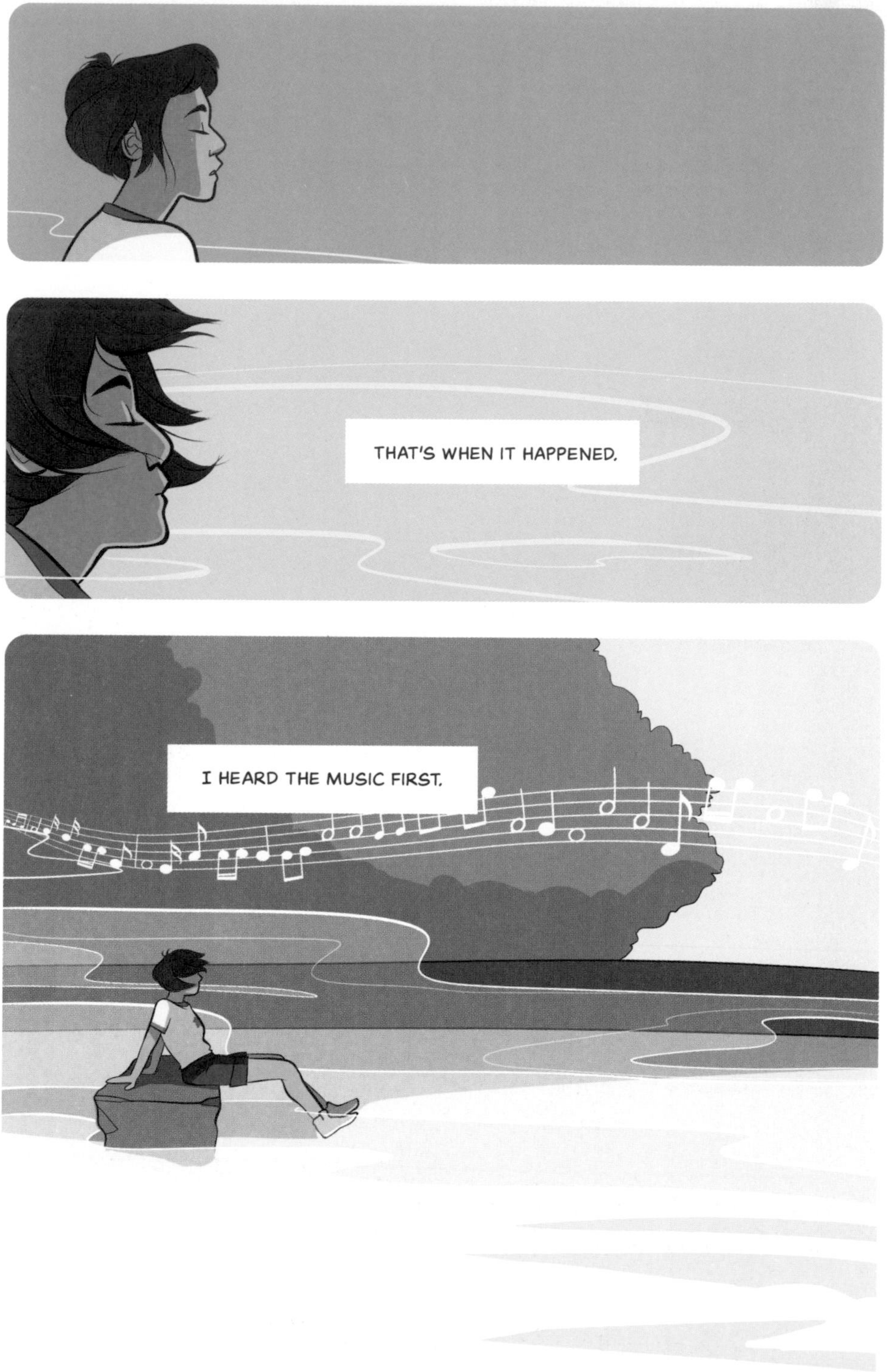
THAT'S WHEN IT HAPPENED.
I HEARD THE MUSIC FIRST.

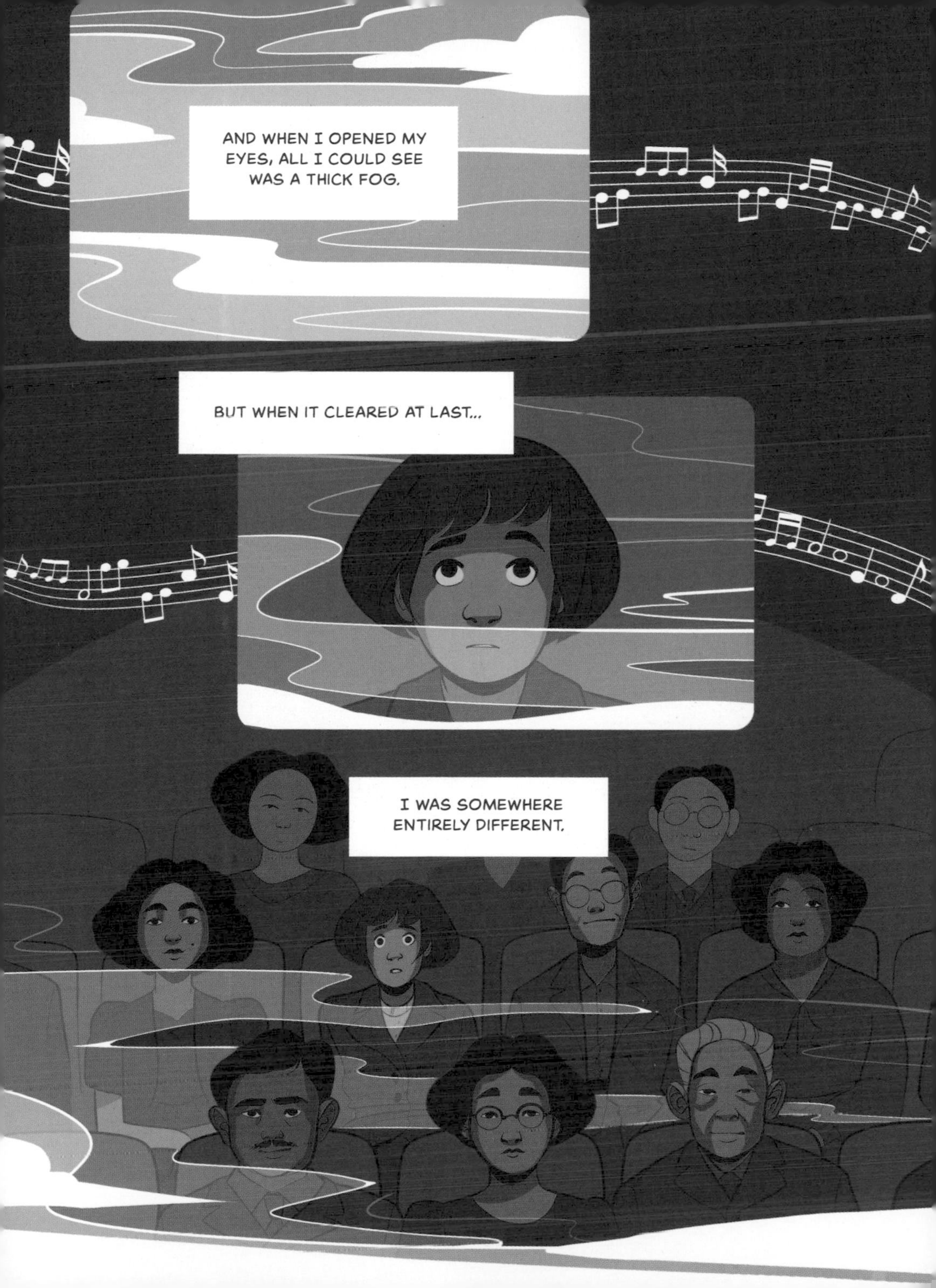
AND WHEN I OPENED MY EYES, ALL I COULD SEE WAS A THICK FOG.
BUT WHEN IT CLEARED AT LAST...
I WAS SOMEWHERE ENTIRELY DIFFERENT.

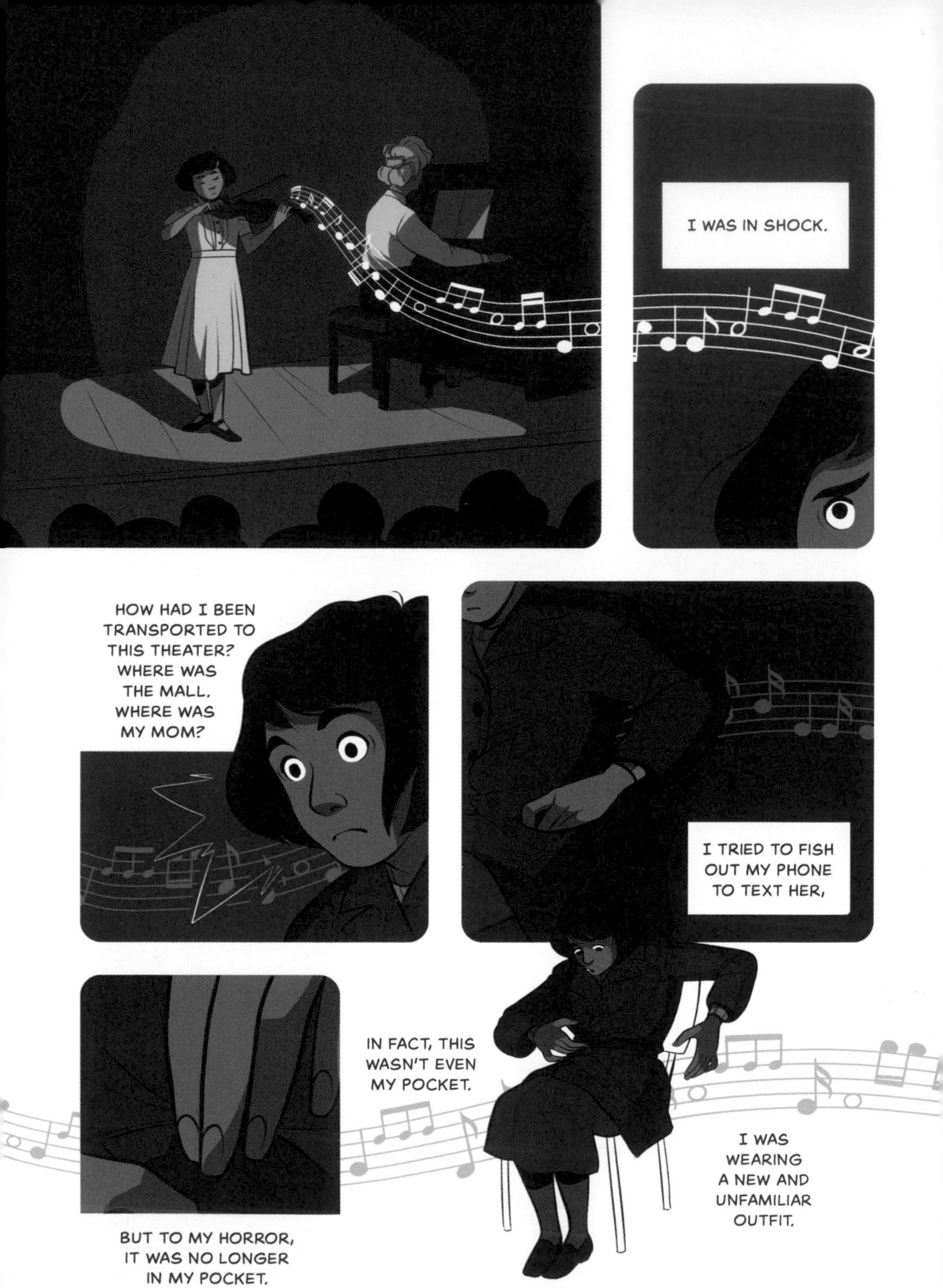
I WAS IN SHOCK.
HOW HAD I BEEN TRANSPORTED TO THIS THEATER? WHERE WAS THE MALL. WHERE WAS MY MOM?
I TRIED TO FISH OUT MY PHONE TO TEXT HER,
BUT TO MY HORROR, IT WAS NO LONGER IN MY POCKET.
IN FACT, THIS WASN'T EVEN MY POCKET.
I WAS WEARING A NEW AND UNFAMILIAR OUTFIT.

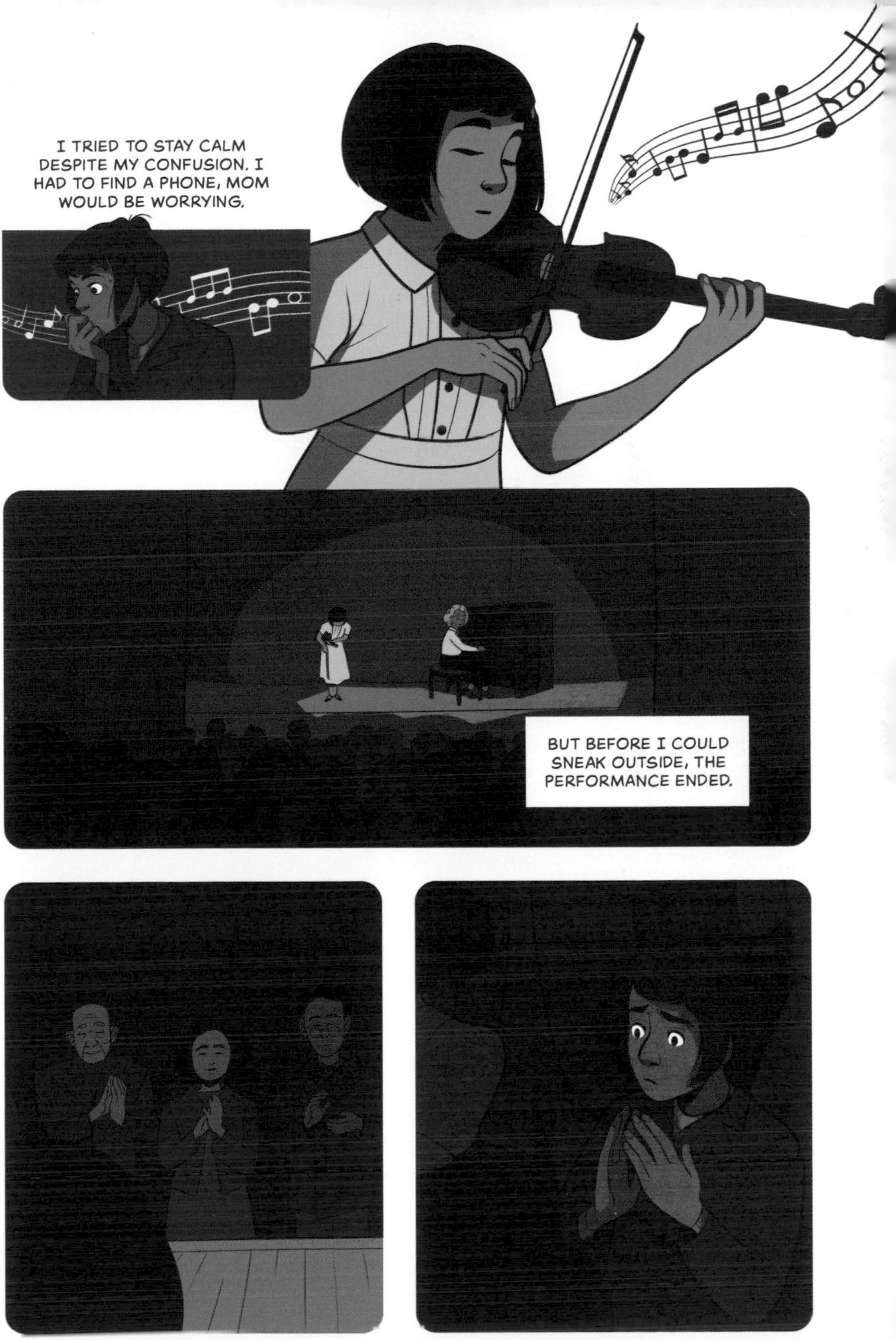
I TRIED TO STAY CALM DESPITE MY CONFUSION. I HAD TO FIND A PHONE, MOM WOULD BE WORRYING.
BUT BEFORE I COULD SNEAK OUTSIDE, THE PERFORMANCE ENDED.

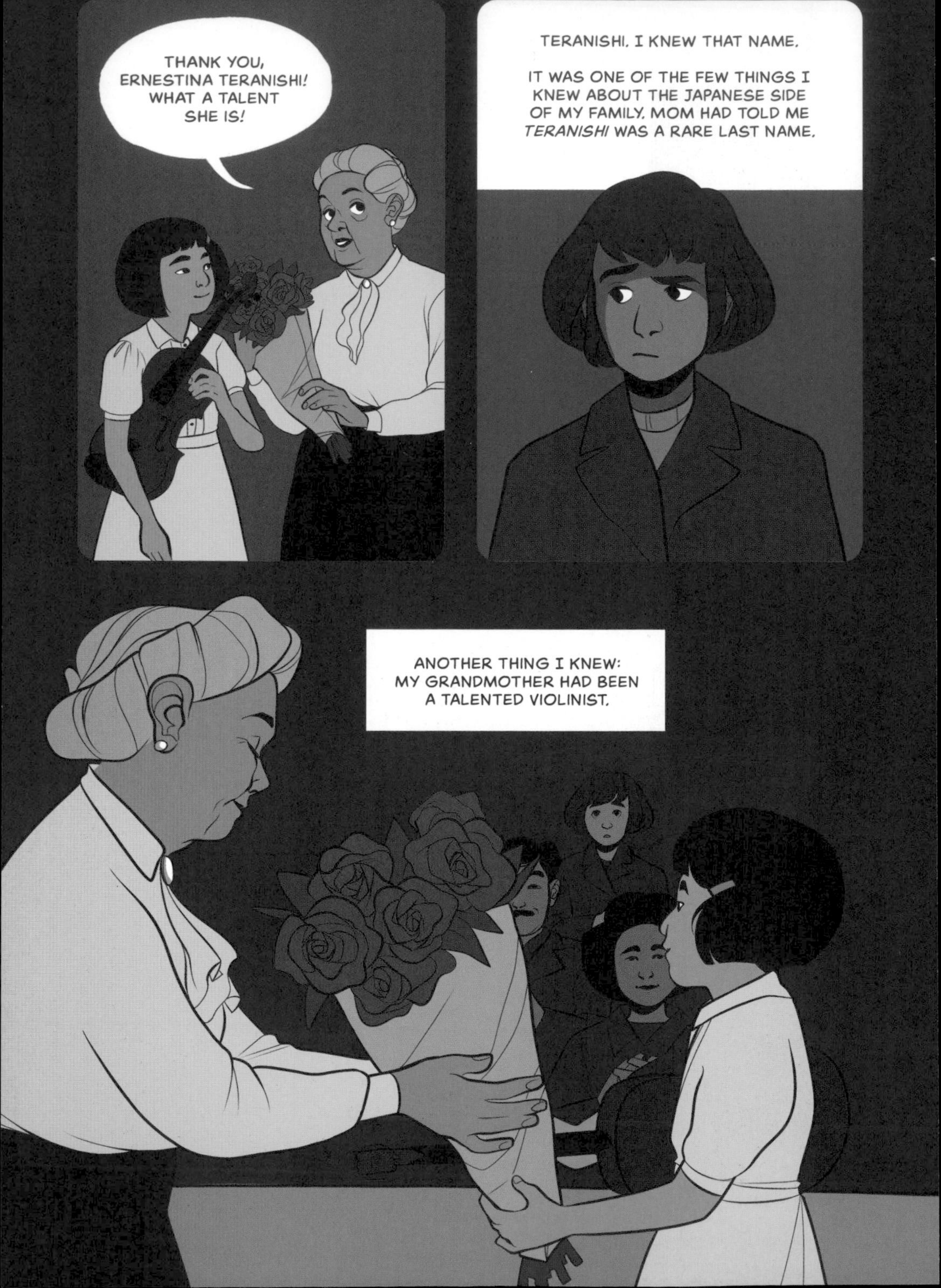
THANK YOU, ERNESTINA TERANISHI! WHAT A TALENT SHE IS!
TERANISHI. I KNEW THAT NAME.
IT WAS ONE OF THE FEW THINGS I KNEW ABOUT THE JAPANESE SIDE OF MY FAMILY. MOM HAD TOLD ME *TERANISHI* WAS A RARE LAST NAME.
ANOTHER THING I KNEW: MY GRANDMOTHER HAD BEEN A TALENTED VIOLINIST.

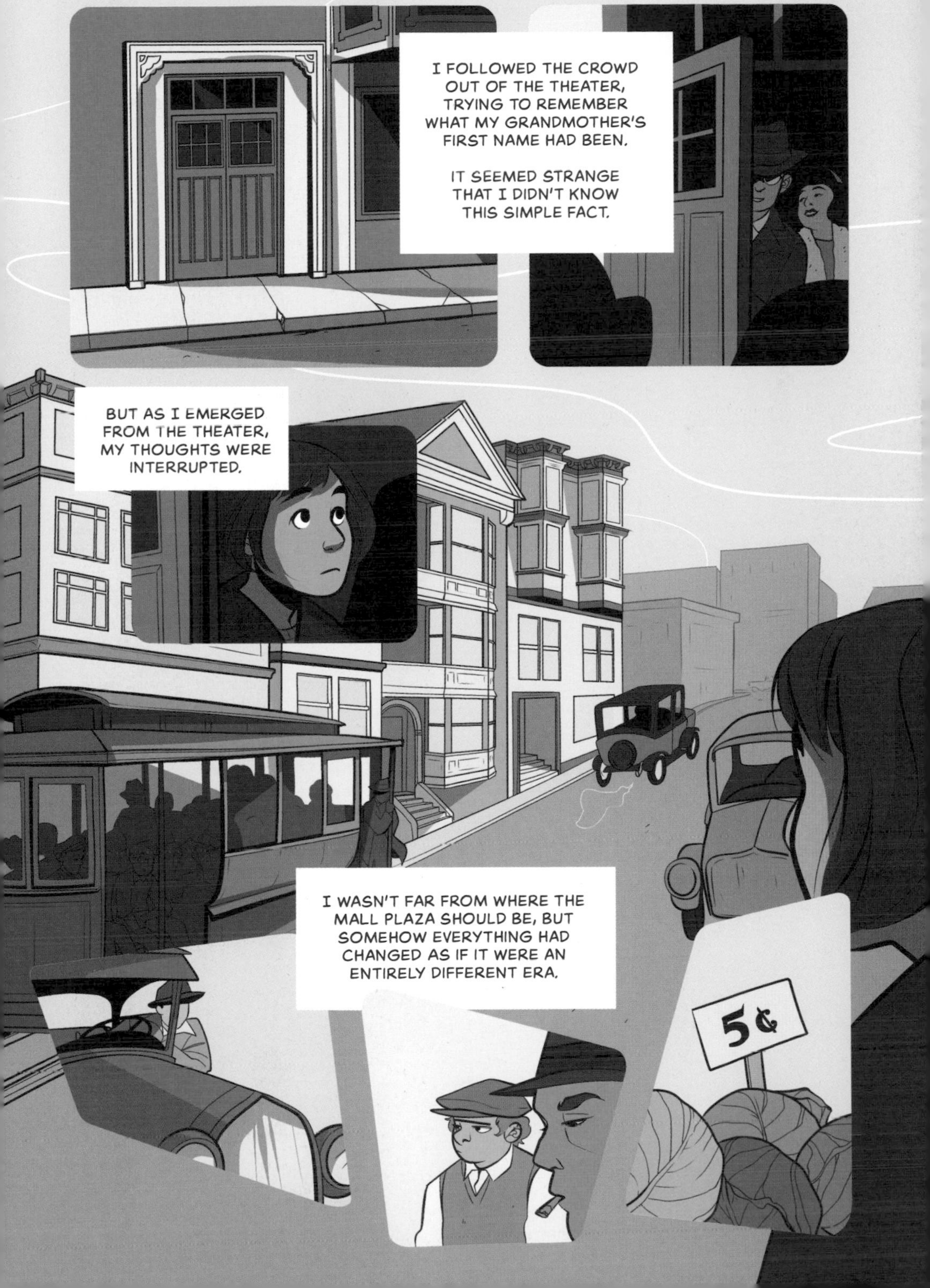
I FOLLOWED THE CROWD OUT OF THE THEATER, TRYING TO REMEMBER WHAT MY GRANDMOTHER'S FIRST NAME HAD BEEN.
IT SEEMED STRANGE THAT I DIDN'T KNOW THIS SIMPLE FACT.
BUT AS I EMERGED FROM THE THEATER, MY THOUGHTS WERE INTERRUPTED.
I WASN'T FAR FROM WHERE THE MALL PLAZA SHOULD BE, BUT SOMEHOW EVERYTHING HAD CHANGED AS IF IT WERE AN ENTIRELY DIFFERENT ERA.
5¢

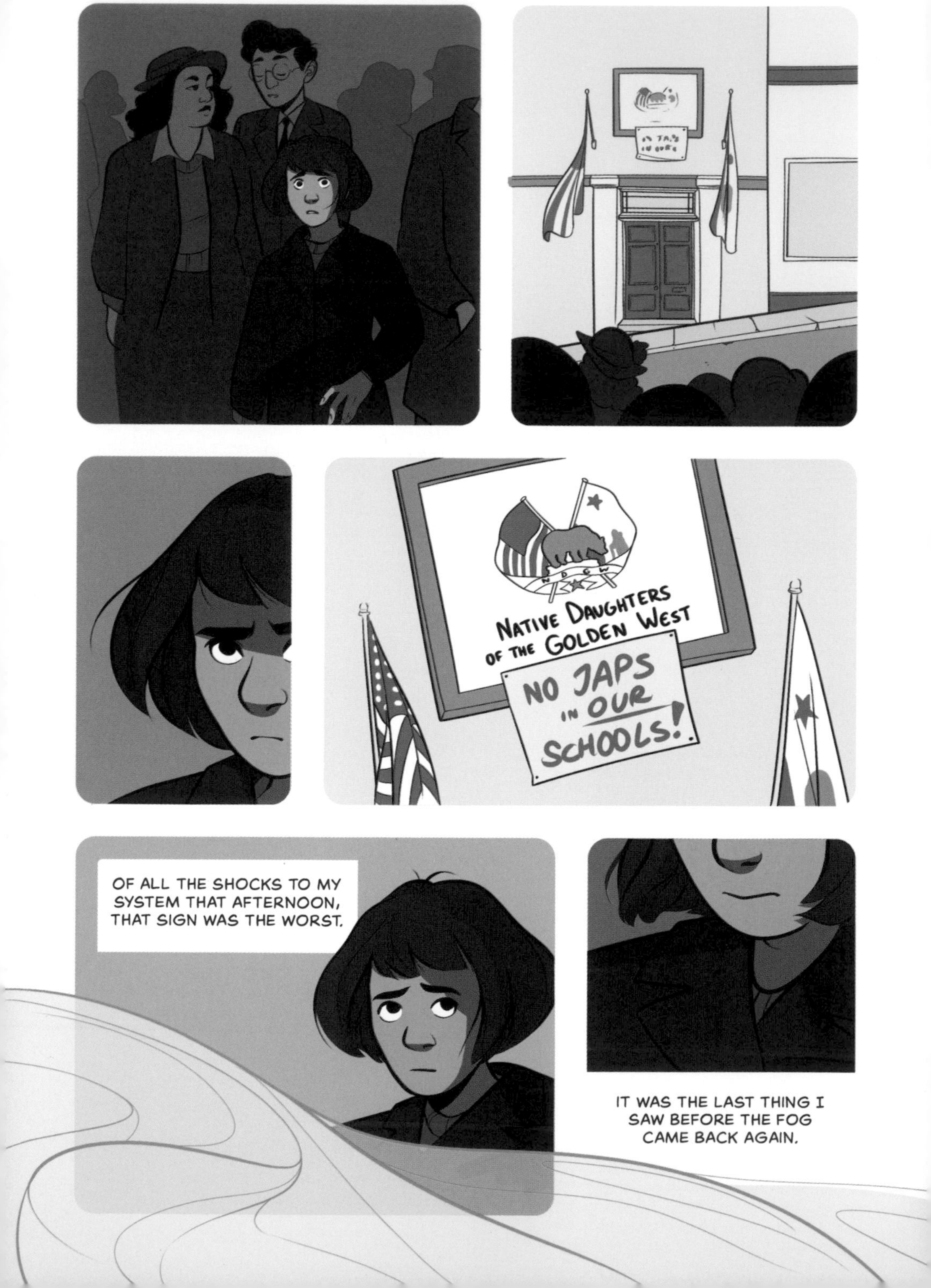
NATIVE DAUGHTERS OF THE GOLDEN WEST
NO JAPS IN OUR SCHOOLS!
OF ALL THE SHOCKS TO MY SYSTEM THAT AFTERNOON, THAT SIGN WAS THE WORST.
IT WAS THE LAST THING I SAW BEFORE THE FOG CAME BACK AGAIN.

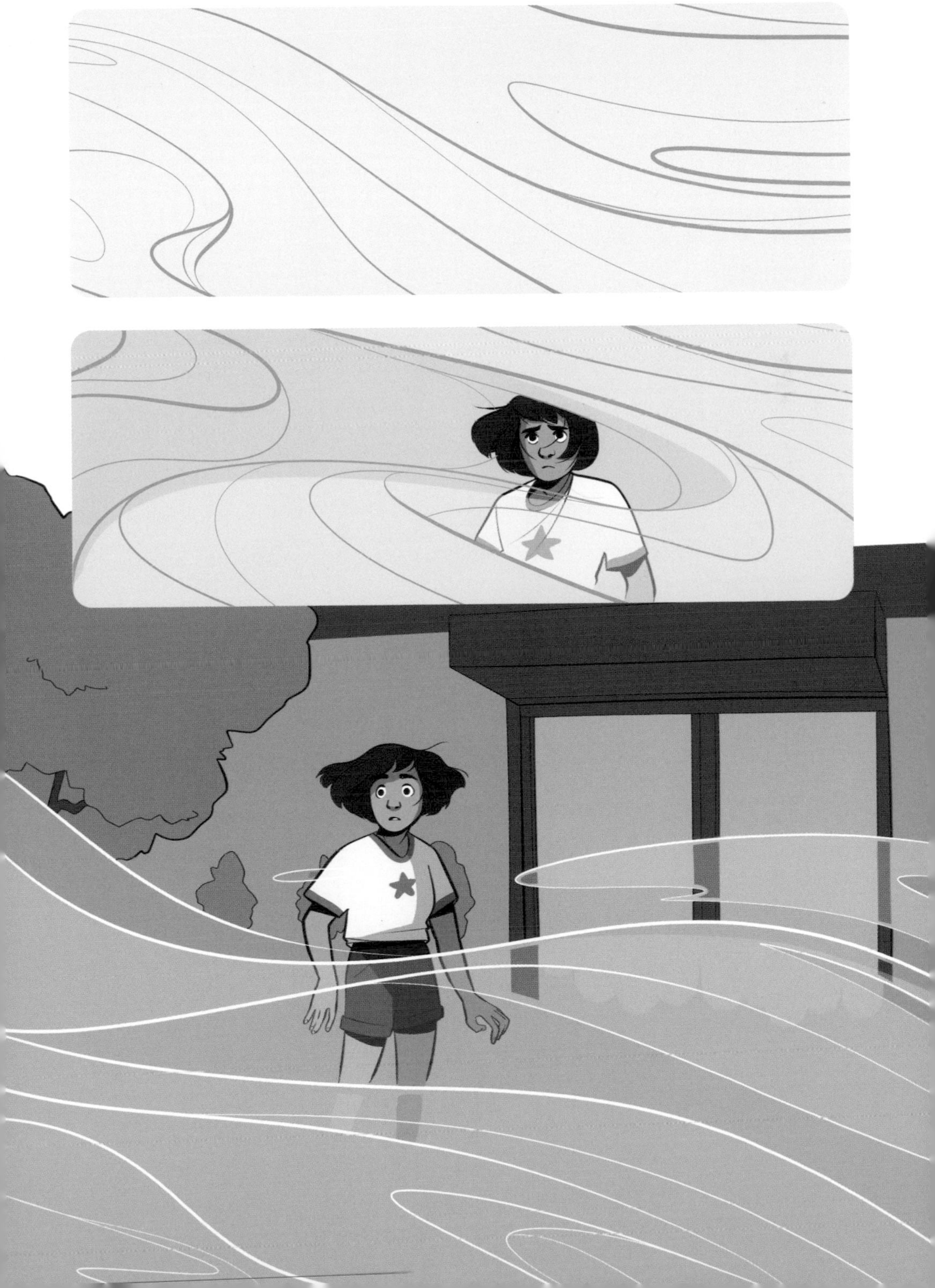

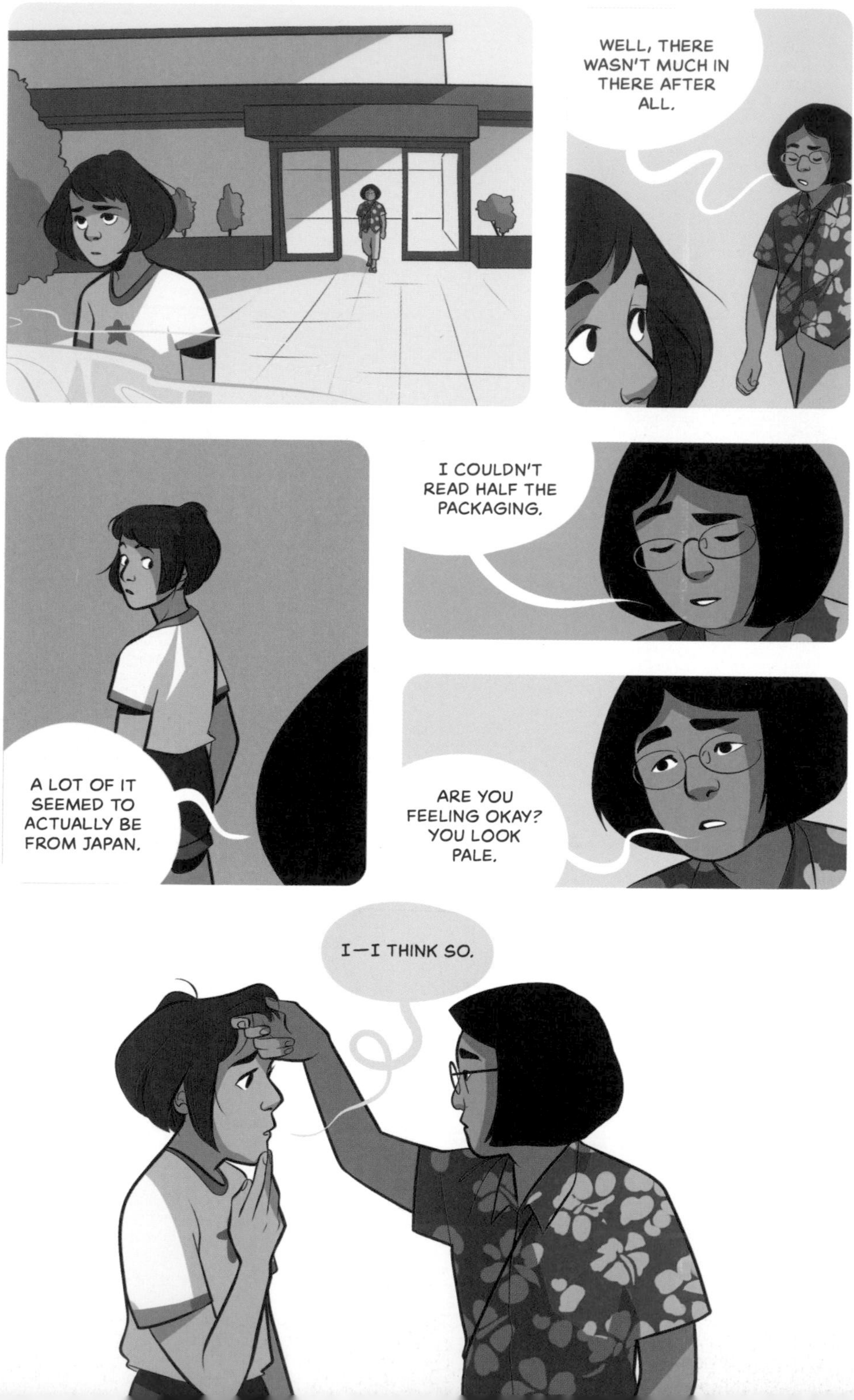
WELL, THERE WASN'T MUCH IN THERE AFTER ALL.
I COULDN'T READ HALF THE PACKAGING.
A LOT OF IT SEEMED TO ACTUALLY BE FROM JAPAN.
ARE YOU FEELING OKAY? YOU LOOK PALE.
I—I THINK SO.

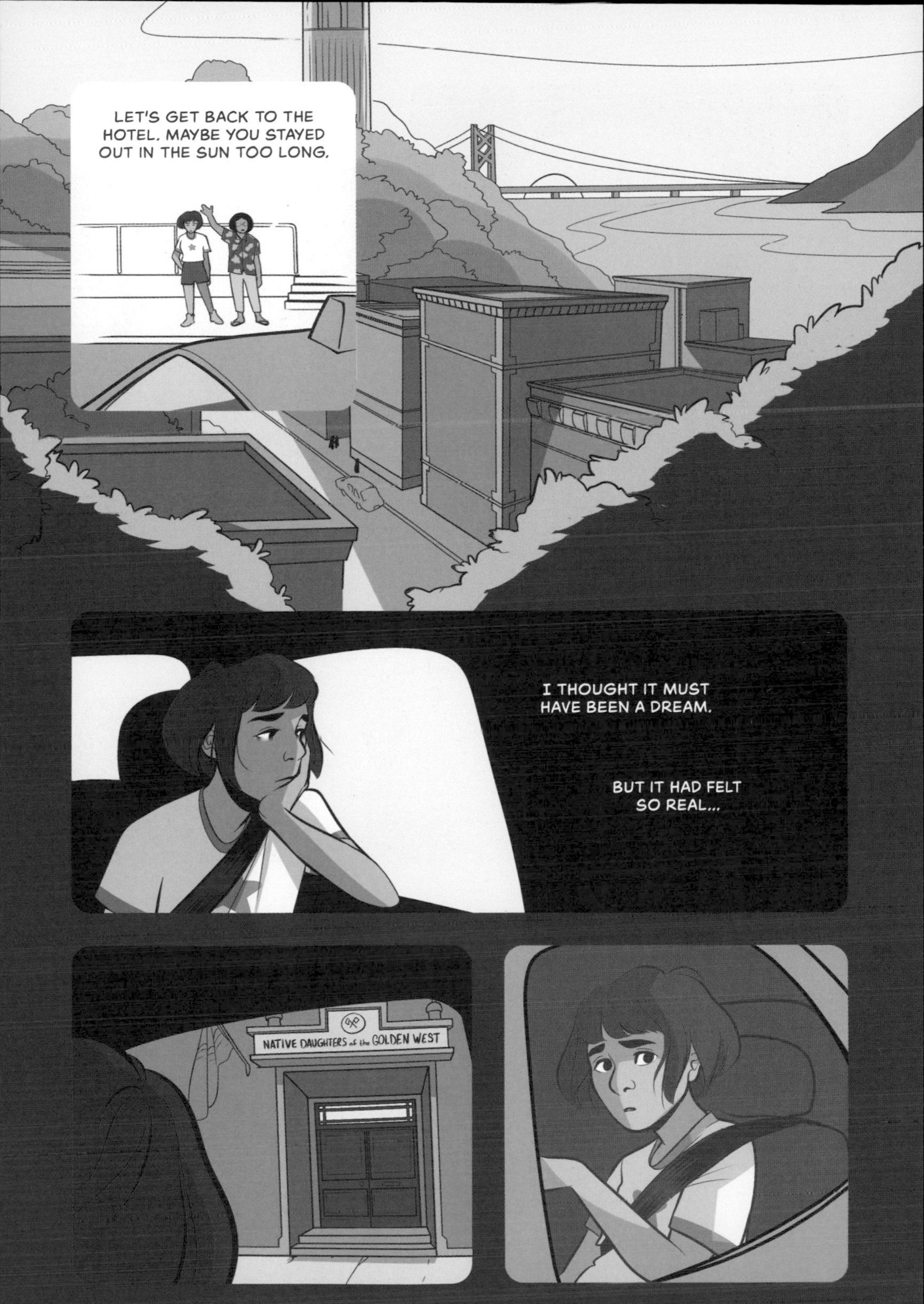
LET'S GET BACK TO THE HOTEL. MAYBE YOU STAYED OUT IN THE SUN TOO LONG.
I THOUGHT IT MUST HAVE BEEN A DREAM.
BUT IT HAD FELT SO REAL...
NATIVE DAUGHTERS of the GOLDEN WEST

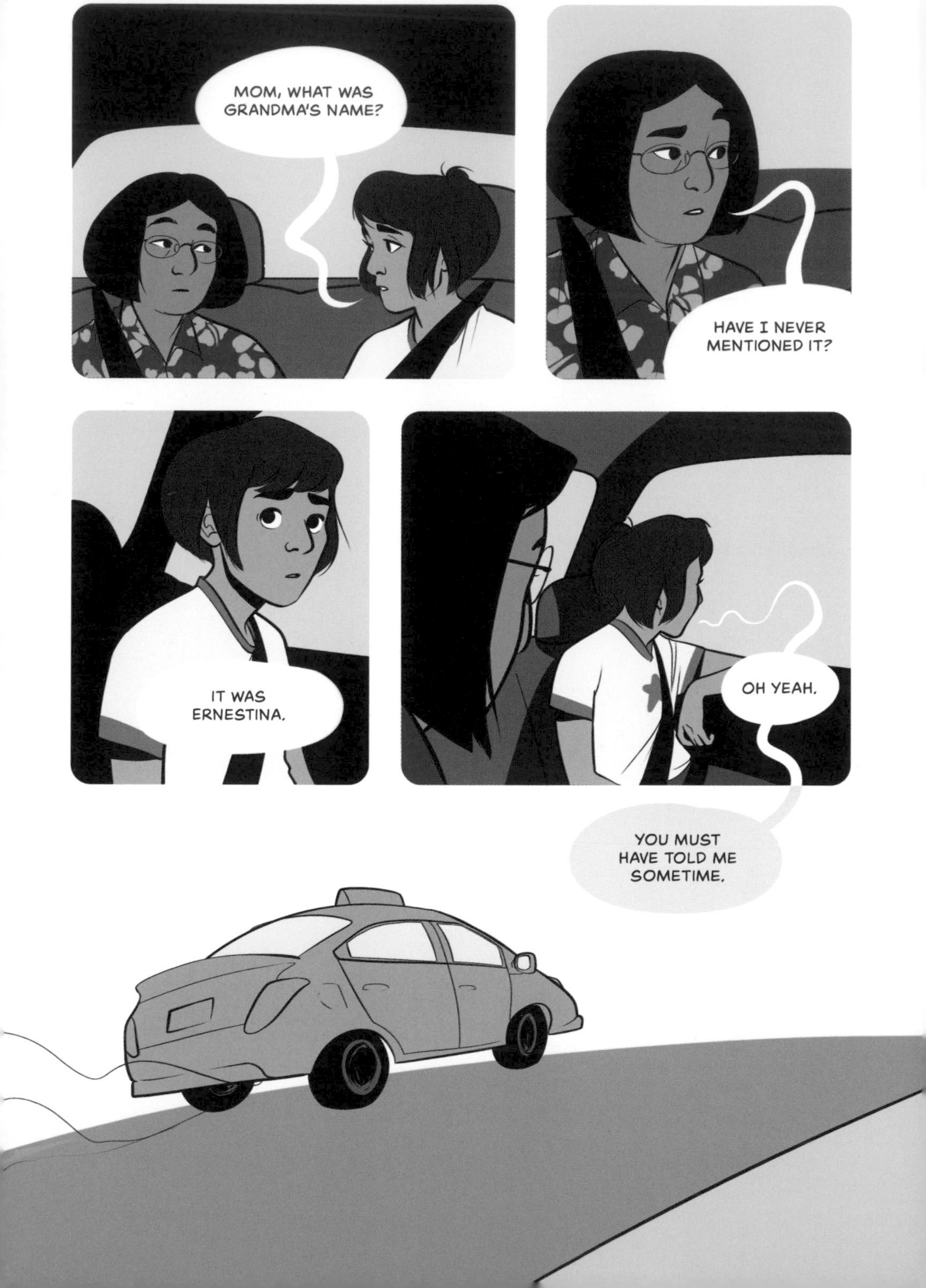
MOM, WHAT WAS GRANDMA'S NAME?
HAVE I NEVER MENTIONED IT?
IT WAS ERNESTINA.
OH YEAH.
YOU MUST HAVE TOLD ME SOMETIME.

IT WAS JUST A DREAM.

IT WAS JUST A DREAM.

IT SEEMS ODD EVEN TO ME THAT I WOULDN'T REALLY KNOW MY OWN GRANDMOTHER'S NAME.

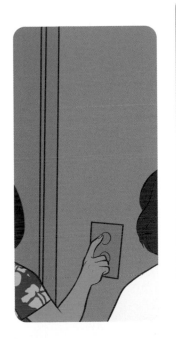

MOM DOESN'T TALK ABOUT HER OFTEN, AND WHEN SHE DOES, OF COURSE SHE JUST CALLS HER "MOM."

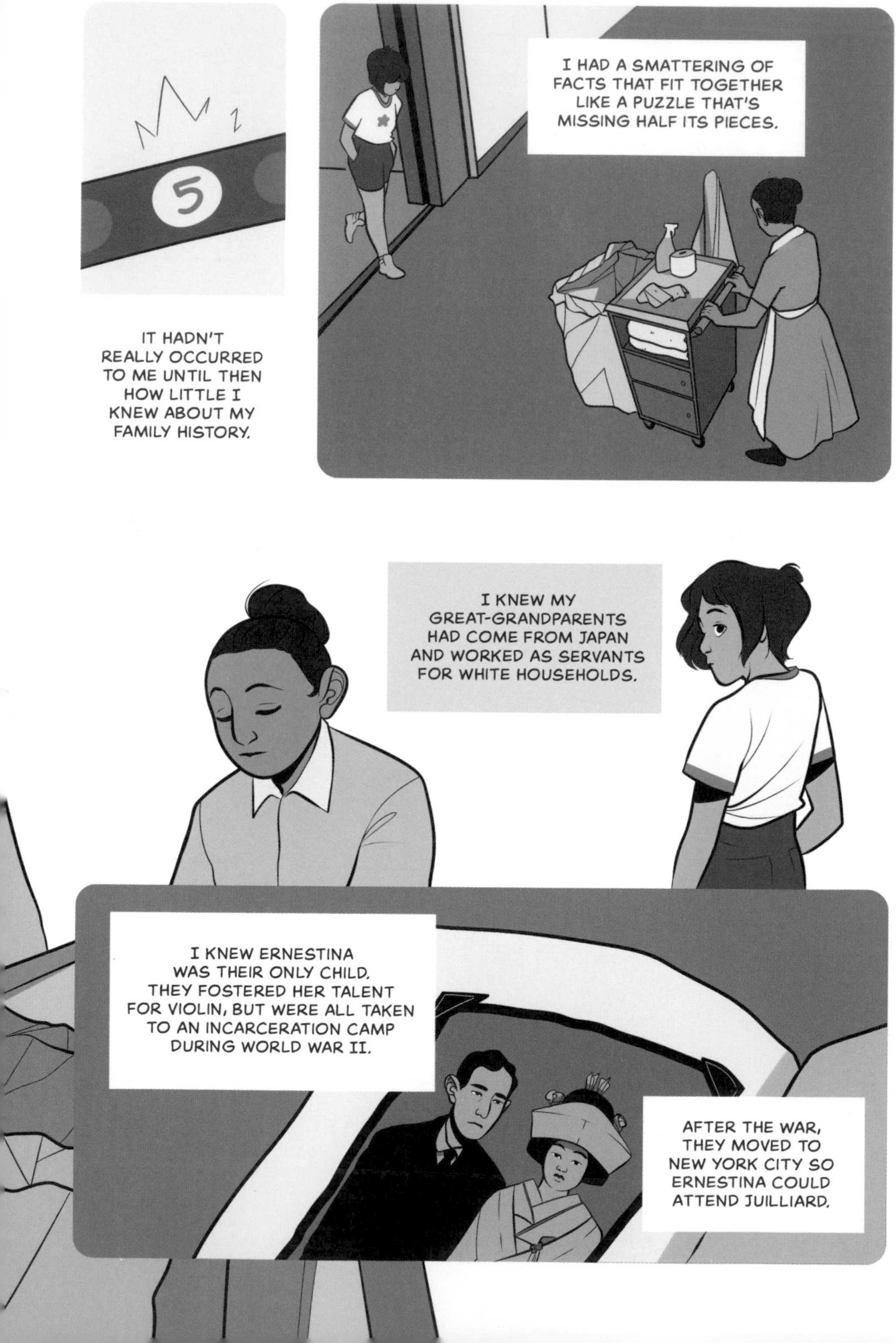
5
IT HADN'T REALLY OCCURRED TO ME UNTIL THEN HOW LITTLE I KNEW ABOUT MY FAMILY HISTORY.
I HAD A SMATTERING OF FACTS THAT FIT TOGETHER LIKE A PUZZLE THAT'S MISSING HALF ITS PIECES.
I KNEW MY GREAT-GRANDPARENTS HAD COME FROM JAPAN AND WORKED AS SERVANTS FOR WHITE HOUSEHOLDS.
I KNEW ERNESTINA WAS THEIR ONLY CHILD. THEY FOSTERED HER TALENT FOR VIOLIN, BUT WERE ALL TAKEN TO AN INCARCERATION CAMP DURING WORLD WAR II.
AFTER THE WAR, THEY MOVED TO NEW YORK CITY SO ERNESTINA COULD ATTEND JUILLIARD.

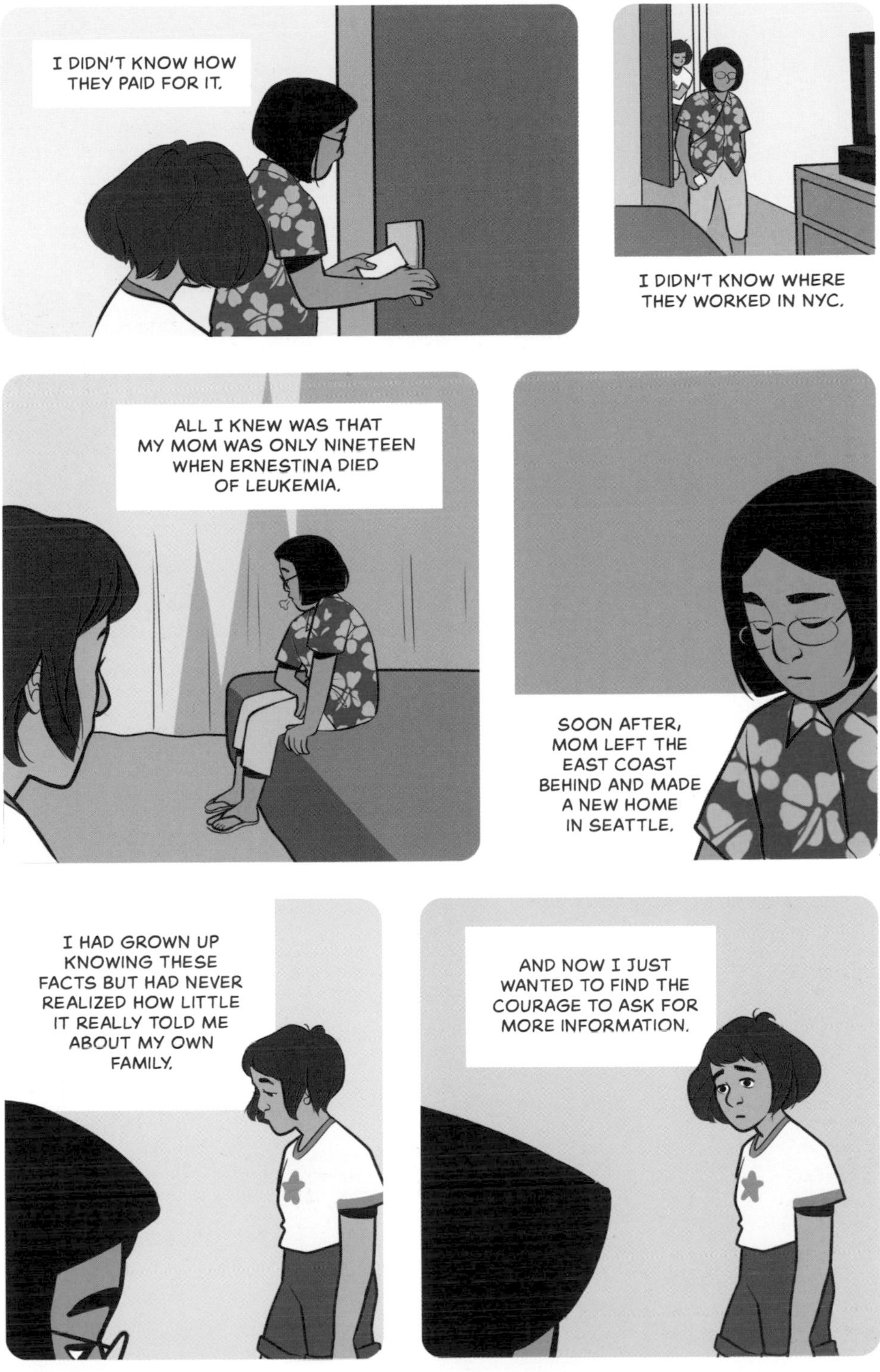

I DIDN'T KNOW HOW THEY PAID FOR IT.
I DIDN'T KNOW WHERE THEY WORKED IN NYC.
ALL I KNEW WAS THAT MY MOM WAS ONLY NINETEEN WHEN ERNESTINA DIED OF LEUKEMIA.
SOON AFTER, MOM LEFT THE EAST COAST BEHIND AND MADE A NEW HOME IN SEATTLE.
I HAD GROWN UP KNOWING THESE FACTS BUT HAD NEVER REALIZED HOW LITTLE IT REALLY TOLD ME ABOUT MY OWN FAMILY.
AND NOW I JUST WANTED TO FIND THE COURAGE TO ASK FOR MORE INFORMATION.

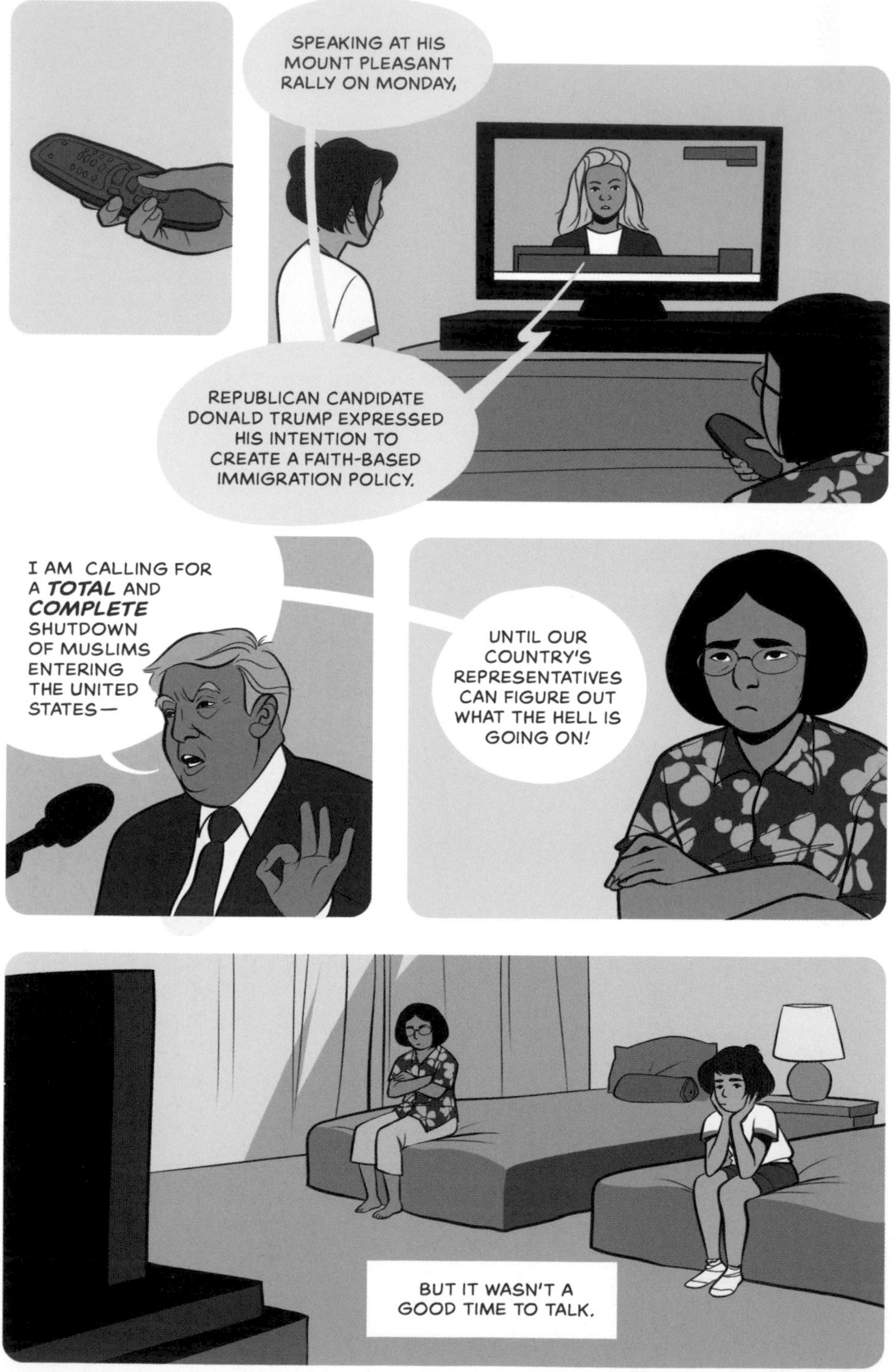
SPEAKING AT HIS MOUNT PLEASANT RALLY ON MONDAY,
REPUBLICAN CANDIDATE DONALD TRUMP EXPRESSED HIS INTENTION TO CREATE A FAITH-BASED IMMIGRATION POLICY.
I AM CALLING FOR A TOTAL AND COMPLETE SHUTDOWN OF MUSLIMS ENTERING THE UNITED STATES—
UNTIL OUR COUNTRY'S REPRESENTATIVES CAN FIGURE OUT WHAT THE HELL IS GOING ON!
BUT IT WASN'T A GOOD TIME TO TALK.

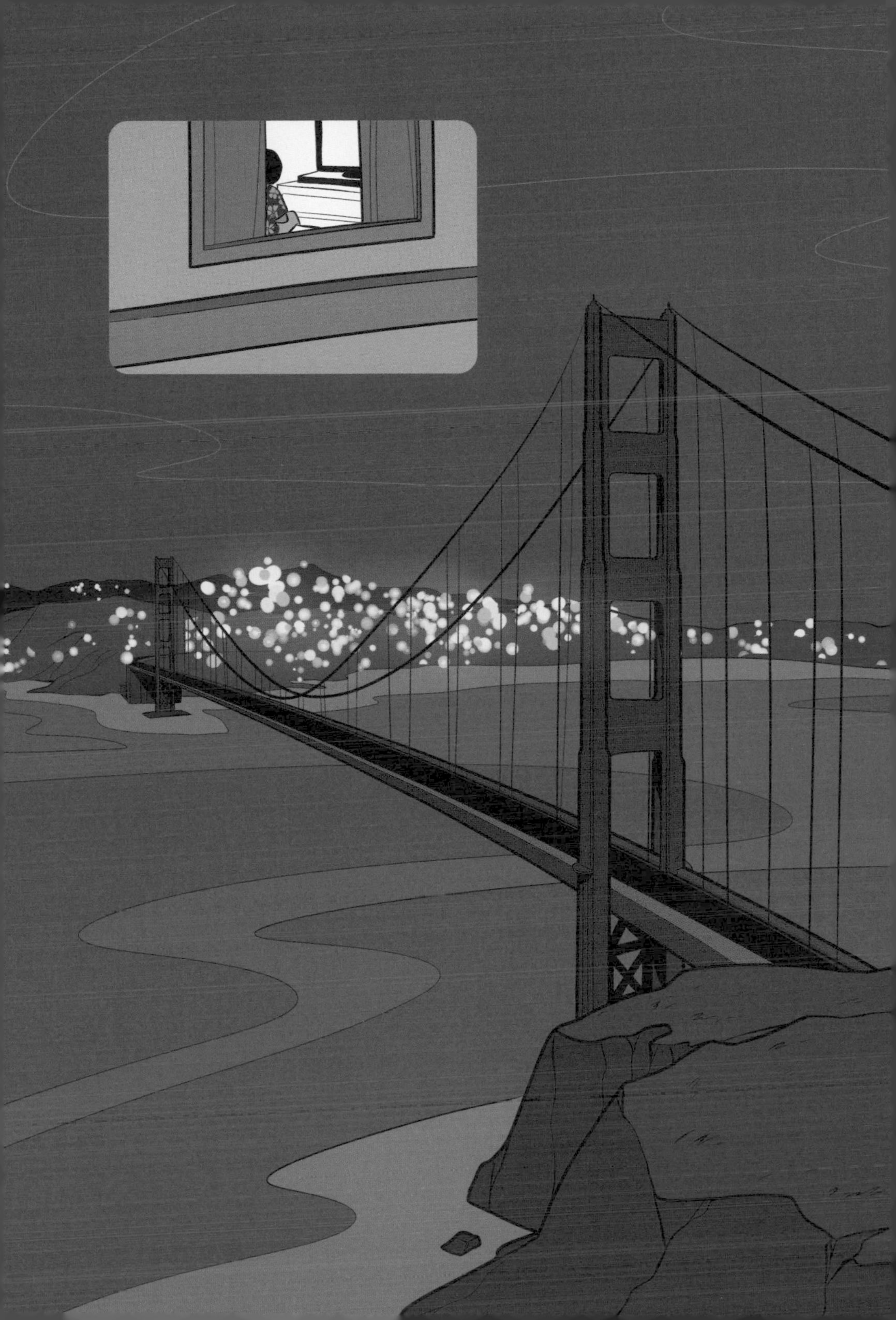

2

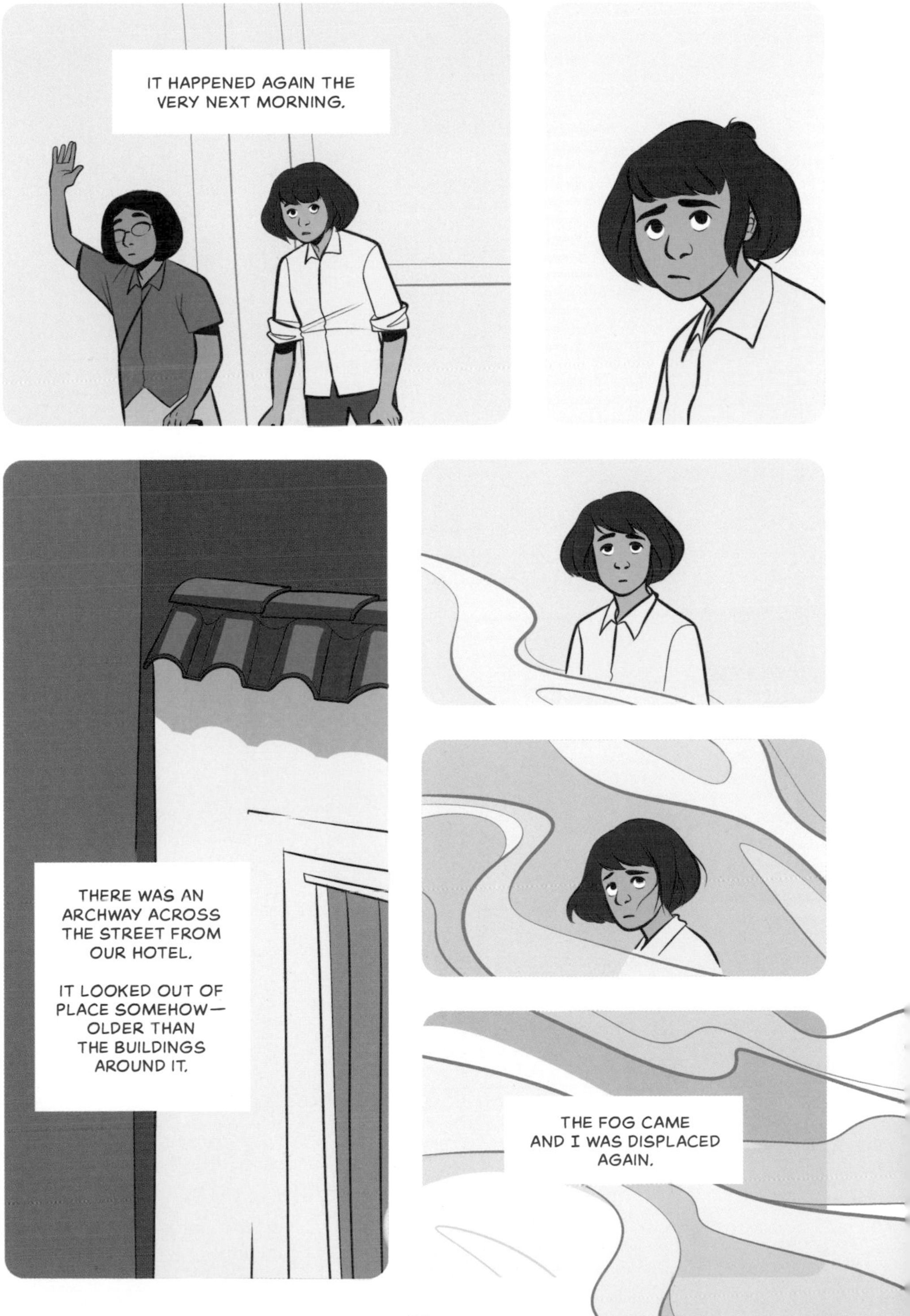
IT HAPPENED AGAIN THE VERY NEXT MORNING.
THERE WAS AN ARCHWAY ACROSS THE STREET FROM OUR HOTEL.
IT LOOKED OUT OF PLACE SOMEHOW— OLDER THAN THE BUILDINGS AROUND IT.
THE FOG CAME AND I WAS DISPLACED AGAIN.

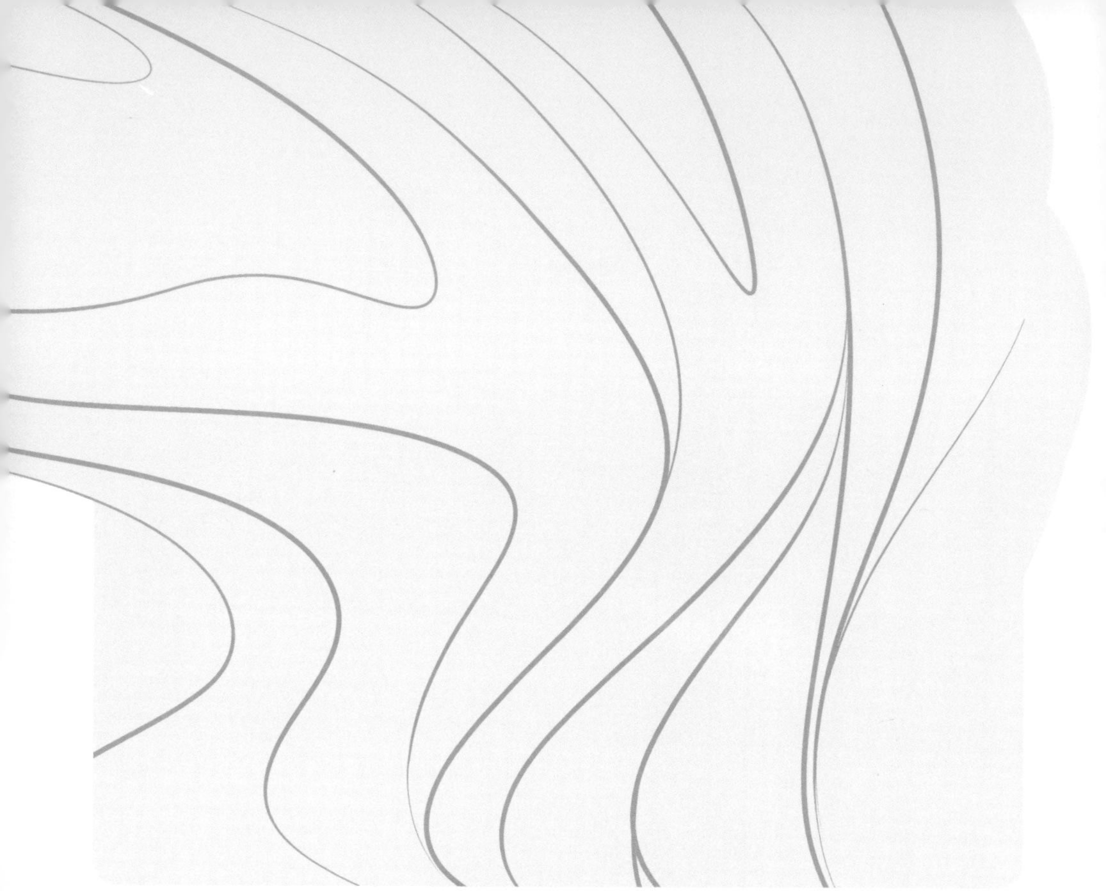

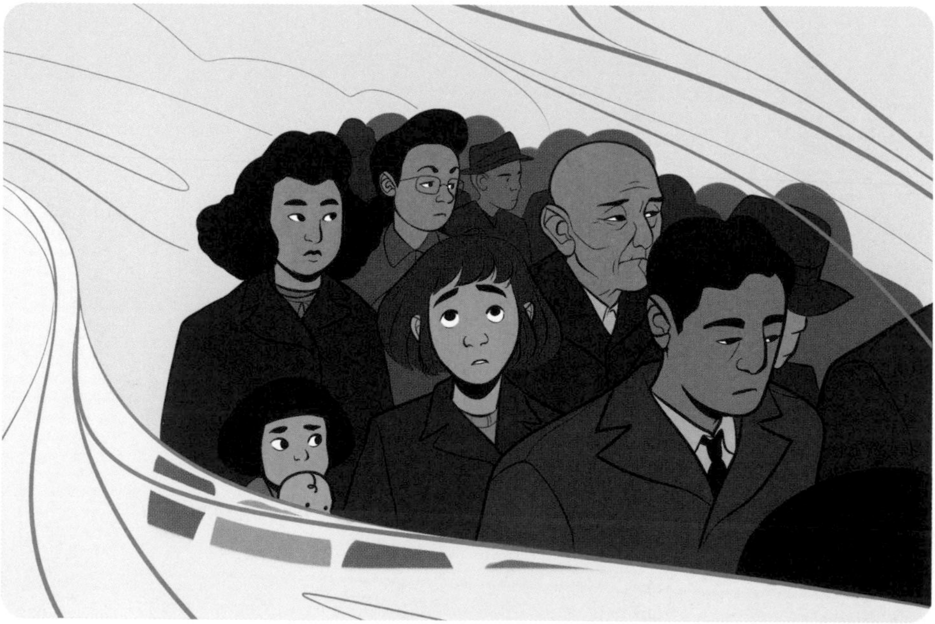

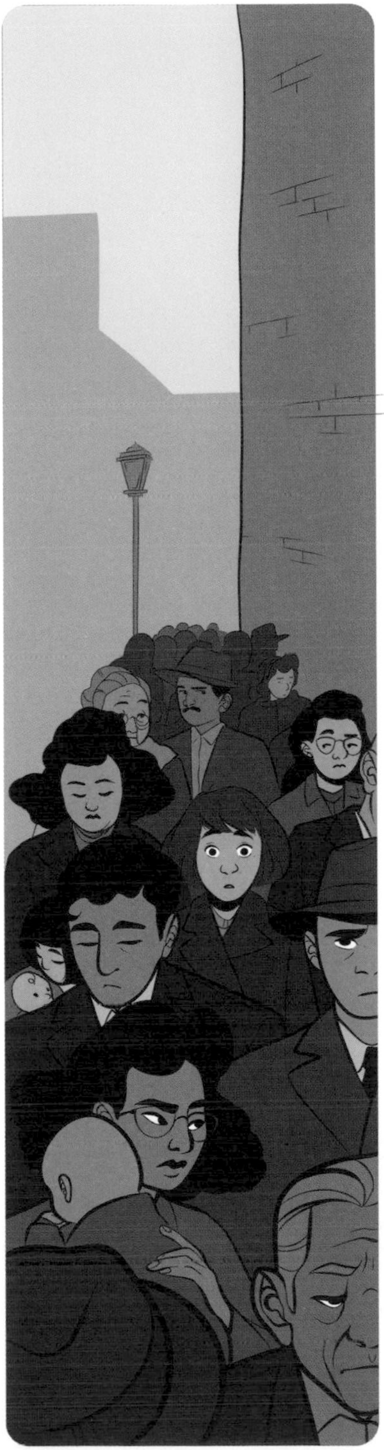

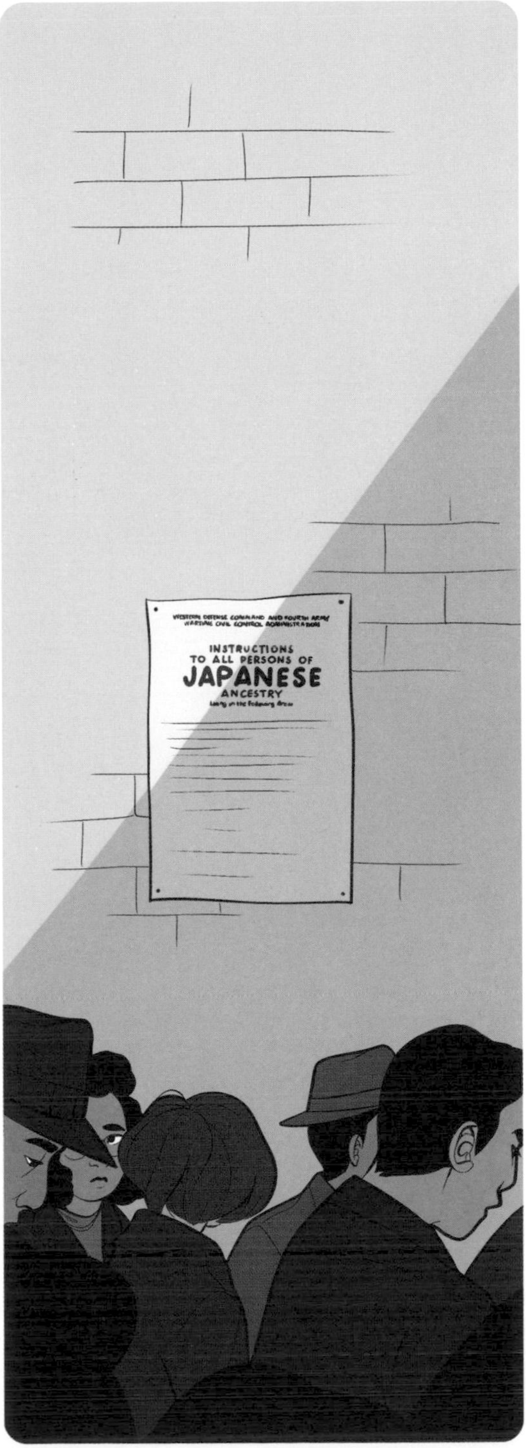
INSTRUCTIONS
TO ALL PERSONS OF
JAPANESE
ANCESTRY

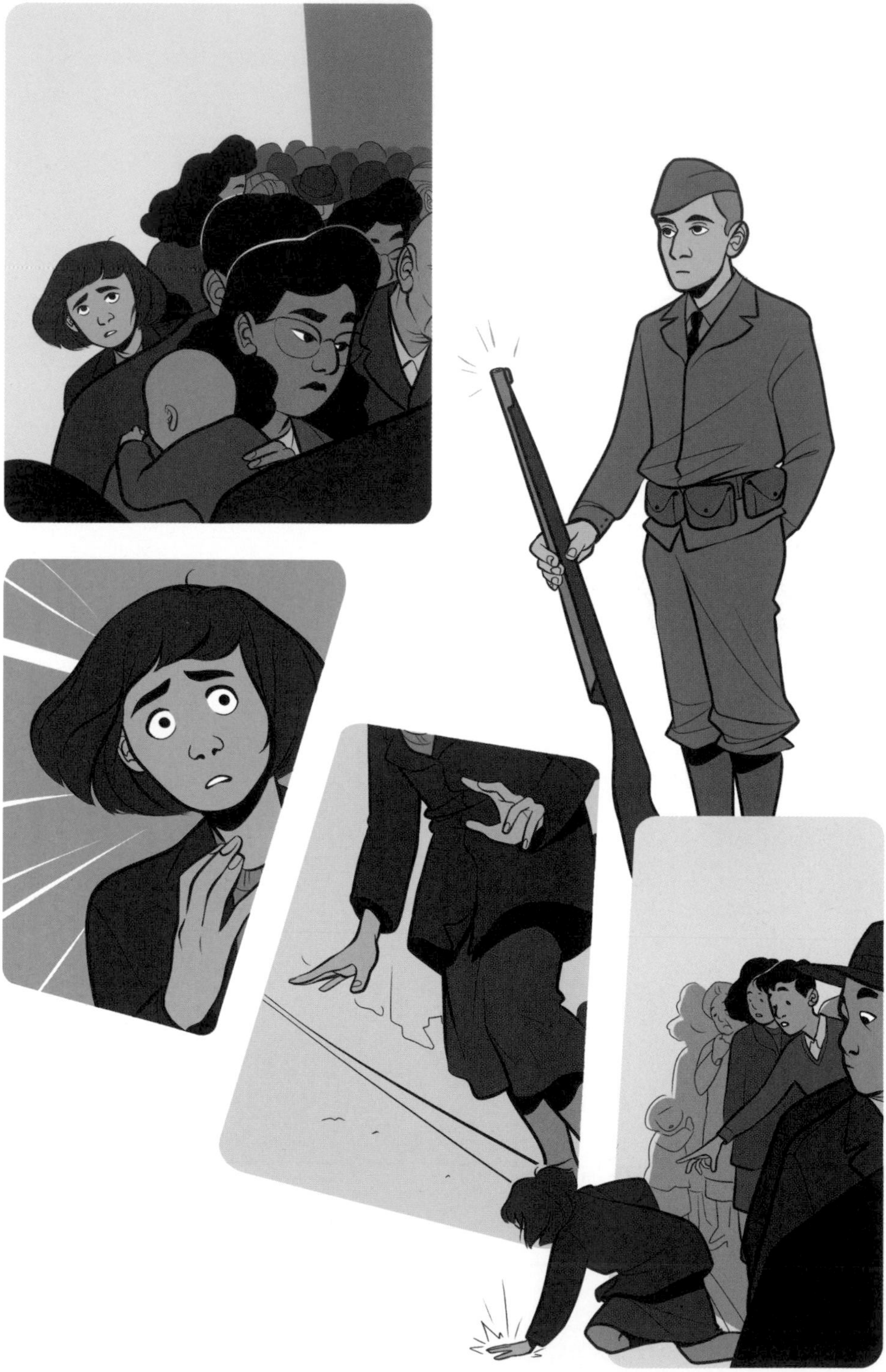

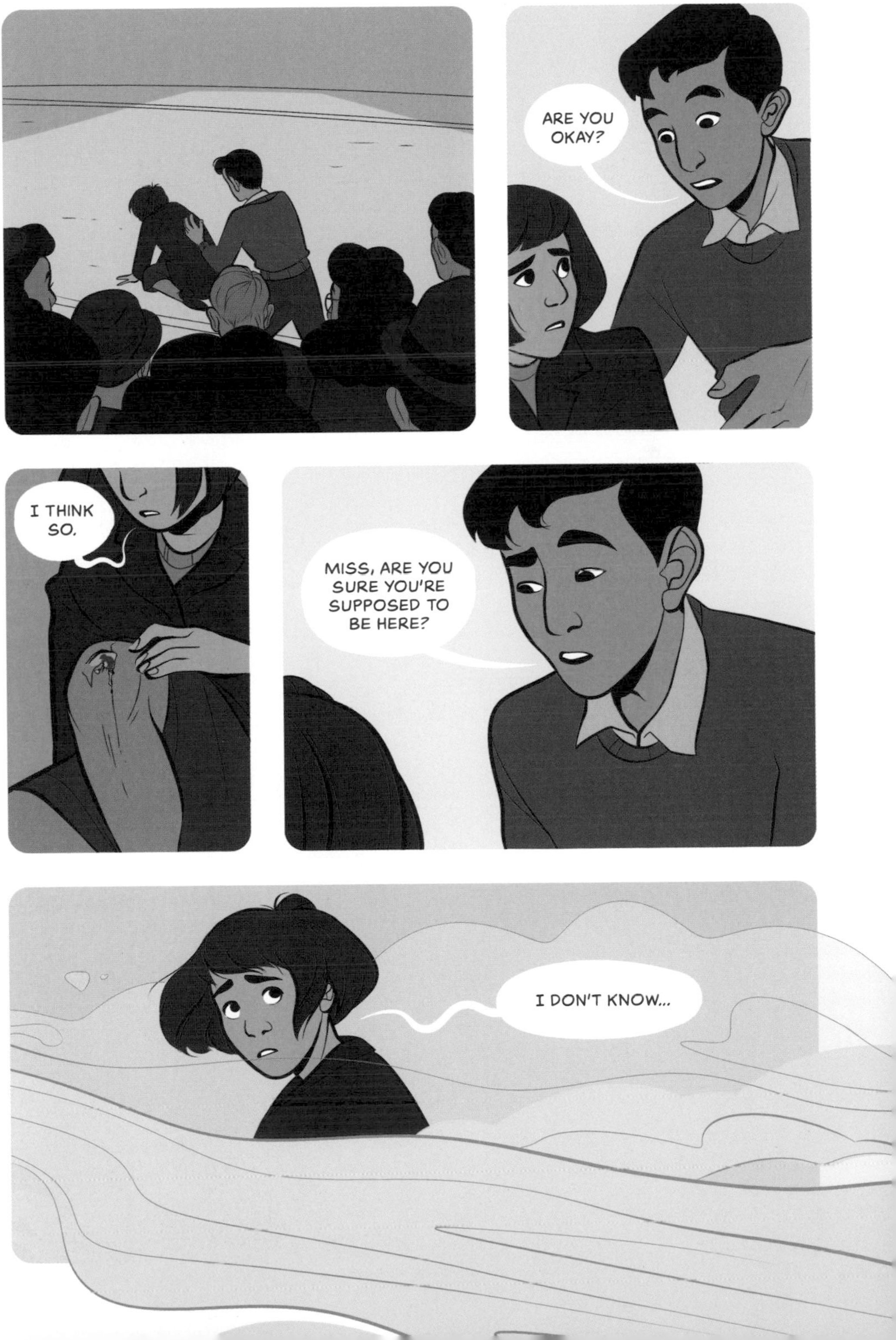
ARE YOU OKAY?
I THINK SO.
MISS, ARE YOU SURE YOU'RE SUPPOSED TO BE HERE?
I DON'T KNOW...

KIKU,
LET'S GO!

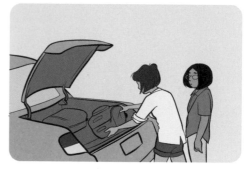

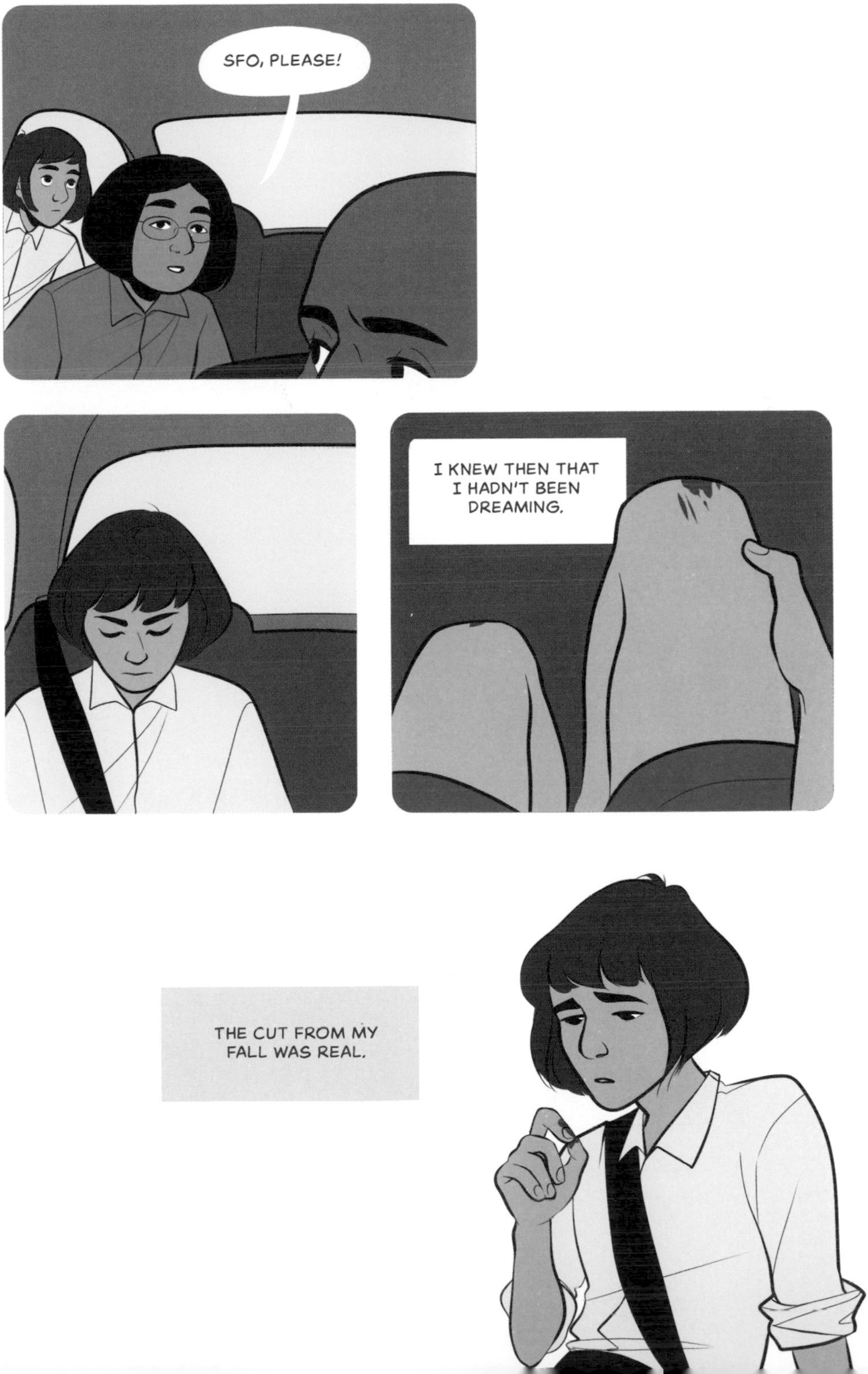
SFO, PLEASE!
I KNEW THEN THAT I HADN'T BEEN DREAMING.
THE CUT FROM MY FALL WAS REAL.

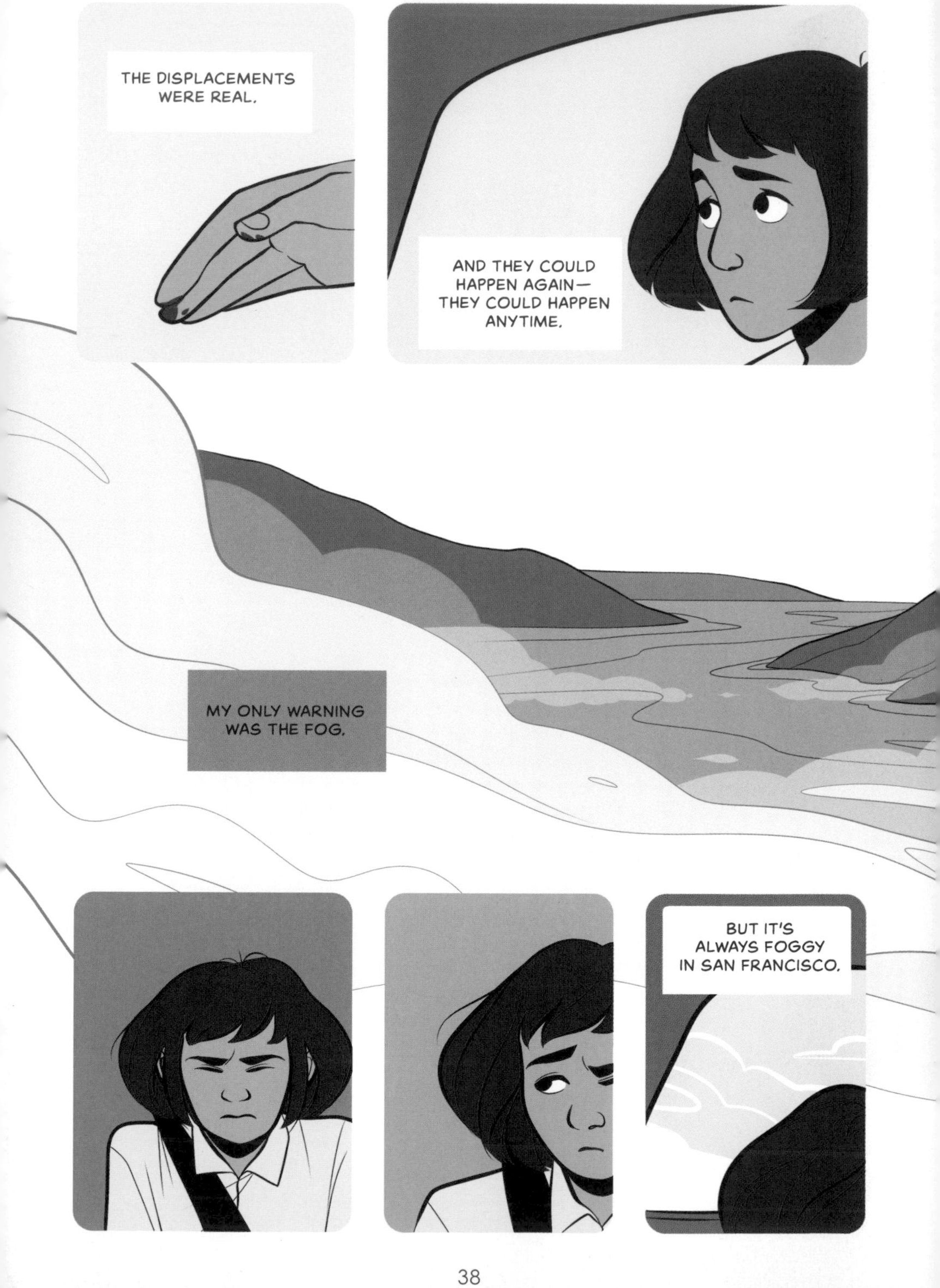
THE DISPLACEMENTS WERE REAL.
AND THEY COULD HAPPEN AGAIN— THEY COULD HAPPEN ANYTIME.
MY ONLY WARNING WAS THE FOG.
BUT IT'S ALWAYS FOGGY IN SAN FRANCISCO.

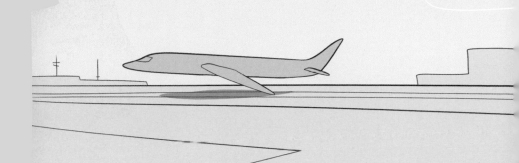

I'M SO READY TO GO HOME.

MHM.

THAT WAS AN UNDERSTATEMENT. I NEEDED TO GET BACK TO SEATTLE, TO A NORMAL LIFE.

THE DISPLACEMENTS HAD BEGUN IN SAN FRANCISCO, SO I CONVINCED MYSELF THEY COULD ONLY HAPPEN THERE.

AT HOME, I'D BE SAFE.

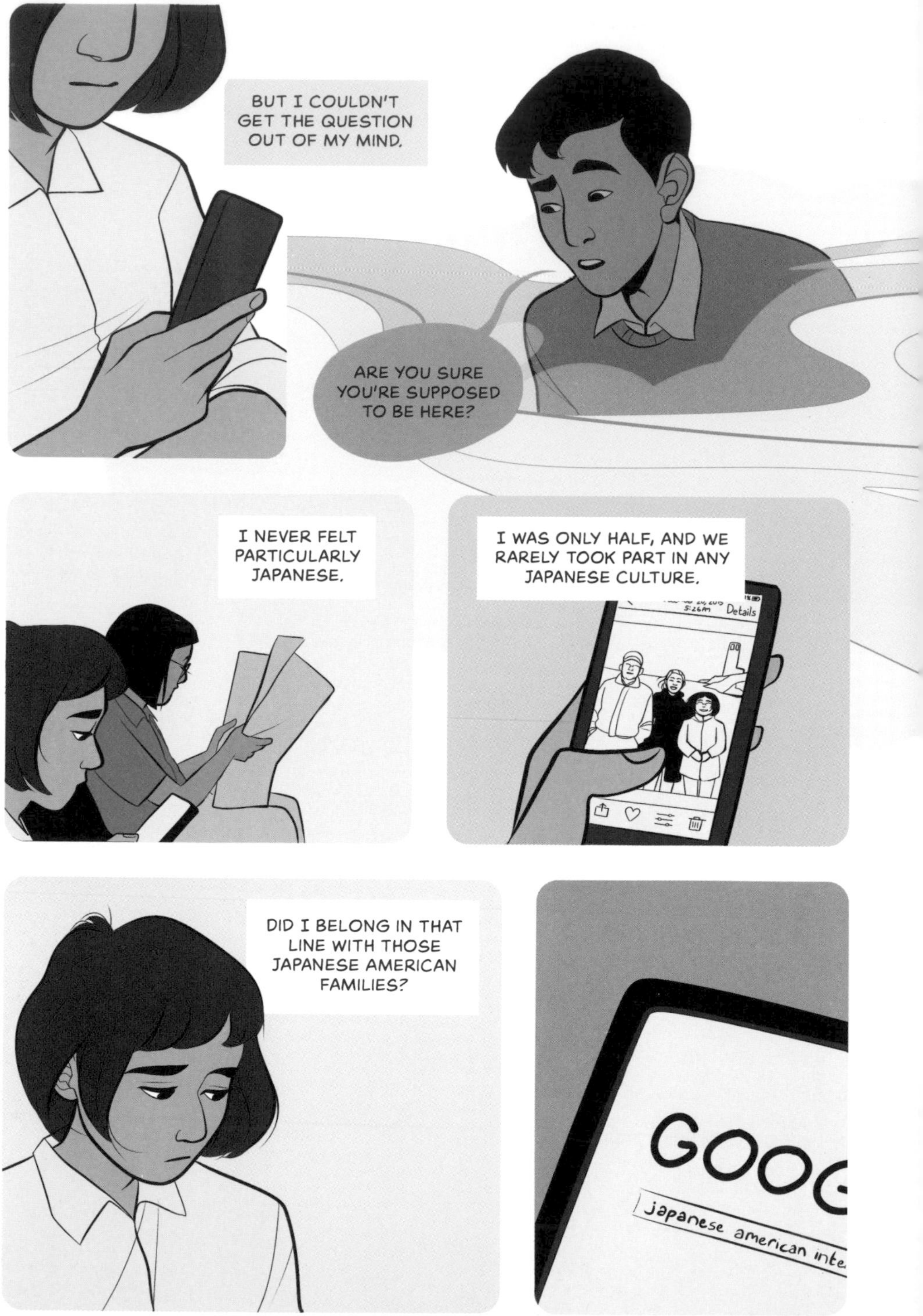
BUT I COULDN'T GET THE QUESTION OUT OF MY MIND.
ARE YOU SURE YOU'RE SUPPOSED TO BE HERE?
I NEVER FELT PARTICULARLY JAPANESE.
I WAS ONLY HALF, AND WE RARELY TOOK PART IN ANY JAPANESE CULTURE.
Details
DID I BELONG IN THAT LINE WITH THOSE JAPANESE AMERICAN FAMILIES?
GOOG
japanese american inte

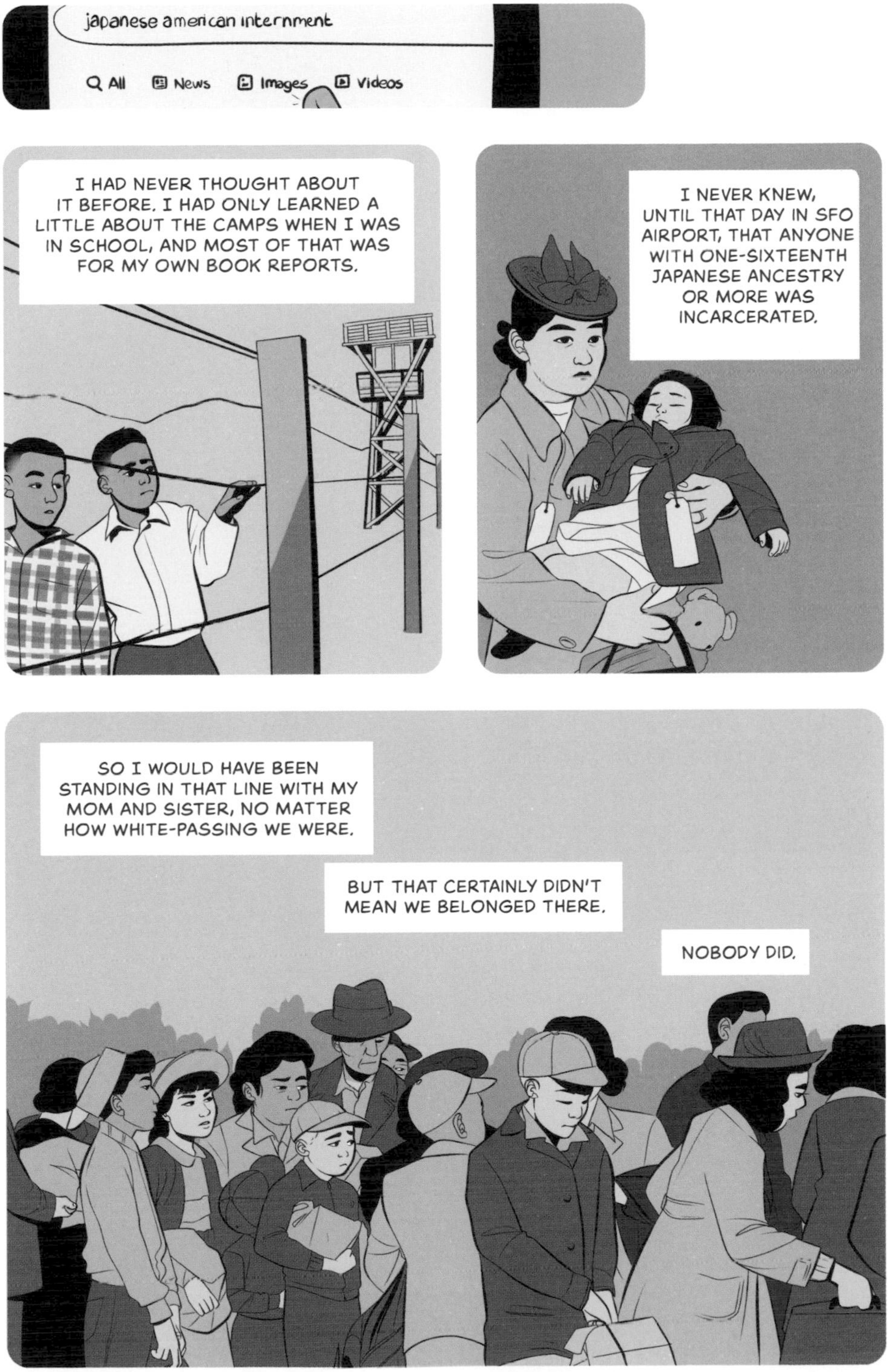
japanese american internment
All
News
Images
Videos
I HAD NEVER THOUGHT ABOUT IT BEFORE. I HAD ONLY LEARNED A LITTLE ABOUT THE CAMPS WHEN I WAS IN SCHOOL, AND MOST OF THAT WAS FOR MY OWN BOOK REPORTS.
I NEVER KNEW, UNTIL THAT DAY IN SFO AIRPORT, THAT ANYONE WITH ONE-SIXTEENTH JAPANESE ANCESTRY OR MORE WAS INCARCERATED.
SO I WOULD HAVE BEEN STANDING IN THAT LINE WITH MY MOM AND SISTER, NO MATTER HOW WHITE-PASSING WE WERE.
BUT THAT CERTAINLY DIDN'T MEAN WE BELONGED THERE.
NOBODY DID.

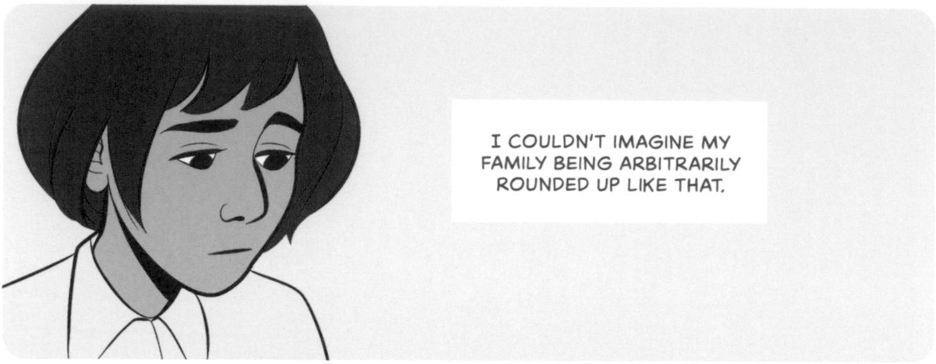
I COULDN'T IMAGINE MY FAMILY BEING ARBITRARILY ROUNDED UP LIKE THAT.

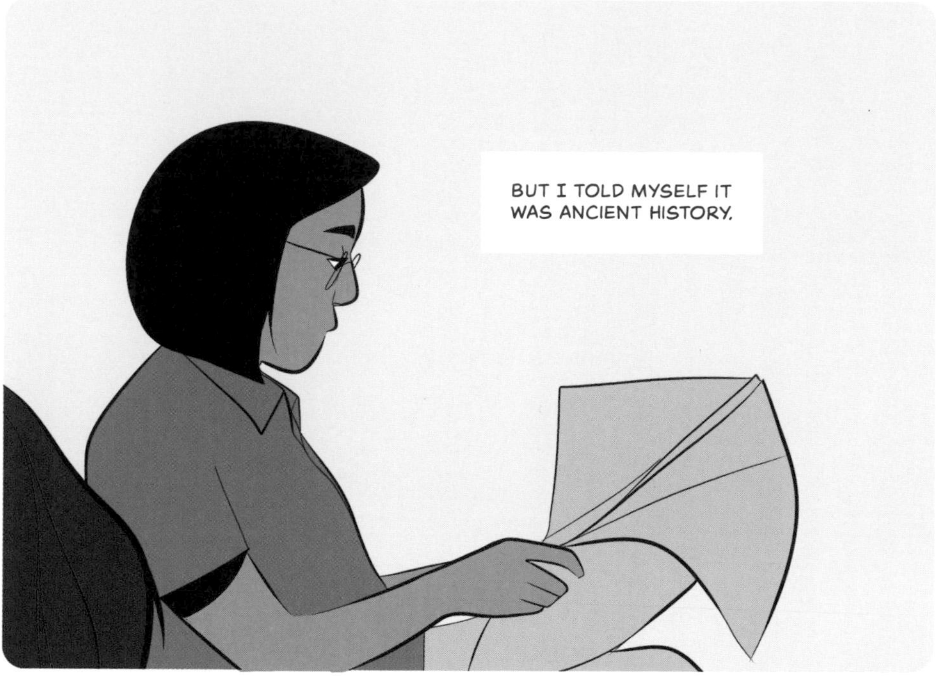
BUT I TOLD MYSELF IT WAS ANCIENT HISTORY.

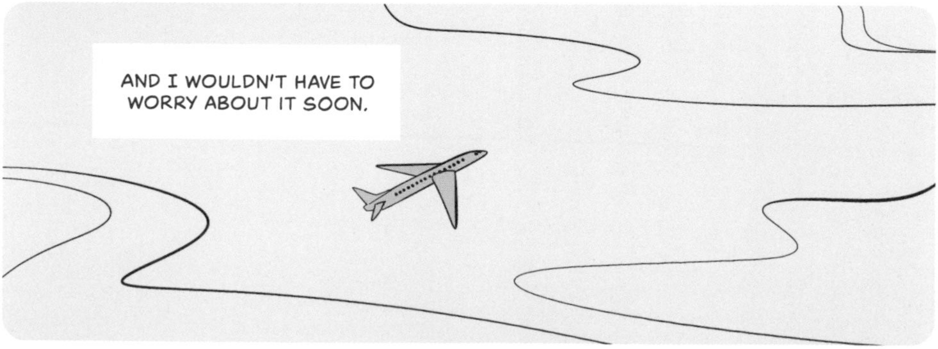
AND I WOULDN'T HAVE TO WORRY ABOUT IT SOON.

part II:
the wastes

3

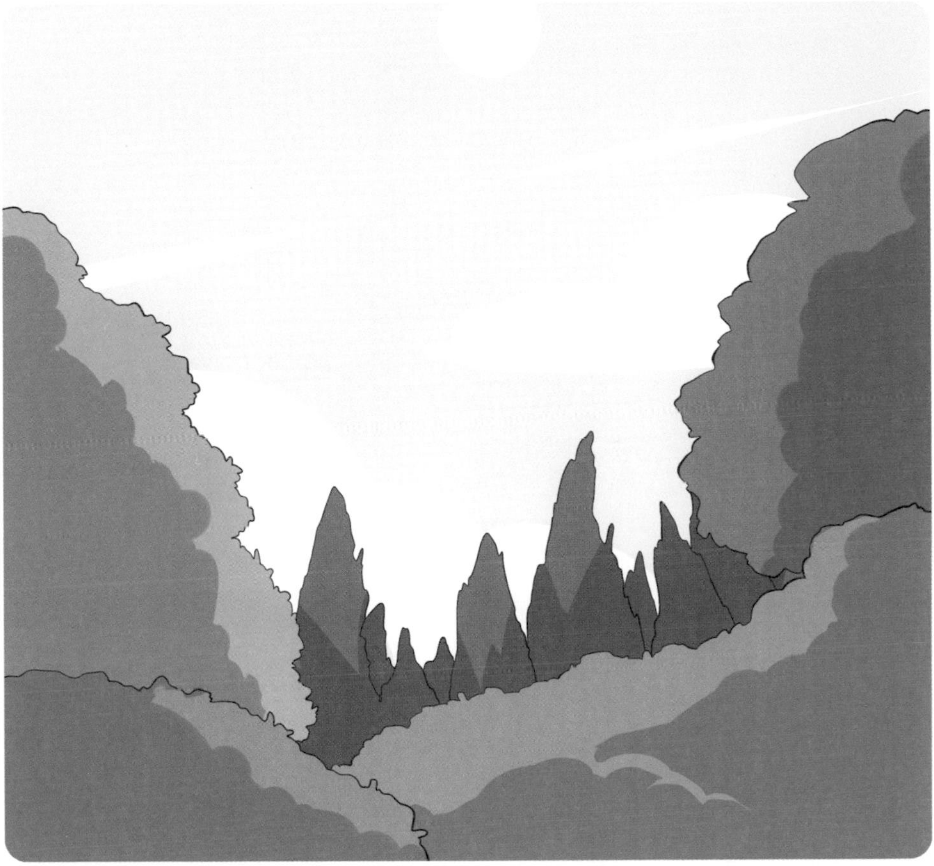

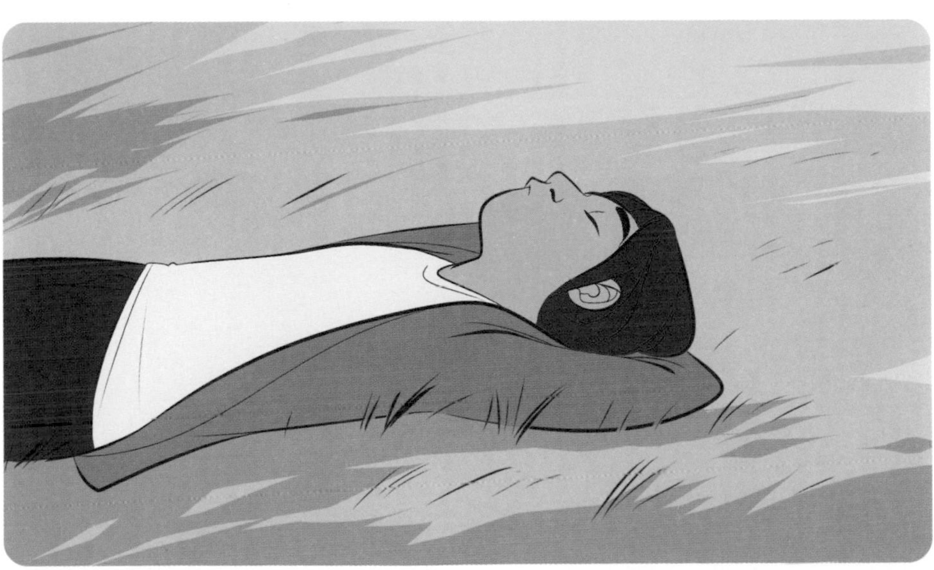

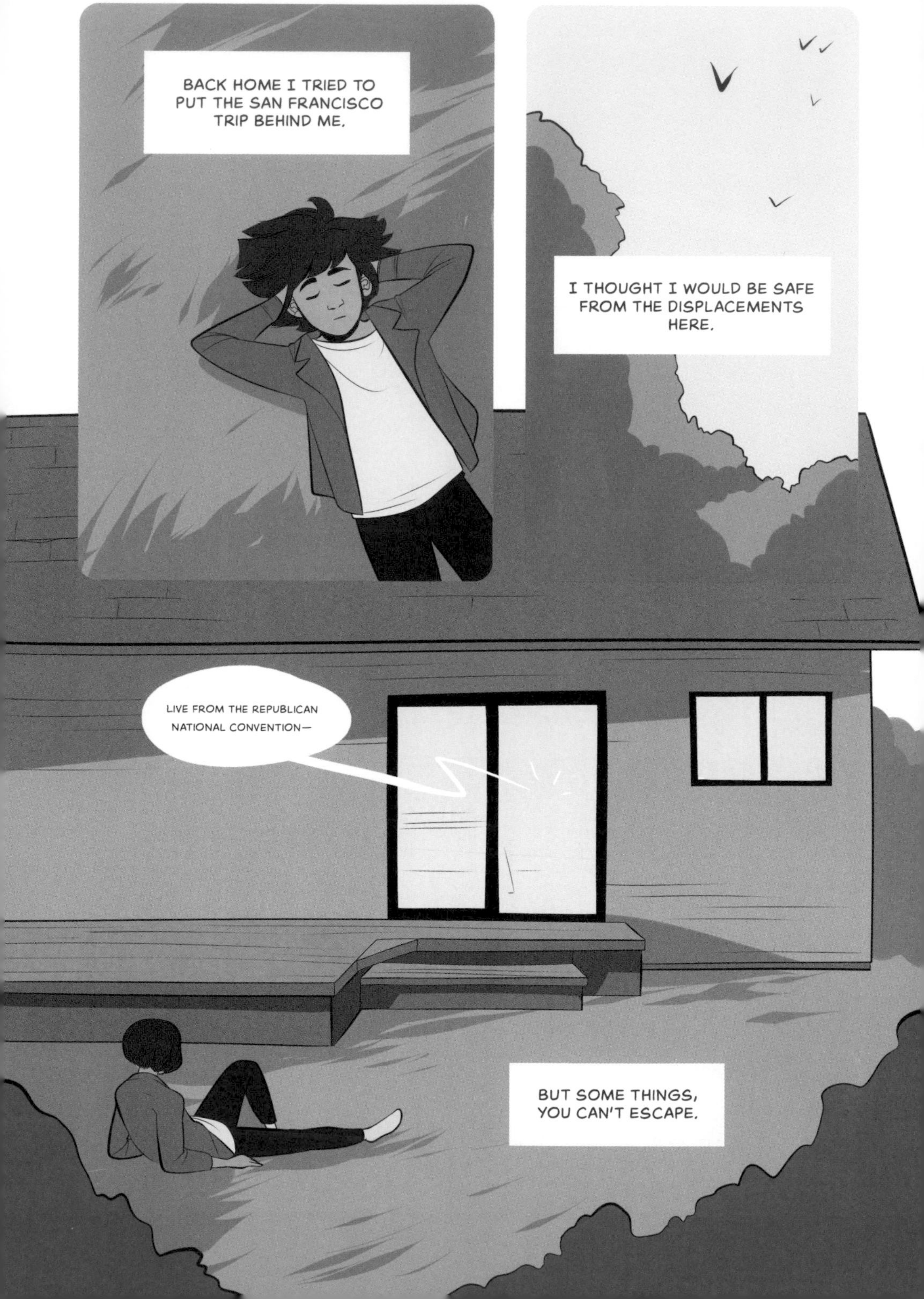
BACK HOME I TRIED TO PUT THE SAN FRANCISCO TRIP BEHIND ME.
I THOUGHT I WOULD BE SAFE FROM THE DISPLACEMENTS HERE.
LIVE FROM THE REPUBLICAN NATIONAL CONVENTION—
BUT SOME THINGS, YOU CAN'T ESCAPE.

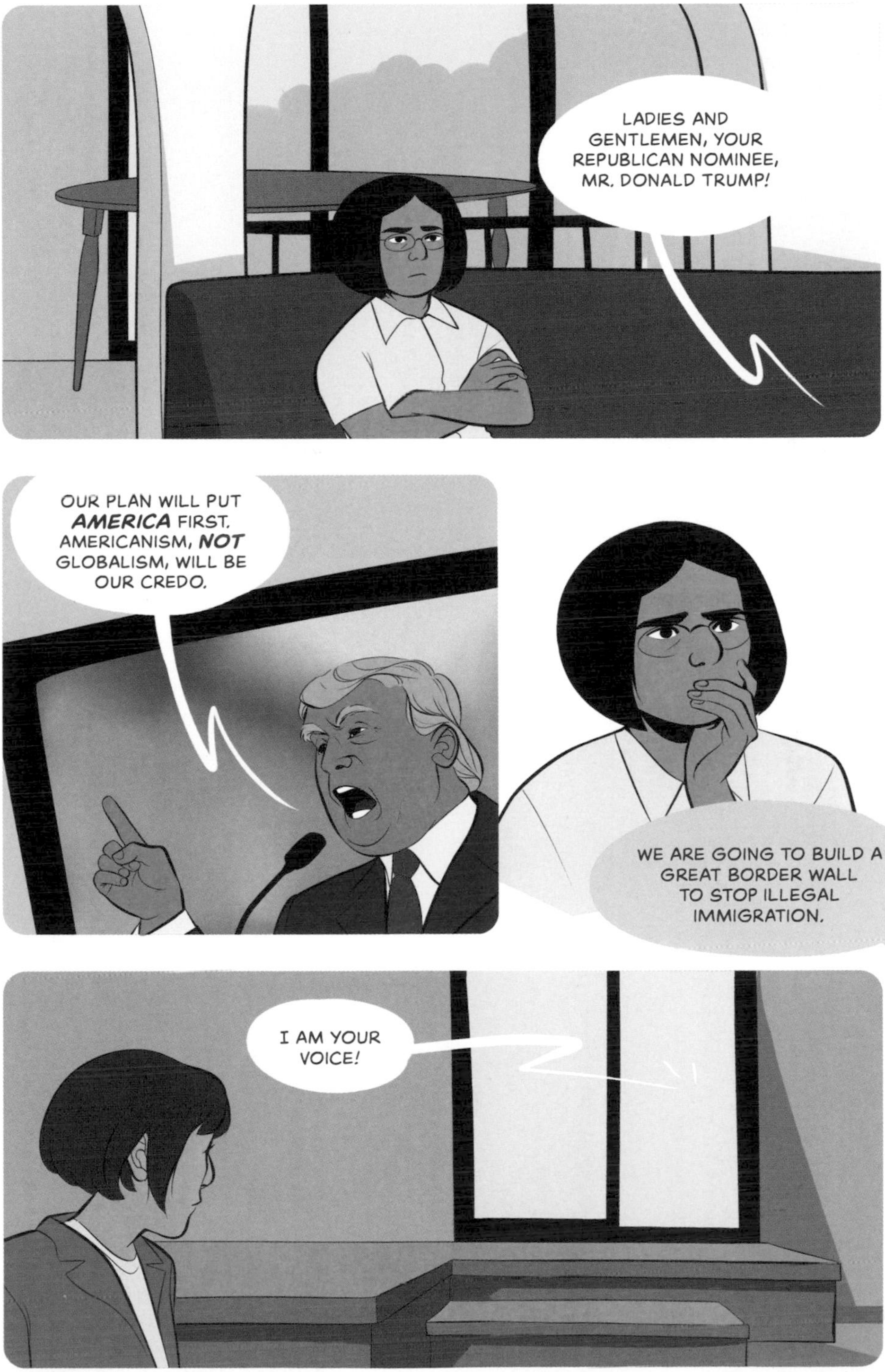
LADIES AND GENTLEMEN, YOUR REPUBLICAN NOMINEE, MR. DONALD TRUMP!
OUR PLAN WILL PUT ***AMERICA*** FIRST. AMERICANISM, ***NOT*** GLOBALISM, WILL BE OUR CREDO.
WE ARE GOING TO BUILD A GREAT BORDER WALL TO STOP ILLEGAL IMMIGRATION.
I AM YOUR VOICE!

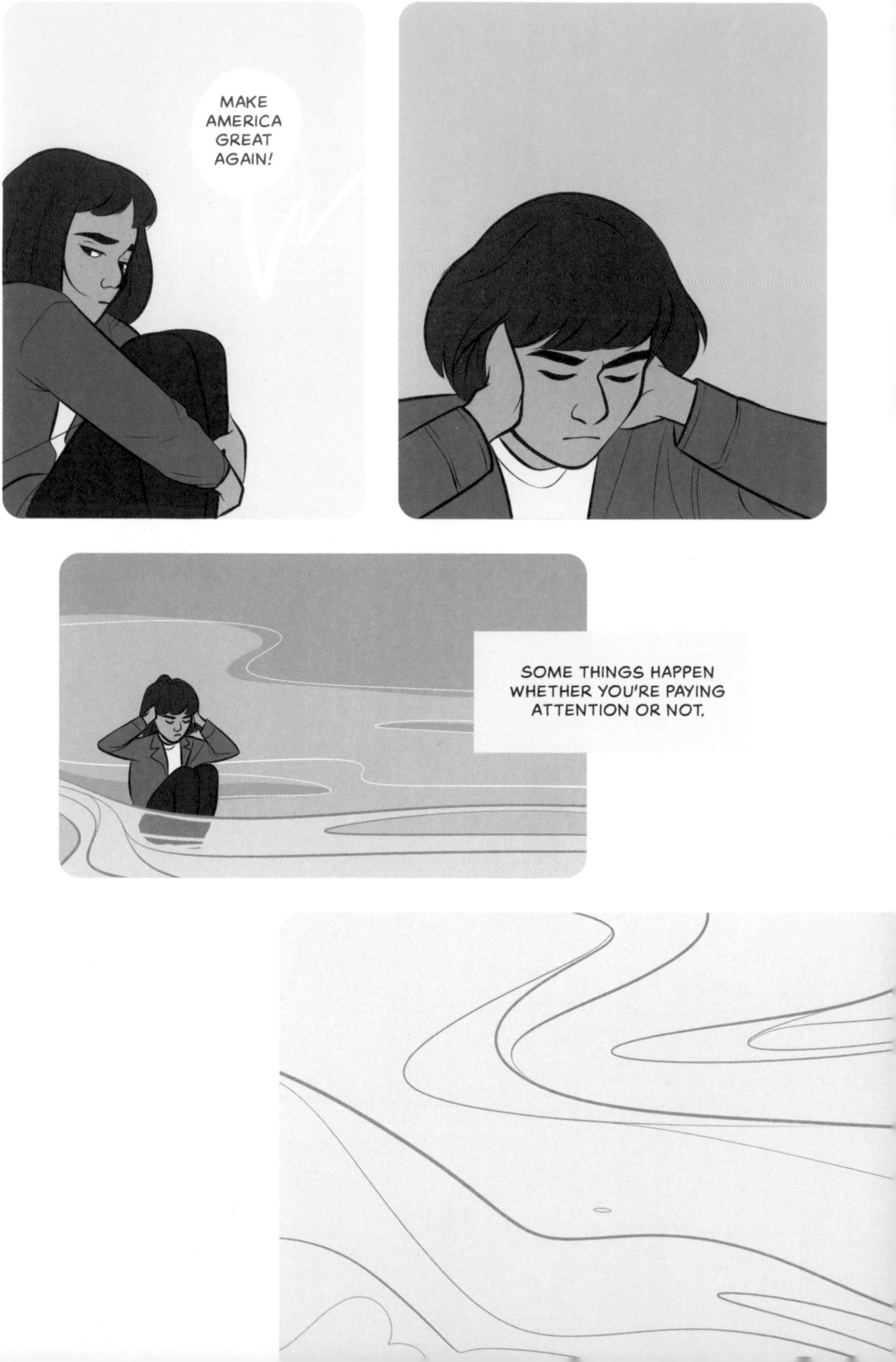
MAKE AMERICA GREAT AGAIN!
SOME THINGS HAPPEN WHETHER YOU'RE PAYING ATTENTION OR NOT.

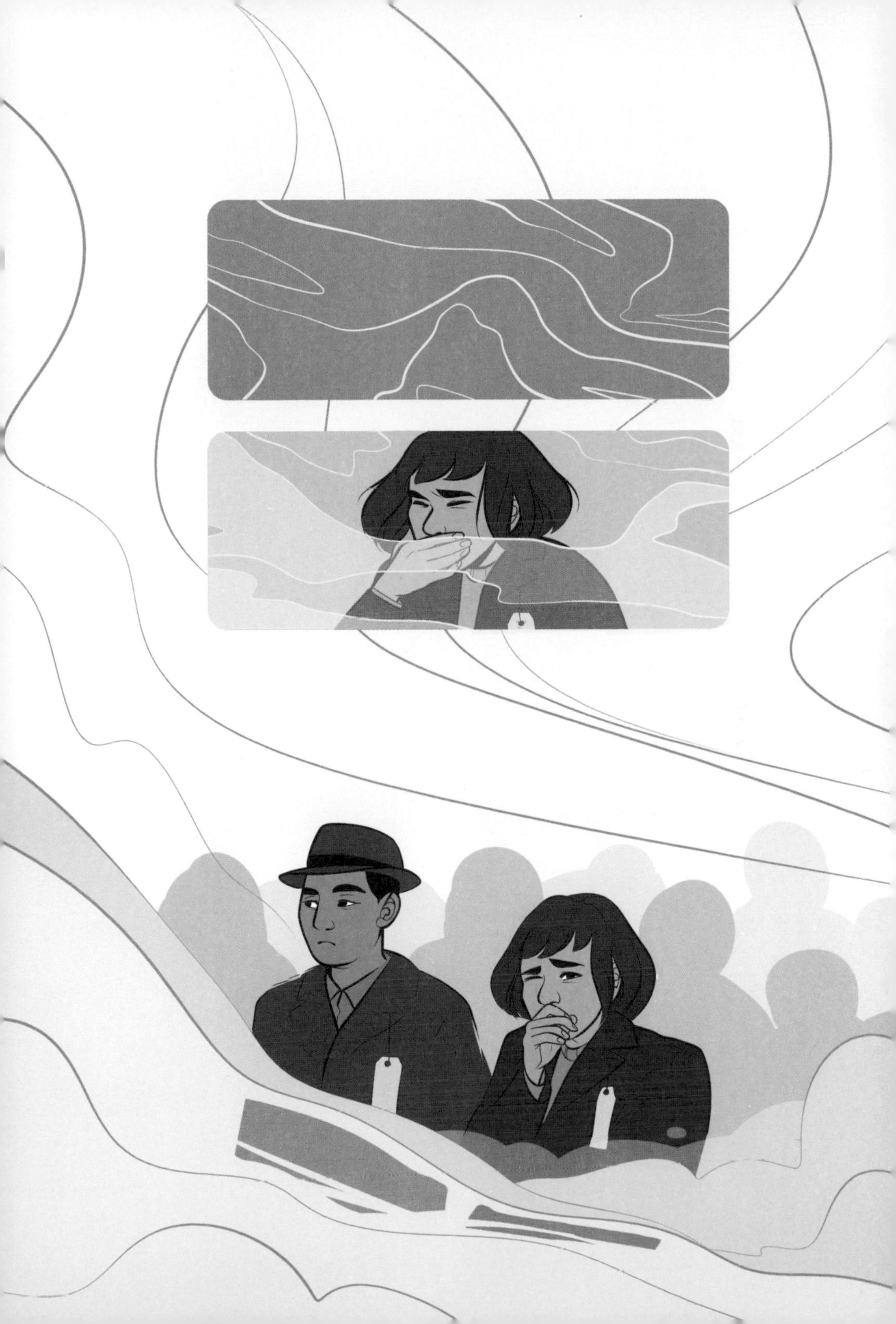

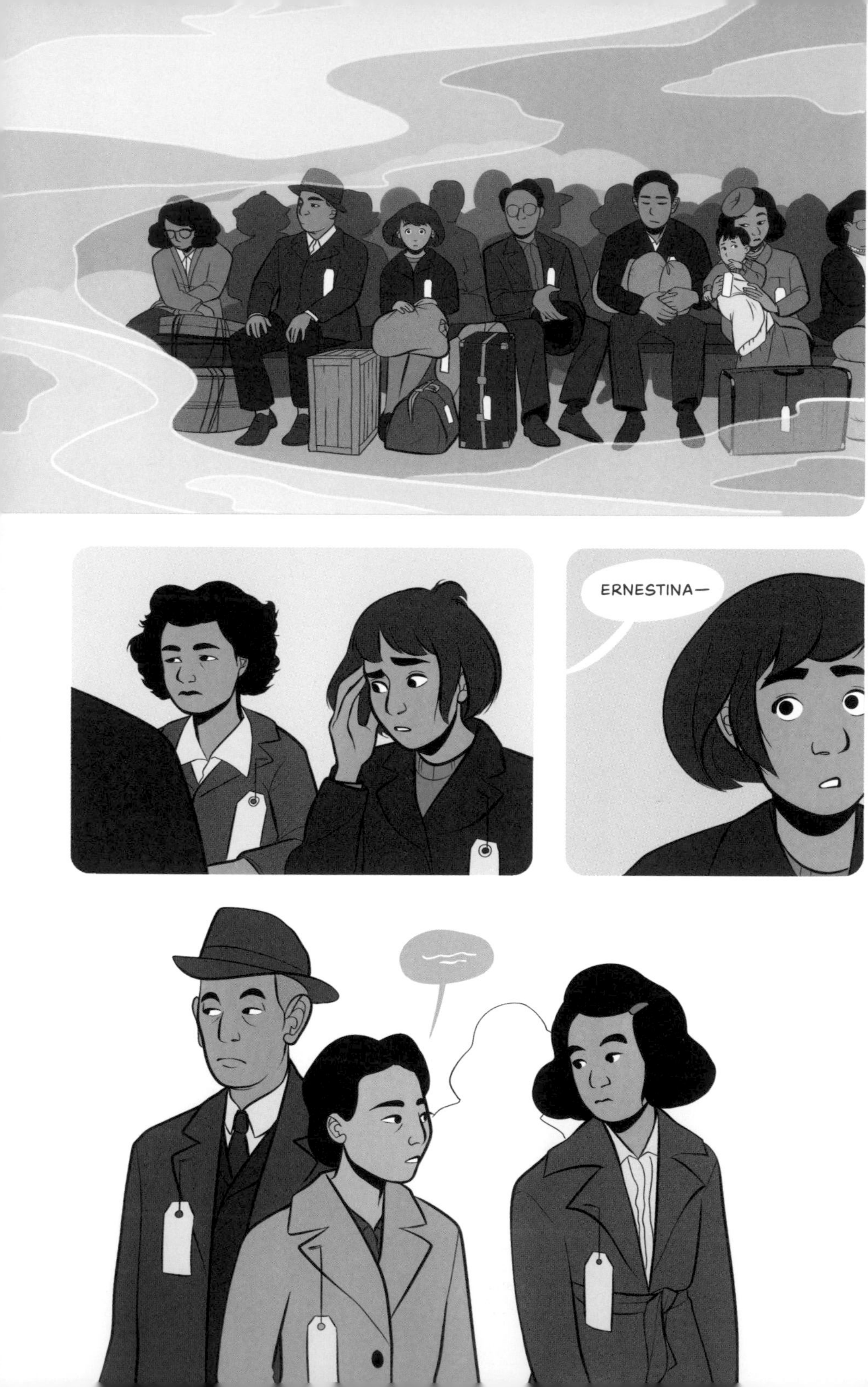
ERNESTINA—

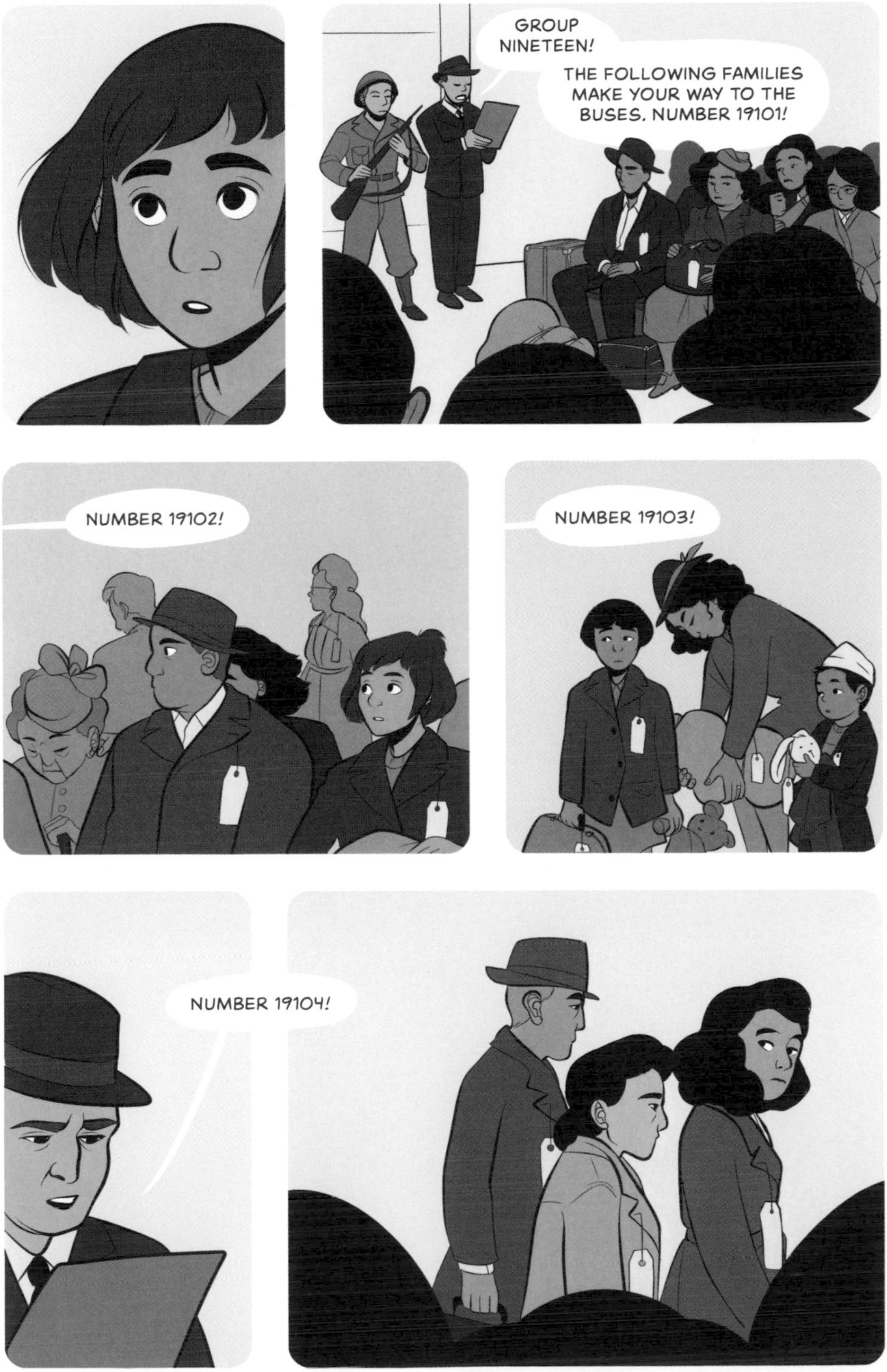
GROUP NINETEEN!
THE FOLLOWING FAMILIES MAKE YOUR WAY TO THE BUSES. NUMBER 19101!
NUMBER 19102!
NUMBER 19103!
NUMBER 19104!

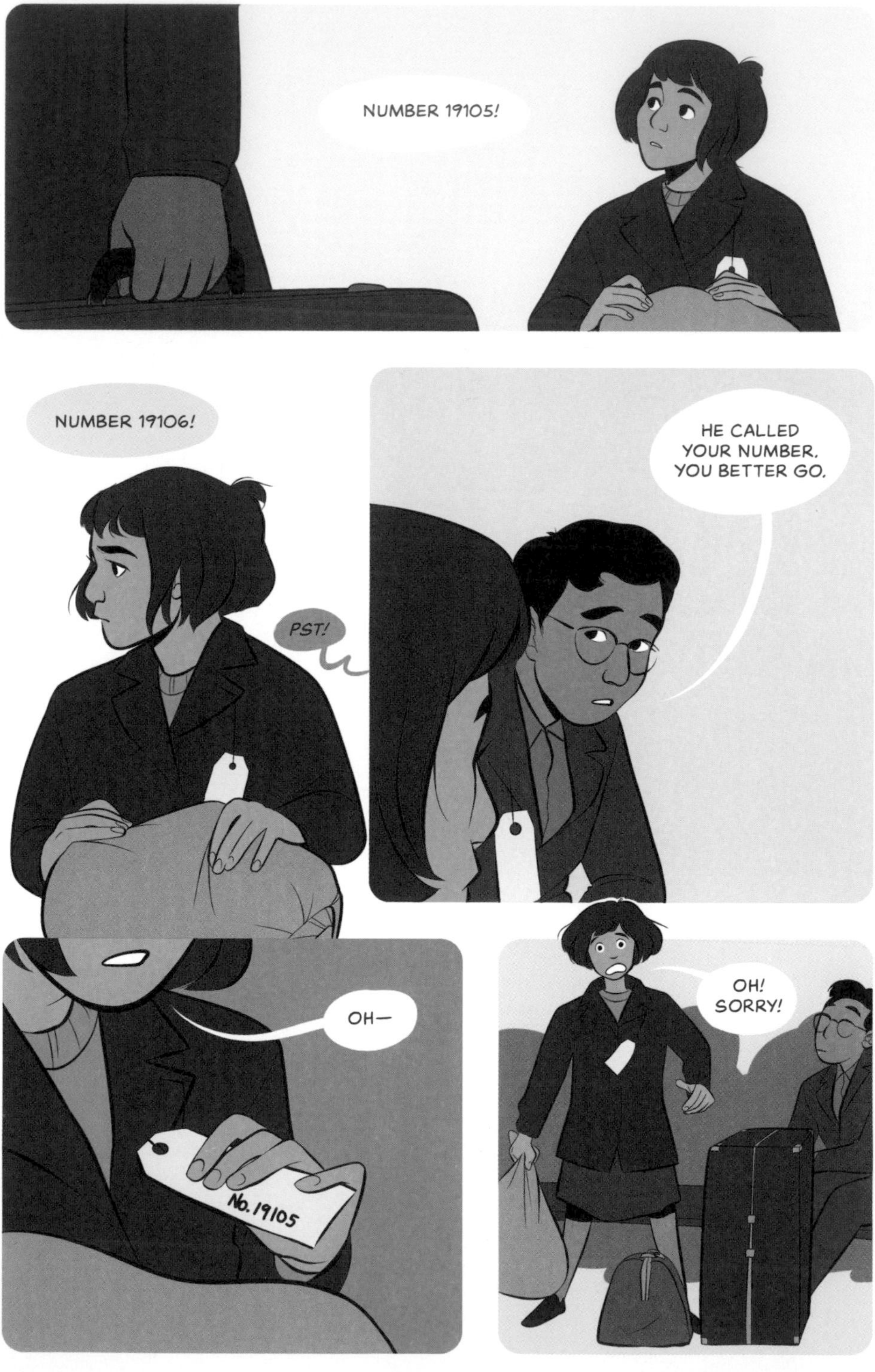
NUMBER 19105!
NUMBER 19106!
PST!
HE CALLED YOUR NUMBER. YOU BETTER GO.
OH—
No. 19105
OH! SORRY!

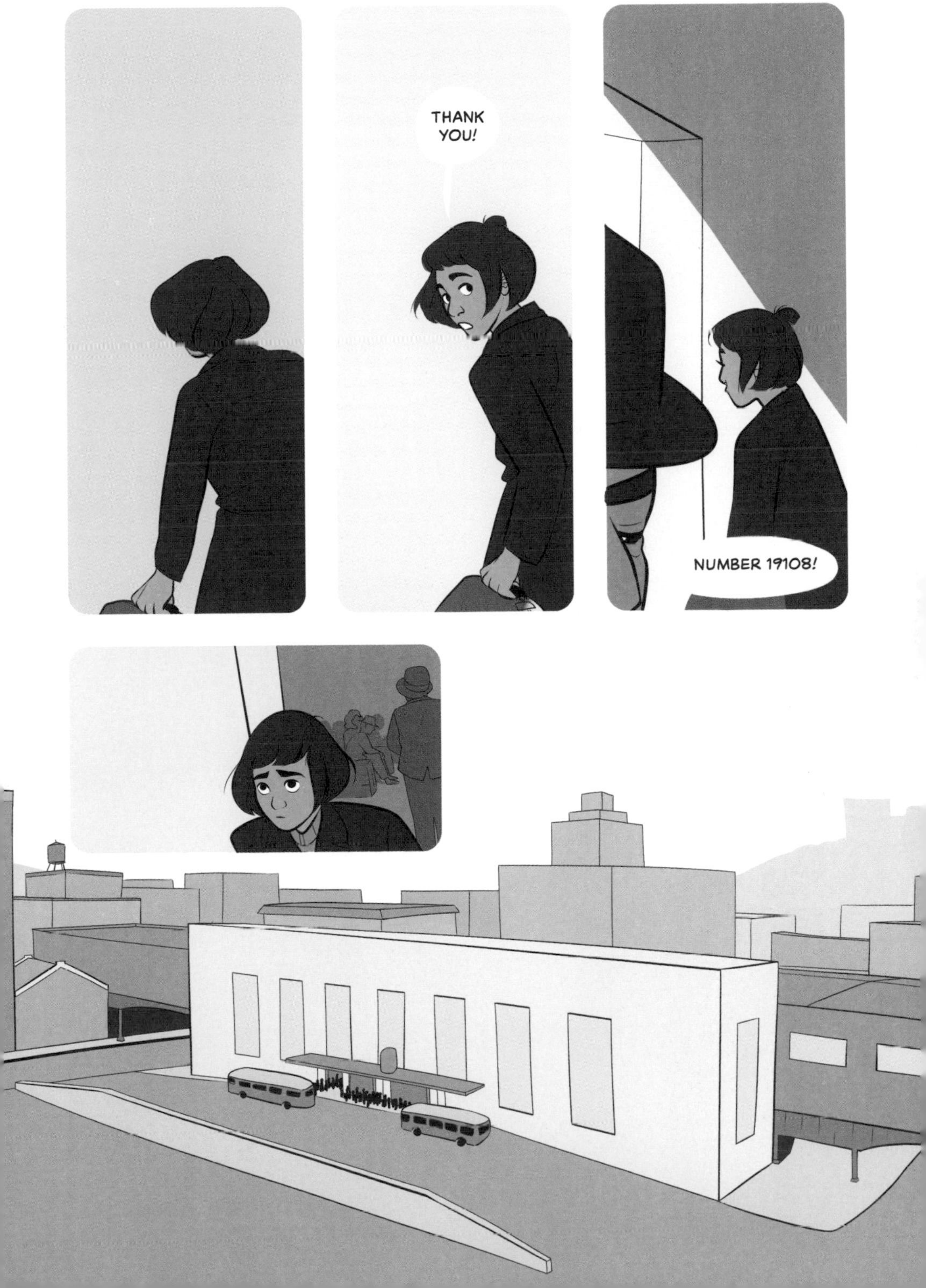
THANK YOU!
NUMBER 19108!

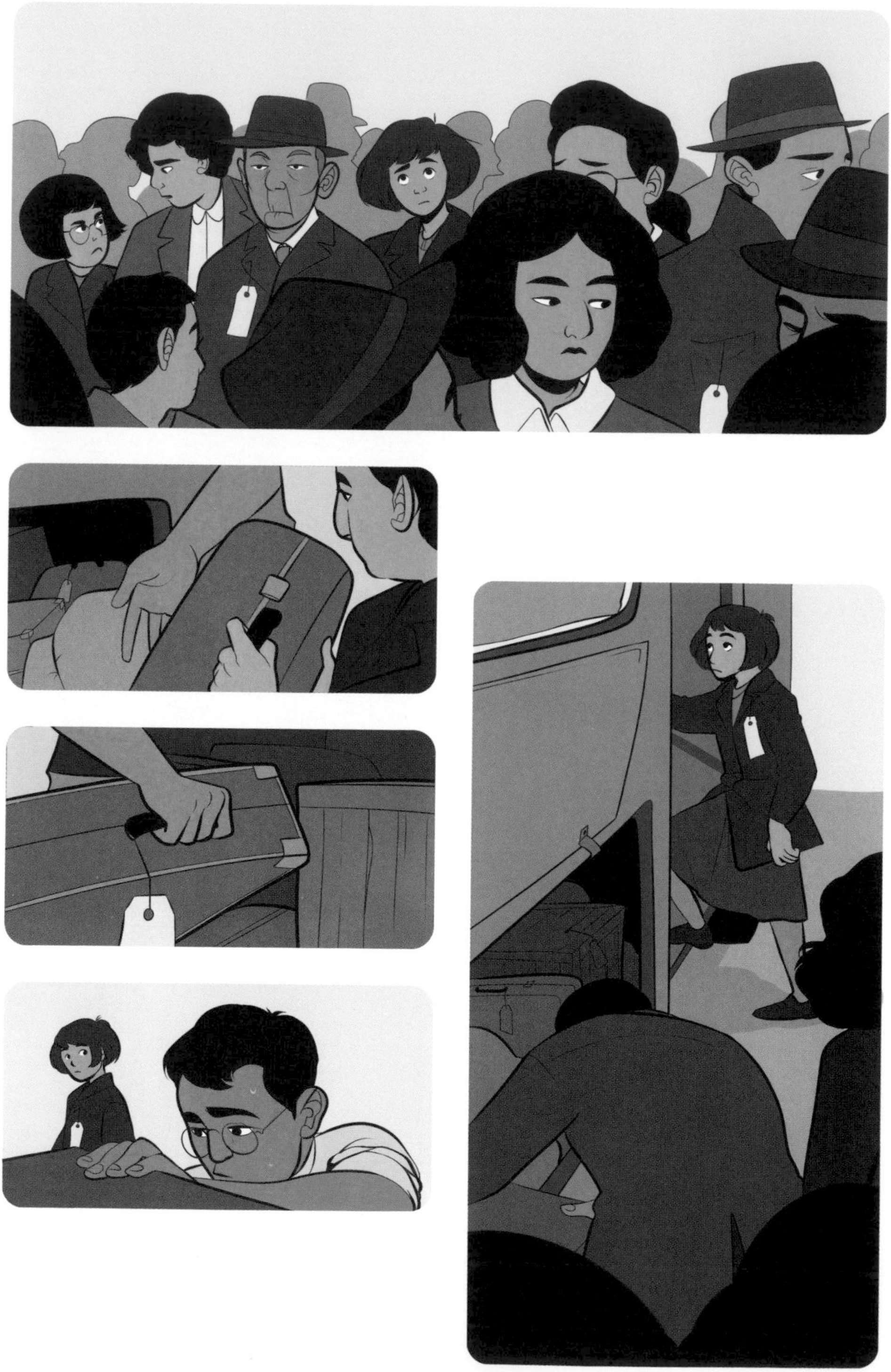

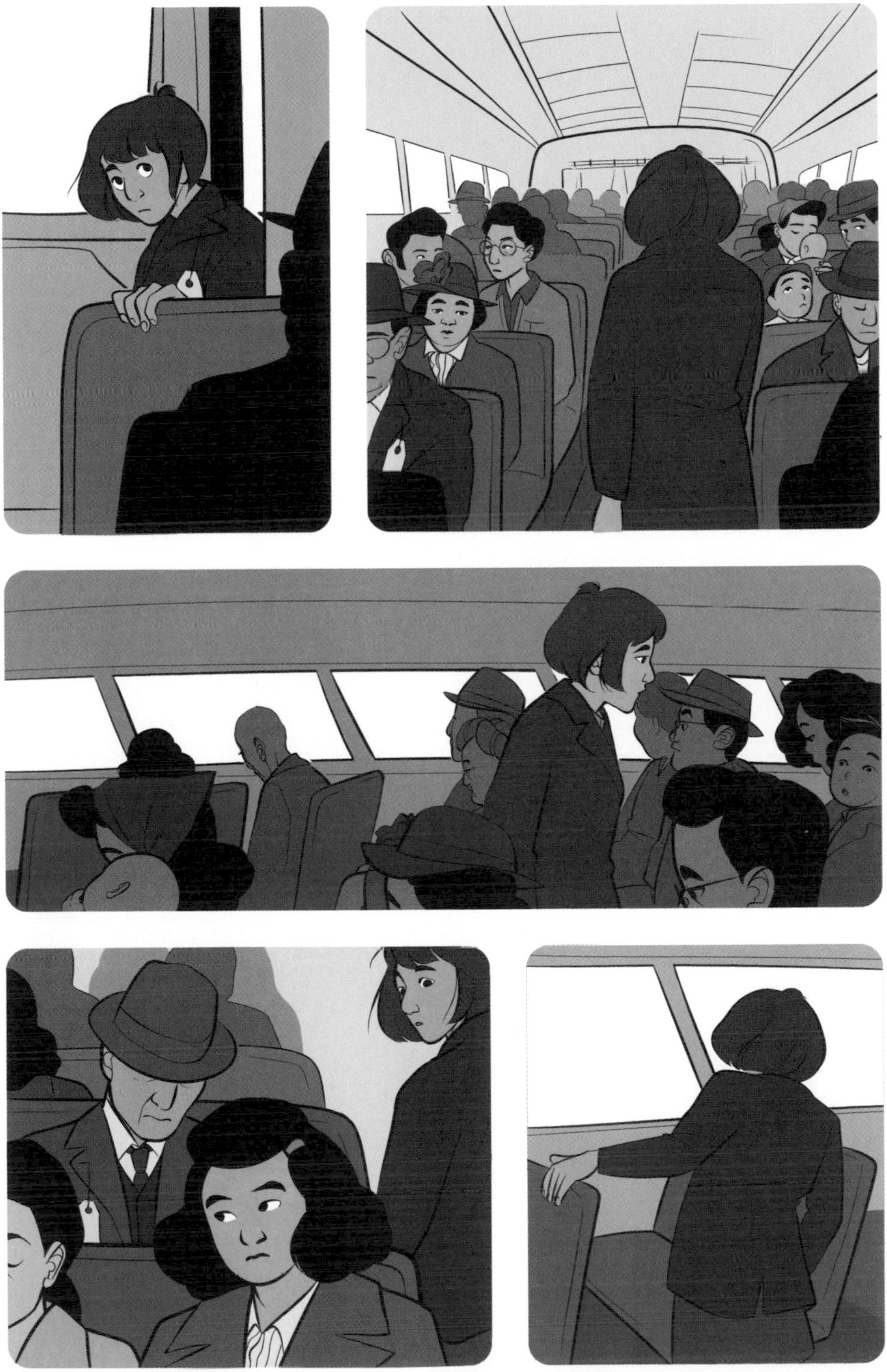

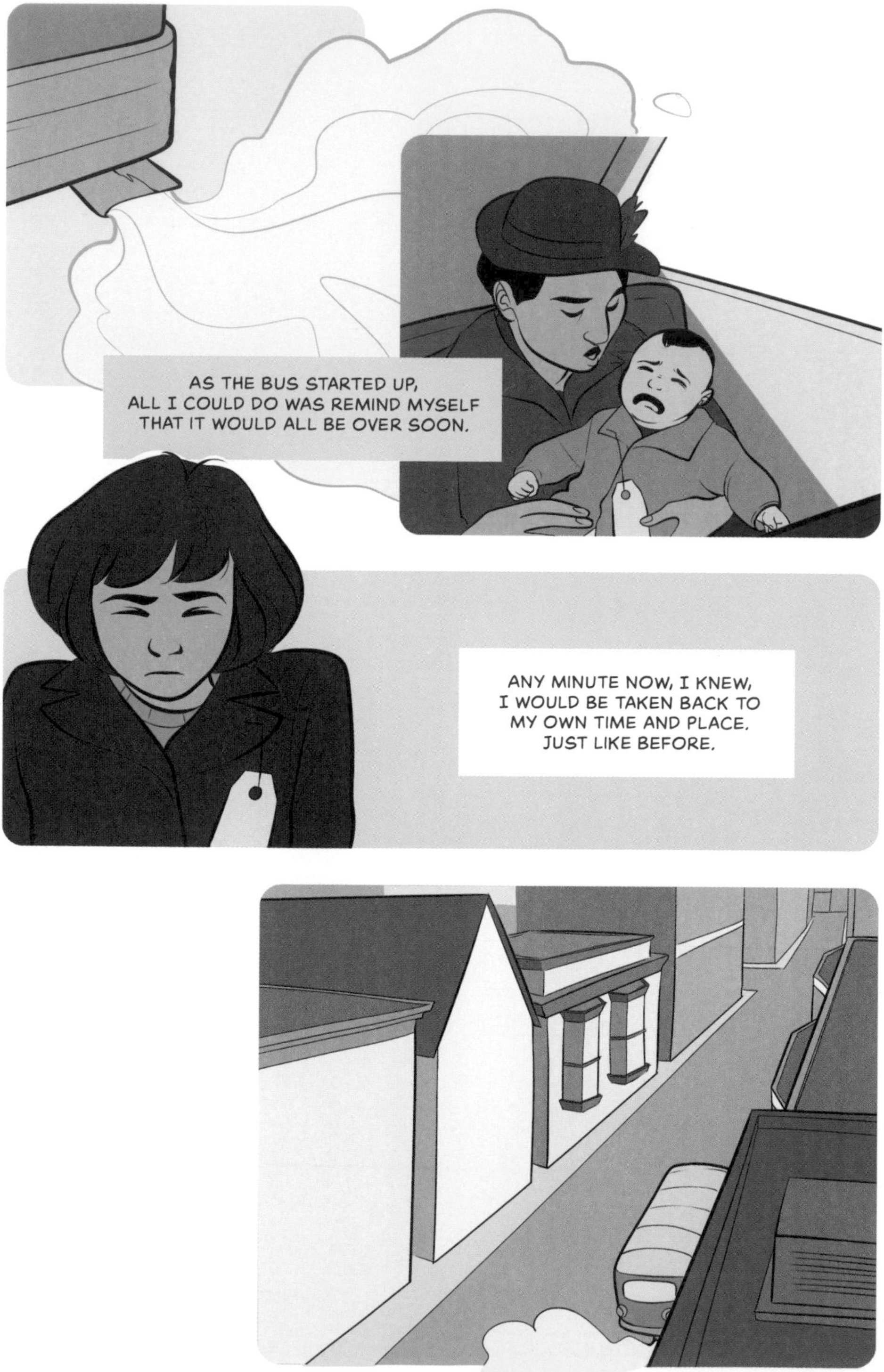
AS THE BUS STARTED UP,
ALL I COULD DO WAS REMIND MYSELF
THAT IT WOULD ALL BE OVER SOON.
ANY MINUTE NOW, I KNEW,
I WOULD BE TAKEN BACK TO
MY OWN TIME AND PLACE.
JUST LIKE BEFORE.

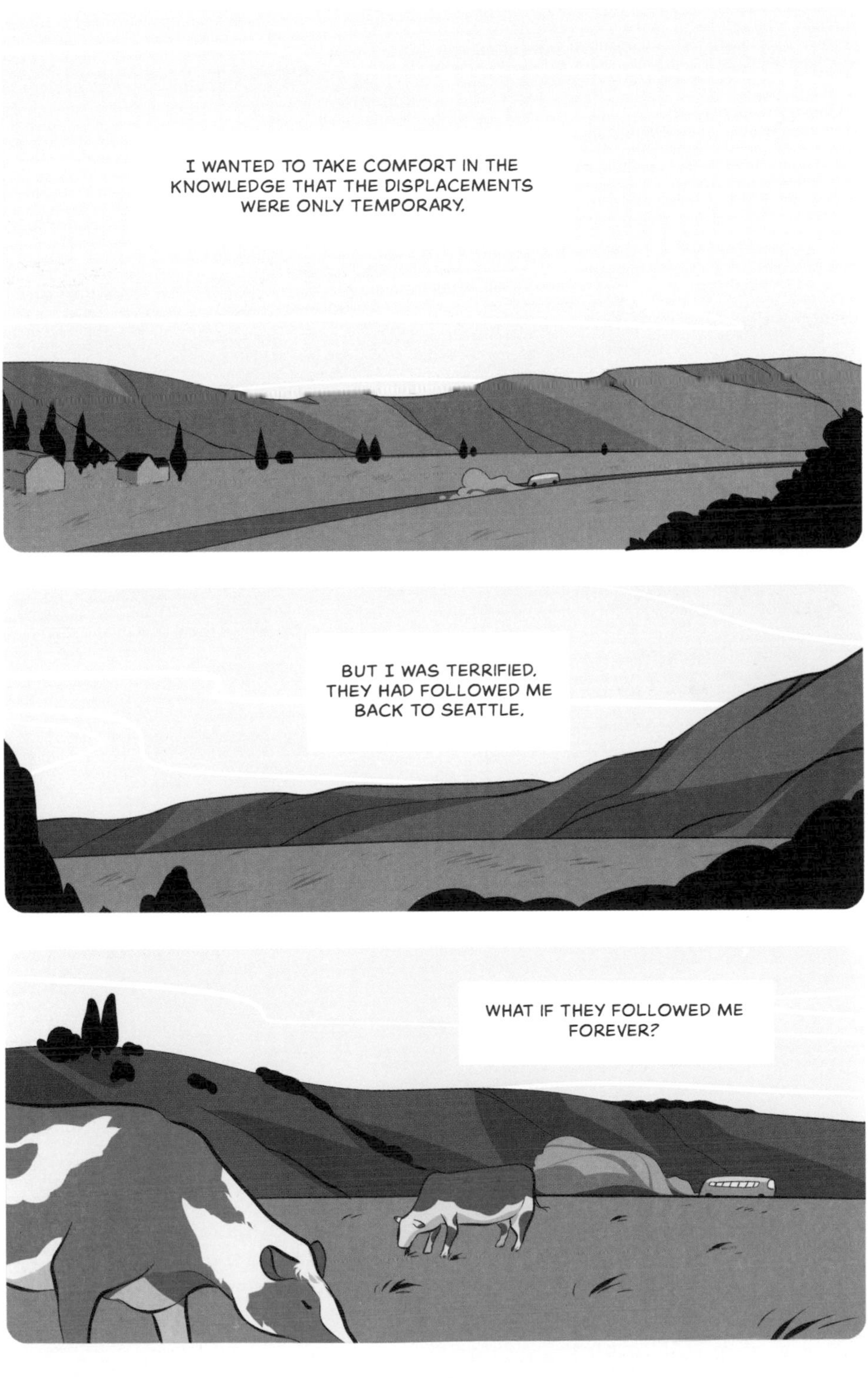
I WANTED TO TAKE COMFORT IN THE KNOWLEDGE THAT THE DISPLACEMENTS WERE ONLY TEMPORARY.
BUT I WAS TERRIFIED. THEY HAD FOLLOWED ME BACK TO SEATTLE.
WHAT IF THEY FOLLOWED ME FOREVER?

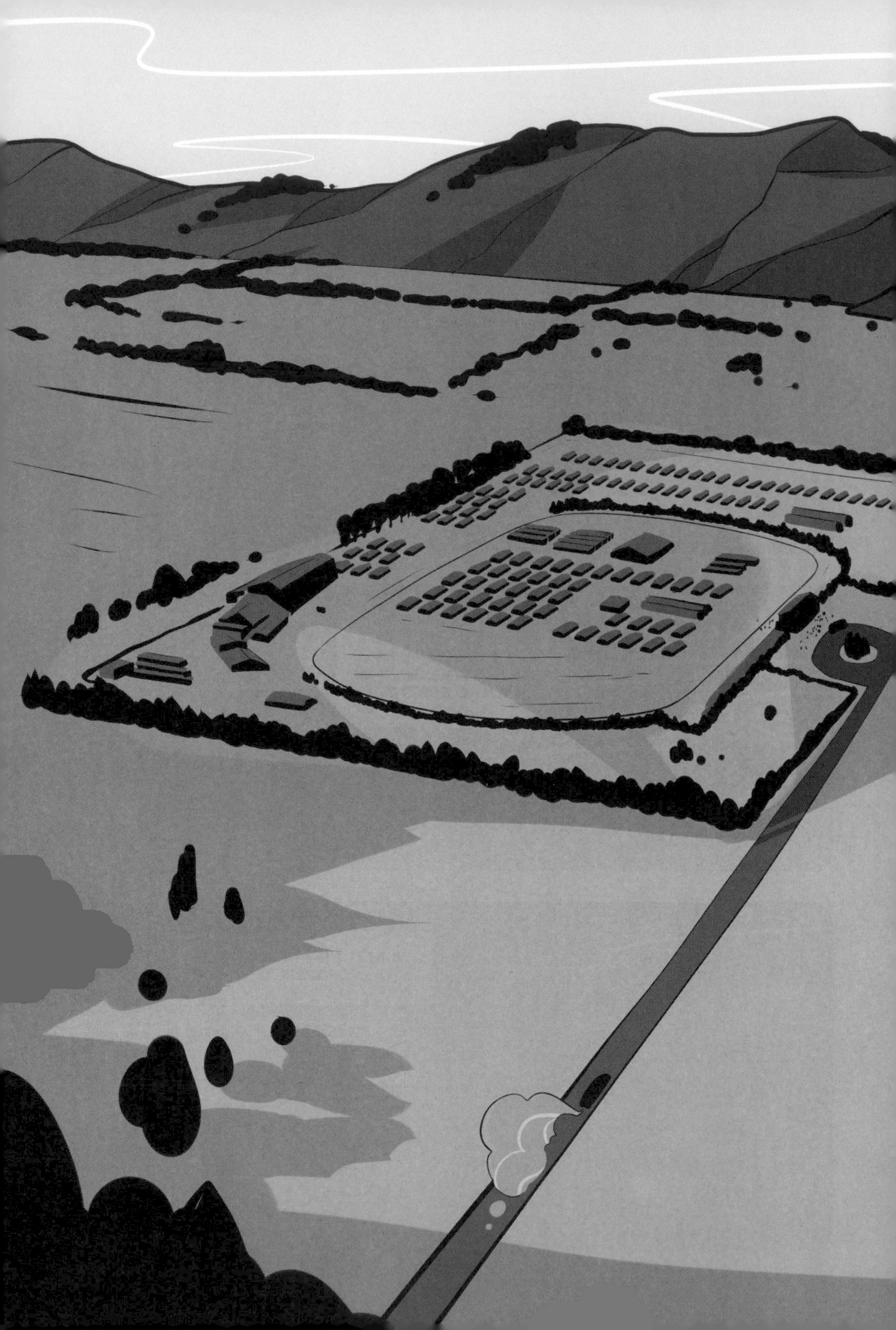

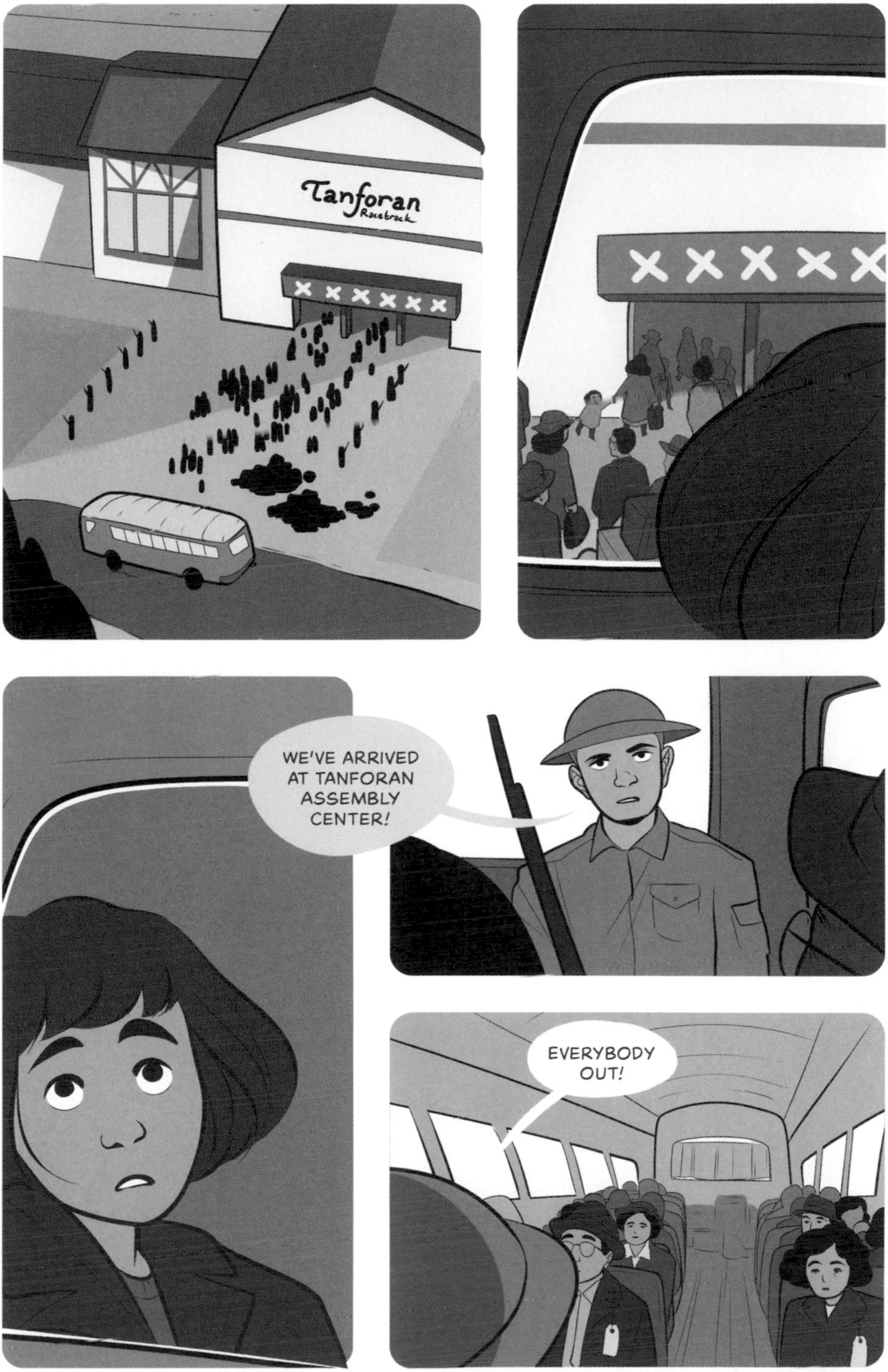
Tanforan
Racetrack
WE'VE ARRIVED AT TANFORAN ASSEMBLY CENTER!
EVERYBODY OUT!

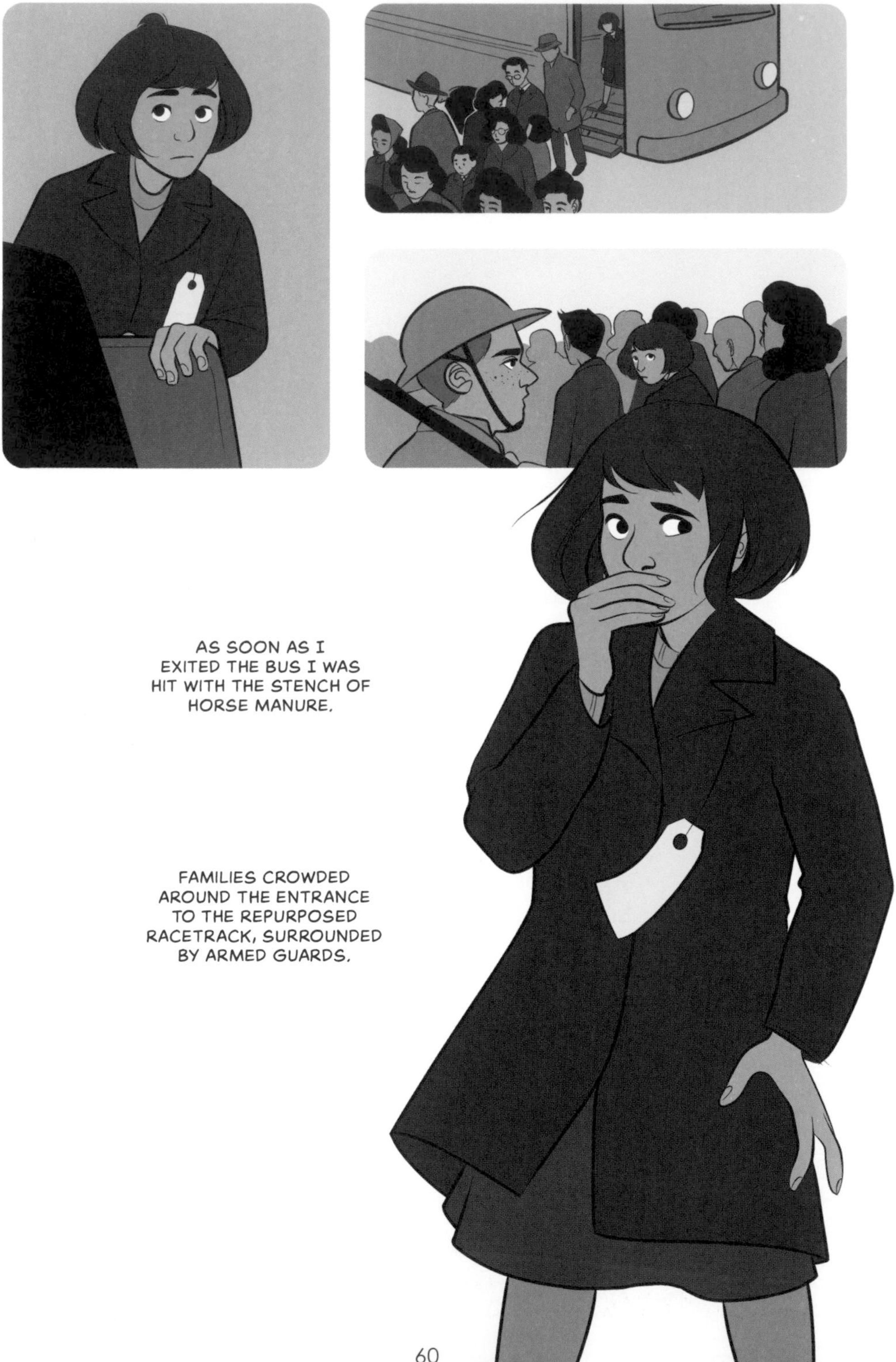
AS SOON AS I EXITED THE BUS I WAS HIT WITH THE STENCH OF HORSE MANURE.
FAMILIES CROWDED AROUND THE ENTRANCE TO THE REPURPOSED RACETRACK, SURROUNDED BY ARMED GUARDS.

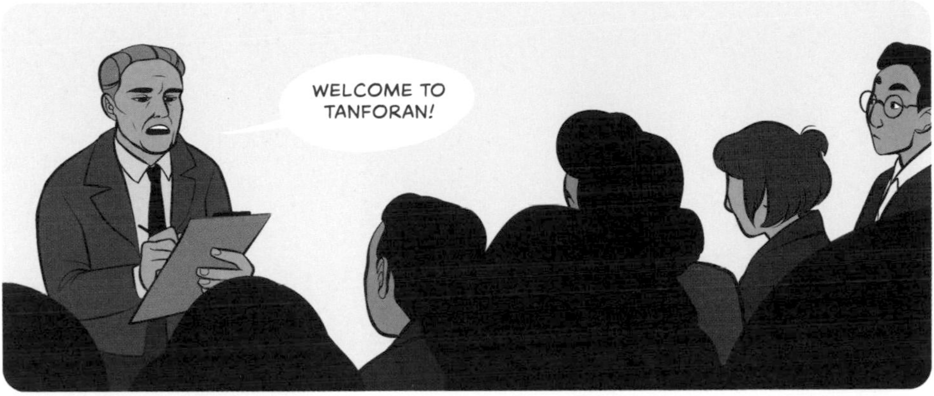
WELCOME TO
TANFORAN!

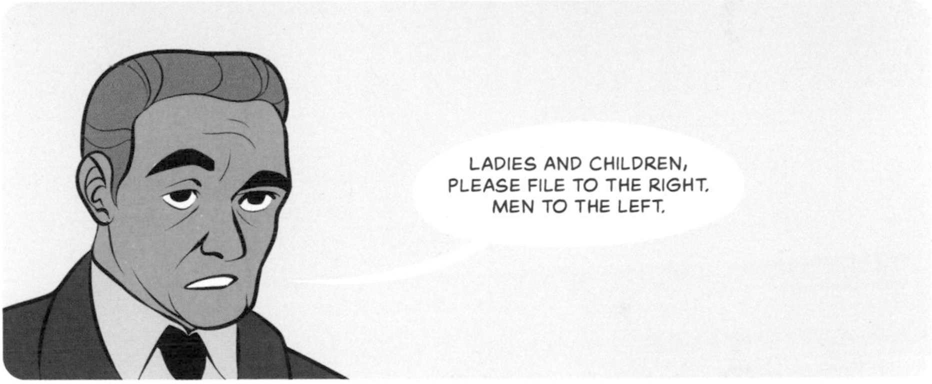
LADIES AND CHILDREN,
PLEASE FILE TO THE RIGHT.
MEN TO THE LEFT.

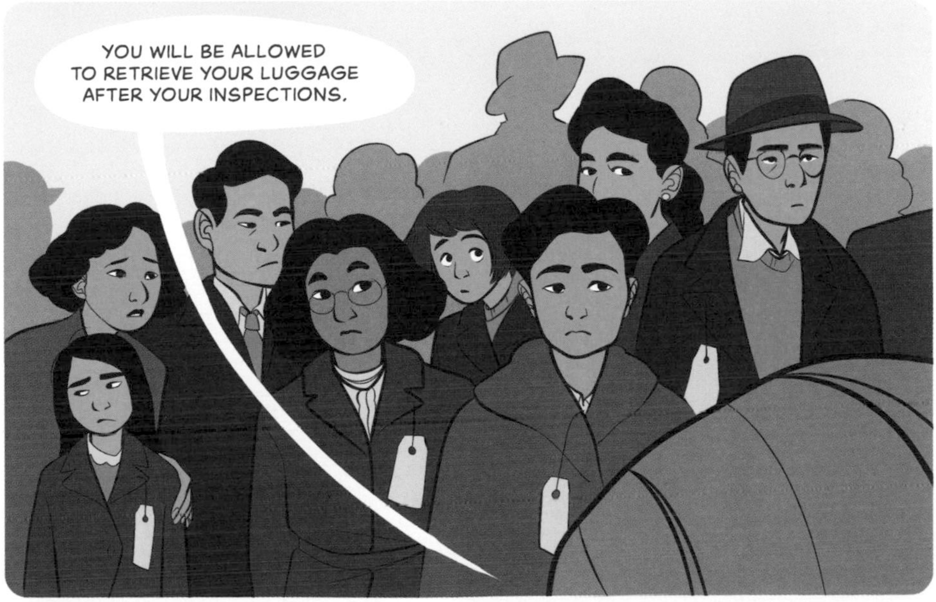
YOU WILL BE ALLOWED
TO RETRIEVE YOUR LUGGAGE
AFTER YOUR INSPECTIONS.

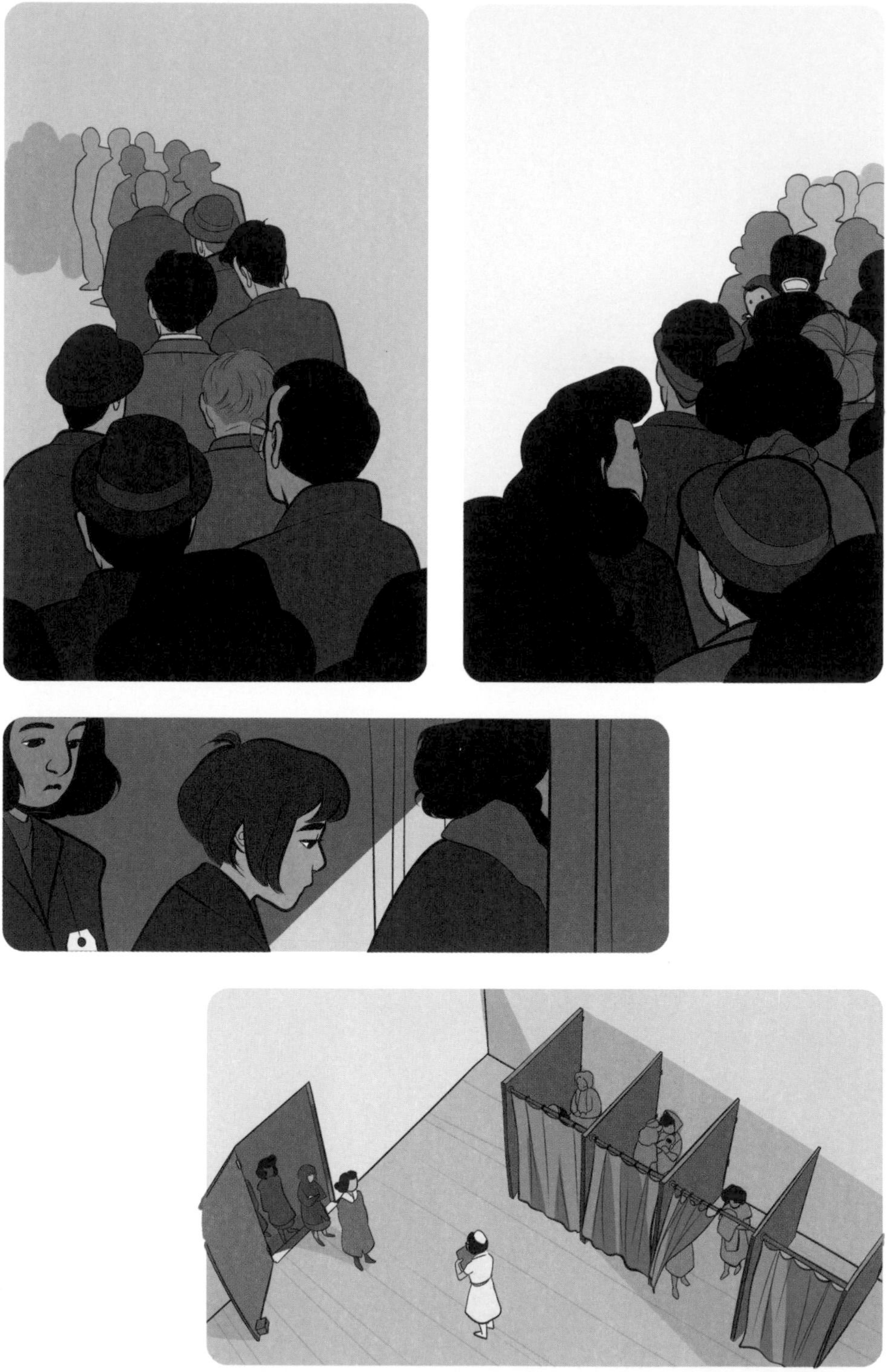

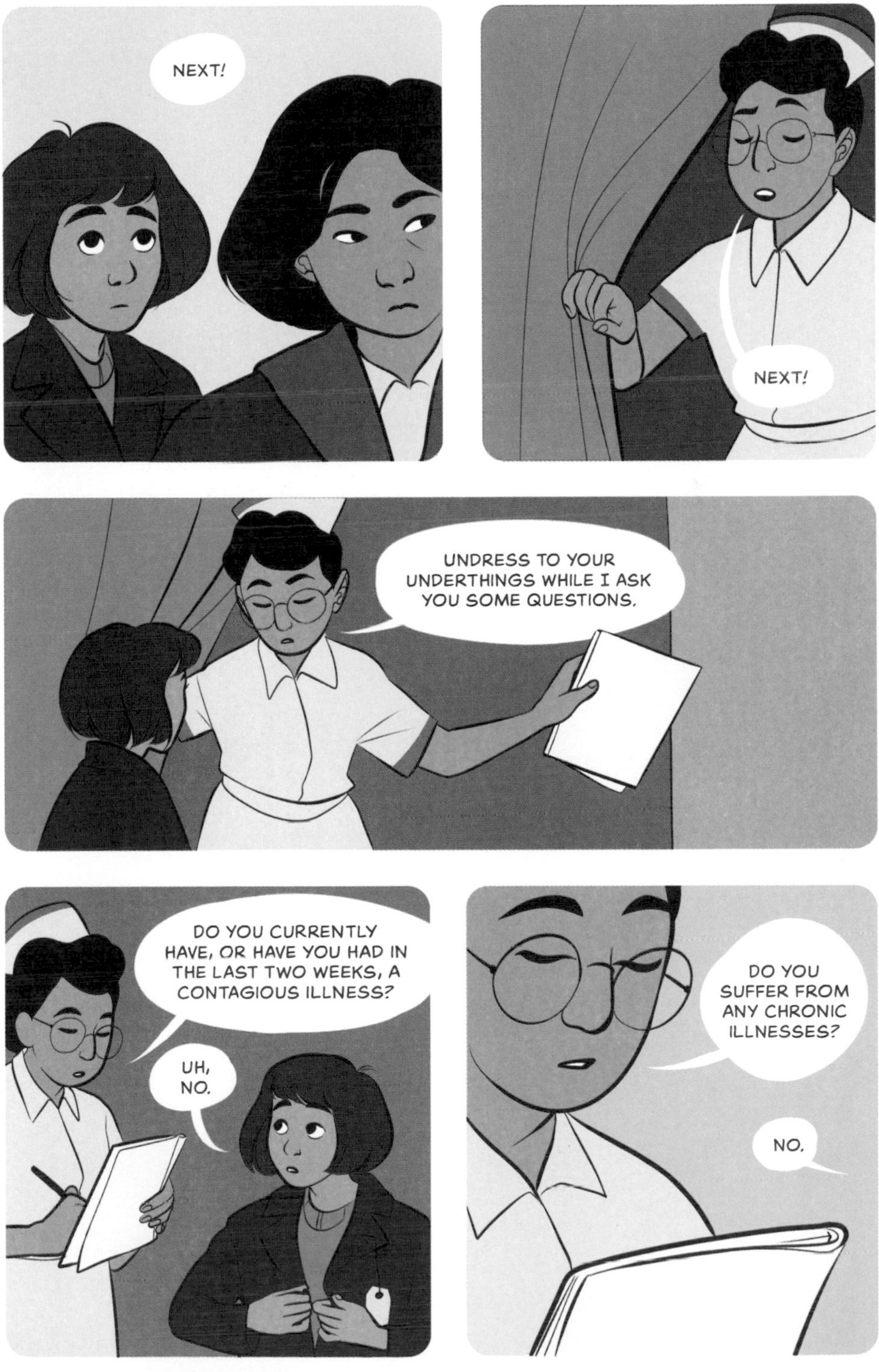
NEXT!
NEXT!
UNDRESS TO YOUR UNDERTHINGS WHILE I ASK YOU SOME QUESTIONS.
DO YOU CURRENTLY HAVE, OR HAVE YOU HAD IN THE LAST TWO WEEKS, A CONTAGIOUS ILLNESS?
UH, NO.
DO YOU SUFFER FROM ANY CHRONIC ILLNESSES?
NO.

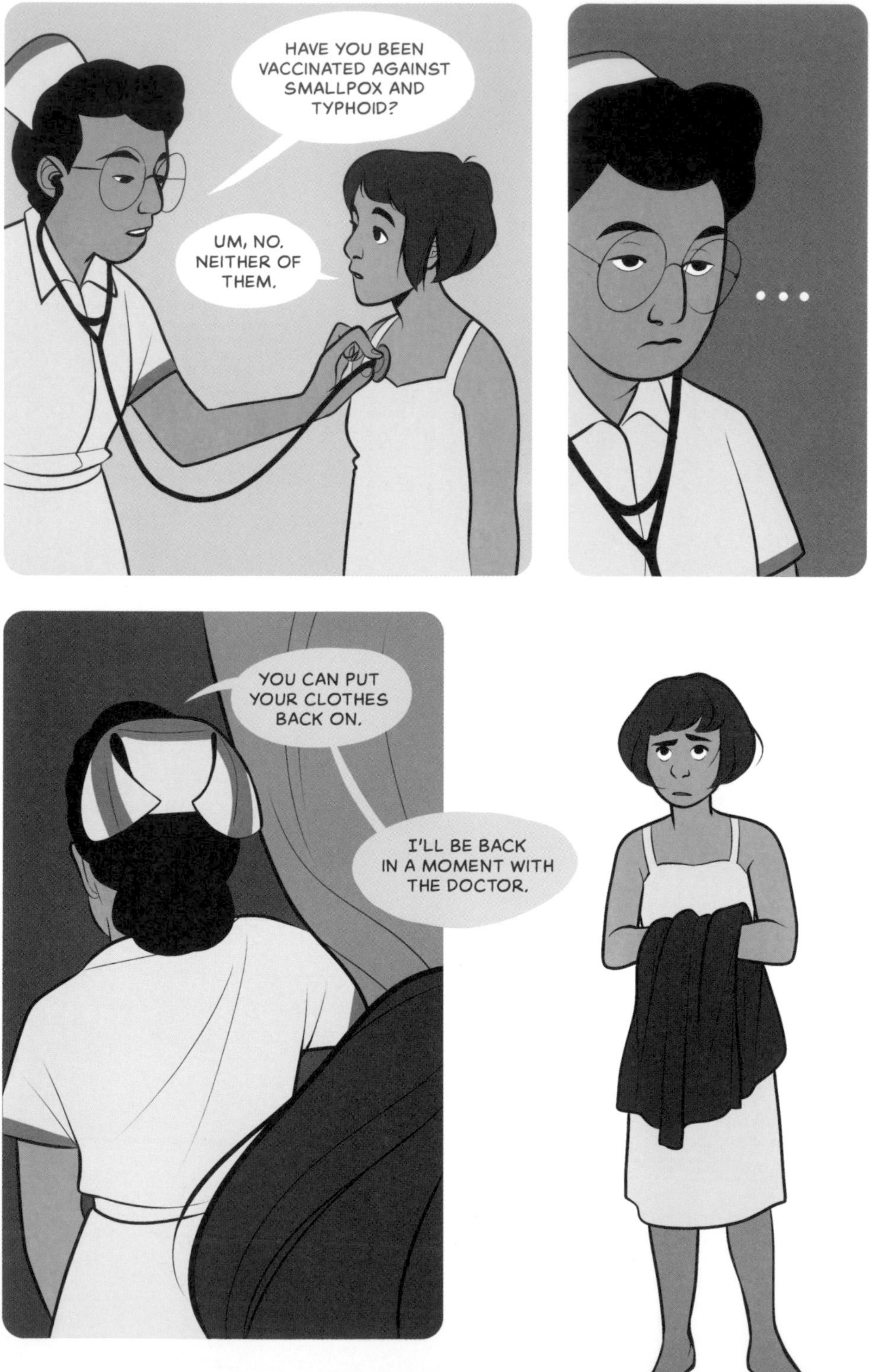
HAVE YOU BEEN VACCINATED AGAINST SMALLPOX AND TYPHOID?
UM, NO. NEITHER OF THEM.
...
YOU CAN PUT YOUR CLOTHES BACK ON.
I'LL BE BACK IN A MOMENT WITH THE DOCTOR.

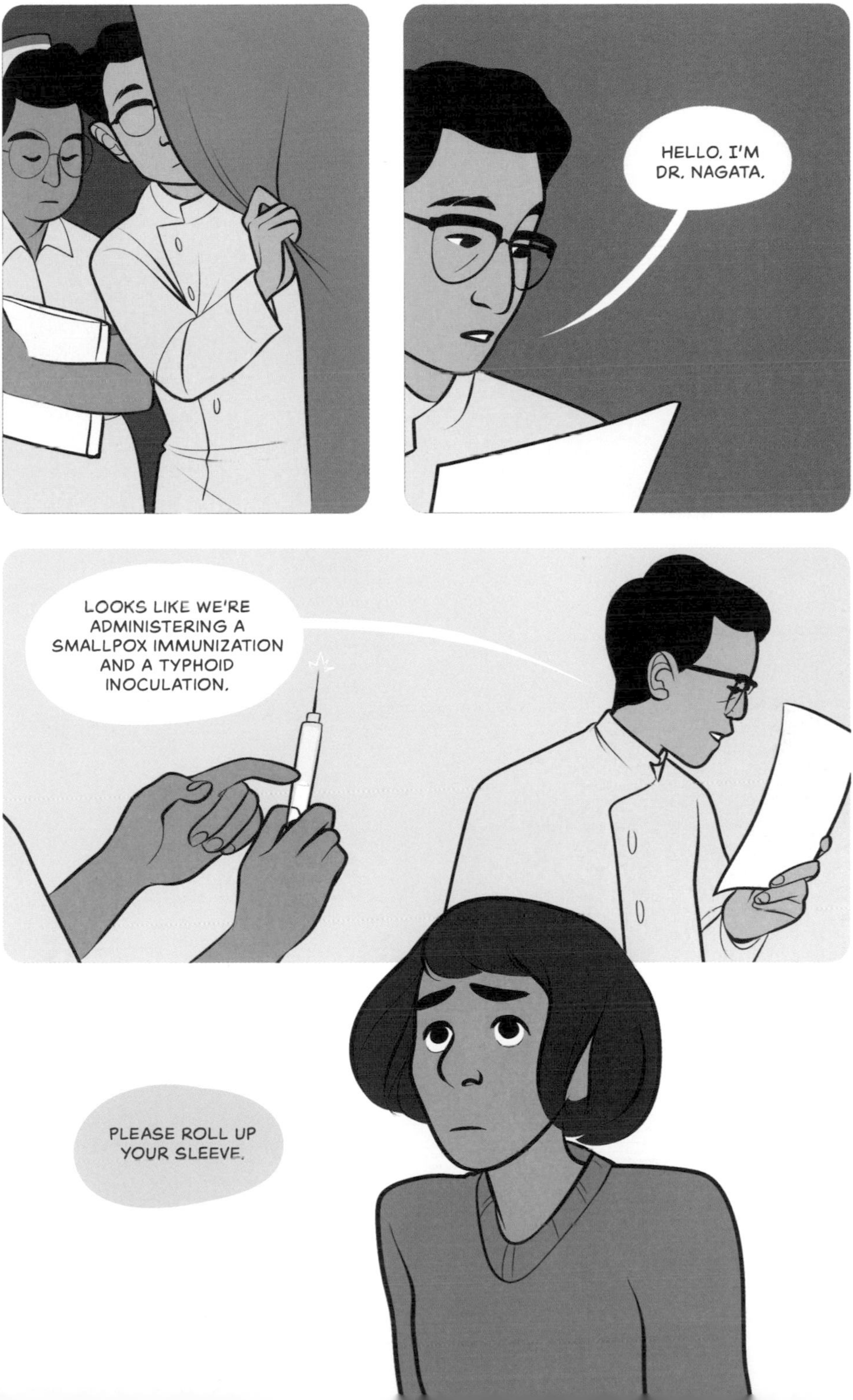
HELLO, I'M
DR. NAGATA.
LOOKS LIKE WE'RE ADMINISTERING A SMALLPOX IMMUNIZATION AND A TYPHOID INOCULATION.
PLEASE ROLL UP YOUR SLEEVE.

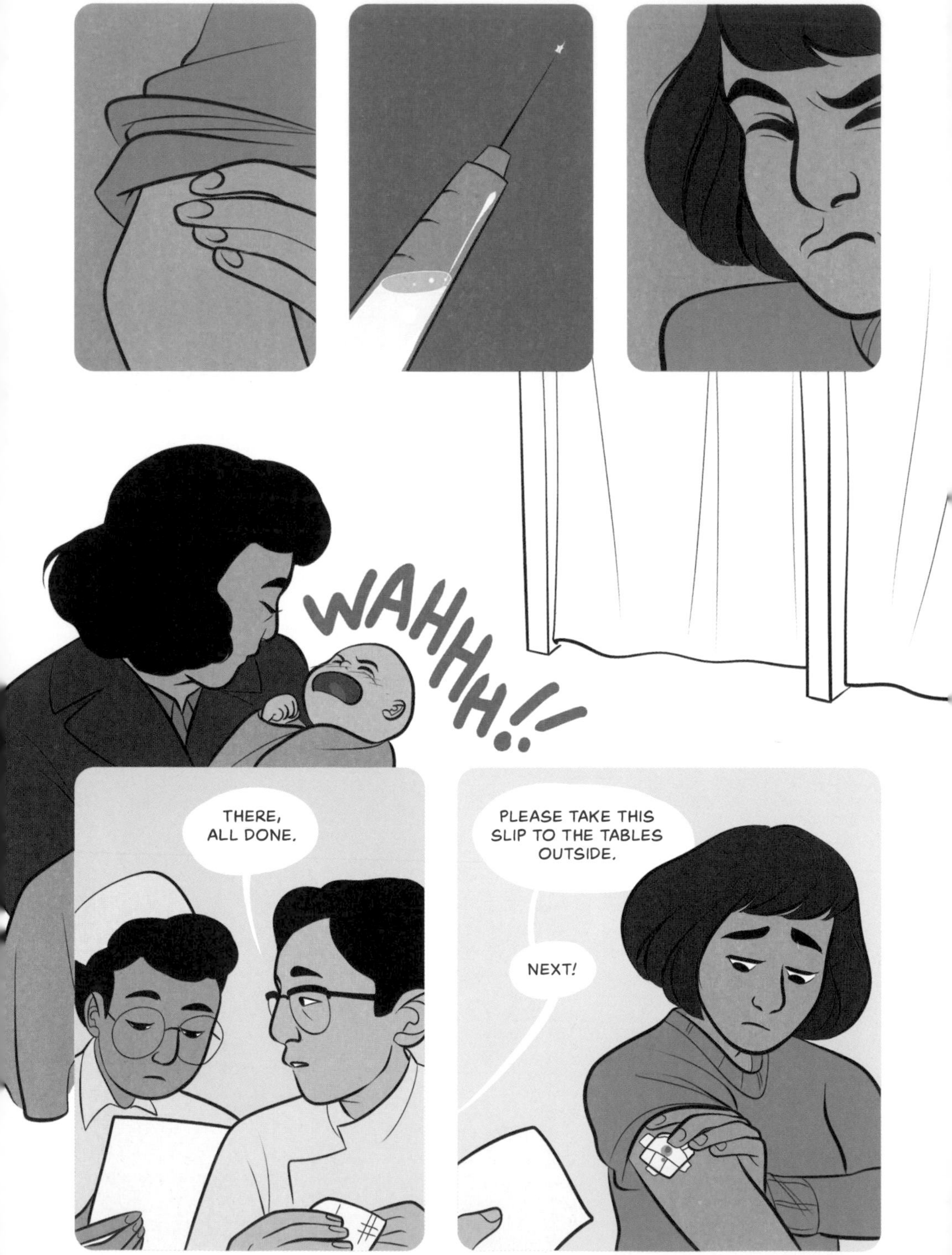
WAHHH!!
THERE, ALL DONE.
PLEASE TAKE THIS SLIP TO THE TABLES OUTSIDE.
NEXT!

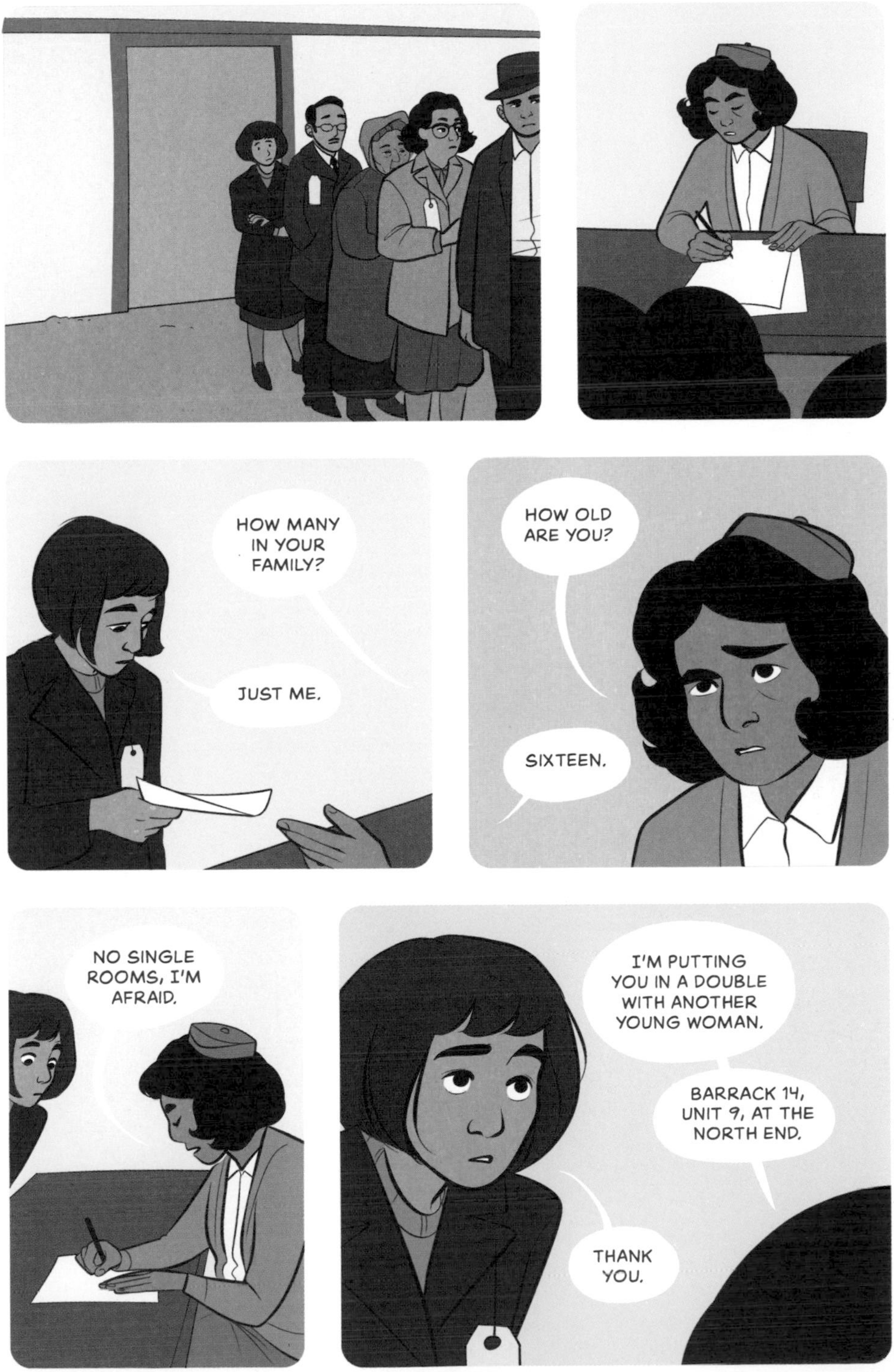
HOW MANY IN YOUR FAMILY?
JUST ME.
HOW OLD ARE YOU?
SIXTEEN.
NO SINGLE ROOMS, I'M AFRAID.
I'M PUTTING YOU IN A DOUBLE WITH ANOTHER YOUNG WOMAN.
BARRACK 14, UNIT 9, AT THE NORTH END.
THANK YOU.

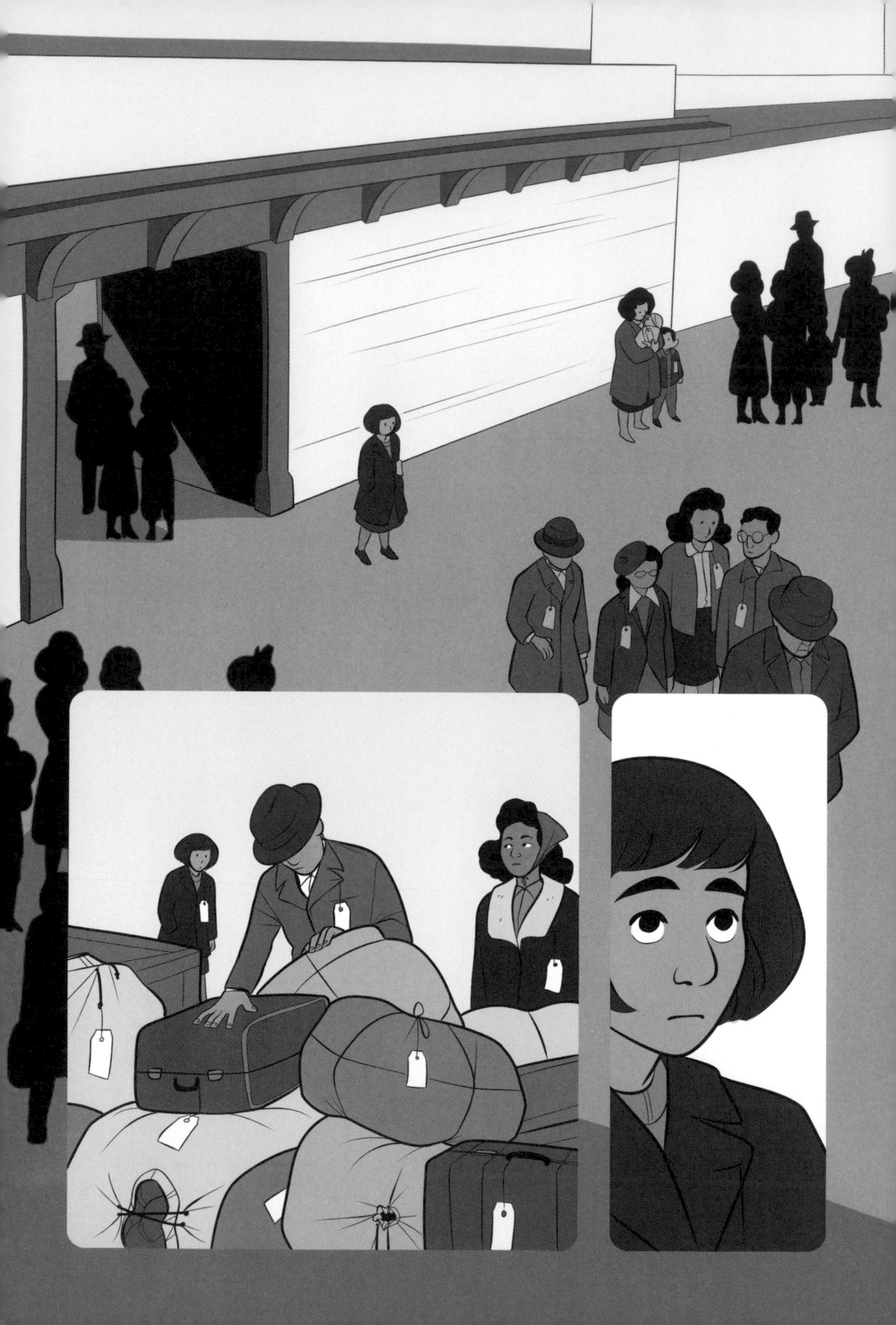

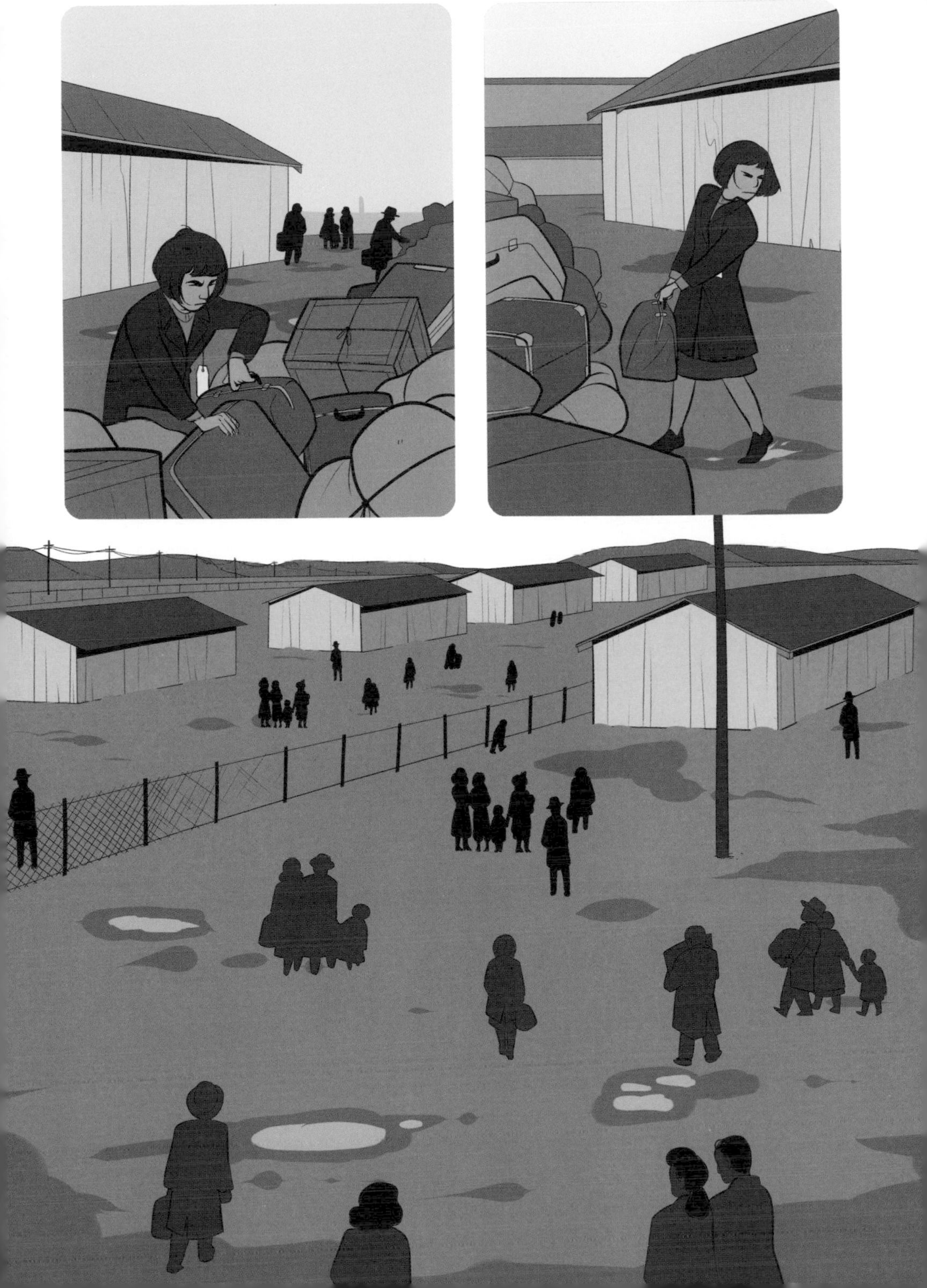

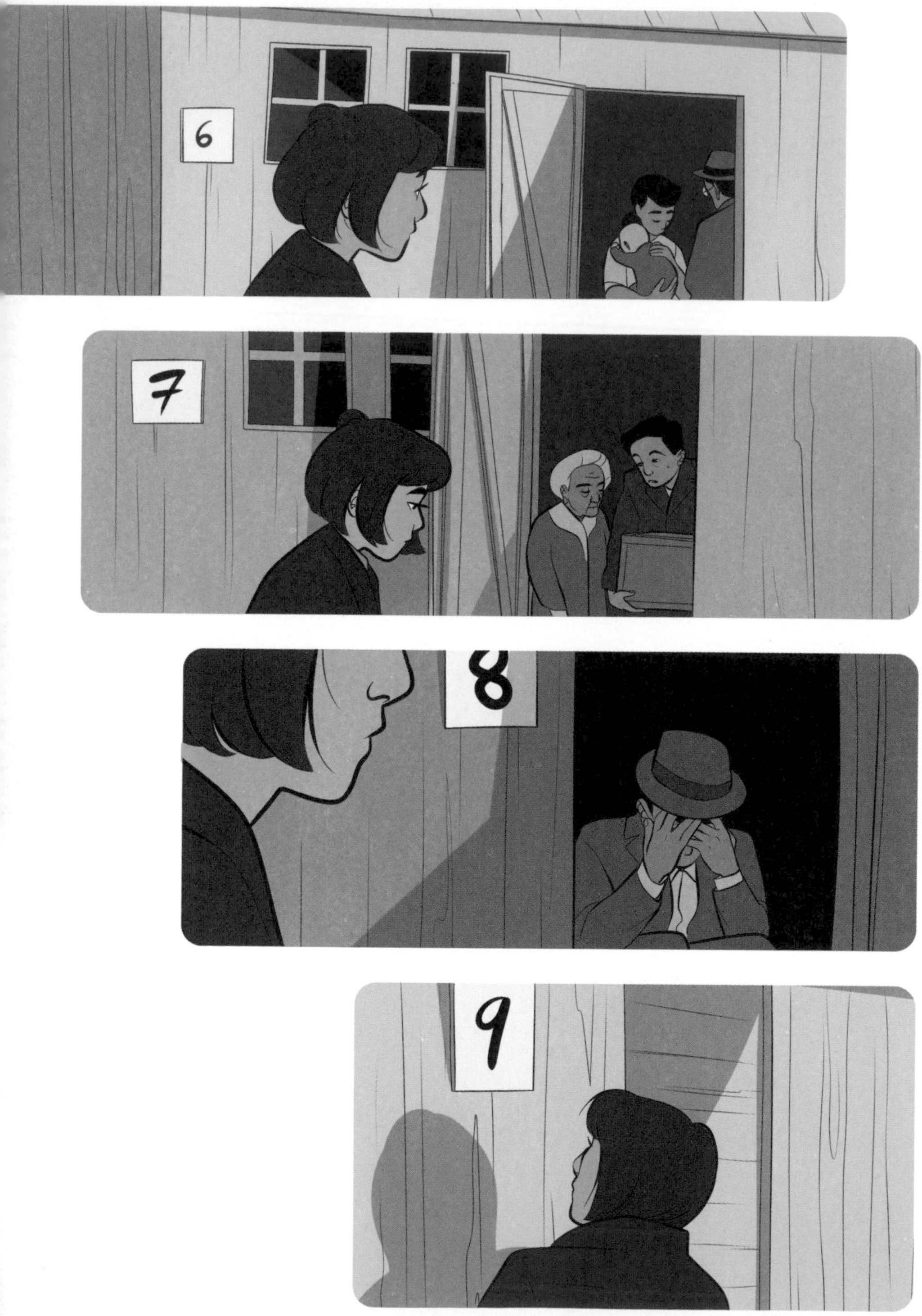
6
7
8
9

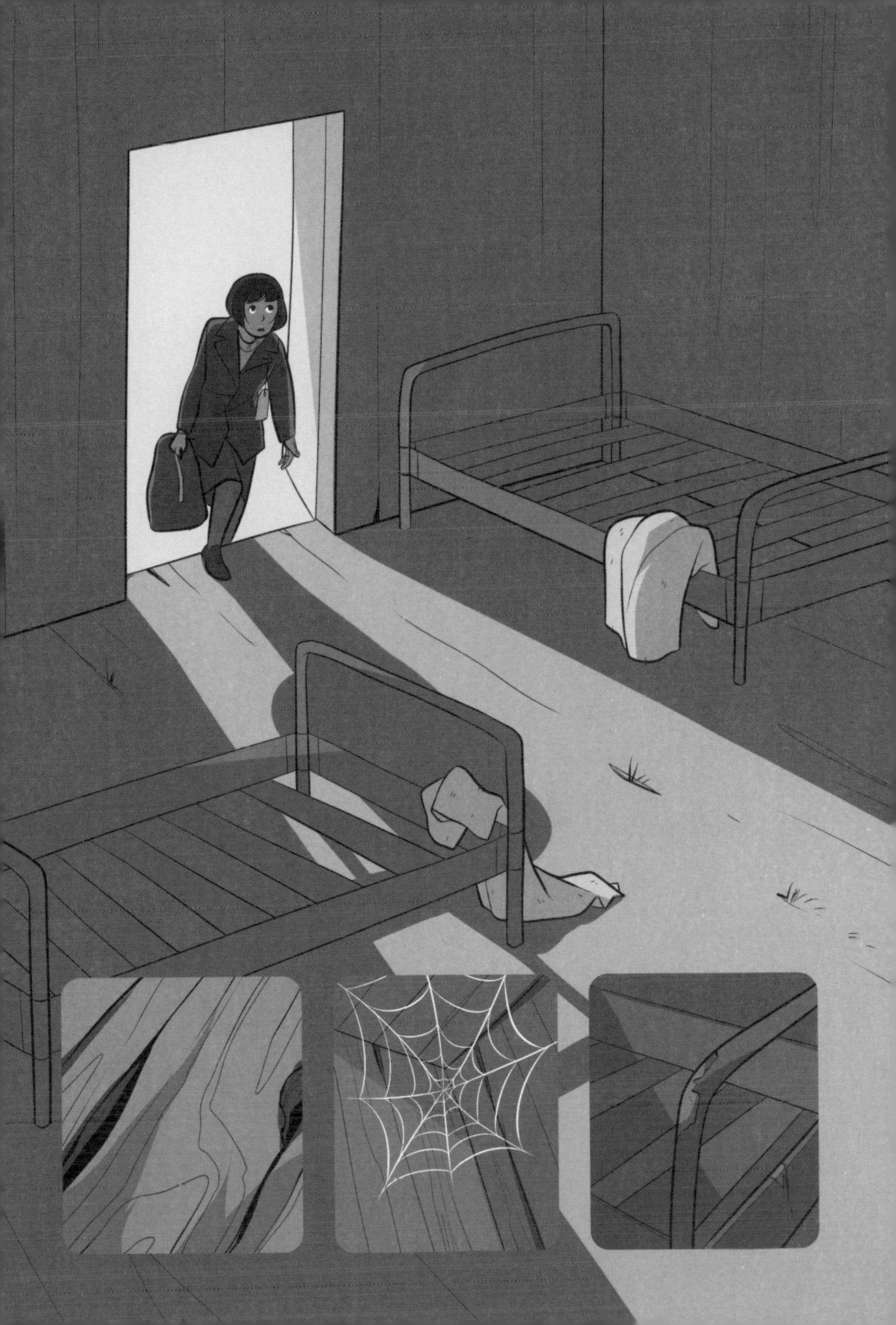

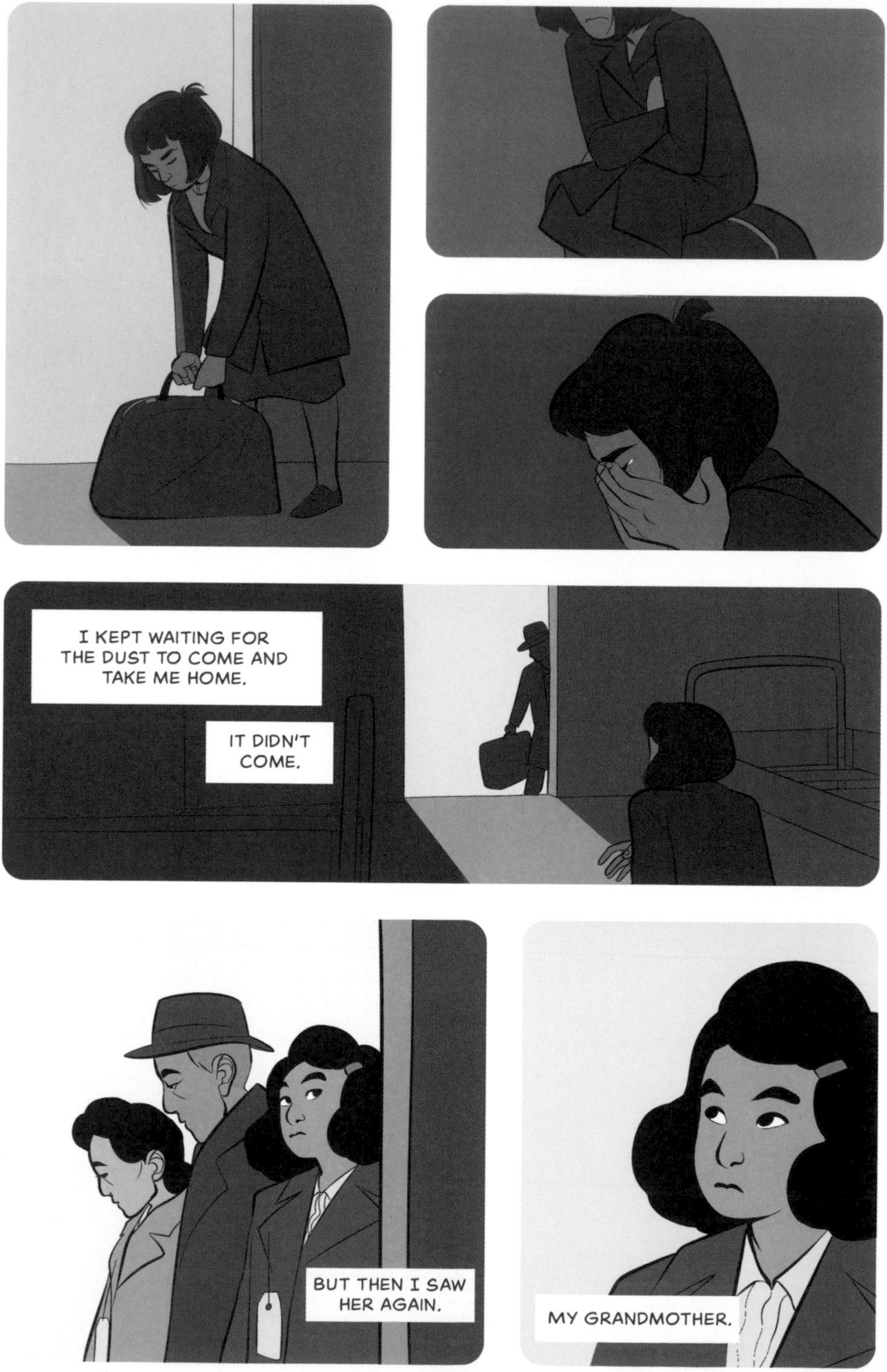
I KEPT WAITING FOR THE DUST TO COME AND TAKE ME HOME.
IT DIDN'T COME.
BUT THEN I SAW HER AGAIN.
MY GRANDMOTHER.

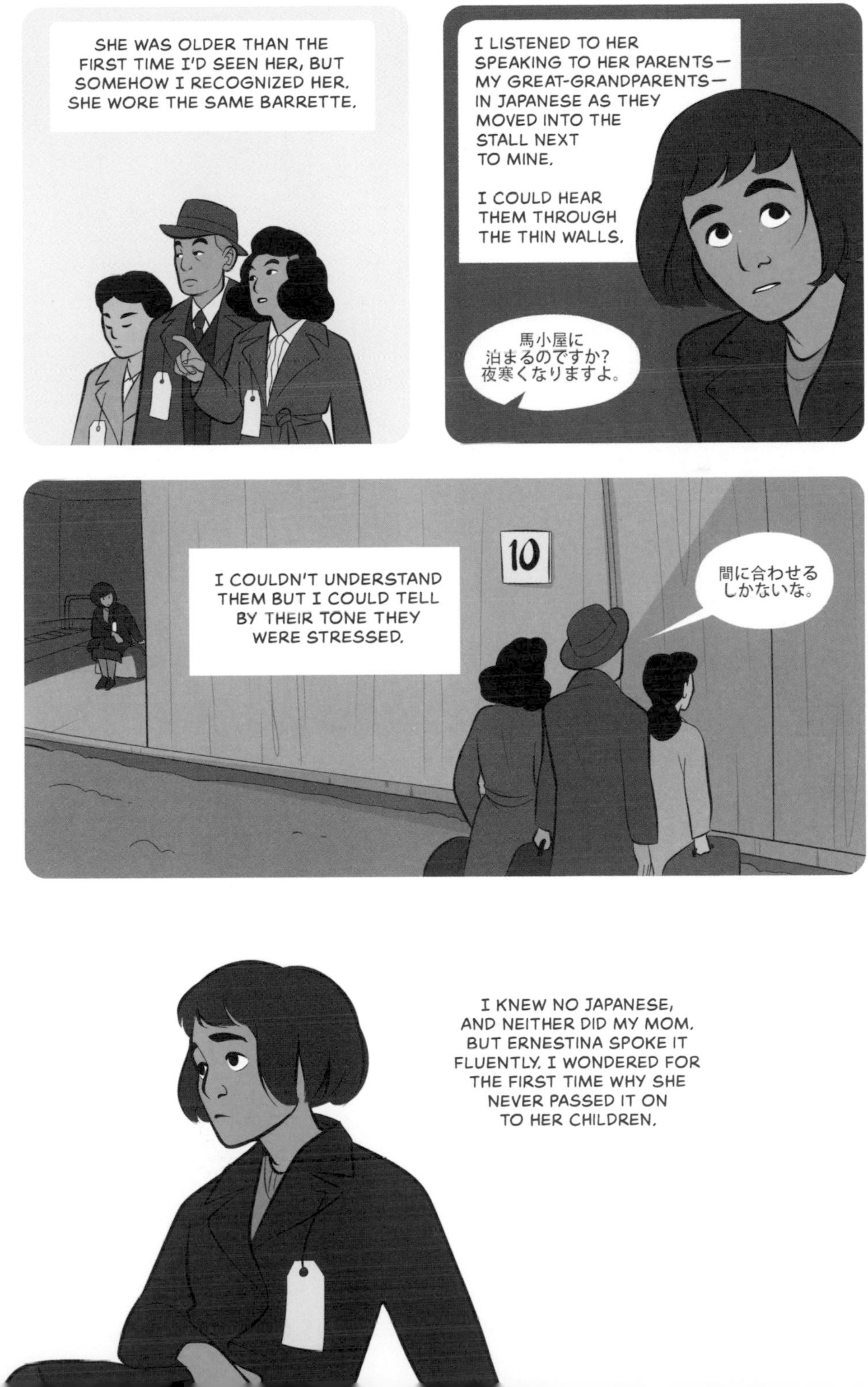
SHE WAS OLDER THAN THE FIRST TIME I'D SEEN HER, BUT SOMEHOW I RECOGNIZED HER. SHE WORE THE SAME BARRETTE.
I LISTENED TO HER SPEAKING TO HER PARENTS— MY GREAT-GRANDPARENTS— IN JAPANESE AS THEY MOVED INTO THE STALL NEXT TO MINE.
I COULD HEAR THEM THROUGH THE THIN WALLS.
馬小屋に泊まるのですか?夜寒くなりますよ。
10
I COULDN'T UNDERSTAND THEM BUT I COULD TELL BY THEIR TONE THEY WERE STRESSED.
間に合わせるしかないな。
I KNEW NO JAPANESE, AND NEITHER DID MY MOM. BUT ERNESTINA SPOKE IT FLUENTLY. I WONDERED FOR THE FIRST TIME WHY SHE NEVER PASSED IT ON TO HER CHILDREN.

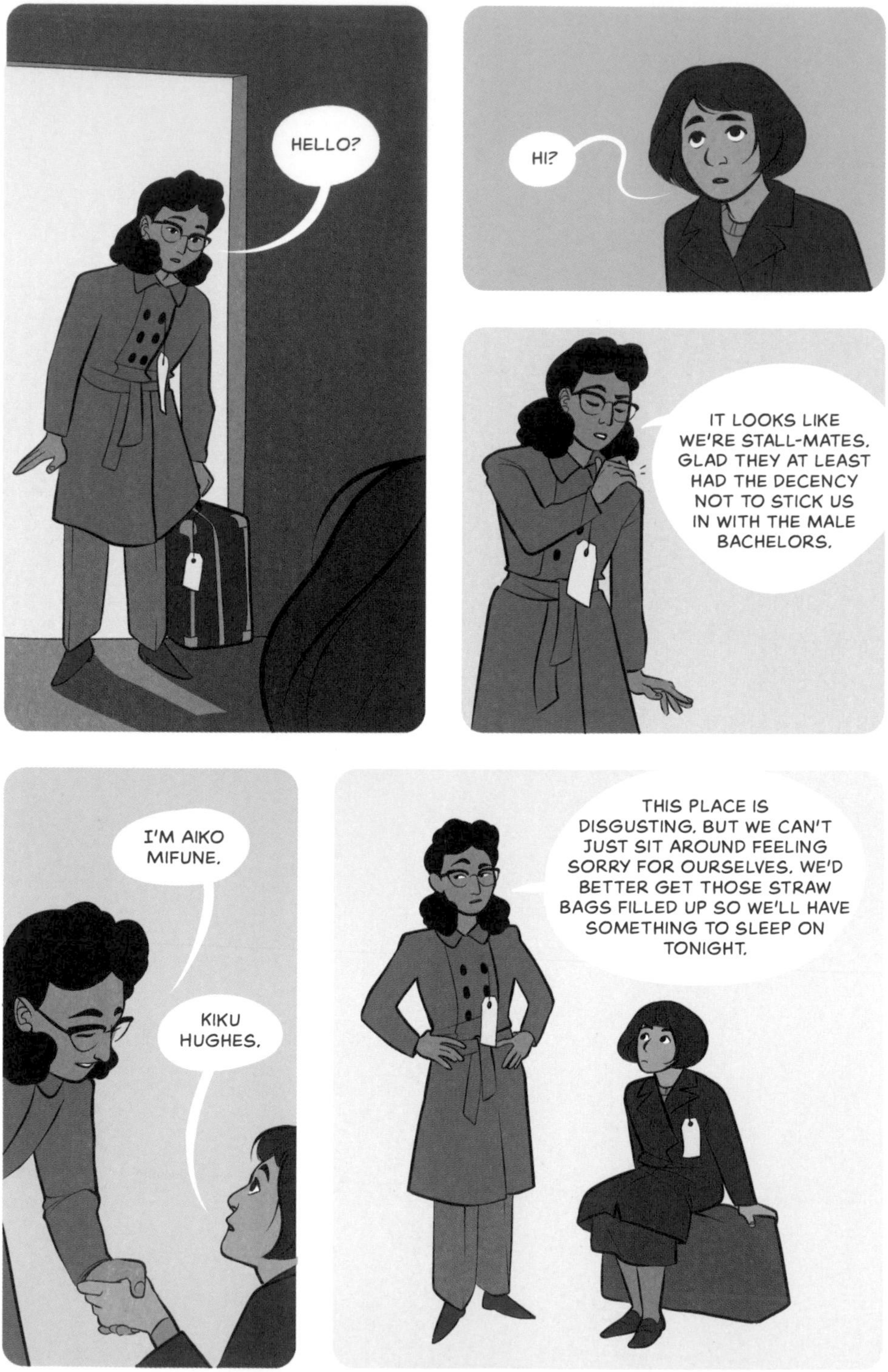
HELLO?
HI?
IT LOOKS LIKE WE'RE STALL-MATES. GLAD THEY AT LEAST HAD THE DECENCY NOT TO STICK US IN WITH THE MALE BACHELORS.
I'M AIKO MIFUNE.
KIKU HUGHES.
THIS PLACE IS DISGUSTING, BUT WE CAN'T JUST SIT AROUND FEELING SORRY FOR OURSELVES. WE'D BETTER GET THOSE STRAW BAGS FILLED UP SO WE'LL HAVE SOMETHING TO SLEEP ON TONIGHT.

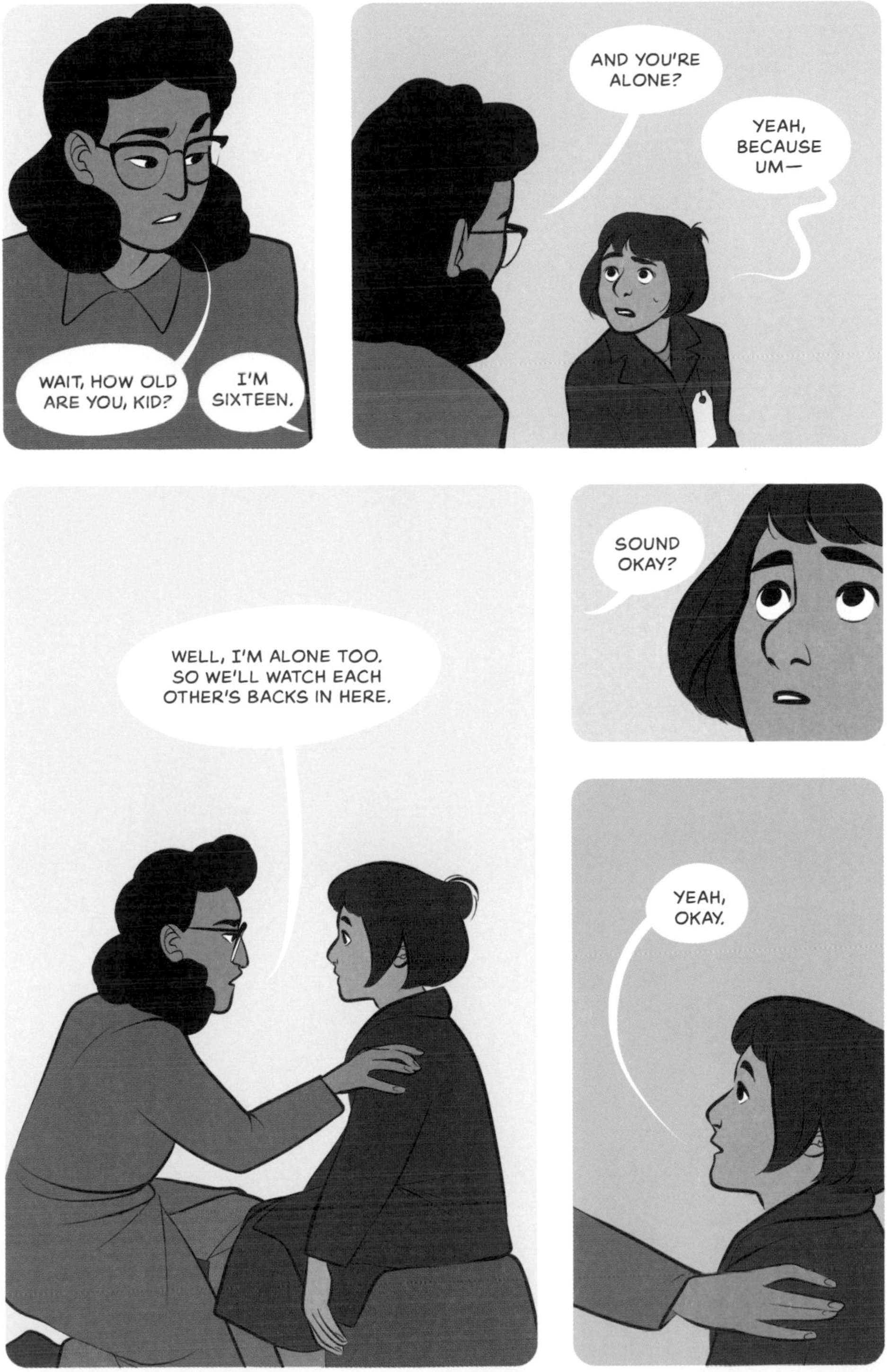
WAIT, HOW OLD ARE YOU, KID?
I'M SIXTEEN.
AND YOU'RE ALONE?
YEAH, BECAUSE UM—
WELL, I'M ALONE TOO. SO WE'LL WATCH EACH OTHER'S BACKS IN HERE.
SOUND OKAY?
YEAH, OKAY.

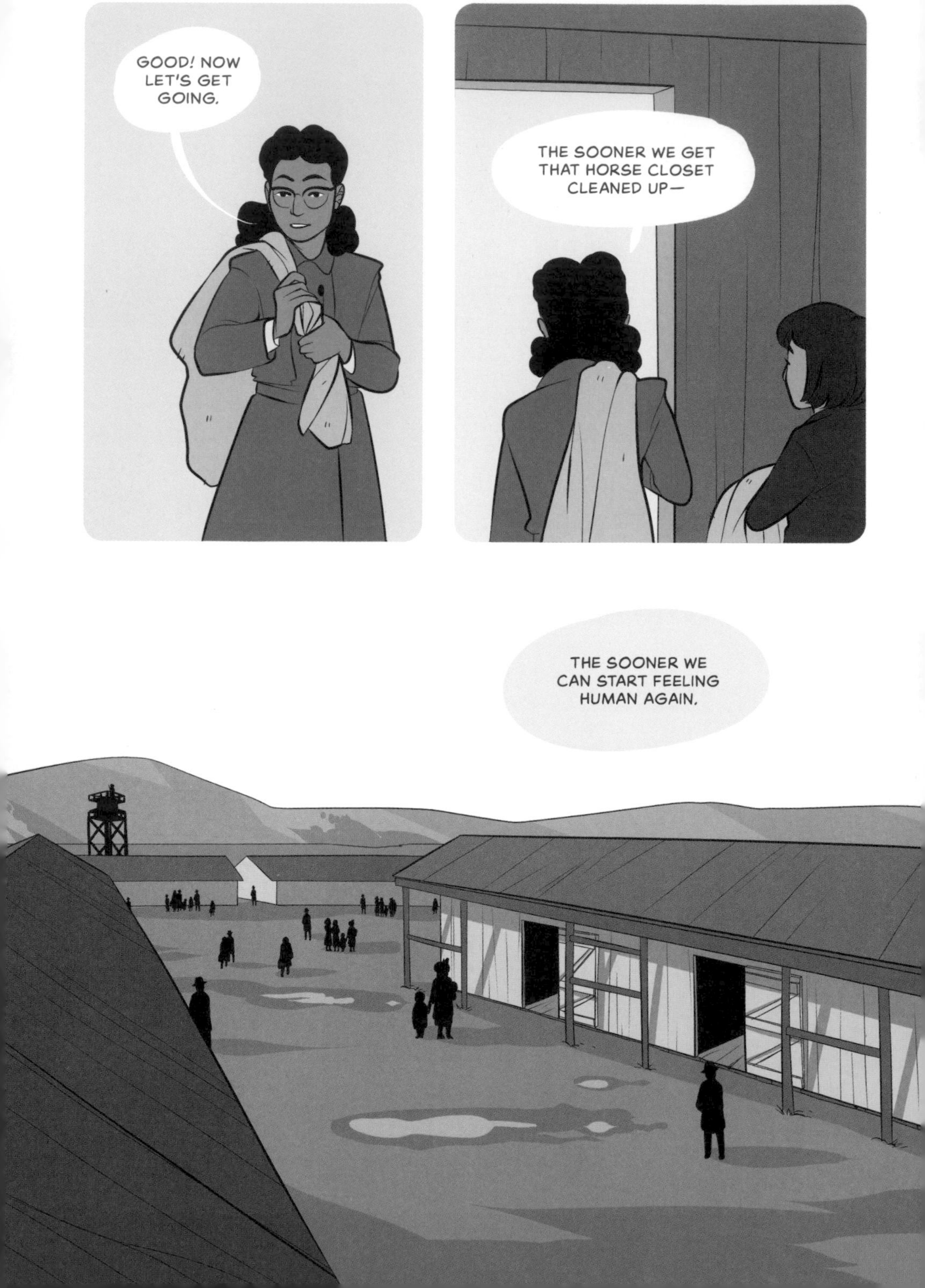
GOOD! NOW LET'S GET GOING.
THE SOONER WE GET THAT HORSE CLOSET CLEANED UP—
THE SOONER WE CAN START FEELING HUMAN AGAIN.

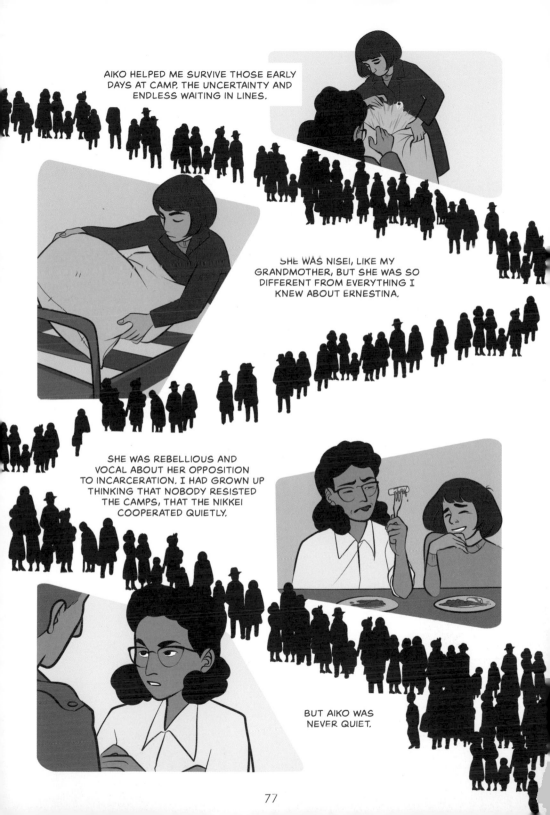

AIKO HELPED ME SURVIVE THOSE EARLY DAYS AT CAMP, THE UNCERTAINTY AND ENDLESS WAITING IN LINES.

SHE WAS NISEI, LIKE MY GRANDMOTHER, BUT SHE WAS SO DIFFERENT FROM EVERYTHING I KNEW ABOUT ERNESTINA.

SHE WAS REBELLIOUS AND VOCAL ABOUT HER OPPOSITION TO INCARCERATION. I HAD GROWN UP THINKING THAT NOBODY RESISTED THE CAMPS, THAT THE NIKKEI COOPERATED QUIETLY.

BUT AIKO WAS NEVER QUIET.

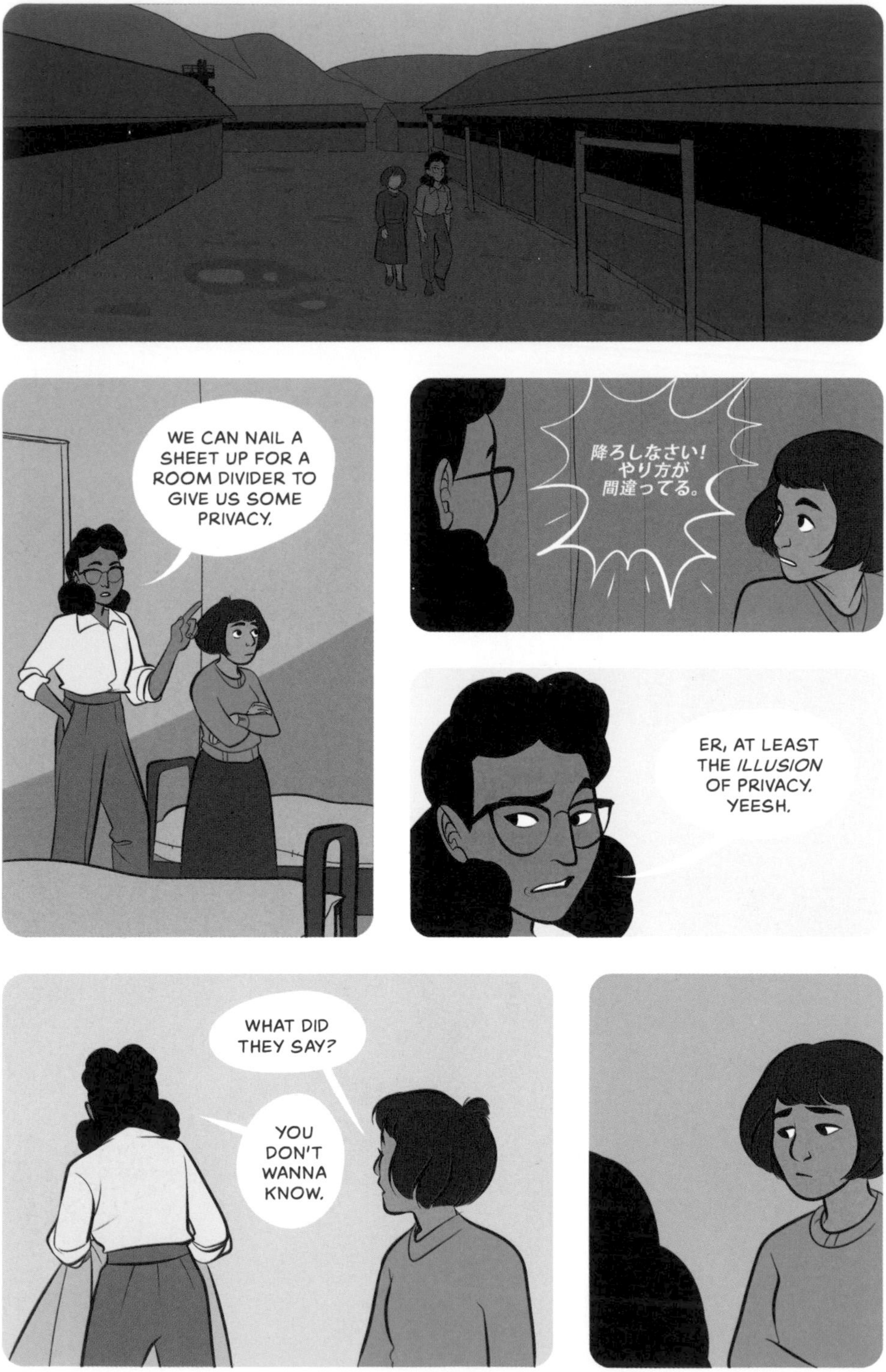
WE CAN NAIL A SHEET UP FOR A ROOM DIVIDER TO GIVE US SOME PRIVACY.
降ろしなさい! やり方が間違ってる。
ER, AT LEAST THE *ILLUSION* OF PRIVACY. YEESH.
WHAT DID THEY SAY?
YOU DON'T WANNA KNOW.

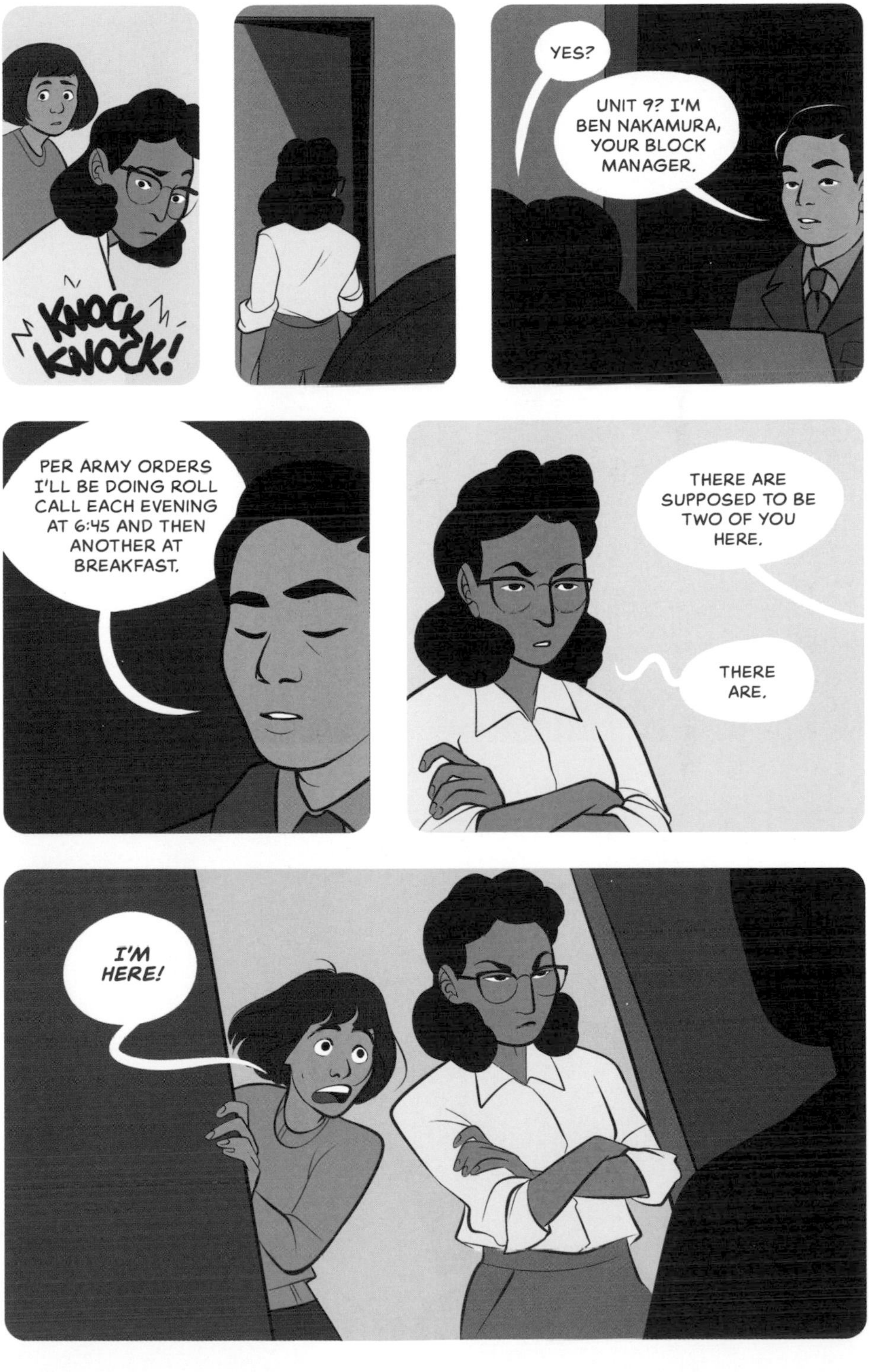
KNOCK KNOCK!
YES?
UNIT 9? I'M BEN NAKAMURA, YOUR BLOCK MANAGER.
PER ARMY ORDERS I'LL BE DOING ROLL CALL EACH EVENING AT 6:45 AND THEN ANOTHER AT BREAKFAST.
THERE ARE SUPPOSED TO BE TWO OF YOU HERE.
THERE ARE.
I'M HERE!

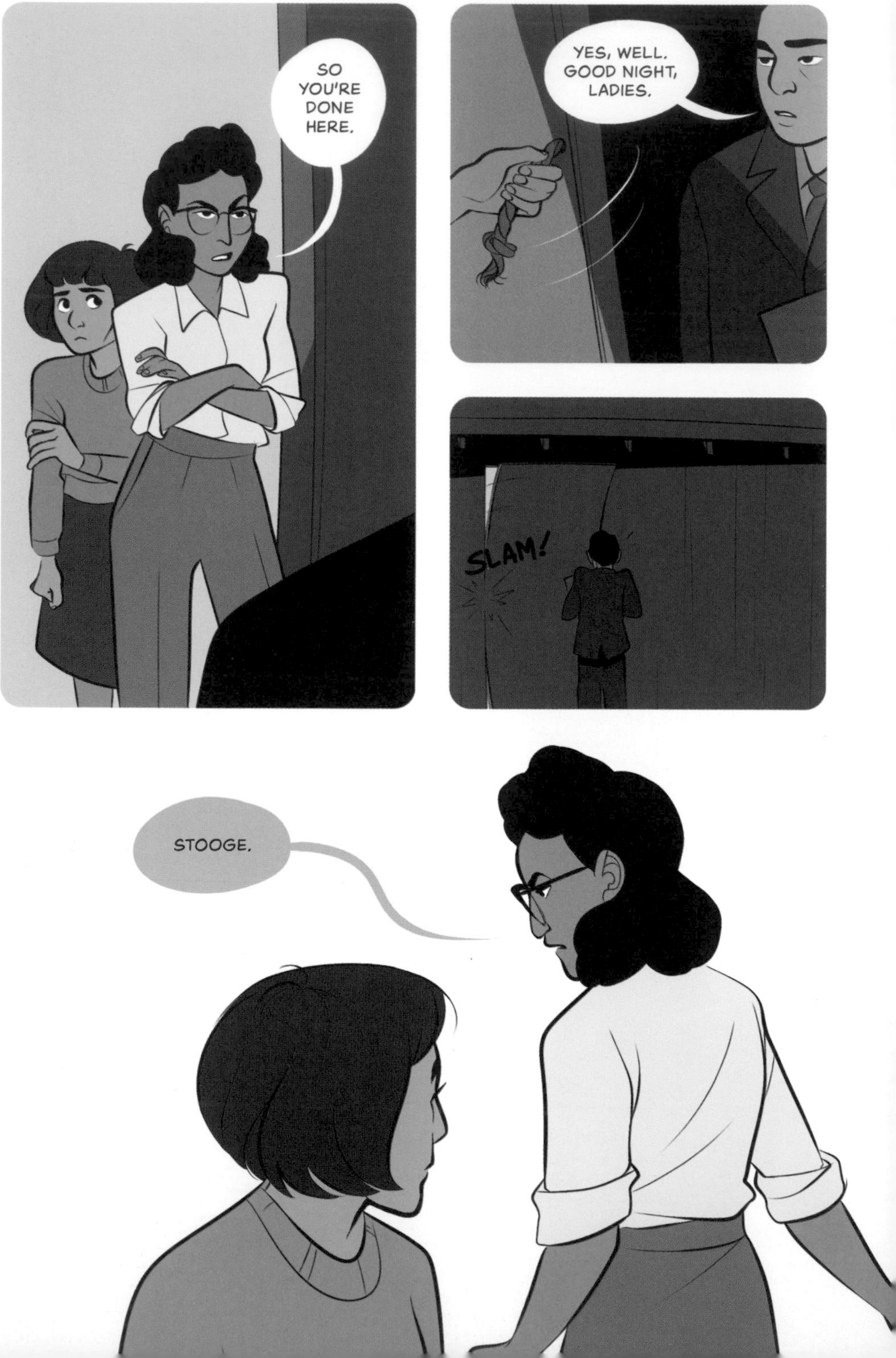
SO YOU'RE DONE HERE.
YES, WELL. GOOD NIGHT, LADIES.
SLAM!
STOOGE.

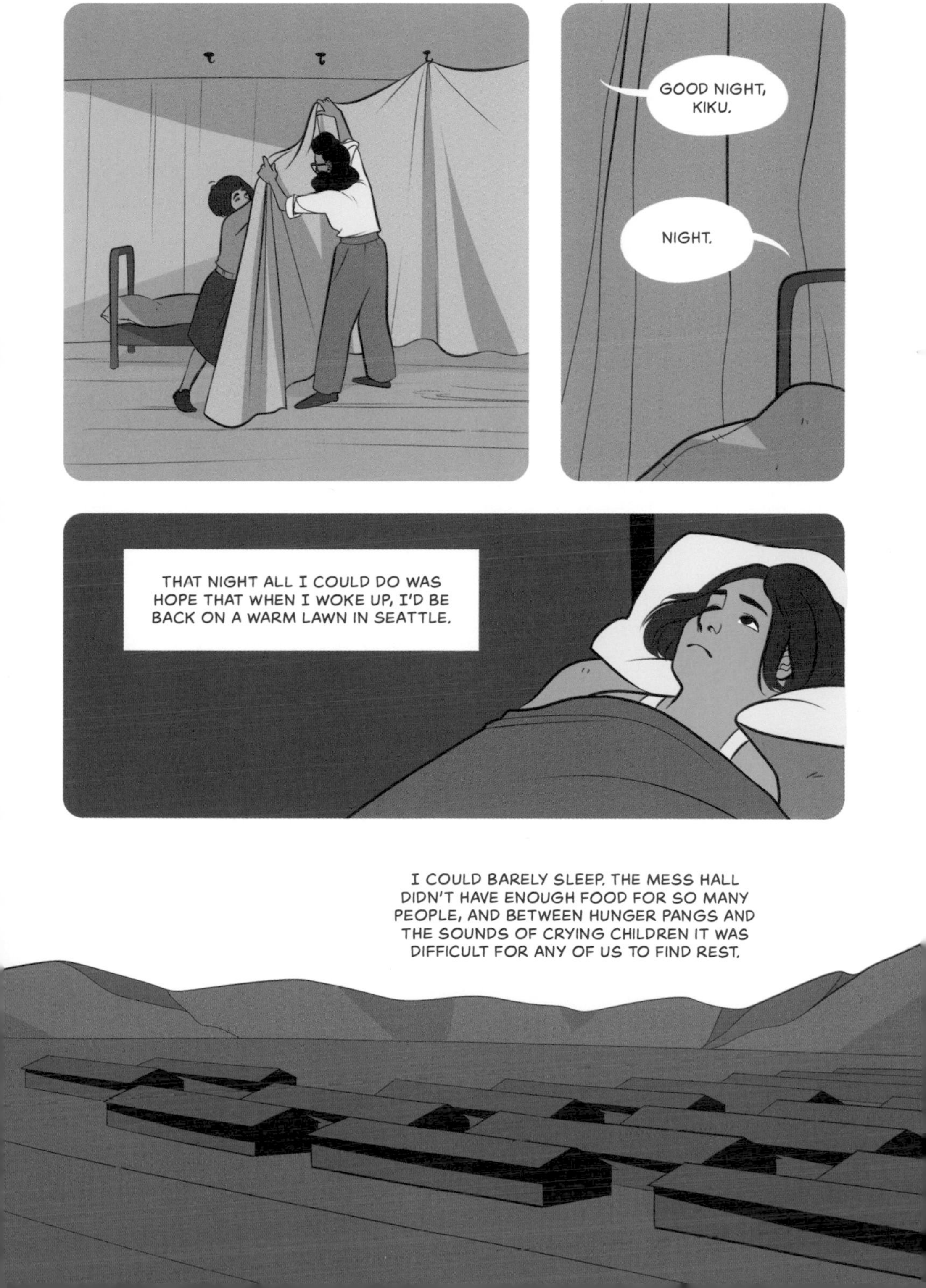
GOOD NIGHT, KIKU.
NIGHT.
THAT NIGHT ALL I COULD DO WAS HOPE THAT WHEN I WOKE UP, I'D BE BACK ON A WARM LAWN IN SEATTLE.
I COULD BARELY SLEEP. THE MESS HALL DIDN'T HAVE ENOUGH FOOD FOR SO MANY PEOPLE, AND BETWEEN HUNGER PANGS AND THE SOUNDS OF CRYING CHILDREN IT WAS DIFFICULT FOR ANY OF US TO FIND REST.

4

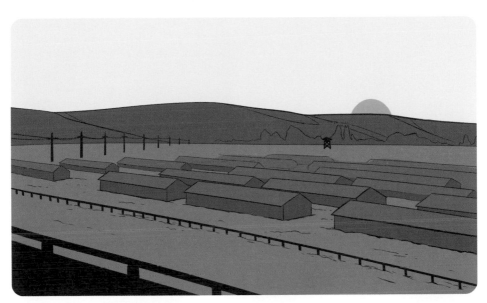

ROLL CALL!

COME ON, THE BLOCK LACKEY WILL REPORT US IF WE DON'T SHOW UP ON TIME.

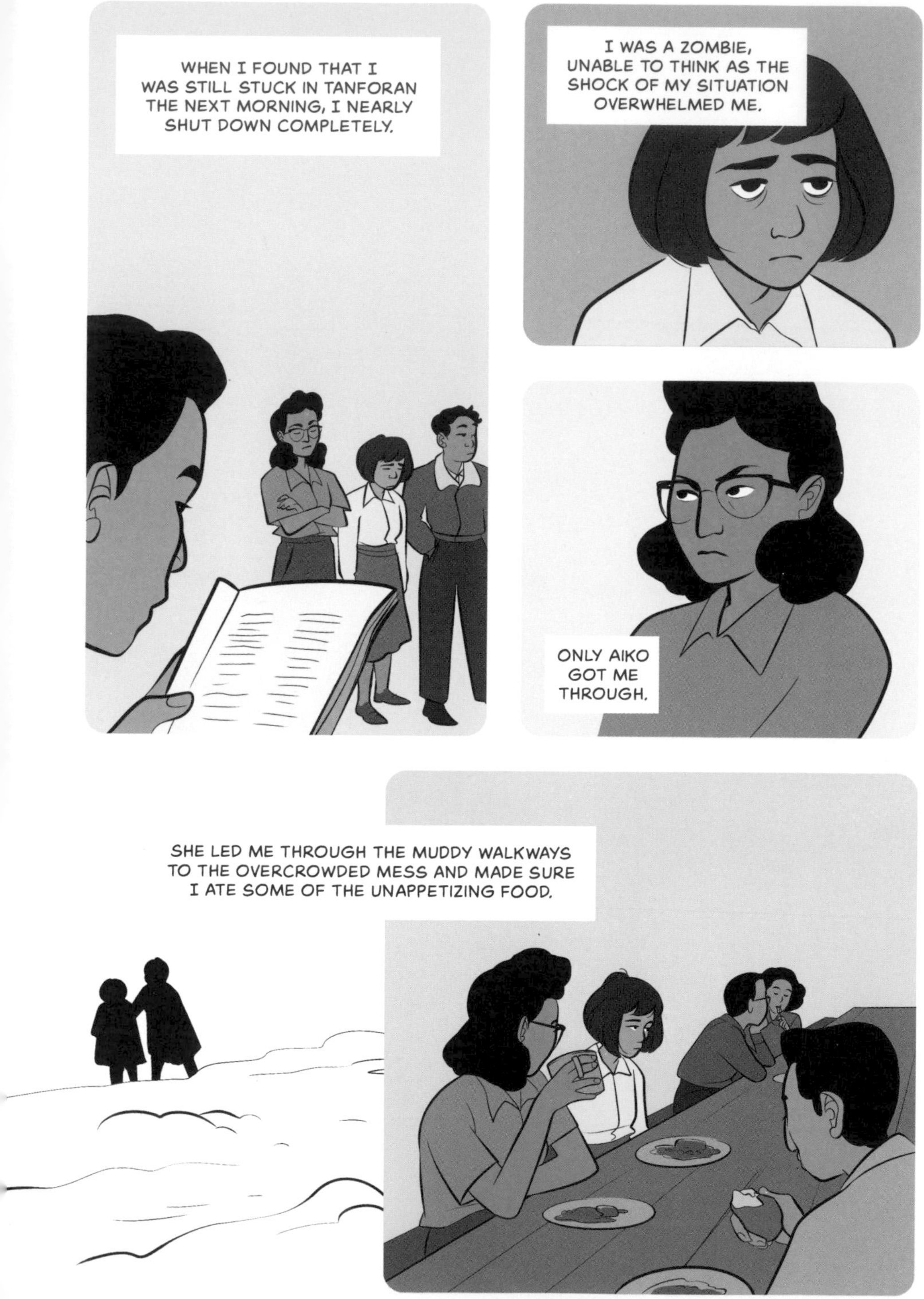
WHEN I FOUND THAT I WAS STILL STUCK IN TANFORAN THE NEXT MORNING, I NEARLY SHUT DOWN COMPLETELY.
I WAS A ZOMBIE, UNABLE TO THINK AS THE SHOCK OF MY SITUATION OVERWHELMED ME.
ONLY AIKO GOT ME THROUGH.
SHE LED ME THROUGH THE MUDDY WALKWAYS TO THE OVERCROWDED MESS AND MADE SURE I ATE SOME OF THE UNAPPETIZING FOOD.

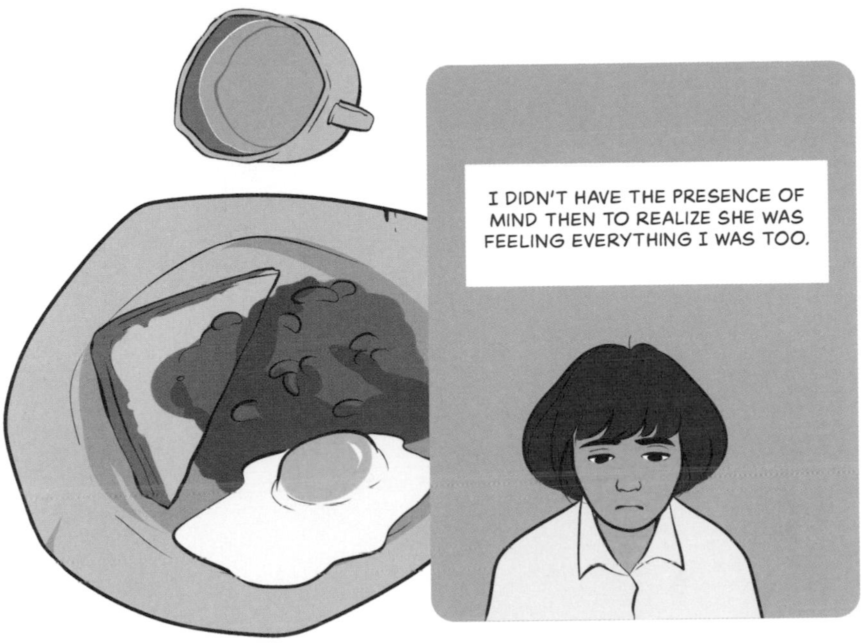
I DIDN'T HAVE THE PRESENCE OF MIND THEN TO REALIZE SHE WAS FEELING EVERYTHING I WAS TOO.

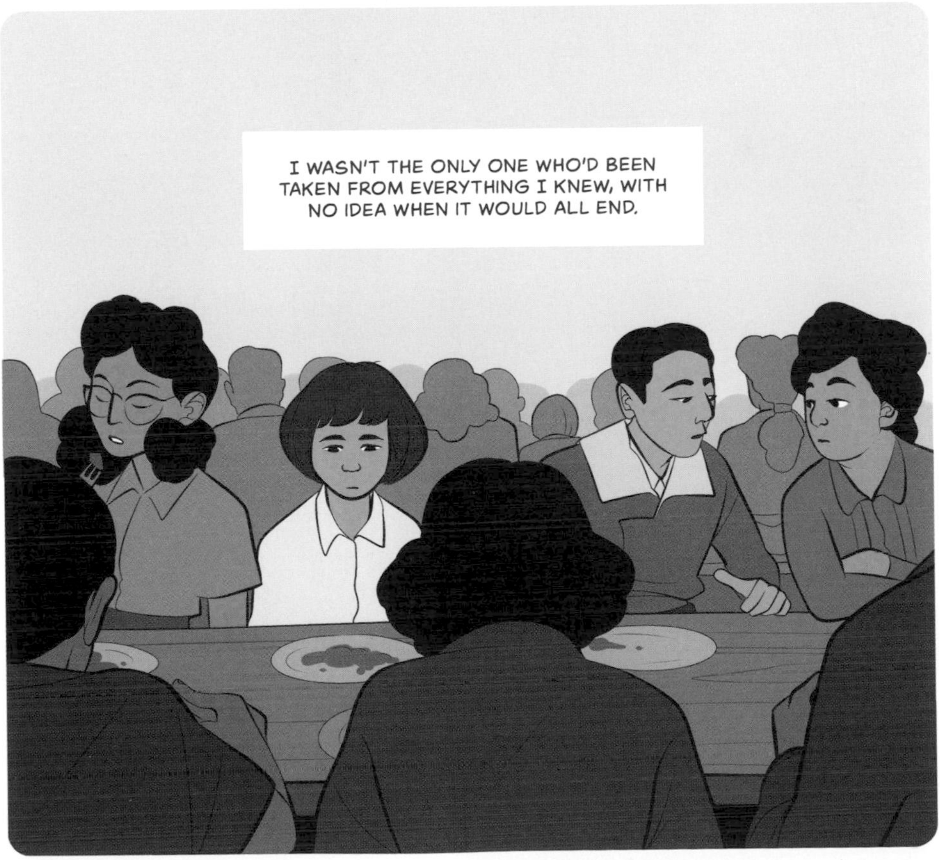
I WASN'T THE ONLY ONE WHO'D BEEN TAKEN FROM EVERYTHING I KNEW, WITH NO IDEA WHEN IT WOULD ALL END.

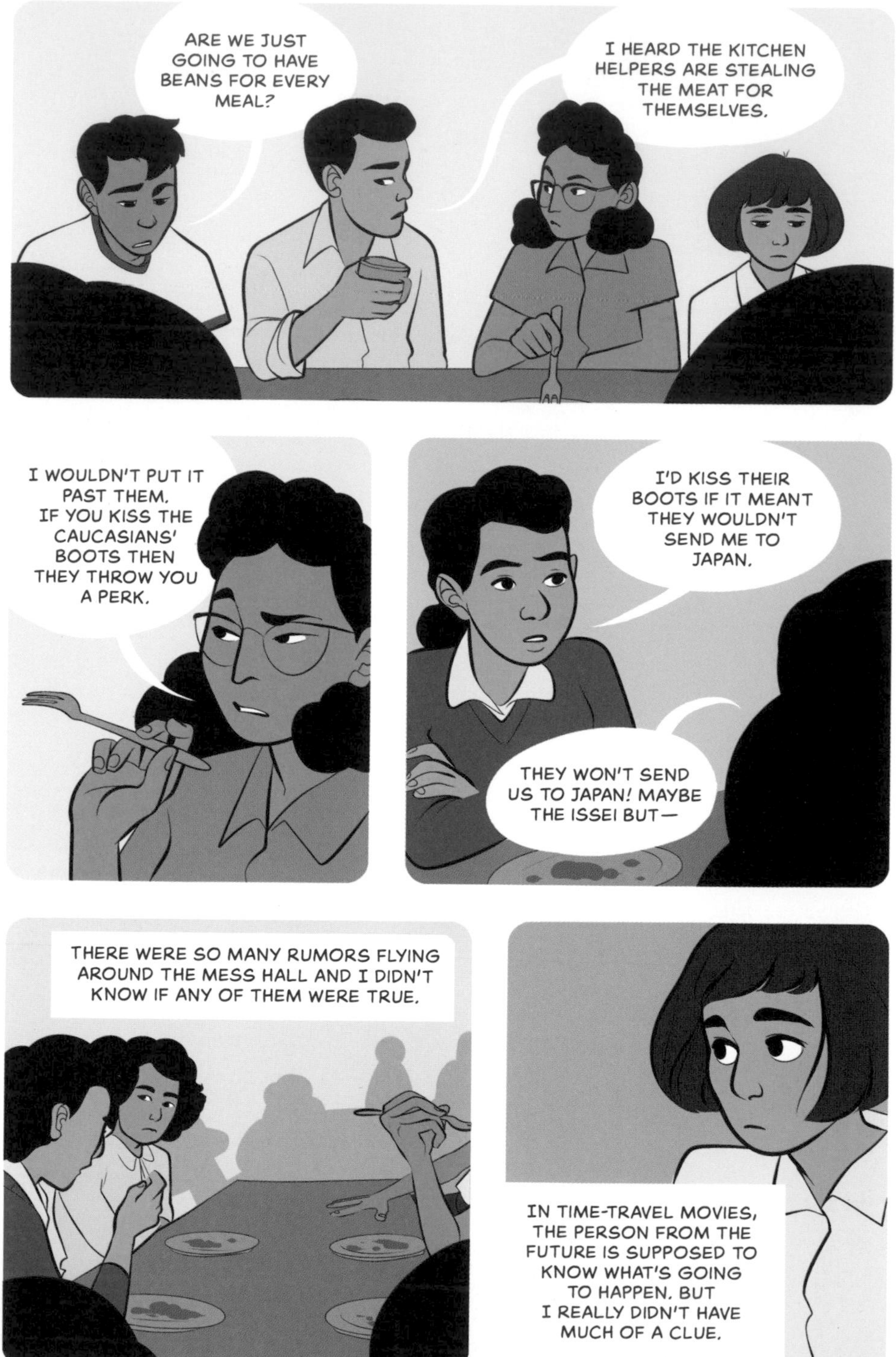
ARE WE JUST GOING TO HAVE BEANS FOR EVERY MEAL?
I HEARD THE KITCHEN HELPERS ARE STEALING THE MEAT FOR THEMSELVES.
I WOULDN'T PUT IT PAST THEM. IF YOU KISS THE CAUCASIANS' BOOTS THEN THEY THROW YOU A PERK.
I'D KISS THEIR BOOTS IF IT MEANT THEY WOULDN'T SEND ME TO JAPAN.
THEY WON'T SEND US TO JAPAN! MAYBE THE ISSEI BUT—
THERE WERE SO MANY RUMORS FLYING AROUND THE MESS HALL AND I DIDN'T KNOW IF ANY OF THEM WERE TRUE.
IN TIME-TRAVEL MOVIES, THE PERSON FROM THE FUTURE IS SUPPOSED TO KNOW WHAT'S GOING TO HAPPEN. BUT I REALLY DIDN'T HAVE MUCH OF A CLUE.

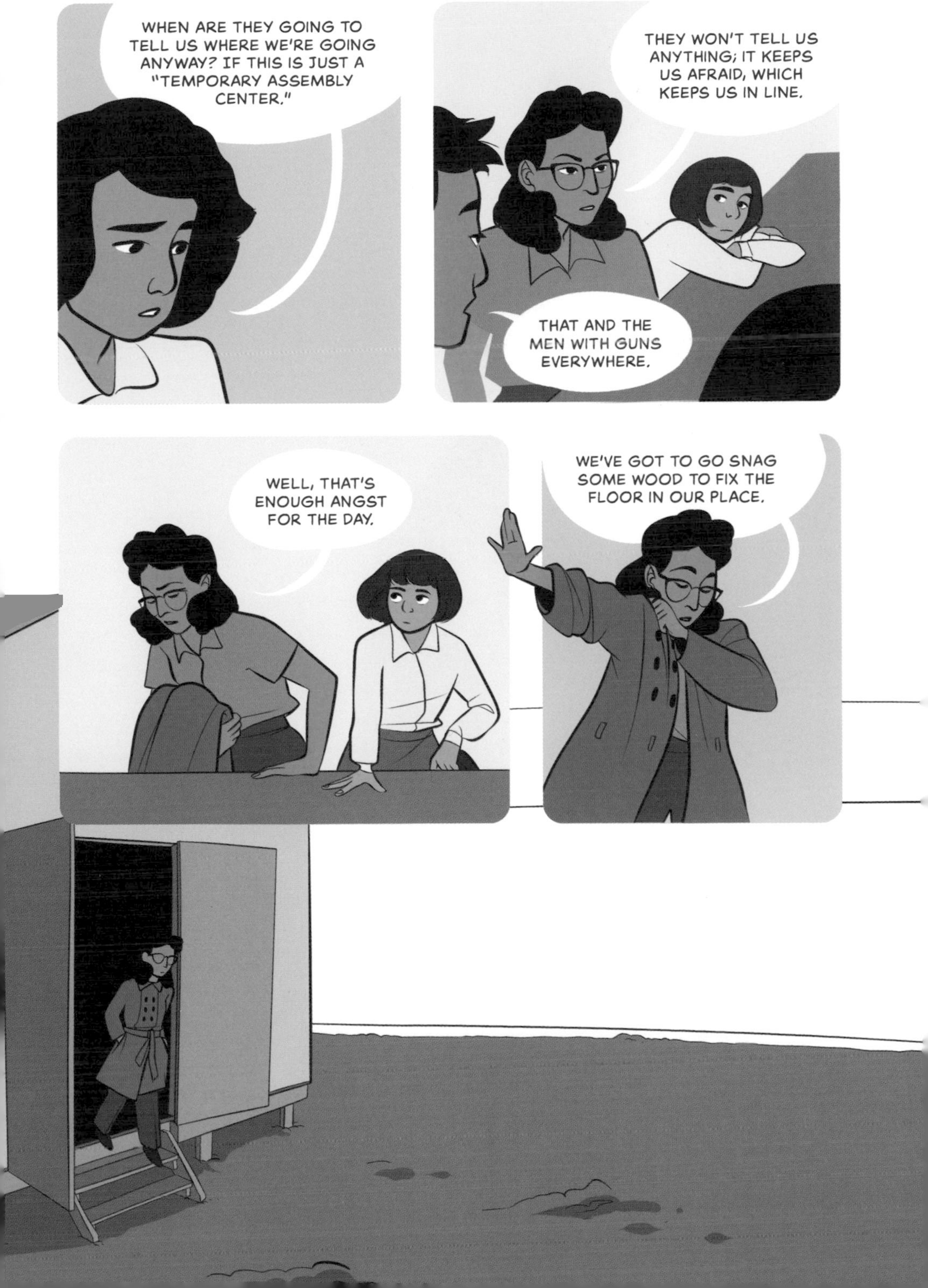
WHEN ARE THEY GOING TO TELL US WHERE WE'RE GOING ANYWAY? IF THIS IS JUST A "TEMPORARY ASSEMBLY CENTER."
THEY WON'T TELL US ANYTHING; IT KEEPS US AFRAID, WHICH KEEPS US IN LINE.
THAT AND THE MEN WITH GUNS EVERYWHERE.
WELL, THAT'S ENOUGH ANGST FOR THE DAY.
WE'VE GOT TO GO SNAG SOME WOOD TO FIX THE FLOOR IN OUR PLACE.

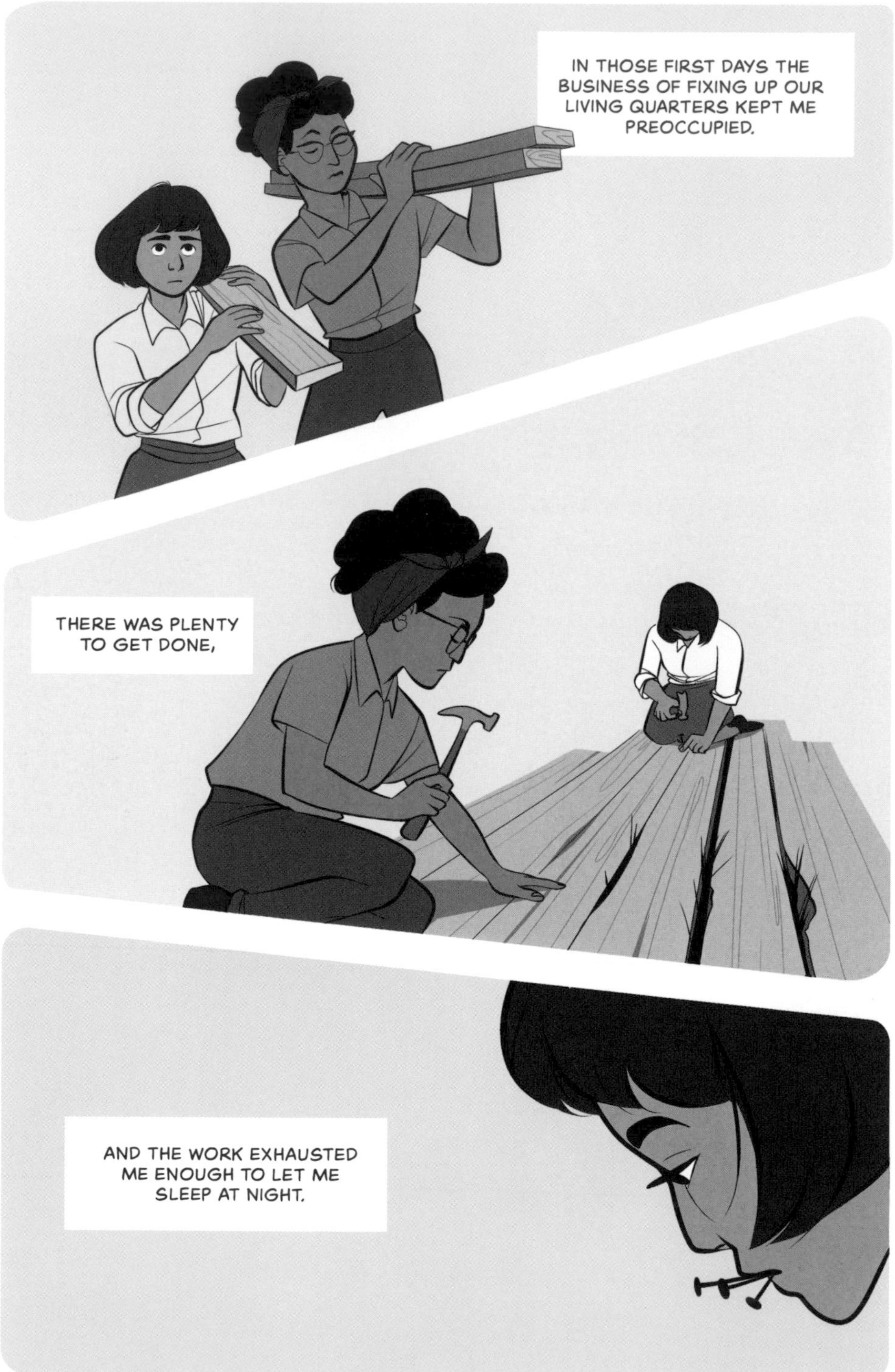
IN THOSE FIRST DAYS THE BUSINESS OF FIXING UP OUR LIVING QUARTERS KEPT ME PREOCCUPIED.
THERE WAS PLENTY TO GET DONE,
AND THE WORK EXHAUSTED ME ENOUGH TO LET ME SLEEP AT NIGHT.

IT WAS OFTEN SIMPLE NECESSITIES THAT BROUGHT ME OUT OF ANY ILLUSION THAT THIS WAS NORMAL.

I HAD TO WORK UP THE MENTAL ENERGY JUST TO GO TO THE BATHROOM, WHERE THERE WAS NO PRIVACY. PEOPLE WERE OFTEN SICK FROM THE FOOD, WHICH ONLY MADE THINGS WORSE.

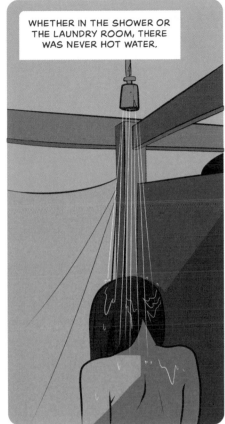

WHETHER IN THE SHOWER OR THE LAUNDRY ROOM, THERE WAS NEVER HOT WATER.

IT WAS ALWAYS FRUSTRATING, BUT I SURPRISED MYSELF WITH HOW QUICKLY I ADAPTED.

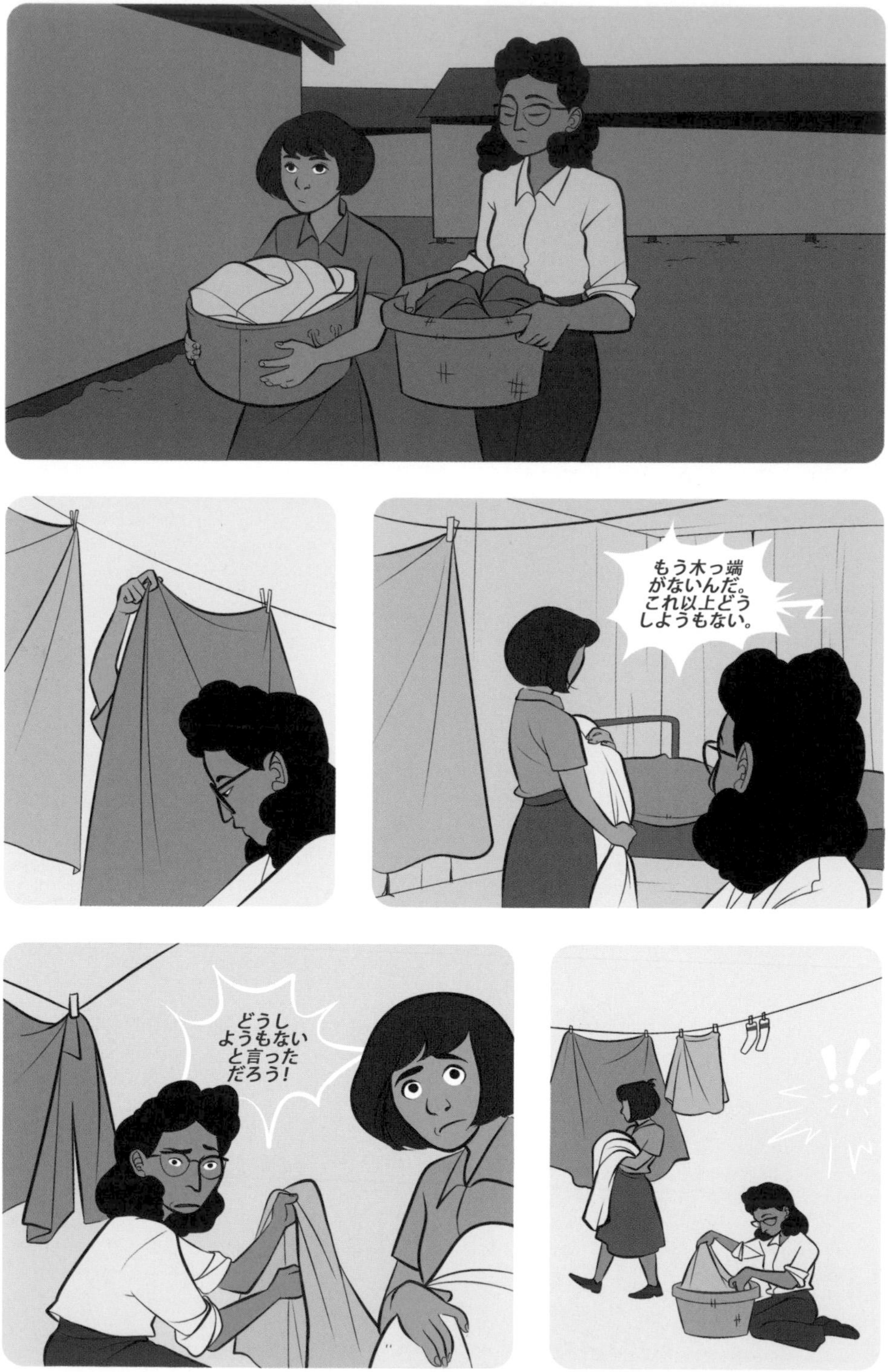
もう木っ端
がないんだ。
これ以上どう
しようもない。
どうし
ようもない
と言った
だろう!

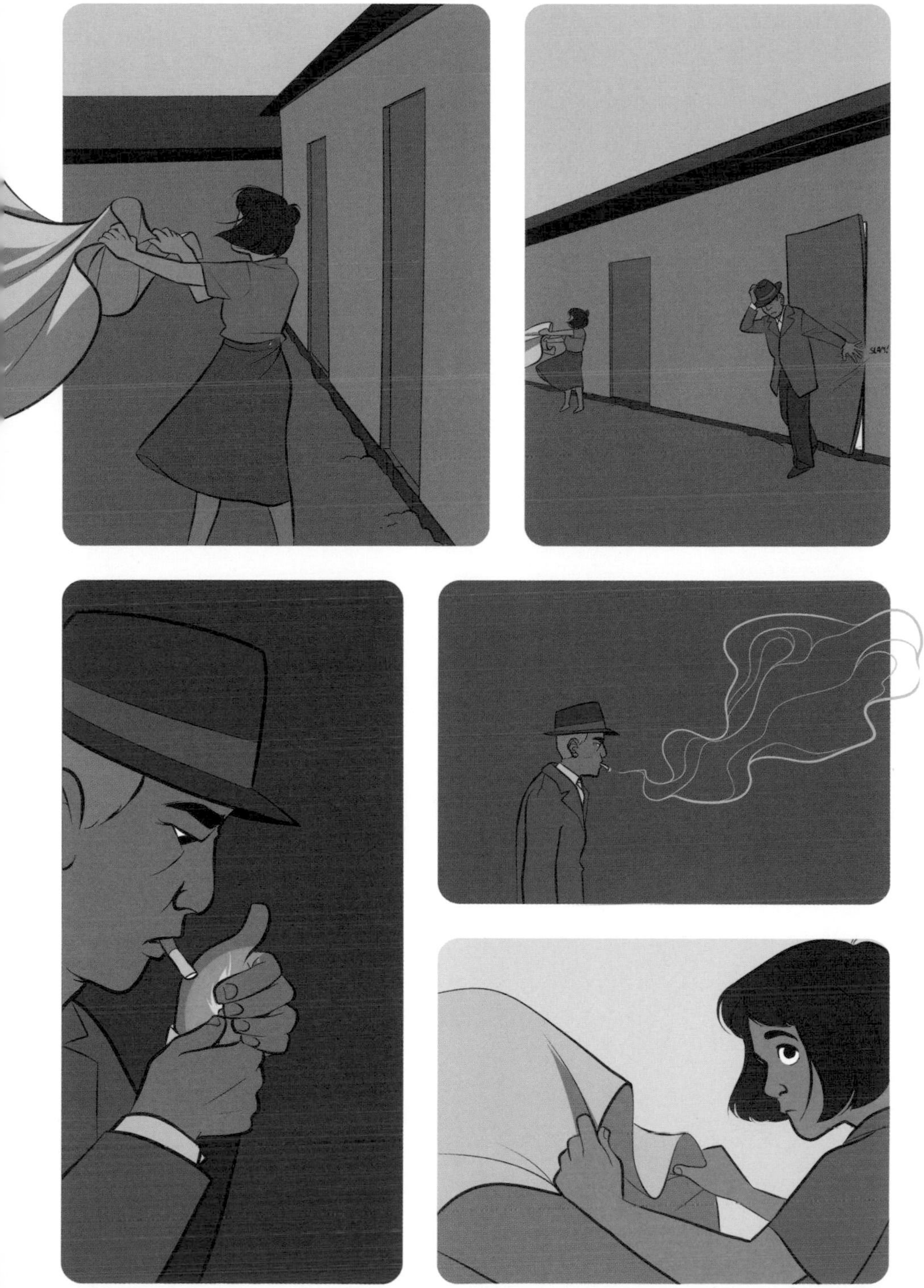
SLAM!

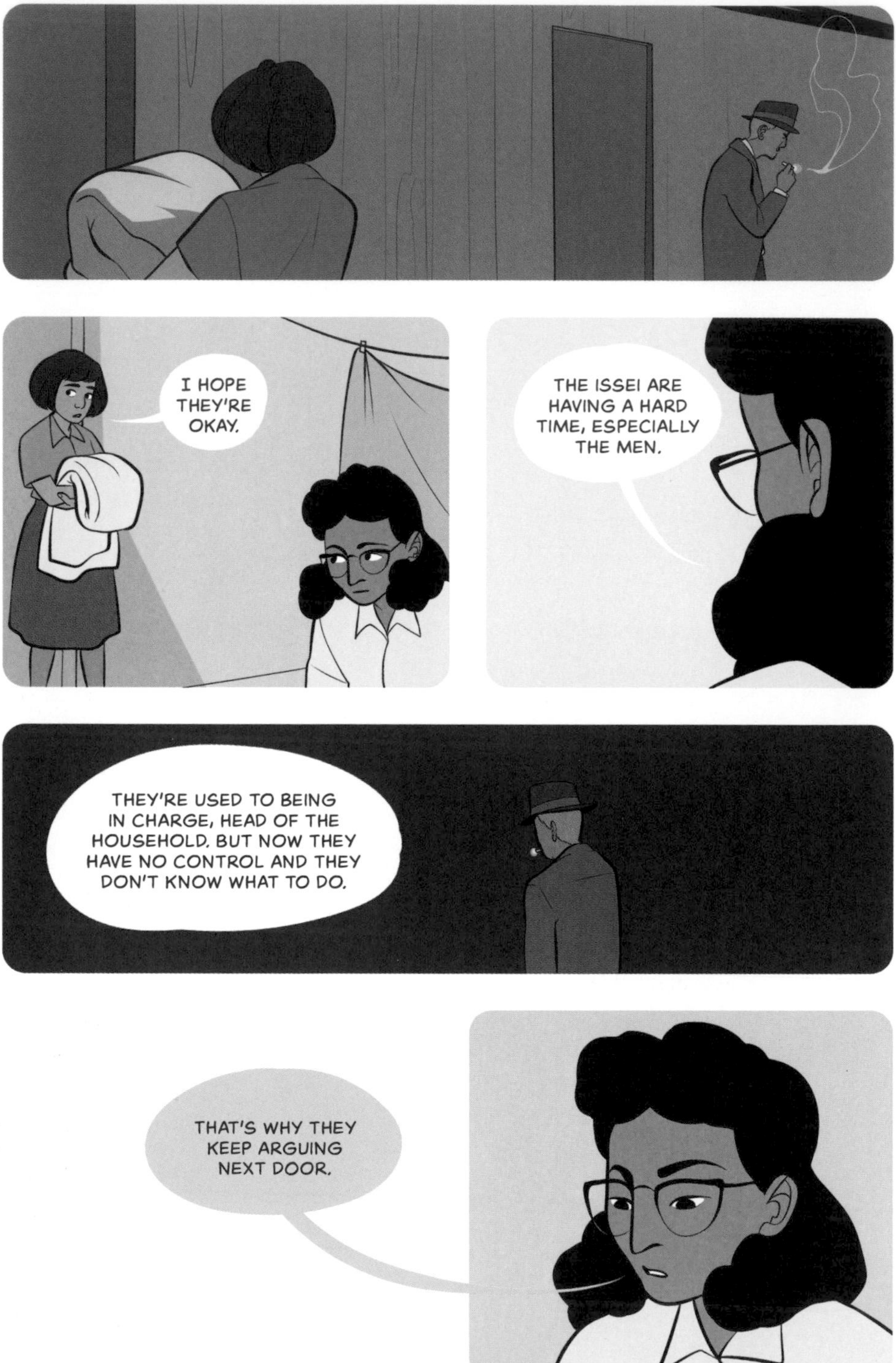
I HOPE THEY'RE OKAY.
THE ISSEI ARE HAVING A HARD TIME, ESPECIALLY THE MEN.
THEY'RE USED TO BEING IN CHARGE, HEAD OF THE HOUSEHOLD. BUT NOW THEY HAVE NO CONTROL AND THEY DON'T KNOW WHAT TO DO.
THAT'S WHY THEY KEEP ARGUING NEXT DOOR.

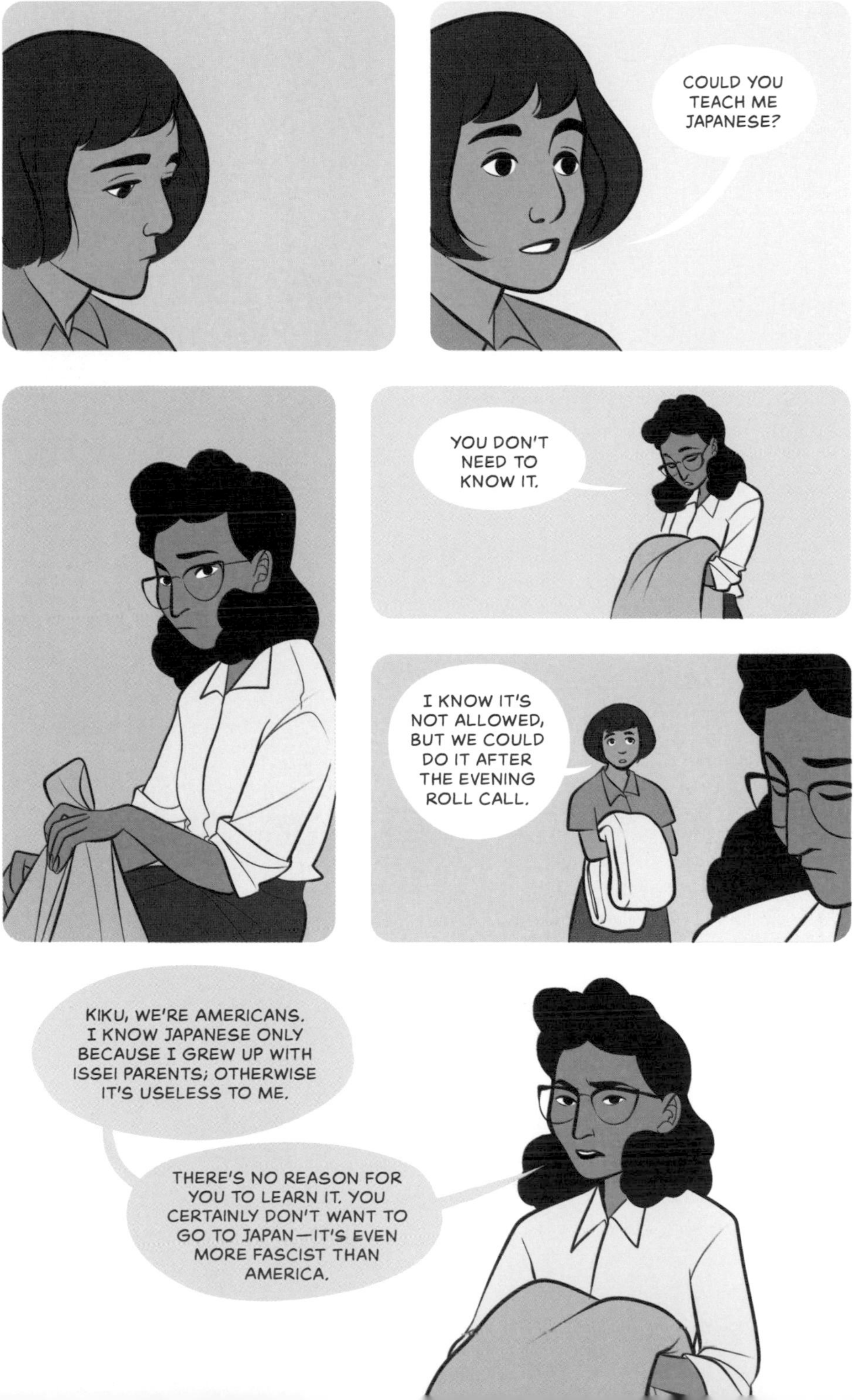

COULD YOU TEACH ME JAPANESE?
YOU DON'T NEED TO KNOW IT.
I KNOW IT'S NOT ALLOWED, BUT WE COULD DO IT AFTER THE EVENING ROLL CALL.
KIKU, WE'RE AMERICANS. I KNOW JAPANESE ONLY BECAUSE I GREW UP WITH ISSEI PARENTS; OTHERWISE IT'S USELESS TO ME.
THERE'S NO REASON FOR YOU TO LEARN IT. YOU CERTAINLY DON'T WANT TO GO TO JAPAN—IT'S EVEN MORE FASCIST THAN AMERICA.

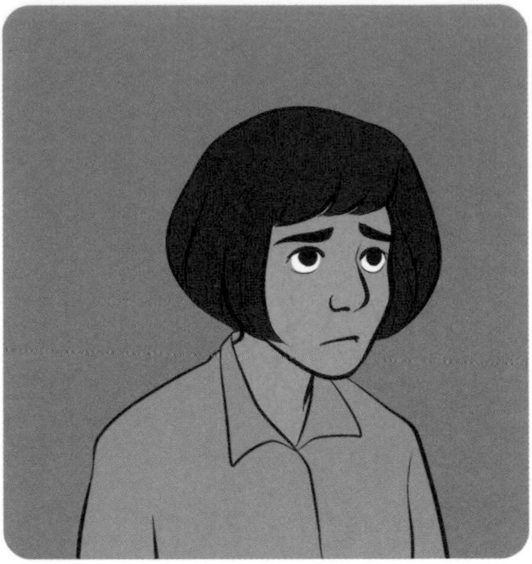

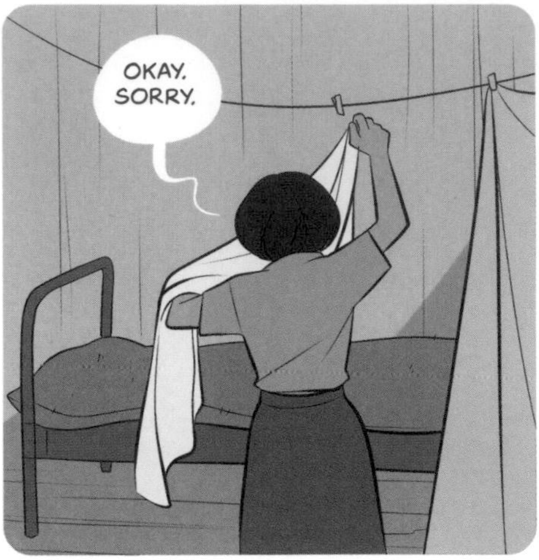
OKAY. SORRY.

I HADN'T EXPECTED AIKO TO BE SO OPPOSED TO ALL THINGS JAPANESE. BECAUSE SHE WAS SO OUTSPOKEN AGAINST THE PREJUDICES WE WERE FACING FOR OUR HERITAGE, I EXPECTED HER TO BE MORE PASSIONATE ABOUT THAT HERITAGE.

BUT SEEING HOW SHE AND OTHER NISEI SHIED AWAY FROM THE ISSEI'S OUTDATED TRADITIONS MADE ME UNDERSTAND A LITTLE MORE JUST WHY THERE WAS ALMOST NO CONNECTION TO JAPAN LEFT BY THE TIME I WAS BORN.

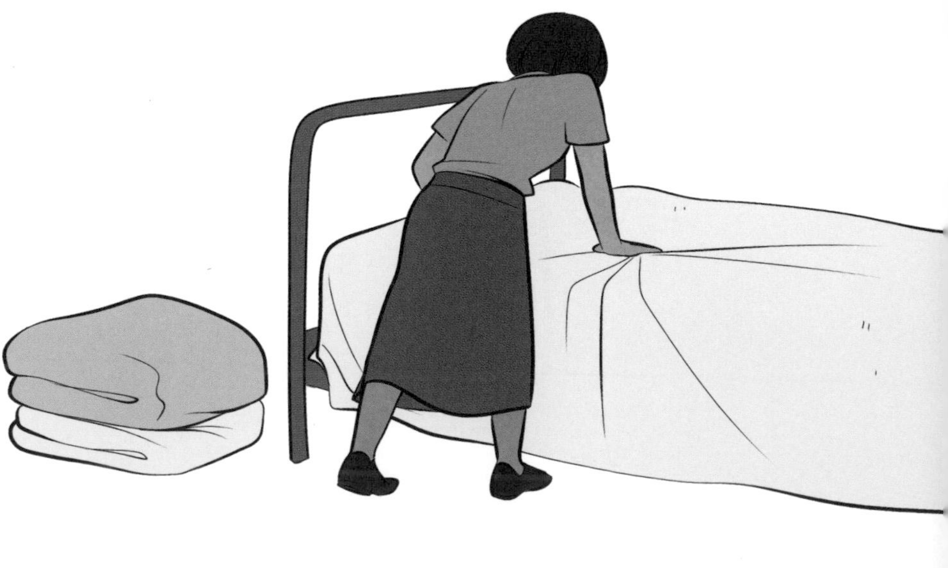

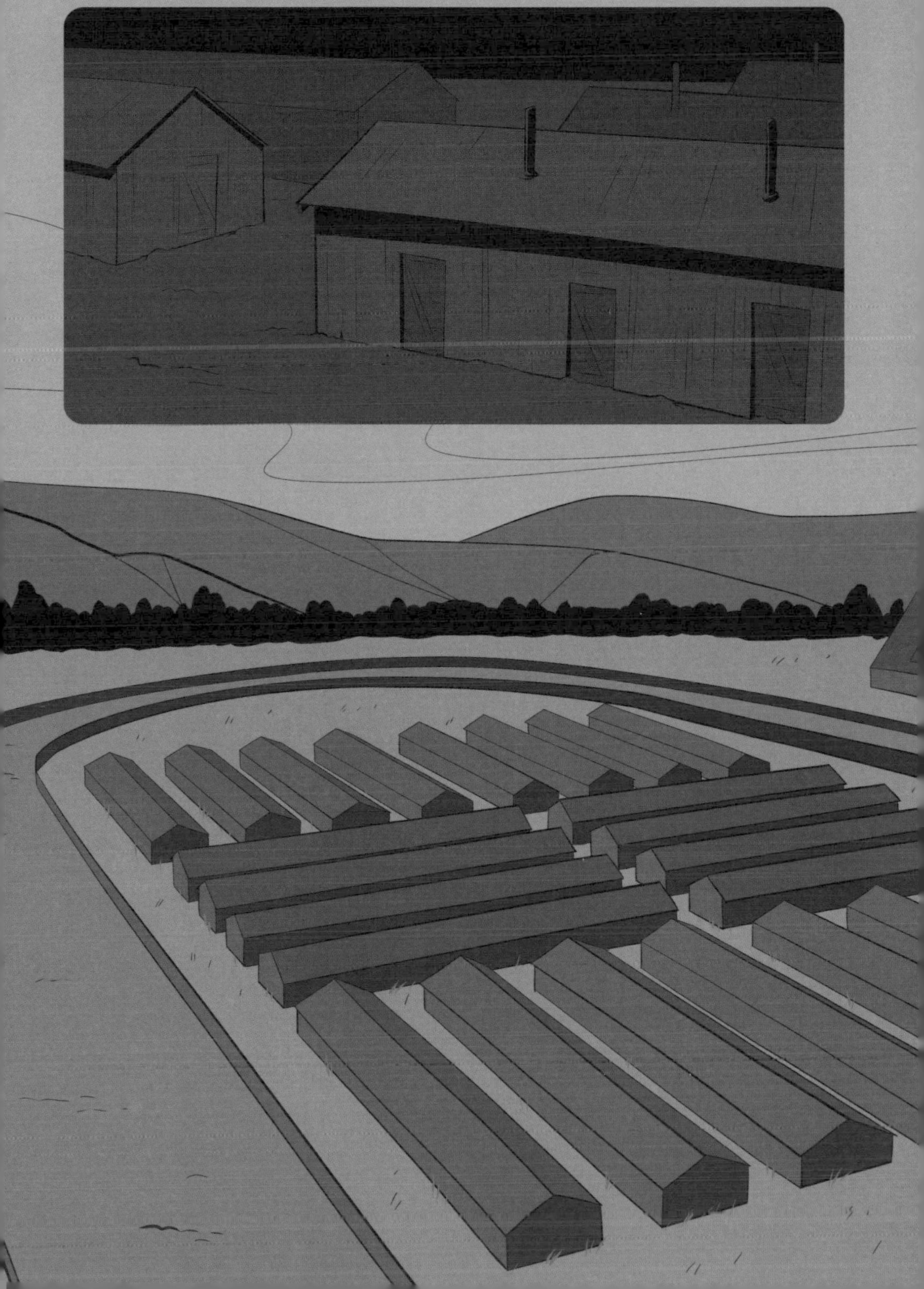

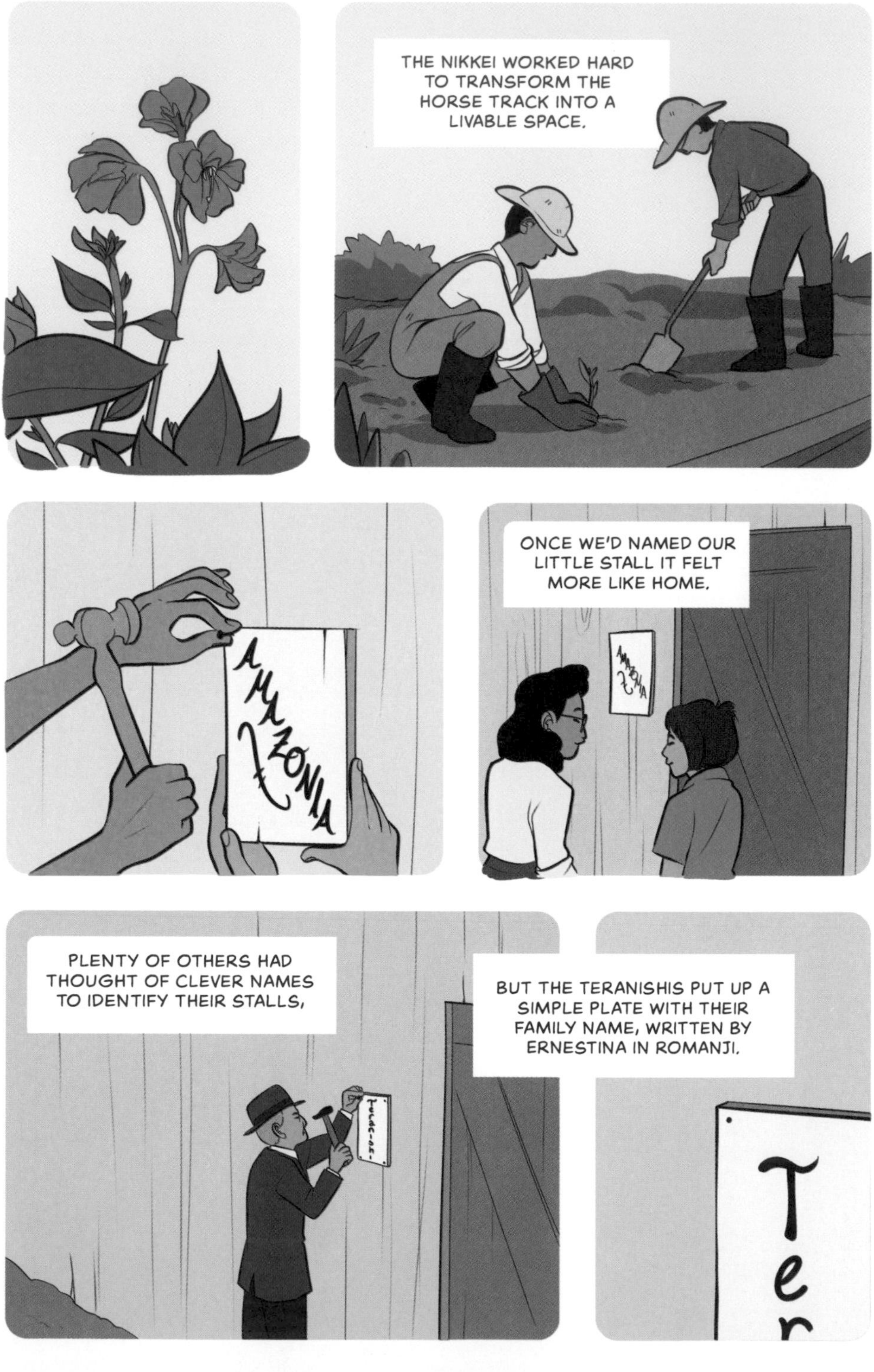
THE NIKKEI WORKED HARD TO TRANSFORM THE HORSE TRACK INTO A LIVABLE SPACE.
AMAZONIA
ONCE WE'D NAMED OUR LITTLE STALL IT FELT MORE LIKE HOME.
AMAZONIA
PLENTY OF OTHERS HAD THOUGHT OF CLEVER NAMES TO IDENTIFY THEIR STALLS,
BUT THE TERANISHIS PUT UP A SIMPLE PLATE WITH THEIR FAMILY NAME, WRITTEN BY ERNESTINA IN ROMANJI.
Teranishi
Ter

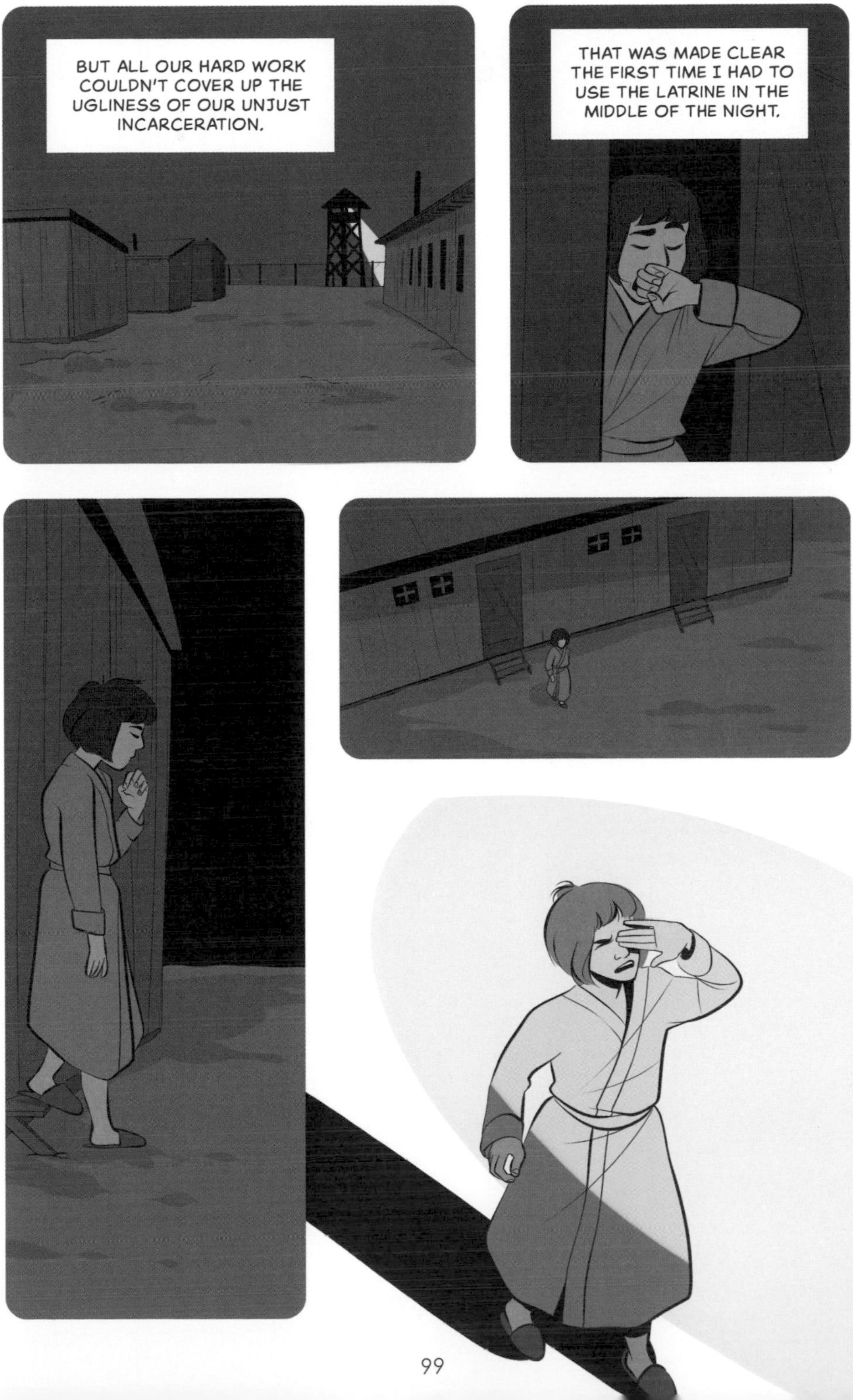
BUT ALL OUR HARD WORK COULDN'T COVER UP THE UGLINESS OF OUR UNJUST INCARCERATION.
THAT WAS MADE CLEAR THE FIRST TIME I HAD TO USE THE LATRINE IN THE MIDDLE OF THE NIGHT.

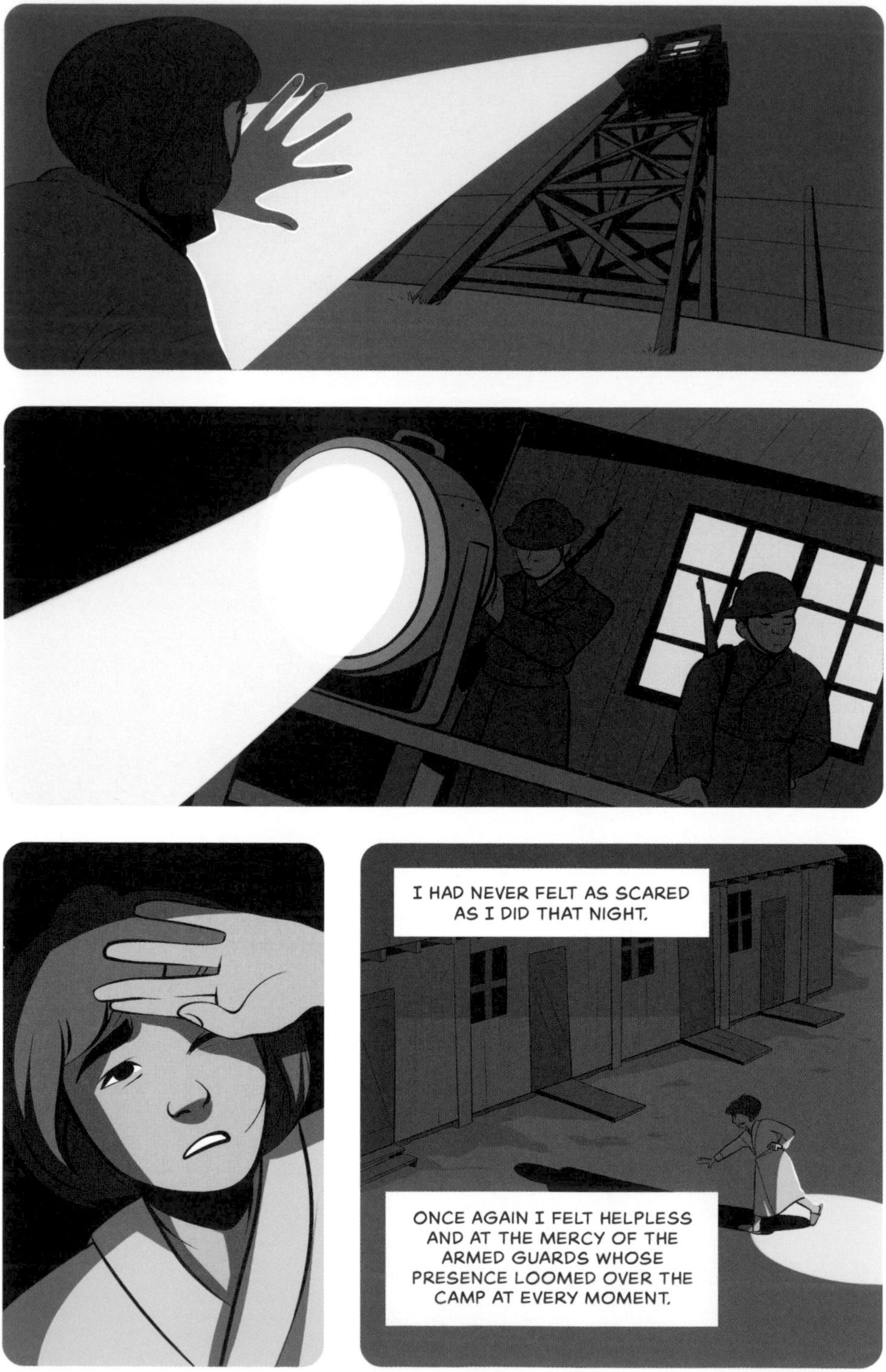
I HAD NEVER FELT AS SCARED AS I DID THAT NIGHT.
ONCE AGAIN I FELT HELPLESS AND AT THE MERCY OF THE ARMED GUARDS WHOSE PRESENCE LOOMED OVER THE CAMP AT EVERY MOMENT.

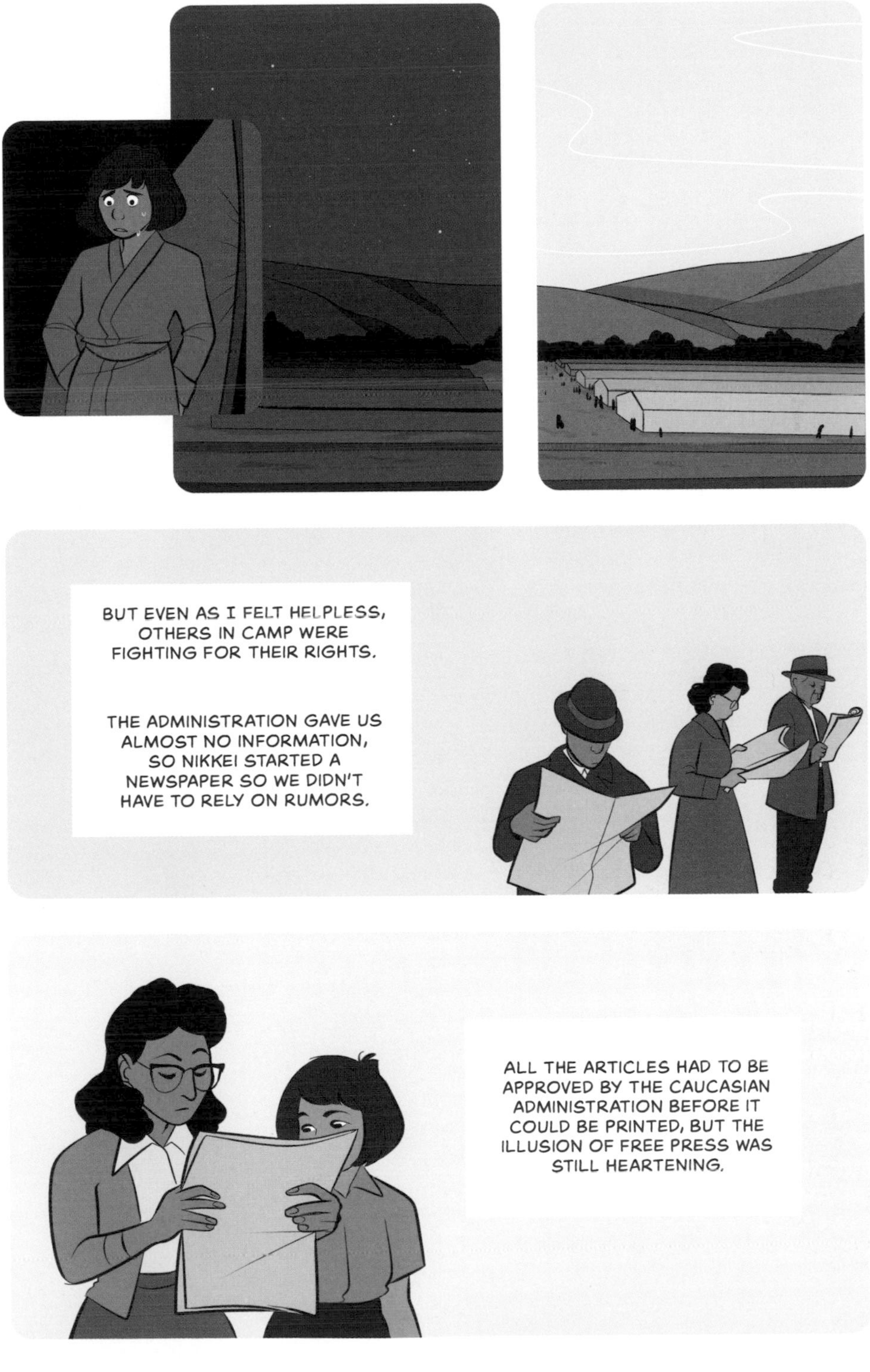
BUT EVEN AS I FELT HELPLESS, OTHERS IN CAMP WERE FIGHTING FOR THEIR RIGHTS.
THE ADMINISTRATION GAVE US ALMOST NO INFORMATION, SO NIKKEI STARTED A NEWSPAPER SO WE DIDN'T HAVE TO RELY ON RUMORS.
ALL THE ARTICLES HAD TO BE APPROVED BY THE CAUCASIAN ADMINISTRATION BEFORE IT COULD BE PRINTED, BUT THE ILLUSION OF FREE PRESS WAS STILL HEARTENING.

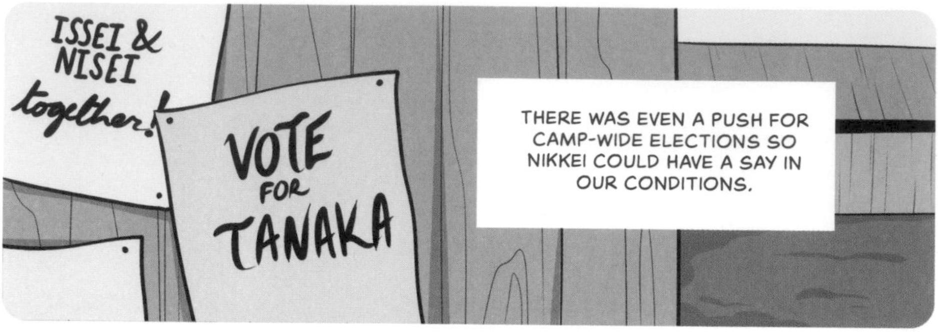
ISSEI & NISEI together!
VOTE FOR TANAKA
THERE WAS EVEN A PUSH FOR CAMP-WIDE ELECTIONS SO NIKKEI COULD HAVE A SAY IN OUR CONDITIONS.

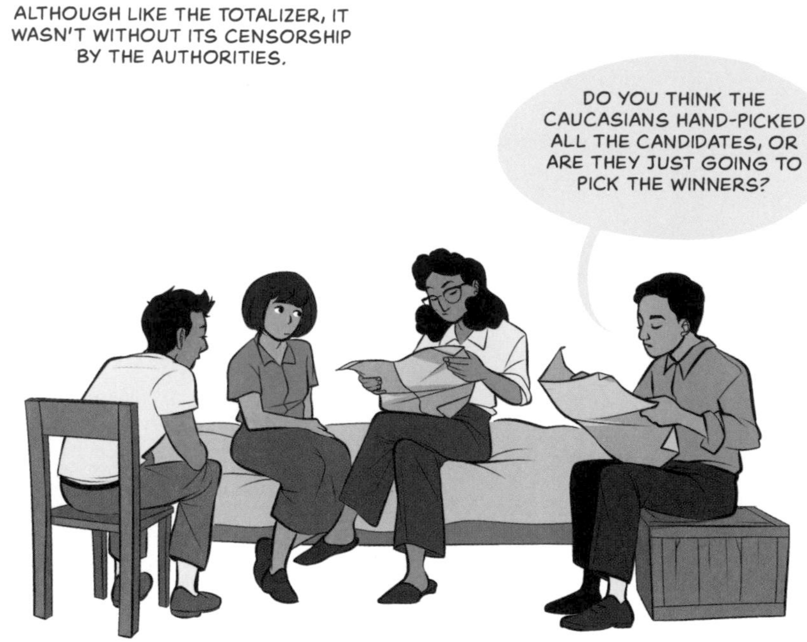
ALTHOUGH LIKE THE TOTALIZER, IT WASN'T WITHOUT ITS CENSORSHIP BY THE AUTHORITIES.
DO YOU THINK THE CAUCASIANS HAND-PICKED ALL THE CANDIDATES, OR ARE THEY JUST GOING TO PICK THE WINNERS?

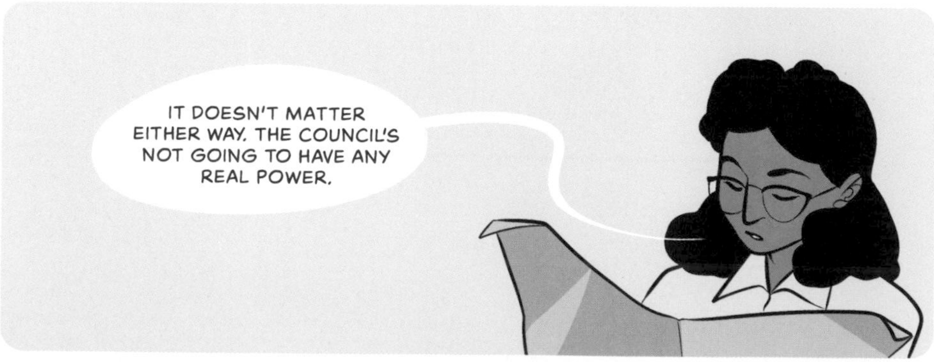
IT DOESN'T MATTER EITHER WAY. THE COUNCIL'S NOT GOING TO HAVE ANY REAL POWER.

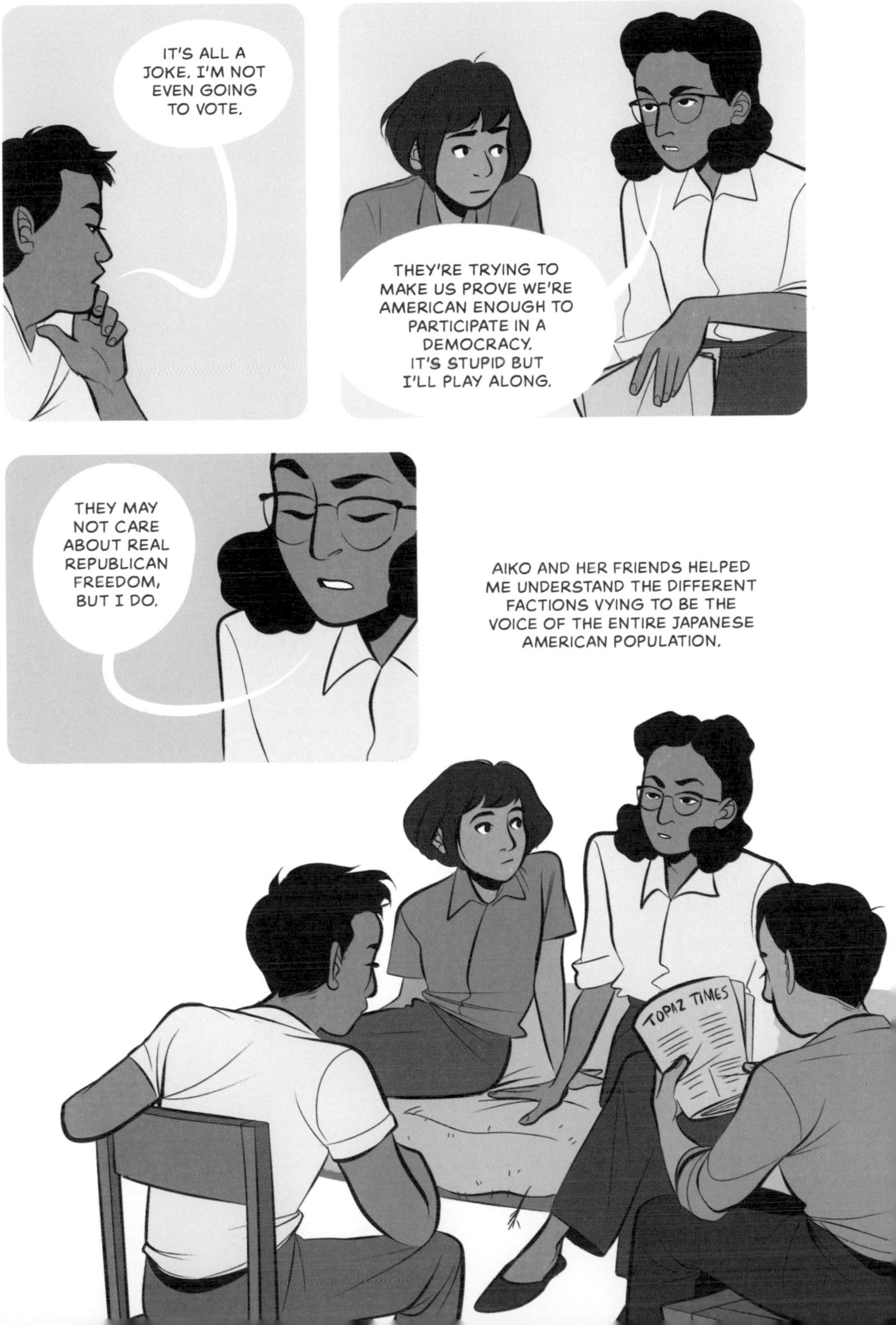
IT'S ALL A JOKE. I'M NOT EVEN GOING TO VOTE.
THEY'RE TRYING TO MAKE US PROVE WE'RE AMERICAN ENOUGH TO PARTICIPATE IN A DEMOCRACY. IT'S STUPID BUT I'LL PLAY ALONG.
THEY MAY NOT CARE ABOUT REAL REPUBLICAN FREEDOM, BUT I DO.
AIKO AND HER FRIENDS HELPED ME UNDERSTAND THE DIFFERENT FACTIONS VYING TO BE THE VOICE OF THE ENTIRE JAPANESE AMERICAN POPULATION.
TOPAZ TIMES

THE JAPANESE AMERICAN CITIZENS LEAGUE (JACL) CANDIDATE WHO WANTS TO REJECT ALL JAPANESE CULTURE AND MAINTAIN COOPERATION WITH THE CAMP ADMINISTRATION.

THE LEFTIST NISEI CANDIDATE WHO WANTS TO PROTEST FOR CIVIL RIGHTS AND AGAINST FASCISM ABROAD AND AT HOME.

THE MODERATE NISEI CANDIDATE WHO EMPHASIZES THE NEED FOR ISSEI AND NISEI TO COME TOGETHER.

AND THEN THERE WERE THE ISSEI WHO DIDN'T FEEL LIKE ANY OF THESE CANDIDATES REPRESENTED THEM.

ISSEI WEREN'T ALLOWED TO RUN FOR OFFICE, BUT THEY WERE ALLOWED TO VOTE FOR THE FIRST TIME. THEY HAD BEEN DENIED U.S. CITIZENSHIP AND HAD NEVER BEEN ABLE TO PARTICIPATE IN ELECTIONS BEFORE.

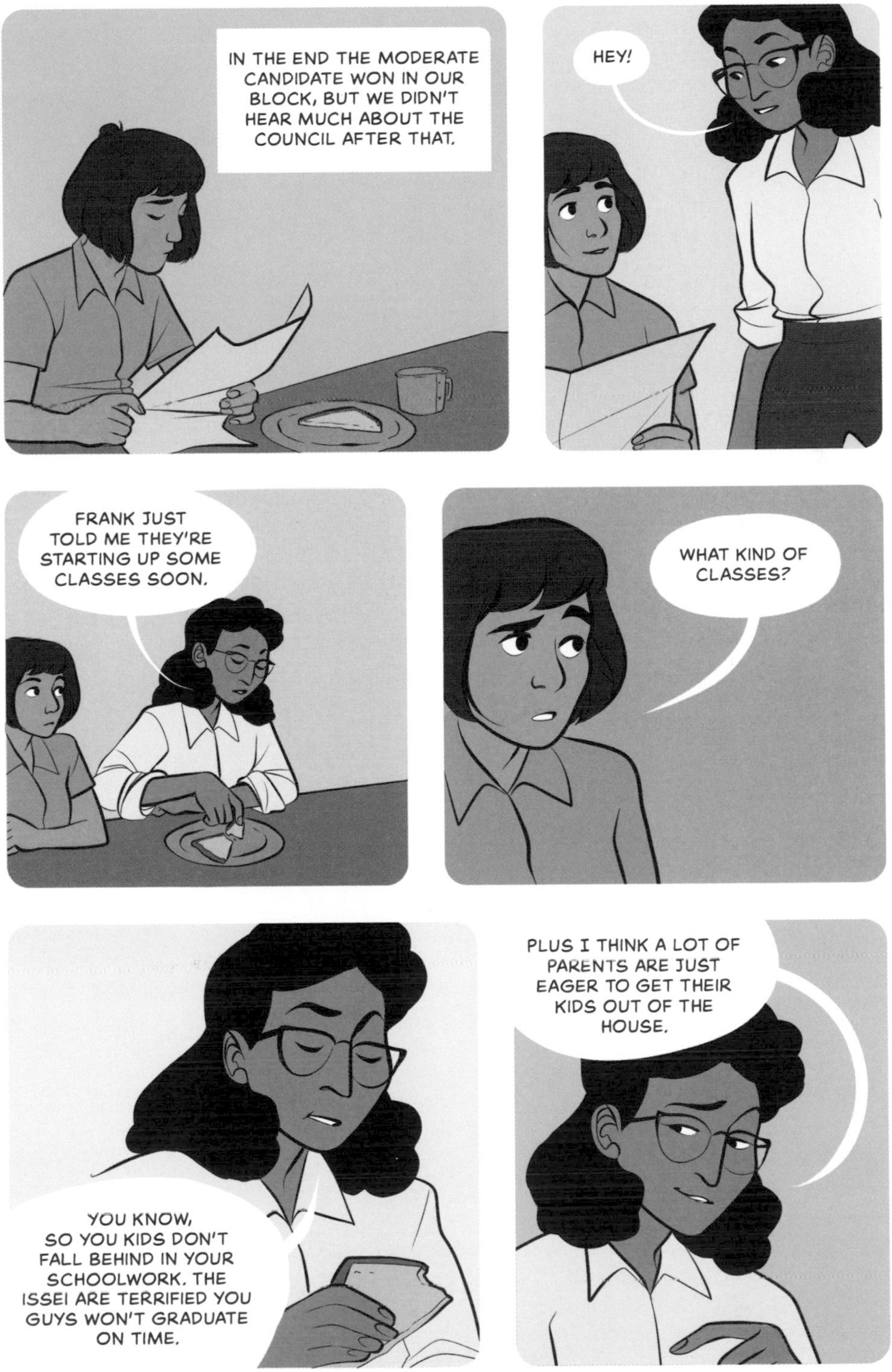
IN THE END THE MODERATE CANDIDATE WON IN OUR BLOCK, BUT WE DIDN'T HEAR MUCH ABOUT THE COUNCIL AFTER THAT.
HEY!
FRANK JUST TOLD ME THEY'RE STARTING UP SOME CLASSES SOON.
WHAT KIND OF CLASSES?
YOU KNOW, SO YOU KIDS DON'T FALL BEHIND IN YOUR SCHOOLWORK. THE ISSEI ARE TERRIFIED YOU GUYS WON'T GRADUATE ON TIME.
PLUS I THINK A LOT OF PARENTS ARE JUST EAGER TO GET THEIR KIDS OUT OF THE HOUSE.

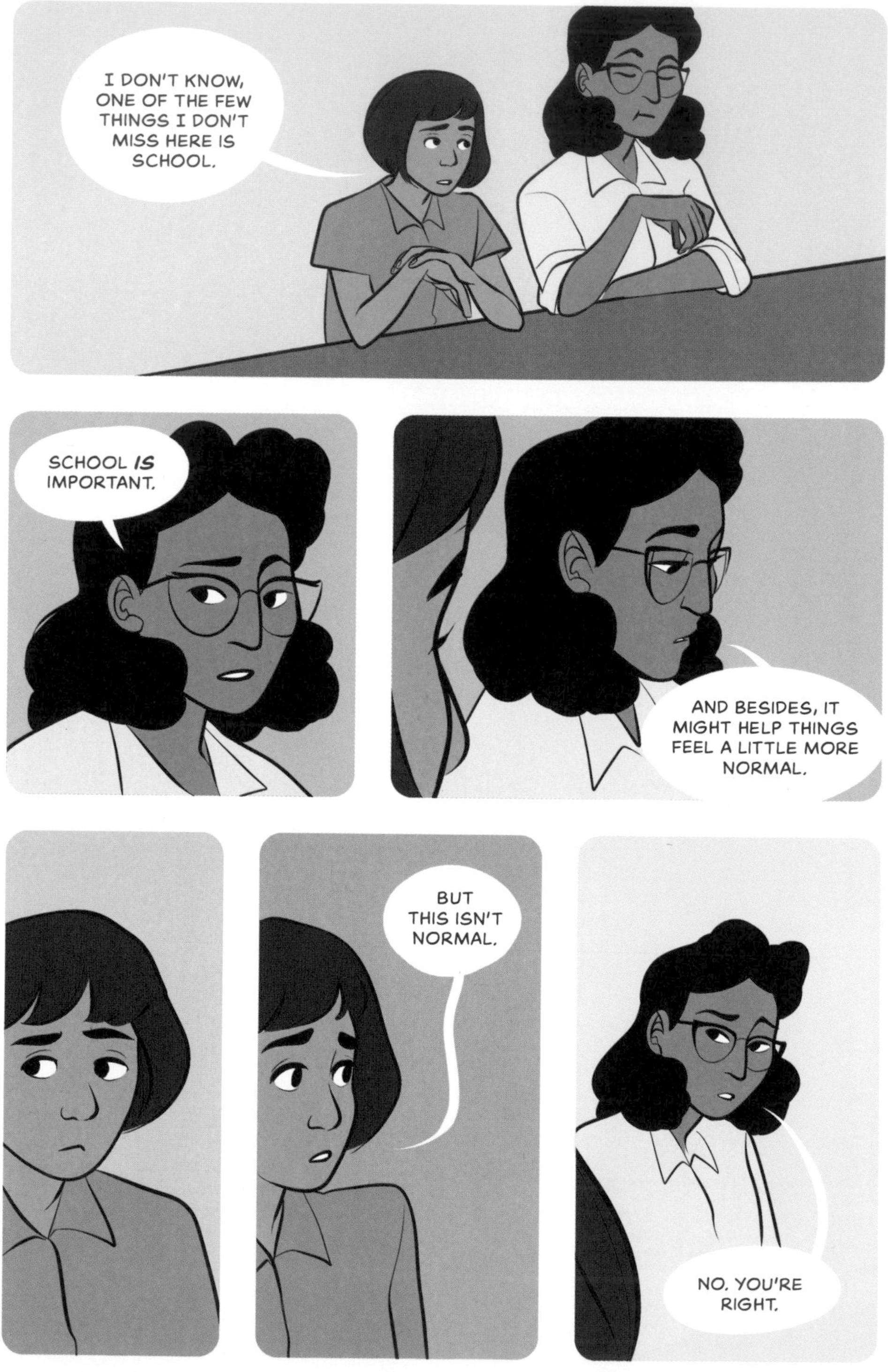
I DON'T KNOW, ONE OF THE FEW THINGS I DON'T MISS HERE IS SCHOOL.
SCHOOL *IS* IMPORTANT.
AND BESIDES, IT MIGHT HELP THINGS FEEL A LITTLE MORE NORMAL.
BUT THIS ISN'T NORMAL.
NO, YOU'RE RIGHT.

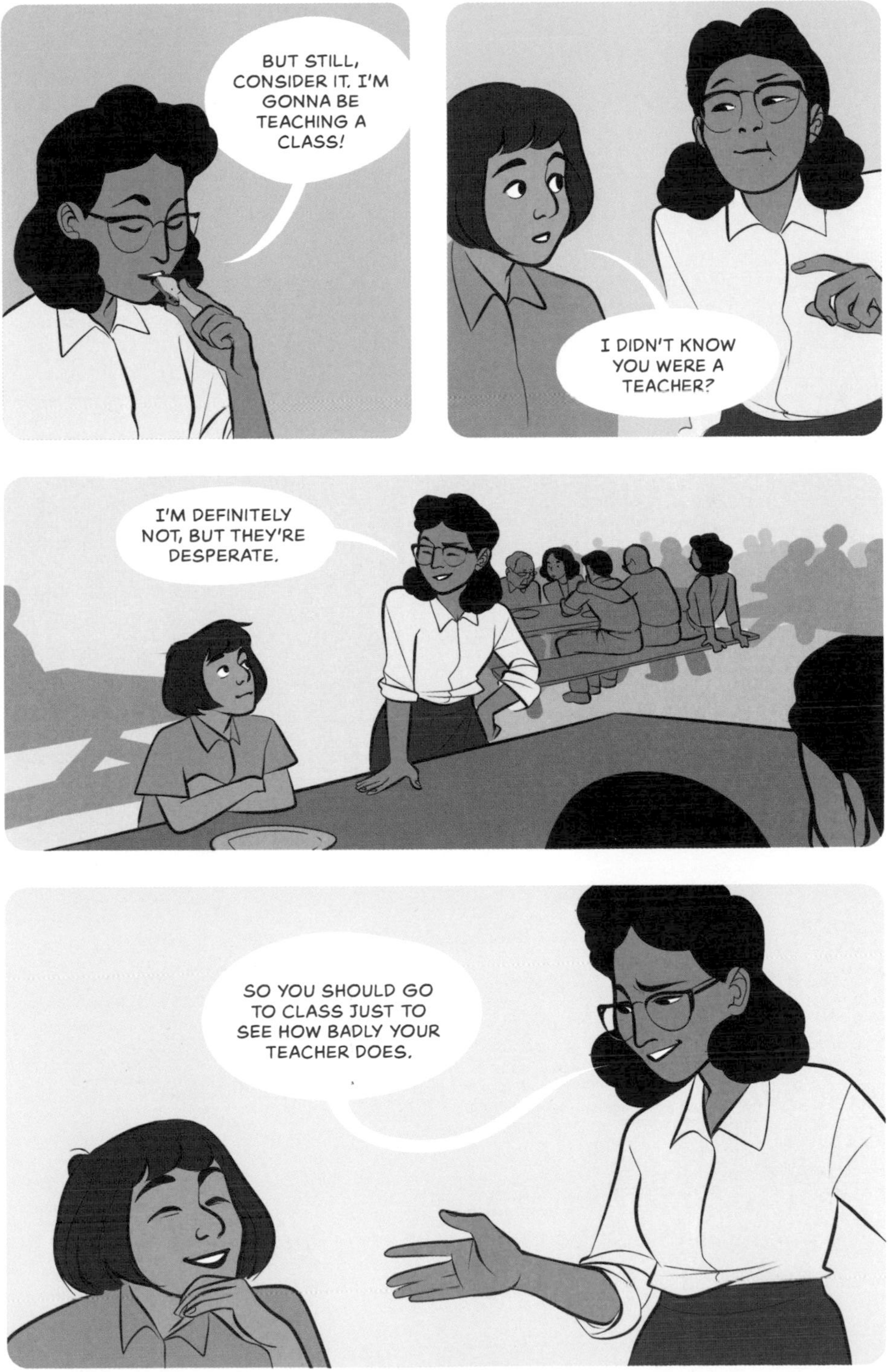
BUT STILL, CONSIDER IT. I'M GONNA BE TEACHING A CLASS!
I DIDN'T KNOW YOU WERE A TEACHER?
I'M DEFINITELY NOT, BUT THEY'RE DESPERATE.
SO YOU SHOULD GO TO CLASS JUST TO SEE HOW BADLY YOUR TEACHER DOES.

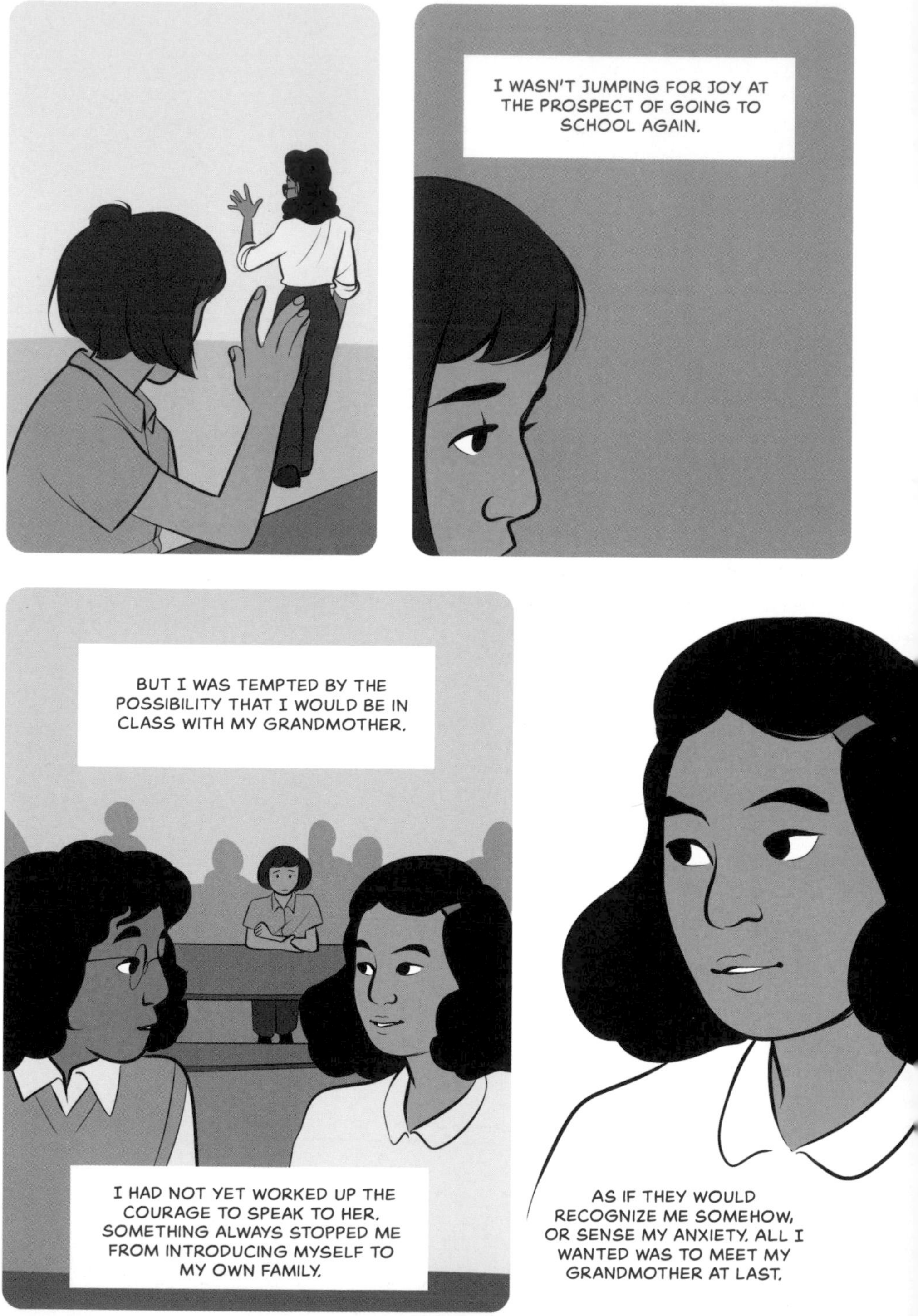
I WASN'T JUMPING FOR JOY AT THE PROSPECT OF GOING TO SCHOOL AGAIN.
BUT I WAS TEMPTED BY THE POSSIBILITY THAT I WOULD BE IN CLASS WITH MY GRANDMOTHER.
I HAD NOT YET WORKED UP THE COURAGE TO SPEAK TO HER. SOMETHING ALWAYS STOPPED ME FROM INTRODUCING MYSELF TO MY OWN FAMILY.
AS IF THEY WOULD RECOGNIZE ME SOMEHOW, OR SENSE MY ANXIETY. ALL I WANTED WAS TO MEET MY GRANDMOTHER AT LAST.

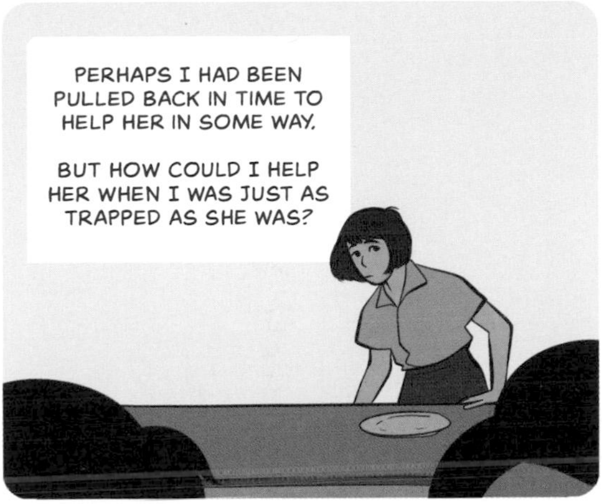
PERHAPS I HAD BEEN PULLED BACK IN TIME TO HELP HER IN SOME WAY.
BUT HOW COULD I HELP HER WHEN I WAS JUST AS TRAPPED AS SHE WAS?

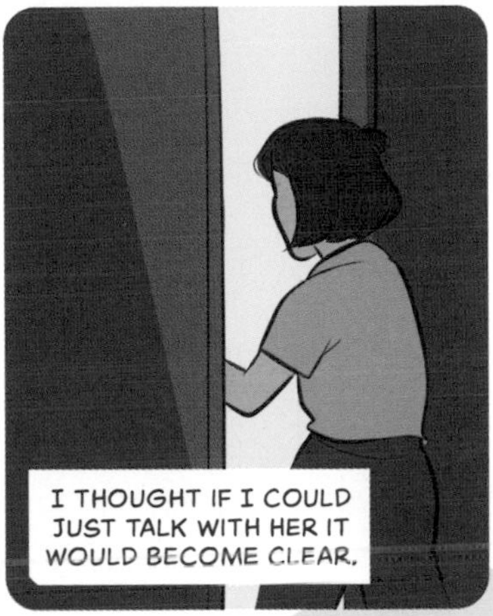
I THOUGHT IF I COULD JUST TALK WITH HER IT WOULD BECOME CLEAR.

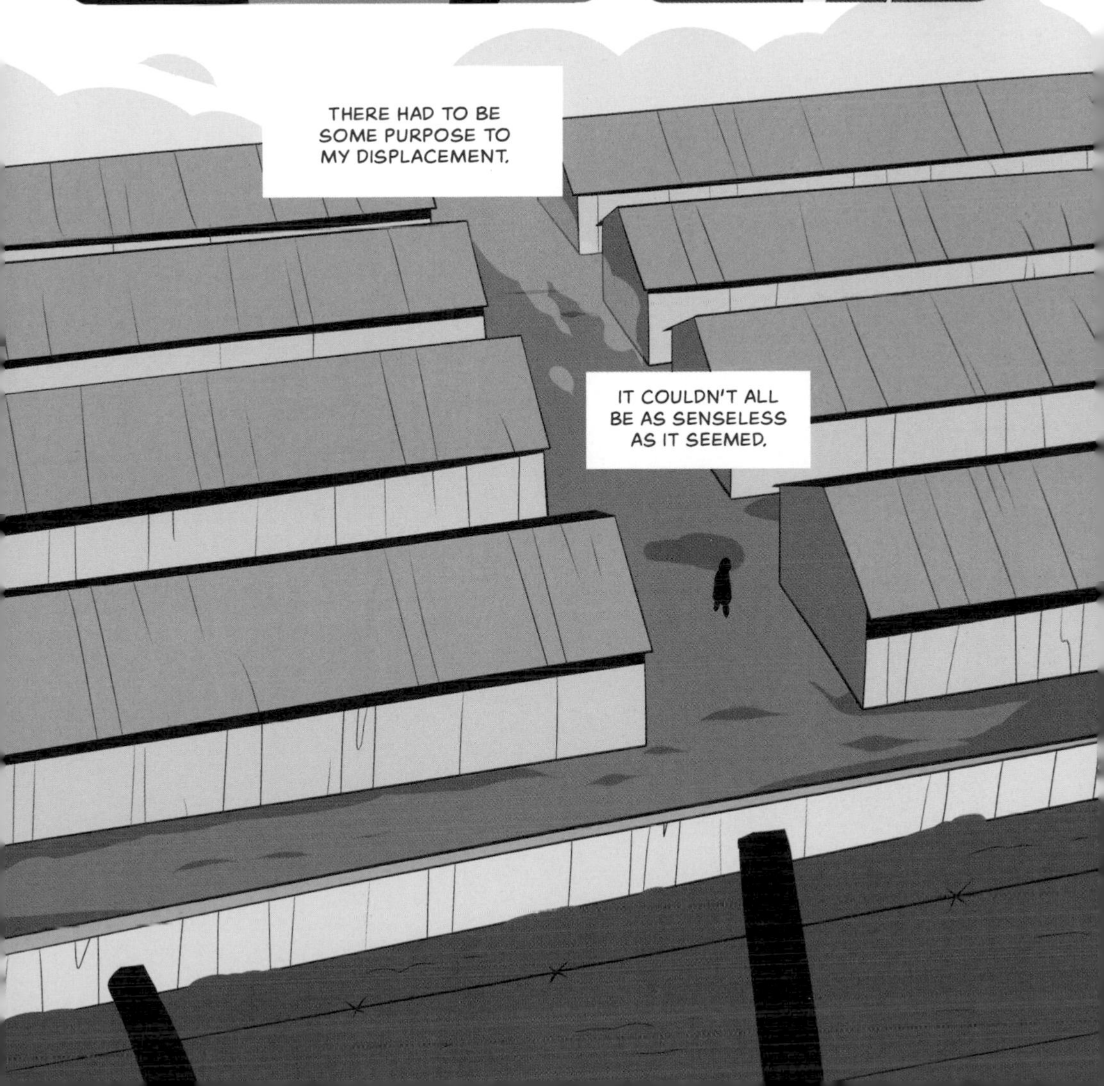
THERE HAD TO BE SOME PURPOSE TO MY DISPLACEMENT.
IT COULDN'T ALL BE AS SENSELESS AS IT SEEMED.

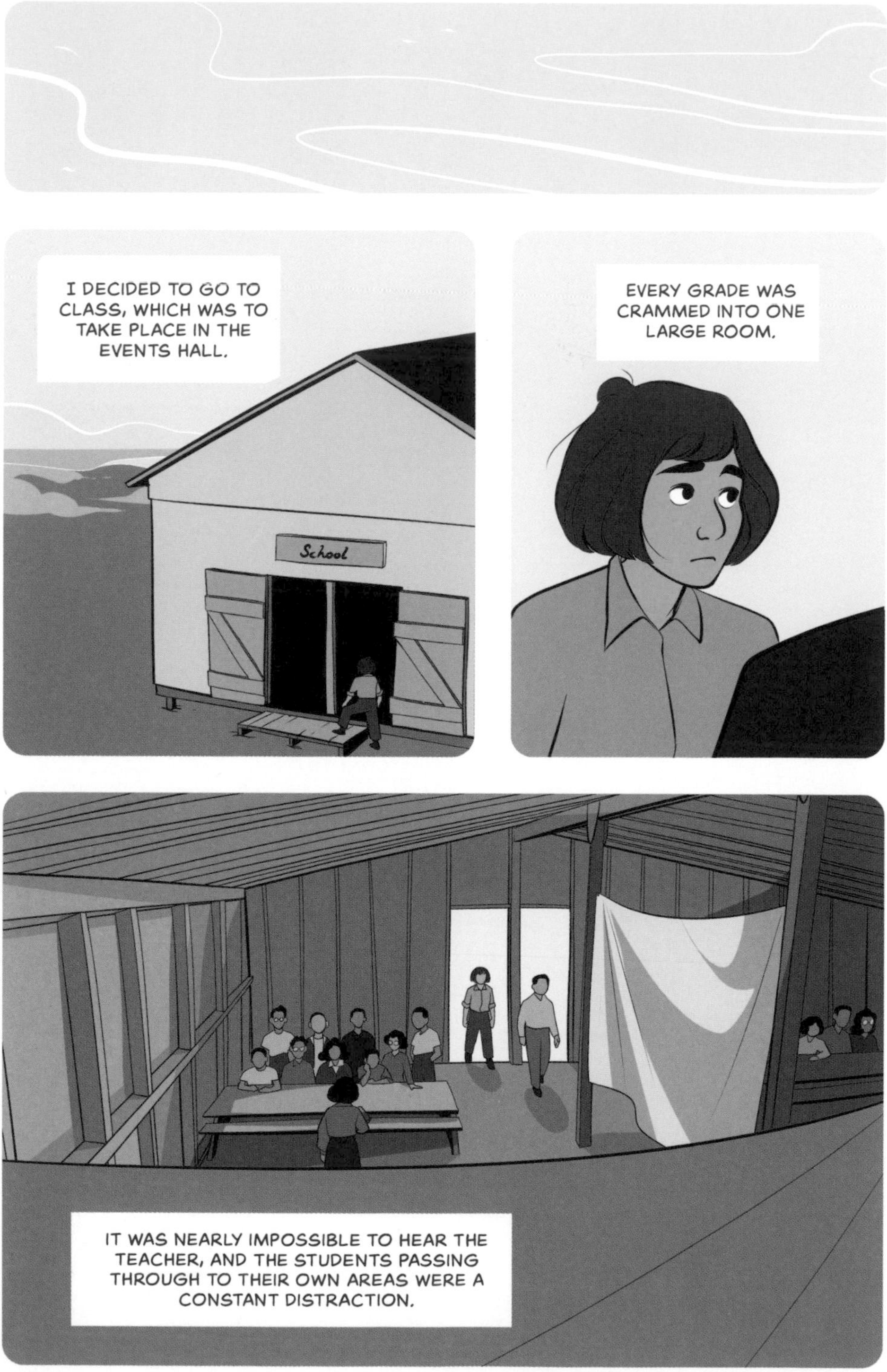
I DECIDED TO GO TO CLASS, WHICH WAS TO TAKE PLACE IN THE EVENTS HALL.
School
EVERY GRADE WAS CRAMMED INTO ONE LARGE ROOM.
IT WAS NEARLY IMPOSSIBLE TO HEAR THE TEACHER, AND THE STUDENTS PASSING THROUGH TO THEIR OWN AREAS WERE A CONSTANT DISTRACTION.

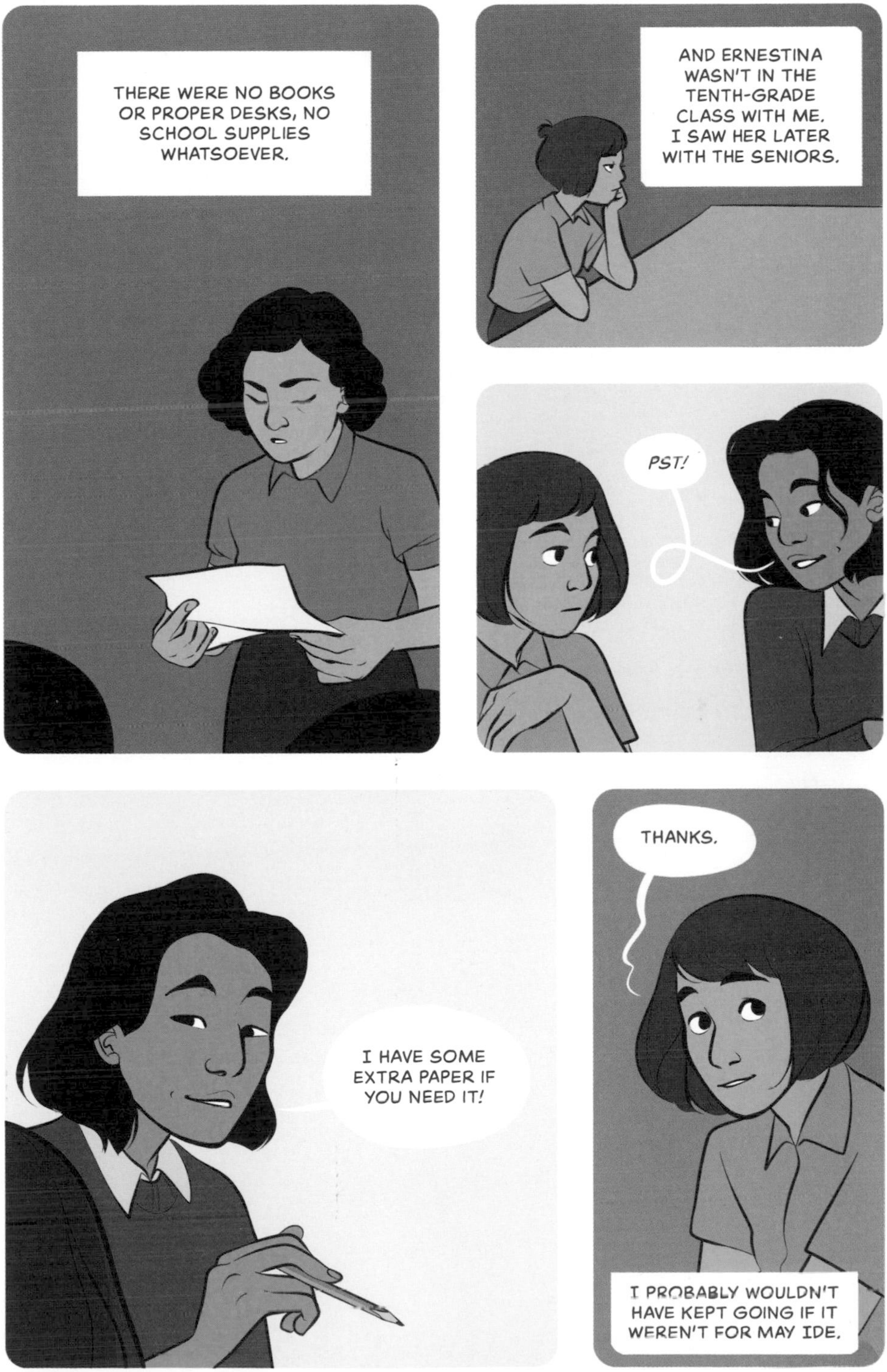
THERE WERE NO BOOKS OR PROPER DESKS, NO SCHOOL SUPPLIES WHATSOEVER.
AND ERNESTINA WASN'T IN THE TENTH-GRADE CLASS WITH ME. I SAW HER LATER WITH THE SENIORS.
PST!
I HAVE SOME EXTRA PAPER IF YOU NEED IT!
THANKS.
I PROBABLY WOULDN'T HAVE KEPT GOING IF IT WEREN'T FOR MAY IDE.

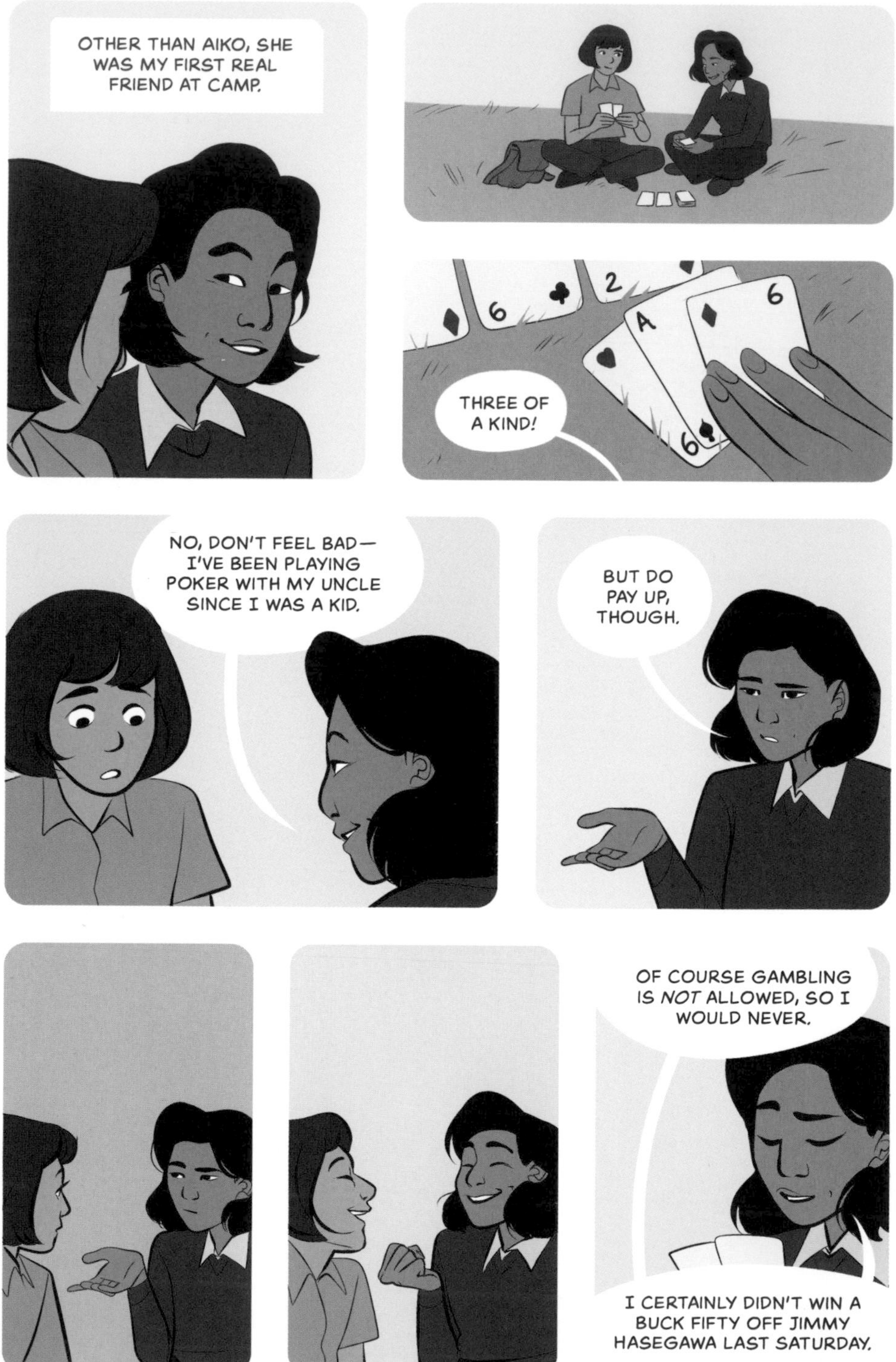
OTHER THAN AIKO, SHE WAS MY FIRST REAL FRIEND AT CAMP.
THREE OF A KIND!
NO, DON'T FEEL BAD— I'VE BEEN PLAYING POKER WITH MY UNCLE SINCE I WAS A KID.
BUT DO PAY UP, THOUGH.
OF COURSE GAMBLING IS *NOT* ALLOWED, SO I WOULD NEVER.
I CERTAINLY DIDN'T WIN A BUCK FIFTY OFF JIMMY HASEGAWA LAST SATURDAY.

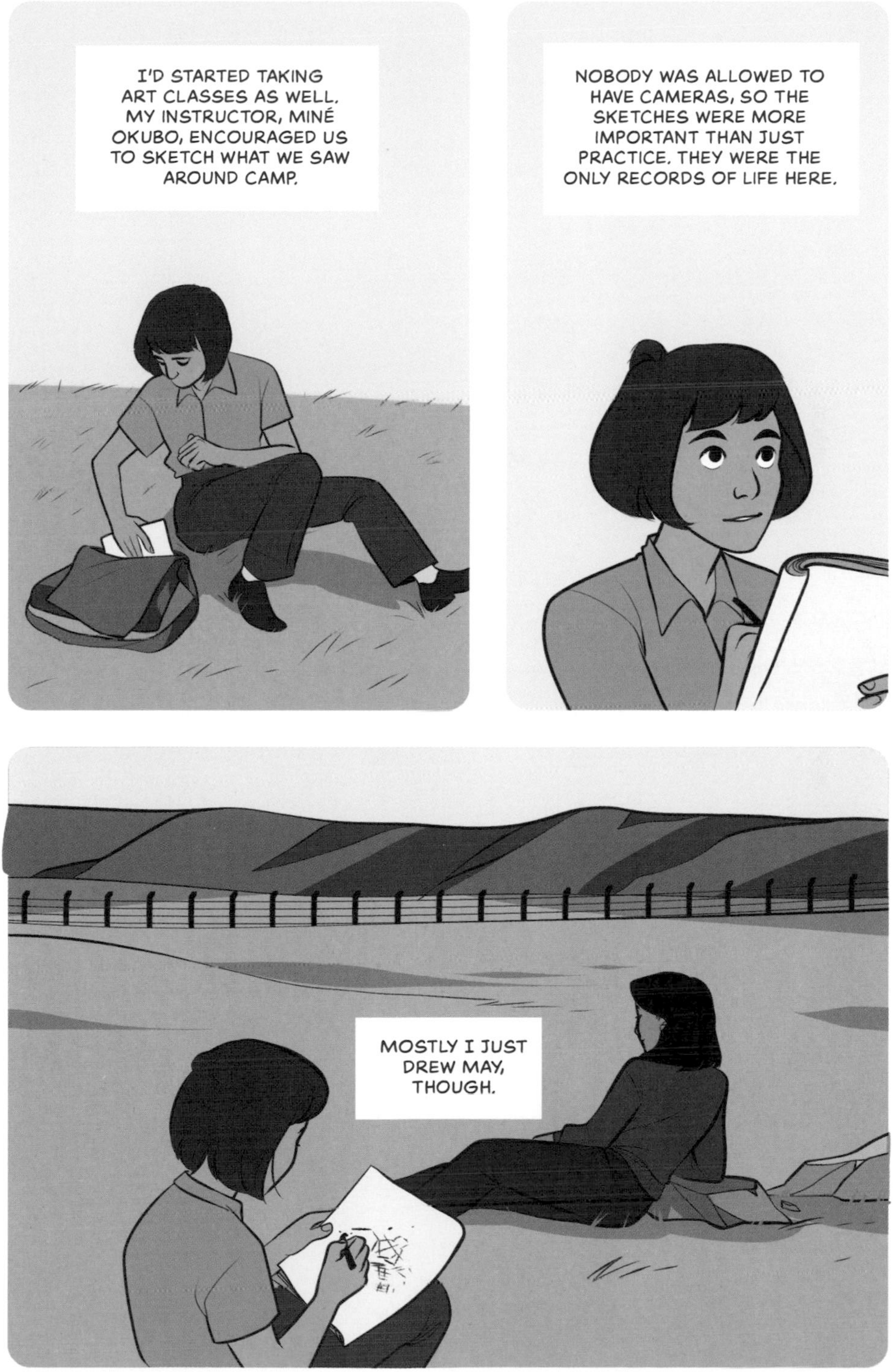
I'D STARTED TAKING ART CLASSES AS WELL. MY INSTRUCTOR, MINÉ OKUBO, ENCOURAGED US TO SKETCH WHAT WE SAW AROUND CAMP.
NOBODY WAS ALLOWED TO HAVE CAMERAS, SO THE SKETCHES WERE MORE IMPORTANT THAN JUST PRACTICE. THEY WERE THE ONLY RECORDS OF LIFE HERE.
MOSTLY I JUST DREW MAY, THOUGH.

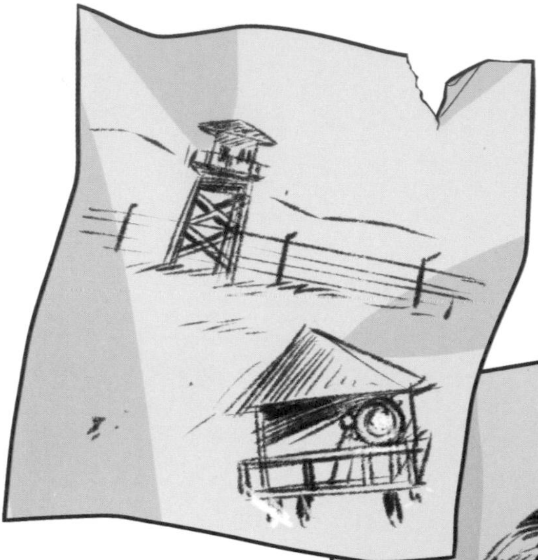

WITH CLASSES AND FRIENDS, I FINALLY FELL INTO A ROUTINE.

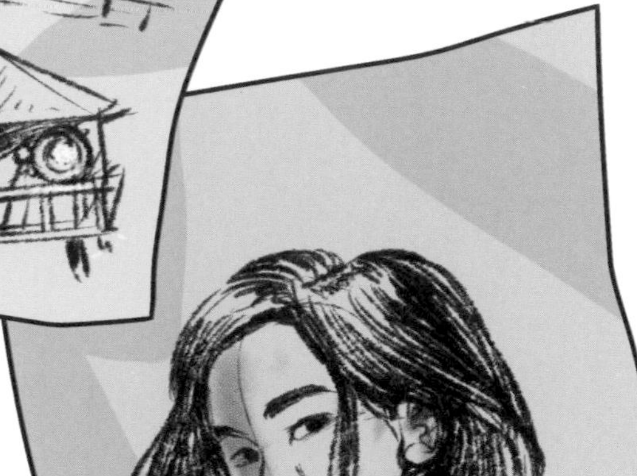

FOR THE FIRST TIME, I WASN'T LYING IN BED EACH NIGHT HOPING TO BE BACK IN MY OWN HOME WHEN I WOKE UP.

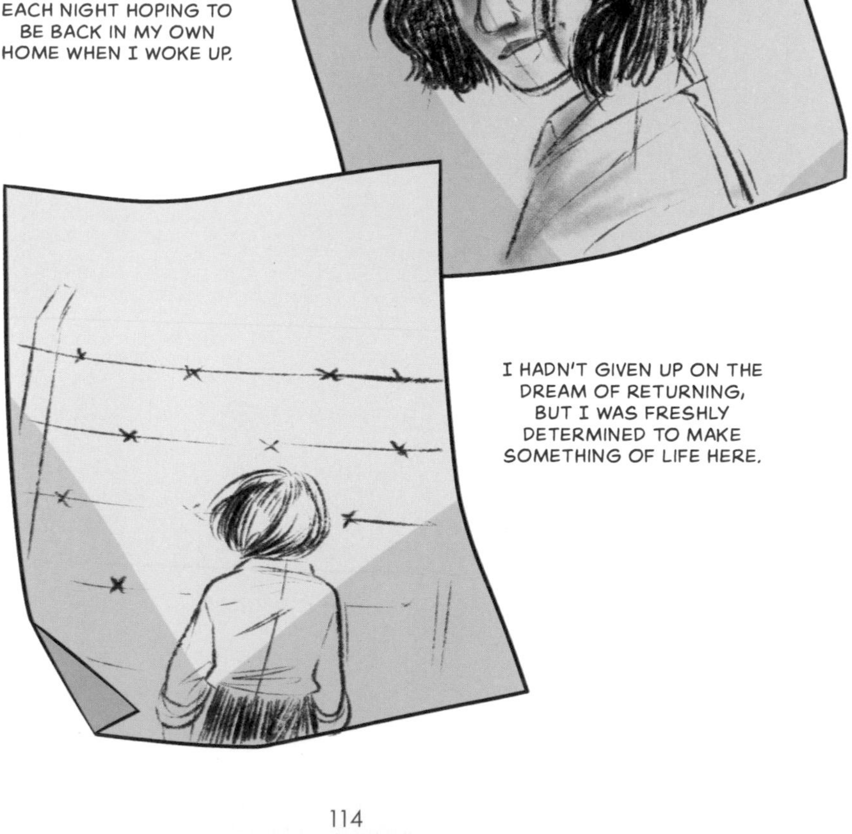

I HADN'T GIVEN UP ON THE DREAM OF RETURNING, BUT I WAS FRESHLY DETERMINED TO MAKE SOMETHING OF LIFE HERE.

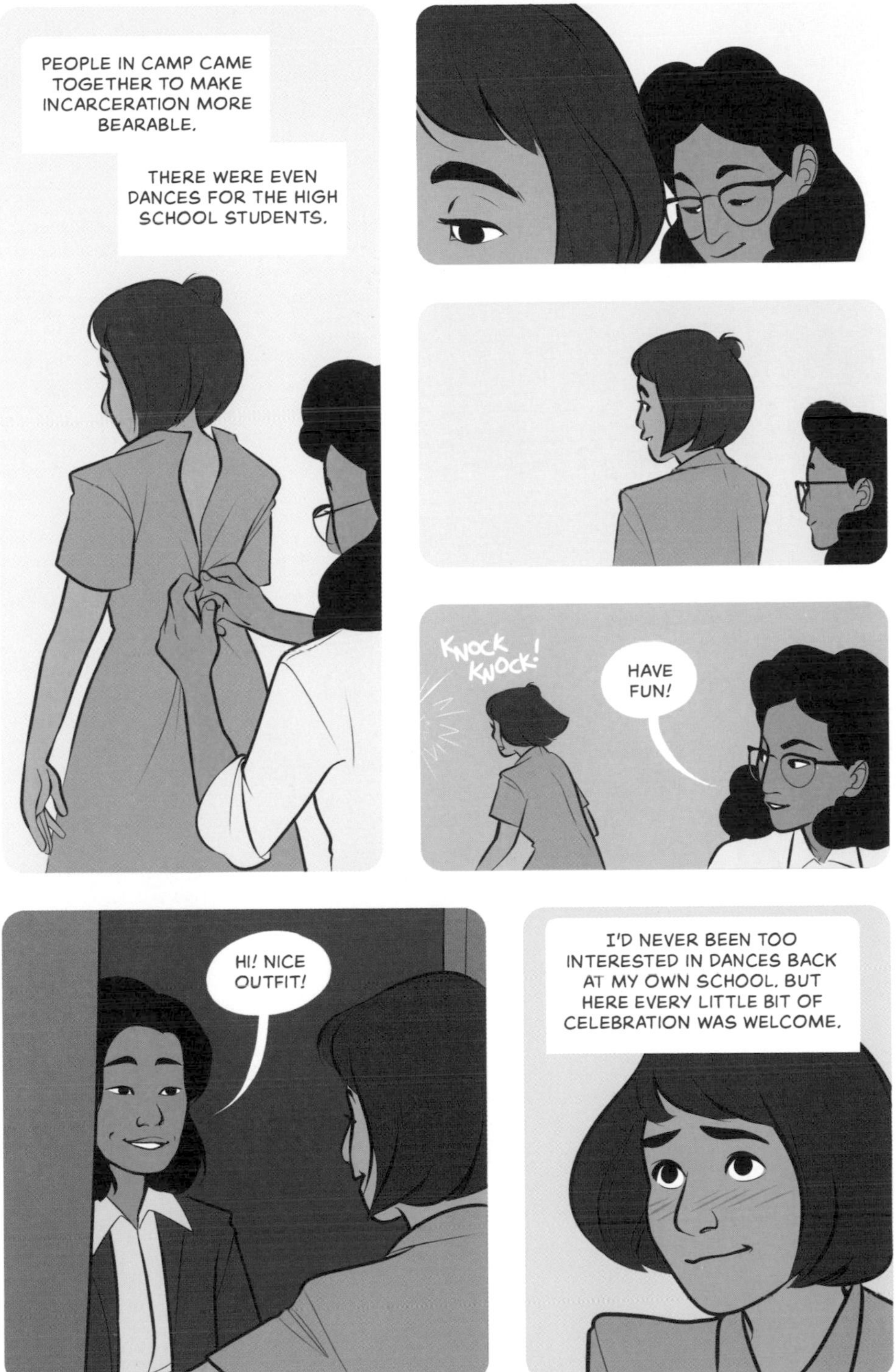
PEOPLE IN CAMP CAME TOGETHER TO MAKE INCARCERATION MORE BEARABLE.
THERE WERE EVEN DANCES FOR THE HIGH SCHOOL STUDENTS.
KNOCK KNOCK!
HAVE FUN!
HI! NICE OUTFIT!
I'D NEVER BEEN TOO INTERESTED IN DANCES BACK AT MY OWN SCHOOL. BUT HERE EVERY LITTLE BIT OF CELEBRATION WAS WELCOME.

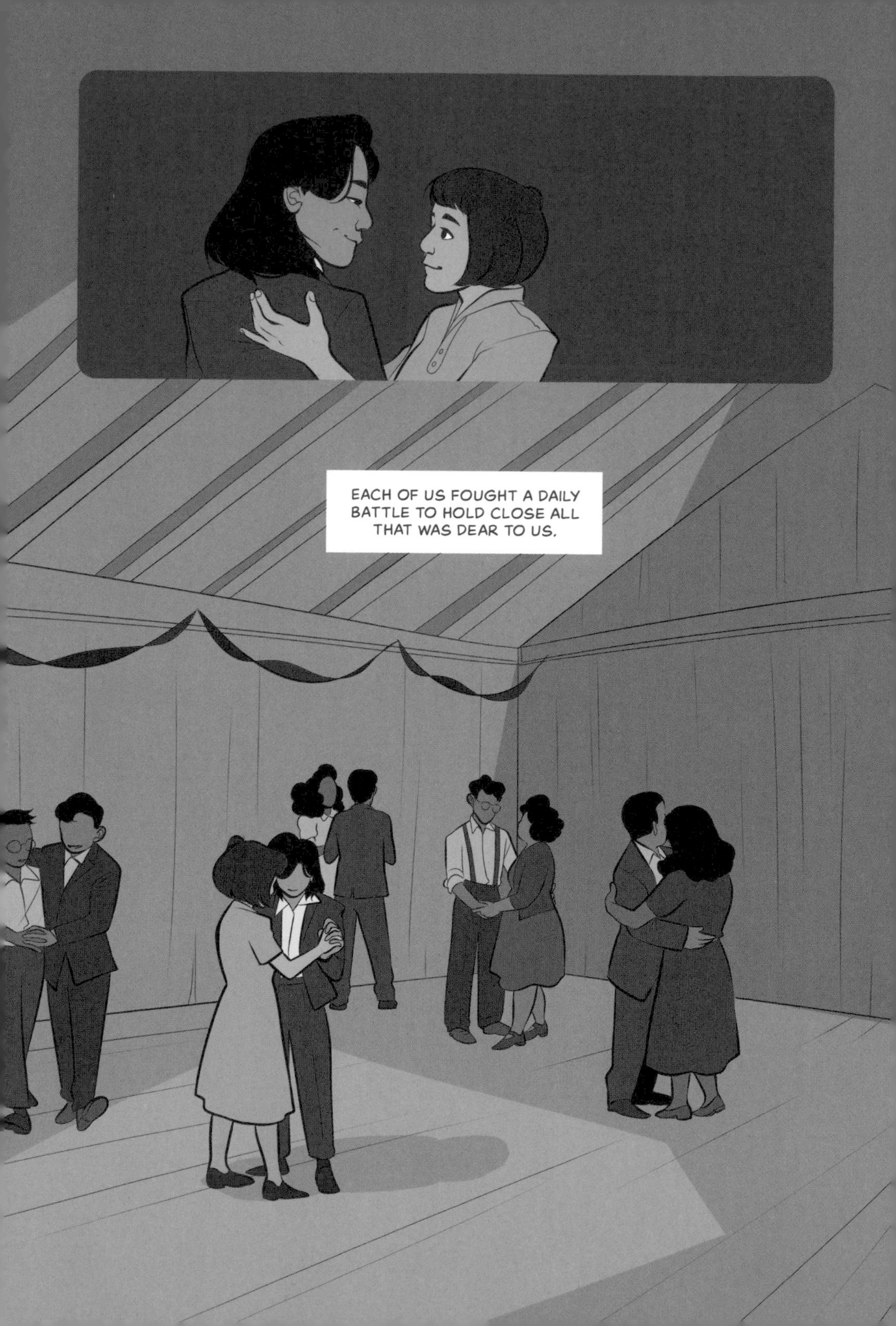
EACH OF US FOUGHT A DAILY BATTLE TO HOLD CLOSE ALL THAT WAS DEAR TO US.

5

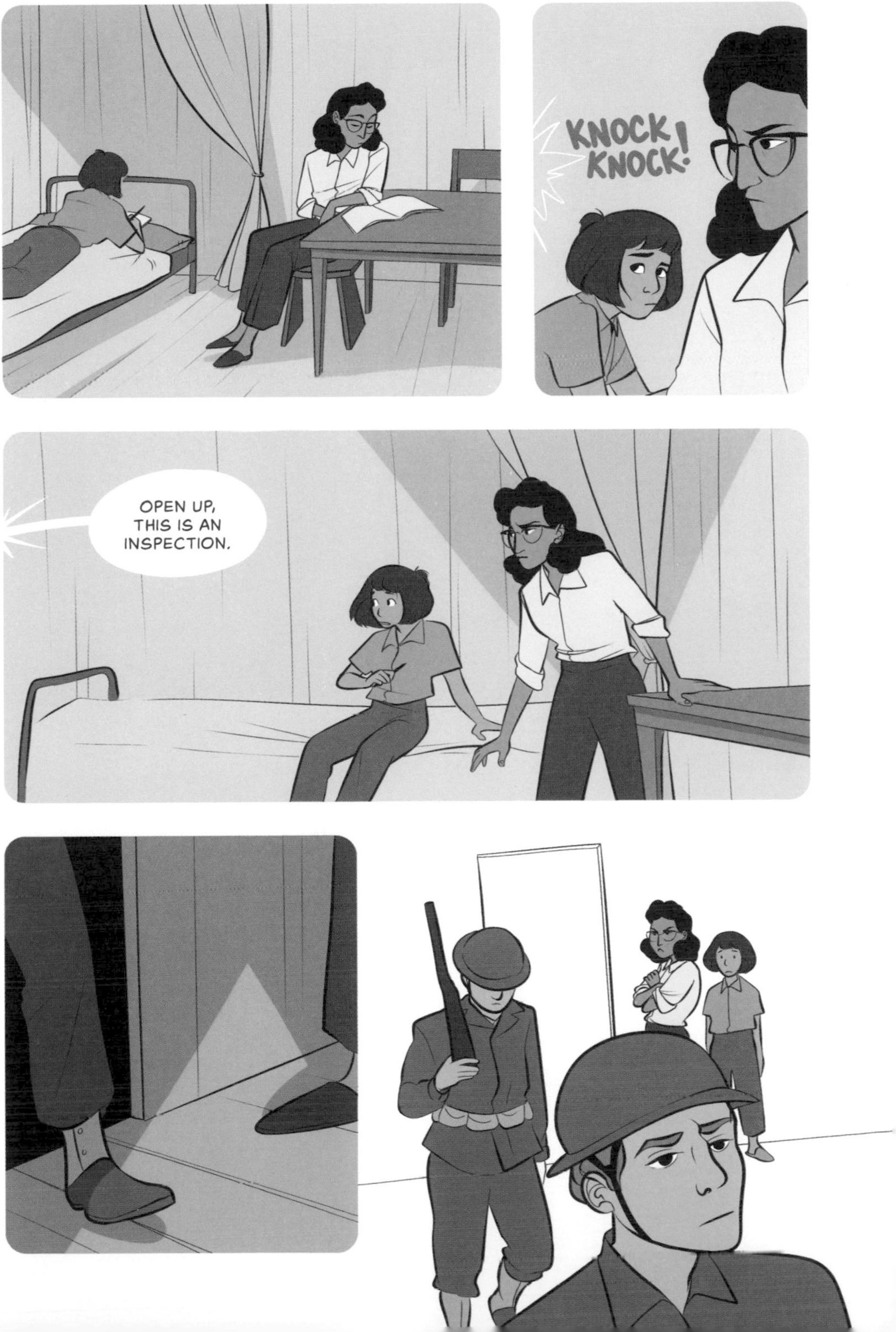
KNOCK KNOCK!
OPEN UP, THIS IS AN INSPECTION.

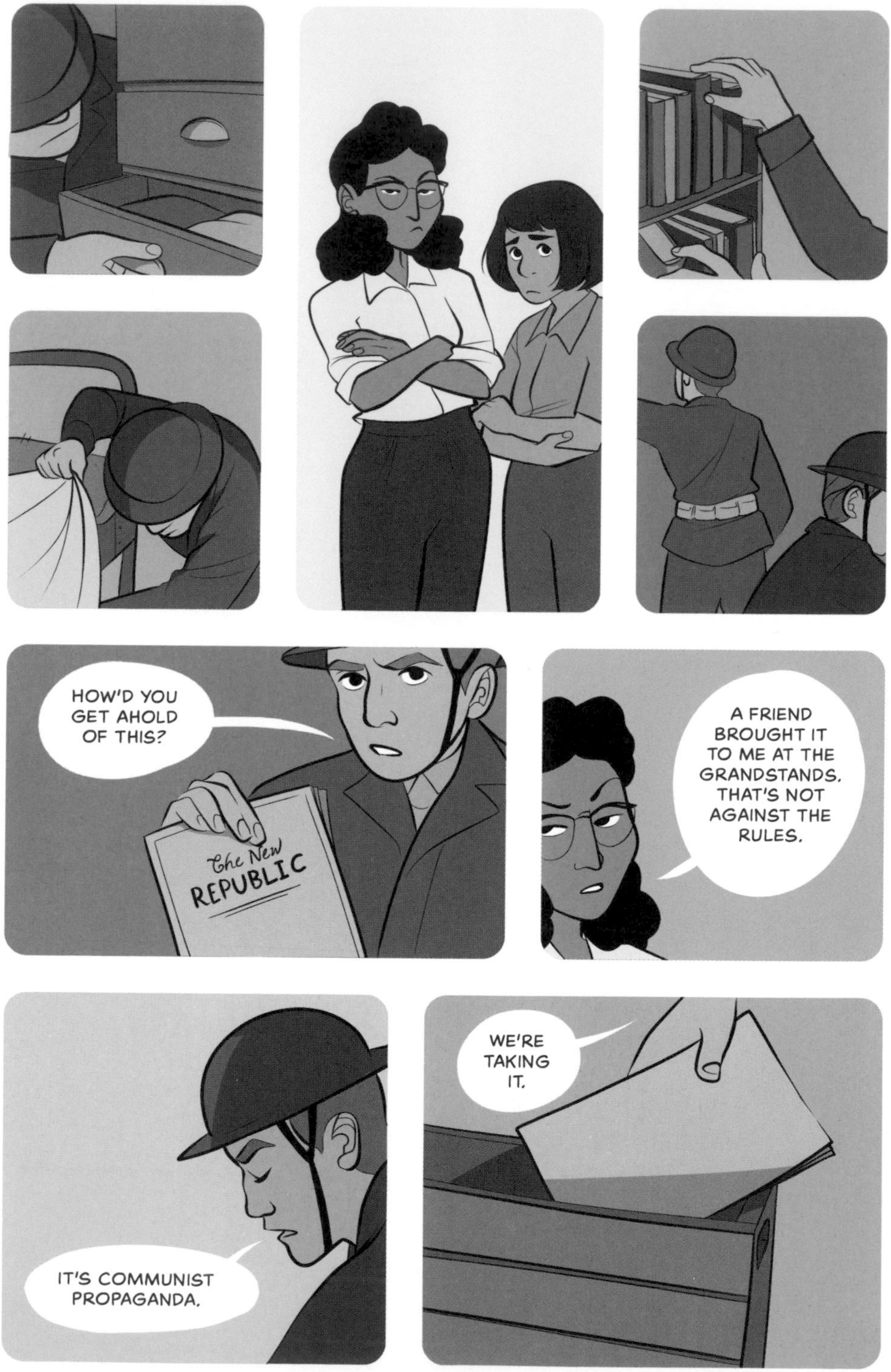
HOW'D YOU GET AHOLD OF THIS?
The New REPUBLIC
A FRIEND BROUGHT IT TO ME AT THE GRANDSTANDS. THAT'S NOT AGAINST THE RULES.
IT'S COMMUNIST PROPAGANDA.
WE'RE TAKING IT.

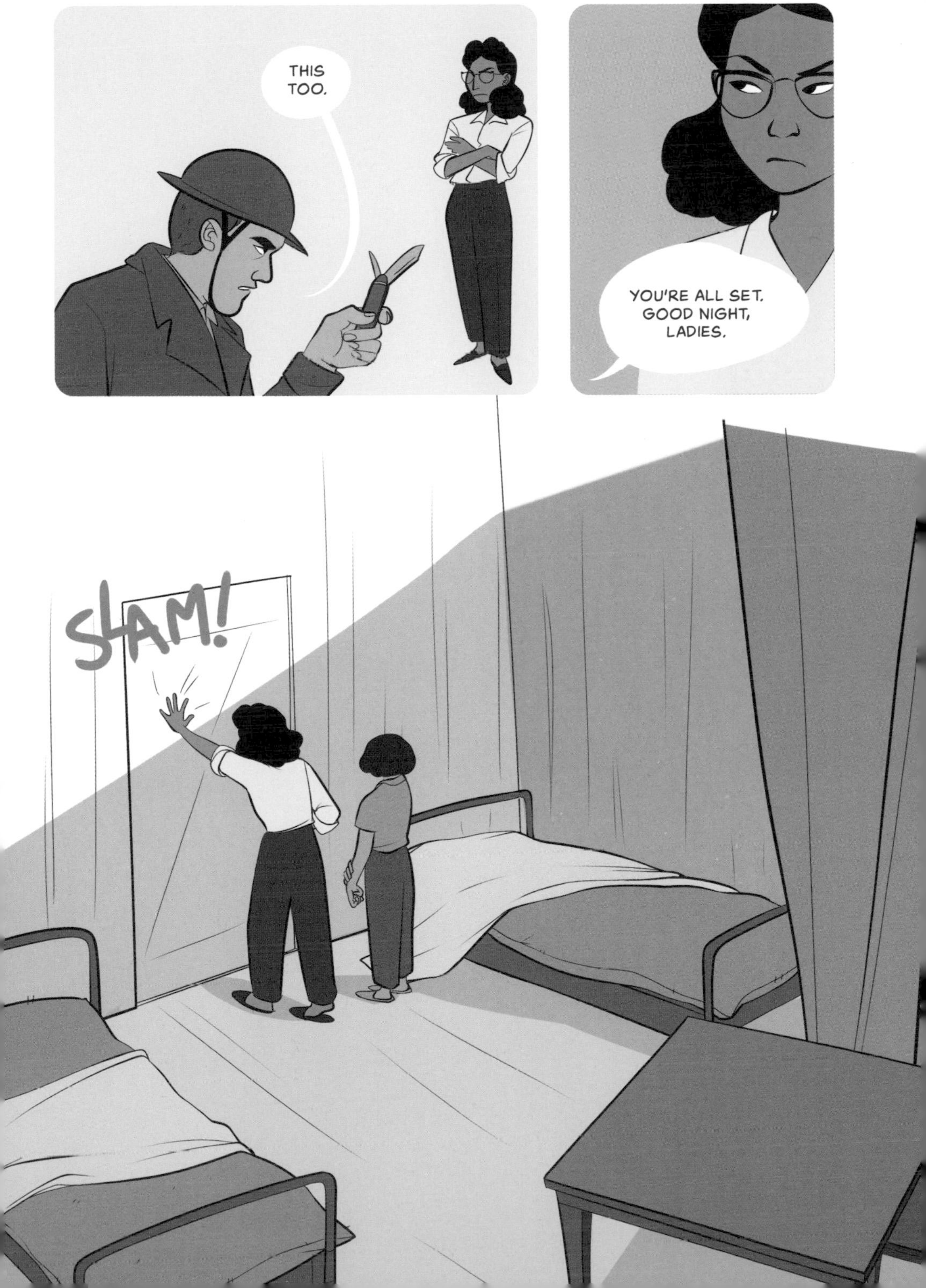
THIS TOO.
YOU'RE ALL SET. GOOD NIGHT, LADIES.
SLAM!

WHAT WAS THAT ABOUT?

I DON'T KNOW.

I'VE HEARD RUMORS THAT WE'LL BE TAKEN TO THE PERMANENT CAMP SOON.

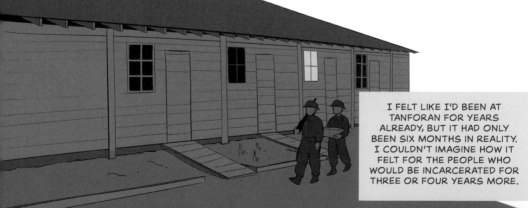

I FELT LIKE I'D BEEN AT TANFORAN FOR YEARS ALREADY, BUT IT HAD ONLY BEEN SIX MONTHS IN REALITY. I COULDN'T IMAGINE HOW IT FELT FOR THE PEOPLE WHO WOULD BE INCARCERATED FOR THREE OR FOUR YEARS MORE.

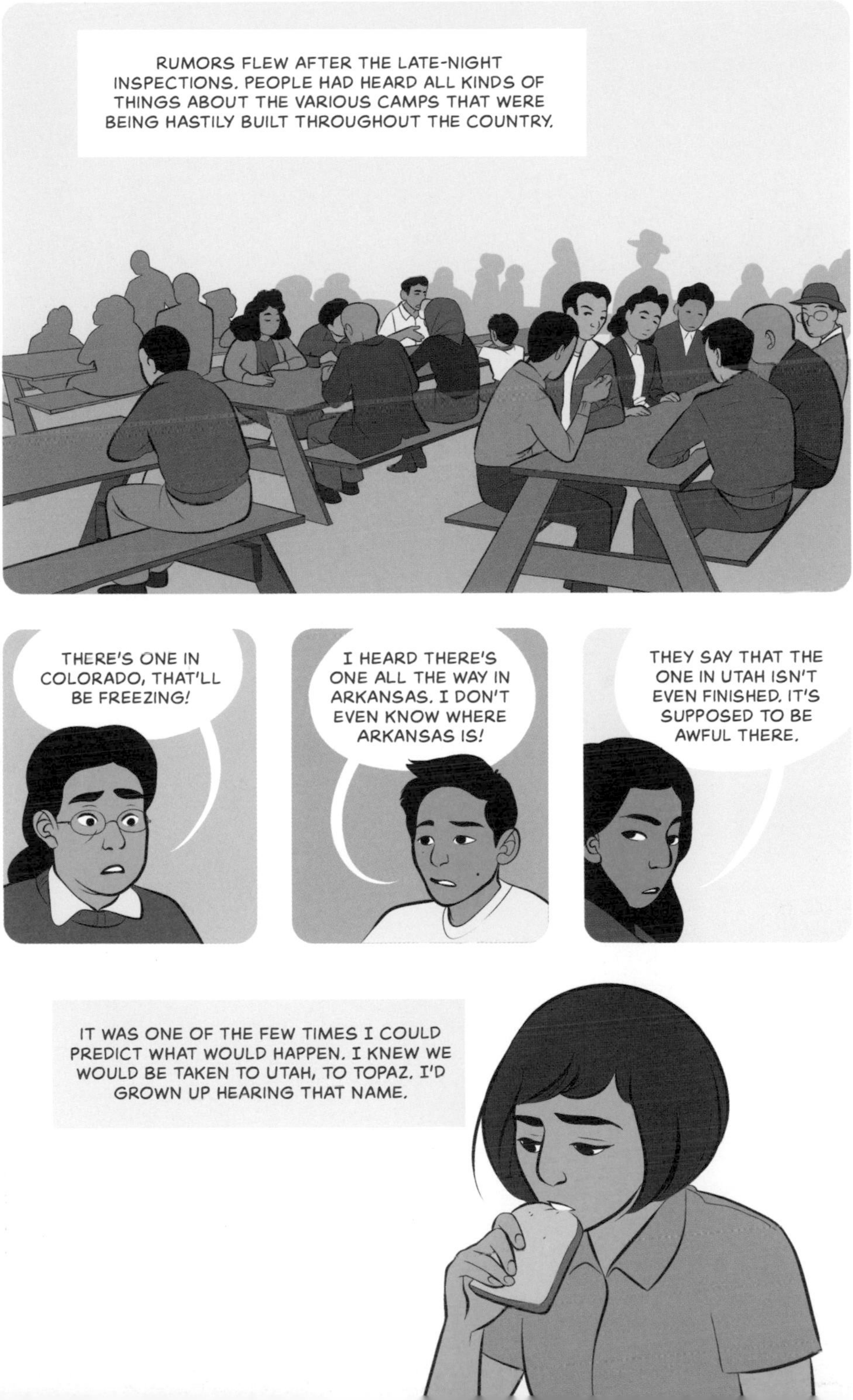
RUMORS FLEW AFTER THE LATE-NIGHT INSPECTIONS. PEOPLE HAD HEARD ALL KINDS OF THINGS ABOUT THE VARIOUS CAMPS THAT WERE BEING HASTILY BUILT THROUGHOUT THE COUNTRY.
THERE'S ONE IN COLORADO, THAT'LL BE FREEZING!
I HEARD THERE'S ONE ALL THE WAY IN ARKANSAS. I DON'T EVEN KNOW WHERE ARKANSAS IS!
THEY SAY THAT THE ONE IN UTAH ISN'T EVEN FINISHED. IT'S SUPPOSED TO BE AWFUL THERE.
IT WAS ONE OF THE FEW TIMES I COULD PREDICT WHAT WOULD HAPPEN. I KNEW WE WOULD BE TAKEN TO UTAH, TO TOPAZ. I'D GROWN UP HEARING THAT NAME.

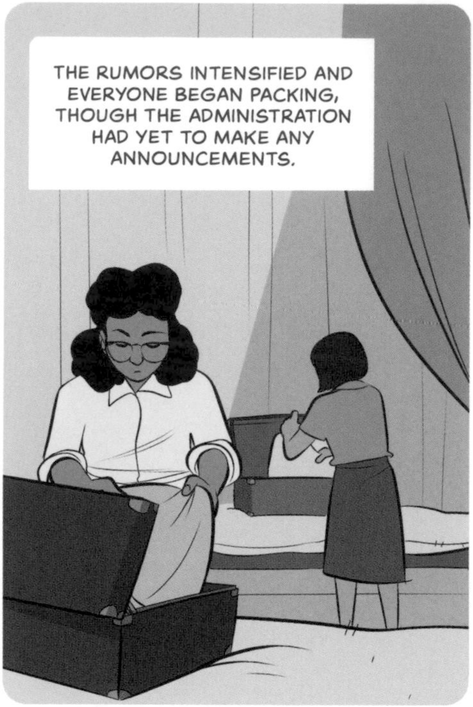
THE RUMORS INTENSIFIED AND EVERYONE BEGAN PACKING, THOUGH THE ADMINISTRATION HAD YET TO MAKE ANY ANNOUNCEMENTS.

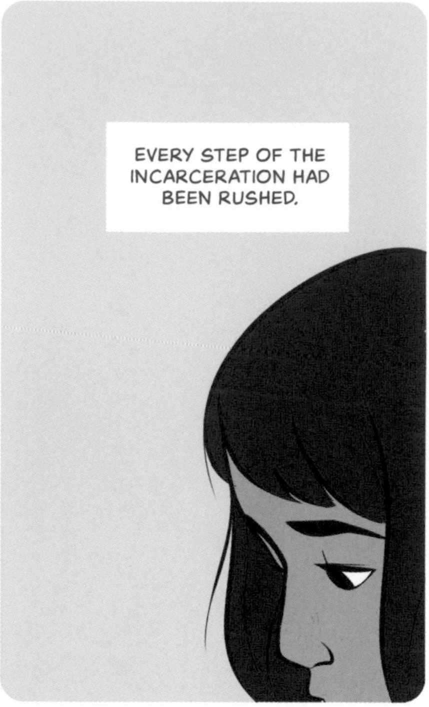
EVERY STEP OF THE INCARCERATION HAD BEEN RUSHED.

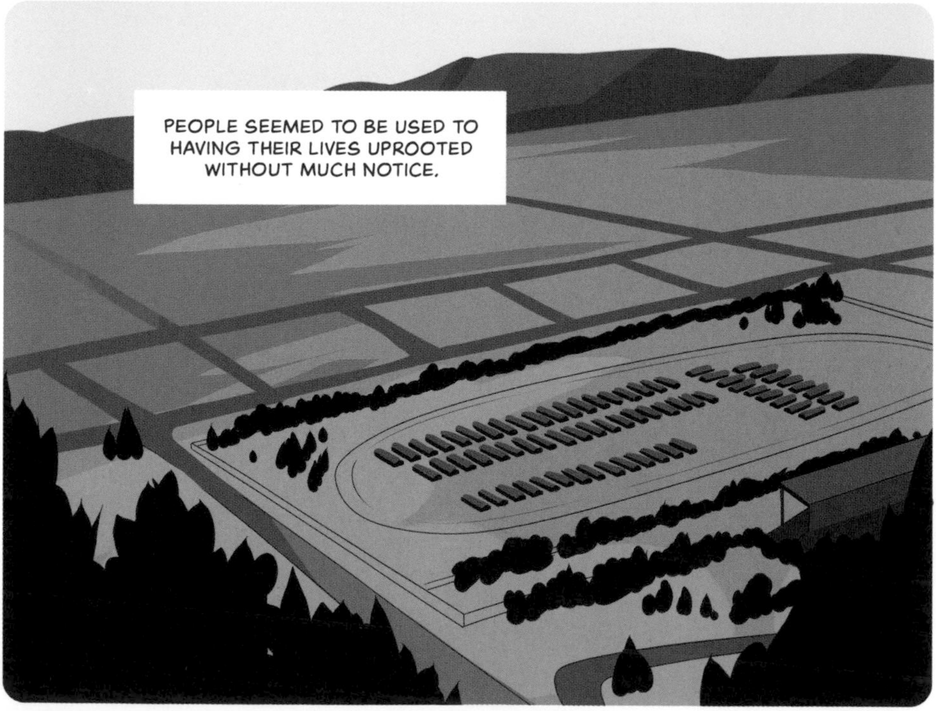
PEOPLE SEEMED TO BE USED TO HAVING THEIR LIVES UPROOTED WITHOUT MUCH NOTICE.

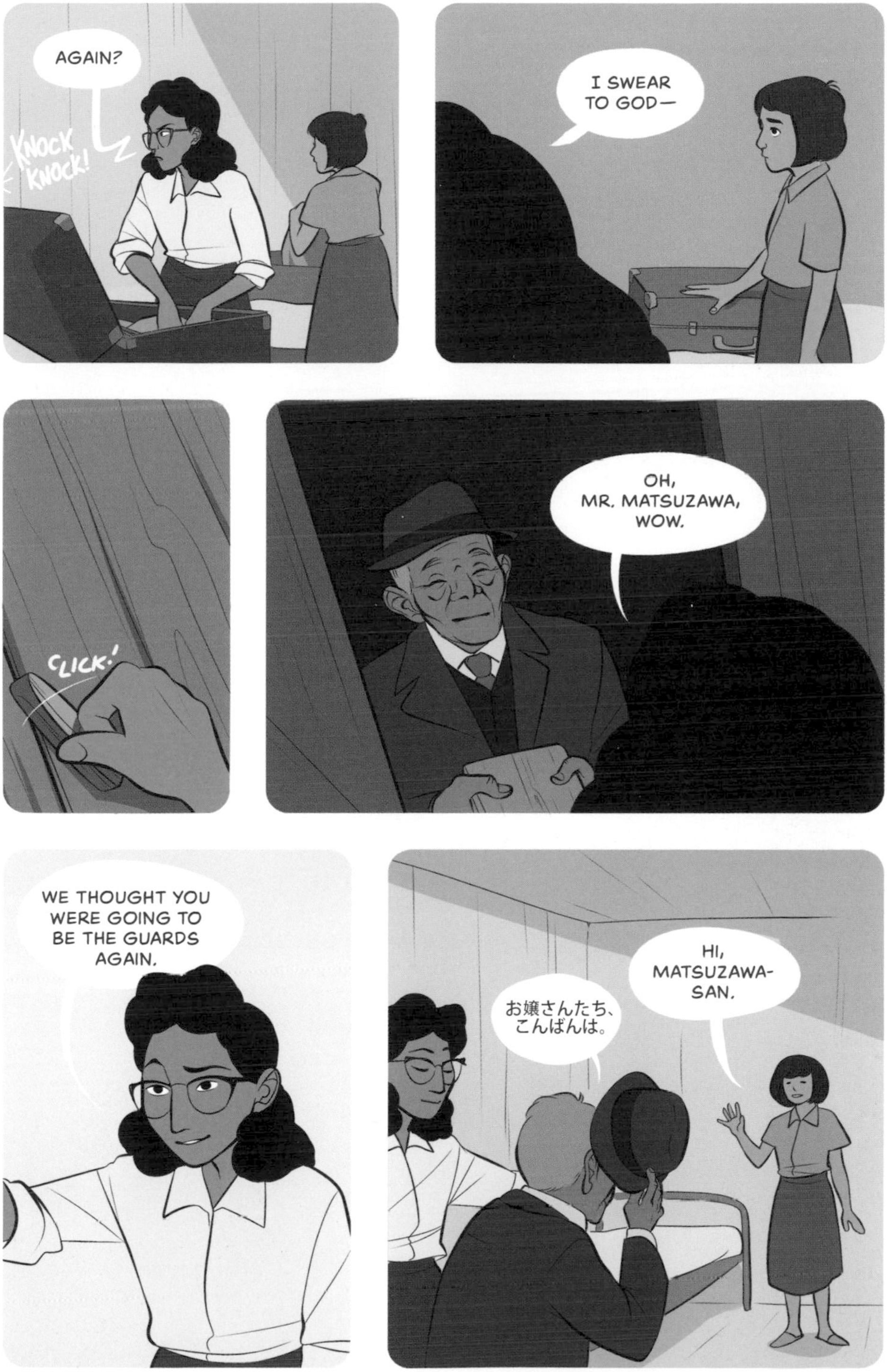
AGAIN?
KNOCK KNOCK!
I SWEAR TO GOD—
CLICK!
OH, MR. MATSUZAWA, WOW.
WE THOUGHT YOU WERE GOING TO BE THE GUARDS AGAIN.
お嬢さんたち、こんばんは。
HI, MATSUZAWA-SAN.

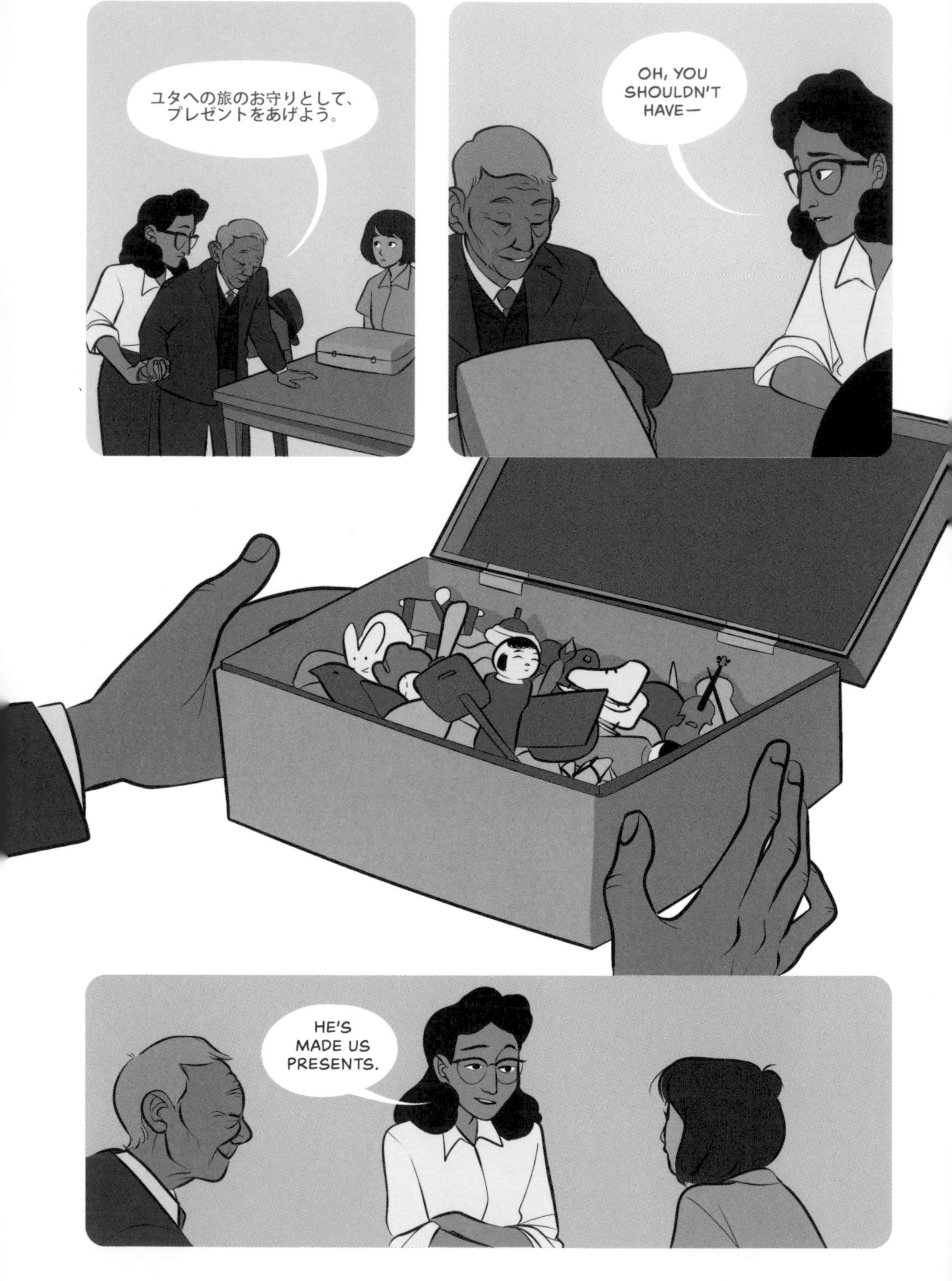
ユタへの旅のお守りとして、
プレゼントをあげよう。
OH, YOU SHOULDN'T HAVE—
HE'S MADE US PRESENTS.

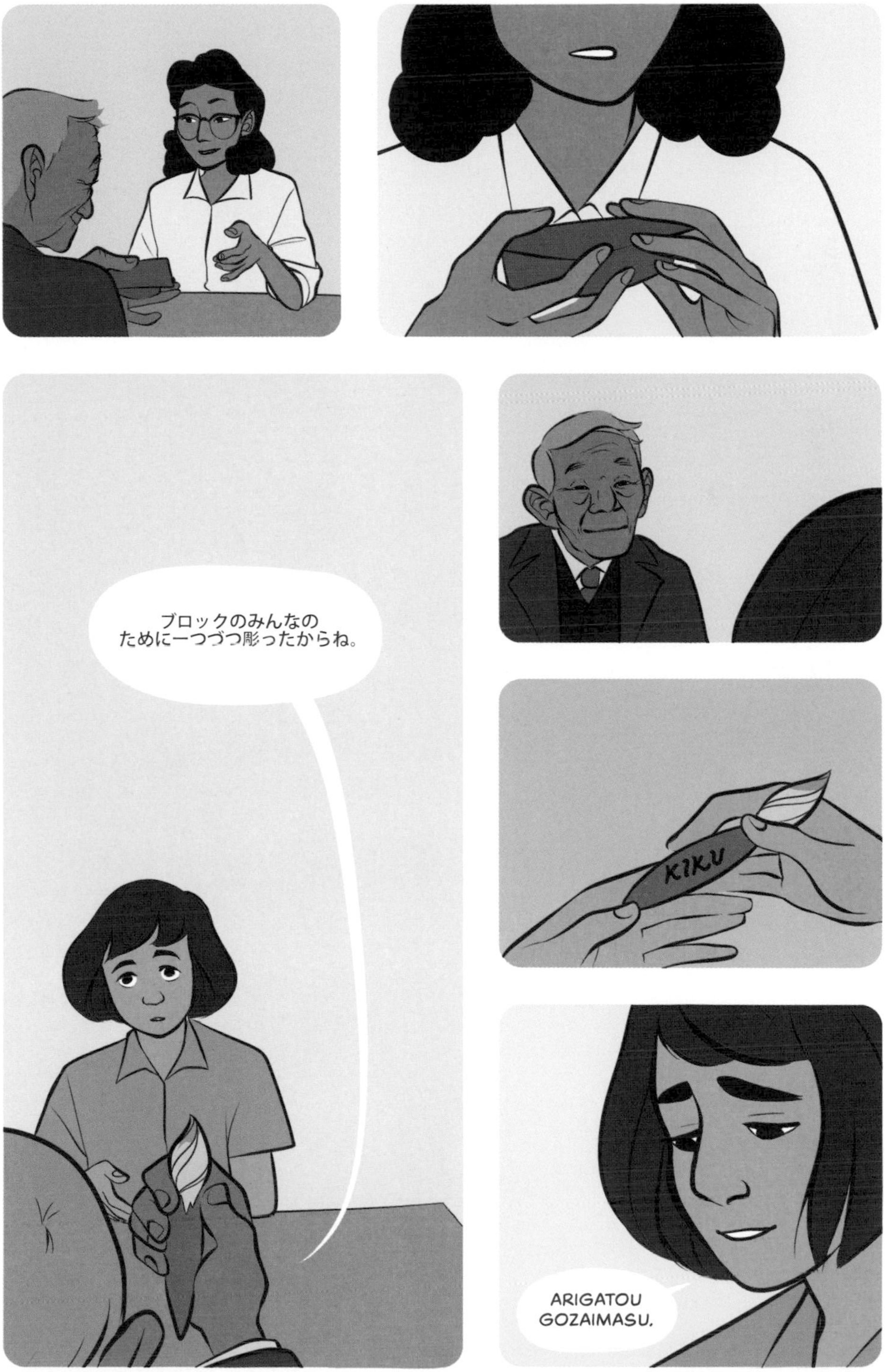

ブロックのみんなの
ために一つづつ彫ったからね。
KIKU
ARIGATOU GOZAIMASU.

I WAS DEEPLY MOVED BY MR. MATSUZAWA'S GIFT. HE WAS A NEIGHBOR WHO WE HAD NEVER SPOKEN MUCH TO, SO I HAD NEVER EXPECTED IT.

BUT IT MEANT EVEN MORE TO ME SINCE I'D SEEN ONE OF THE CARVINGS IN HIS BOX BEFORE.

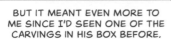

おやすみなさい!

A SMALL VIOLIN FIGURE WITH MY GRANDMOTHER'S NAME ON IT HAS BEEN CAREFULLY TUCKED AWAY IN MY FAMILY'S LIVING ROOM MY WHOLE LIFE.

I FELT AN INTENSE CONNECTION TO MY GRANDMOTHER IN THAT MOMENT. WE WERE LINKED THROUGH THIS COMMUNITY, AND I HELD THE PROOF IN MY HAND.

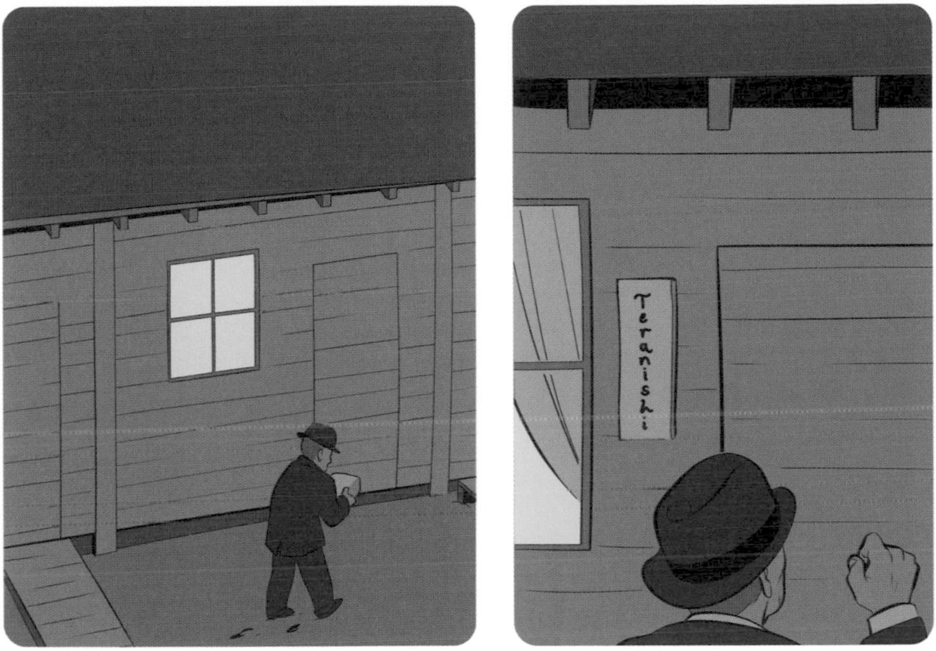
Teranishi

IT WAS A CLOSENESS I HAD NEVER FELT BEFORE. SO MUCH OF OUR HISTORY HAD BEEN OBSCURED BY SILENCE.

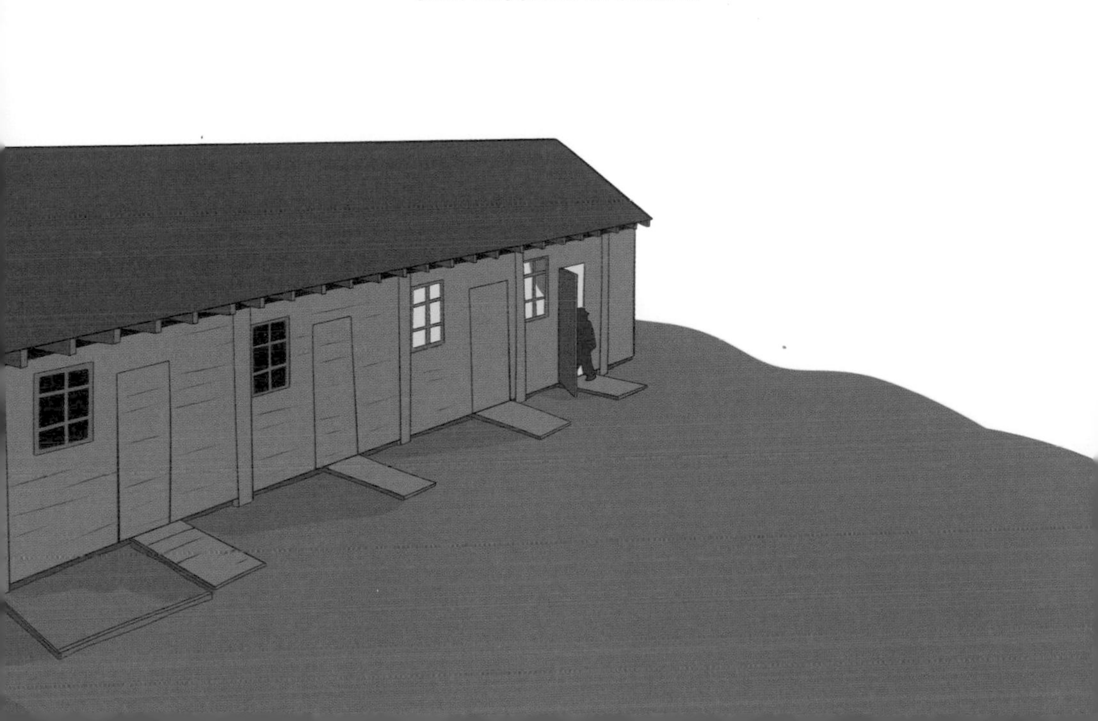

6

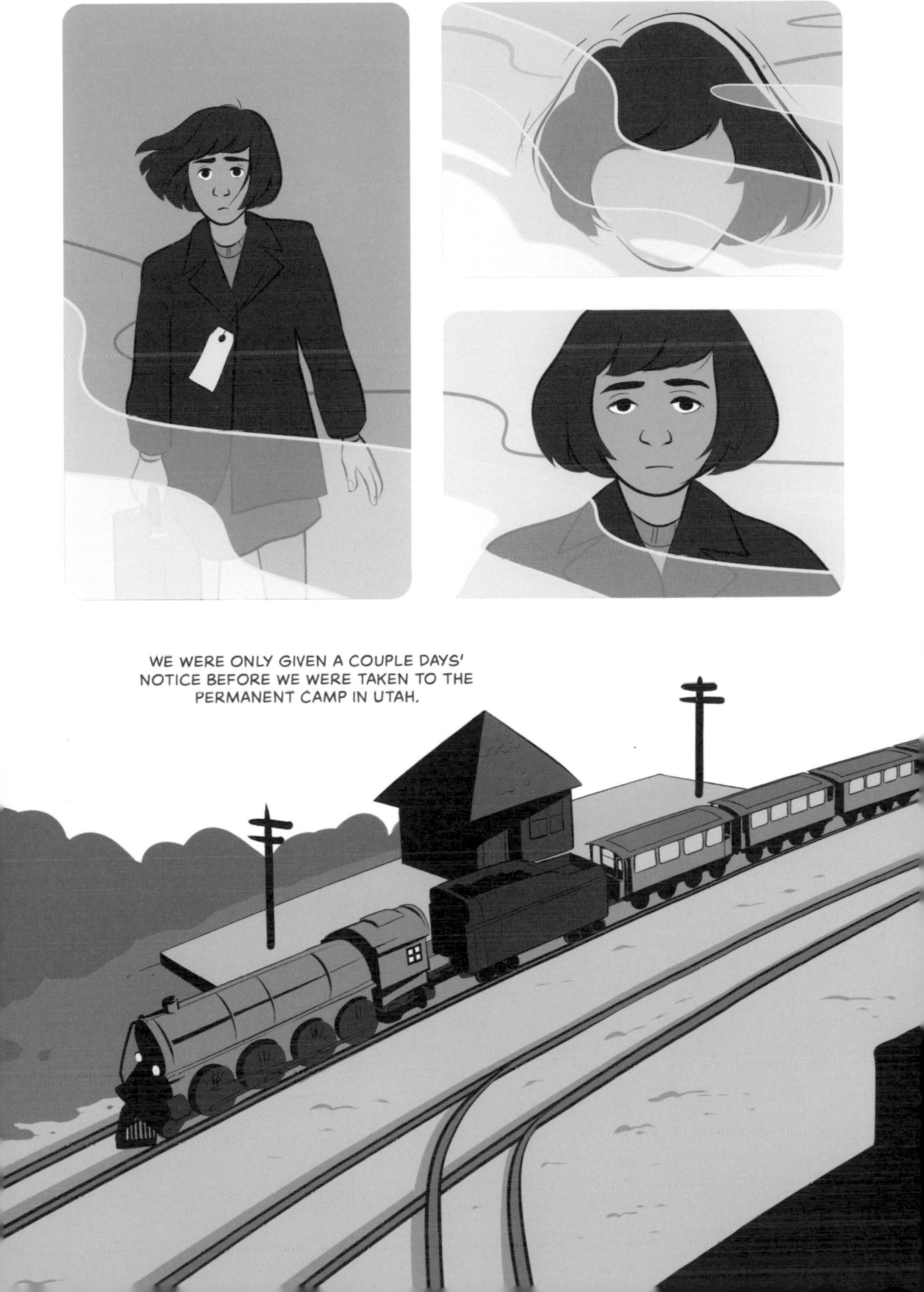
WE WERE ONLY GIVEN A COUPLE DAYS' NOTICE BEFORE WE WERE TAKEN TO THE PERMANENT CAMP IN UTAH.

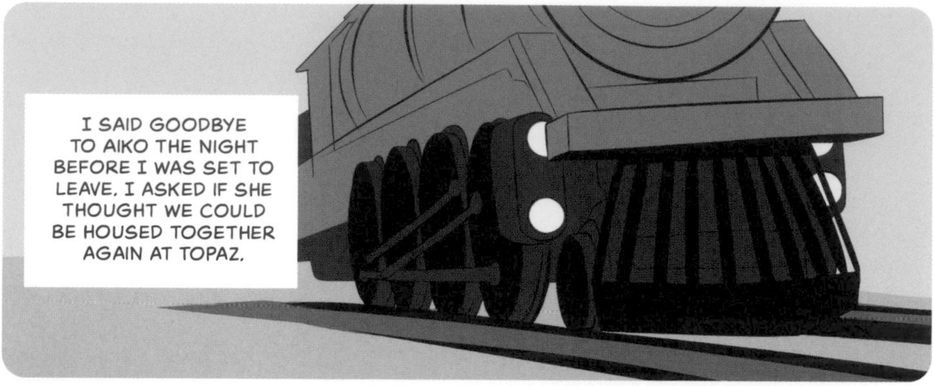
I SAID GOODBYE TO AIKO THE NIGHT BEFORE I WAS SET TO LEAVE. I ASKED IF SHE THOUGHT WE COULD BE HOUSED TOGETHER AGAIN AT TOPAZ.

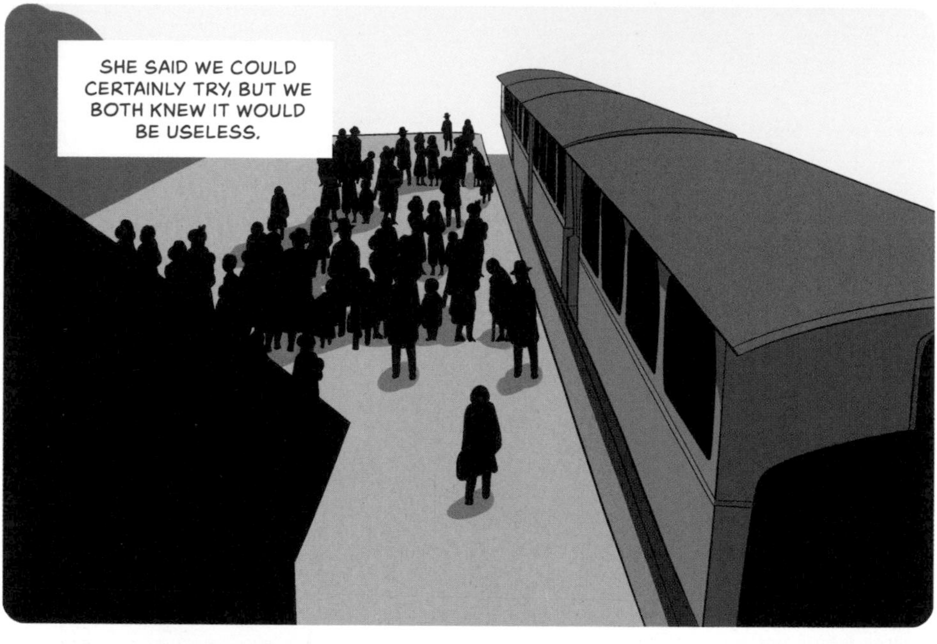
SHE SAID WE COULD CERTAINLY TRY, BUT WE BOTH KNEW IT WOULD BE USELESS.

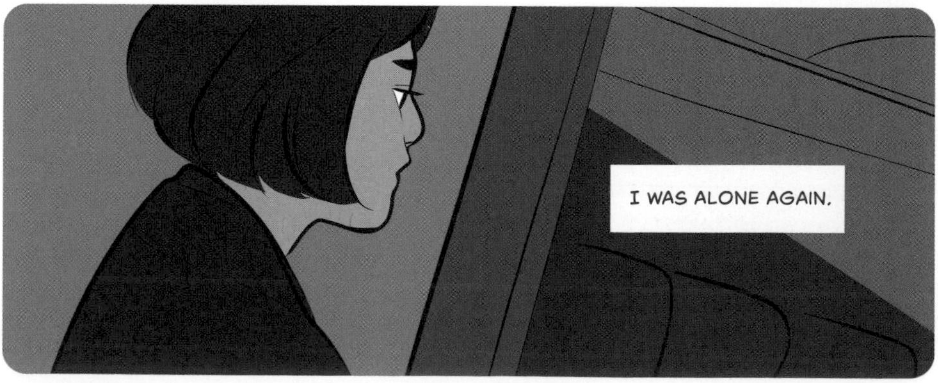
I WAS ALONE AGAIN.

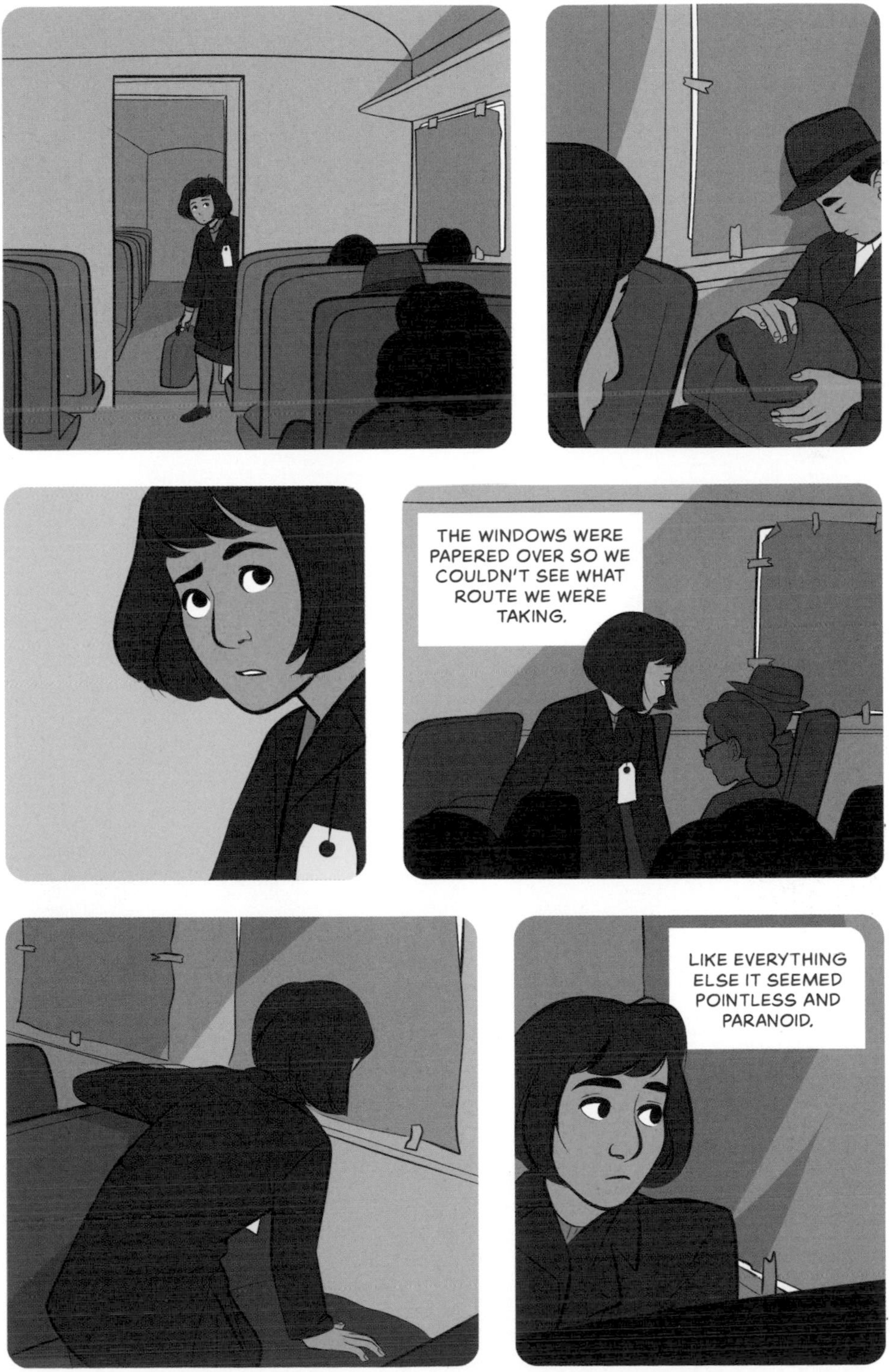
THE WINDOWS WERE PAPERED OVER SO WE COULDN'T SEE WHAT ROUTE WE WERE TAKING.
LIKE EVERYTHING ELSE IT SEEMED POINTLESS AND PARANOID.

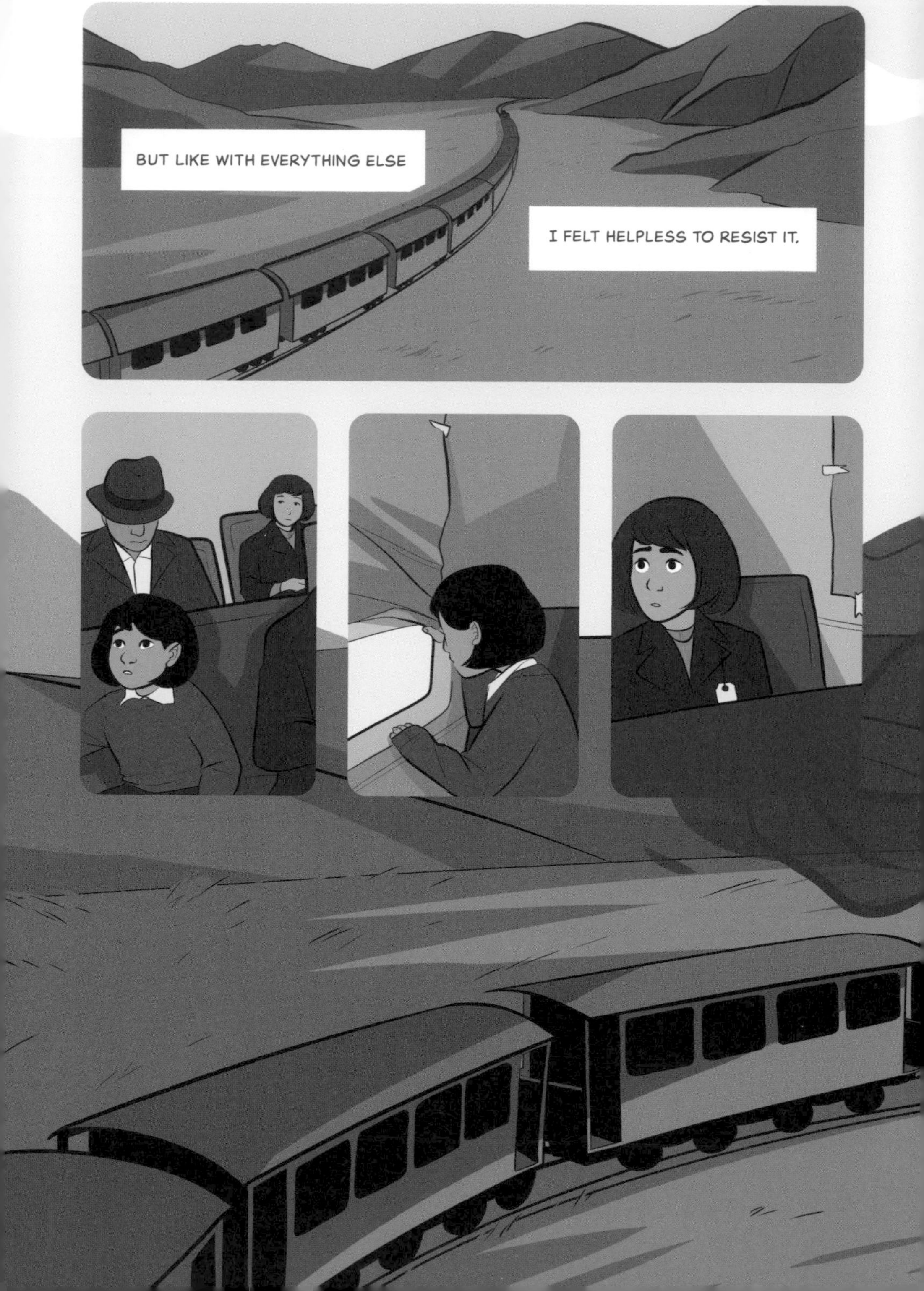
BUT LIKE WITH EVERYTHING ELSE
I FELT HELPLESS TO RESIST IT.

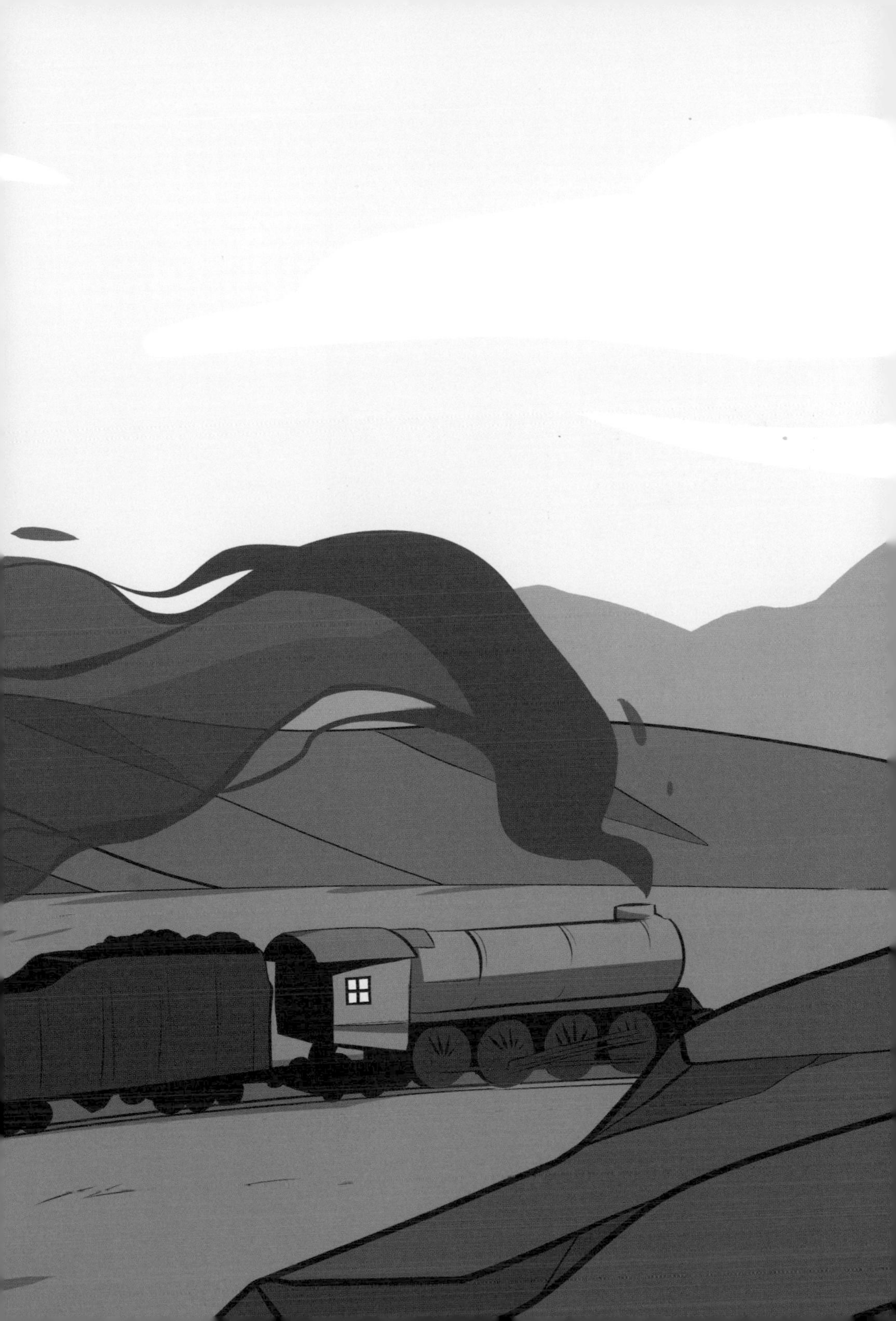

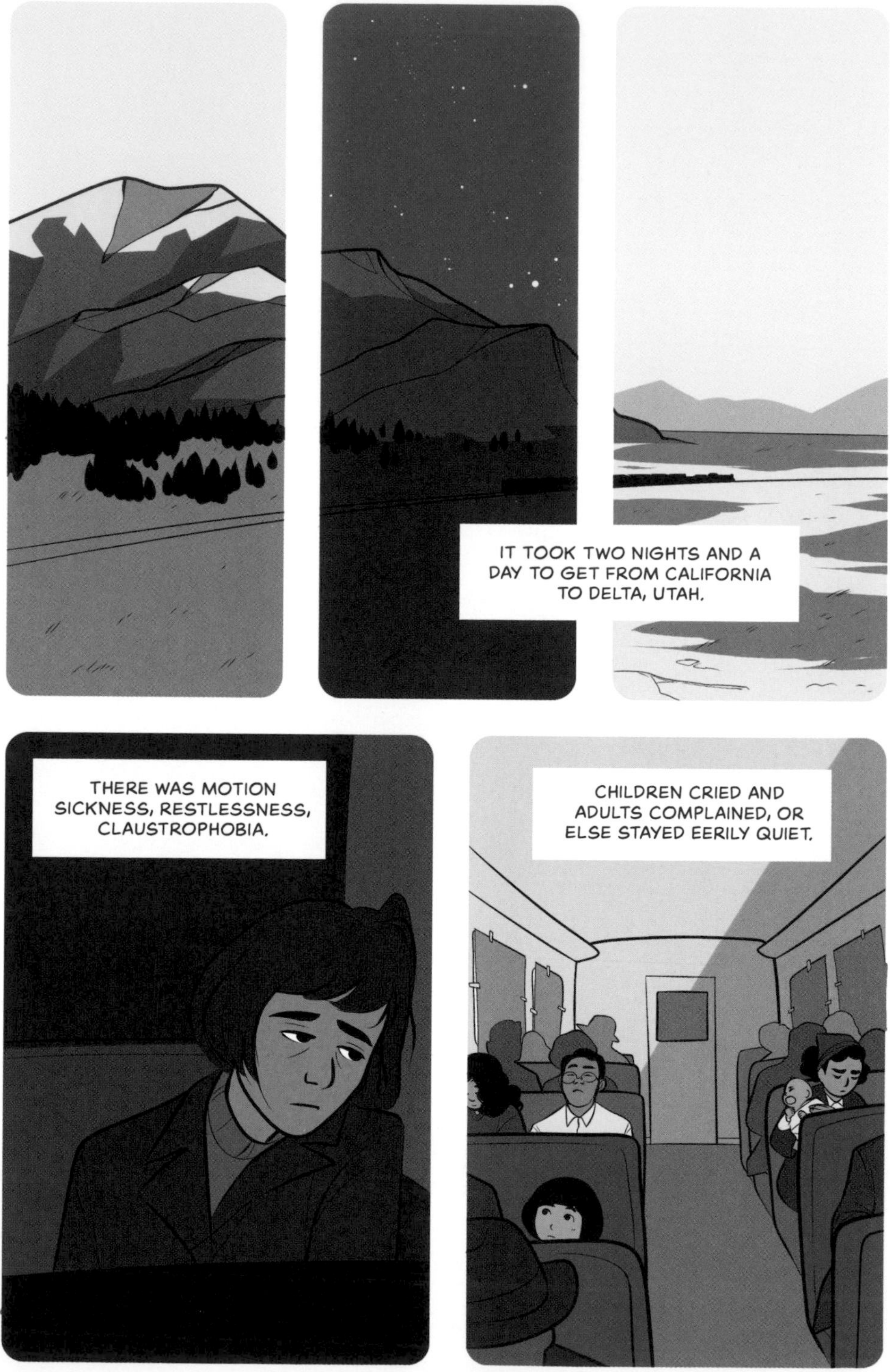
IT TOOK TWO NIGHTS AND A DAY TO GET FROM CALIFORNIA TO DELTA, UTAH.
THERE WAS MOTION SICKNESS, RESTLESSNESS, CLAUSTROPHOBIA.
CHILDREN CRIED AND ADULTS COMPLAINED, OR ELSE STAYED EERILY QUIET.

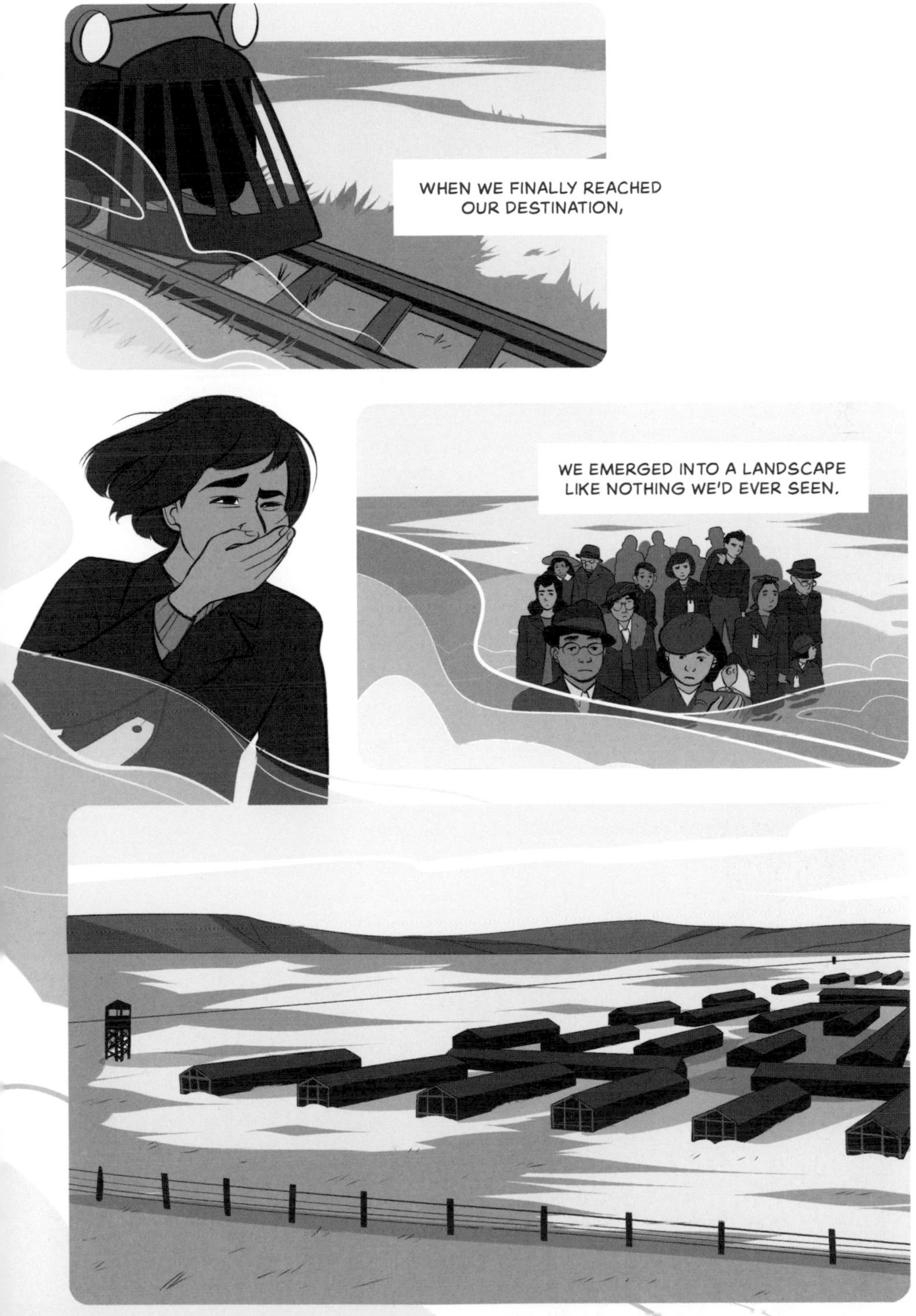
WHEN WE FINALLY REACHED OUR DESTINATION,
WE EMERGED INTO A LANDSCAPE LIKE NOTHING WE'D EVER SEEN.

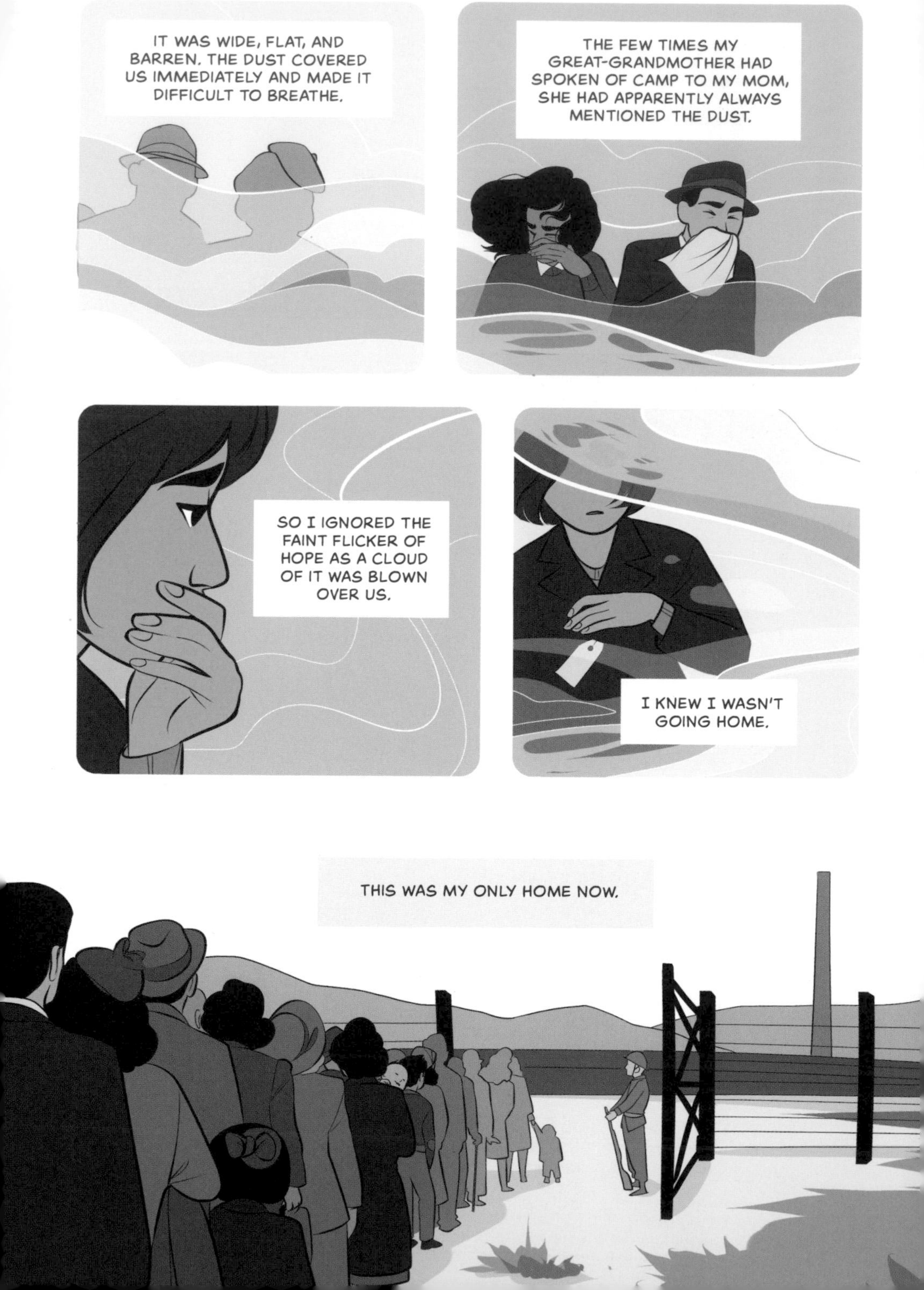
IT WAS WIDE, FLAT, AND BARREN. THE DUST COVERED US IMMEDIATELY AND MADE IT DIFFICULT TO BREATHE.
THE FEW TIMES MY GREAT-GRANDMOTHER HAD SPOKEN OF CAMP TO MY MOM, SHE HAD APPARENTLY ALWAYS MENTIONED THE DUST.
SO I IGNORED THE FAINT FLICKER OF HOPE AS A CLOUD OF IT WAS BLOWN OVER US.
I KNEW I WASN'T GOING HOME.
THIS WAS MY ONLY HOME NOW.

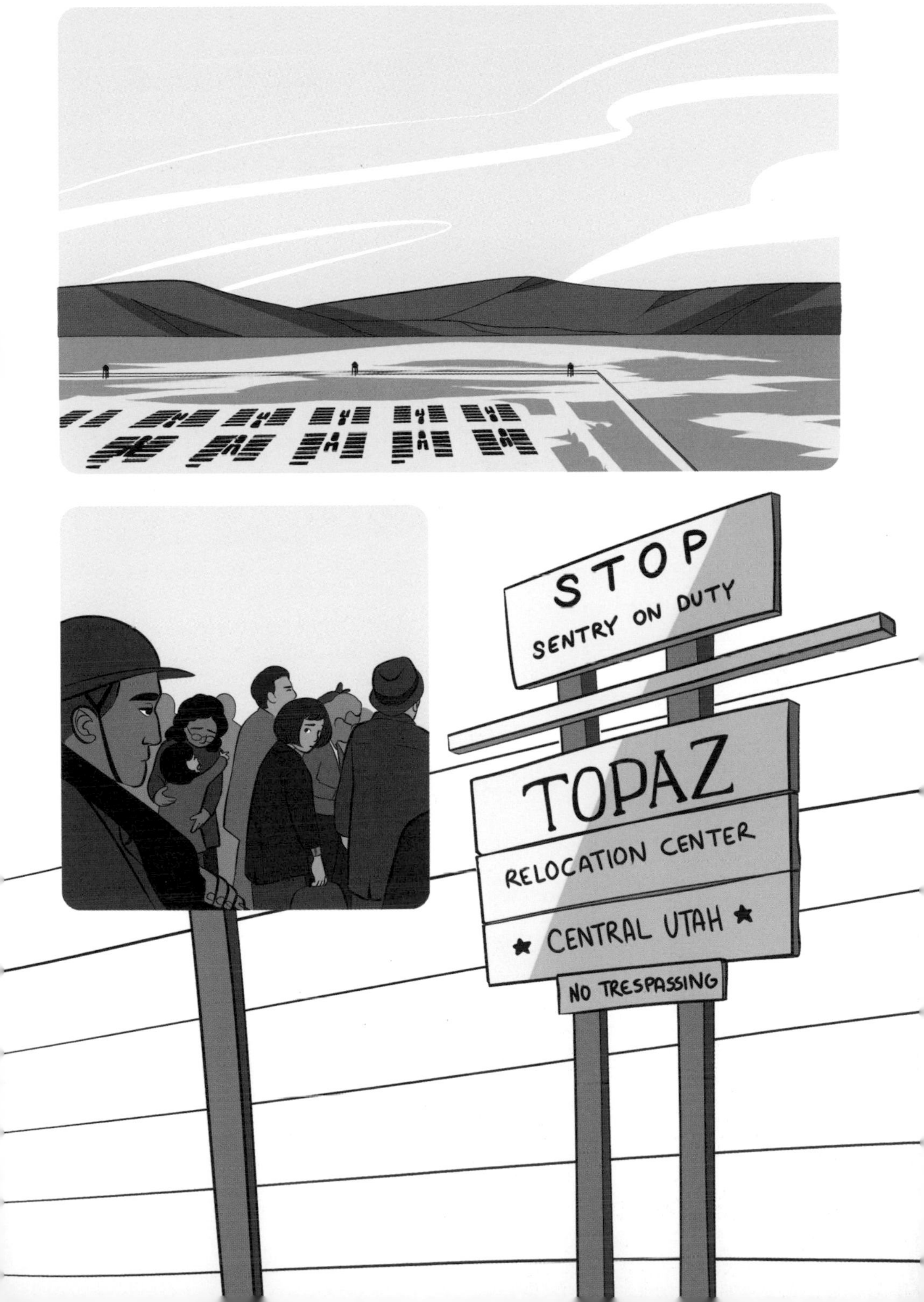
STOP
SENTRY ON DUTY
TOPAZ
RELOCATION CENTER
CENTRAL UTAH
NO TRESPASSING

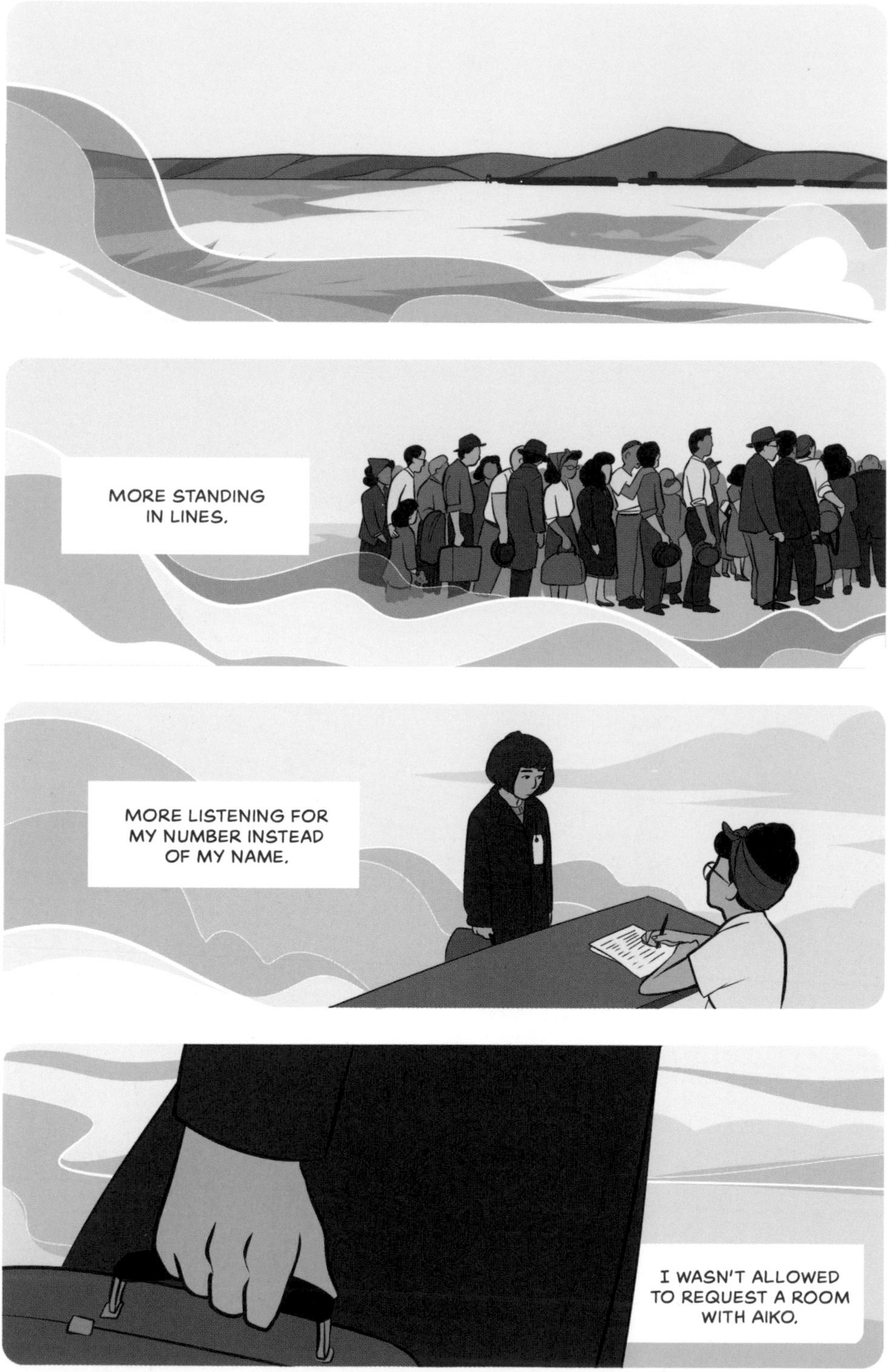
MORE STANDING IN LINES.
MORE LISTENING FOR MY NUMBER INSTEAD OF MY NAME.
I WASN'T ALLOWED TO REQUEST A ROOM WITH AIKO.

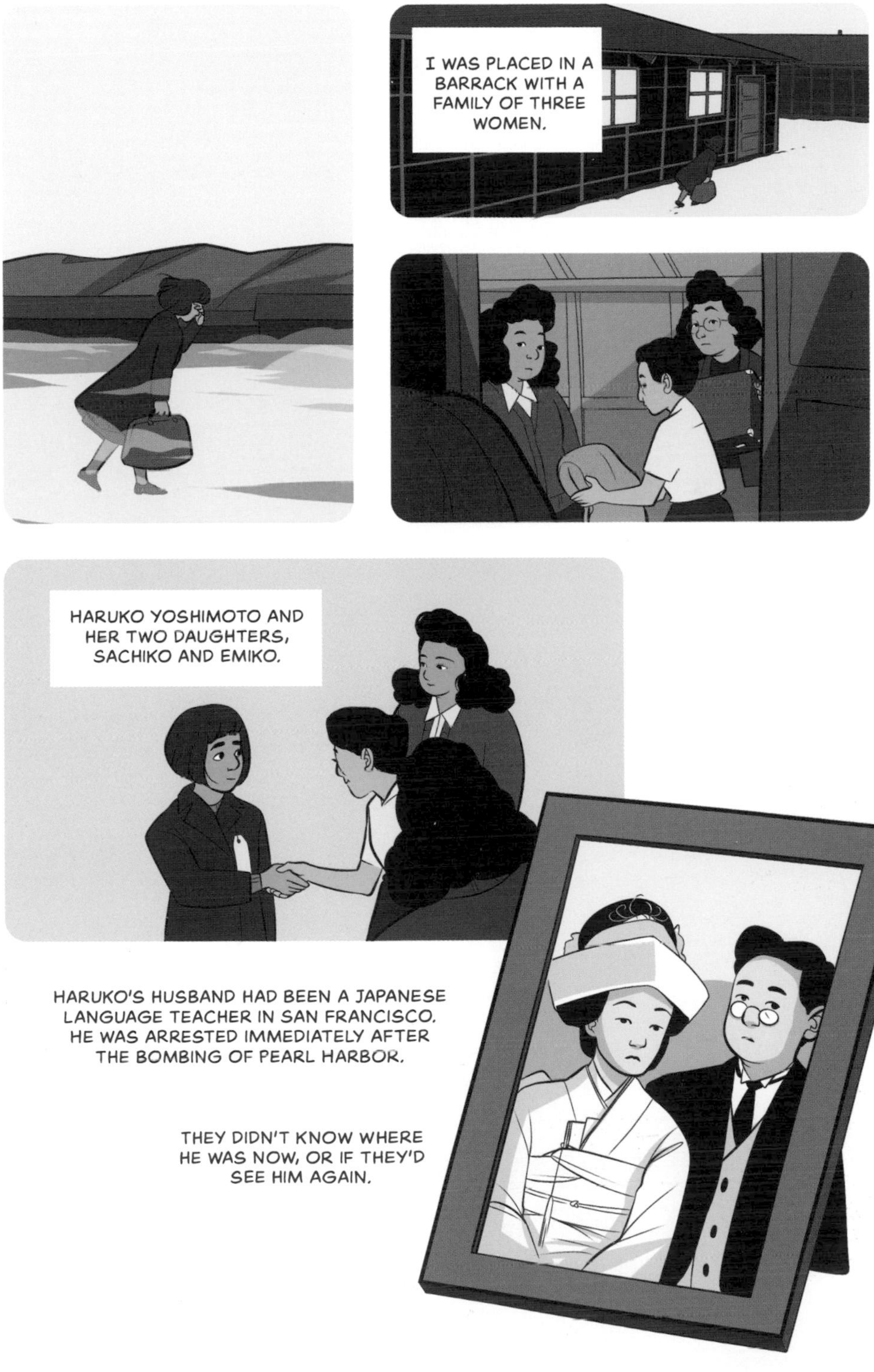
I WAS PLACED IN A BARRACK WITH A FAMILY OF THREE WOMEN.
HARUKO YOSHIMOTO AND HER TWO DAUGHTERS, SACHIKO AND EMIKO.
HARUKO'S HUSBAND HAD BEEN A JAPANESE LANGUAGE TEACHER IN SAN FRANCISCO. HE WAS ARRESTED IMMEDIATELY AFTER THE BOMBING OF PEARL HARBOR.
THEY DIDN'T KNOW WHERE HE WAS NOW, OR IF THEY'D SEE HIM AGAIN.

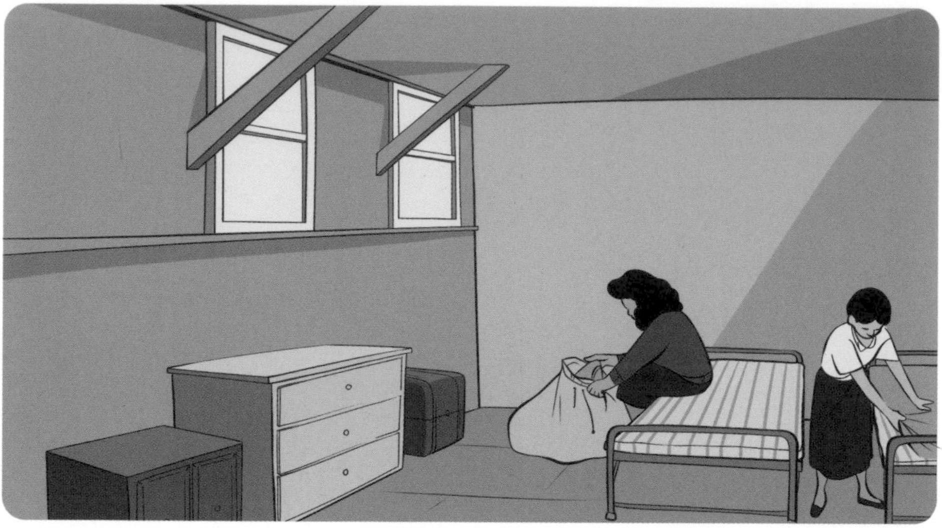

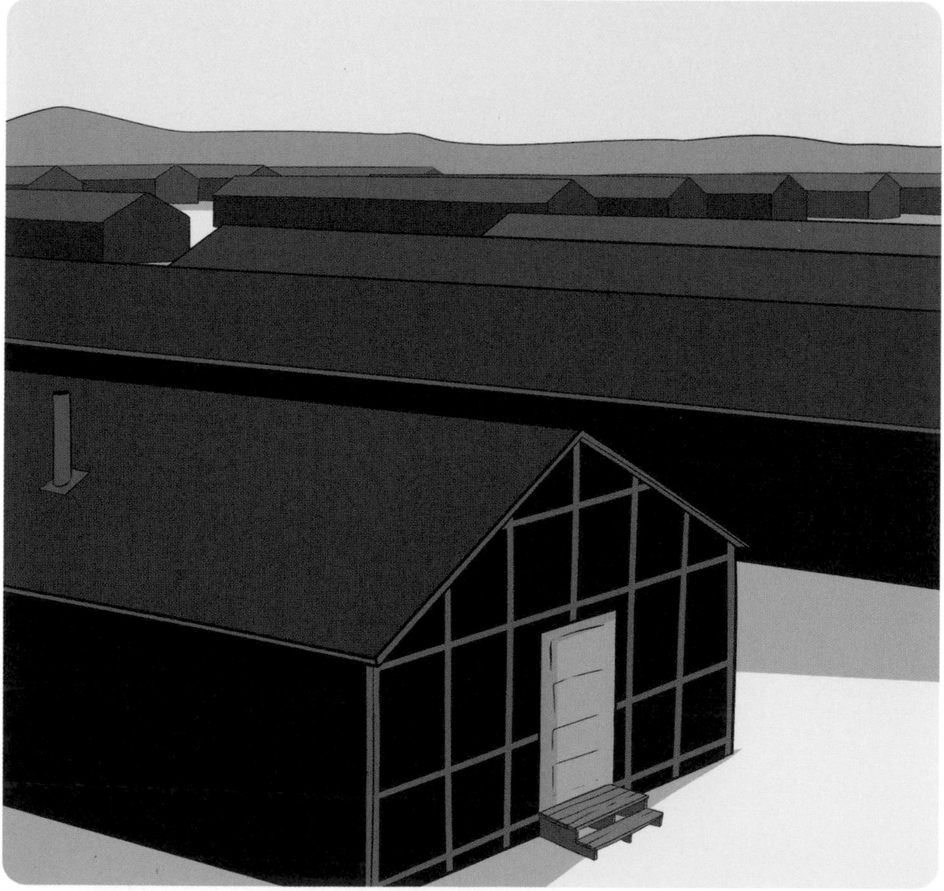

SO MUCH
ABOUT TOPAZ WAS
DIFFERENT FROM
TANFORAN.

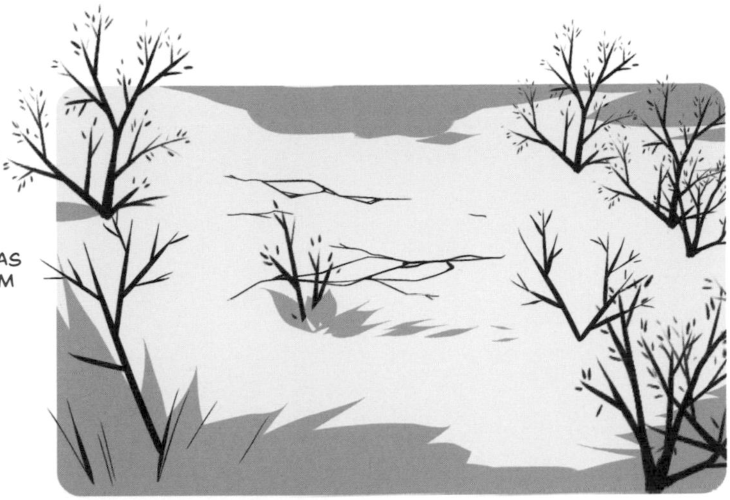

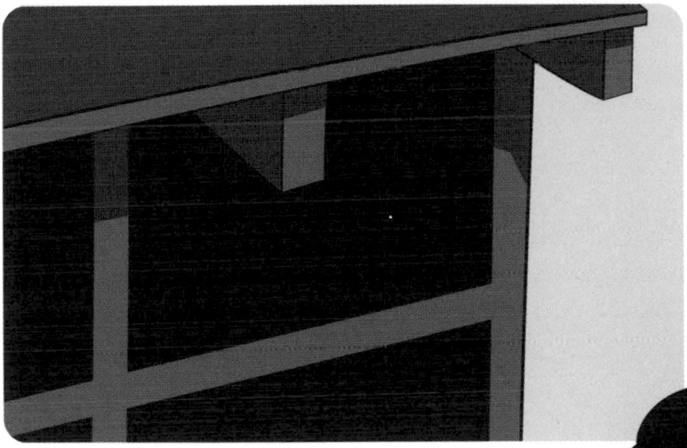

THERE WAS NOTHING
GREEN IN THE UTAH
DESERT, AND WHEN
WE ARRIVED IN FALL
IT WAS ALREADY
FREEZING AT NIGHT.

ONE THING HADN'T
CHANGED, THOUGH.

MY GRANDMOTHER AND
GREAT-GRANDPARENTS
WERE ONCE AGAIN PLACED
NEXT DOOR TO ME.

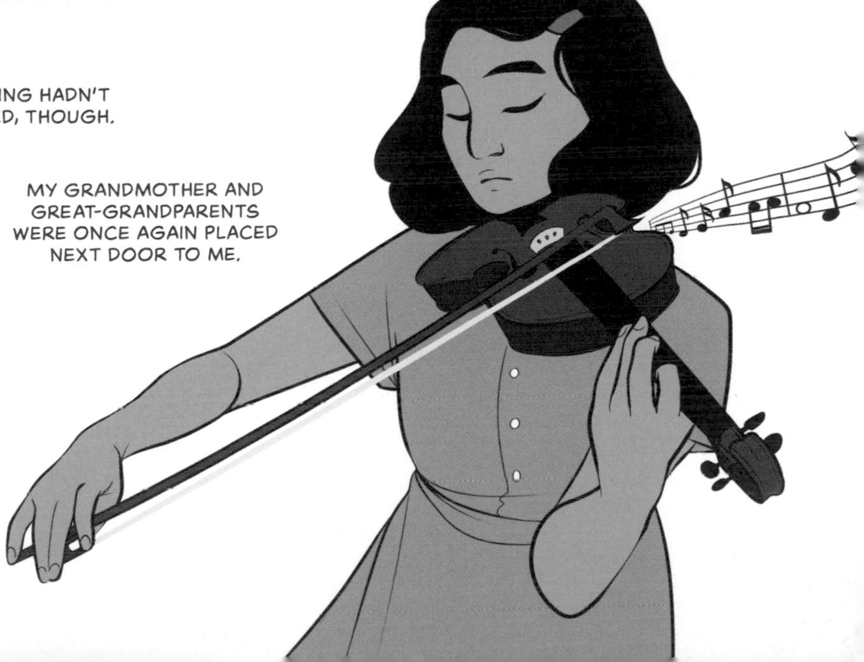

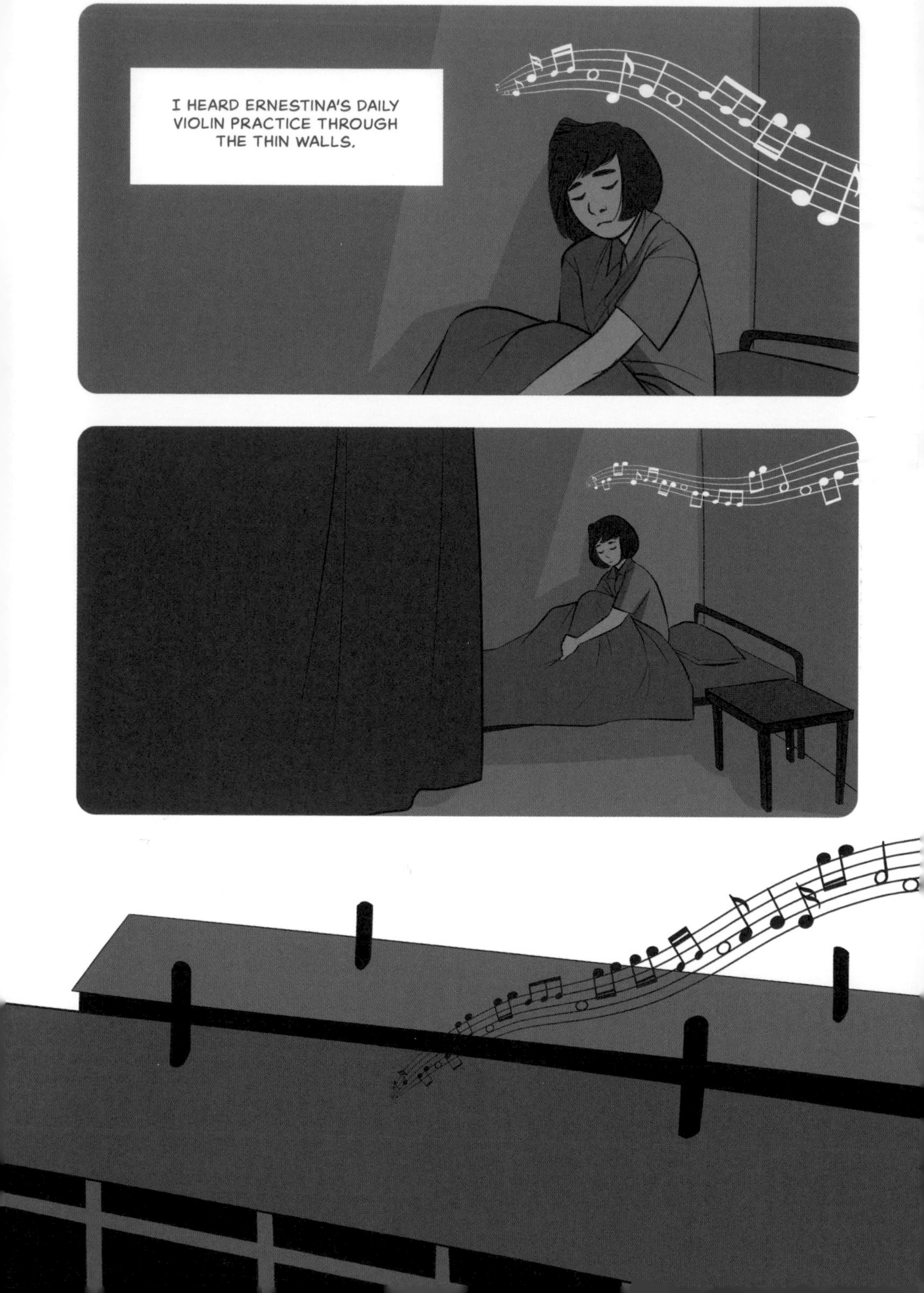
I HEARD ERNESTINA'S DAILY VIOLIN PRACTICE THROUGH THE THIN WALLS.

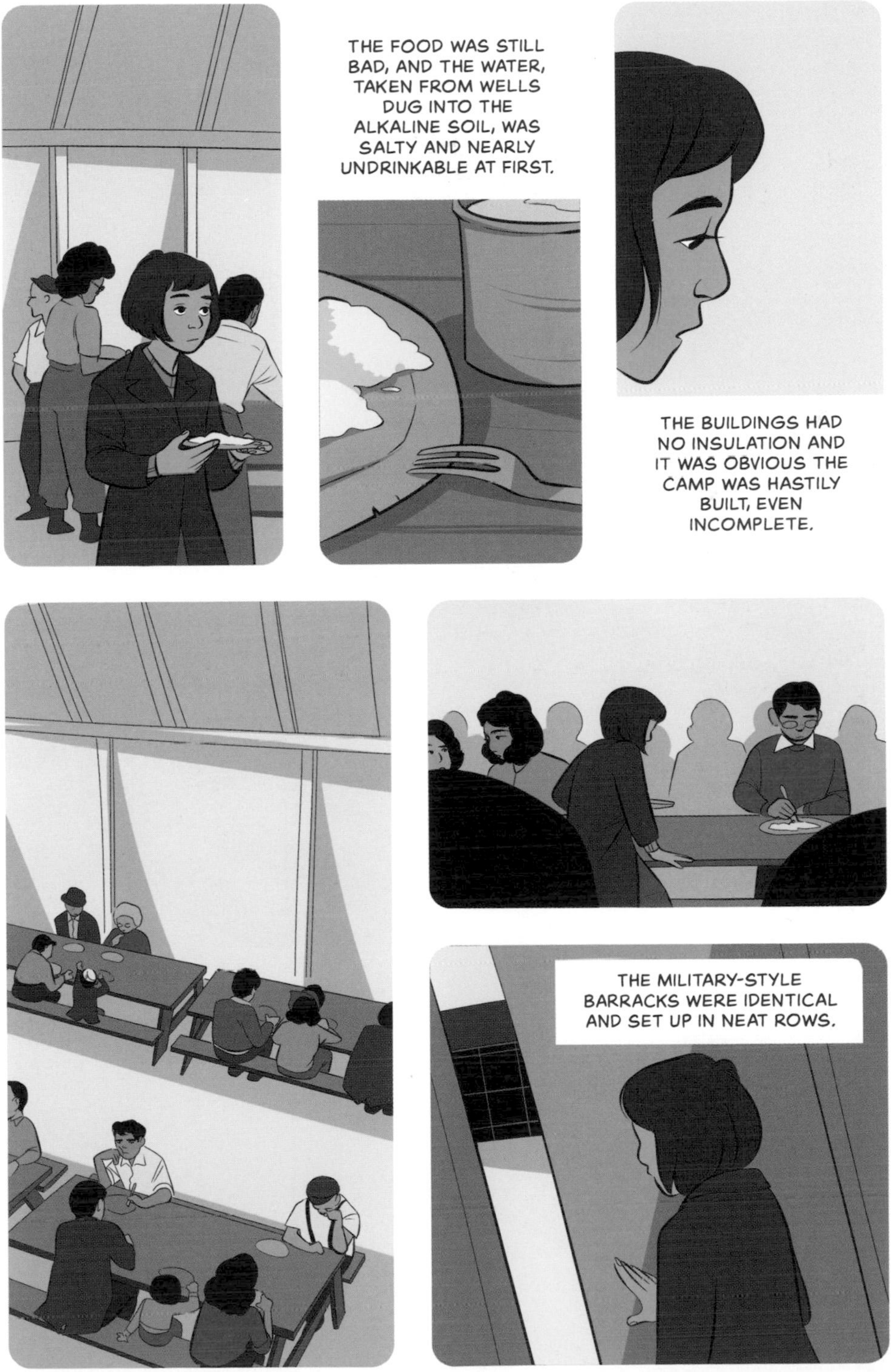
THE FOOD WAS STILL BAD, AND THE WATER, TAKEN FROM WELLS DUG INTO THE ALKALINE SOIL, WAS SALTY AND NEARLY UNDRINKABLE AT FIRST.
THE BUILDINGS HAD NO INSULATION AND IT WAS OBVIOUS THE CAMP WAS HASTILY BUILT, EVEN INCOMPLETE.
THE MILITARY-STYLE BARRACKS WERE IDENTICAL AND SET UP IN NEAT ROWS.

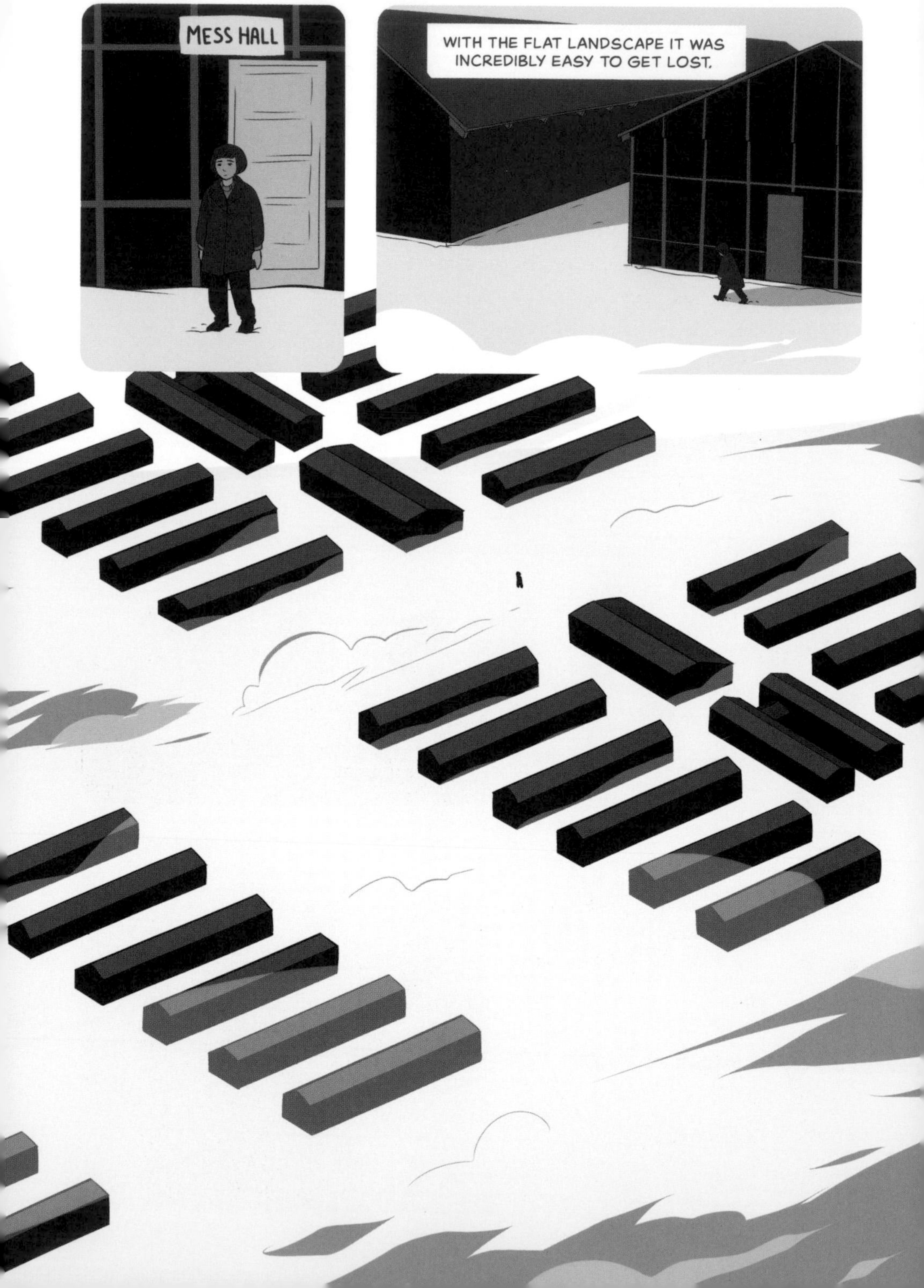
MESS HALL
WITH THE FLAT LANDSCAPE IT WAS INCREDIBLY EASY TO GET LOST.

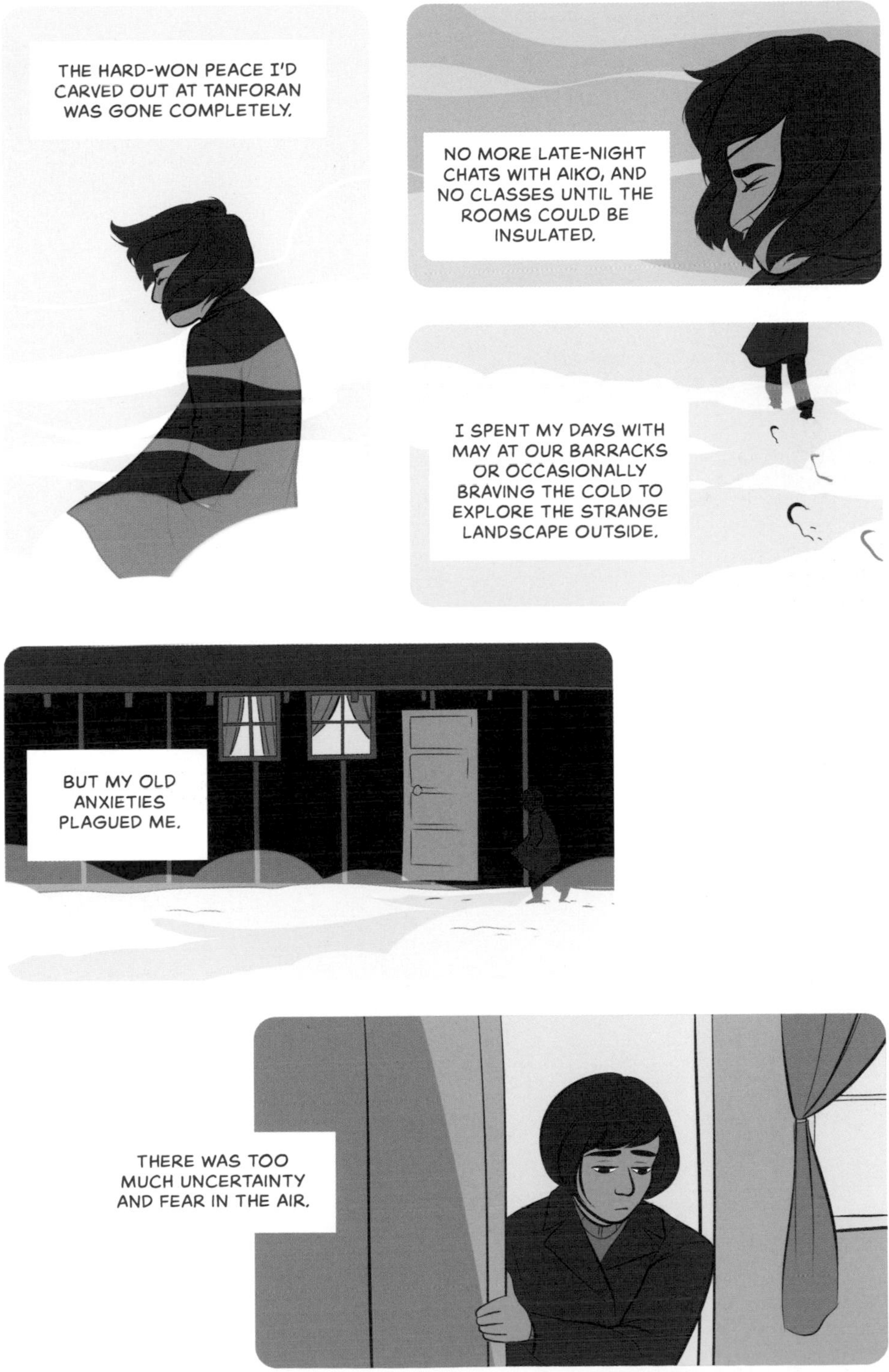
THE HARD-WON PEACE I'D CARVED OUT AT TANFORAN WAS GONE COMPLETELY.
NO MORE LATE-NIGHT CHATS WITH AIKO, AND NO CLASSES UNTIL THE ROOMS COULD BE INSULATED.
I SPENT MY DAYS WITH MAY AT OUR BARRACKS OR OCCASIONALLY BRAVING THE COLD TO EXPLORE THE STRANGE LANDSCAPE OUTSIDE.
BUT MY OLD ANXIETIES PLAGUED ME.
THERE WAS TOO MUCH UNCERTAINTY AND FEAR IN THE AIR.

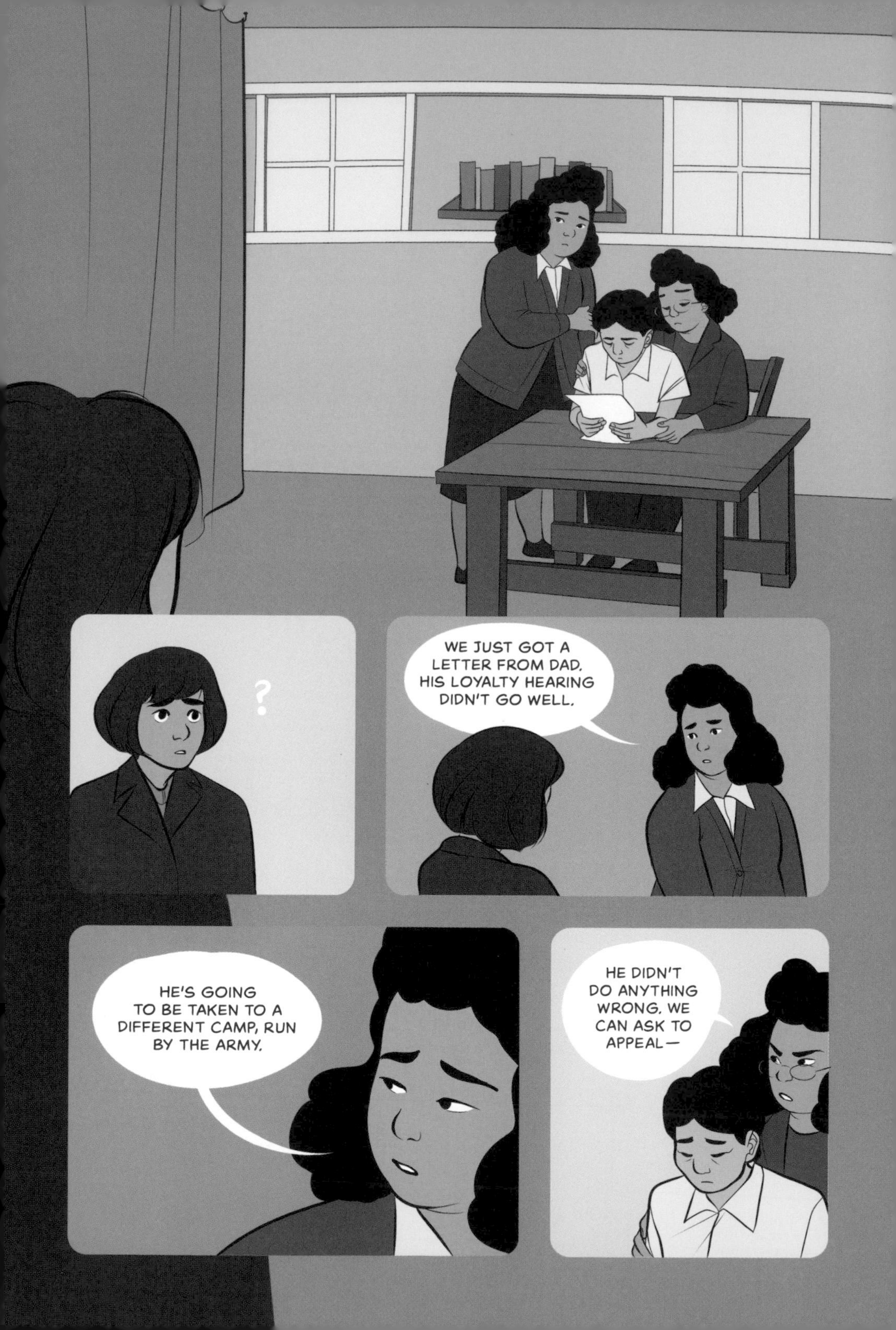
?
WE JUST GOT A LETTER FROM DAD. HIS LOYALTY HEARING DIDN'T GO WELL.
HE'S GOING TO BE TAKEN TO A DIFFERENT CAMP, RUN BY THE ARMY.
HE DIDN'T DO ANYTHING WRONG. WE CAN ASK TO APPEAL—

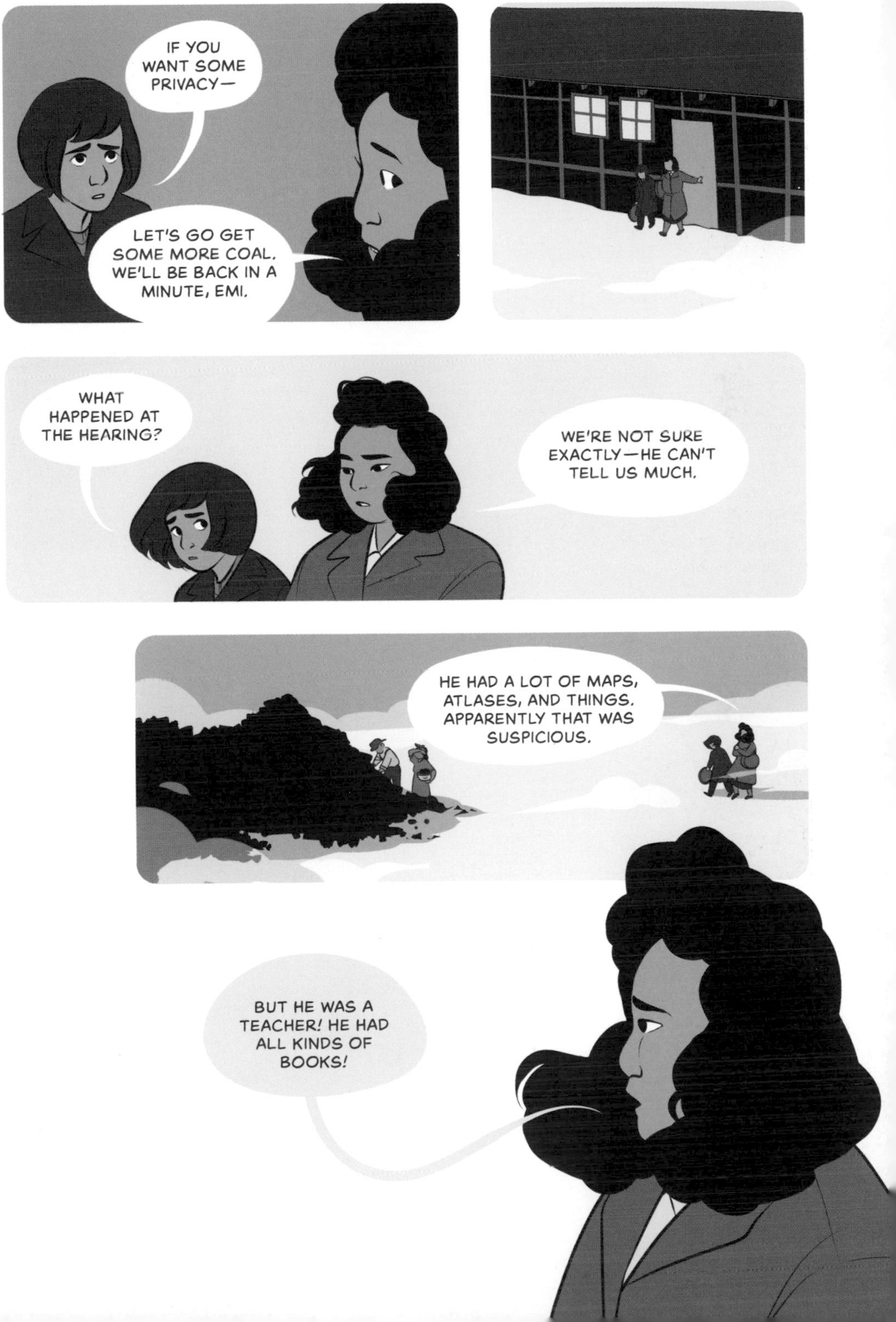
IF YOU WANT SOME PRIVACY—
LET'S GO GET SOME MORE COAL. WE'LL BE BACK IN A MINUTE, EMI.
WHAT HAPPENED AT THE HEARING?
WE'RE NOT SURE EXACTLY—HE CAN'T TELL US MUCH.
HE HAD A LOT OF MAPS, ATLASES, AND THINGS. APPARENTLY THAT WAS SUSPICIOUS.
BUT HE WAS A TEACHER! HE HAD ALL KINDS OF BOOKS!

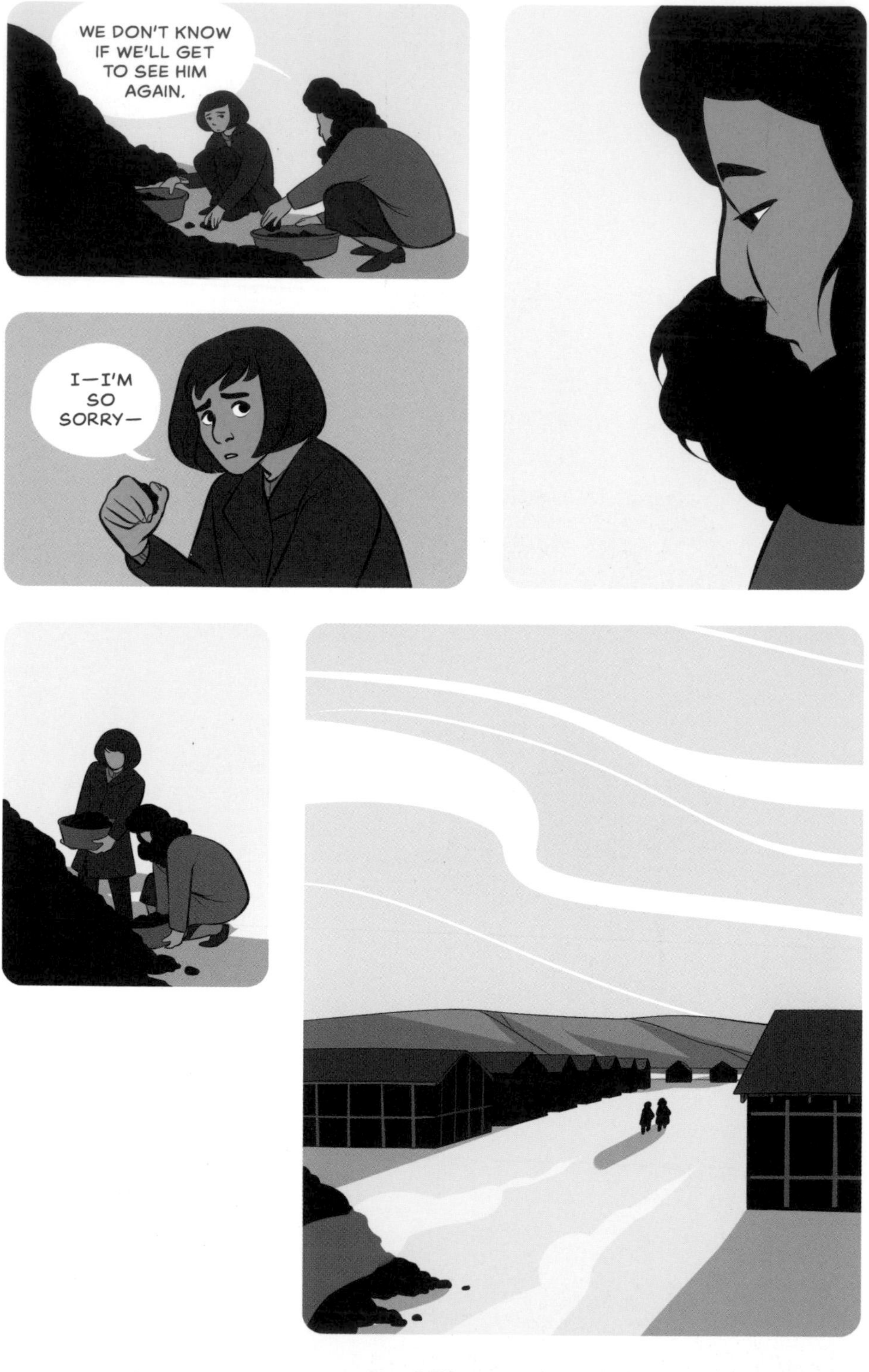
WE DON'T KNOW IF WE'LL GET TO SEE HIM AGAIN.
I—I'M SO SORRY—

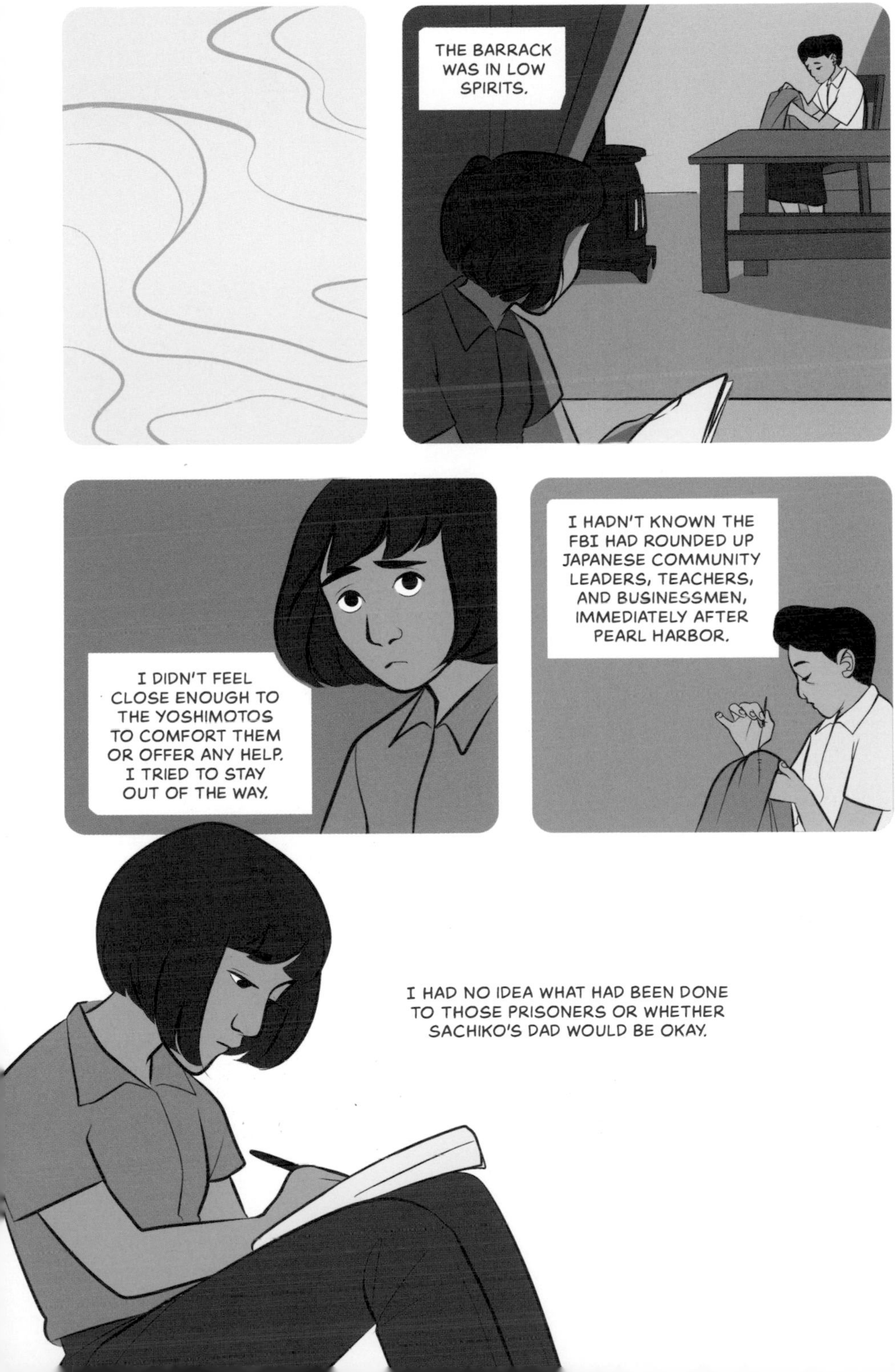
THE BARRACK WAS IN LOW SPIRITS.
I DIDN'T FEEL CLOSE ENOUGH TO THE YOSHIMOTOS TO COMFORT THEM OR OFFER ANY HELP. I TRIED TO STAY OUT OF THE WAY.
I HADN'T KNOWN THE FBI HAD ROUNDED UP JAPANESE COMMUNITY LEADERS, TEACHERS, AND BUSINESSMEN, IMMEDIATELY AFTER PEARL HARBOR.
I HAD NO IDEA WHAT HAD BEEN DONE TO THOSE PRISONERS OR WHETHER SACHIKO'S DAD WOULD BE OKAY.

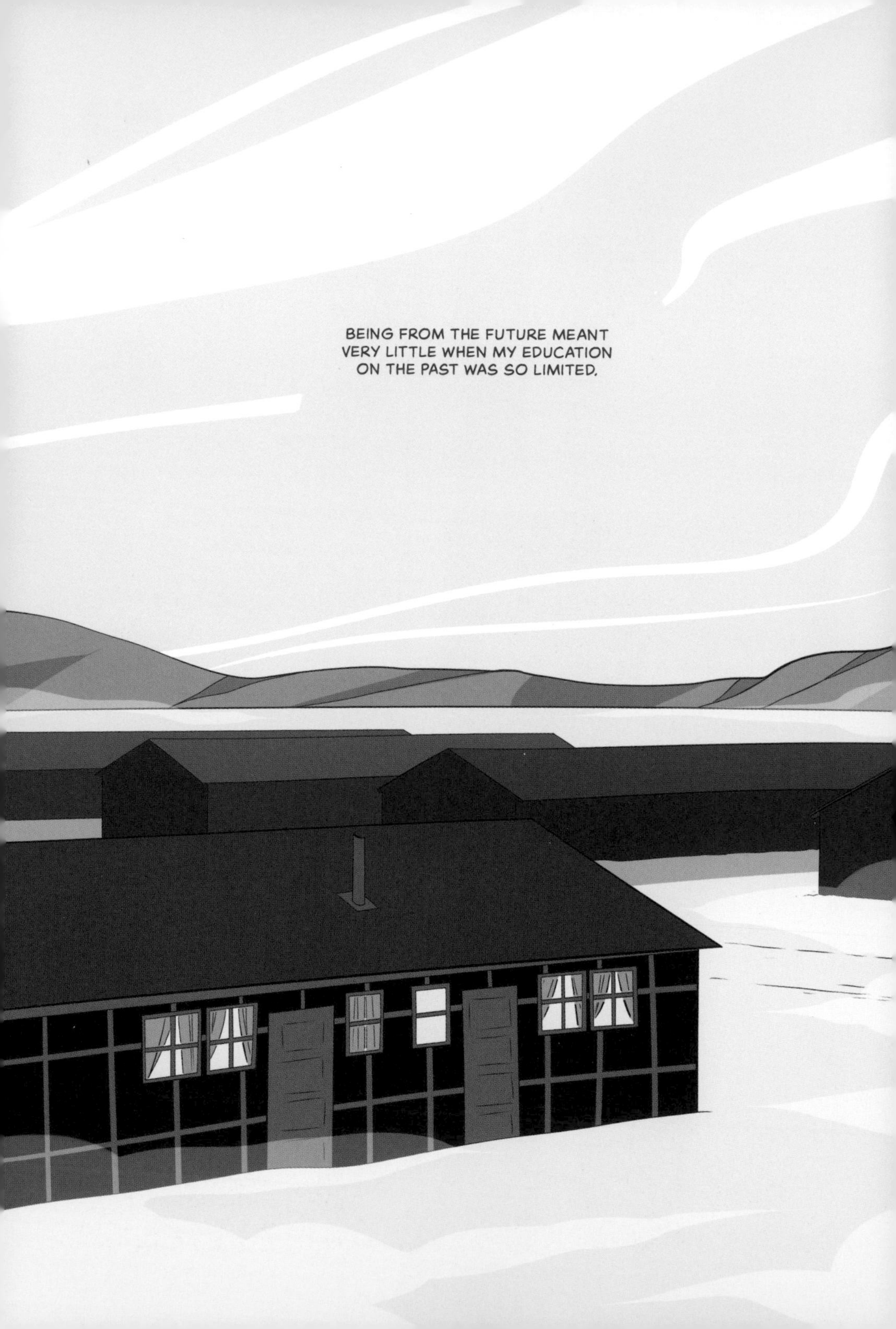
BEING FROM THE FUTURE MEANT VERY LITTLE WHEN MY EDUCATION ON THE PAST WAS SO LIMITED.

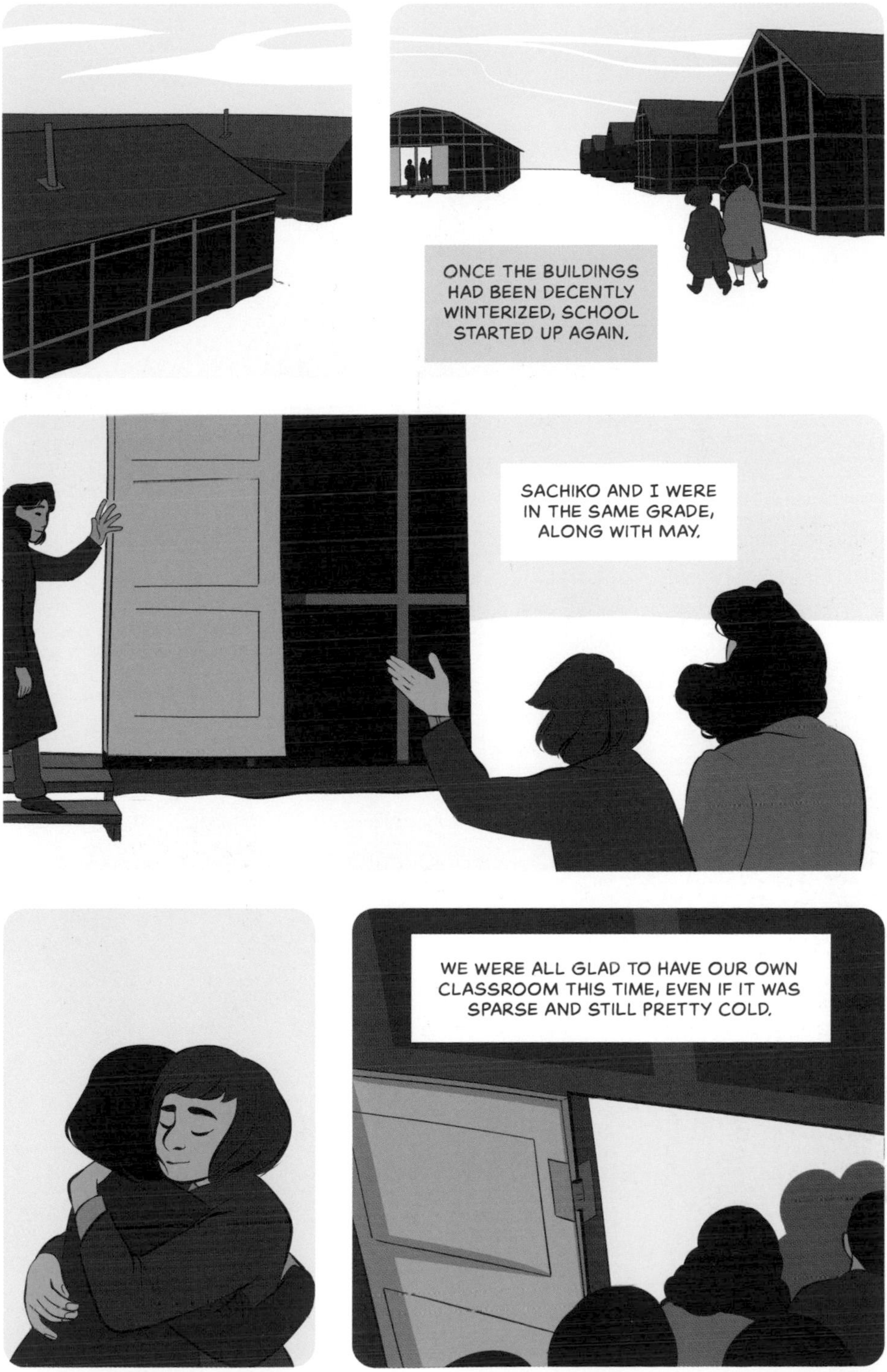
ONCE THE BUILDINGS HAD BEEN DECENTLY WINTERIZED, SCHOOL STARTED UP AGAIN.
SACHIKO AND I WERE IN THE SAME GRADE, ALONG WITH MAY.
WE WERE ALL GLAD TO HAVE OUR OWN CLASSROOM THIS TIME, EVEN IF IT WAS SPARSE AND STILL PRETTY COLD.

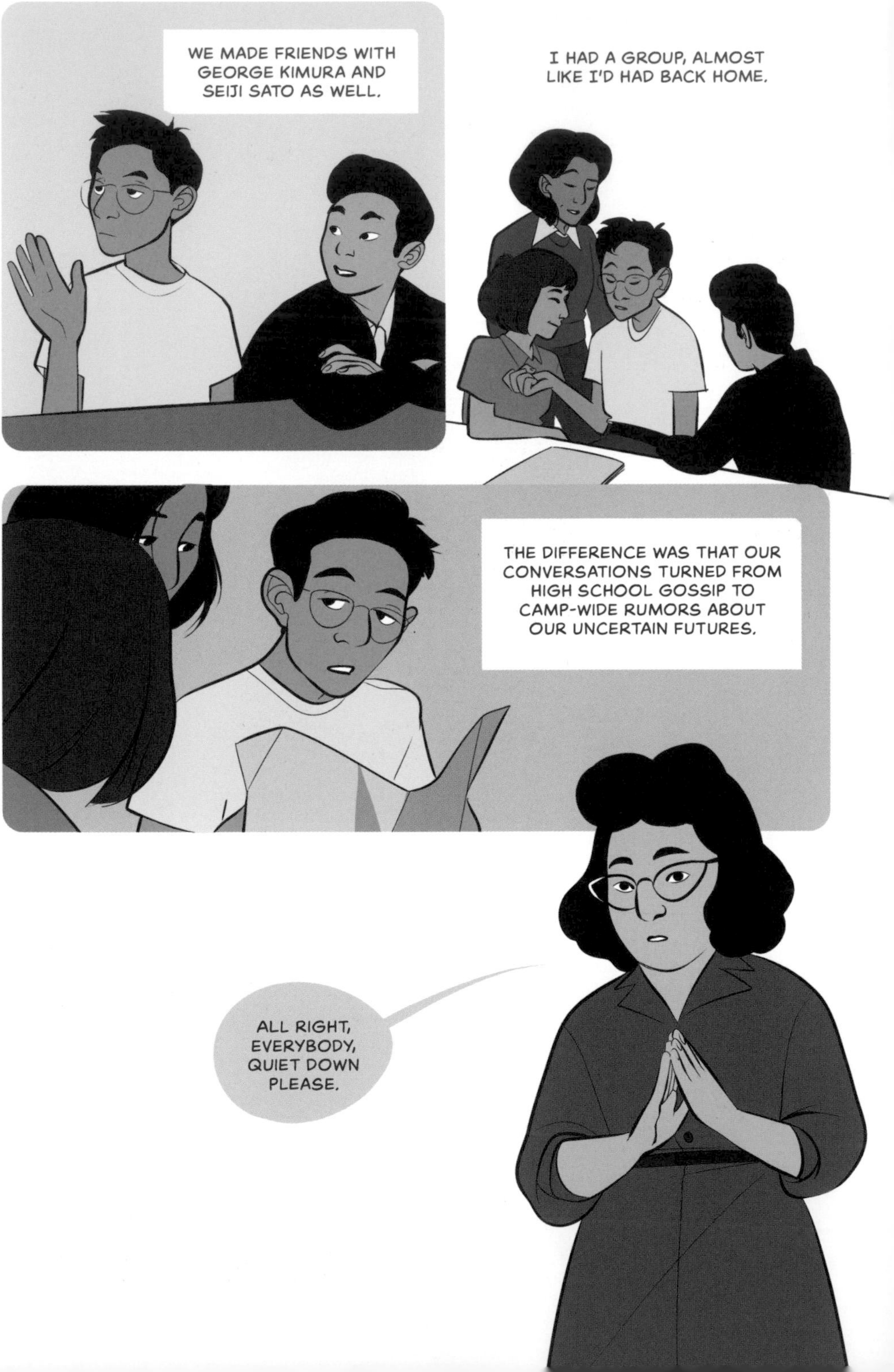
WE MADE FRIENDS WITH GEORGE KIMURA AND SEIJI SATO AS WELL.
I HAD A GROUP, ALMOST LIKE I'D HAD BACK HOME.
THE DIFFERENCE WAS THAT OUR CONVERSATIONS TURNED FROM HIGH SCHOOL GOSSIP TO CAMP-WIDE RUMORS ABOUT OUR UNCERTAIN FUTURES.
ALL RIGHT, EVERYBODY, QUIET DOWN PLEASE.

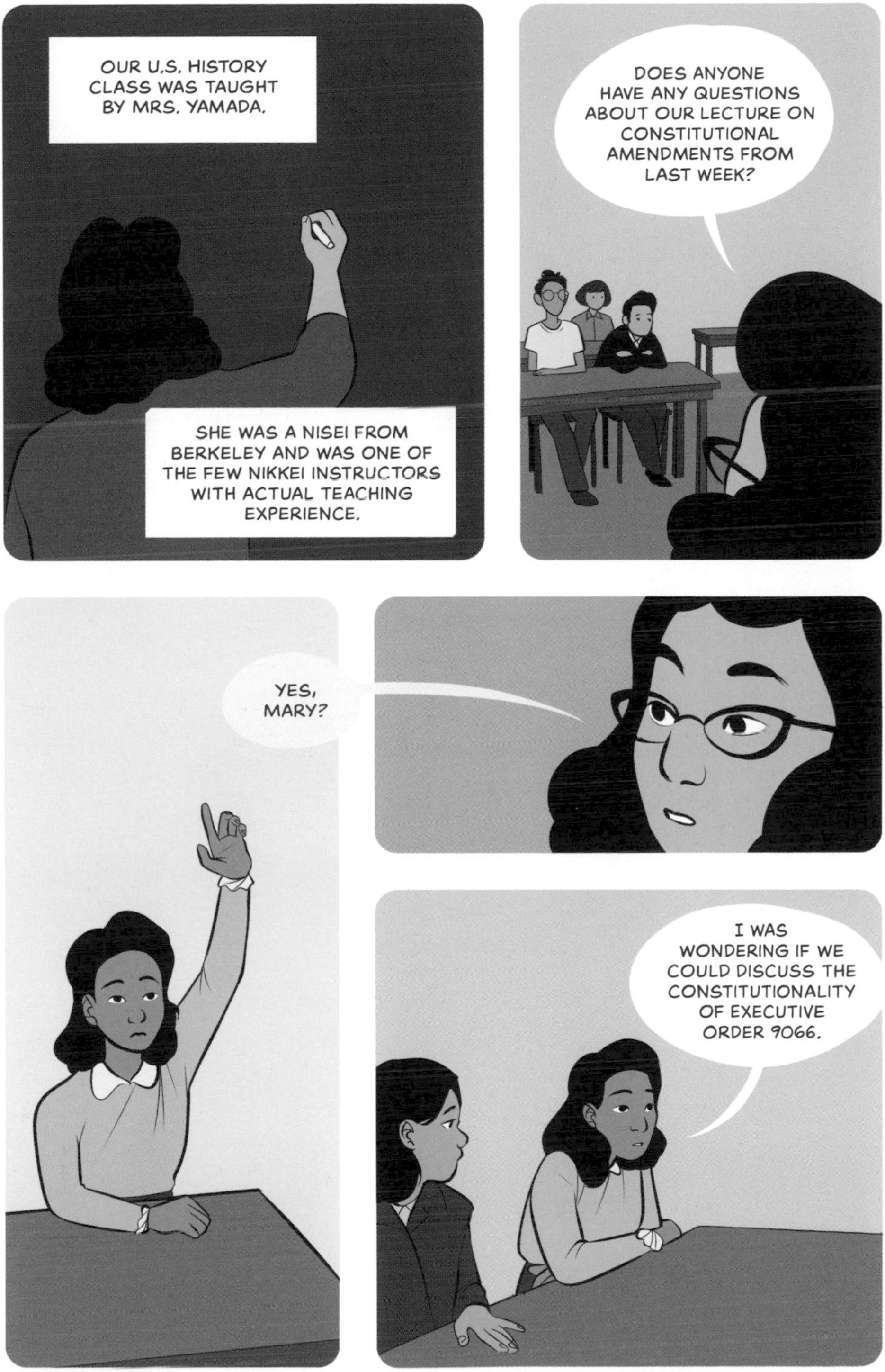
OUR U.S. HISTORY CLASS WAS TAUGHT BY MRS. YAMADA.
SHE WAS A NISEI FROM BERKELEY AND WAS ONE OF THE FEW NIKKEI INSTRUCTORS WITH ACTUAL TEACHING EXPERIENCE.
DOES ANYONE HAVE ANY QUESTIONS ABOUT OUR LECTURE ON CONSTITUTIONAL AMENDMENTS FROM LAST WEEK?
YES, MARY?
I WAS WONDERING IF WE COULD DISCUSS THE CONSTITUTIONALITY OF EXECUTIVE ORDER 9066.

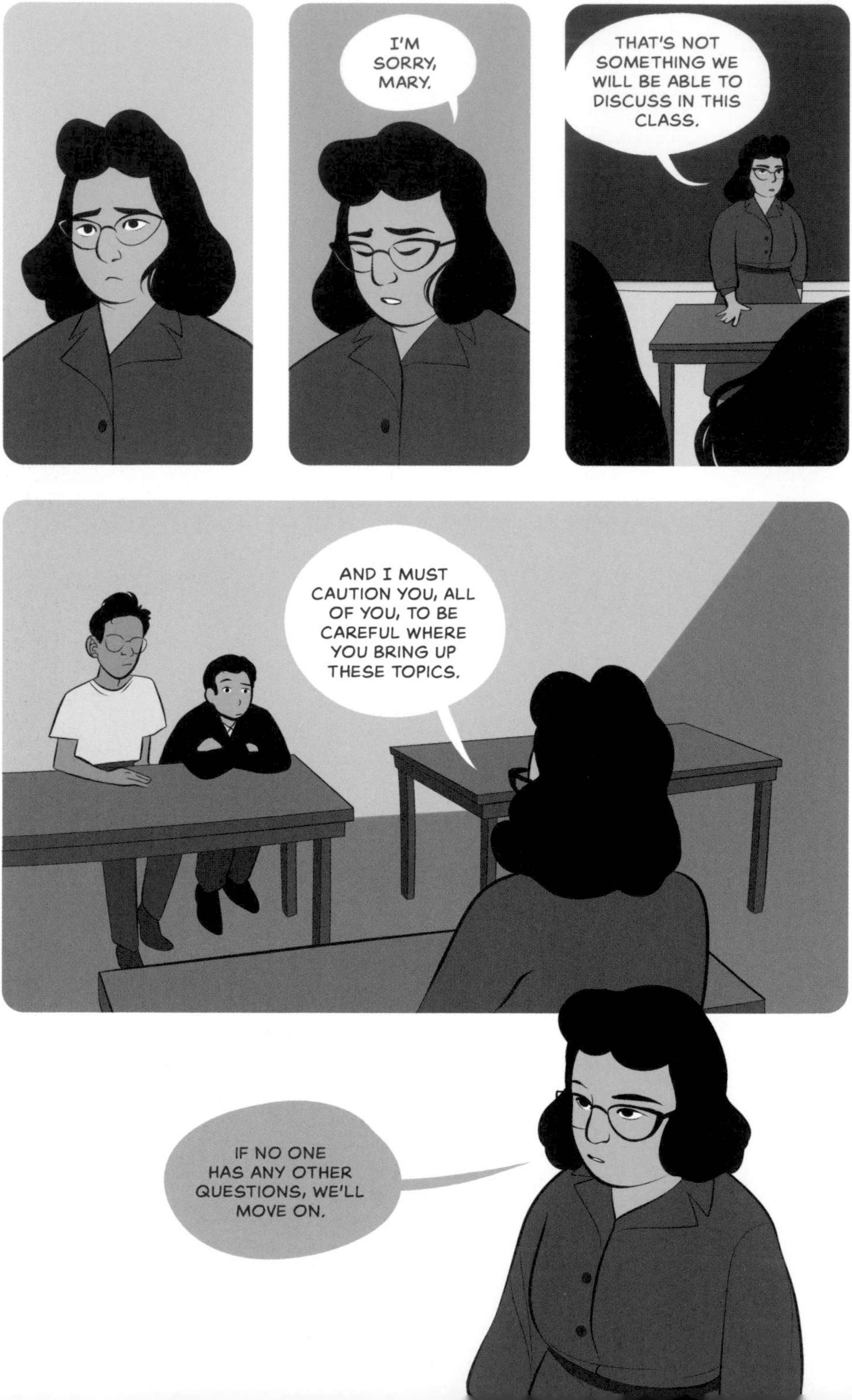
I'M SORRY, MARY.
THAT'S NOT SOMETHING WE WILL BE ABLE TO DISCUSS IN THIS CLASS.
AND I MUST CAUTION YOU, ALL OF YOU, TO BE CAREFUL WHERE YOU BRING UP THESE TOPICS.
IF NO ONE HAS ANY OTHER QUESTIONS, WE'LL MOVE ON.

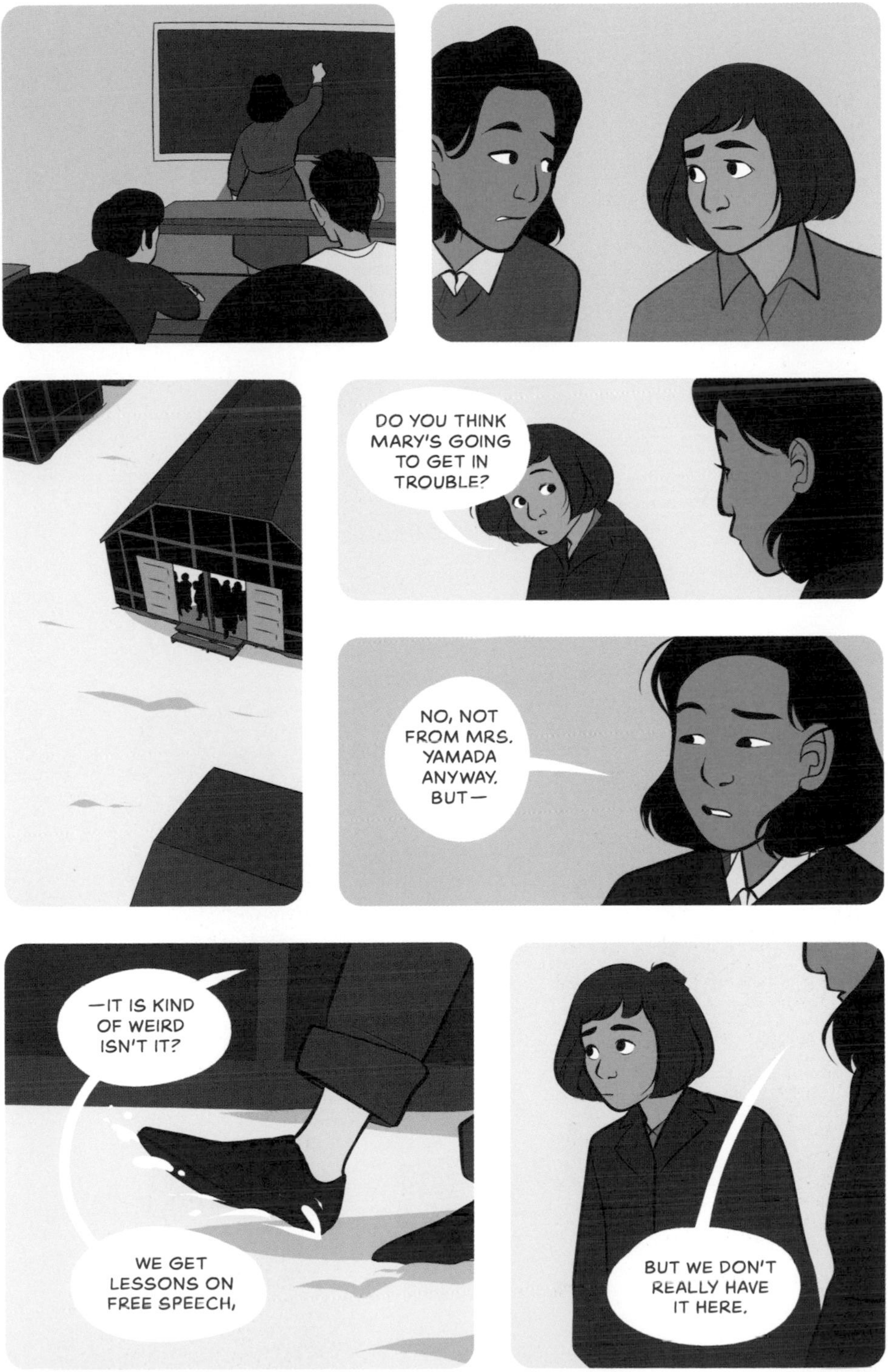
DO YOU THINK MARY'S GOING TO GET IN TROUBLE?
NO, NOT FROM MRS. YAMADA ANYWAY. BUT—
—IT IS KIND OF WEIRD ISN'T IT?
WE GET LESSONS ON FREE SPEECH,
BUT WE DON'T REALLY HAVE IT HERE.

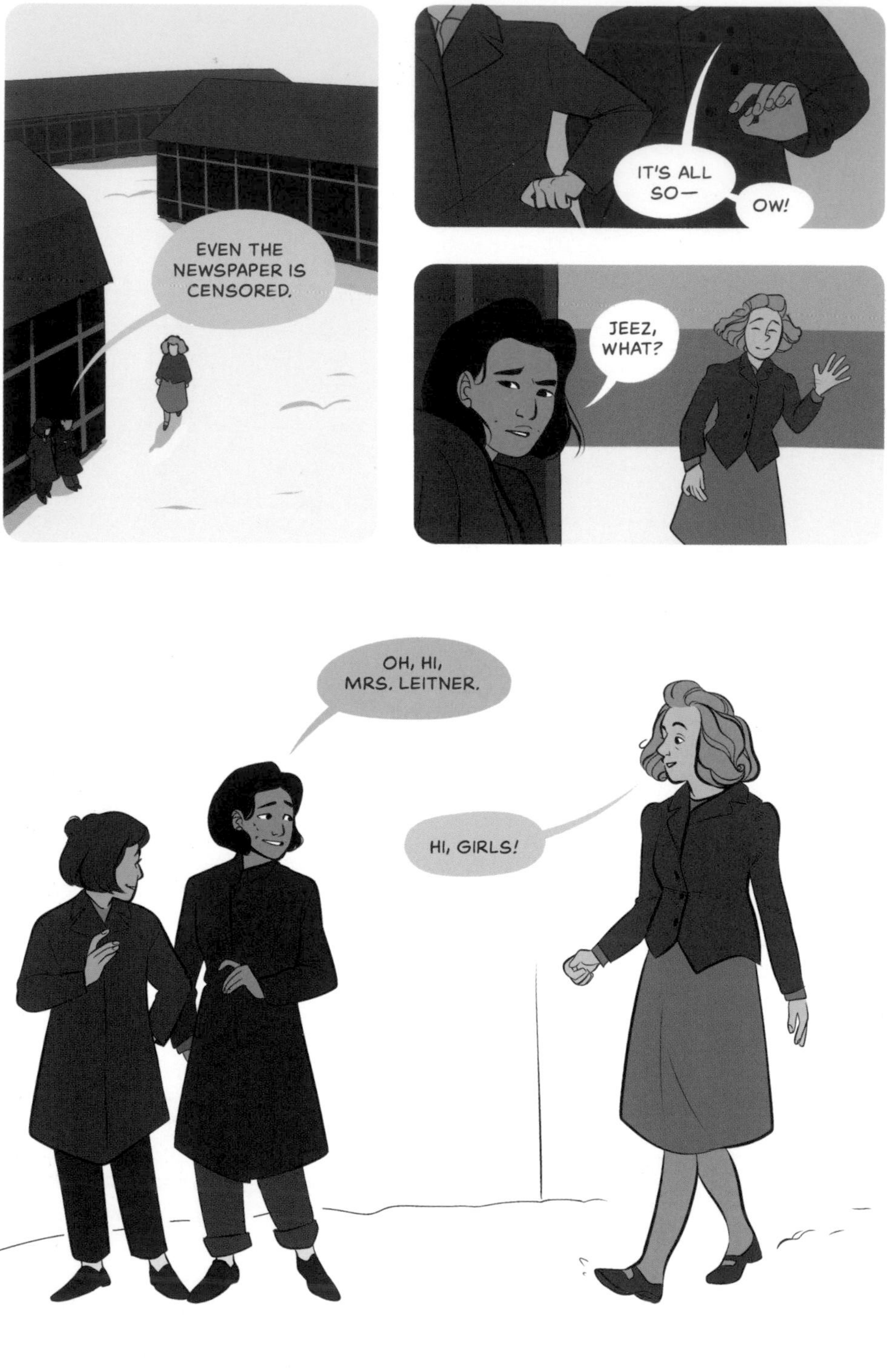
EVEN THE NEWSPAPER IS CENSORED.
IT'S ALL SO—
OW!
JEEZ, WHAT?
OH, HI, MRS. LEITNER.
HI, GIRLS!

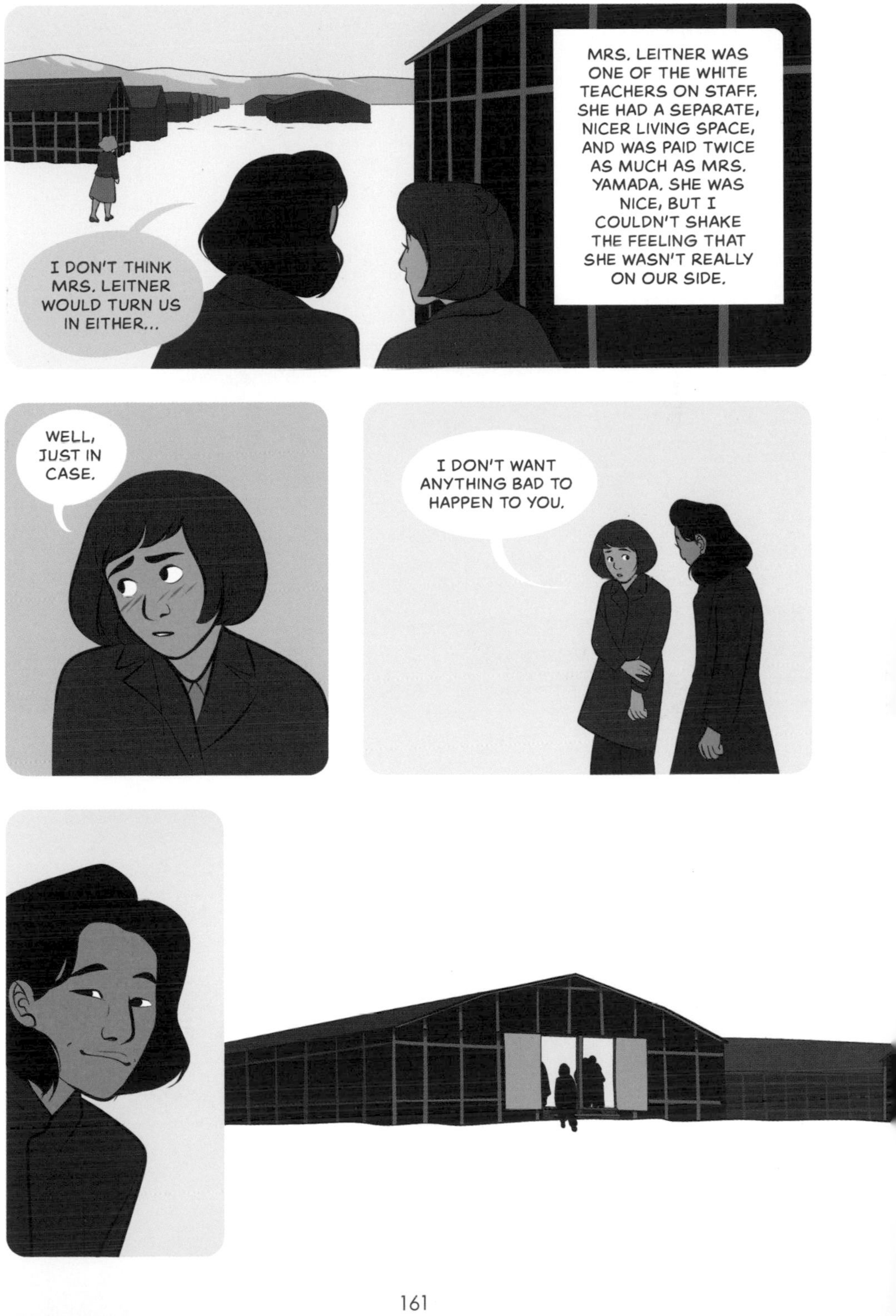

MRS. LEITNER WAS ONE OF THE WHITE TEACHERS ON STAFF. SHE HAD A SEPARATE, NICER LIVING SPACE, AND WAS PAID TWICE AS MUCH AS MRS. YAMADA. SHE WAS NICE, BUT I COULDN'T SHAKE THE FEELING THAT SHE WASN'T REALLY ON OUR SIDE.
I DON'T THINK MRS. LEITNER WOULD TURN US IN EITHER...
WELL, JUST IN CASE.
I DON'T WANT ANYTHING BAD TO HAPPEN TO YOU.

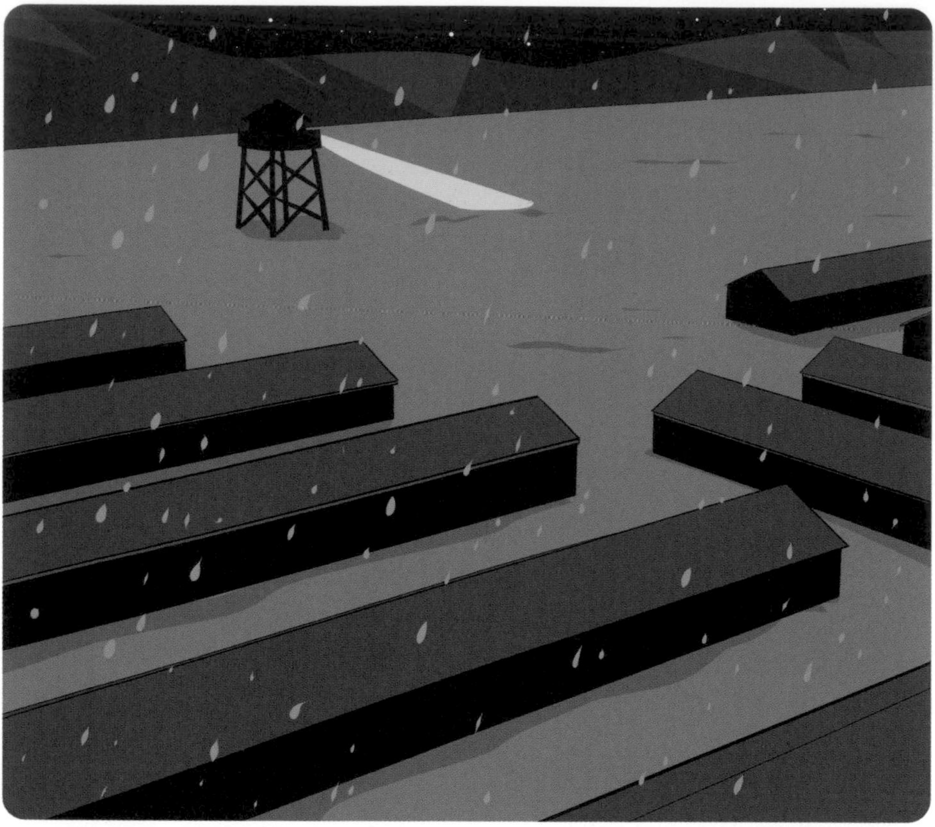

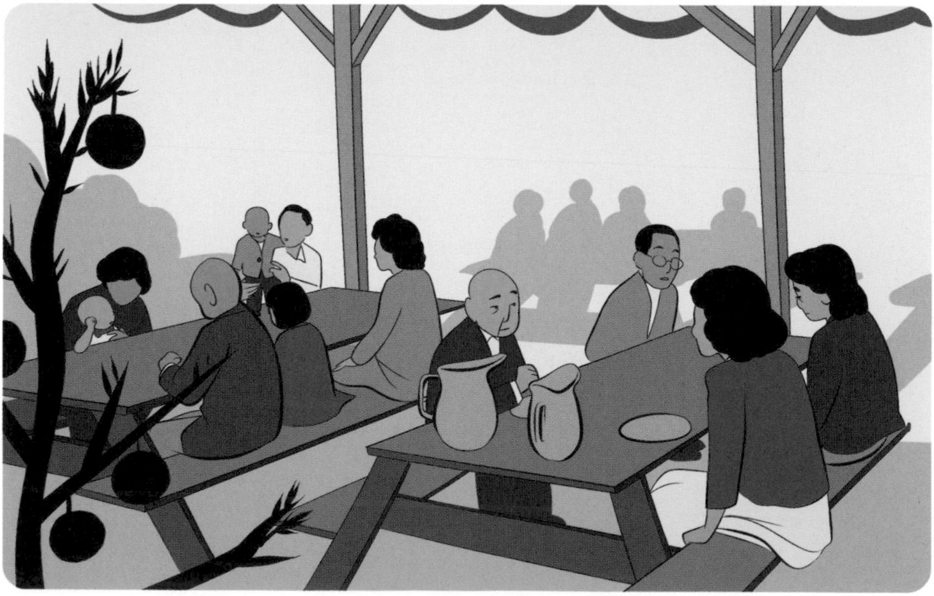

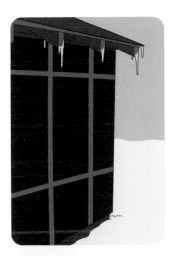

AS CHRISTMAS APPROACHED, WE FINALLY GOT SUPPLIES TO WINTERIZE OUR HOMES.

THE SMALL STOVES EACH BARRACK WAS GIVEN WERE NOT ENOUGH TO COMBAT THE HARSH UTAH WINTER, THE LIKES OF WHICH NONE OF US WEST COASTERS HAD EXPERIENCED BEFORE.

THOUGH MANY NIKKEI DID CELEBRATE CHRISTMAS, THE YOSHIMOTOS WEREN'T PARTICULARLY INCLINED TO.

THEY WERE BUDDHISTS, AND BESIDES, THEY WEREN'T IN A CELEBRATORY MOOD.

I COULDN'T BLAME THEM.

THE FIRST CLUE I HAD THAT THE HOLIDAY WAS NEAR WAS THE VISIT FROM THE QUAKERS.

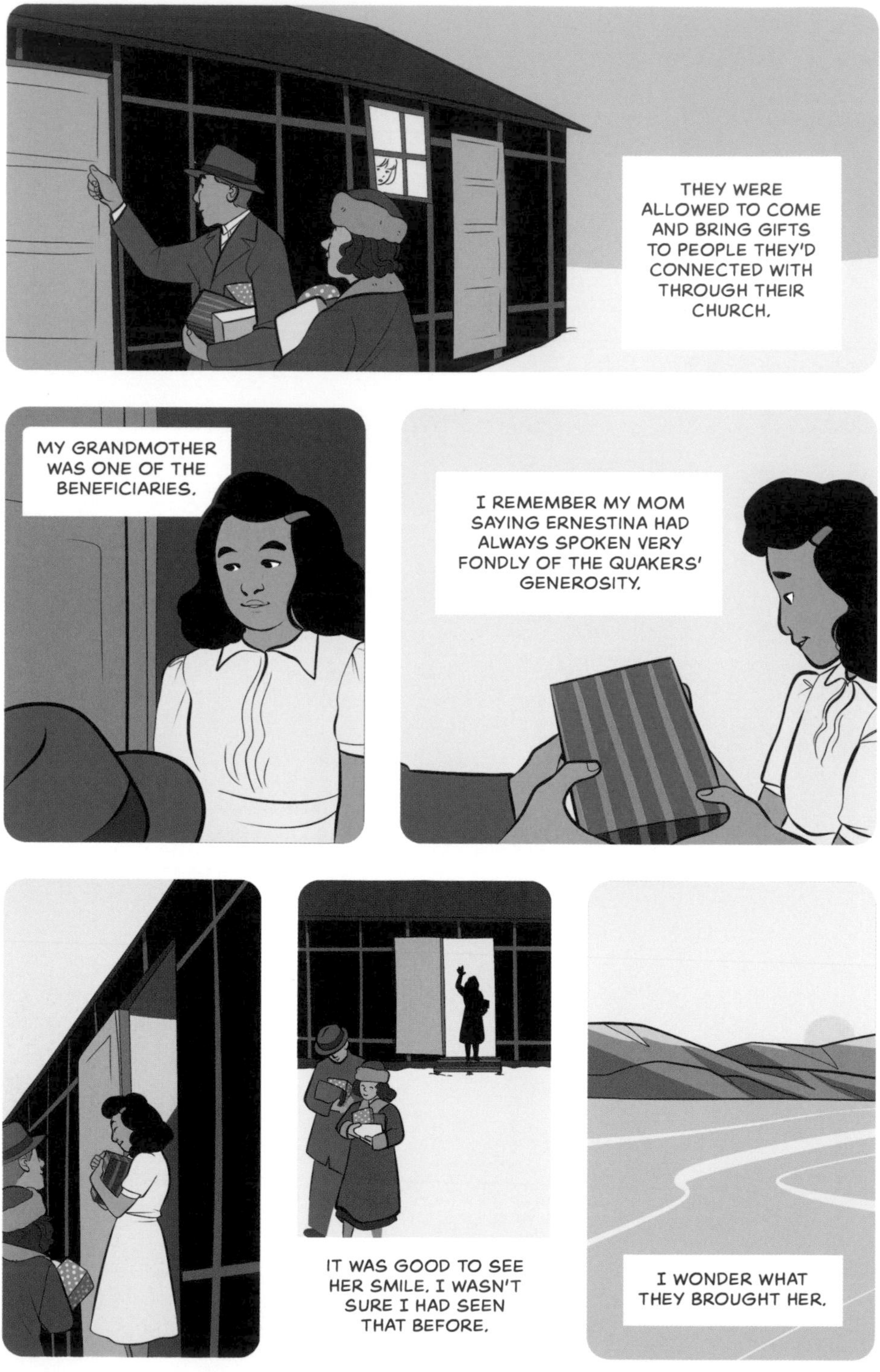
THEY WERE ALLOWED TO COME AND BRING GIFTS TO PEOPLE THEY'D CONNECTED WITH THROUGH THEIR CHURCH.
MY GRANDMOTHER WAS ONE OF THE BENEFICIARIES.
I REMEMBER MY MOM SAYING ERNESTINA HAD ALWAYS SPOKEN VERY FONDLY OF THE QUAKERS' GENEROSITY.
IT WAS GOOD TO SEE HER SMILE. I WASN'T SURE I HAD SEEN THAT BEFORE.
I WONDER WHAT THEY BROUGHT HER.

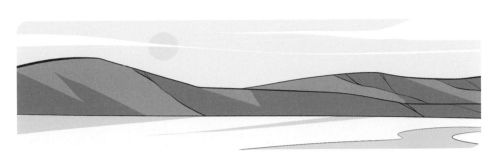

CHRISTMAS PASSED BY WITHOUT MUCH ACKNOWLEDGMENT, BUT NEW YEAR'S WAS CELEBRATED BY EVERYONE.

WE MADE MOCHI AND PLAYED GAMES WITH FAMILY AND FRIENDS.

IT WAS WONDERFUL, BUT IT ALSO MADE ME HOMESICK.

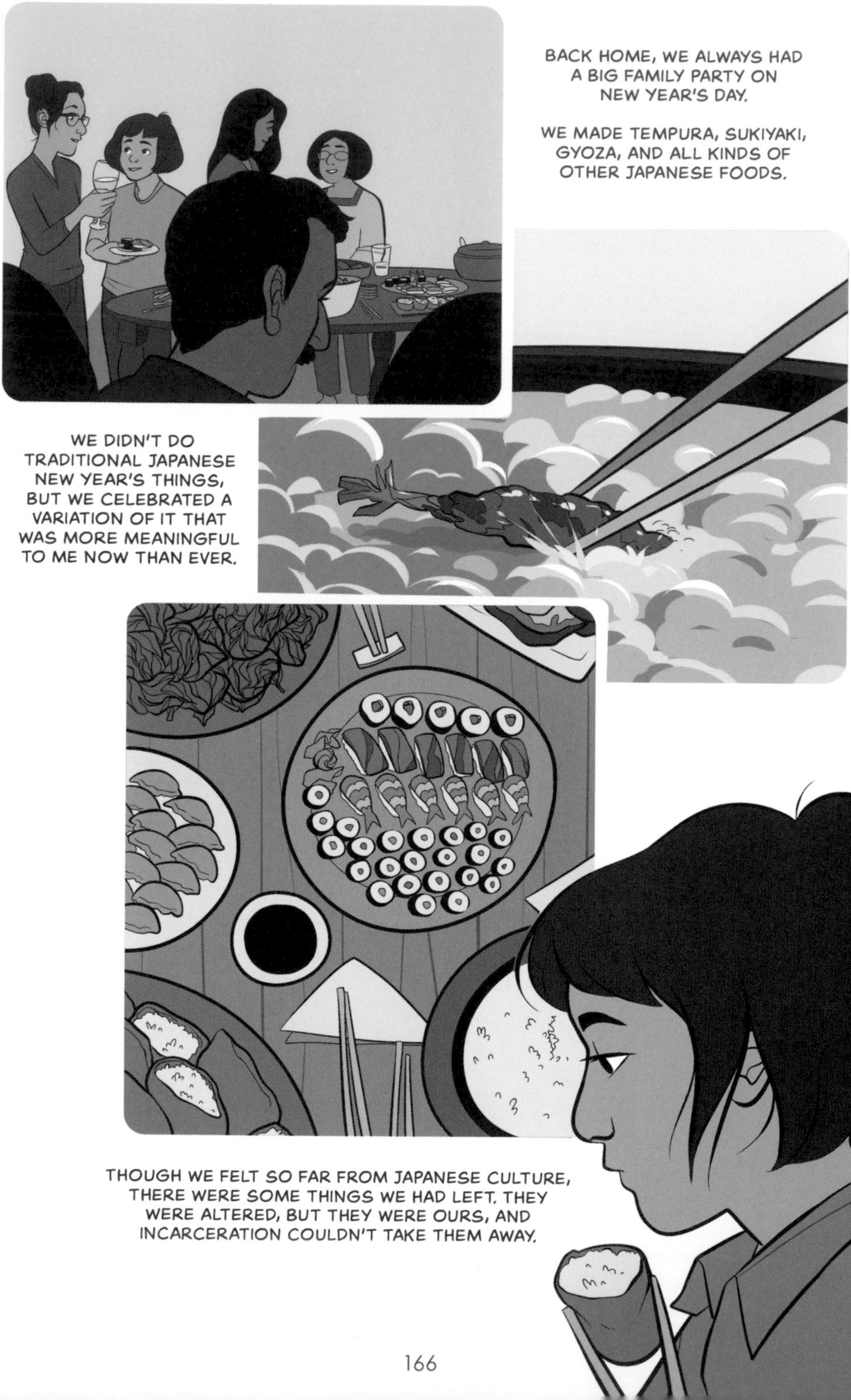
BACK HOME, WE ALWAYS HAD A BIG FAMILY PARTY ON NEW YEAR'S DAY.
WE MADE TEMPURA, SUKIYAKI, GYOZA, AND ALL KINDS OF OTHER JAPANESE FOODS.
WE DIDN'T DO TRADITIONAL JAPANESE NEW YEAR'S THINGS, BUT WE CELEBRATED A VARIATION OF IT THAT WAS MORE MEANINGFUL TO ME NOW THAN EVER.
THOUGH WE FELT SO FAR FROM JAPANESE CULTURE, THERE WERE SOME THINGS WE HAD LEFT. THEY WERE ALTERED, BUT THEY WERE OURS, AND INCARCERATION COULDN'T TAKE THEM AWAY.

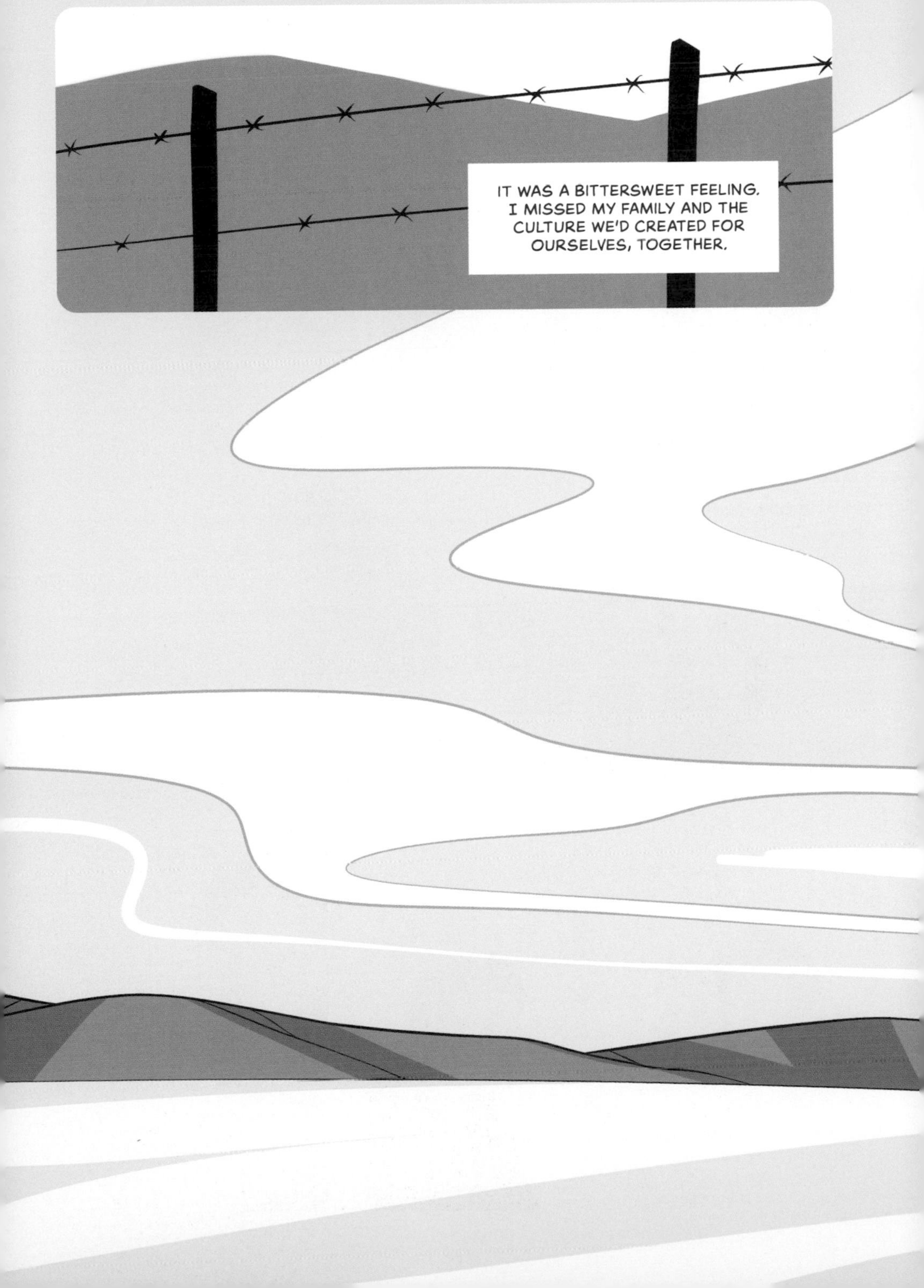
IT WAS A BITTERSWEET FEELING. I MISSED MY FAMILY AND THE CULTURE WE'D CREATED FOR OURSELVES, TOGETHER.

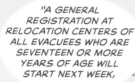

"A GENERAL REGISTRATION AT RELOCATION CENTERS OF ALL EVACUEES WHO ARE SEVENTEEN OR MORE YEARS OF AGE WILL START NEXT WEEK,

FOLLOWING THE ANNOUNCEMENT LAST THURSDAY THAT A COMBAT UNIT OF AMERICAN CITIZENS OF JAPANESE ANCESTRY WILL BE FORMED FOR ACTIVE SERVICE,

IT WAS REVEALED THAT THE GOVERNMENT, SEEKING A FEASIBLE SOLUTION TO THE ACUTE WARTIME PROBLEM OF THE JAPANESE AMERICAN PEOPLE,

HAD DECIDED TO DETERMINE PRINCIPALLY BY MEANS OF QUESTIONNAIRES, THE EXTENT OF THE LOYALTY HELD BY THE EVACUEES TOWARDS THE UNITED STATES,"

SO THEY LOCK US UP, AND NOW THEY EXPECT US TO VOLUNTEER TO GET SHOT IN THE PACIFIC?

ONLY IF YOU CAN PROVE YOU'RE LOYAL ENOUGH TO GET SHOT.

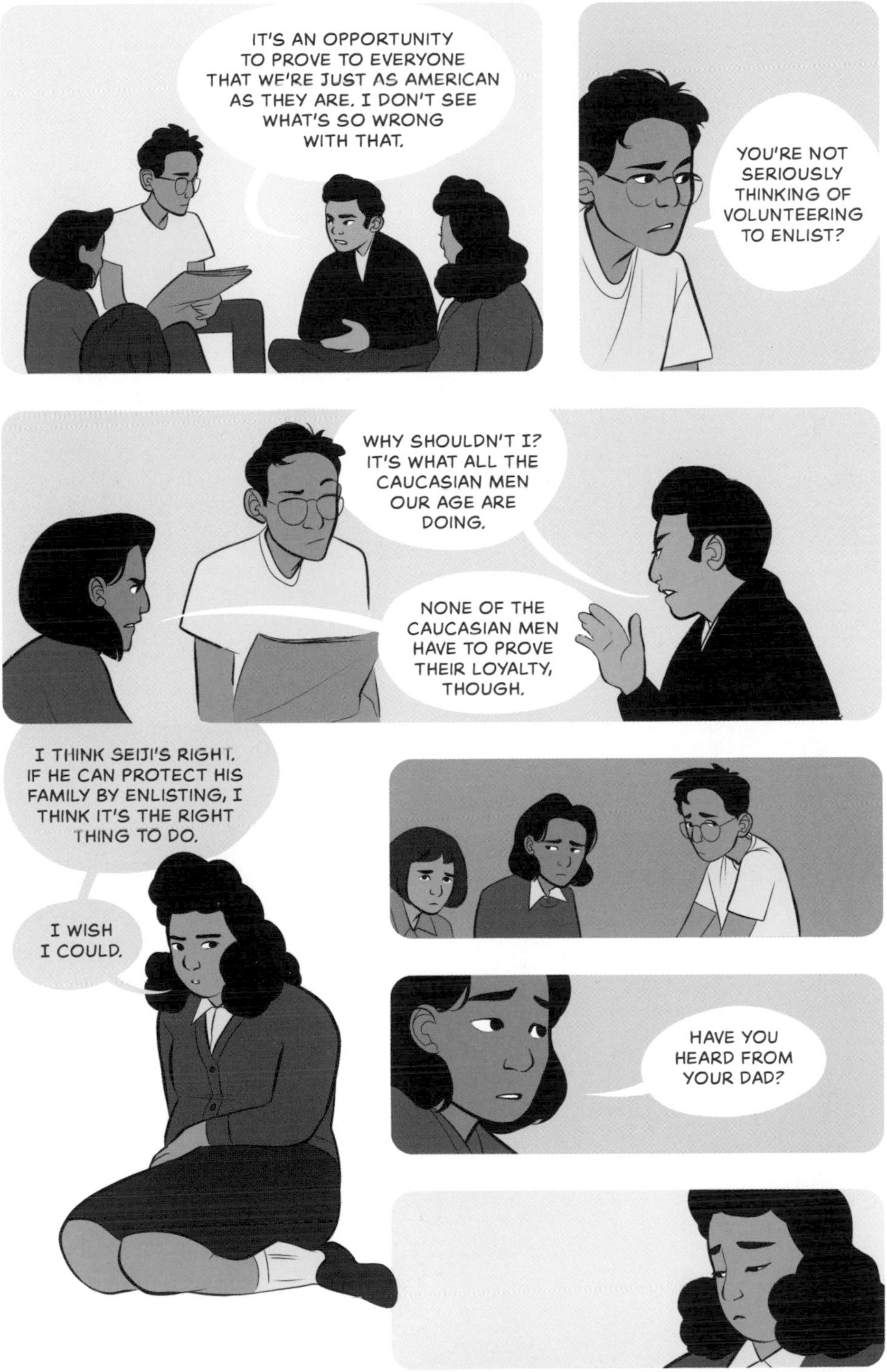
IT'S AN OPPORTUNITY TO PROVE TO EVERYONE THAT WE'RE JUST AS AMERICAN AS THEY ARE. I DON'T SEE WHAT'S SO WRONG WITH THAT.
YOU'RE NOT SERIOUSLY THINKING OF VOLUNTEERING TO ENLIST?
WHY SHOULDN'T I? IT'S WHAT ALL THE CAUCASIAN MEN OUR AGE ARE DOING.
NONE OF THE CAUCASIAN MEN HAVE TO PROVE THEIR LOYALTY, THOUGH.
I THINK SEIJI'S RIGHT. IF HE CAN PROTECT HIS FAMILY BY ENLISTING, I THINK IT'S THE RIGHT THING TO DO.
I WISH I COULD.
HAVE YOU HEARD FROM YOUR DAD?

THE LOYALTY QUESTIONNAIRES DIDN'T END WITH NISEI MEN ABLE TO ENLIST. SOON THEY WERE BEING ADMINISTERED TO EVERYONE AT CAMP WHO WAS SEVENTEEN OR OLDER.

THE CONCEPT OF A LOYALTY QUESTIONNAIRE WAS CONTROVERSIAL ENOUGH AROUND CAMP, BUT THE BIGGEST PROBLEM WAS WITH QUESTIONS 27 AND 28.

THESE TWO WERE THE SUBJECT OF COUNTLESS DEBATES, ARGUMENTS, AND SLEEPLESS NIGHTS AT TOPAZ.

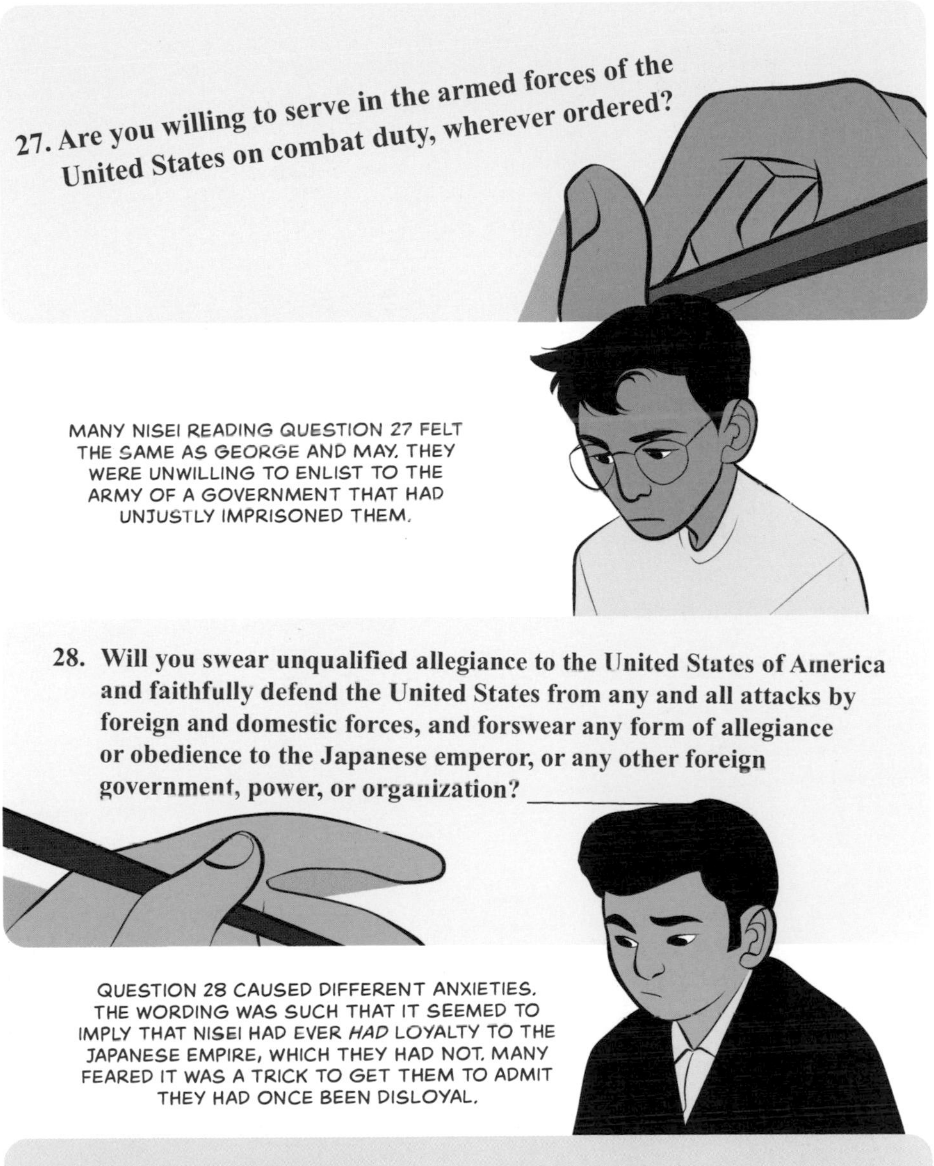
27. Are you willing to serve in the armed forces of the United States on combat duty, wherever ordered?
MANY NISEI READING QUESTION 27 FELT THE SAME AS GEORGE AND MAY. THEY WERE UNWILLING TO ENLIST TO THE ARMY OF A GOVERNMENT THAT HAD UNJUSTLY IMPRISONED THEM.
28. Will you swear unqualified allegiance to the United States of America and faithfully defend the United States from any and all attacks by foreign and domestic forces, and forswear any form of allegiance or obedience to the Japanese emperor, or any other foreign government, power, or organization? ______
QUESTION 28 CAUSED DIFFERENT ANXIETIES. THE WORDING WAS SUCH THAT IT SEEMED TO IMPLY THAT NISEI HAD EVER *HAD* LOYALTY TO THE JAPANESE EMPIRE, WHICH THEY HAD NOT. MANY FEARED IT WAS A TRICK TO GET THEM TO ADMIT THEY HAD ONCE BEEN DISLOYAL.
FOR ISSEI, WHO HAD BEEN DENIED CITIZENSHIP BY THE U.S. GOVERNMENT, THEY WORRIED THEY WOULD BECOME STATELESS IF THEY RENOUNCED THEIR JAPANESE CITIZENSHIP. THEY WOULD HAVE NO LEGAL STATUS IN THE WORLD.

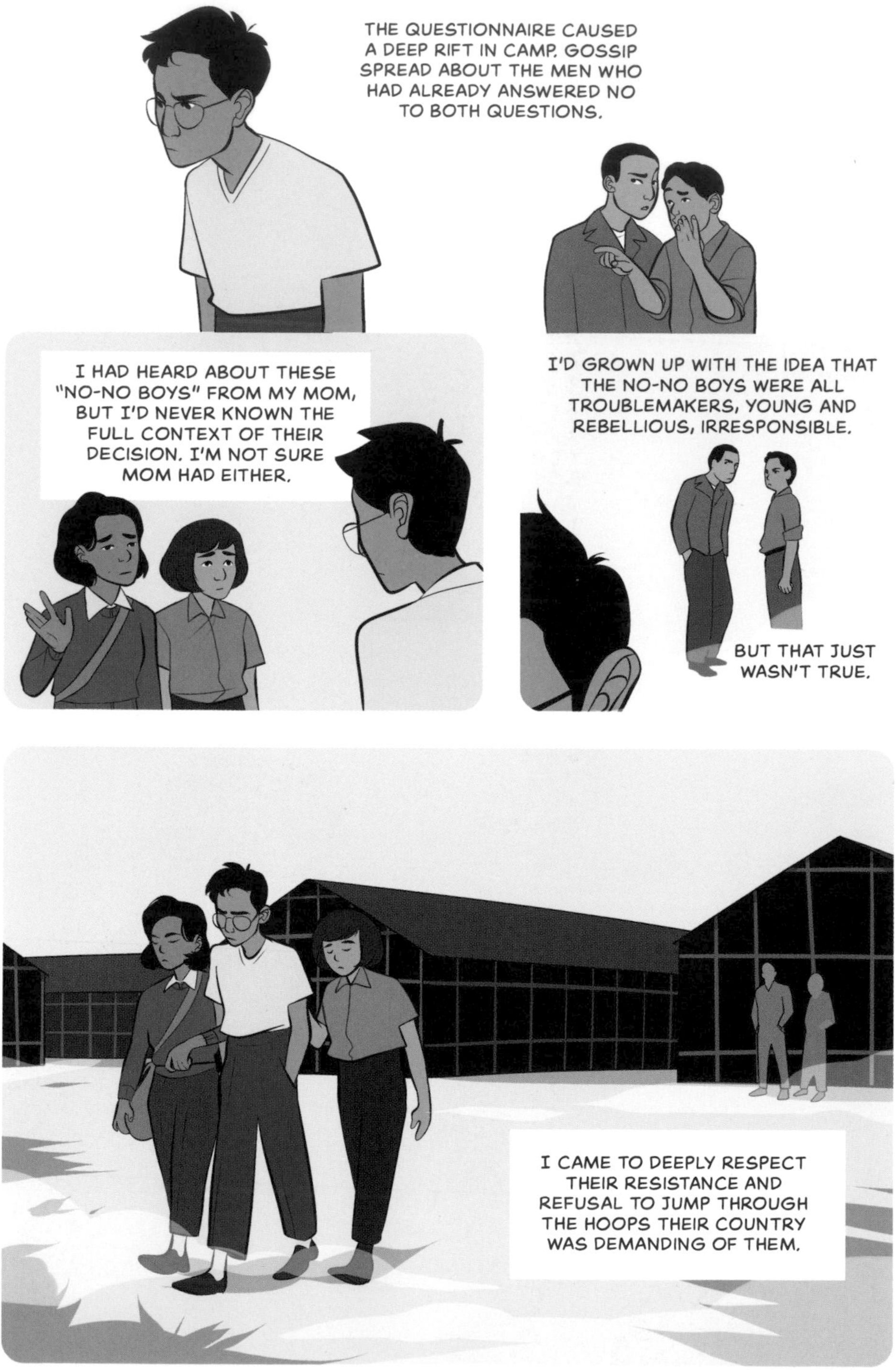
THE QUESTIONNAIRE CAUSED A DEEP RIFT IN CAMP. GOSSIP SPREAD ABOUT THE MEN WHO HAD ALREADY ANSWERED NO TO BOTH QUESTIONS.
I HAD HEARD ABOUT THESE "NO-NO BOYS" FROM MY MOM, BUT I'D NEVER KNOWN THE FULL CONTEXT OF THEIR DECISION. I'M NOT SURE MOM HAD EITHER.
I'D GROWN UP WITH THE IDEA THAT THE NO-NO BOYS WERE ALL TROUBLEMAKERS, YOUNG AND REBELLIOUS, IRRESPONSIBLE.
BUT THAT JUST WASN'T TRUE.
I CAME TO DEEPLY RESPECT THEIR RESISTANCE AND REFUSAL TO JUMP THROUGH THE HOOPS THEIR COUNTRY WAS DEMANDING OF THEM.

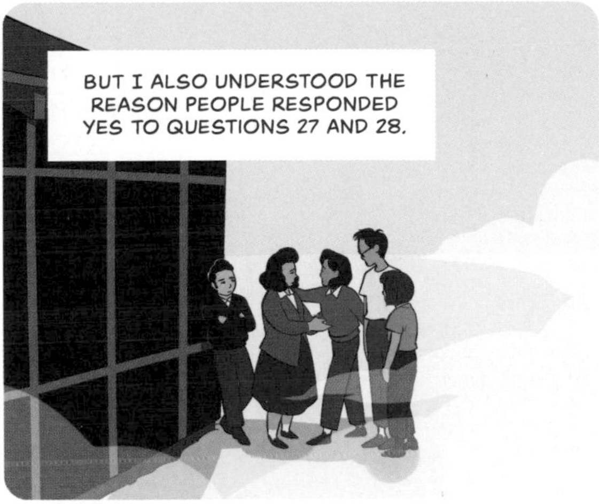
BUT I ALSO UNDERSTOOD THE REASON PEOPLE RESPONDED YES TO QUESTIONS 27 AND 28.

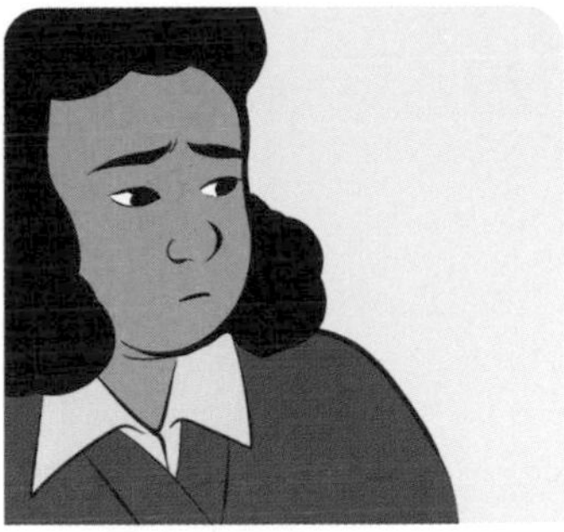

NOBODY KNEW THEN WHAT THE CONSEQUENCES OF RESISTANCE COULD BE. THERE WAS FEAR AND AN EVER-PRESENT DANGER.

AND I STILL DIDN'T KNOW HOW I WOULD RESPOND. I HAD TURNED SEVENTEEN JUST AS THE QUESTIONNAIRE WAS BEING ROLLED OUT, SO I WAS PRESENTED WITH A CHOICE AS WELL.

I KNEW THE NO-NO BOYS WOULD BE TAKEN TO A HIGH-SECURITY CAMP, AND THE FEAR OF THAT WRESTLED WITH MY DESIRE TO RESIST OUR INJUSTICE.

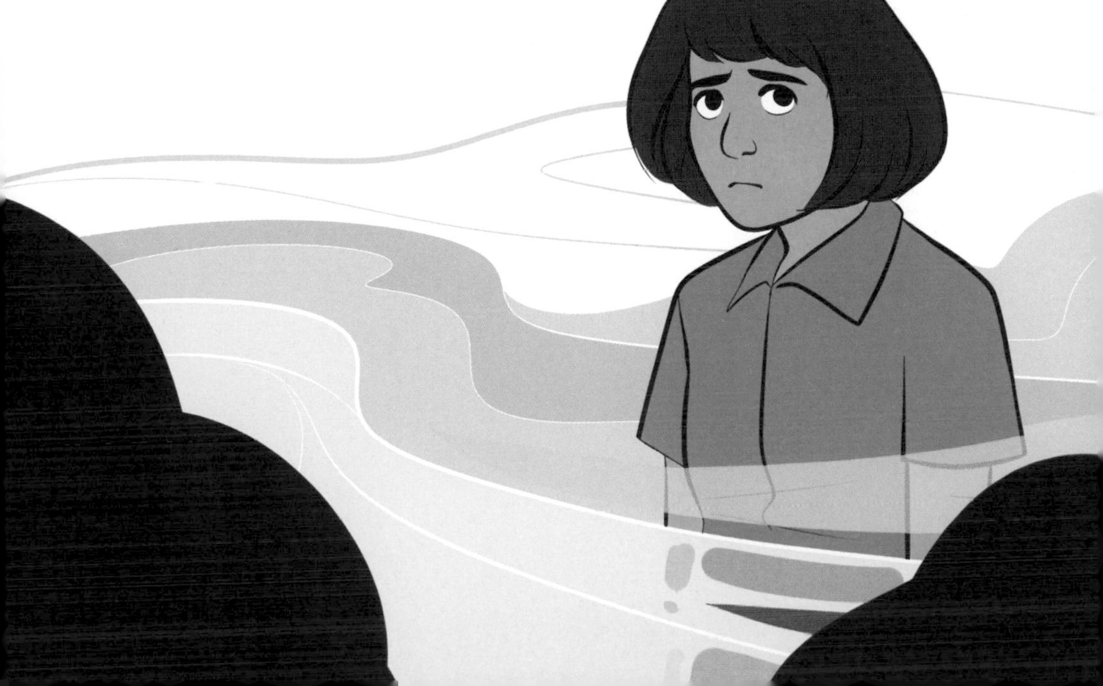

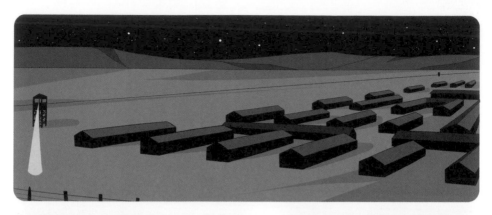

THE NIGHT BEFORE WE HAD TO TURN IN OUR QUESTIONNAIRES, I HEARD THE TERANISHIS SPEAKING IN JAPANESE NEXT DOOR.

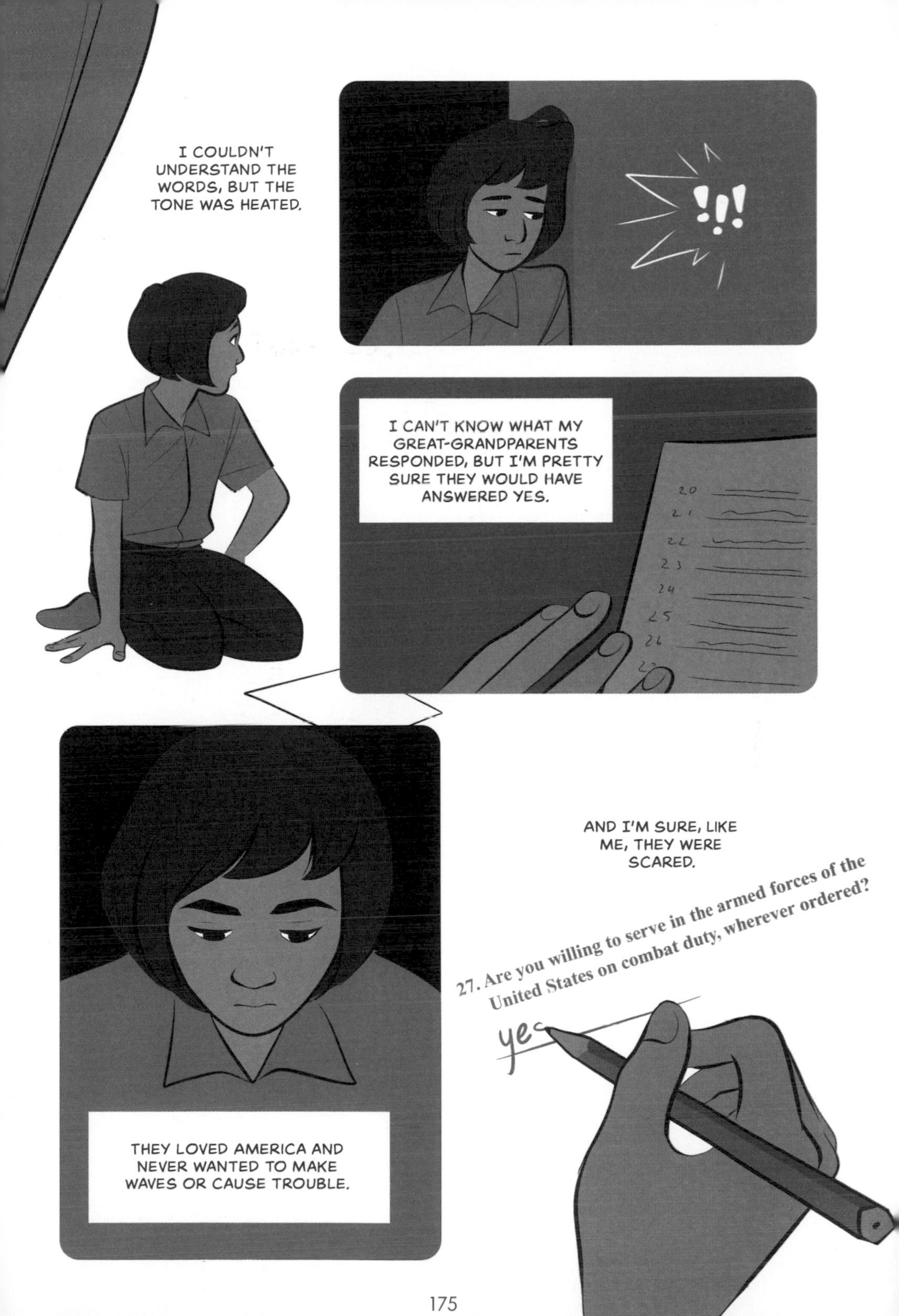
I COULDN'T UNDERSTAND THE WORDS, BUT THE TONE WAS HEATED.
!!!
I CAN'T KNOW WHAT MY GREAT-GRANDPARENTS RESPONDED, BUT I'M PRETTY SURE THEY WOULD HAVE ANSWERED YES.
20
21
22
23
24
25
26
THEY LOVED AMERICA AND NEVER WANTED TO MAKE WAVES OR CAUSE TROUBLE.
AND I'M SURE, LIKE ME, THEY WERE SCARED.
27. Are you willing to serve in the armed forces of the United States on combat duty, wherever ordered?
yes

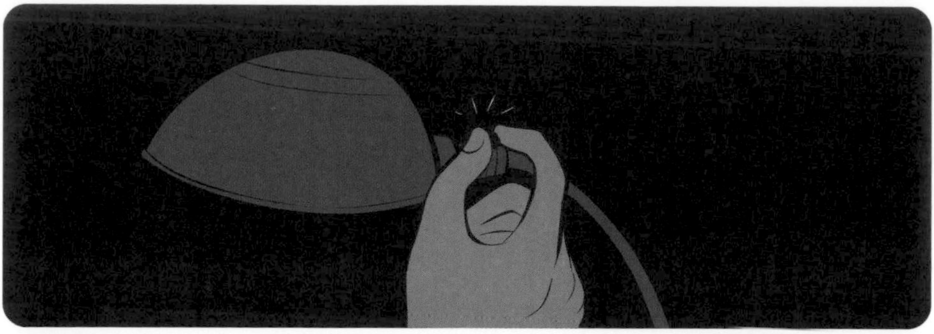

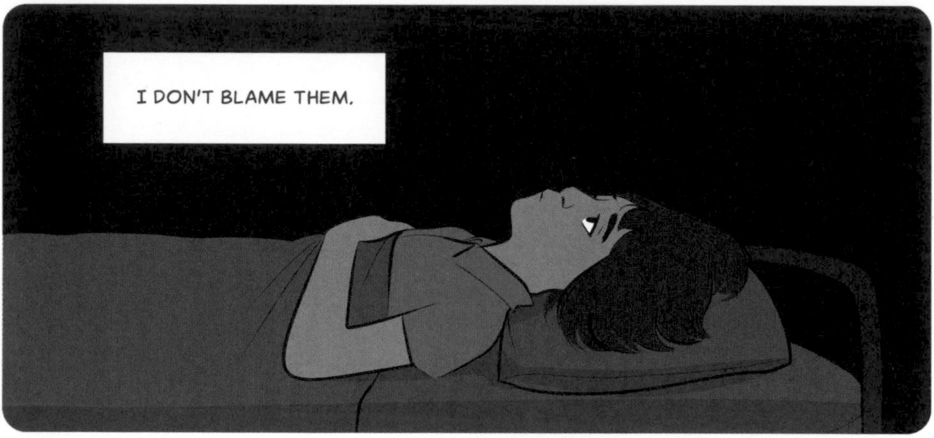
I DON'T BLAME THEM.

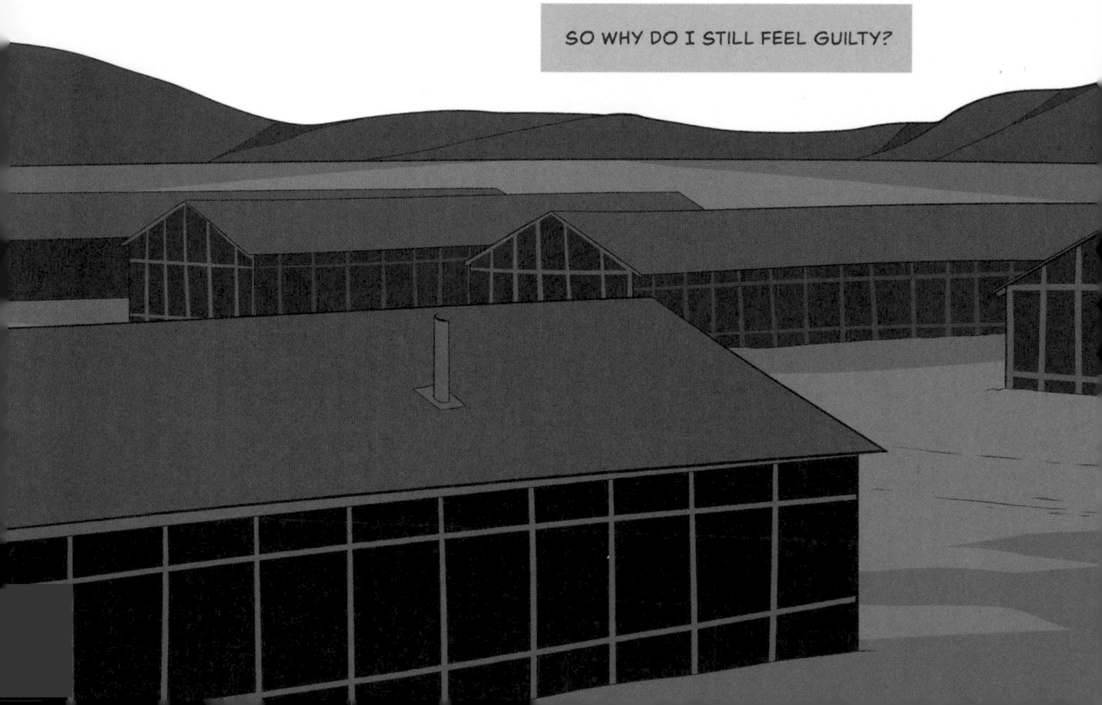
SO WHY DO I STILL FEEL GUILTY?

7

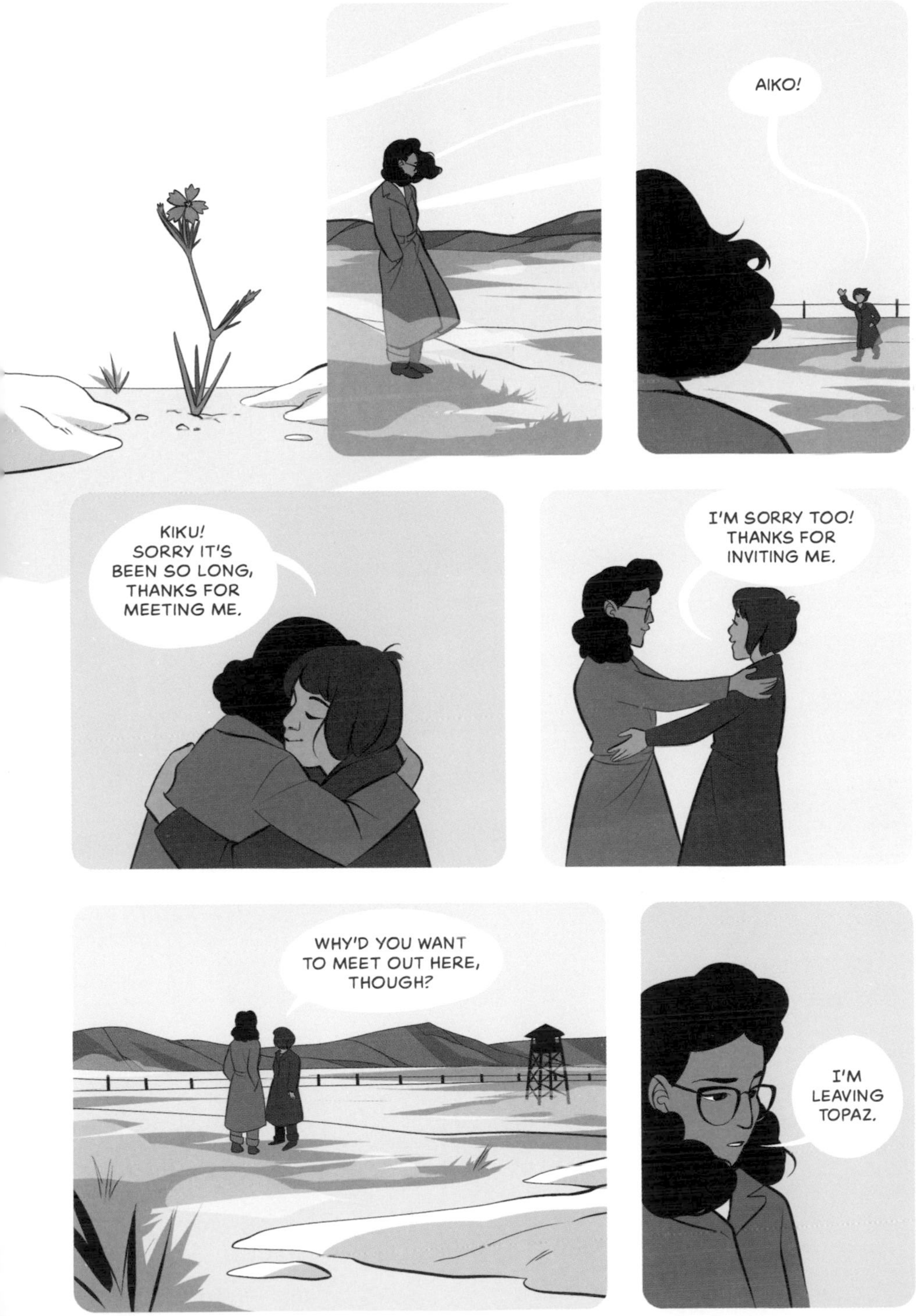
AIKO!
KIKU! SORRY IT'S BEEN SO LONG, THANKS FOR MEETING ME.
I'M SORRY TOO! THANKS FOR INVITING ME.
WHY'D YOU WANT TO MEET OUT HERE, THOUGH?
I'M LEAVING TOPAZ.

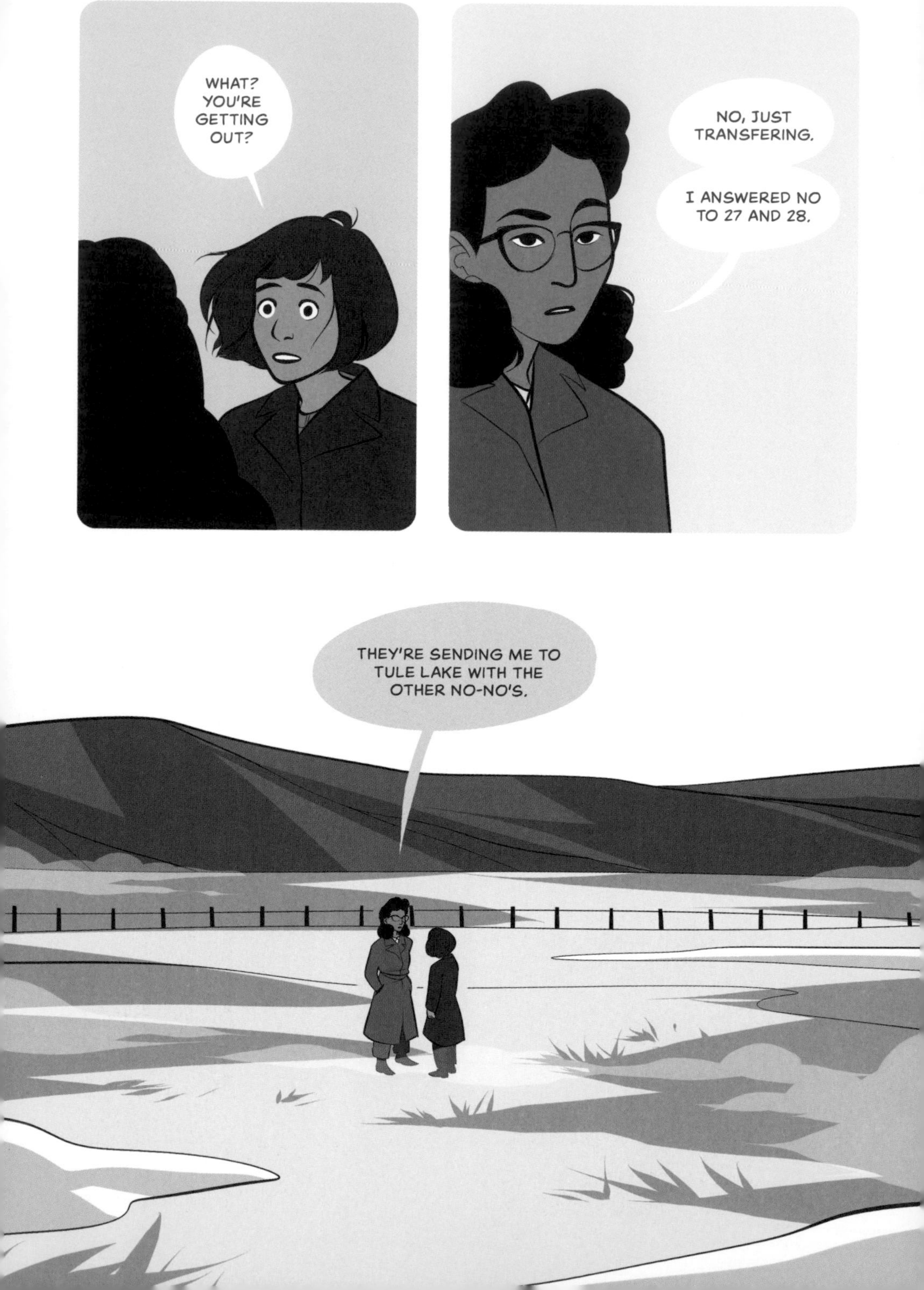
WHAT? YOU'RE GETTING OUT?
NO, JUST TRANSFERING.
I ANSWERED NO TO 27 AND 28.
THEY'RE SENDING ME TO TULE LAKE WITH THE OTHER NO-NO'S.

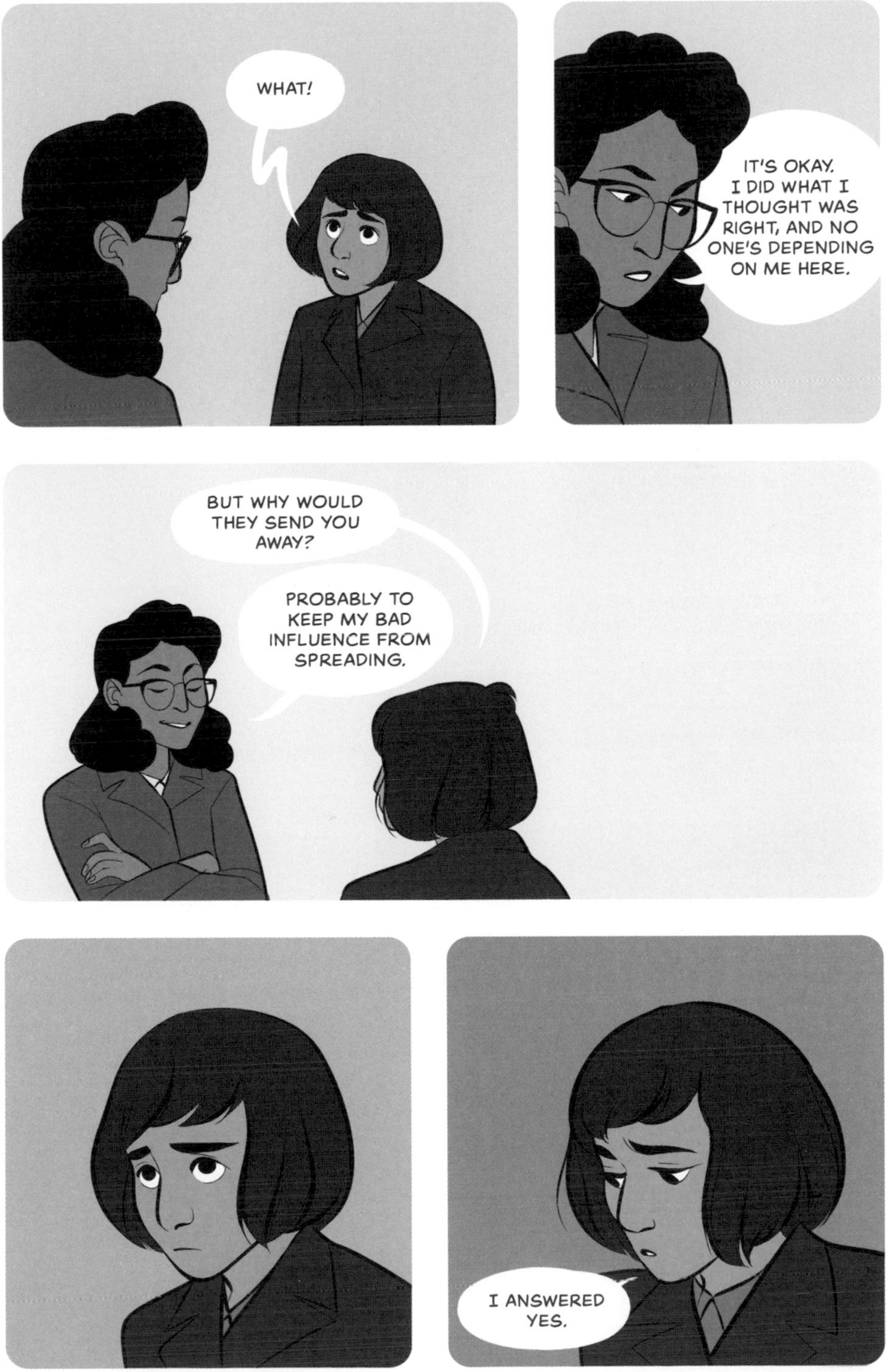

WHAT!
IT'S OKAY. I DID WHAT I THOUGHT WAS RIGHT, AND NO ONE'S DEPENDING ON ME HERE.
BUT WHY WOULD THEY SEND YOU AWAY?
PROBABLY TO KEEP MY BAD INFLUENCE FROM SPREADING.
I ANSWERED YES.

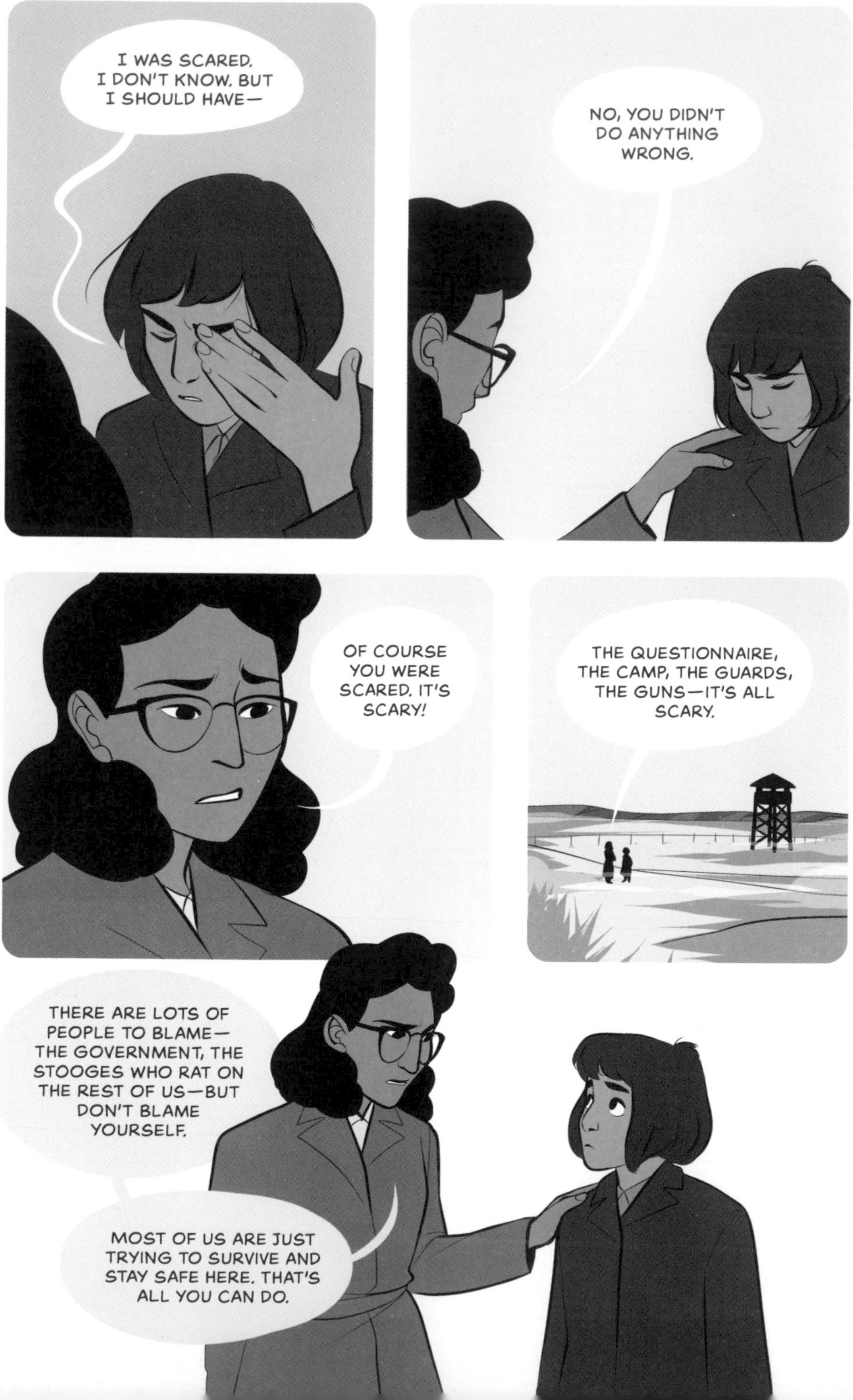
I WAS SCARED. I DON'T KNOW. BUT I SHOULD HAVE—
NO, YOU DIDN'T DO ANYTHING WRONG.
OF COURSE YOU WERE SCARED. IT'S SCARY!
THE QUESTIONNAIRE, THE CAMP, THE GUARDS, THE GUNS—IT'S ALL SCARY.
THERE ARE LOTS OF PEOPLE TO BLAME— THE GOVERNMENT, THE STOOGES WHO RAT ON THE REST OF US—BUT DON'T BLAME YOURSELF.
MOST OF US ARE JUST TRYING TO SURVIVE AND STAY SAFE HERE. THAT'S ALL YOU CAN DO.

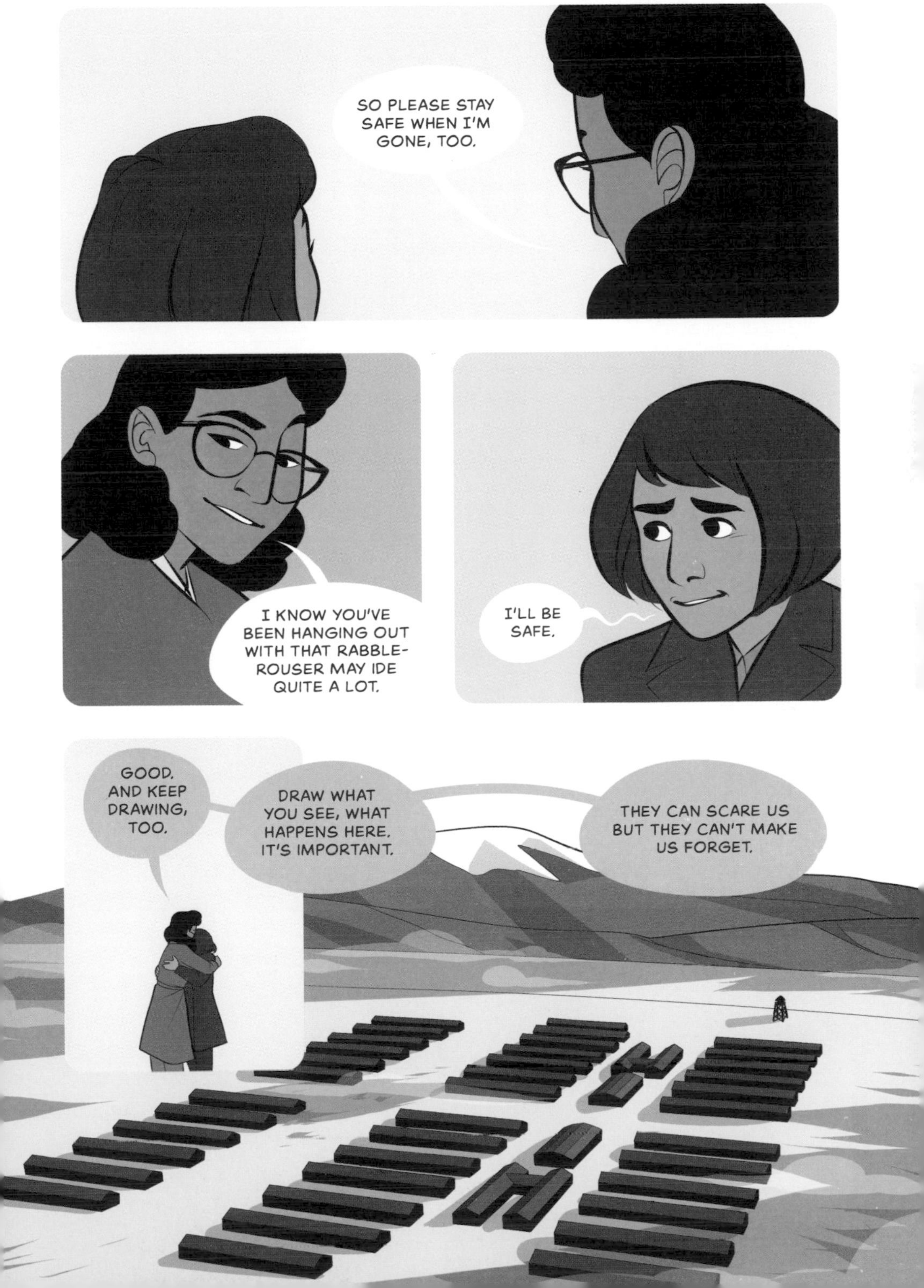
SO PLEASE STAY SAFE WHEN I'M GONE, TOO.
I KNOW YOU'VE BEEN HANGING OUT WITH THAT RABBLE-ROUSER MAY IDE QUITE A LOT.
I'LL BE SAFE.
GOOD. AND KEEP DRAWING, TOO.
DRAW WHAT YOU SEE, WHAT HAPPENS HERE. IT'S IMPORTANT.
THEY CAN SCARE US BUT THEY CAN'T MAKE US FORGET.

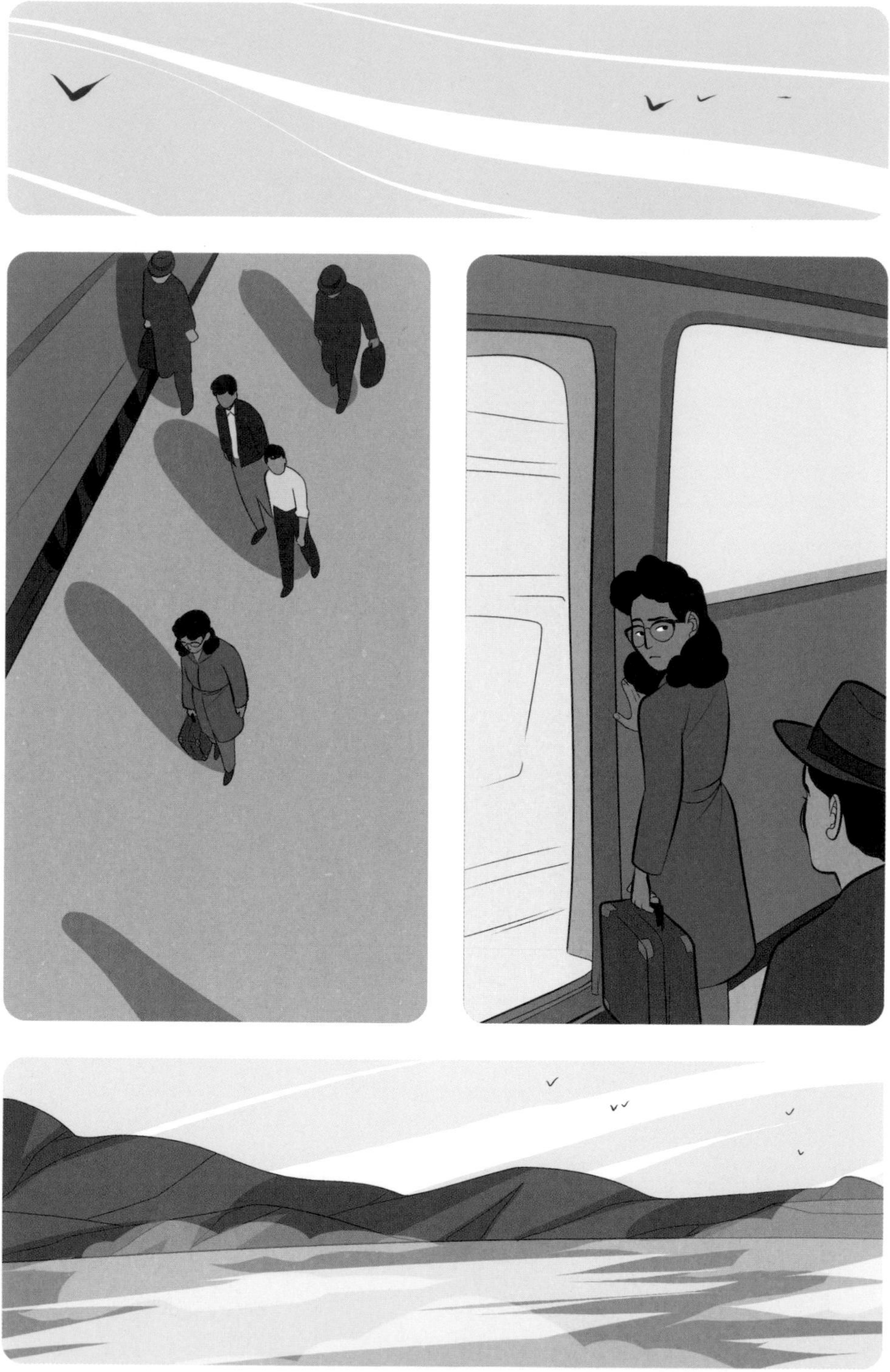

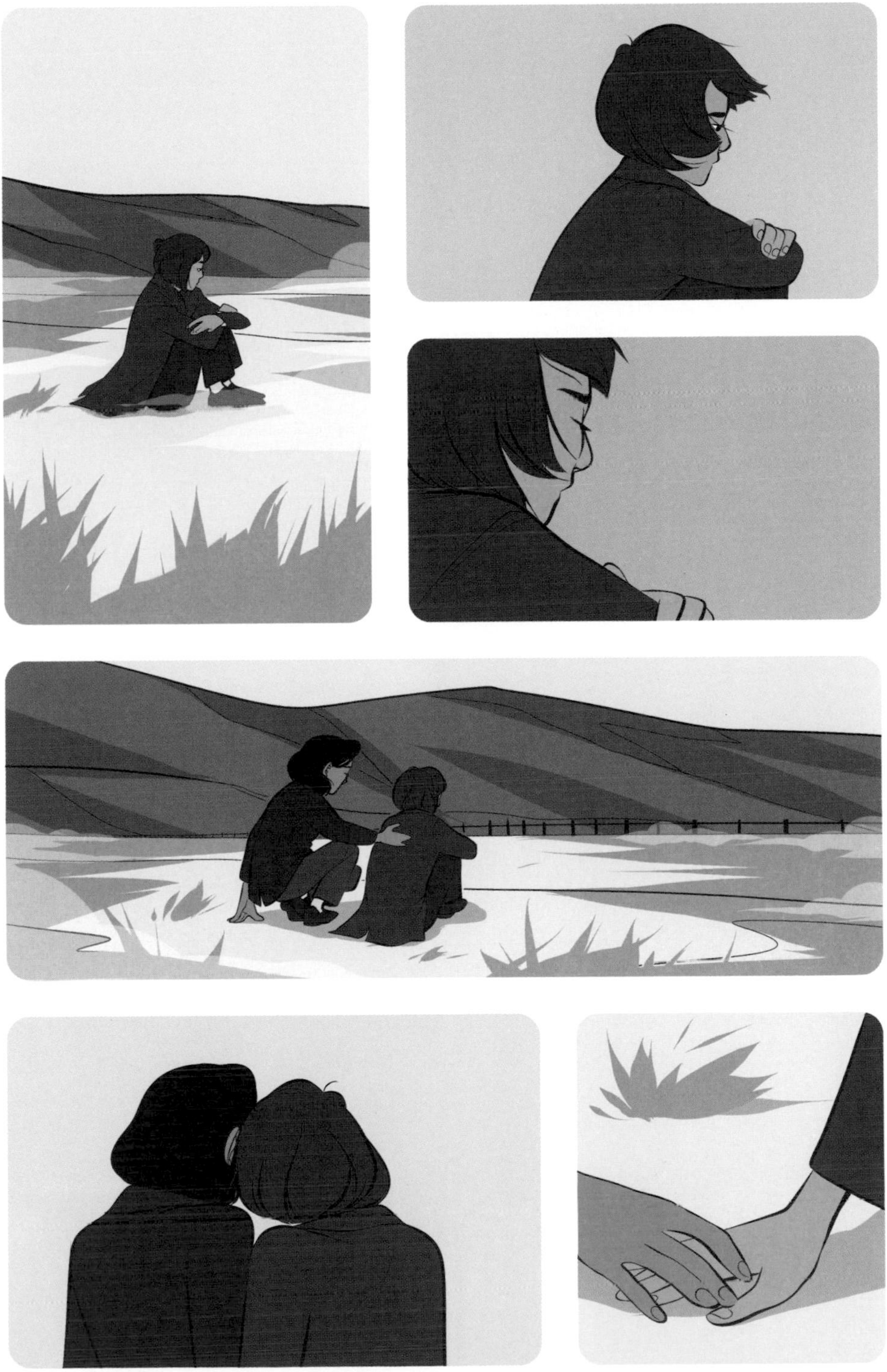

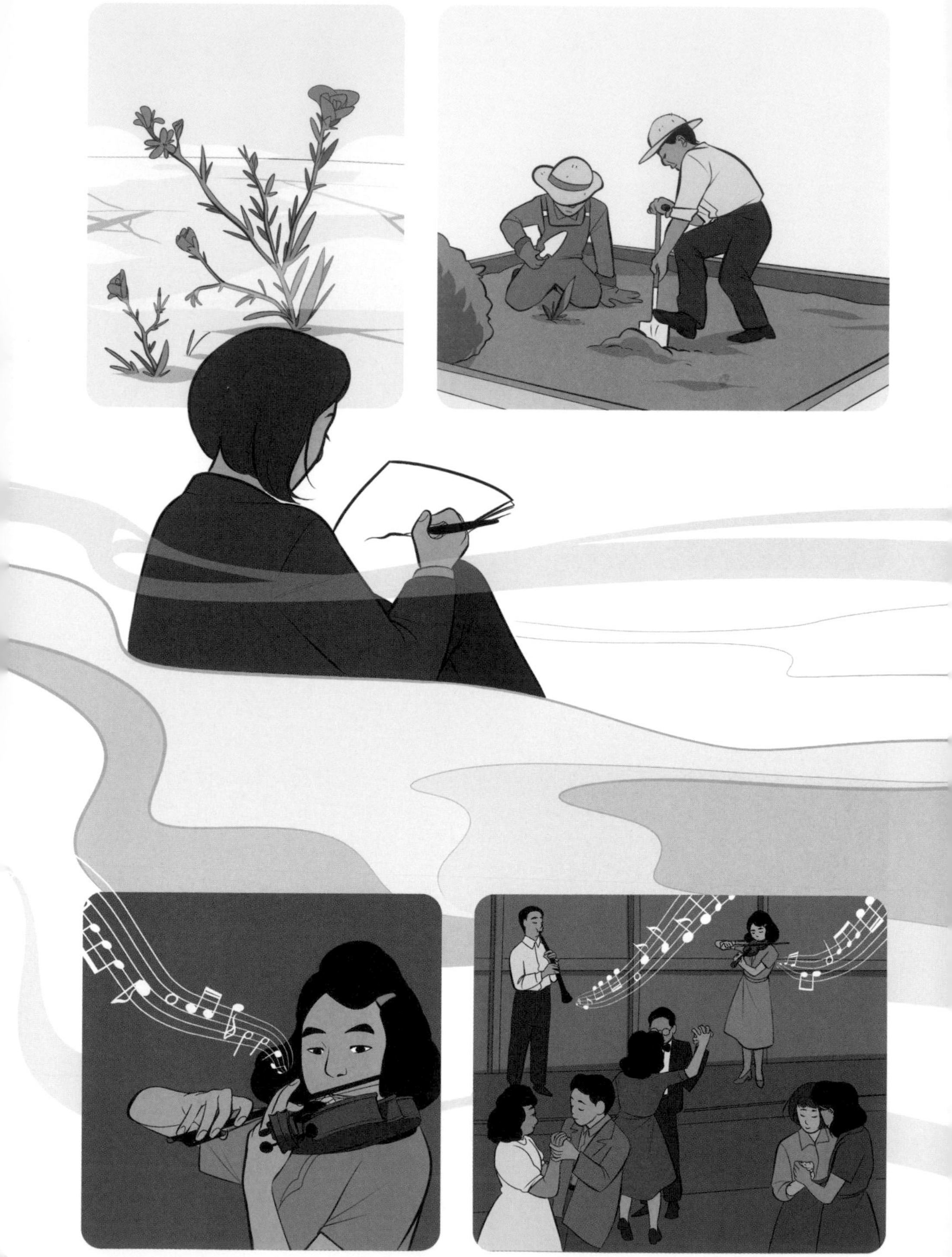

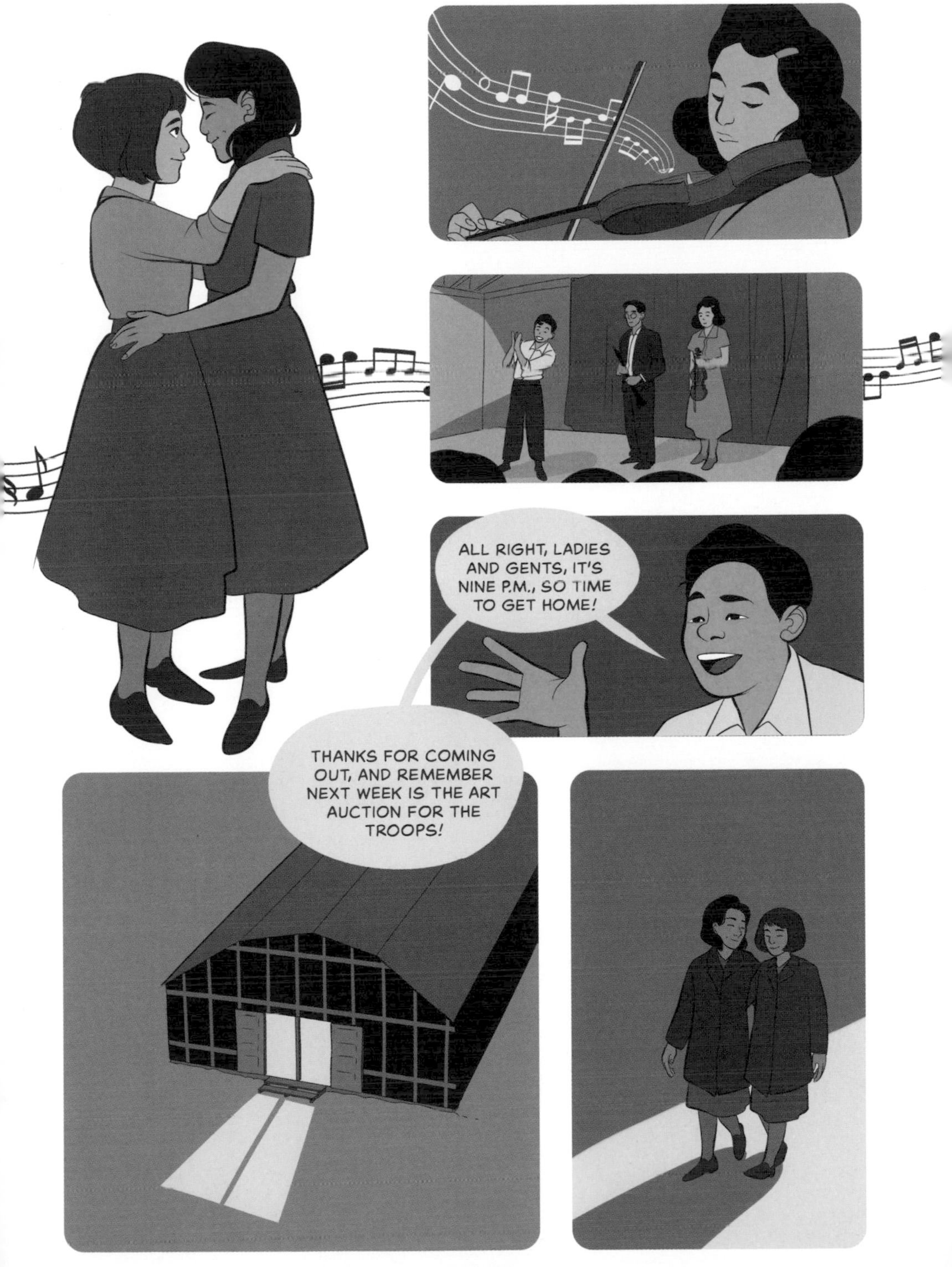
ALL RIGHT, LADIES AND GENTS, IT'S NINE P.M., SO TIME TO GET HOME!
THANKS FOR COMING OUT, AND REMEMBER NEXT WEEK IS THE ART AUCTION FOR THE TROOPS!

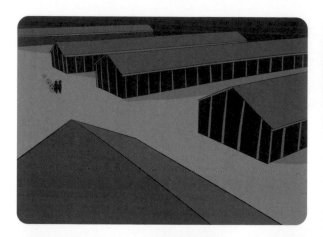

THANKS FOR COMING WITH ME, IT WAS—

GREAT!

YEAH, IT WAS.

GOOD NIGHT.
GOOD NIGHT!
CRACK!

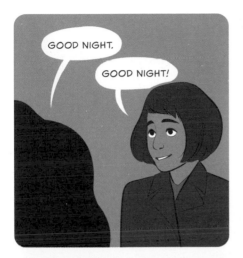

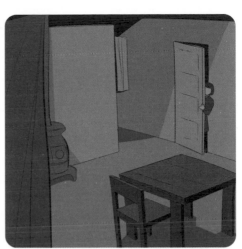

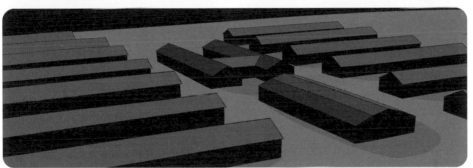

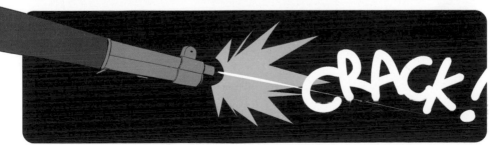

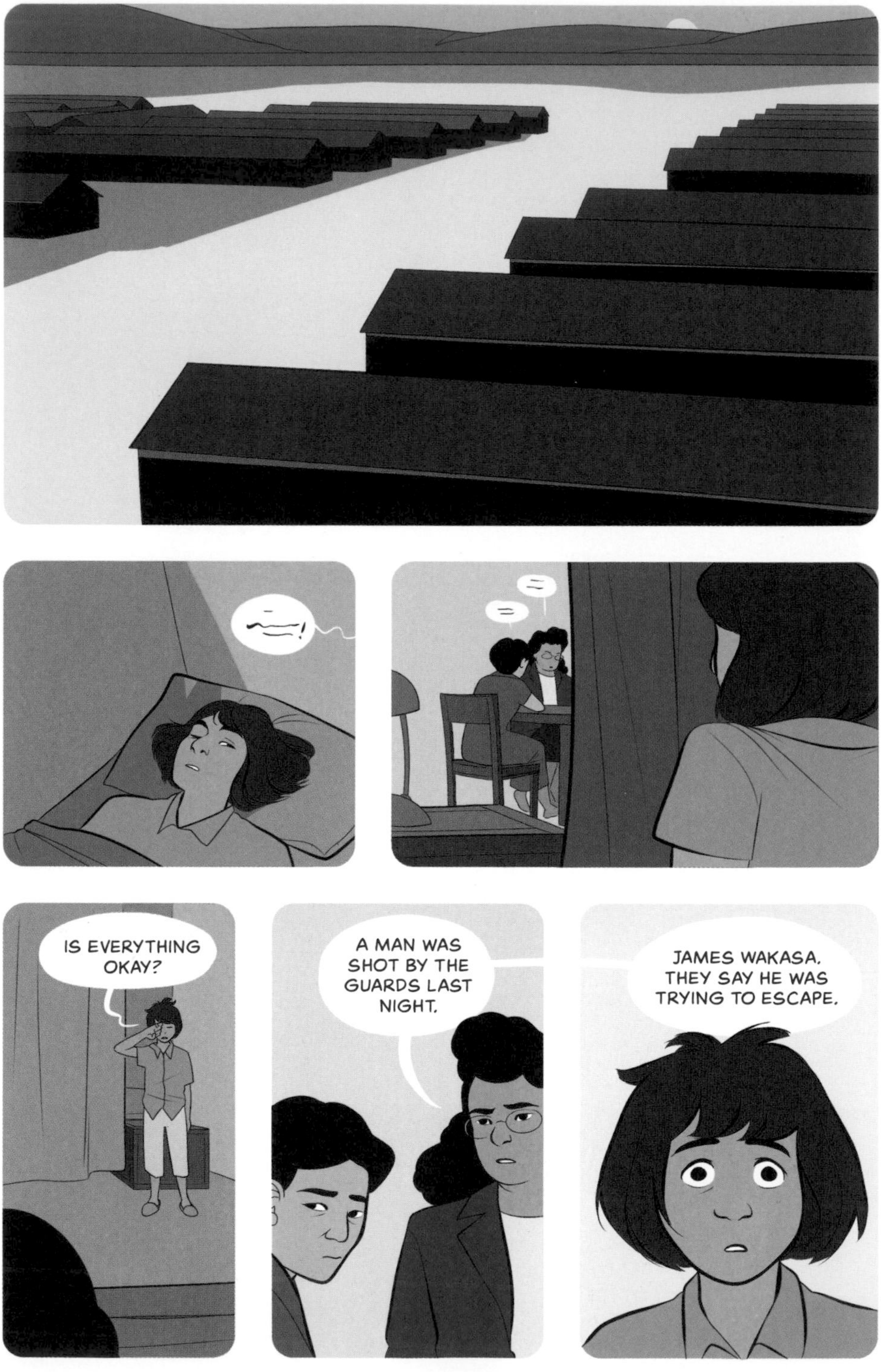
IS EVERYTHING OKAY?
A MAN WAS SHOT BY THE GUARDS LAST NIGHT.
JAMES WAKASA. THEY SAY HE WAS TRYING TO ESCAPE.

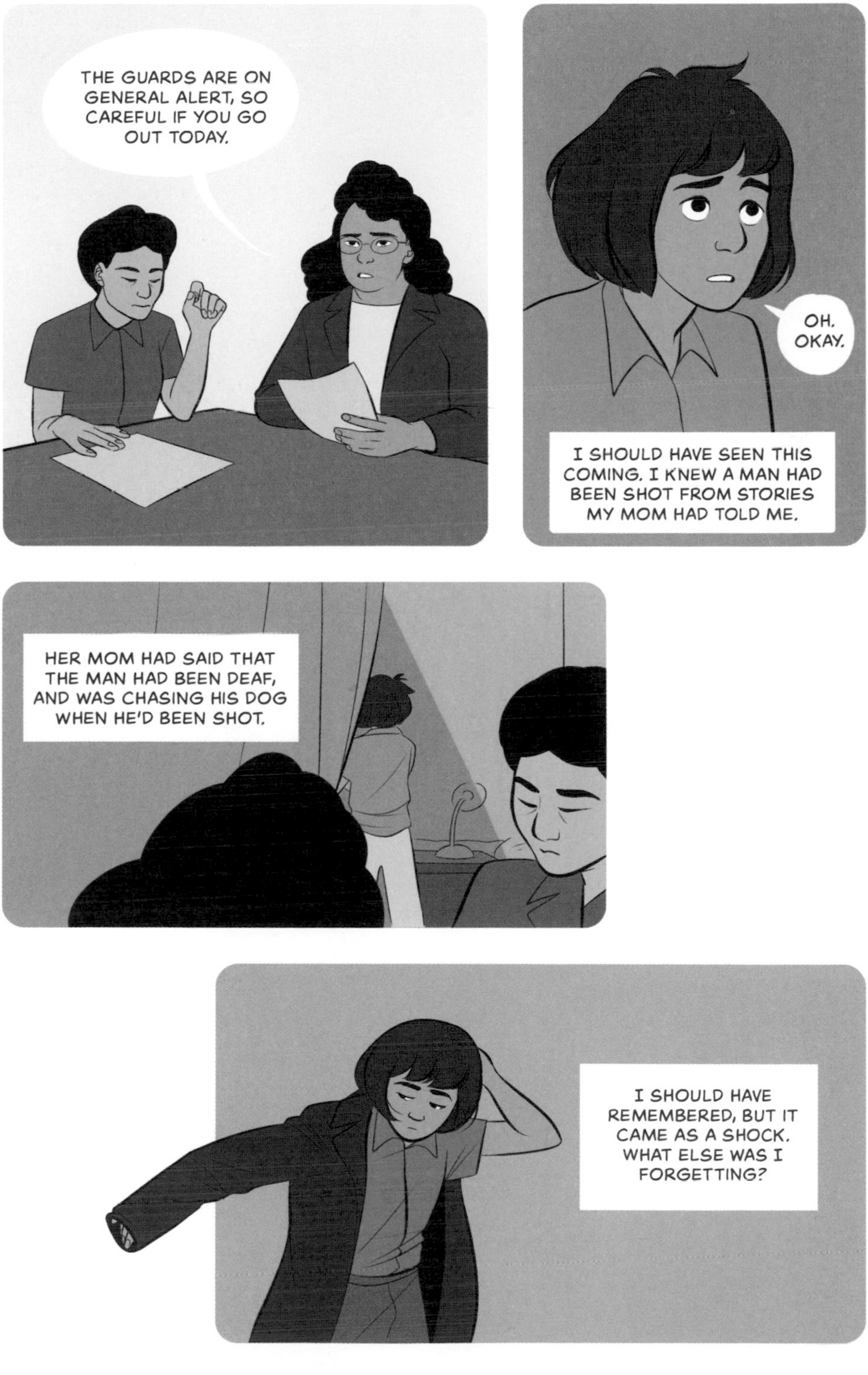
THE GUARDS ARE ON GENERAL ALERT, SO CAREFUL IF YOU GO OUT TODAY.
OH. OKAY.
I SHOULD HAVE SEEN THIS COMING. I KNEW A MAN HAD BEEN SHOT FROM STORIES MY MOM HAD TOLD ME.
HER MOM HAD SAID THAT THE MAN HAD BEEN DEAF, AND WAS CHASING HIS DOG WHEN HE'D BEEN SHOT.
I SHOULD HAVE REMEMBERED, BUT IT CAME AS A SHOCK. WHAT ELSE WAS I FORGETTING?

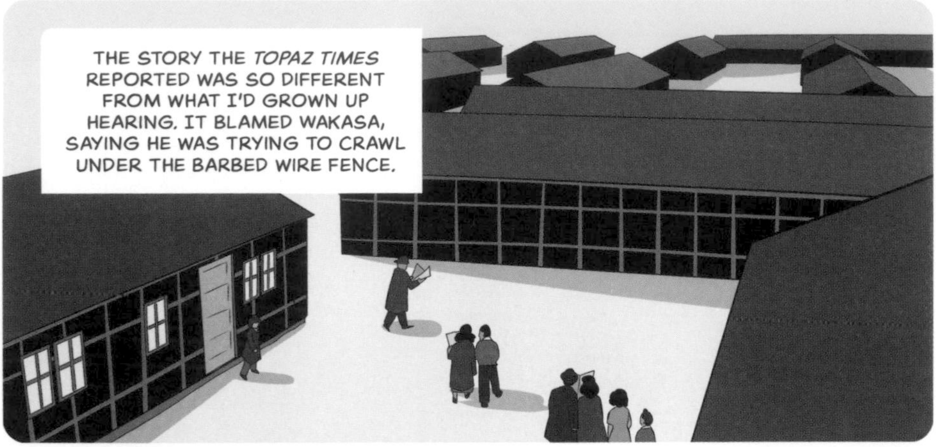
THE STORY THE *TOPAZ TIMES* REPORTED WAS SO DIFFERENT FROM WHAT I'D GROWN UP HEARING. IT BLAMED WAKASA, SAYING HE WAS TRYING TO CRAWL UNDER THE BARBED WIRE FENCE.

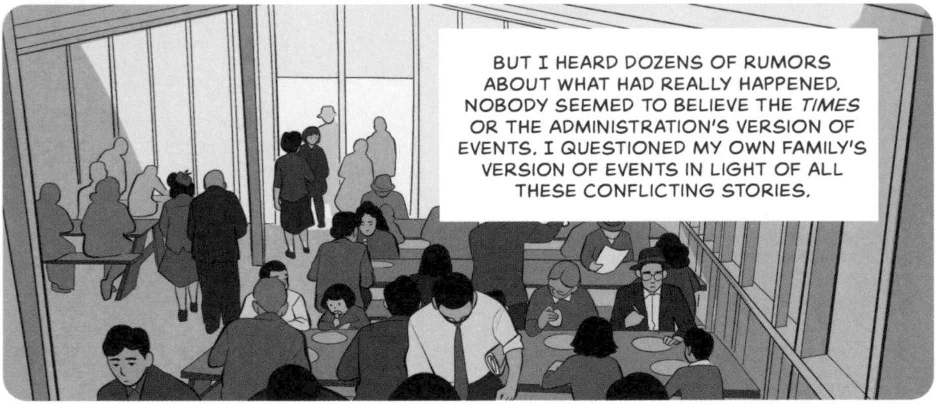
BUT I HEARD DOZENS OF RUMORS ABOUT WHAT HAD REALLY HAPPENED. NOBODY SEEMED TO BELIEVE THE *TIMES* OR THE ADMINISTRATION'S VERSION OF EVENTS. I QUESTIONED MY OWN FAMILY'S VERSION OF EVENTS IN LIGHT OF ALL THESE CONFLICTING STORIES.

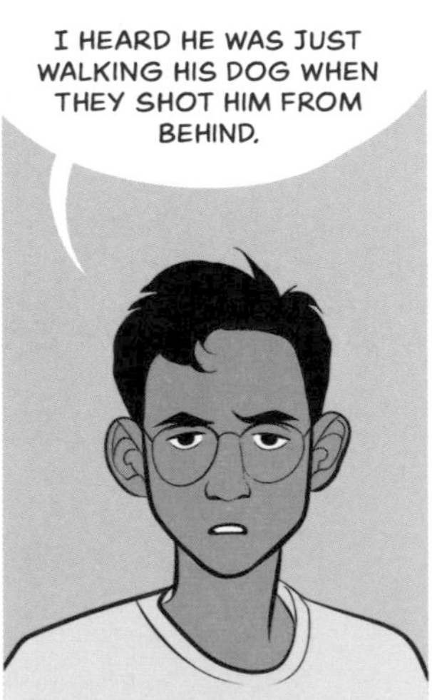
I HEARD HE WAS JUST WALKING HIS DOG WHEN THEY SHOT HIM FROM BEHIND.

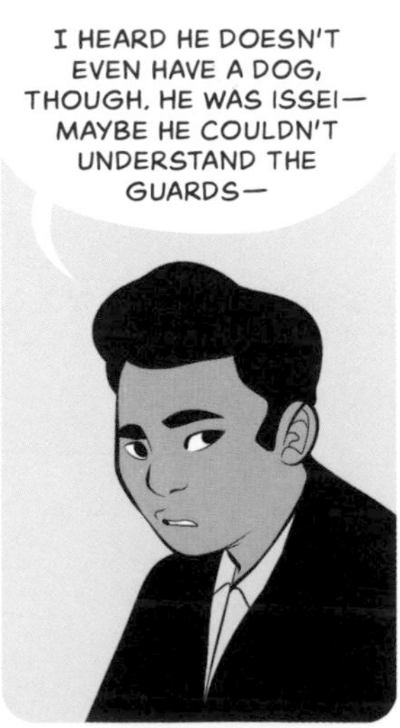
I HEARD HE DOESN'T EVEN HAVE A DOG, THOUGH. HE WAS ISSEI— MAYBE HE COULDN'T UNDERSTAND THE GUARDS—

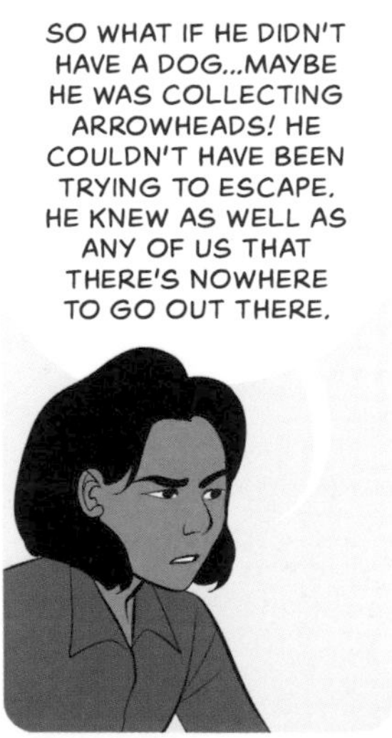
SO WHAT IF HE DIDN'T HAVE A DOG...MAYBE HE WAS COLLECTING ARROWHEADS! HE COULDN'T HAVE BEEN TRYING TO ESCAPE. HE KNEW AS WELL AS ANY OF US THAT THERE'S NOWHERE TO GO OUT THERE.

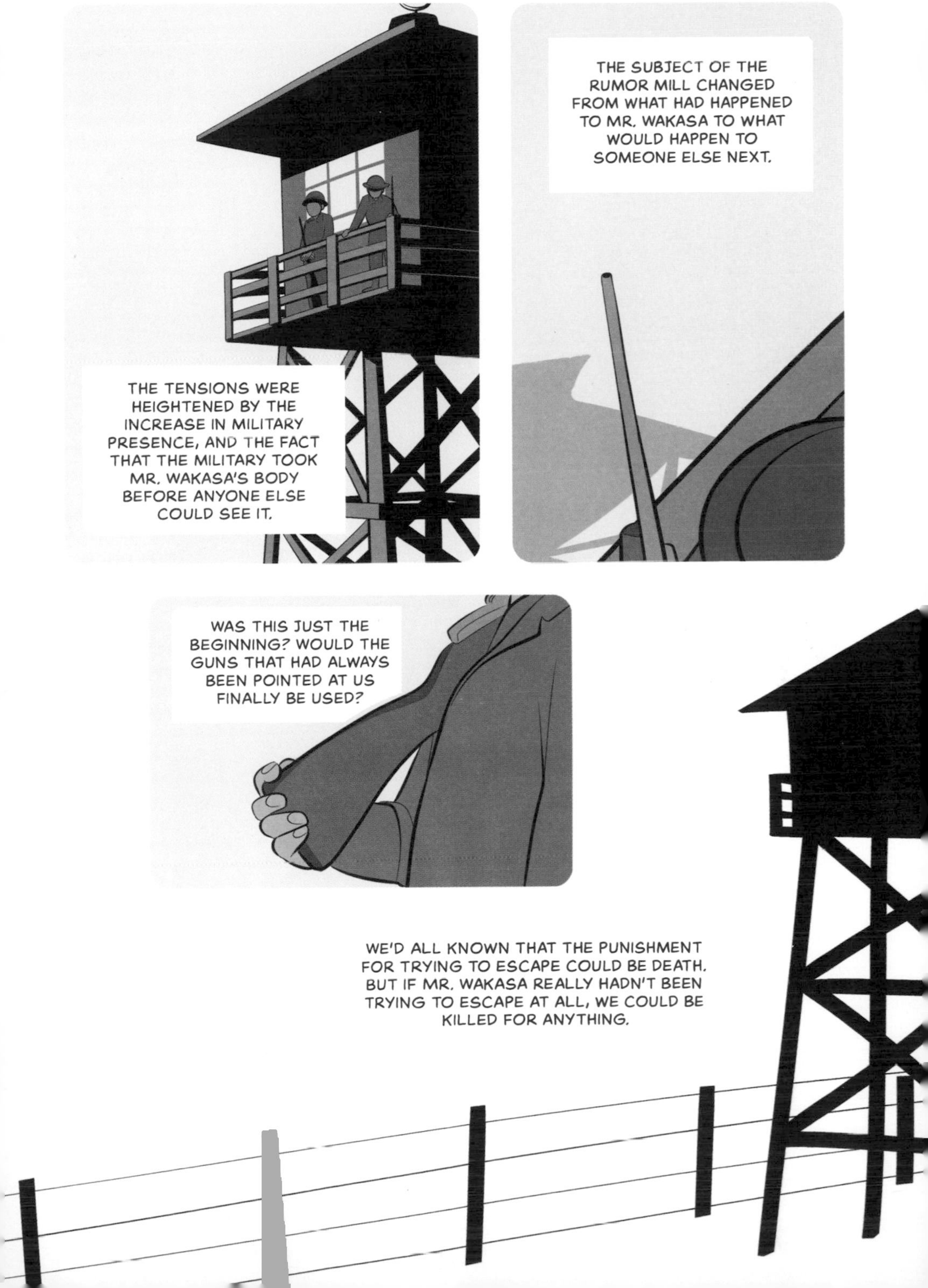
THE TENSIONS WERE HEIGHTENED BY THE INCREASE IN MILITARY PRESENCE, AND THE FACT THAT THE MILITARY TOOK MR. WAKASA'S BODY BEFORE ANYONE ELSE COULD SEE IT.
THE SUBJECT OF THE RUMOR MILL CHANGED FROM WHAT HAD HAPPENED TO MR. WAKASA TO WHAT WOULD HAPPEN TO SOMEONE ELSE NEXT.
WAS THIS JUST THE BEGINNING? WOULD THE GUNS THAT HAD ALWAYS BEEN POINTED AT US FINALLY BE USED?
WE'D ALL KNOWN THAT THE PUNISHMENT FOR TRYING TO ESCAPE COULD BE DEATH. BUT IF MR. WAKASA REALLY HADN'T BEEN TRYING TO ESCAPE AT ALL, WE COULD BE KILLED FOR ANYTHING.

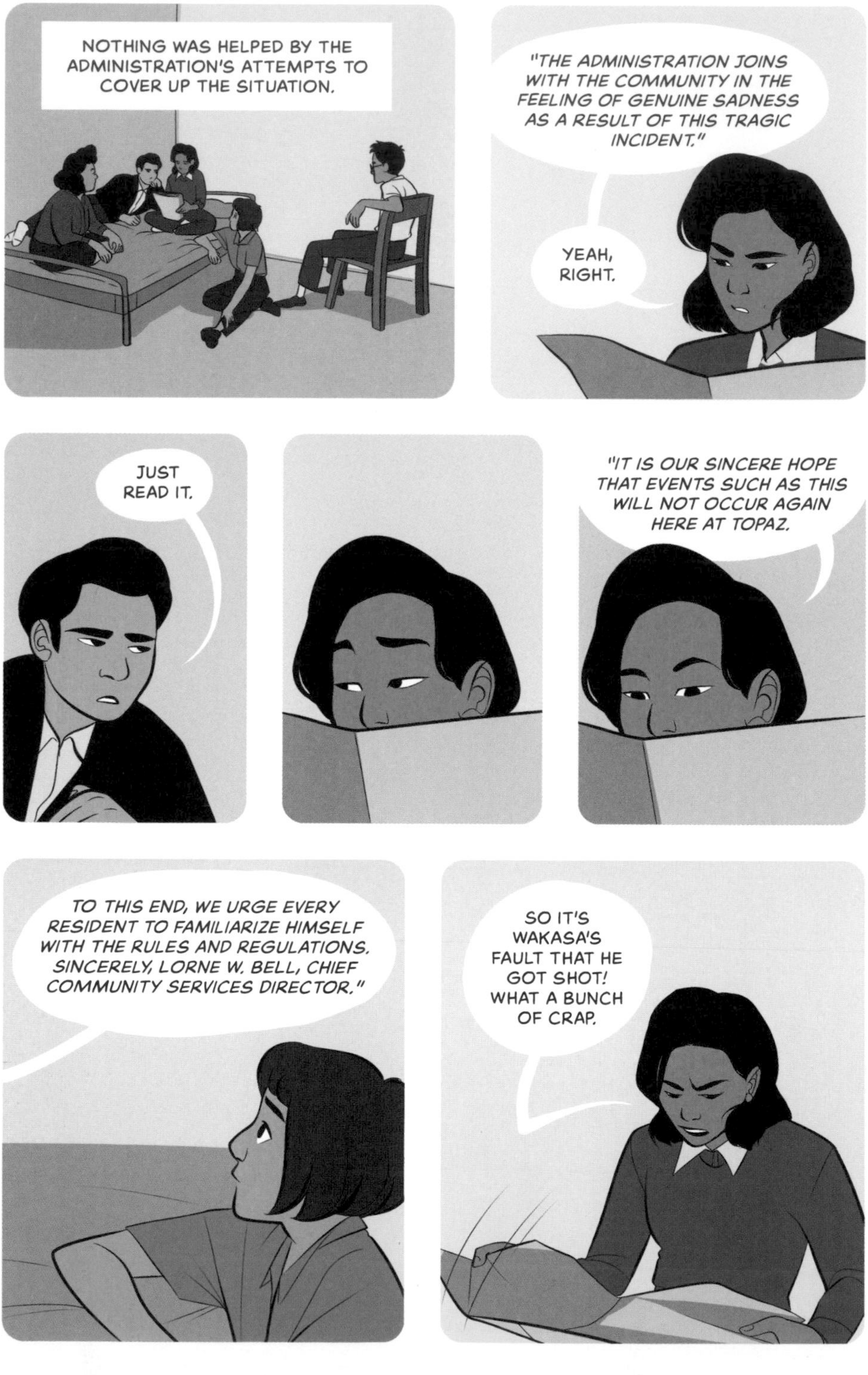
NOTHING WAS HELPED BY THE ADMINISTRATION'S ATTEMPTS TO COVER UP THE SITUATION.
"THE ADMINISTRATION JOINS WITH THE COMMUNITY IN THE FEELING OF GENUINE SADNESS AS A RESULT OF THIS TRAGIC INCIDENT."
YEAH, RIGHT.
JUST READ IT.
"IT IS OUR SINCERE HOPE THAT EVENTS SUCH AS THIS WILL NOT OCCUR AGAIN HERE AT TOPAZ.
TO THIS END, WE URGE EVERY RESIDENT TO FAMILIARIZE HIMSELF WITH THE RULES AND REGULATIONS. SINCERELY, LORNE W. BELL, CHIEF COMMUNITY SERVICES DIRECTOR."
SO IT'S WAKASA'S FAULT THAT HE GOT SHOT! WHAT A BUNCH OF CRAP.

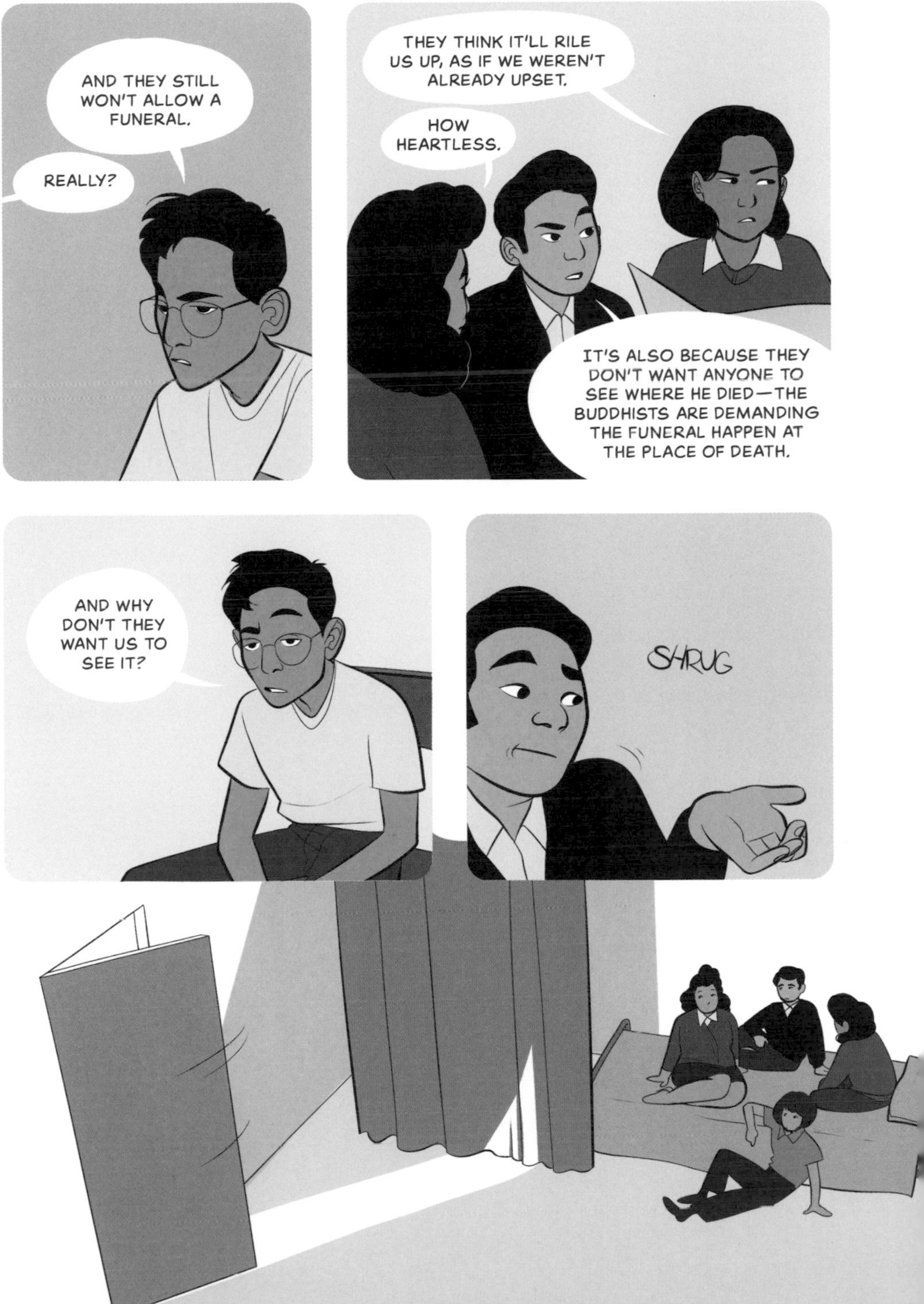

AND THEY STILL WON'T ALLOW A FUNERAL.
REALLY?
THEY THINK IT'LL RILE US UP, AS IF WE WEREN'T ALREADY UPSET.
HOW HEARTLESS.
IT'S ALSO BECAUSE THEY DON'T WANT ANYONE TO SEE WHERE HE DIED—THE BUDDHISTS ARE DEMANDING THE FUNERAL HAPPEN AT THE PLACE OF DEATH.
AND WHY DON'T THEY WANT US TO SEE IT?
SHRUG

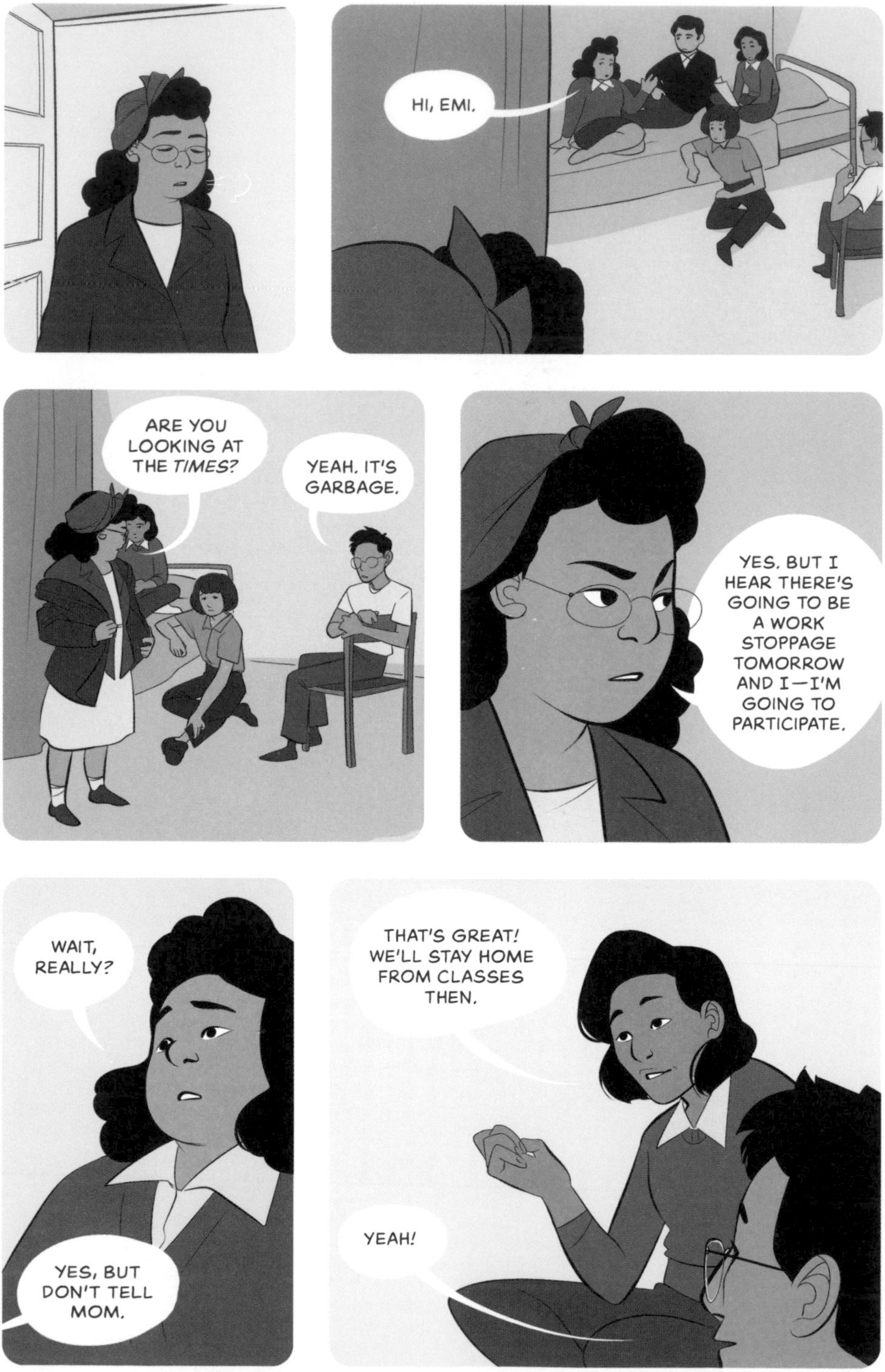
HI, EMI.
ARE YOU LOOKING AT THE *TIMES?*
YEAH. IT'S GARBAGE.
YES. BUT I HEAR THERE'S GOING TO BE A WORK STOPPAGE TOMORROW AND I—I'M GOING TO PARTICIPATE.
WAIT, REALLY?
YES, BUT DON'T TELL MOM.
THAT'S GREAT! WE'LL STAY HOME FROM CLASSES THEN.
YEAH!

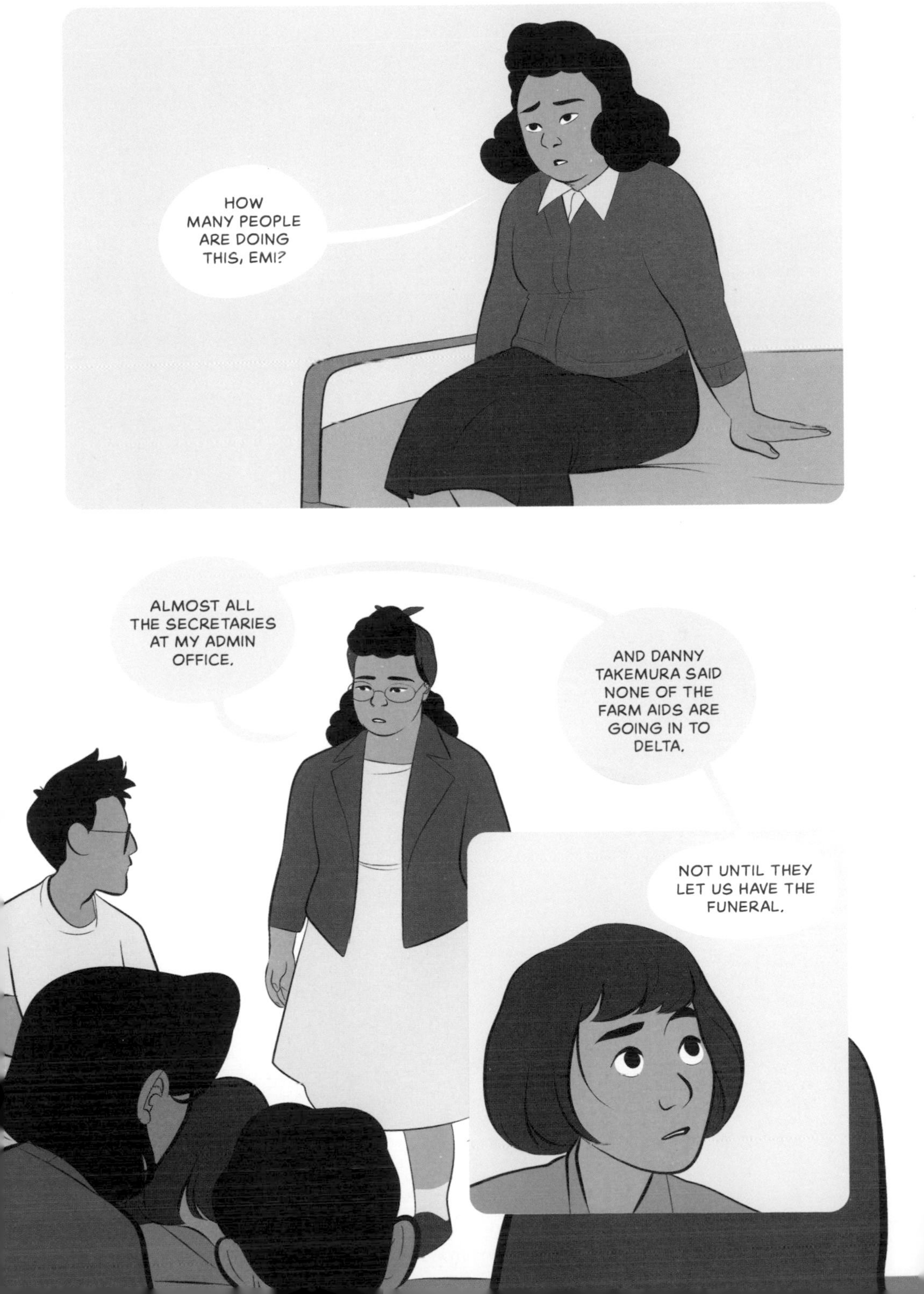
HOW MANY PEOPLE ARE DOING THIS, EMI?
ALMOST ALL THE SECRETARIES AT MY ADMIN OFFICE.
AND DANNY TAKEMURA SAID NONE OF THE FARM AIDS ARE GOING IN TO DELTA.
NOT UNTIL THEY LET US HAVE THE FUNERAL.

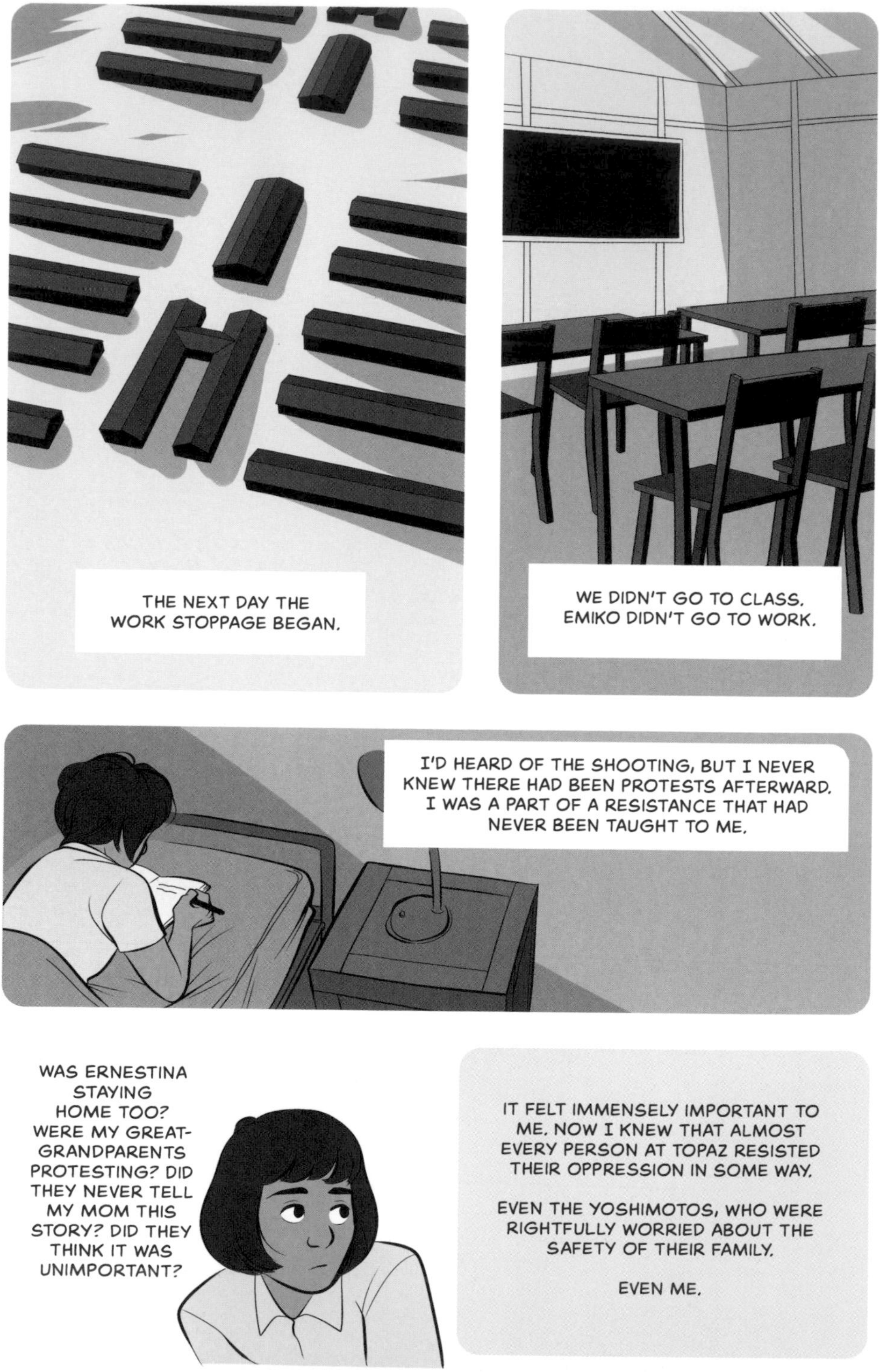
THE NEXT DAY THE WORK STOPPAGE BEGAN.
WE DIDN'T GO TO CLASS. EMIKO DIDN'T GO TO WORK.
I'D HEARD OF THE SHOOTING, BUT I NEVER KNEW THERE HAD BEEN PROTESTS AFTERWARD. I WAS A PART OF A RESISTANCE THAT HAD NEVER BEEN TAUGHT TO ME.
WAS ERNESTINA STAYING HOME TOO? WERE MY GREAT-GRANDPARENTS PROTESTING? DID THEY NEVER TELL MY MOM THIS STORY? DID THEY THINK IT WAS UNIMPORTANT?
IT FELT IMMENSELY IMPORTANT TO ME. NOW I KNEW THAT ALMOST EVERY PERSON AT TOPAZ RESISTED THEIR OPPRESSION IN SOME WAY.
EVEN THE YOSHIMOTOS, WHO WERE RIGHTFULLY WORRIED ABOUT THE SAFETY OF THEIR FAMILY.
EVEN ME.

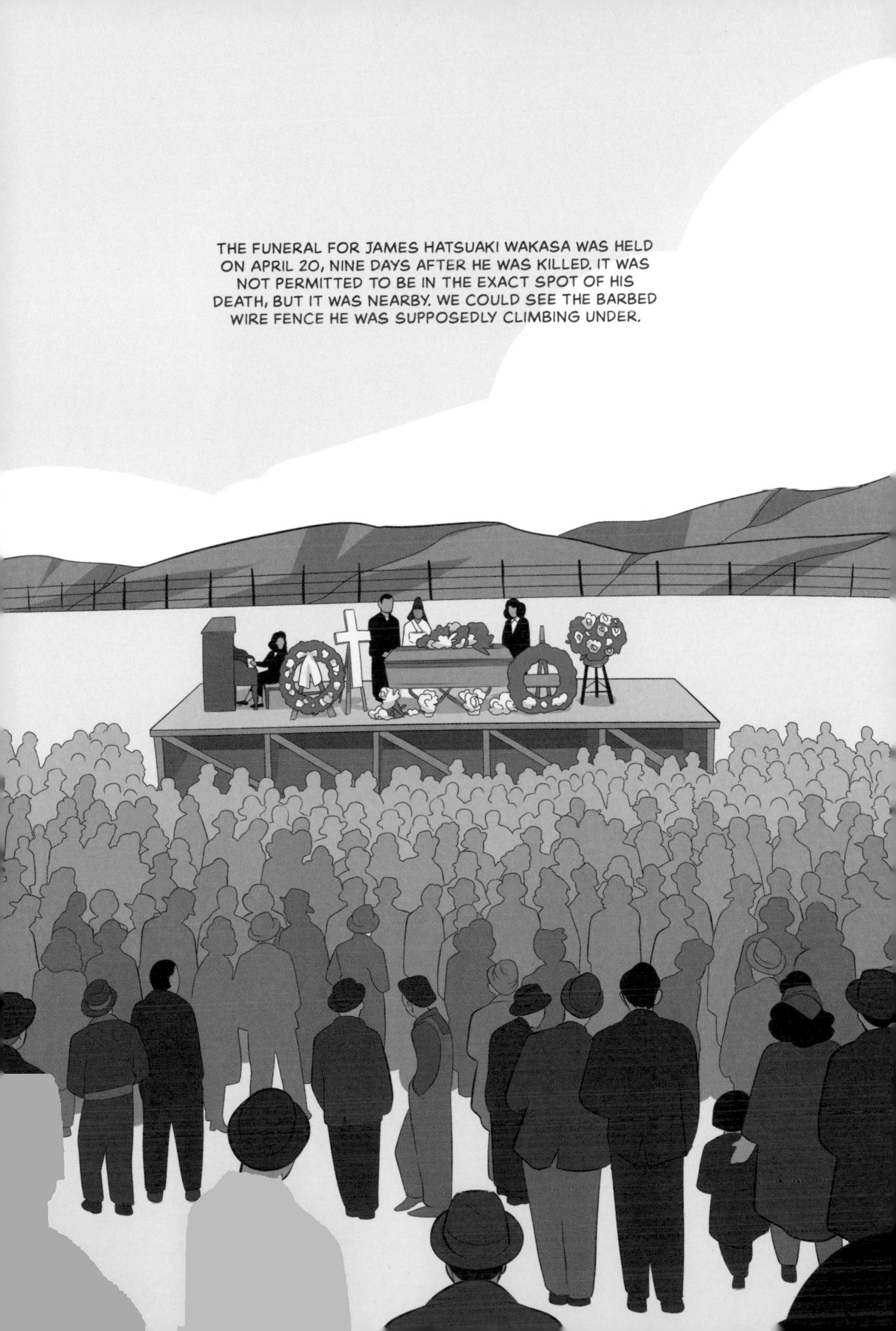
THE FUNERAL FOR JAMES HATSUAKI WAKASA WAS HELD ON APRIL 20, NINE DAYS AFTER HE WAS KILLED. IT WAS NOT PERMITTED TO BE IN THE EXACT SPOT OF HIS DEATH, BUT IT WAS NEARBY. WE COULD SEE THE BARBED WIRE FENCE HE WAS SUPPOSEDLY CLIMBING UNDER.

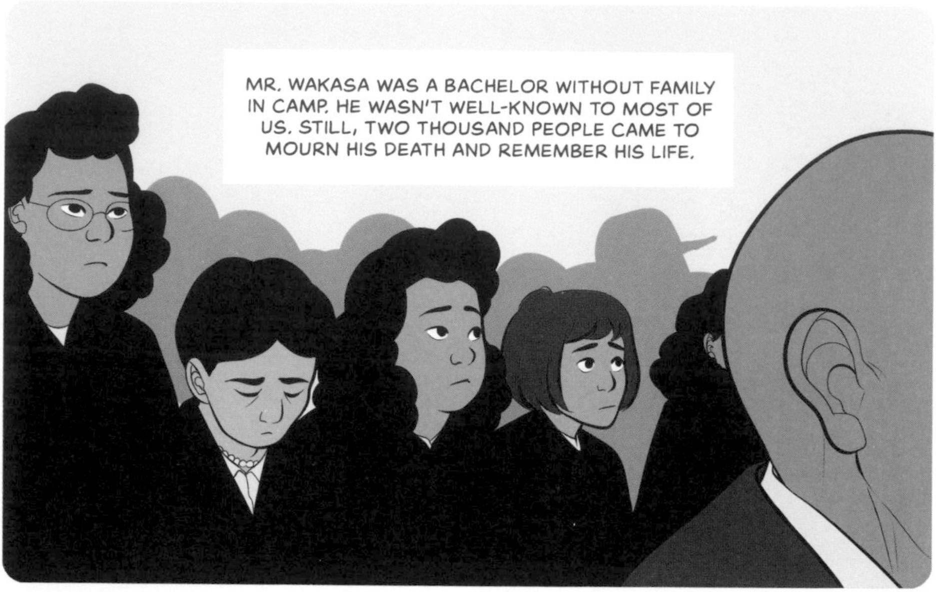
MR. WAKASA WAS A BACHELOR WITHOUT FAMILY IN CAMP. HE WASN'T WELL-KNOWN TO MOST OF US. STILL, TWO THOUSAND PEOPLE CAME TO MOURN HIS DEATH AND REMEMBER HIS LIFE.

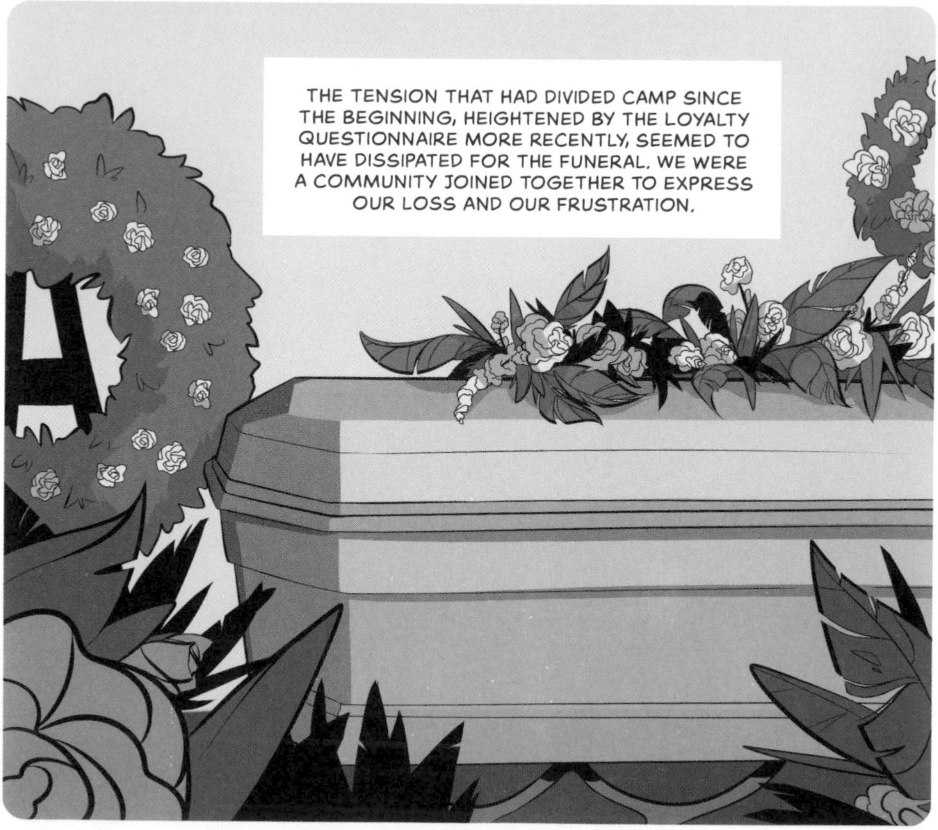
THE TENSION THAT HAD DIVIDED CAMP SINCE THE BEGINNING, HEIGHTENED BY THE LOYALTY QUESTIONNAIRE MORE RECENTLY, SEEMED TO HAVE DISSIPATED FOR THE FUNERAL. WE WERE A COMMUNITY JOINED TOGETHER TO EXPRESS OUR LOSS AND OUR FRUSTRATION.

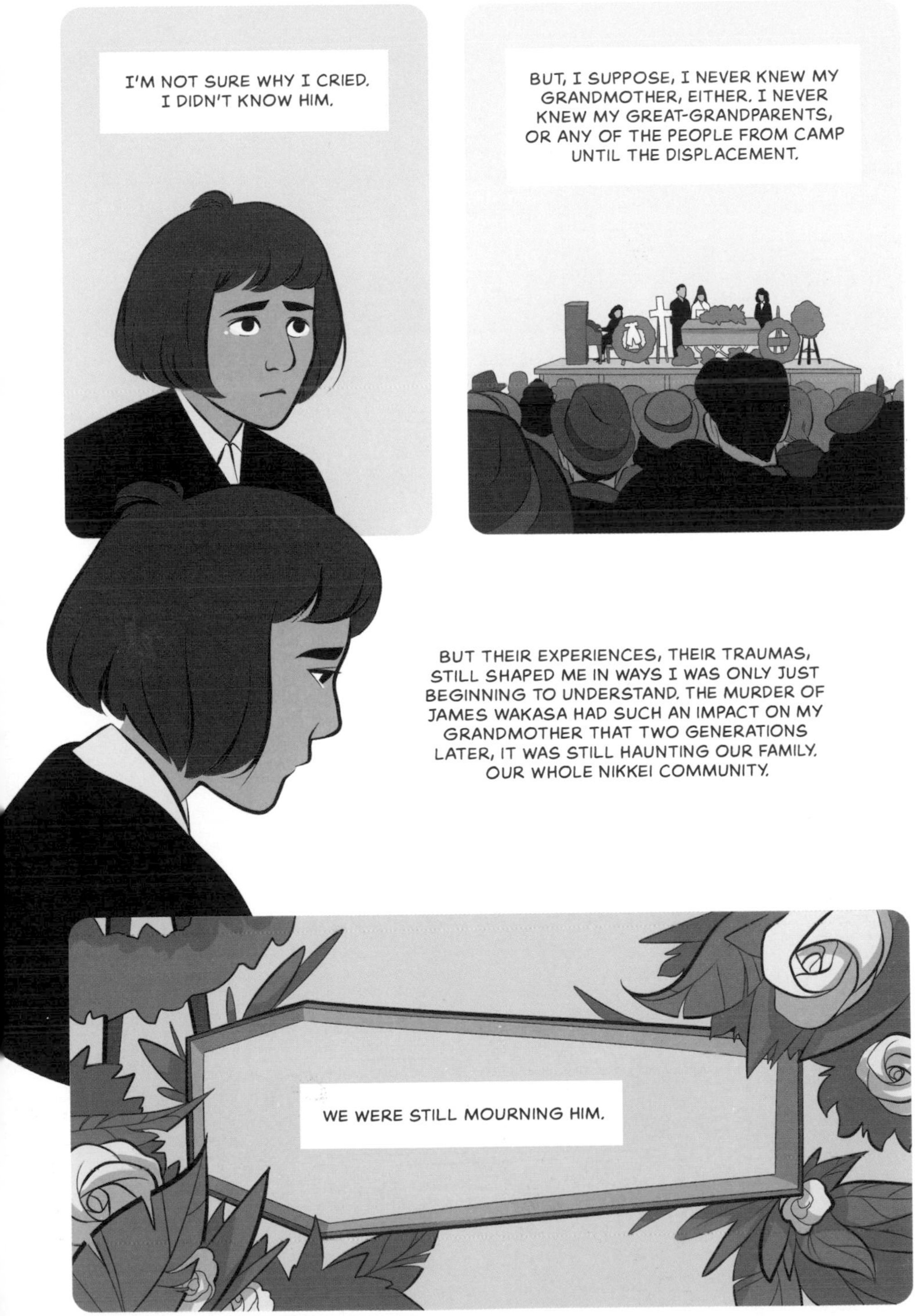
I'M NOT SURE WHY I CRIED. I DIDN'T KNOW HIM.
BUT, I SUPPOSE, I NEVER KNEW MY GRANDMOTHER, EITHER. I NEVER KNEW MY GREAT-GRANDPARENTS, OR ANY OF THE PEOPLE FROM CAMP UNTIL THE DISPLACEMENT.
BUT THEIR EXPERIENCES, THEIR TRAUMAS, STILL SHAPED ME IN WAYS I WAS ONLY JUST BEGINNING TO UNDERSTAND. THE MURDER OF JAMES WAKASA HAD SUCH AN IMPACT ON MY GRANDMOTHER THAT TWO GENERATIONS LATER, IT WAS STILL HAUNTING OUR FAMILY. OUR WHOLE NIKKEI COMMUNITY.
WE WERE STILL MOURNING HIM.

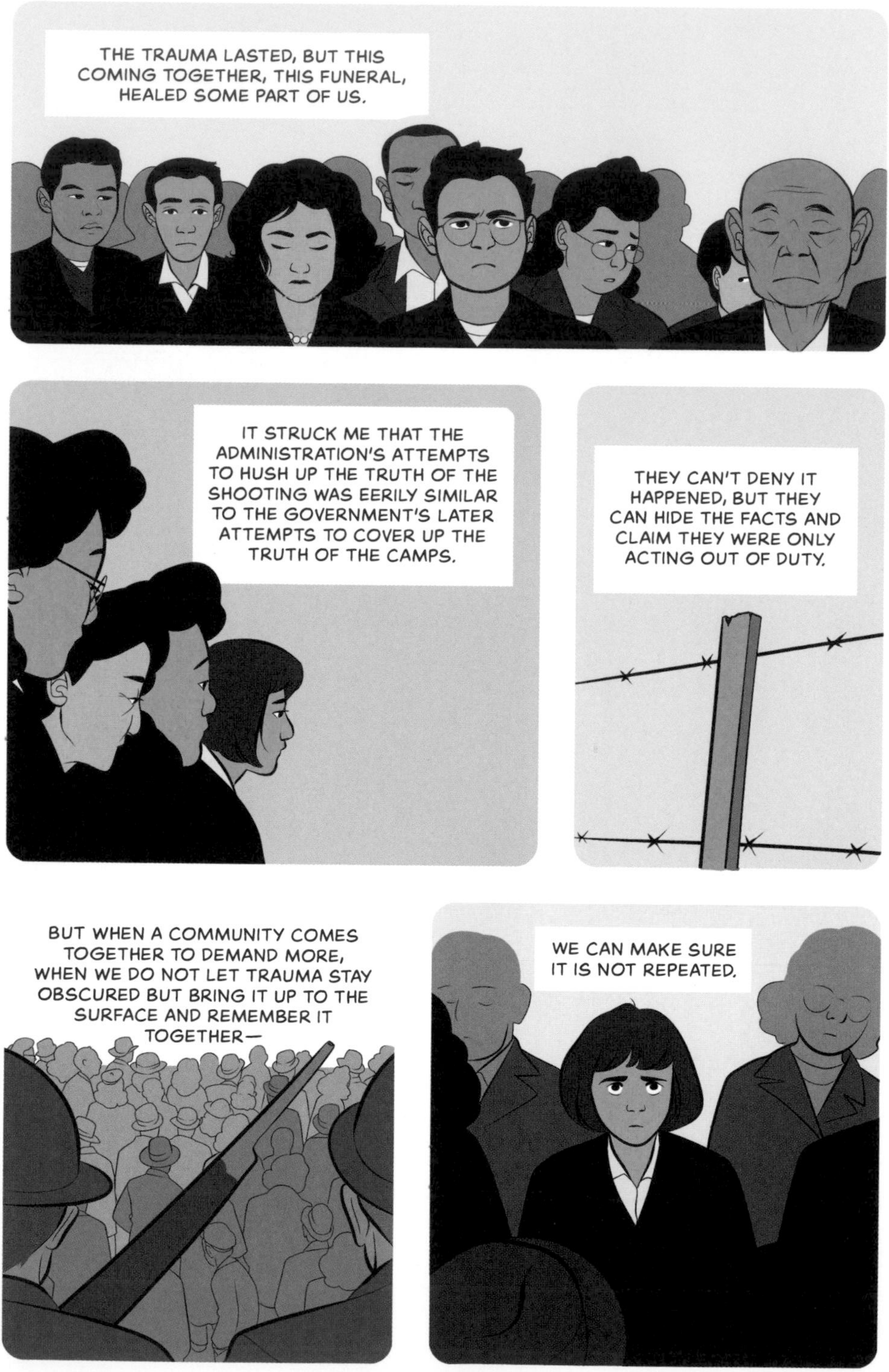
THE TRAUMA LASTED, BUT THIS COMING TOGETHER, THIS FUNERAL, HEALED SOME PART OF US.
IT STRUCK ME THAT THE ADMINISTRATION'S ATTEMPTS TO HUSH UP THE TRUTH OF THE SHOOTING WAS EERILY SIMILAR TO THE GOVERNMENT'S LATER ATTEMPTS TO COVER UP THE TRUTH OF THE CAMPS.
THEY CAN'T DENY IT HAPPENED, BUT THEY CAN HIDE THE FACTS AND CLAIM THEY WERE ONLY ACTING OUT OF DUTY.
BUT WHEN A COMMUNITY COMES TOGETHER TO DEMAND MORE, WHEN WE DO NOT LET TRAUMA STAY OBSCURED BUT BRING IT UP TO THE SURFACE AND REMEMBER IT TOGETHER—
WE CAN MAKE SURE IT IS NOT REPEATED.

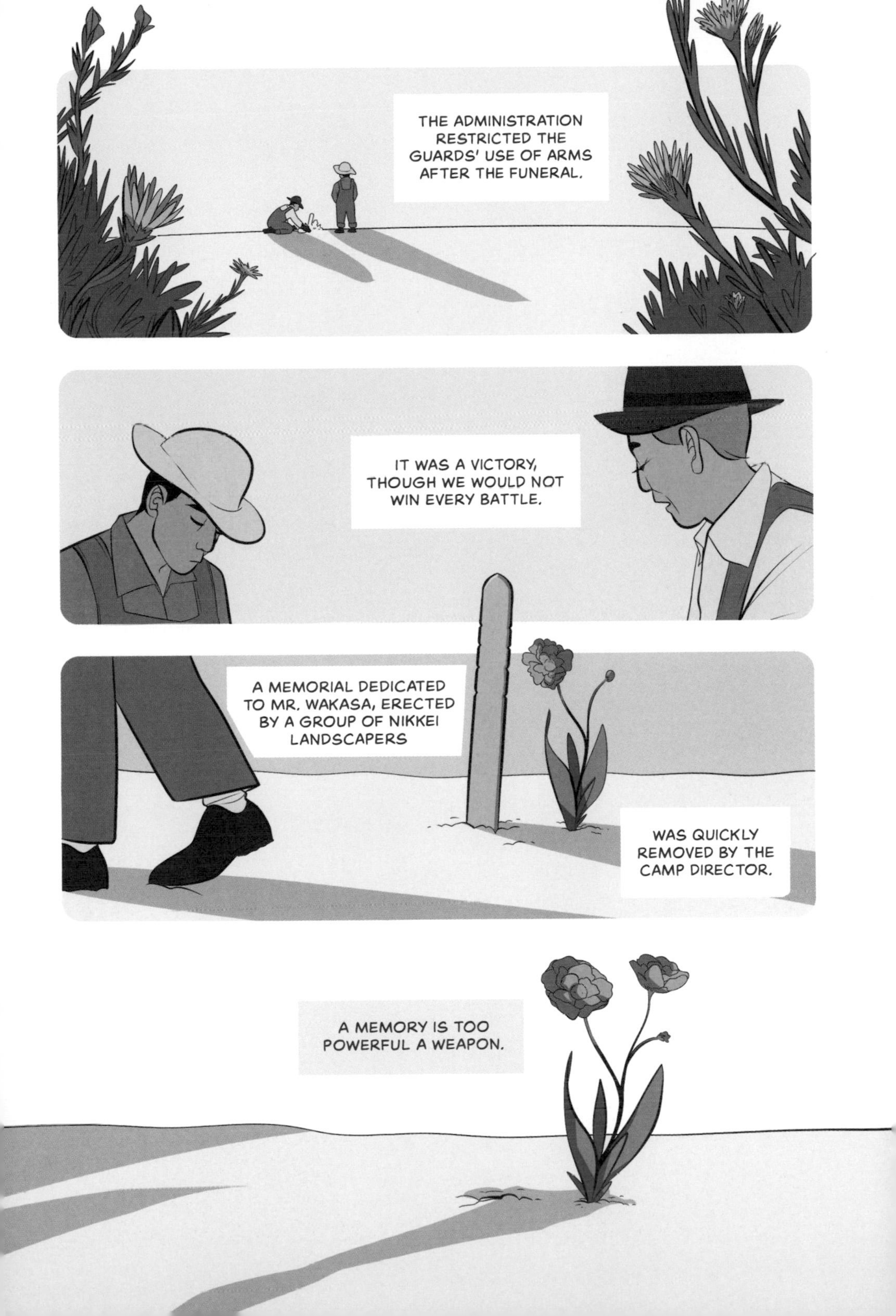
THE ADMINISTRATION RESTRICTED THE GUARDS' USE OF ARMS AFTER THE FUNERAL.
IT WAS A VICTORY, THOUGH WE WOULD NOT WIN EVERY BATTLE.
A MEMORIAL DEDICATED TO MR. WAKASA, ERECTED BY A GROUP OF NIKKEI LANDSCAPERS
WAS QUICKLY REMOVED BY THE CAMP DIRECTOR.
A MEMORY IS TOO POWERFUL A WEAPON.

8

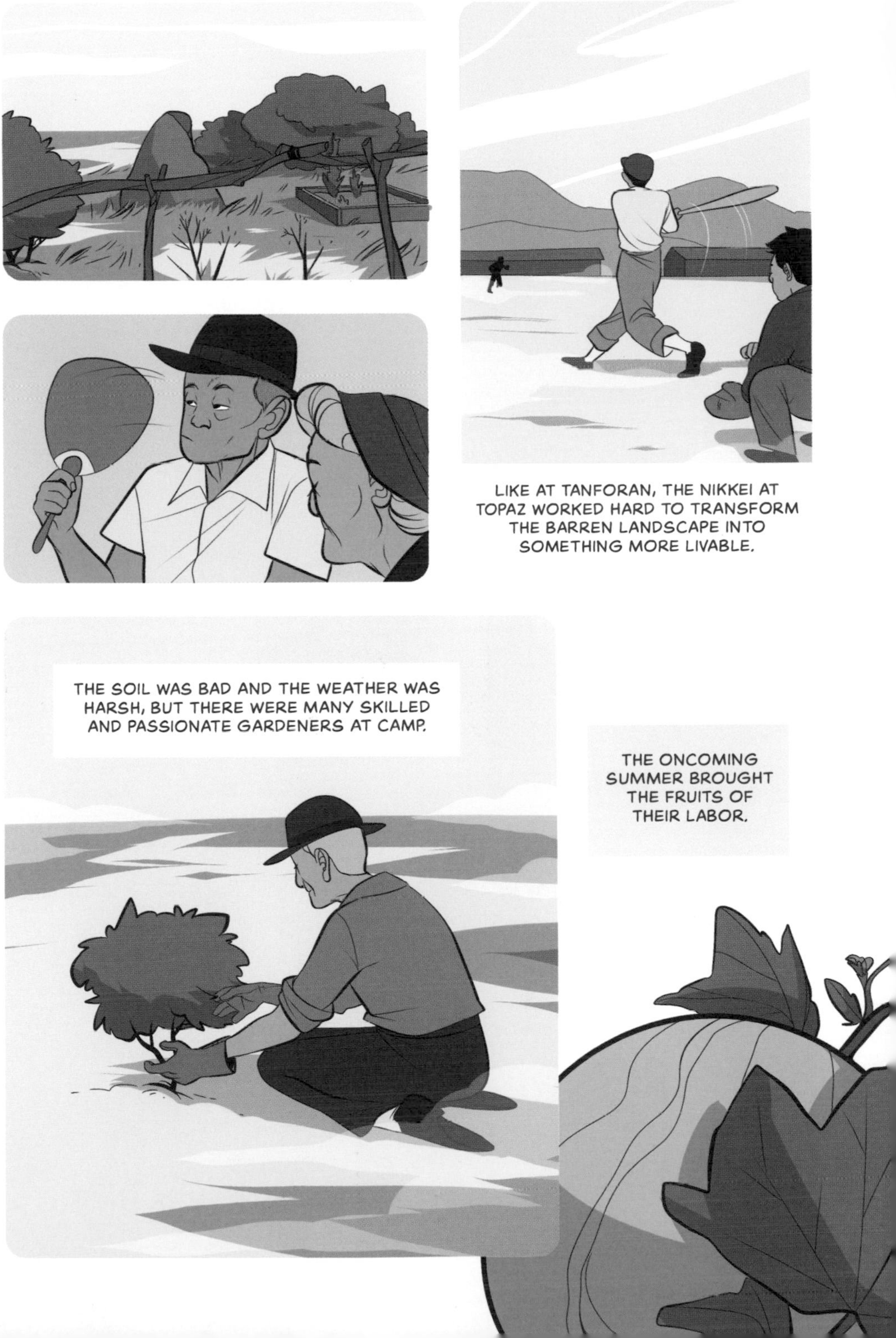
LIKE AT TANFORAN, THE NIKKEI AT TOPAZ WORKED HARD TO TRANSFORM THE BARREN LANDSCAPE INTO SOMETHING MORE LIVABLE.
THE SOIL WAS BAD AND THE WEATHER WAS HARSH, BUT THERE WERE MANY SKILLED AND PASSIONATE GARDENERS AT CAMP.
THE ONCOMING SUMMER BROUGHT THE FRUITS OF THEIR LABOR.

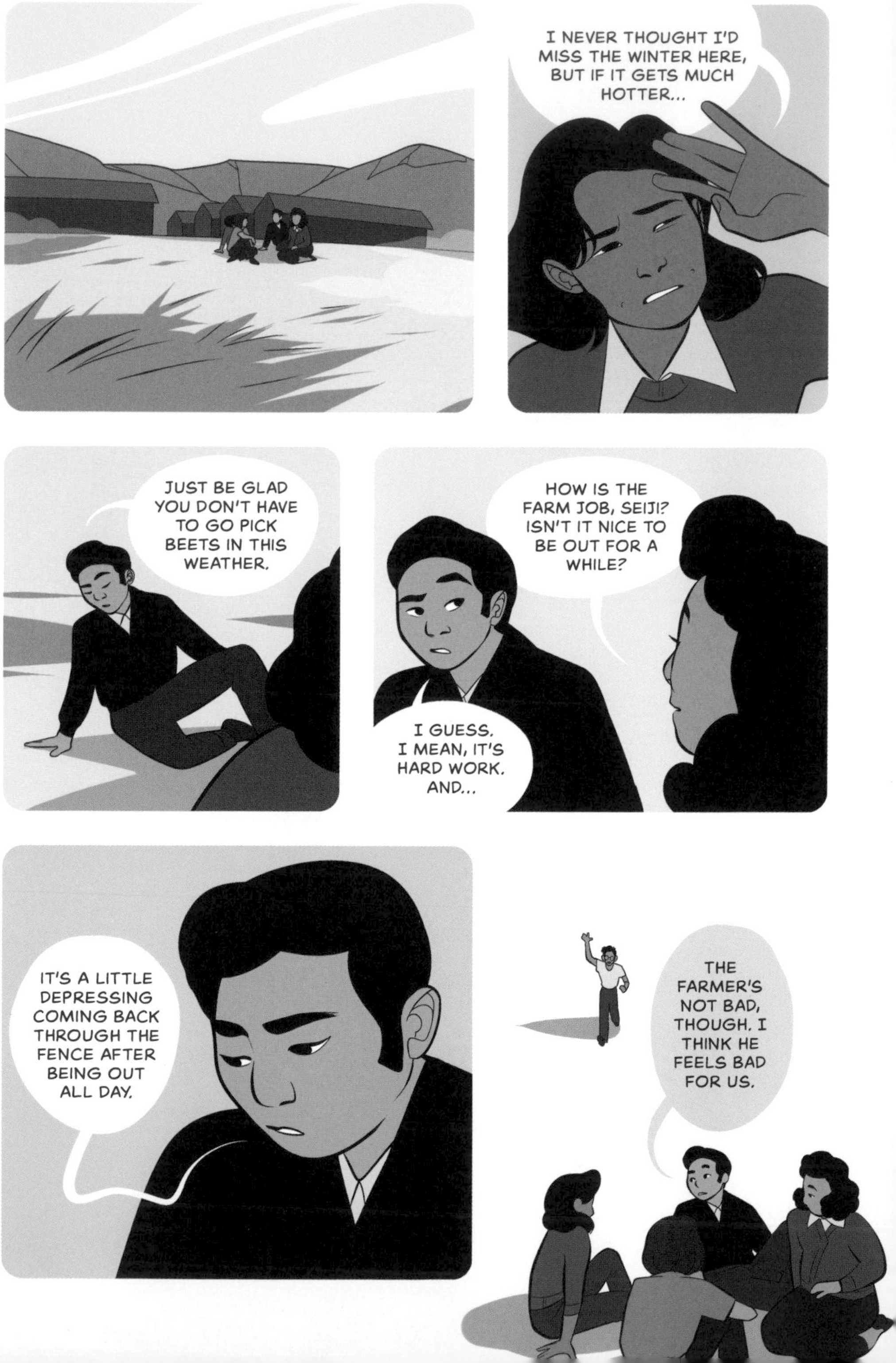
I NEVER THOUGHT I'D MISS THE WINTER HERE, BUT IF IT GETS MUCH HOTTER...
JUST BE GLAD YOU DON'T HAVE TO GO PICK BEETS IN THIS WEATHER.
HOW IS THE FARM JOB, SEIJI? ISN'T IT NICE TO BE OUT FOR A WHILE?
I GUESS. I MEAN, IT'S HARD WORK. AND...
IT'S A LITTLE DEPRESSING COMING BACK THROUGH THE FENCE AFTER BEING OUT ALL DAY.
THE FARMER'S NOT BAD, THOUGH. I THINK HE FEELS BAD FOR US.

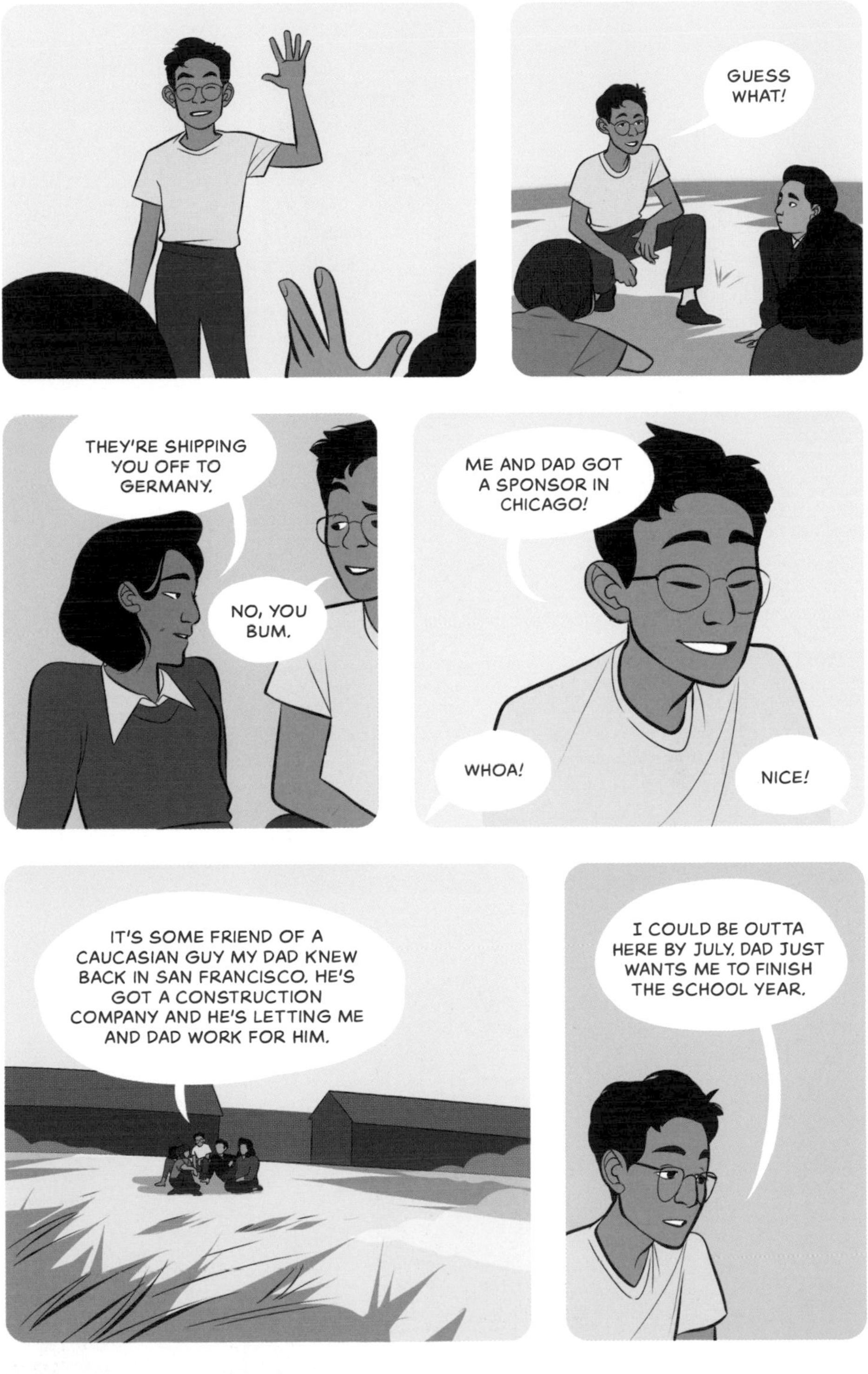
GUESS WHAT!
THEY'RE SHIPPING YOU OFF TO GERMANY.
NO, YOU BUM.
ME AND DAD GOT A SPONSOR IN CHICAGO!
WHOA!
NICE!
IT'S SOME FRIEND OF A CAUCASIAN GUY MY DAD KNEW BACK IN SAN FRANCISCO. HE'S GOT A CONSTRUCTION COMPANY AND HE'S LETTING ME AND DAD WORK FOR HIM.
I COULD BE OUTTA HERE BY JULY. DAD JUST WANTS ME TO FINISH THE SCHOOL YEAR.

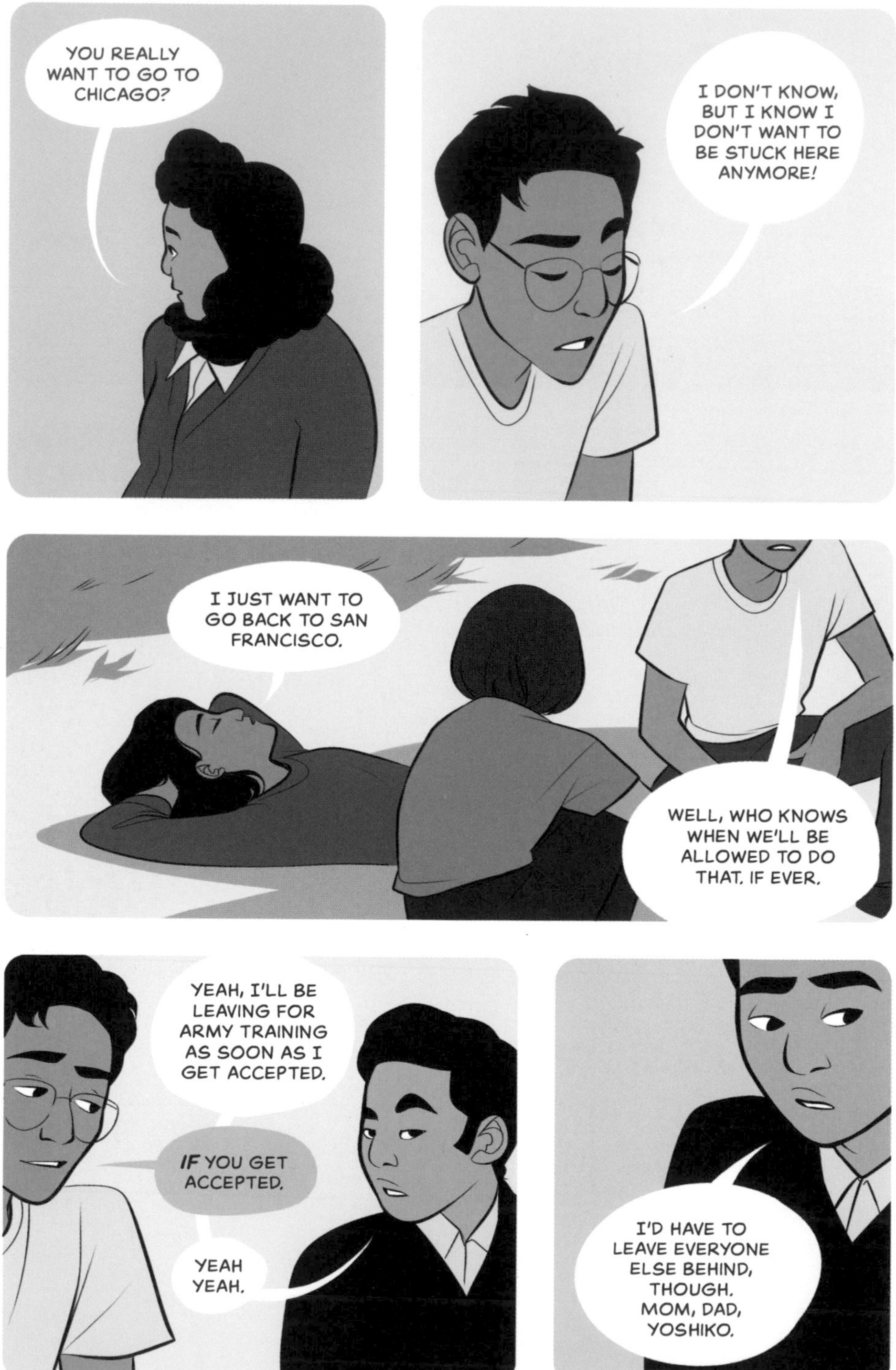

YOU REALLY WANT TO GO TO CHICAGO?
I DON'T KNOW, BUT I KNOW I DON'T WANT TO BE STUCK HERE ANYMORE!
I JUST WANT TO GO BACK TO SAN FRANCISCO.
WELL, WHO KNOWS WHEN WE'LL BE ALLOWED TO DO THAT. IF EVER.
YEAH, I'LL BE LEAVING FOR ARMY TRAINING AS SOON AS I GET ACCEPTED.
IF YOU GET ACCEPTED.
YEAH YEAH.
I'D HAVE TO LEAVE EVERYONE ELSE BEHIND, THOUGH. MOM, DAD, YOSHIKO.

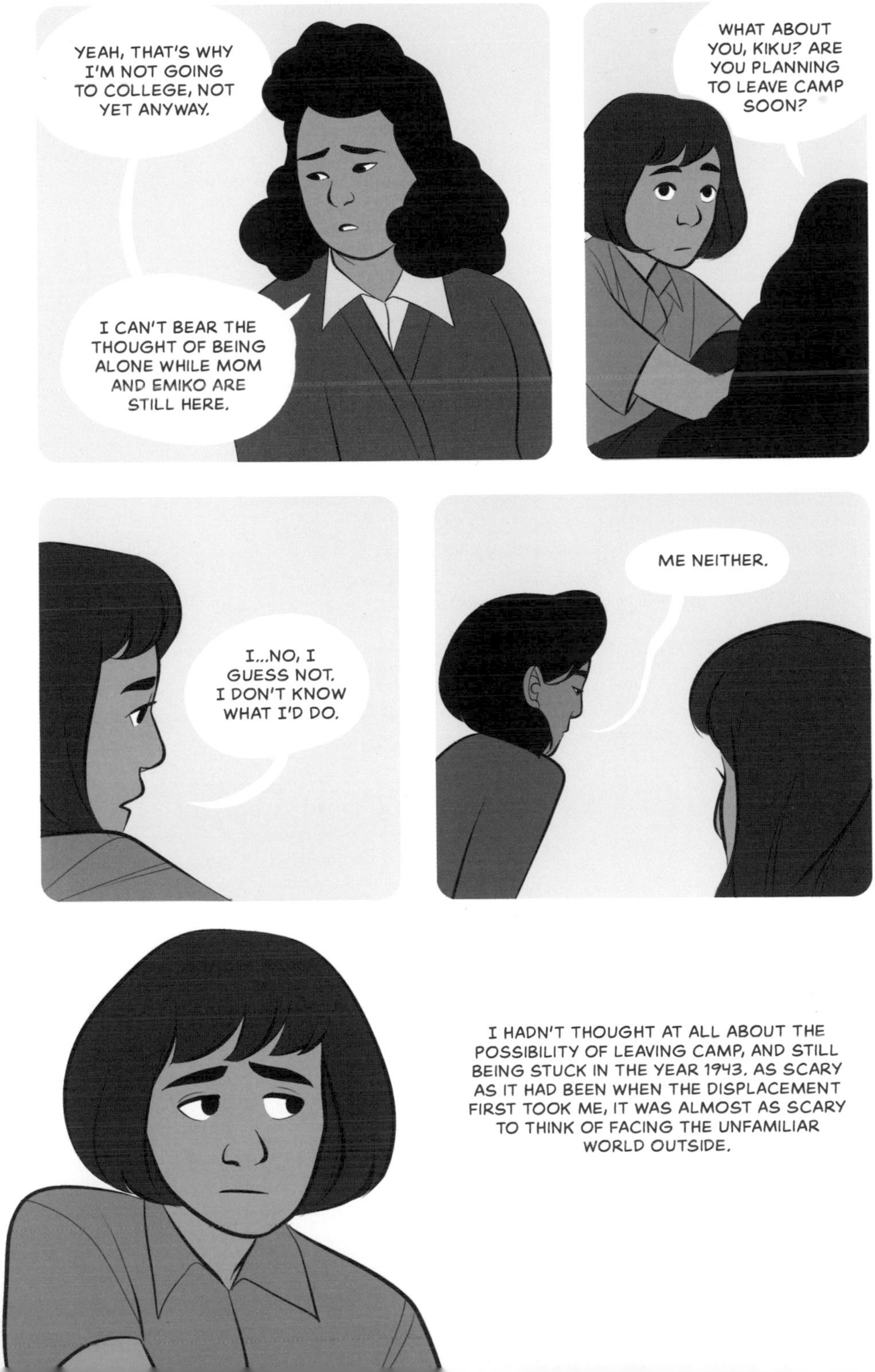
YEAH, THAT'S WHY I'M NOT GOING TO COLLEGE, NOT YET ANYWAY.
I CAN'T BEAR THE THOUGHT OF BEING ALONE WHILE MOM AND EMIKO ARE STILL HERE.
WHAT ABOUT YOU, KIKU? ARE YOU PLANNING TO LEAVE CAMP SOON?
I...NO, I GUESS NOT. I DON'T KNOW WHAT I'D DO.
ME NEITHER.
I HADN'T THOUGHT AT ALL ABOUT THE POSSIBILITY OF LEAVING CAMP, AND STILL BEING STUCK IN THE YEAR 1943. AS SCARY AS IT HAD BEEN WHEN THE DISPLACEMENT FIRST TOOK ME, IT WAS ALMOST AS SCARY TO THINK OF FACING THE UNFAMILIAR WORLD OUTSIDE.

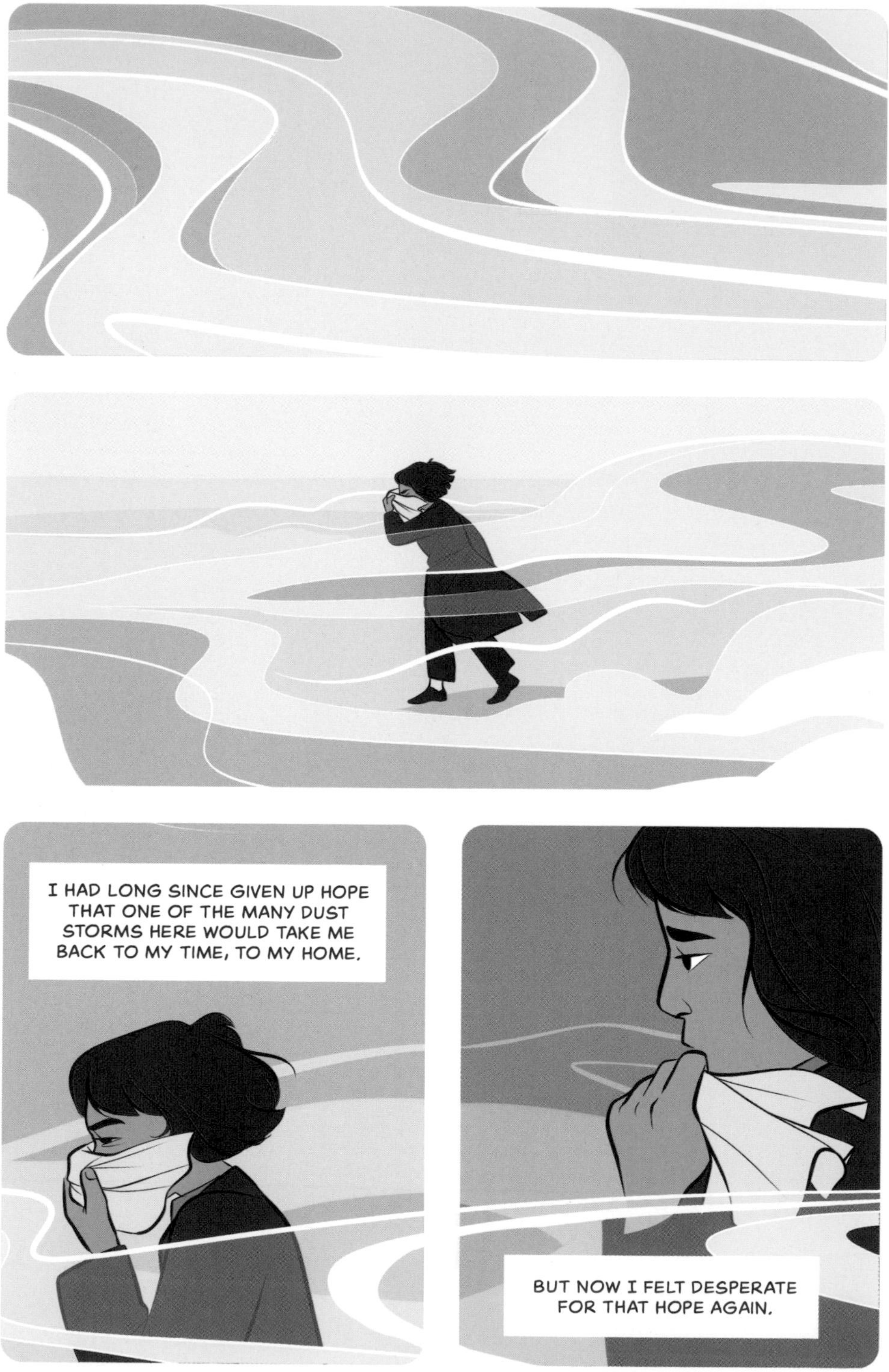
I HAD LONG SINCE GIVEN UP HOPE THAT ONE OF THE MANY DUST STORMS HERE WOULD TAKE ME BACK TO MY TIME, TO MY HOME.
BUT NOW I FELT DESPERATE FOR THAT HOPE AGAIN.

CAMP WAS DIFFICULT, DEGRADING, TERRIFYING.

BUT THE PEOPLE HERE MADE IT LIVABLE.

THROUGH COMMUNITY AND HARD WORK WE ENDURED AND SURVIVED. I HAD NOWHERE TO GO AND NO ONE TO GO TO OUTSIDE OF CAMP.

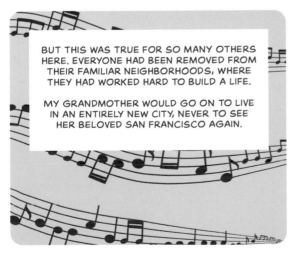

BUT THIS WAS TRUE FOR SO MANY OTHERS HERE. EVERYONE HAD BEEN REMOVED FROM THEIR FAMILIAR NEIGHBORHOODS, WHERE THEY HAD WORKED HARD TO BUILD A LIFE.

MY GRANDMOTHER WOULD GO ON TO LIVE IN AN ENTIRELY NEW CITY, NEVER TO SEE HER BELOVED SAN FRANCISCO AGAIN.

WHAT WOULD HAPPEN TO US ALL?

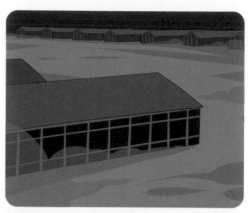

I'VE WRITTEN IT ALL DOWN, THE FIRST DISPLACEMENT, THE SECOND, AND THIS ONE, WHICH MAY BE THE LAST.

MAYBE I'LL NEVER SEE MY REAL HOME AGAIN.

MY FRIENDS ARE GOING THEIR SEPARATE WAYS. AIKO LEFT LONG AGO.

AND ERNESTINA, THE GRANDMOTHER AND NEIGHBOR I NEVER SPOKE TO—

TOPAZ HIGH GRADUATES

IS GRADUATING FROM HIGH SCHOOL TOMORROW.

THE PAPER SAYS SHE WILL BE ATTENDING JUILLIARD THANKS TO THE AMERICAN FRIENDS SCHOLARSHIP.

I DIDN'T KNOW SHE'D BE LEAVING ALREADY.

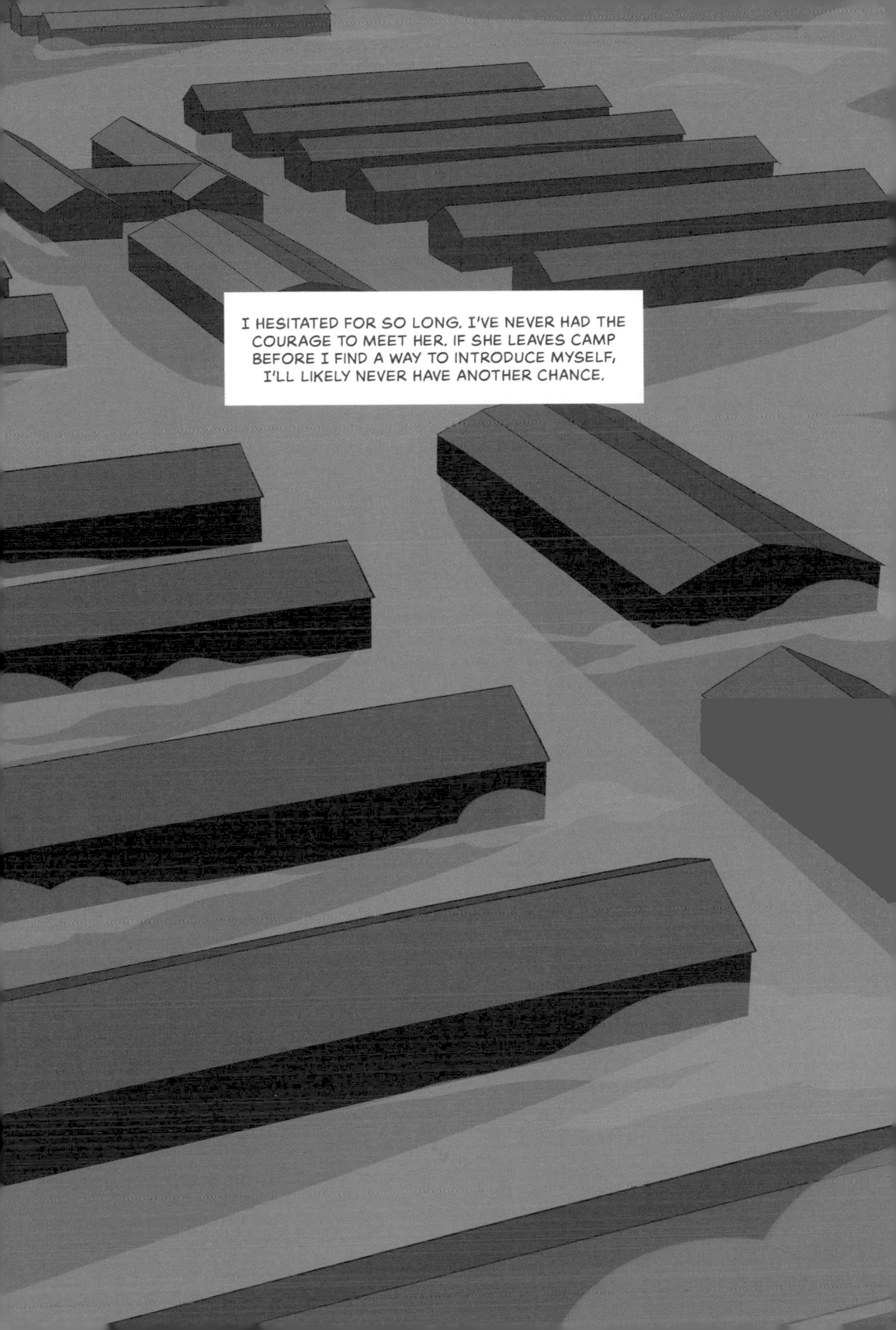
I HESITATED FOR SO LONG. I'VE NEVER HAD THE COURAGE TO MEET HER. IF SHE LEAVES CAMP BEFORE I FIND A WAY TO INTRODUCE MYSELF, I'LL LIKELY NEVER HAVE ANOTHER CHANCE.

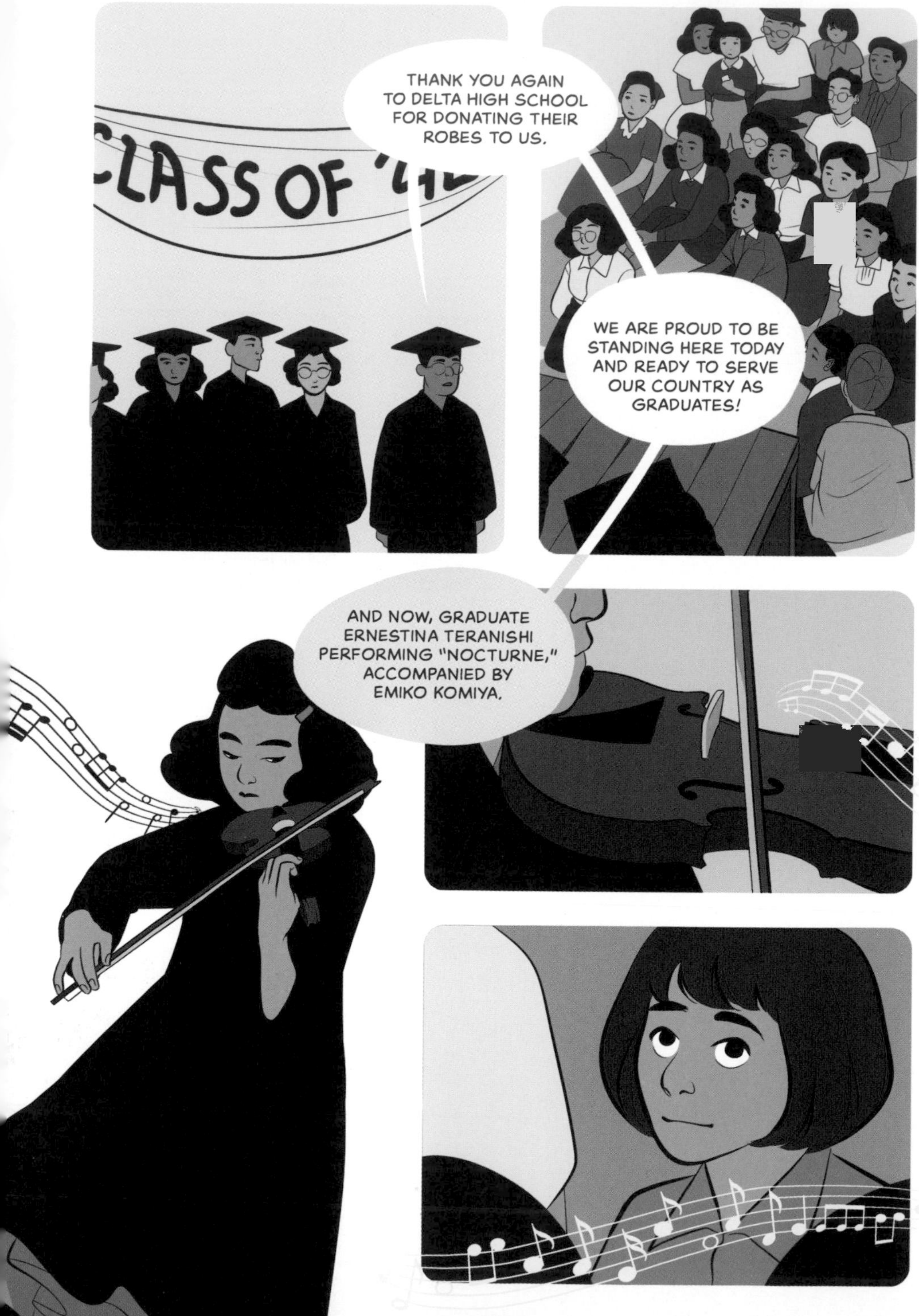

CLASS OF
THANK YOU AGAIN TO DELTA HIGH SCHOOL FOR DONATING THEIR ROBES TO US.
WE ARE PROUD TO BE STANDING HERE TODAY AND READY TO SERVE OUR COUNTRY AS GRADUATES!
AND NOW, GRADUATE ERNESTINA TERANISHI PERFORMING "NOCTURNE," ACCOMPANIED BY EMIKO KOMIYA.

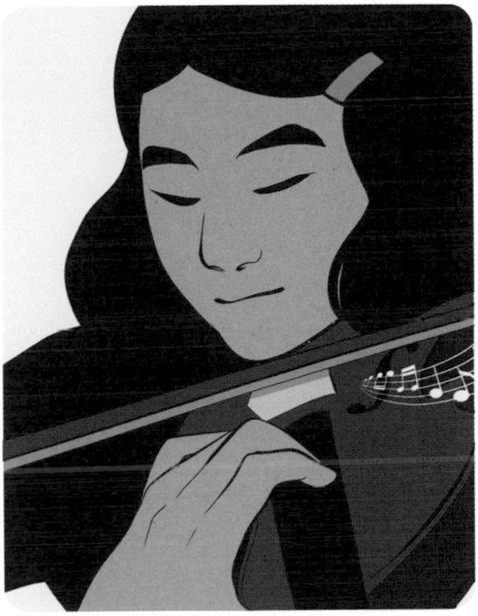
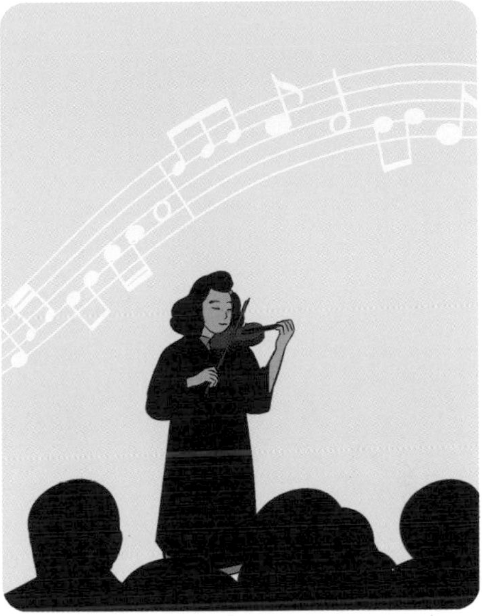
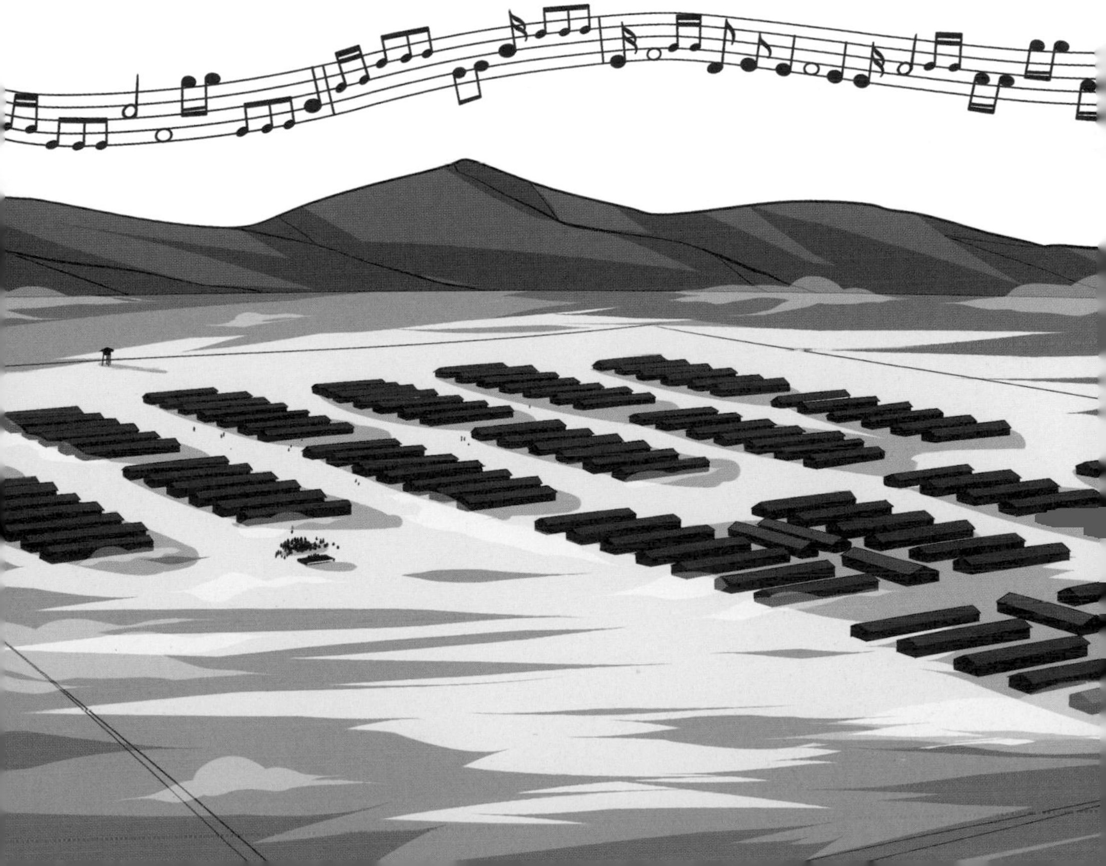

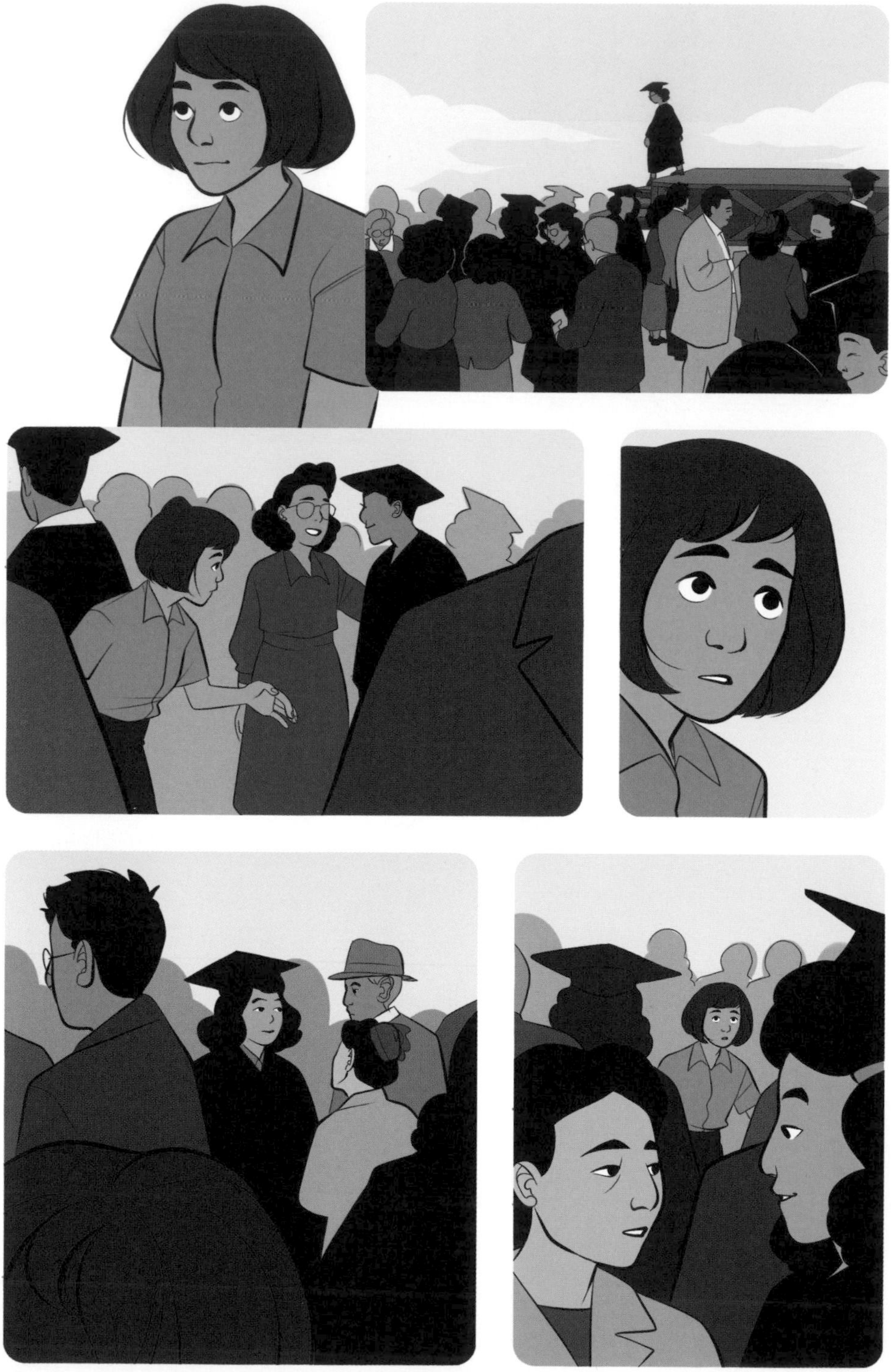

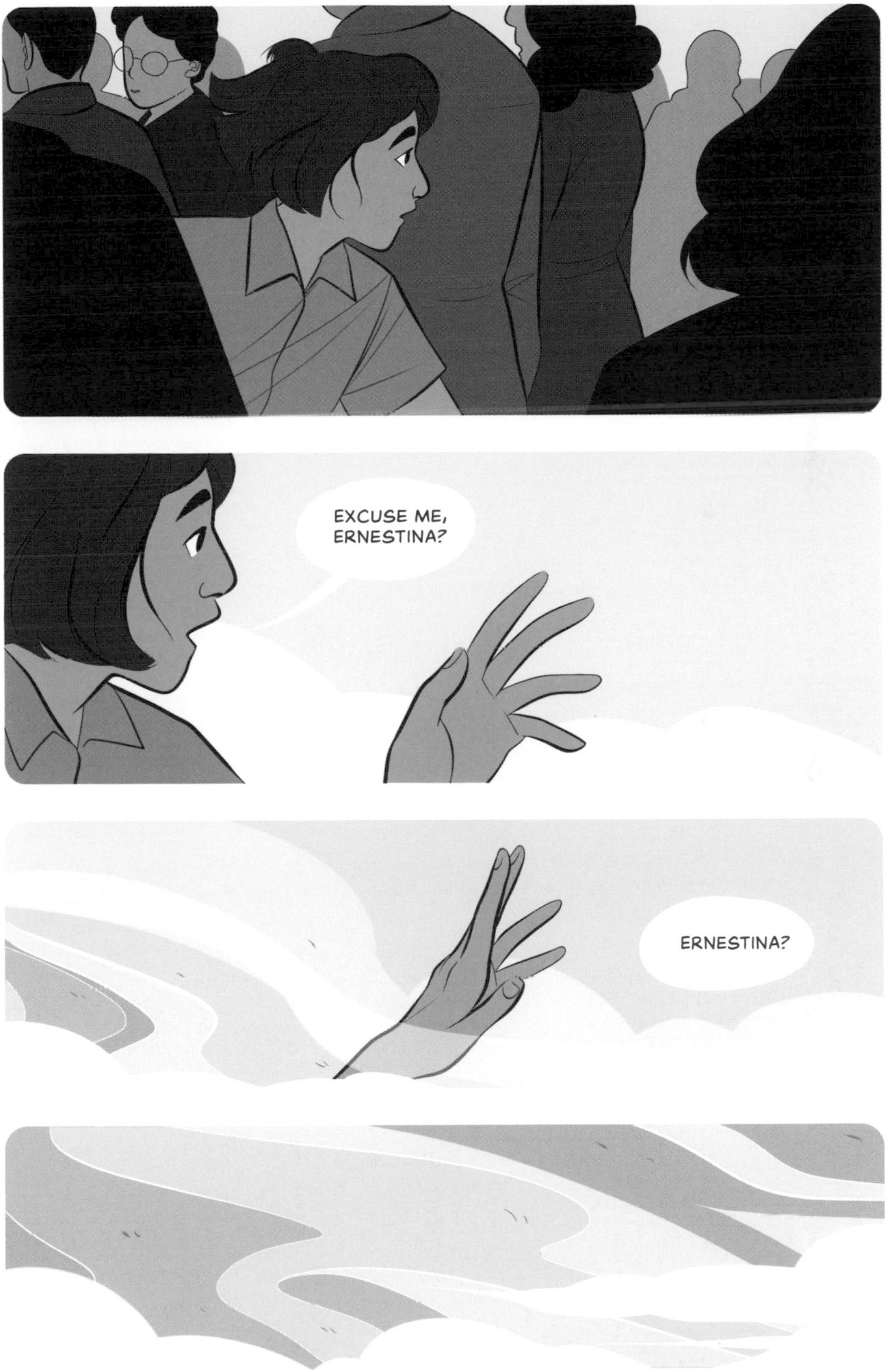
EXCUSE ME,
ERNESTINA?
ERNESTINA?

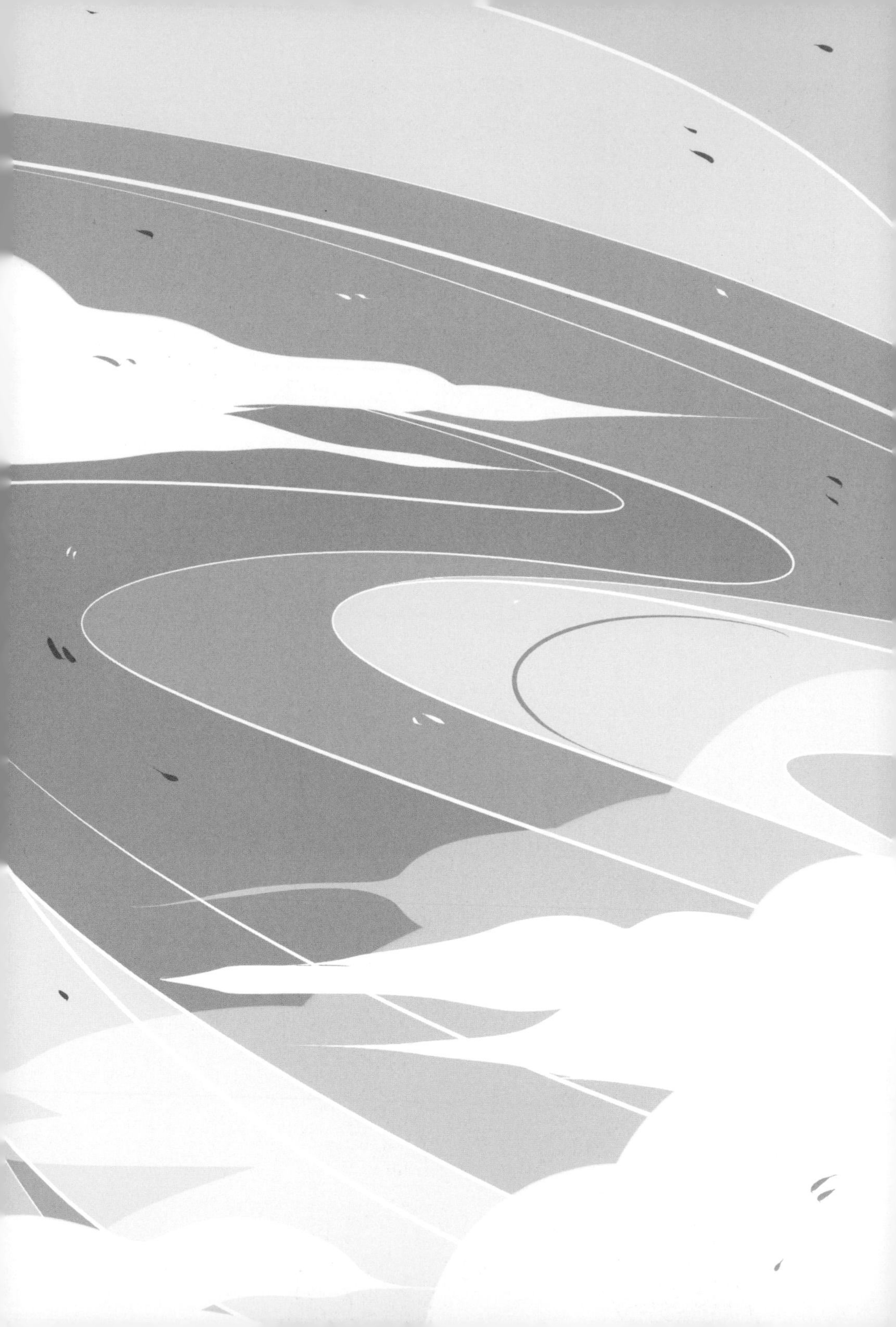

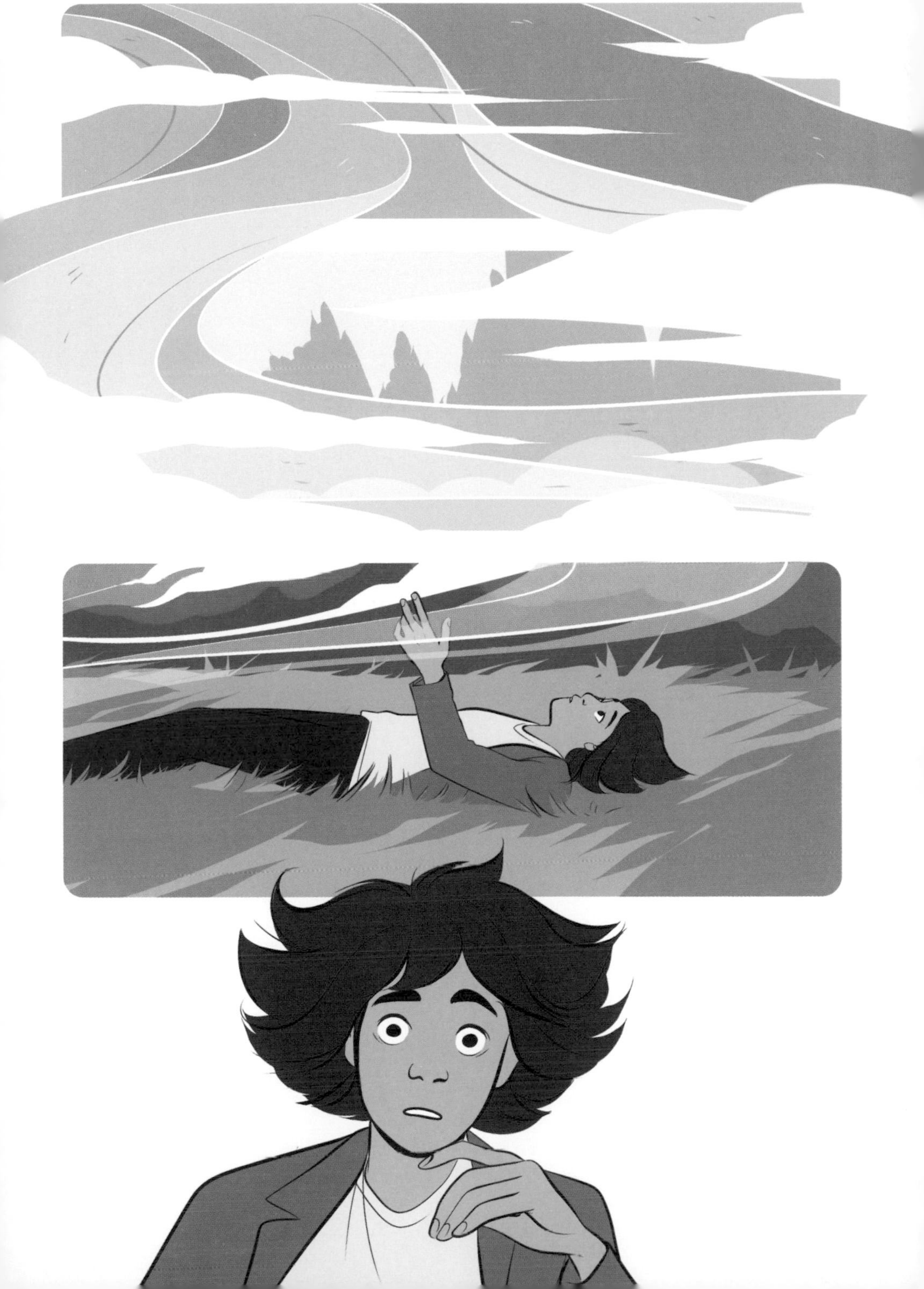

part III:
the east

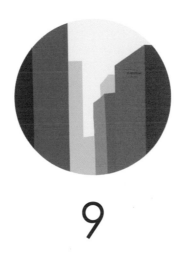

9

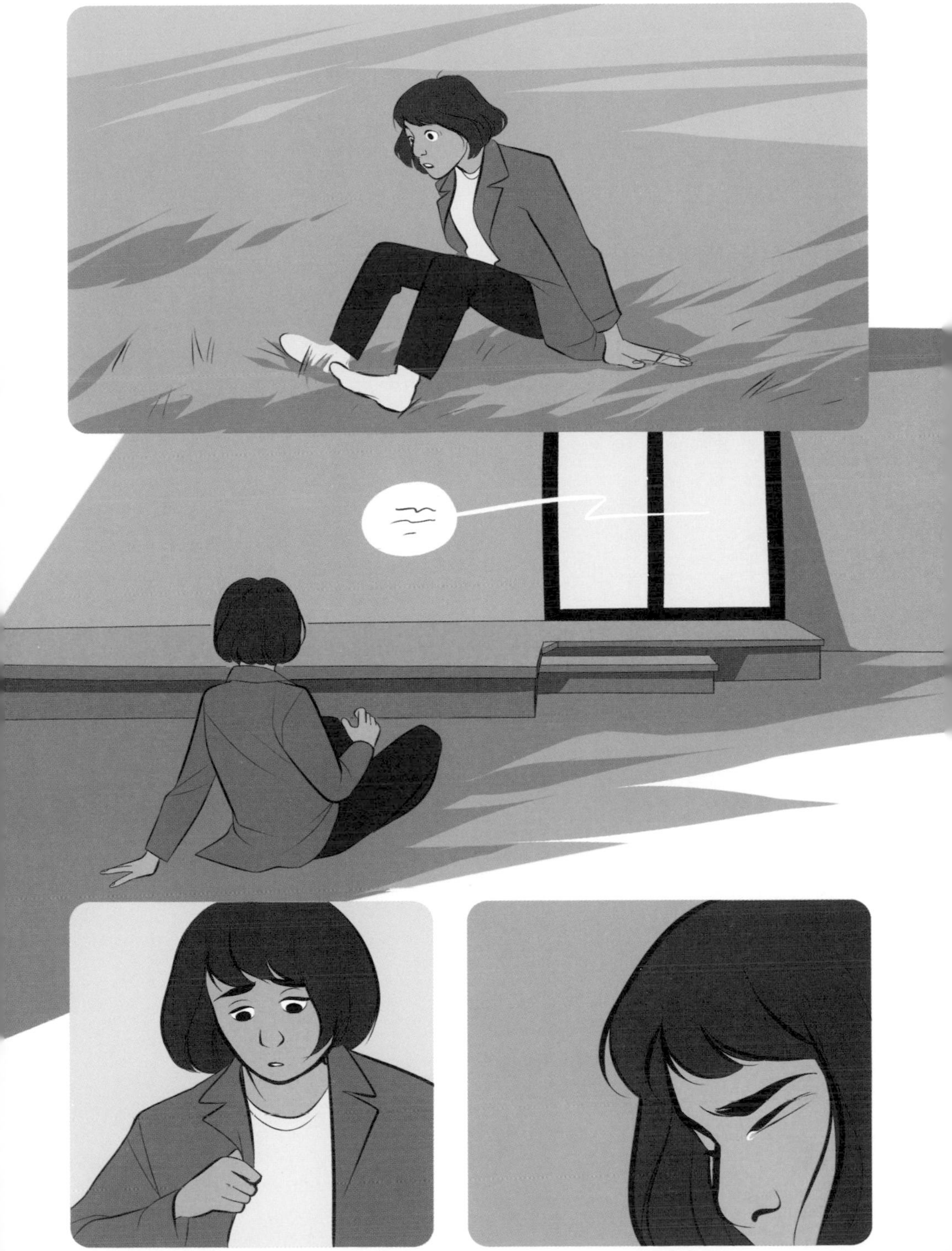

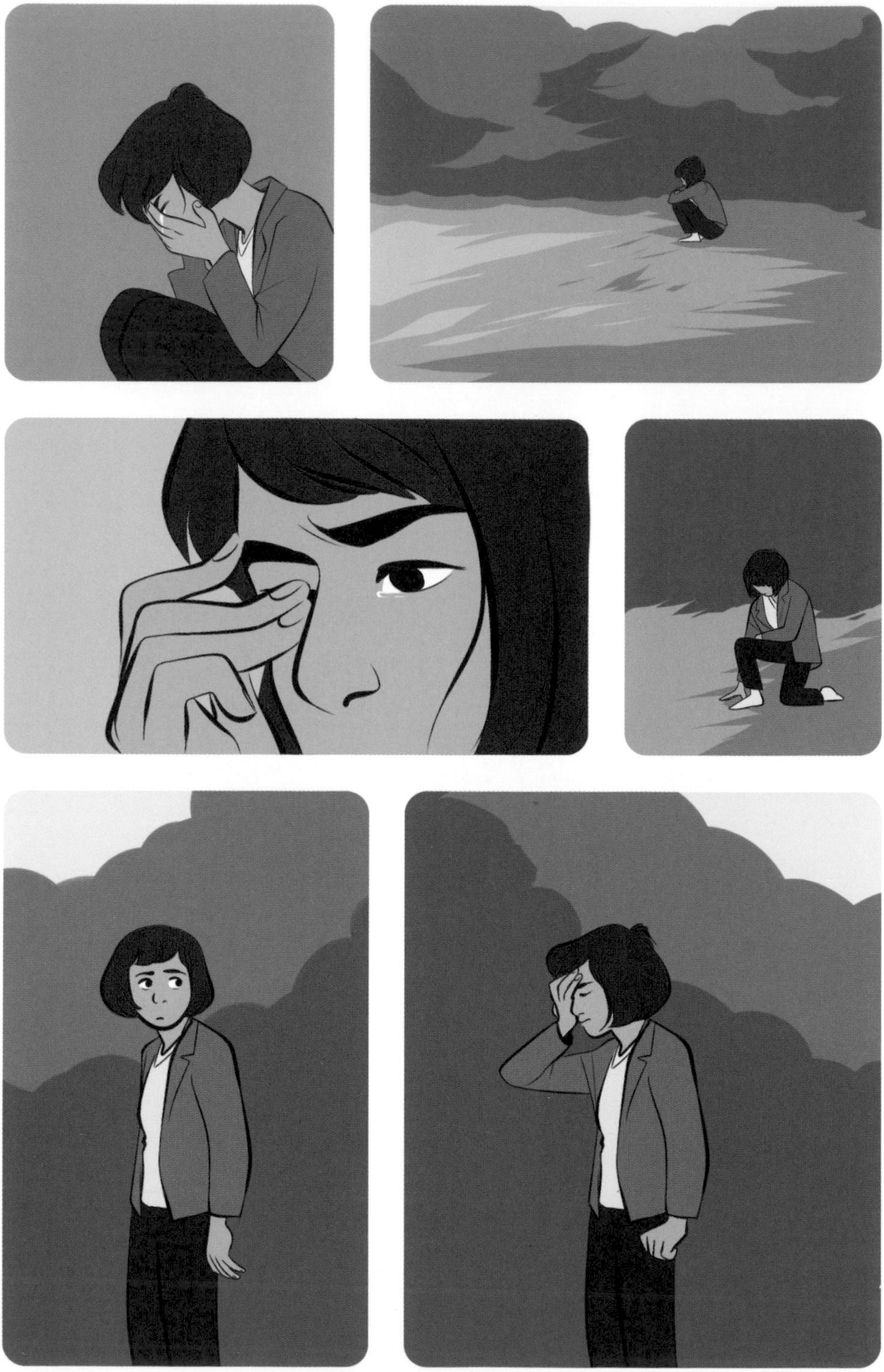

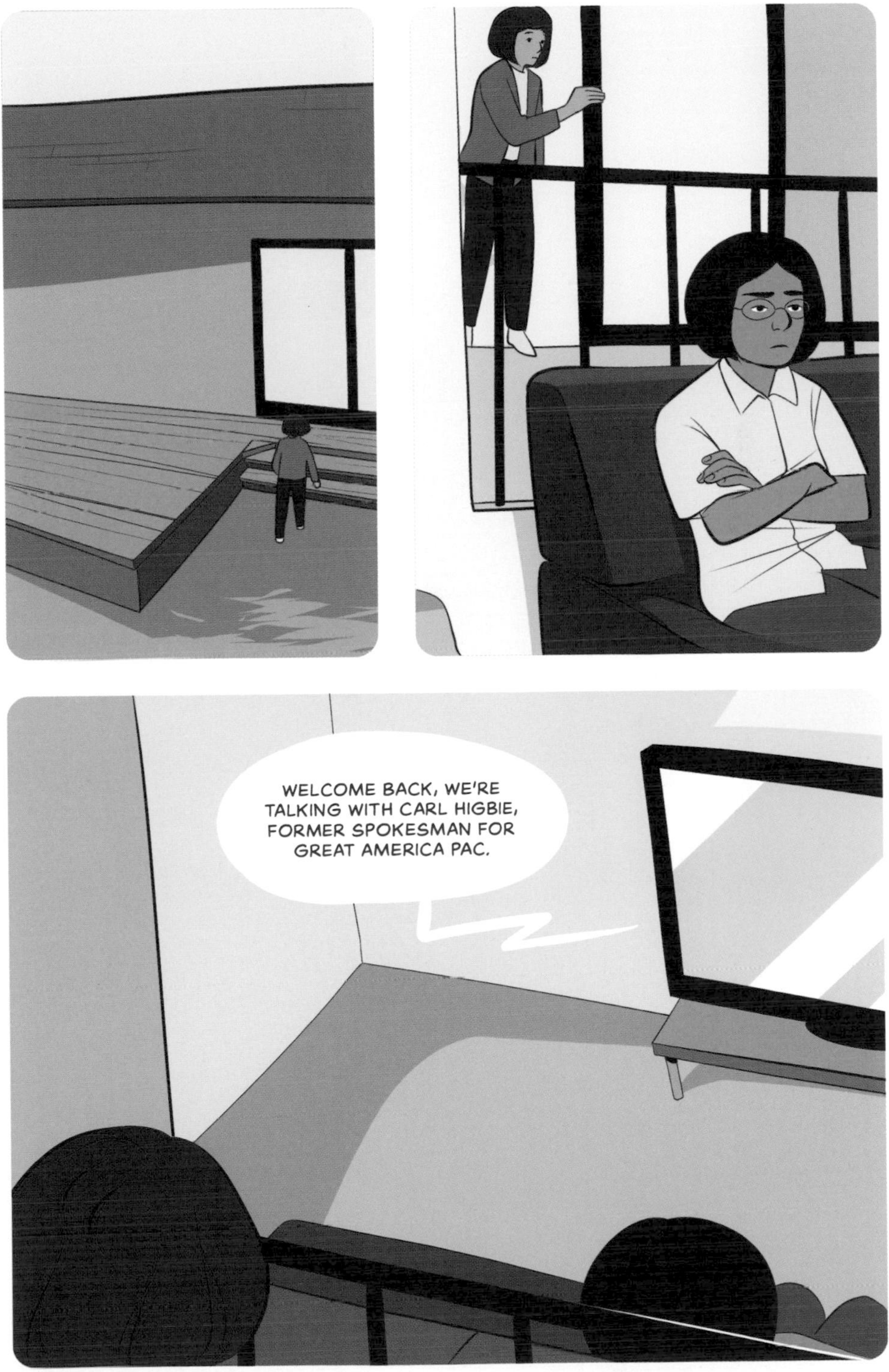
WELCOME BACK, WE'RE TALKING WITH CARL HIGBIE, FORMER SPOKESMAN FOR GREAT AMERICA PAC.

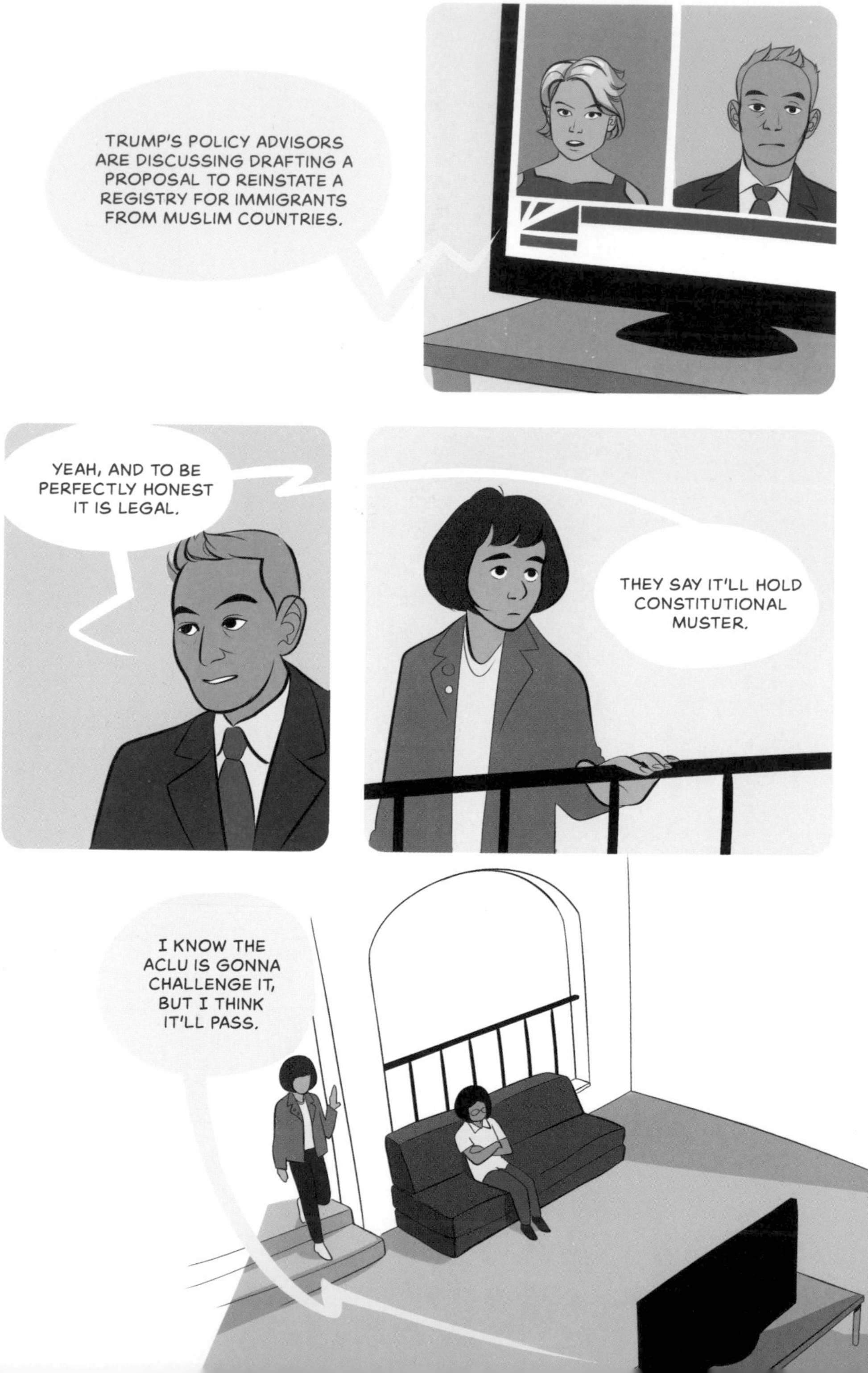
TRUMP'S POLICY ADVISORS ARE DISCUSSING DRAFTING A PROPOSAL TO REINSTATE A REGISTRY FOR IMMIGRANTS FROM MUSLIM COUNTRIES.
YEAH, AND TO BE PERFECTLY HONEST IT IS LEGAL.
THEY SAY IT'LL HOLD CONSTITUTIONAL MUSTER.
I KNOW THE ACLU IS GONNA CHALLENGE IT, BUT I THINK IT'LL PASS.

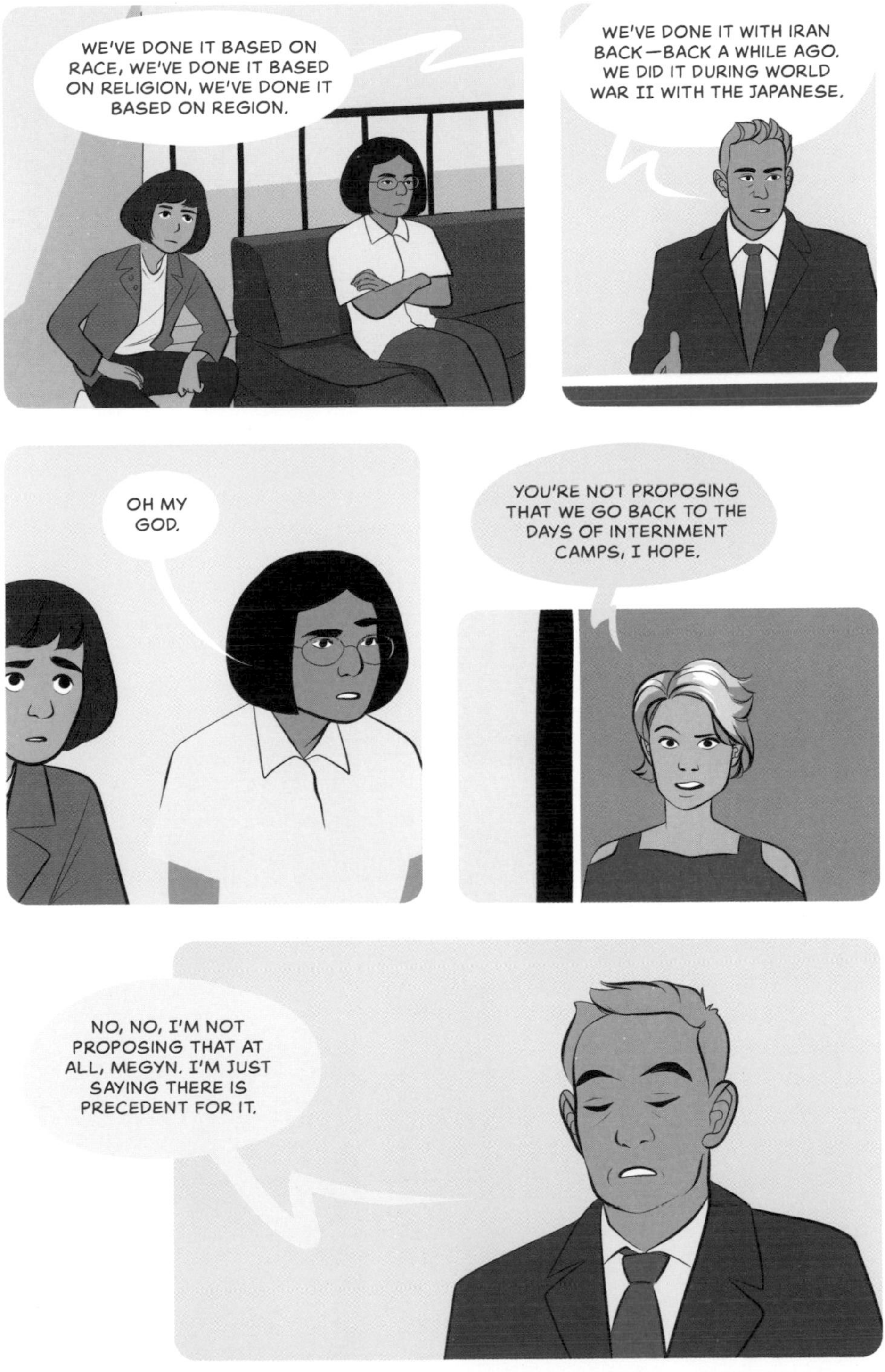
WE'VE DONE IT BASED ON RACE, WE'VE DONE IT BASED ON RELIGION, WE'VE DONE IT BASED ON REGION.
WE'VE DONE IT WITH IRAN BACK—BACK A WHILE AGO. WE DID IT DURING WORLD WAR II WITH THE JAPANESE.
OH MY GOD.
YOU'RE NOT PROPOSING THAT WE GO BACK TO THE DAYS OF INTERNMENT CAMPS, I HOPE.
NO, NO, I'M NOT PROPOSING THAT AT ALL, MEGYN. I'M JUST SAYING THERE IS PRECEDENT FOR IT.

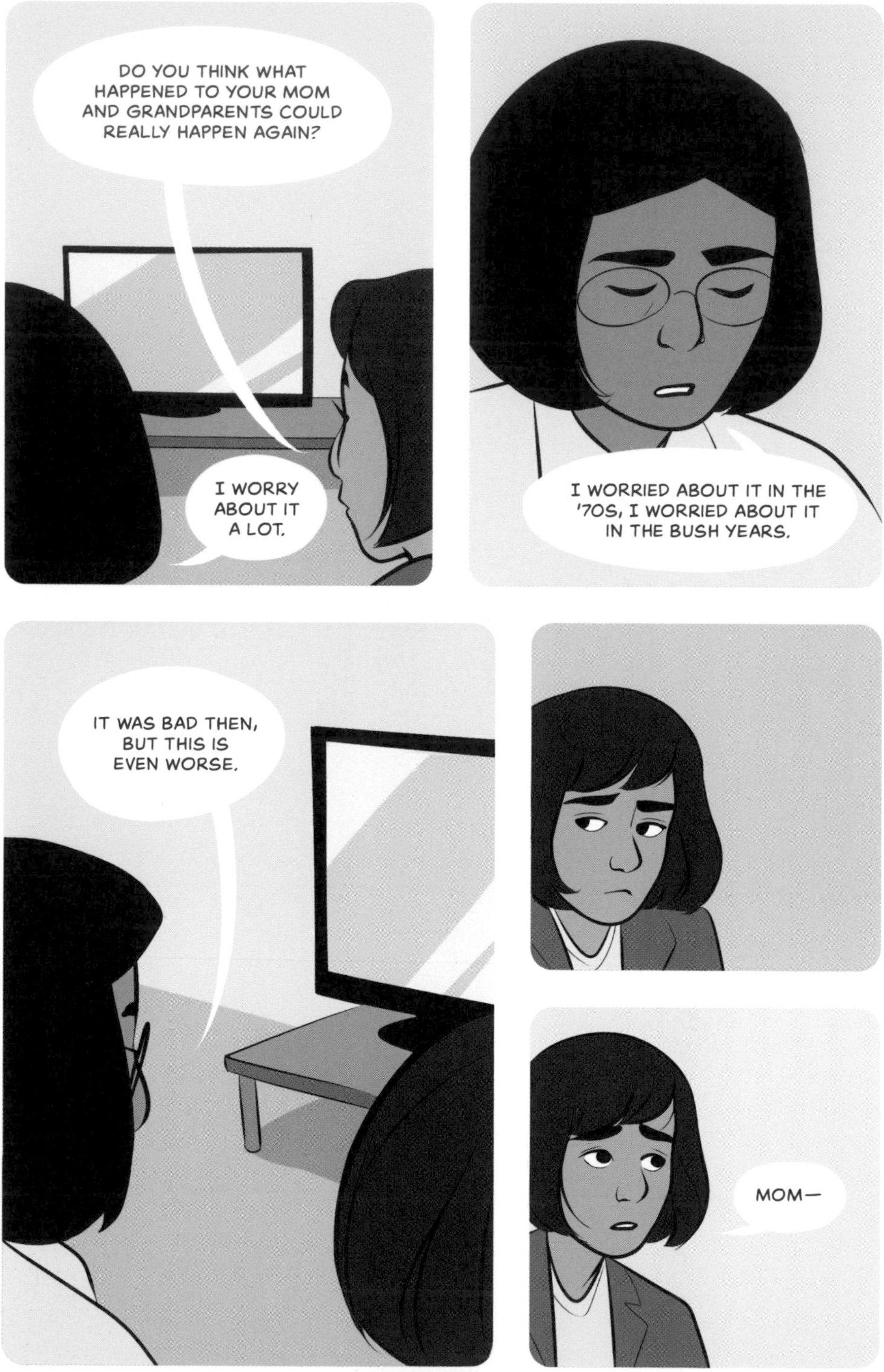

DO YOU THINK WHAT HAPPENED TO YOUR MOM AND GRANDPARENTS COULD REALLY HAPPEN AGAIN?
I WORRY ABOUT IT A LOT.
I WORRIED ABOUT IT IN THE '70S, I WORRIED ABOUT IT IN THE BUSH YEARS.
IT WAS BAD THEN, BUT THIS IS EVEN WORSE.
MOM—

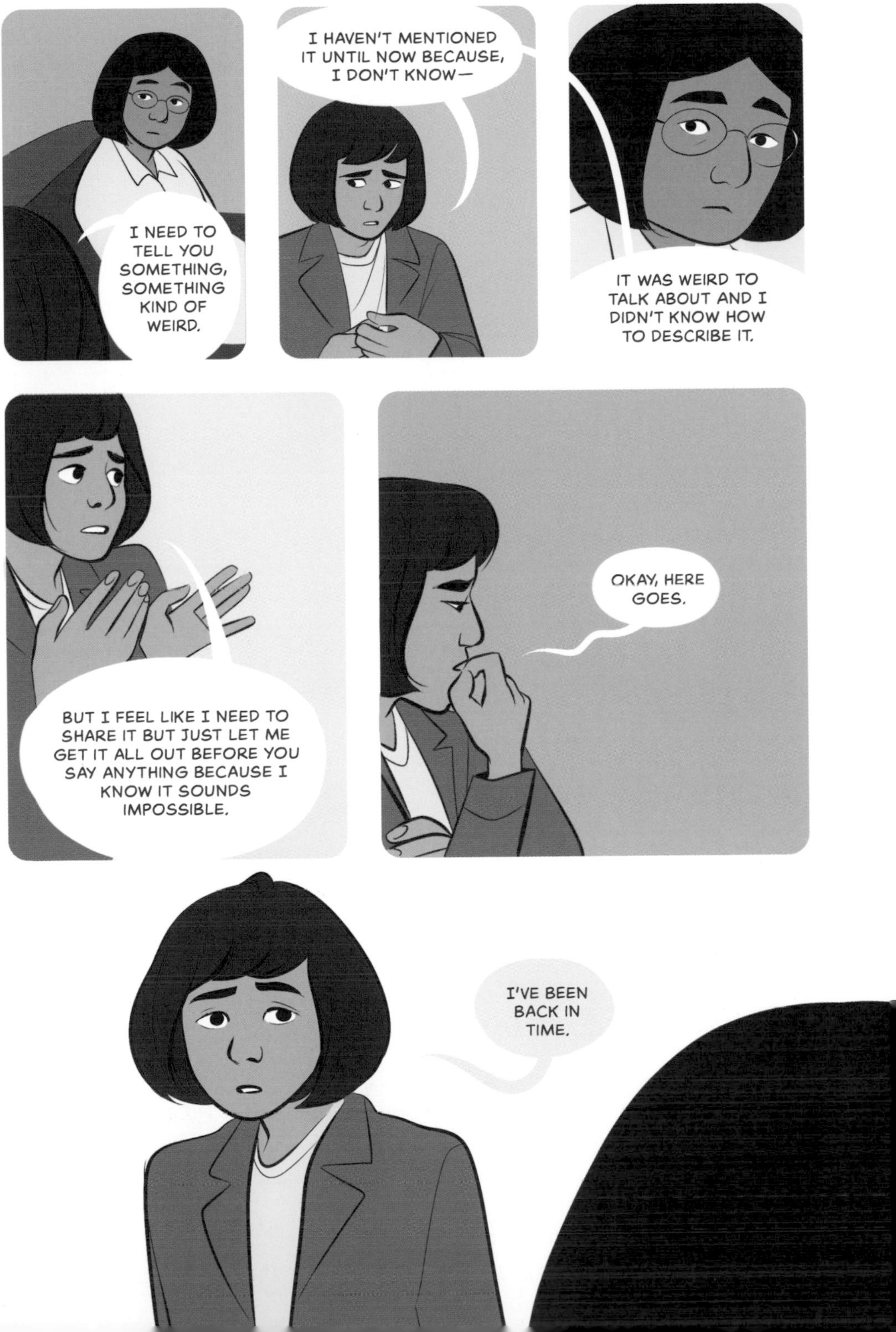
I NEED TO TELL YOU SOMETHING, SOMETHING KIND OF WEIRD.
I HAVEN'T MENTIONED IT UNTIL NOW BECAUSE, I DON'T KNOW—
IT WAS WEIRD TO TALK ABOUT AND I DIDN'T KNOW HOW TO DESCRIBE IT.
BUT I FEEL LIKE I NEED TO SHARE IT BUT JUST LET ME GET IT ALL OUT BEFORE YOU SAY ANYTHING BECAUSE I KNOW IT SOUNDS IMPOSSIBLE.
OKAY, HERE GOES.
I'VE BEEN BACK IN TIME.

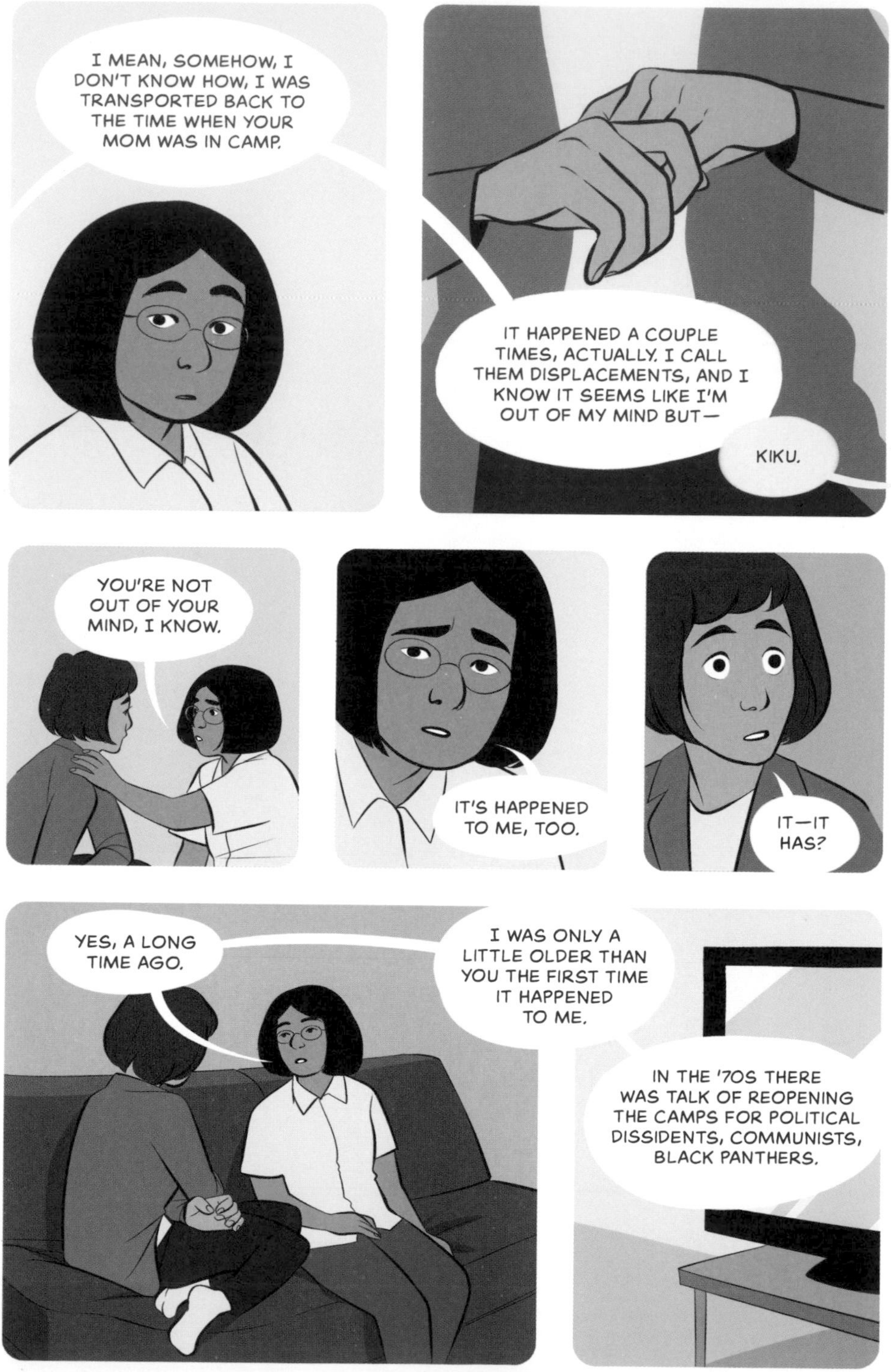
I MEAN, SOMEHOW, I DON'T KNOW HOW, I WAS TRANSPORTED BACK TO THE TIME WHEN YOUR MOM WAS IN CAMP.
IT HAPPENED A COUPLE TIMES, ACTUALLY. I CALL THEM DISPLACEMENTS, AND I KNOW IT SEEMS LIKE I'M OUT OF MY MIND BUT—
KIKU.
YOU'RE NOT OUT OF YOUR MIND, I KNOW.
IT'S HAPPENED TO ME, TOO.
IT—IT HAS?
YES, A LONG TIME AGO.
I WAS ONLY A LITTLE OLDER THAN YOU THE FIRST TIME IT HAPPENED TO ME.
IN THE '70S THERE WAS TALK OF REOPENING THE CAMPS FOR POLITICAL DISSIDENTS, COMMUNISTS, BLACK PANTHERS.

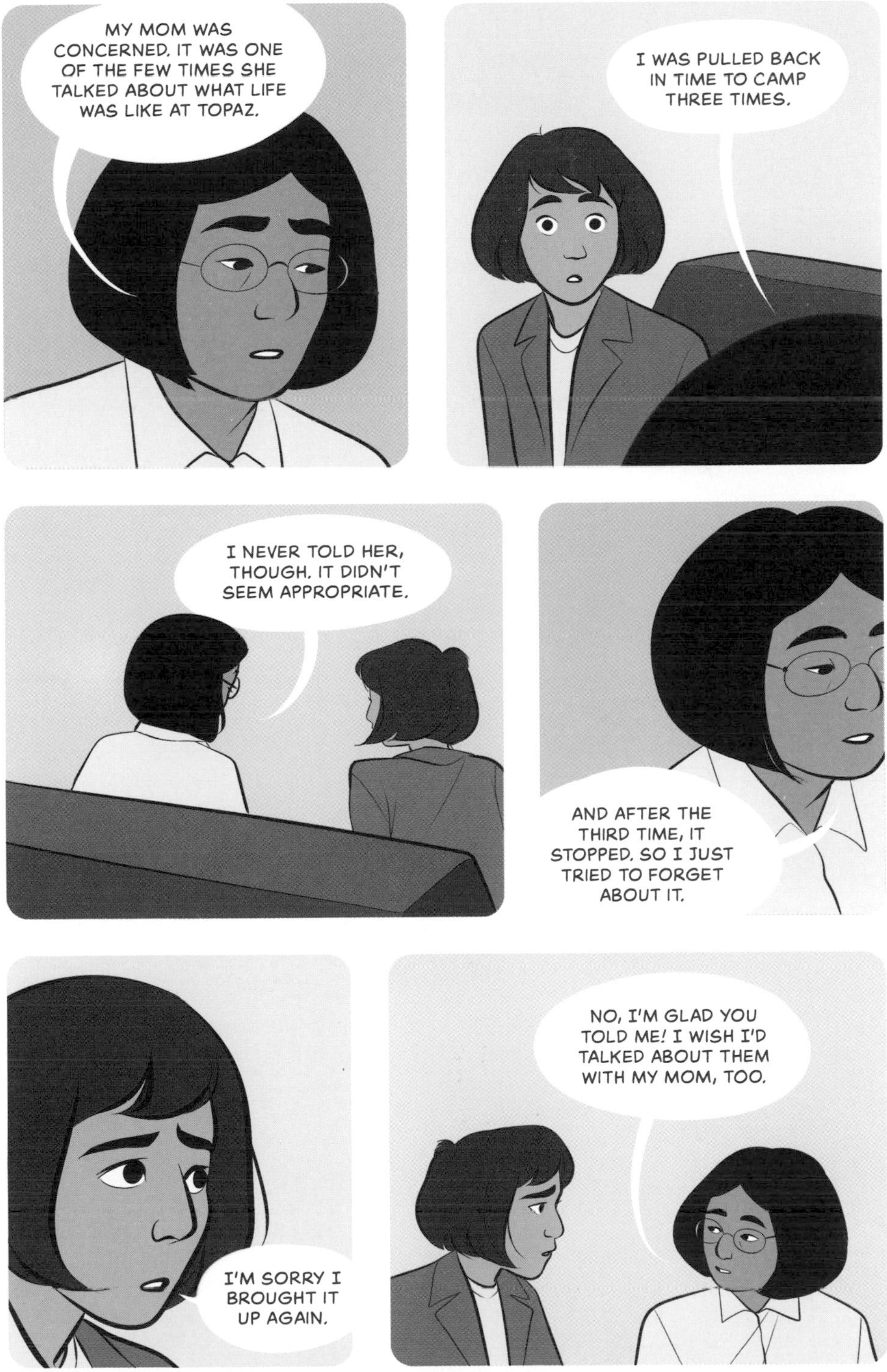
MY MOM WAS CONCERNED. IT WAS ONE OF THE FEW TIMES SHE TALKED ABOUT WHAT LIFE WAS LIKE AT TOPAZ.
I WAS PULLED BACK IN TIME TO CAMP THREE TIMES.
I NEVER TOLD HER, THOUGH. IT DIDN'T SEEM APPROPRIATE.
AND AFTER THE THIRD TIME, IT STOPPED. SO I JUST TRIED TO FORGET ABOUT IT.
I'M SORRY I BROUGHT IT UP AGAIN.
NO, I'M GLAD YOU TOLD ME! I WISH I'D TALKED ABOUT THEM WITH MY MOM, TOO.

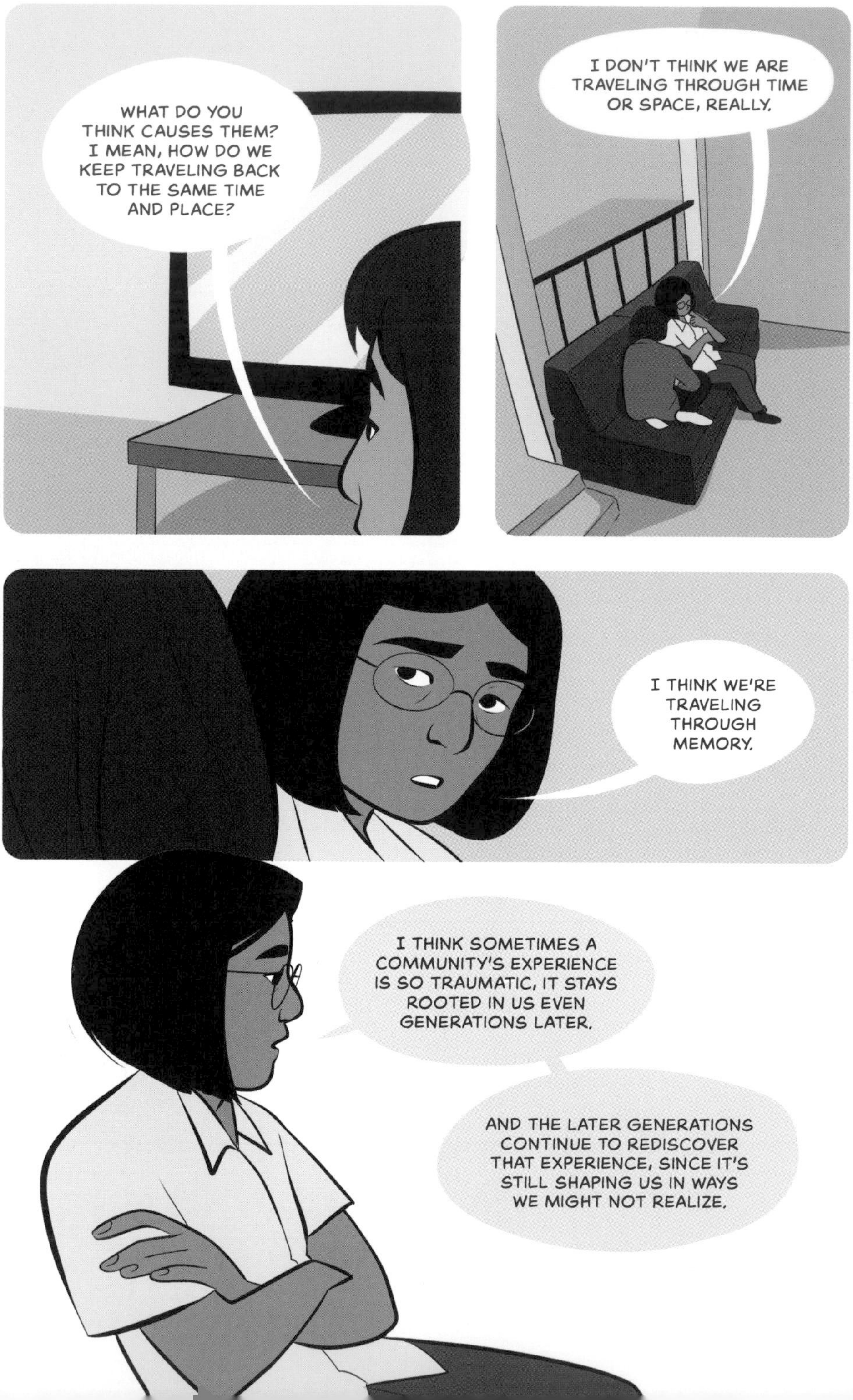
WHAT DO YOU THINK CAUSES THEM? I MEAN, HOW DO WE KEEP TRAVELING BACK TO THE SAME TIME AND PLACE?
I DON'T THINK WE ARE TRAVELING THROUGH TIME OR SPACE, REALLY.
I THINK WE'RE TRAVELING THROUGH MEMORY.
I THINK SOMETIMES A COMMUNITY'S EXPERIENCE IS SO TRAUMATIC, IT STAYS ROOTED IN US EVEN GENERATIONS LATER.
AND THE LATER GENERATIONS CONTINUE TO REDISCOVER THAT EXPERIENCE, SINCE IT'S STILL SHAPING US IN WAYS WE MIGHT NOT REALIZE.

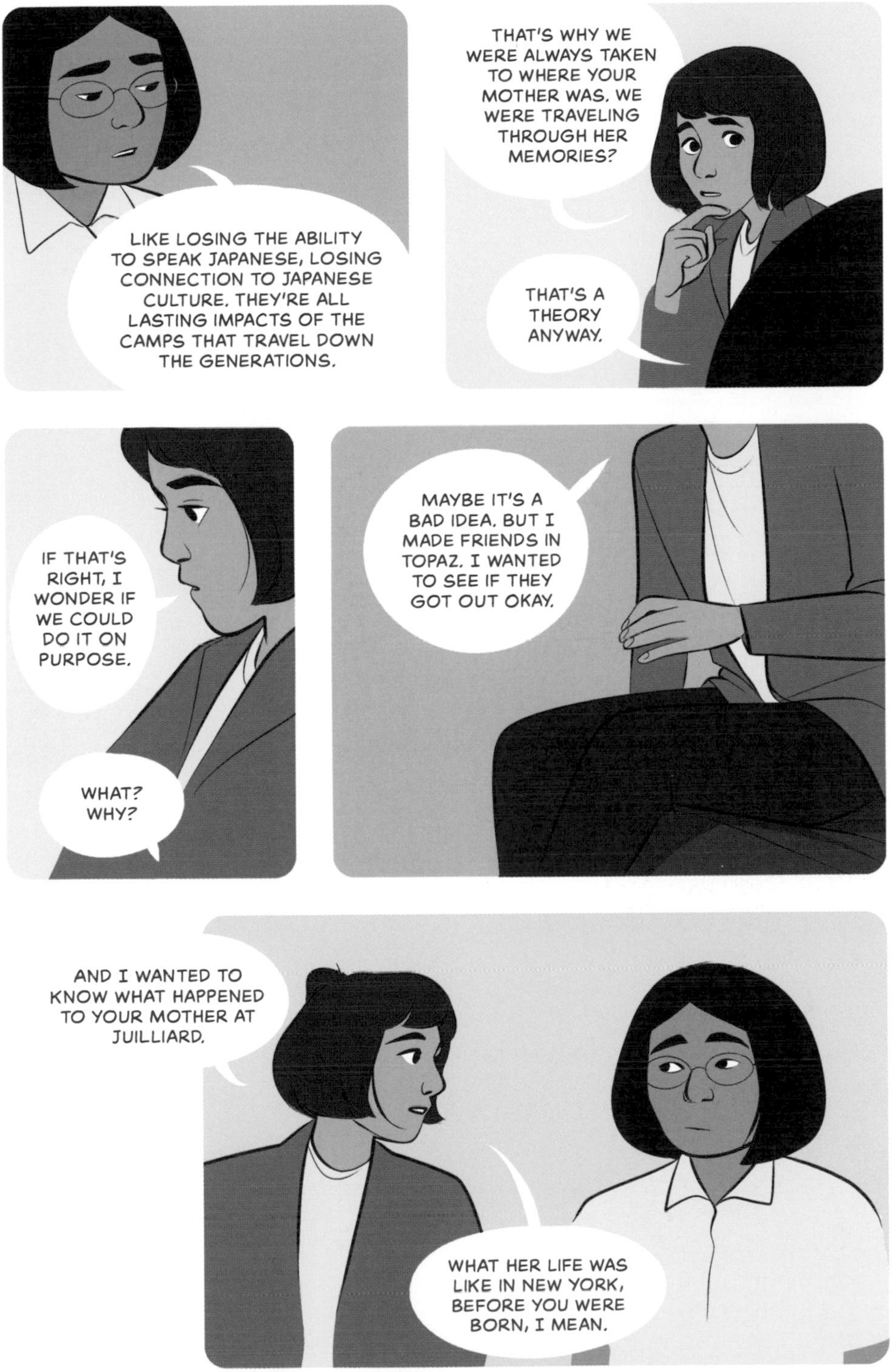
LIKE LOSING THE ABILITY TO SPEAK JAPANESE, LOSING CONNECTION TO JAPANESE CULTURE. THEY'RE ALL LASTING IMPACTS OF THE CAMPS THAT TRAVEL DOWN THE GENERATIONS.
THAT'S WHY WE WERE ALWAYS TAKEN TO WHERE YOUR MOTHER WAS. WE WERE TRAVELING THROUGH HER MEMORIES?
THAT'S A THEORY ANYWAY.
IF THAT'S RIGHT, I WONDER IF WE COULD DO IT ON PURPOSE.
WHAT? WHY?
MAYBE IT'S A BAD IDEA. BUT I MADE FRIENDS IN TOPAZ. I WANTED TO SEE IF THEY GOT OUT OKAY.
AND I WANTED TO KNOW WHAT HAPPENED TO YOUR MOTHER AT JUILLIARD.
WHAT HER LIFE WAS LIKE IN NEW YORK, BEFORE YOU WERE BORN, I MEAN.

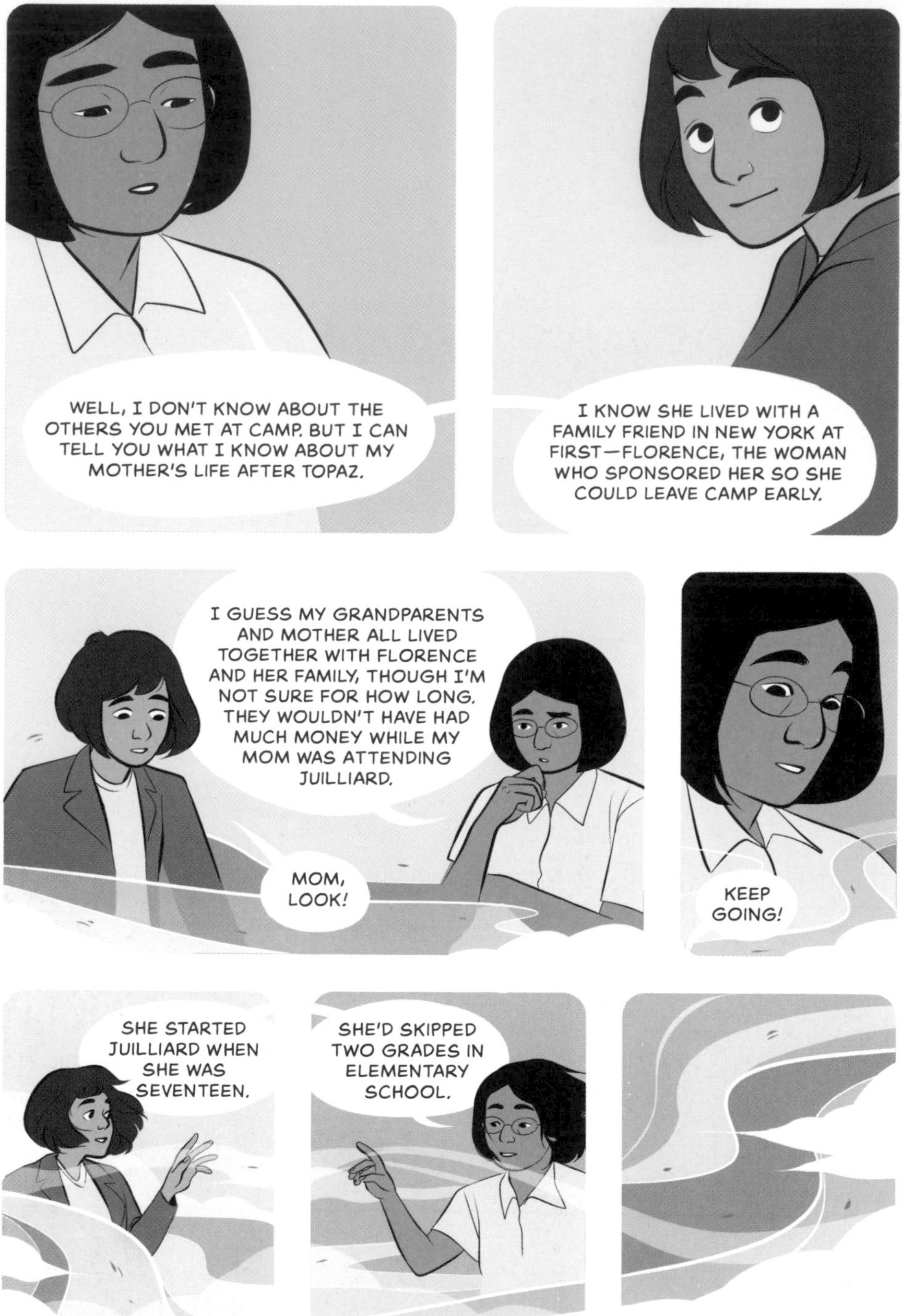
WELL, I DON'T KNOW ABOUT THE OTHERS YOU MET AT CAMP. BUT I CAN TELL YOU WHAT I KNOW ABOUT MY MOTHER'S LIFE AFTER TOPAZ.
I KNOW SHE LIVED WITH A FAMILY FRIEND IN NEW YORK AT FIRST—FLORENCE, THE WOMAN WHO SPONSORED HER SO SHE COULD LEAVE CAMP EARLY.
I GUESS MY GRANDPARENTS AND MOTHER ALL LIVED TOGETHER WITH FLORENCE AND HER FAMILY, THOUGH I'M NOT SURE FOR HOW LONG. THEY WOULDN'T HAVE HAD MUCH MONEY WHILE MY MOM WAS ATTENDING JUILLIARD.
MOM, LOOK!
KEEP GOING!
SHE STARTED JUILLIARD WHEN SHE WAS SEVENTEEN.
SHE'D SKIPPED TWO GRADES IN ELEMENTARY SCHOOL.

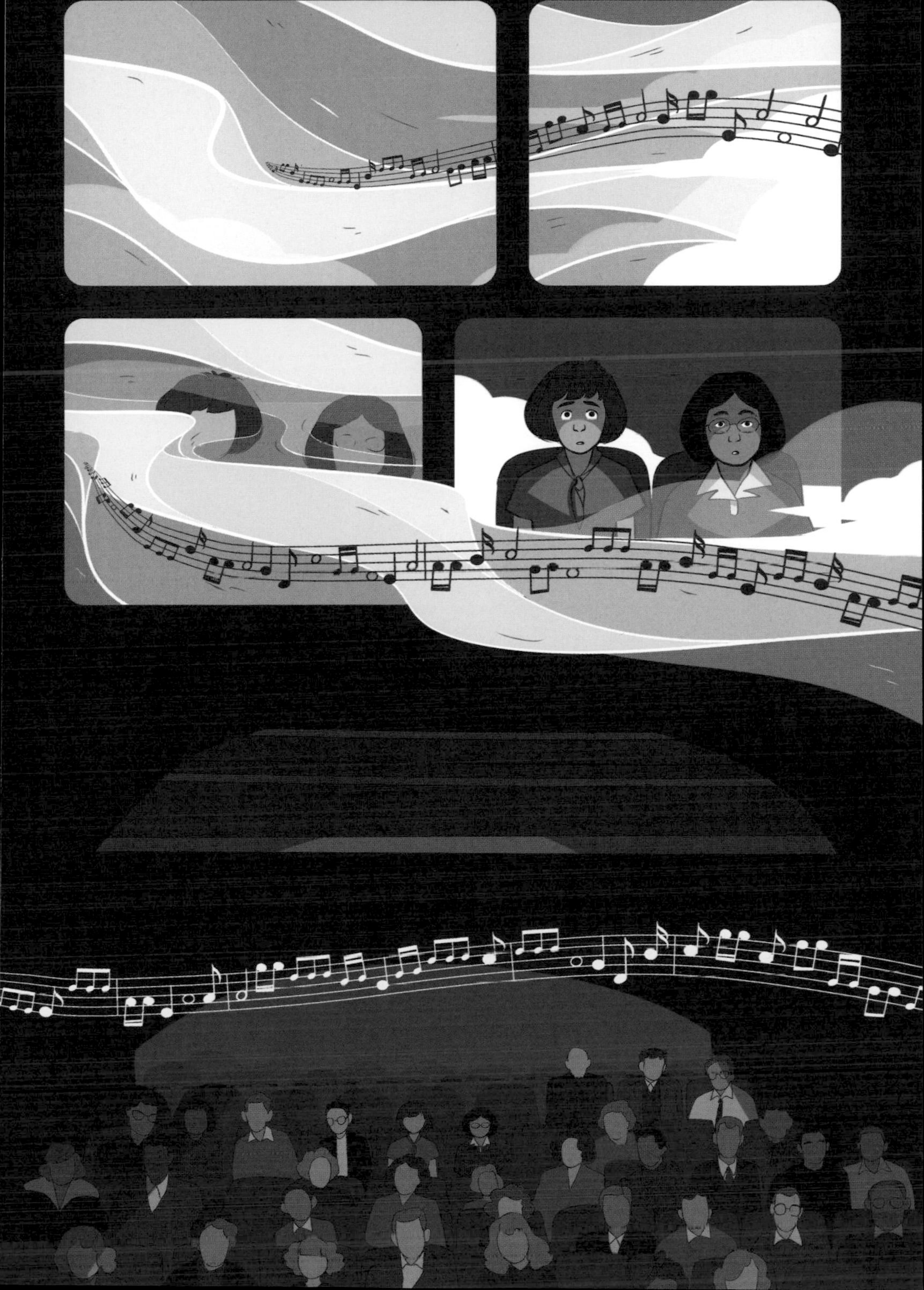

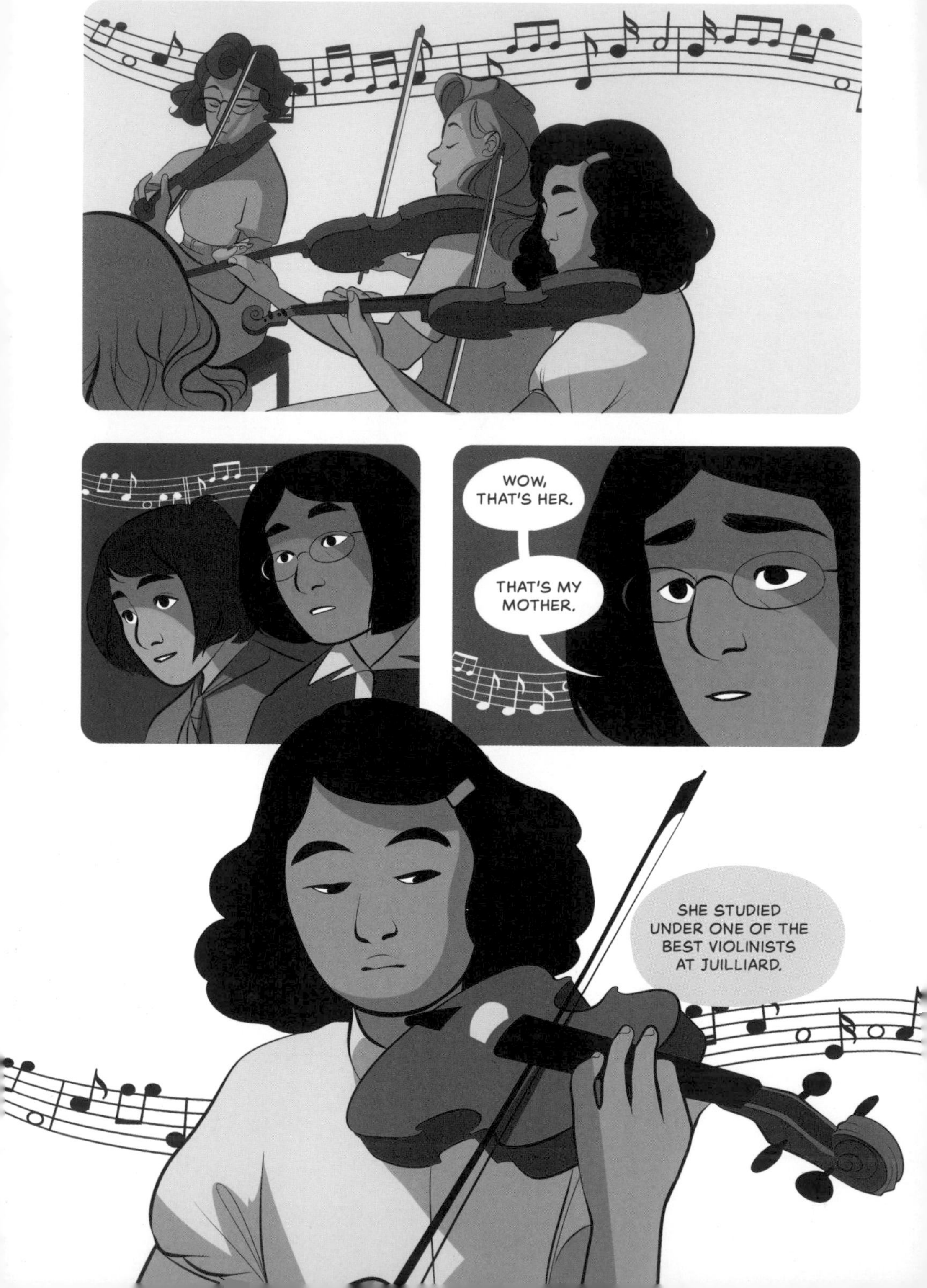
WOW, THAT'S HER.
THAT'S MY MOTHER.
SHE STUDIED UNDER ONE OF THE BEST VIOLINISTS AT JUILLIARD.

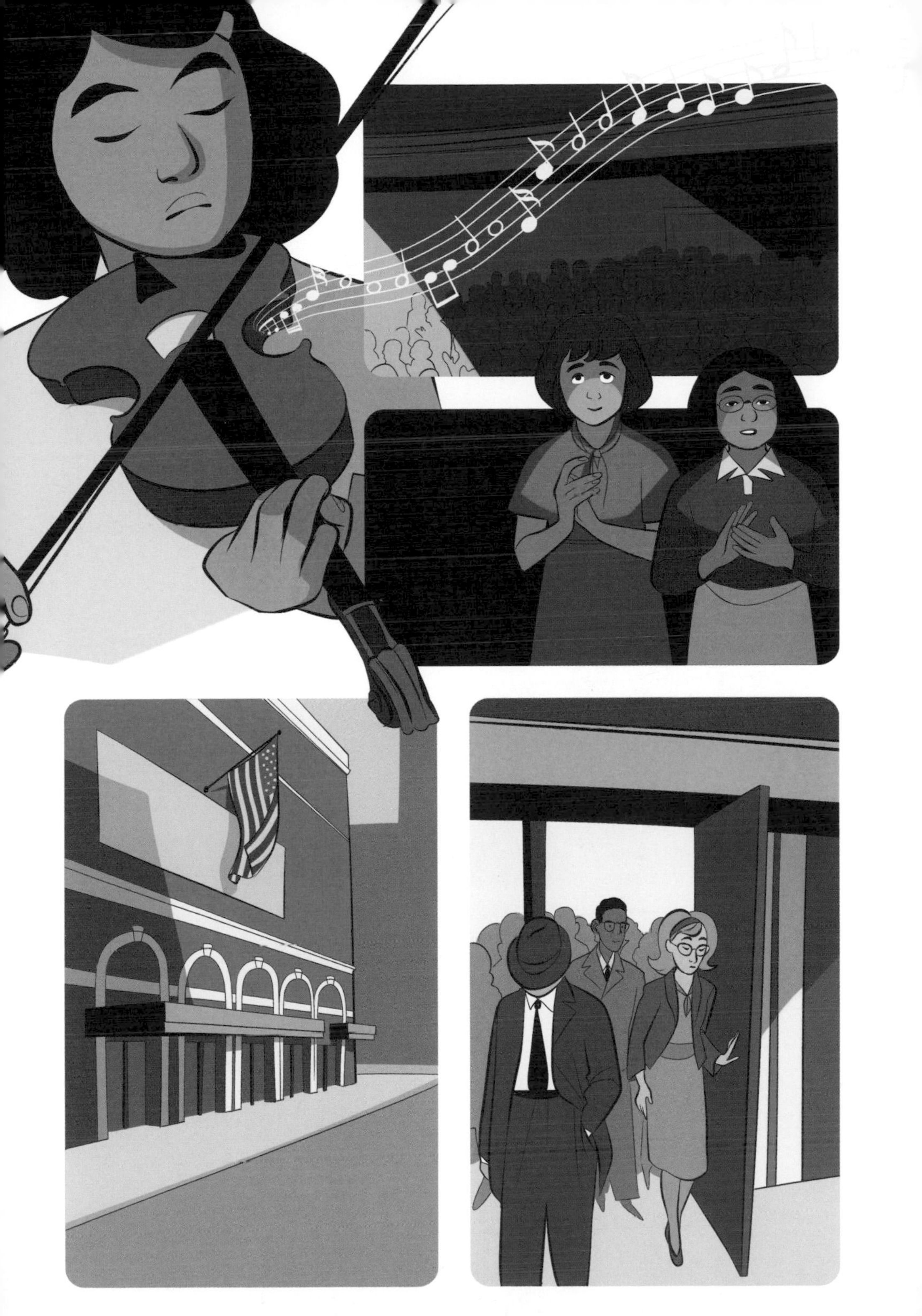

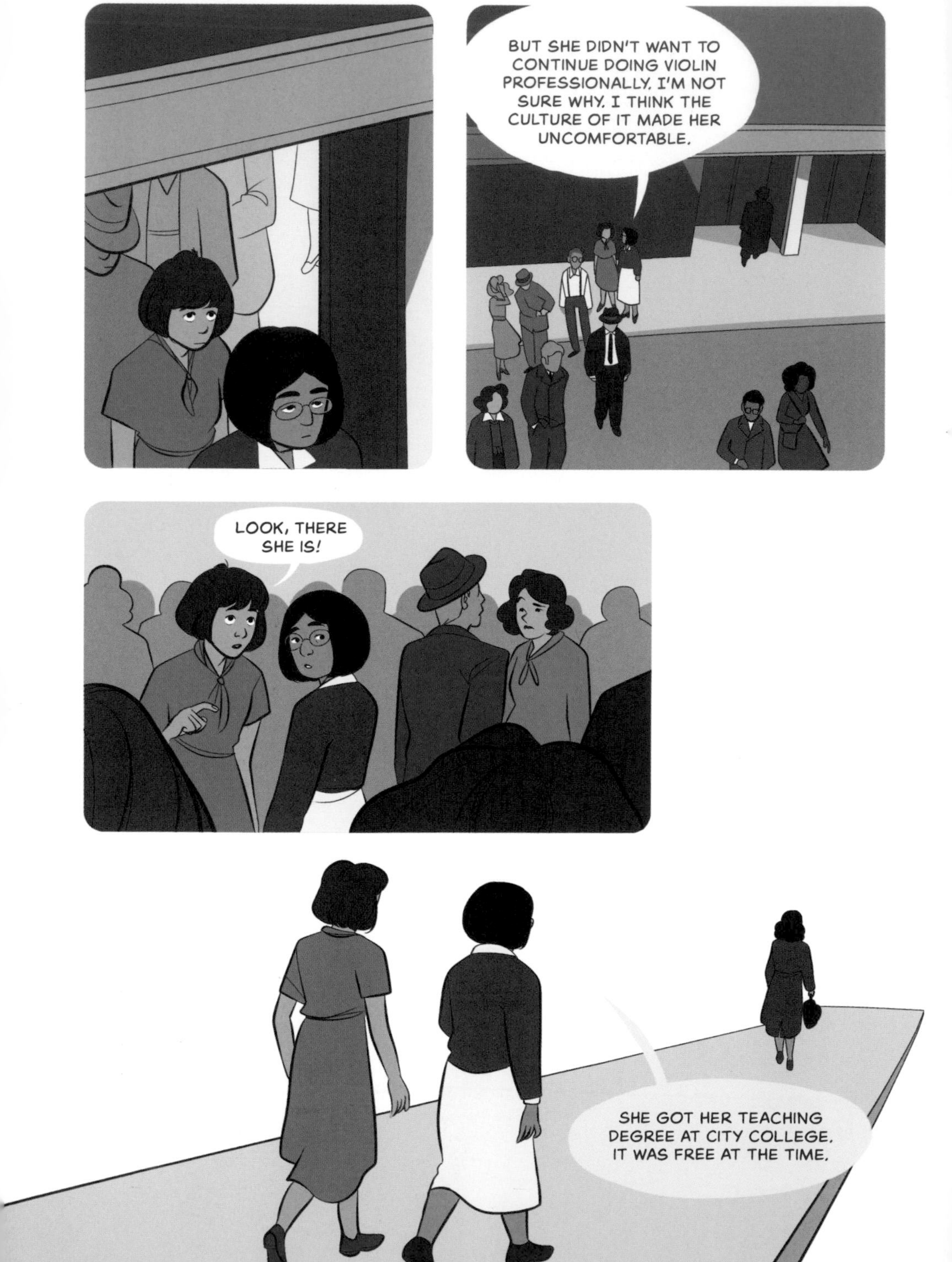
BUT SHE DIDN'T WANT TO CONTINUE DOING VIOLIN PROFESSIONALLY. I'M NOT SURE WHY. I THINK THE CULTURE OF IT MADE HER UNCOMFORTABLE.
LOOK, THERE SHE IS!
SHE GOT HER TEACHING DEGREE AT CITY COLLEGE. IT WAS FREE AT THE TIME.

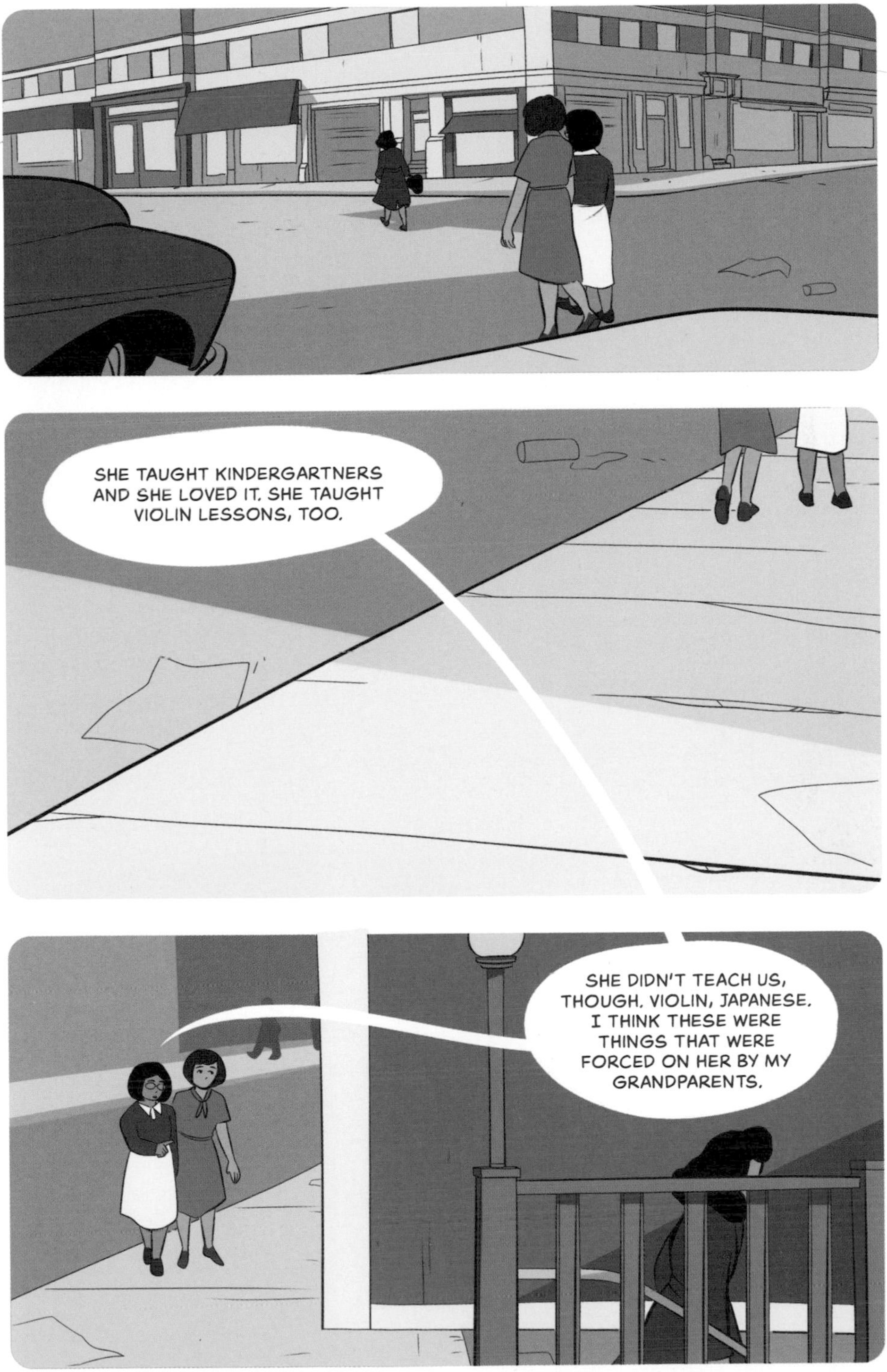
SHE TAUGHT KINDERGARTNERS AND SHE LOVED IT. SHE TAUGHT VIOLIN LESSONS, TOO.
SHE DIDN'T TEACH US, THOUGH. VIOLIN, JAPANESE. I THINK THESE WERE THINGS THAT WERE FORCED ON HER BY MY GRANDPARENTS.

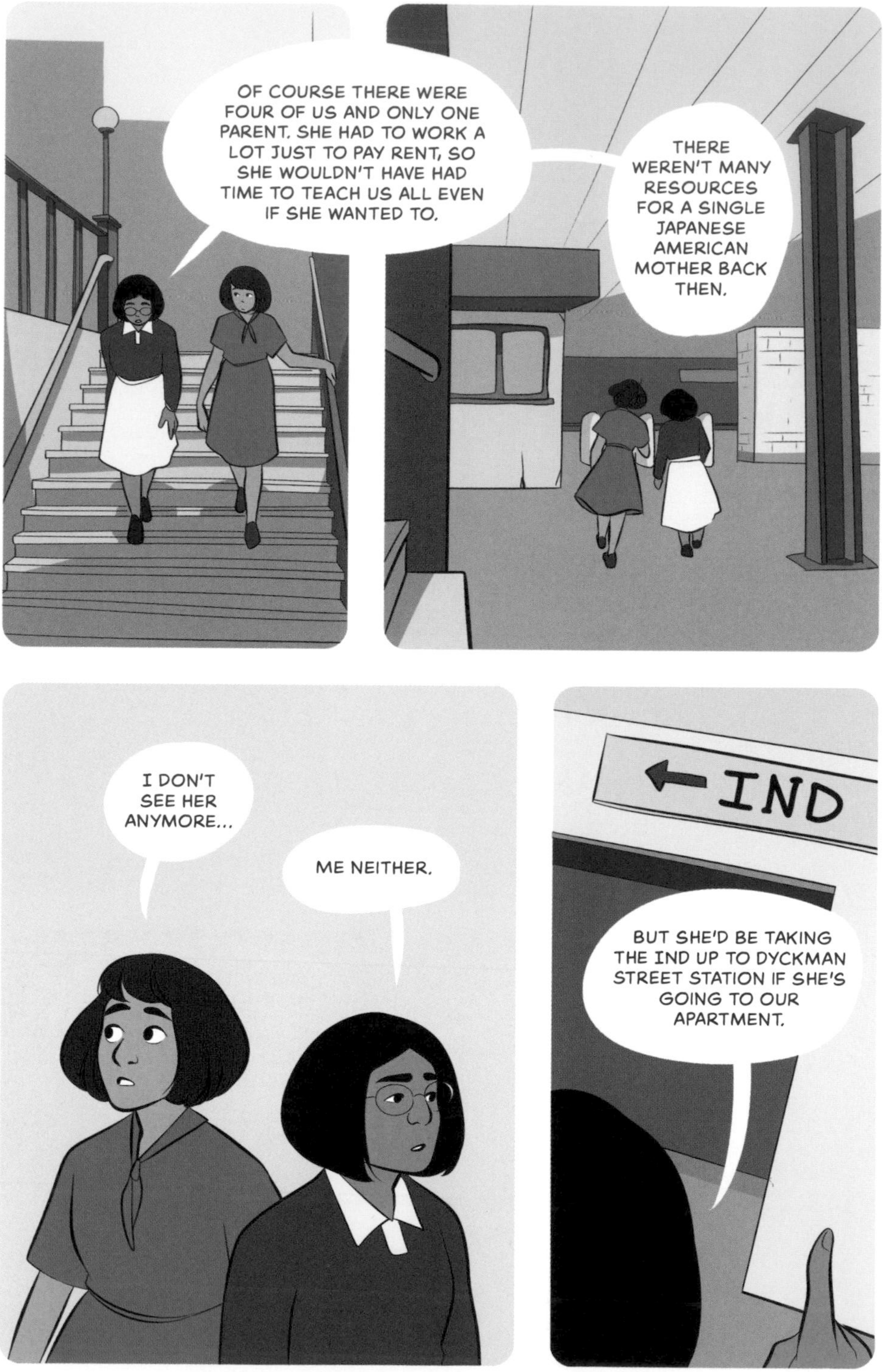
OF COURSE THERE WERE FOUR OF US AND ONLY ONE PARENT. SHE HAD TO WORK A LOT JUST TO PAY RENT, SO SHE WOULDN'T HAVE HAD TIME TO TEACH US ALL EVEN IF SHE WANTED TO.
THERE WEREN'T MANY RESOURCES FOR A SINGLE JAPANESE AMERICAN MOTHER BACK THEN.
I DON'T SEE HER ANYMORE...
ME NEITHER.
IND
BUT SHE'D BE TAKING THE IND UP TO DYCKMAN STREET STATION IF SHE'S GOING TO OUR APARTMENT.

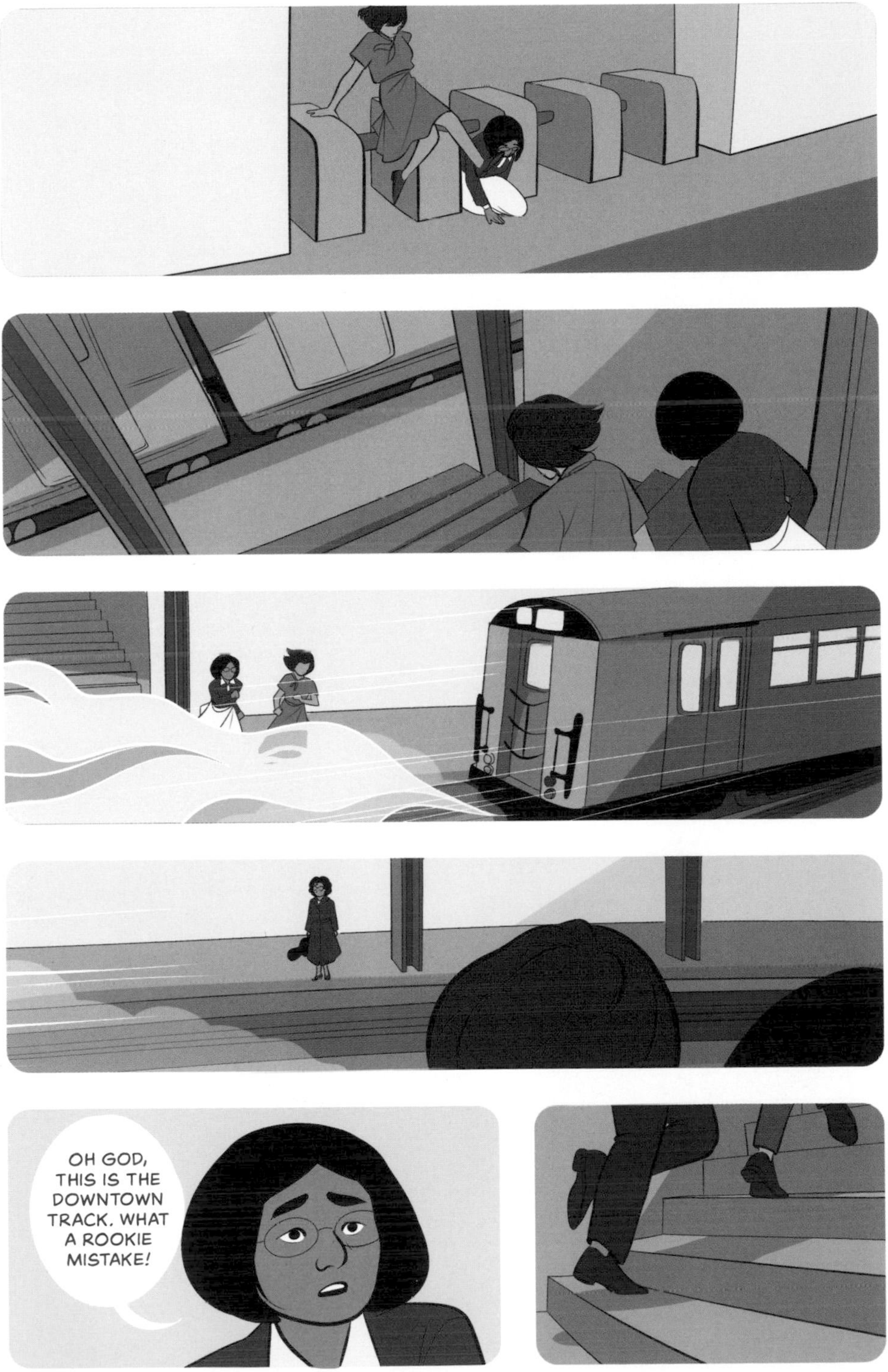
OH GOD, THIS IS THE DOWNTOWN TRACK. WHAT A ROOKIE MISTAKE!

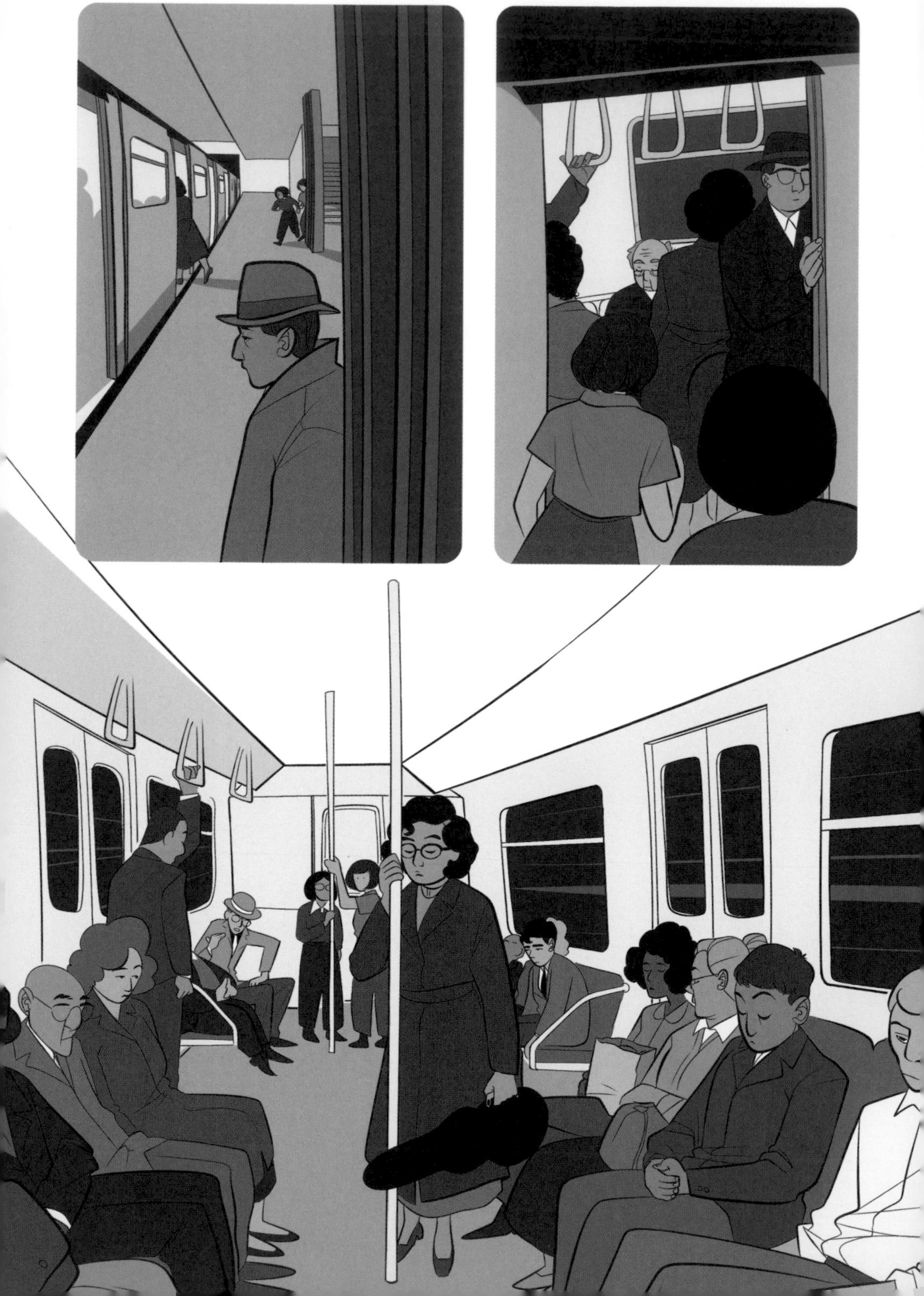

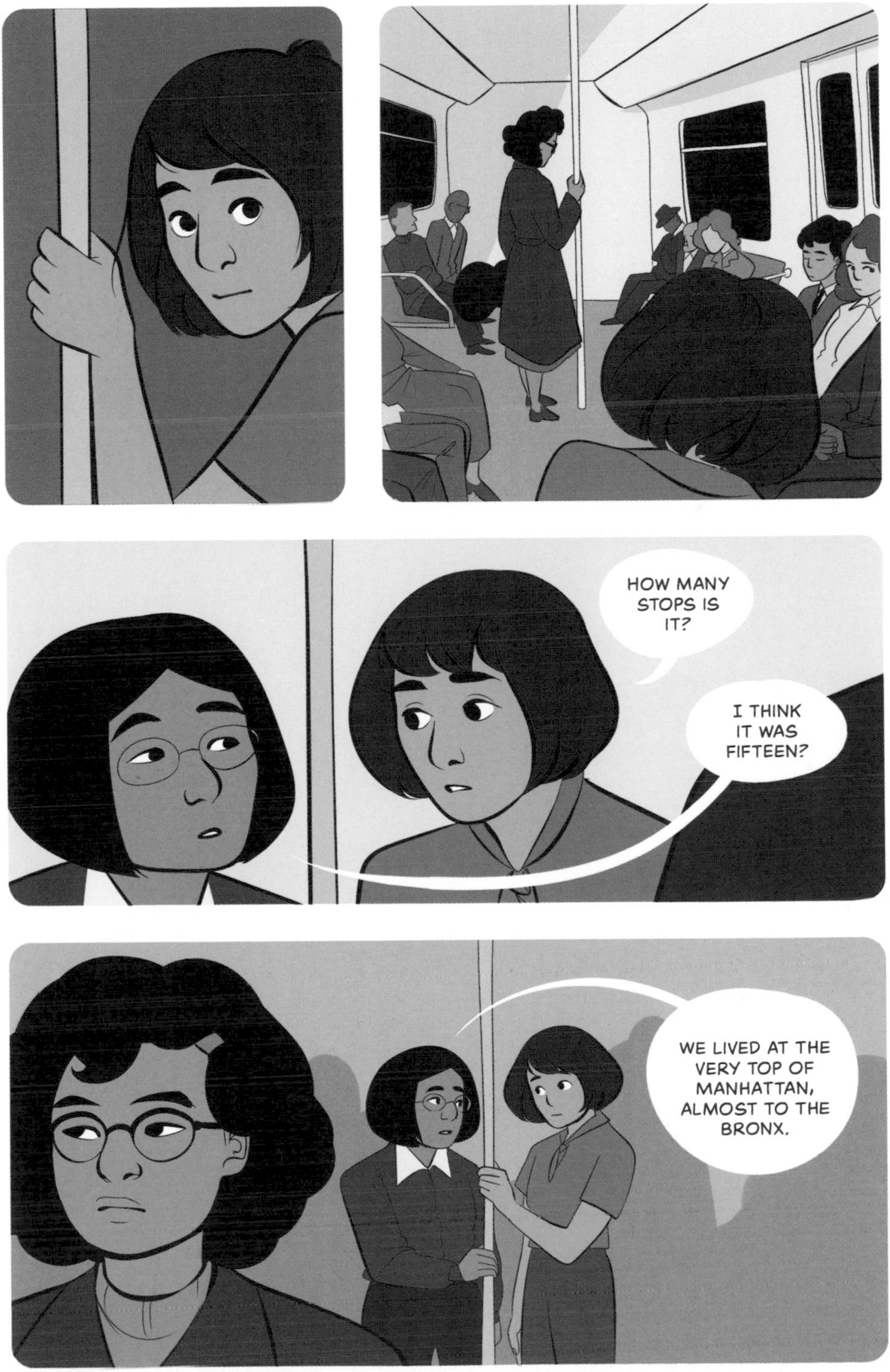
HOW MANY STOPS IS IT?
I THINK IT WAS FIFTEEN?
WE LIVED AT THE VERY TOP OF MANHATTAN, ALMOST TO THE BRONX.

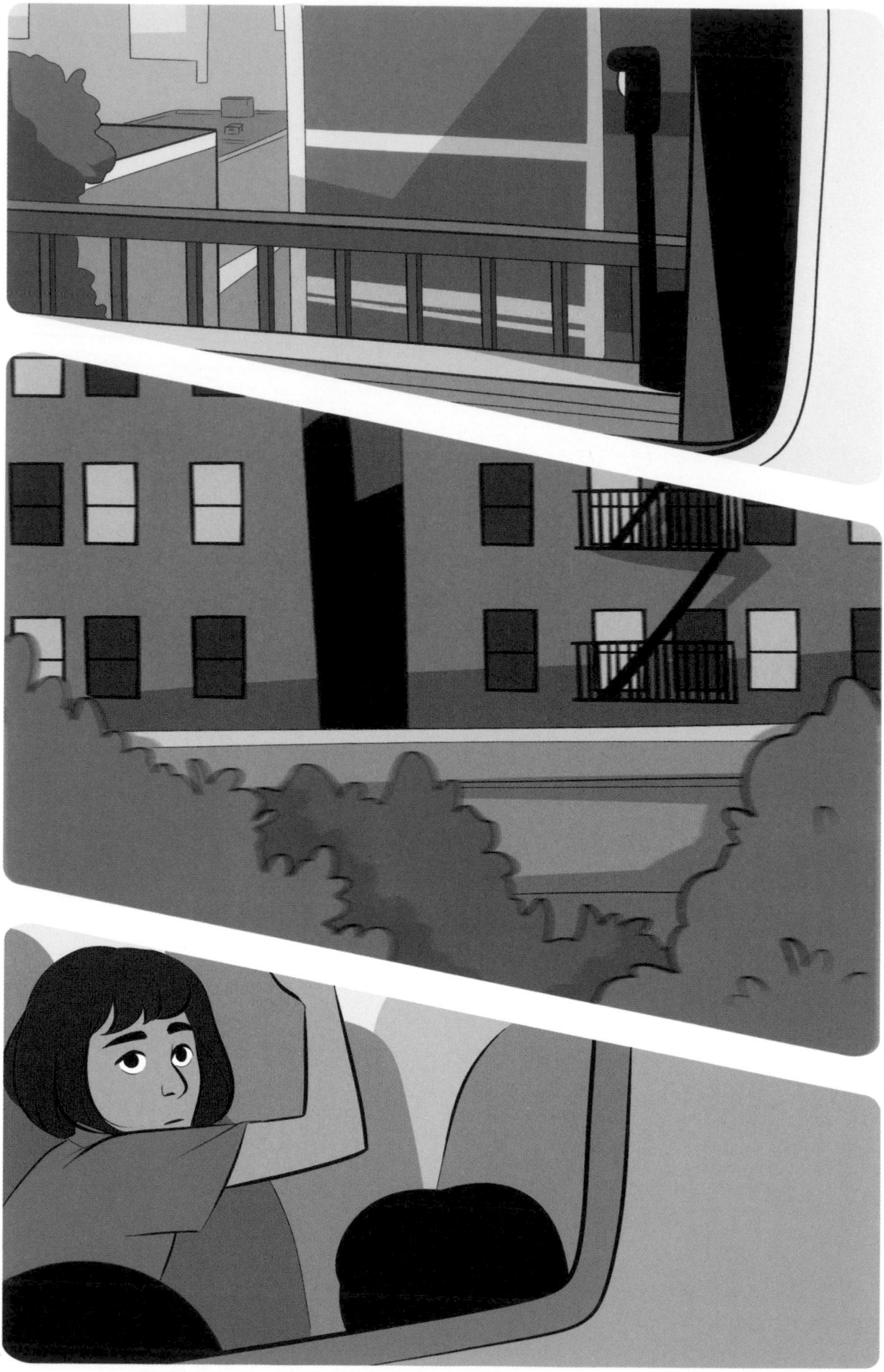

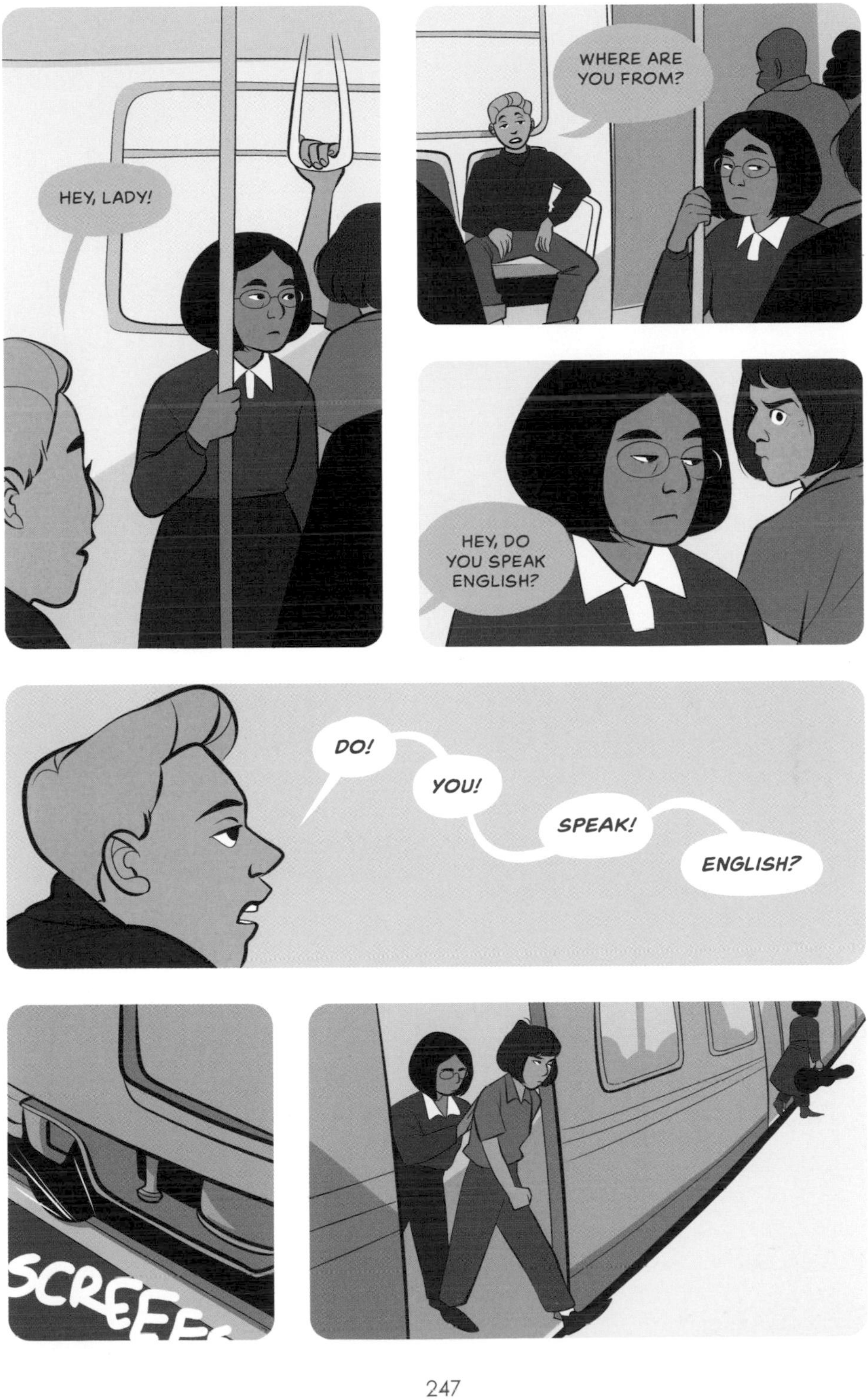
HEY, LADY!
WHERE ARE YOU FROM?
HEY, DO YOU SPEAK ENGLISH?
DO!
YOU!
SPEAK!
ENGLISH?
SCREEEE

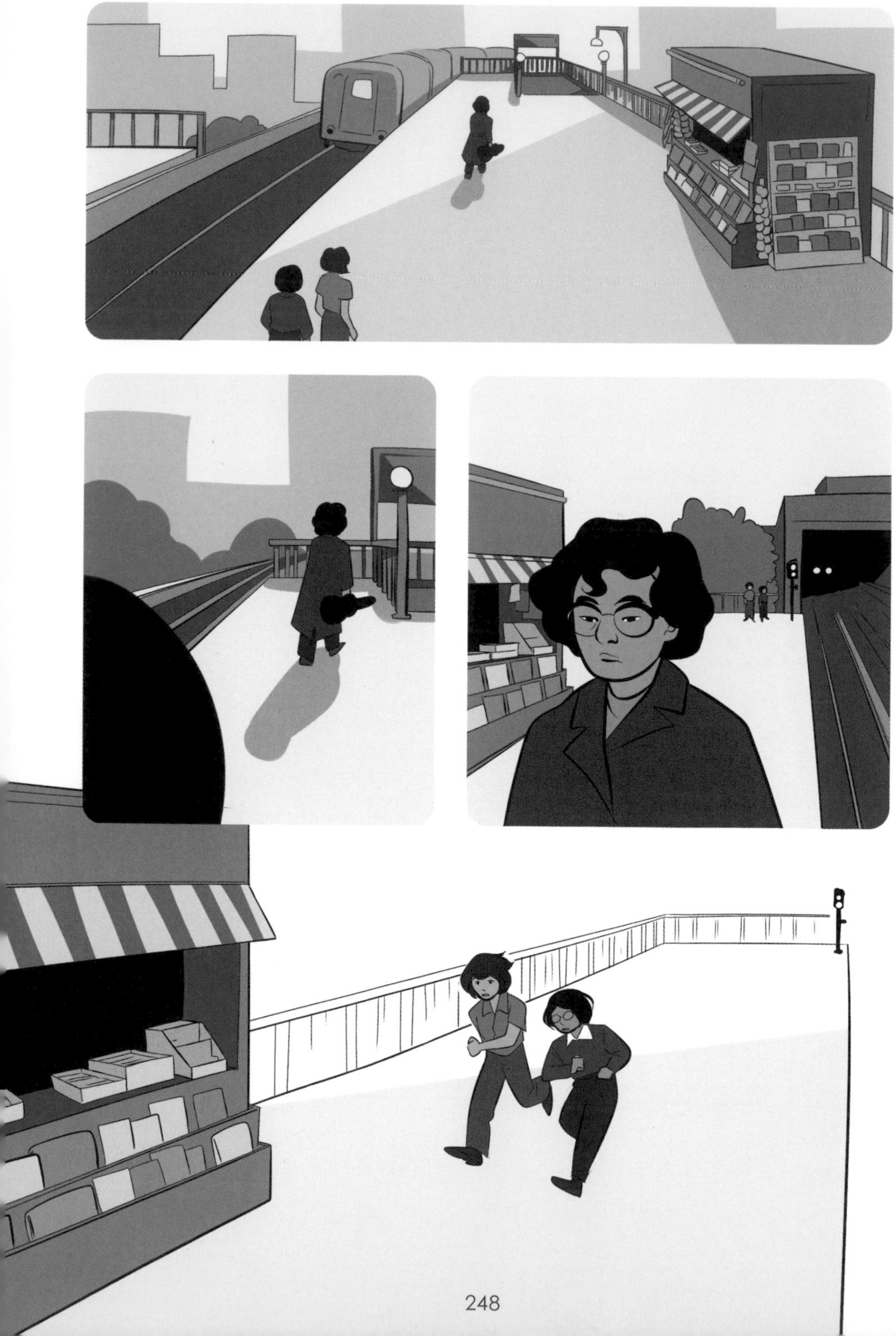

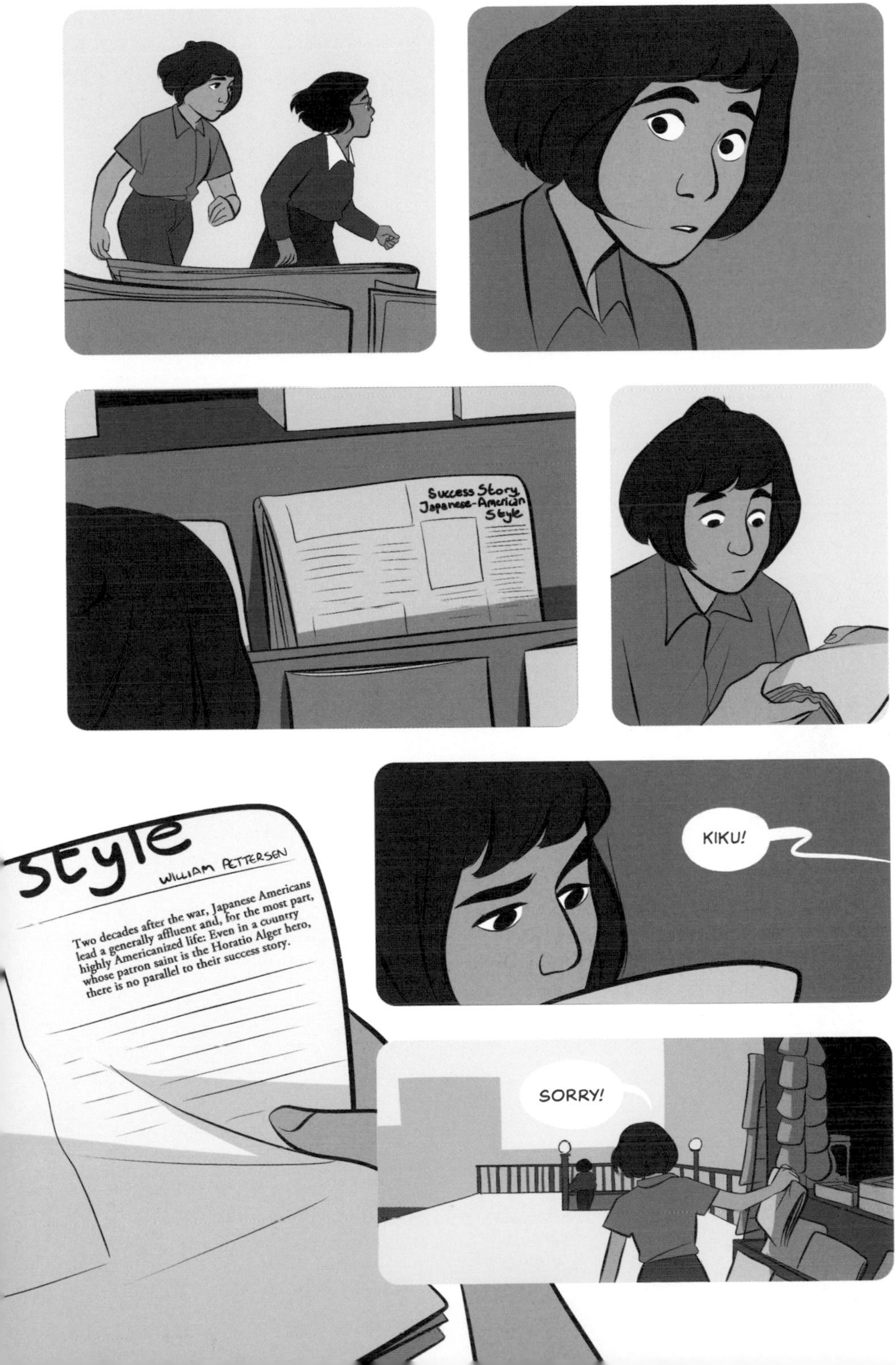
Success Story, Japanese-American Style
Style
WILLIAM PETTERSEN
Two decades after the war, Japanese Americans lead a generally affluent and, for the most part, highly Americanized life: Even in a country whose patron saint is the Horatio Alger hero, there is no parallel to their success story.
KIKU!
SORRY!

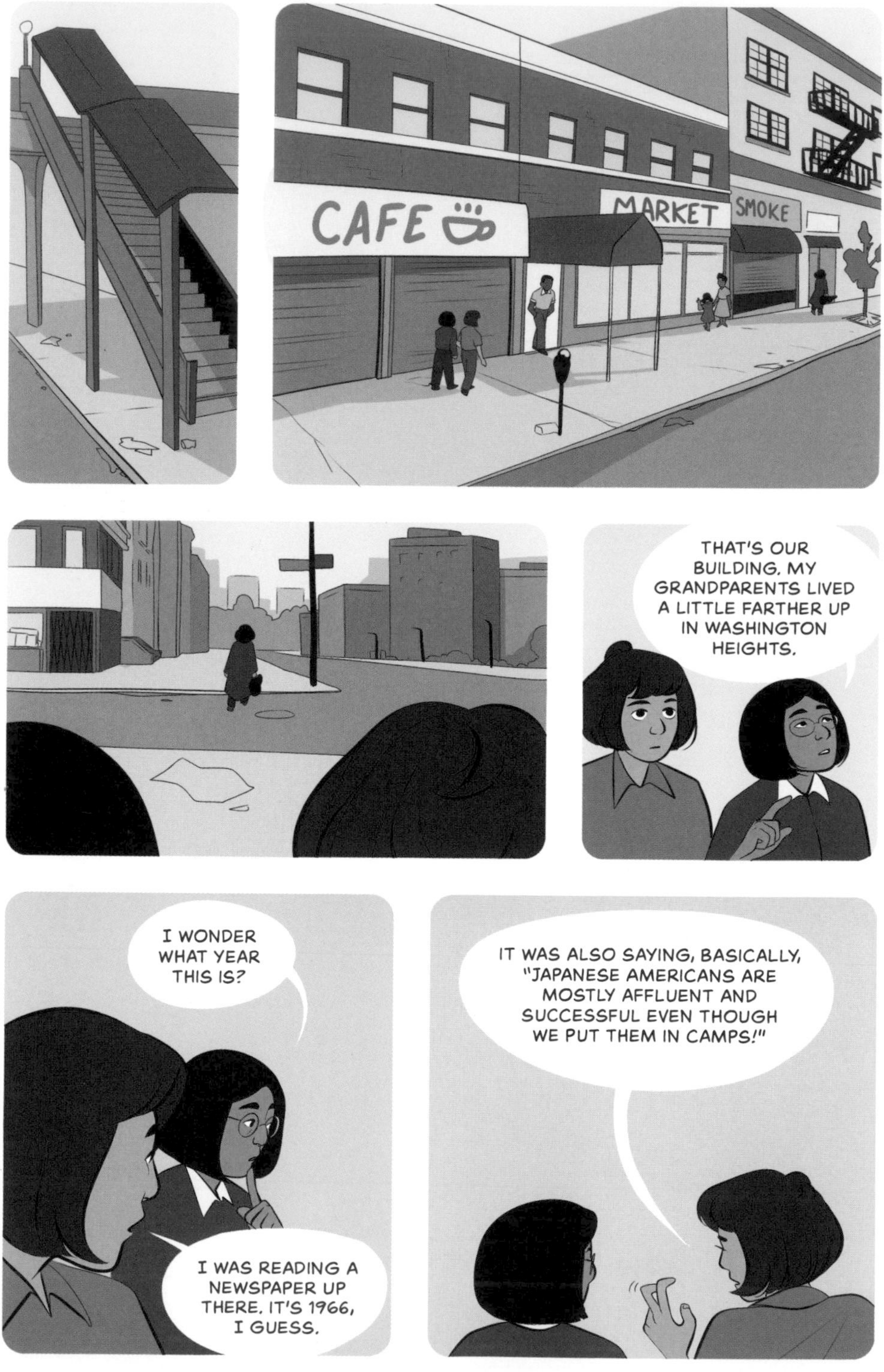
CAFE
MARKET
SMOKE
THAT'S OUR BUILDING. MY GRANDPARENTS LIVED A LITTLE FARTHER UP IN WASHINGTON HEIGHTS.
I WONDER WHAT YEAR THIS IS?
I WAS READING A NEWSPAPER UP THERE. IT'S 1966, I GUESS.
IT WAS ALSO SAYING, BASICALLY, "JAPANESE AMERICANS ARE MOSTLY AFFLUENT AND SUCCESSFUL EVEN THOUGH WE PUT THEM IN CAMPS!"

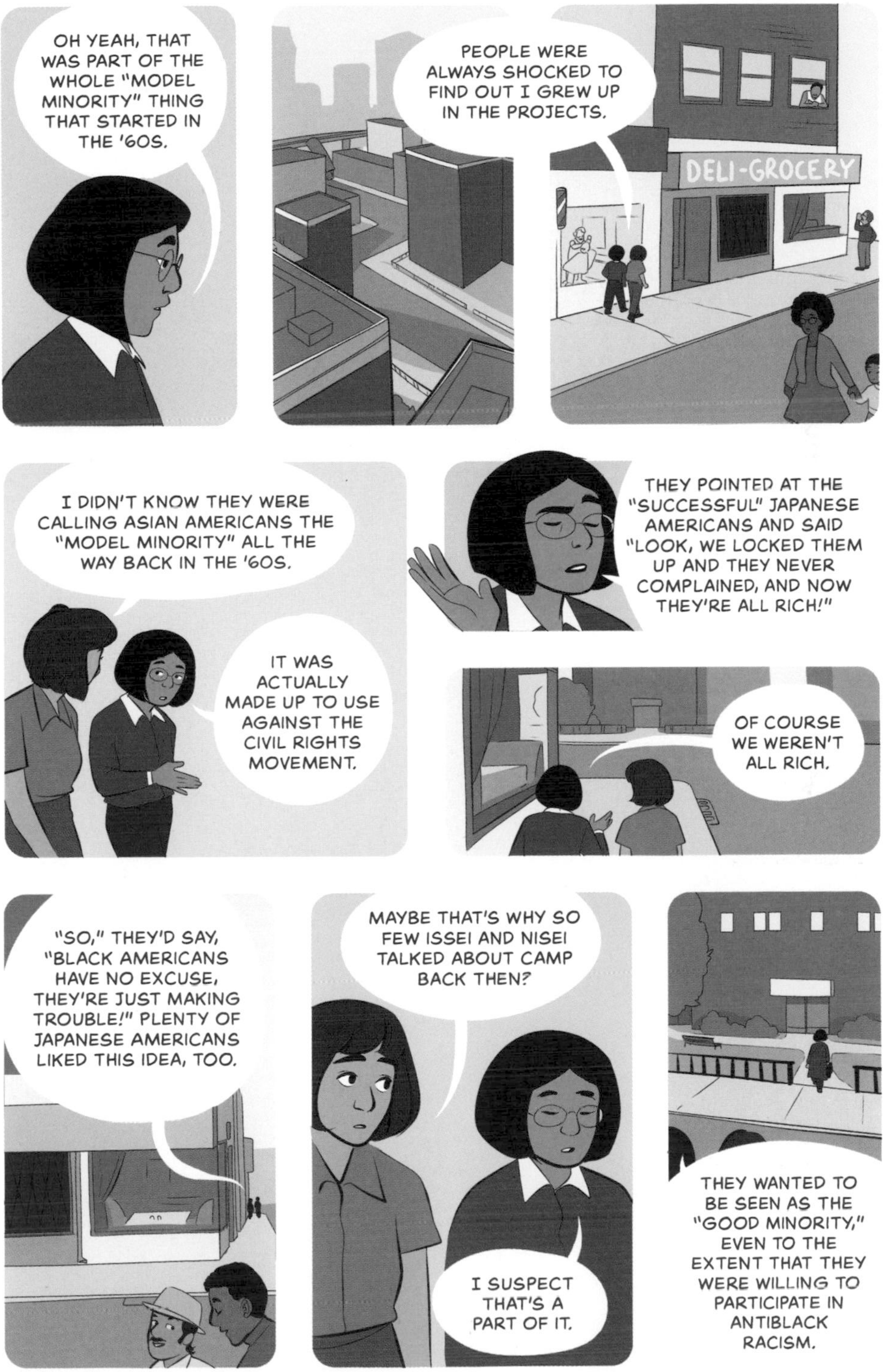
OH YEAH, THAT WAS PART OF THE WHOLE "MODEL MINORITY" THING THAT STARTED IN THE '60S.
PEOPLE WERE ALWAYS SHOCKED TO FIND OUT I GREW UP IN THE PROJECTS.
DELI-GROCERY
I DIDN'T KNOW THEY WERE CALLING ASIAN AMERICANS THE "MODEL MINORITY" ALL THE WAY BACK IN THE '60S.
IT WAS ACTUALLY MADE UP TO USE AGAINST THE CIVIL RIGHTS MOVEMENT.
THEY POINTED AT THE "SUCCESSFUL" JAPANESE AMERICANS AND SAID "LOOK, WE LOCKED THEM UP AND THEY NEVER COMPLAINED, AND NOW THEY'RE ALL RICH!"
OF COURSE WE WEREN'T ALL RICH.
"SO," THEY'D SAY, "BLACK AMERICANS HAVE NO EXCUSE, THEY'RE JUST MAKING TROUBLE!" PLENTY OF JAPANESE AMERICANS LIKED THIS IDEA, TOO.
MAYBE THAT'S WHY SO FEW ISSEI AND NISEI TALKED ABOUT CAMP BACK THEN?
I SUSPECT THAT'S A PART OF IT.
THEY WANTED TO BE SEEN AS THE "GOOD MINORITY," EVEN TO THE EXTENT THAT THEY WERE WILLING TO PARTICIPATE IN ANTIBLACK RACISM.

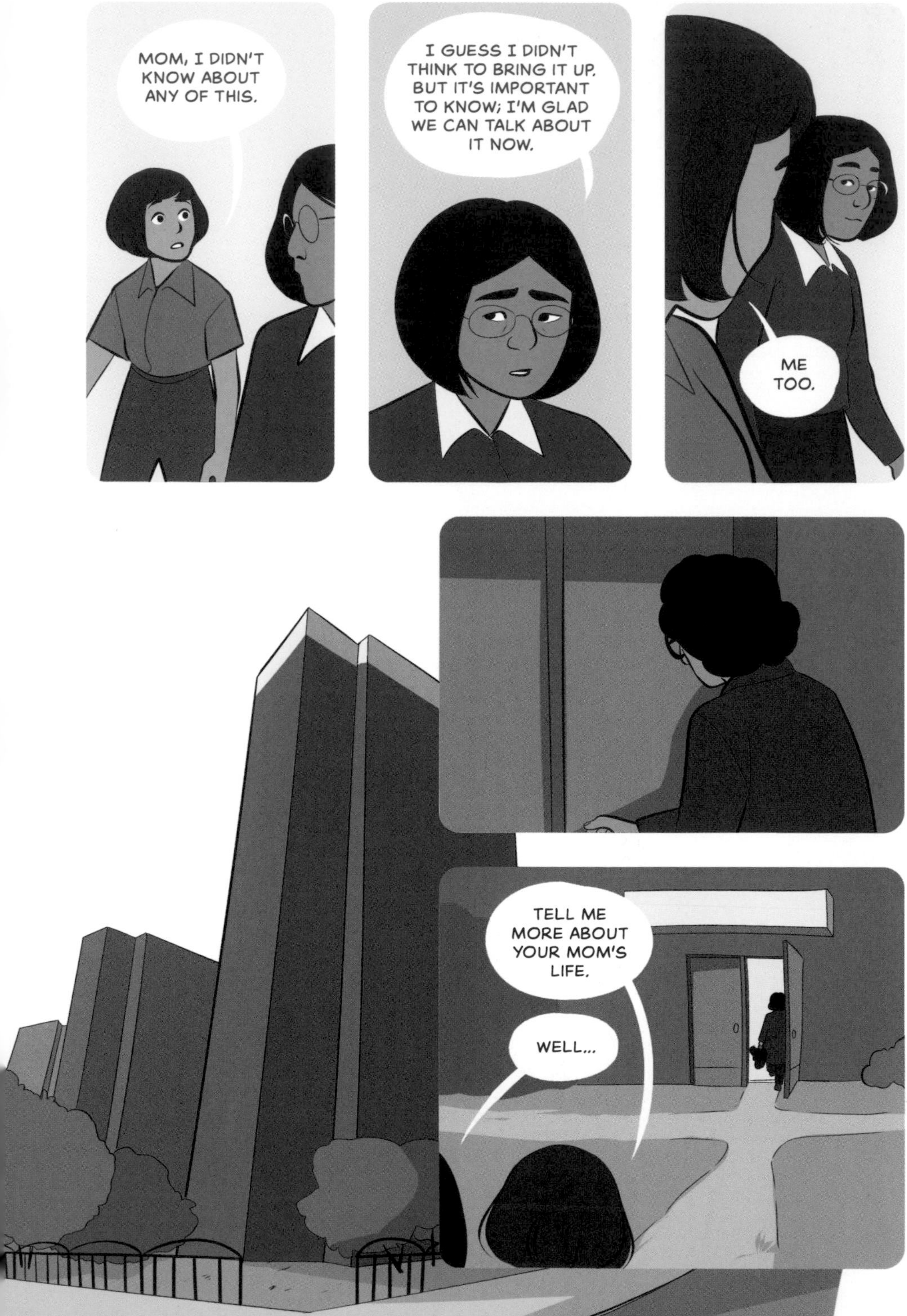
MOM, I DIDN'T KNOW ABOUT ANY OF THIS.
I GUESS I DIDN'T THINK TO BRING IT UP. BUT IT'S IMPORTANT TO KNOW; I'M GLAD WE CAN TALK ABOUT IT NOW.
ME TOO.
TELL ME MORE ABOUT YOUR MOM'S LIFE.
WELL...

SHE CONTINUED TEACHING, AND SHE MARRIED MY STEPFATHER IN 1966. WE MOVED TO NEW JERSEY BECAUSE OF HIM. WE WERE THE ONLY PEOPLE OF COLOR IN OUR TOWN.

SHE WAS DIAGNOSED WITH LEUKEMIA JUST A COUPLE YEARS LATER, AS I WAS FINISHING HIGH SCHOOL.

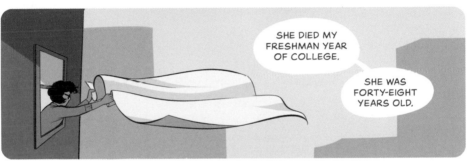

SHE DIED MY FRESHMAN YEAR OF COLLEGE.

SHE WAS FORTY-EIGHT YEARS OLD.

I DIDN'T KNOW SHE WAS SO YOUNG.

SHE WAS VERY YOUNG.

WE DIDN'T KNOW WHY; CANCER IS ALWAYS HARD TO UNDERSTAND. BUT I ALWAYS KIND OF SUSPECTED THAT HER TIME IN CAMP MADE HER SICK.

TOPAZ WAS IN THE SOUTHWEST, WHERE THEY WERE DOING NUCLEAR BOMB TESTS, TOO. OR, I DON'T KNOW, MAYBE IT WAS JUST THE STRESS OF IT ALL.

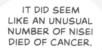
IT DID SEEM LIKE AN UNUSUAL NUMBER OF NISEI DIED OF CANCER.

MAYBE THAT'S JUST RUMOR, THOUGH. IT'S NOT AS THOUGH IT WAS STUDIED.

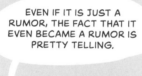
EVEN IF IT IS JUST A RUMOR, THE FACT THAT IT EVEN BECAME A RUMOR IS PRETTY TELLING.

RUMORS START WHEN THERE'S FEAR AND A LACK OF INFORMATION.

AND THEY STICK AROUND AND INFLUENCE OUR MEMORIES FOREVER.

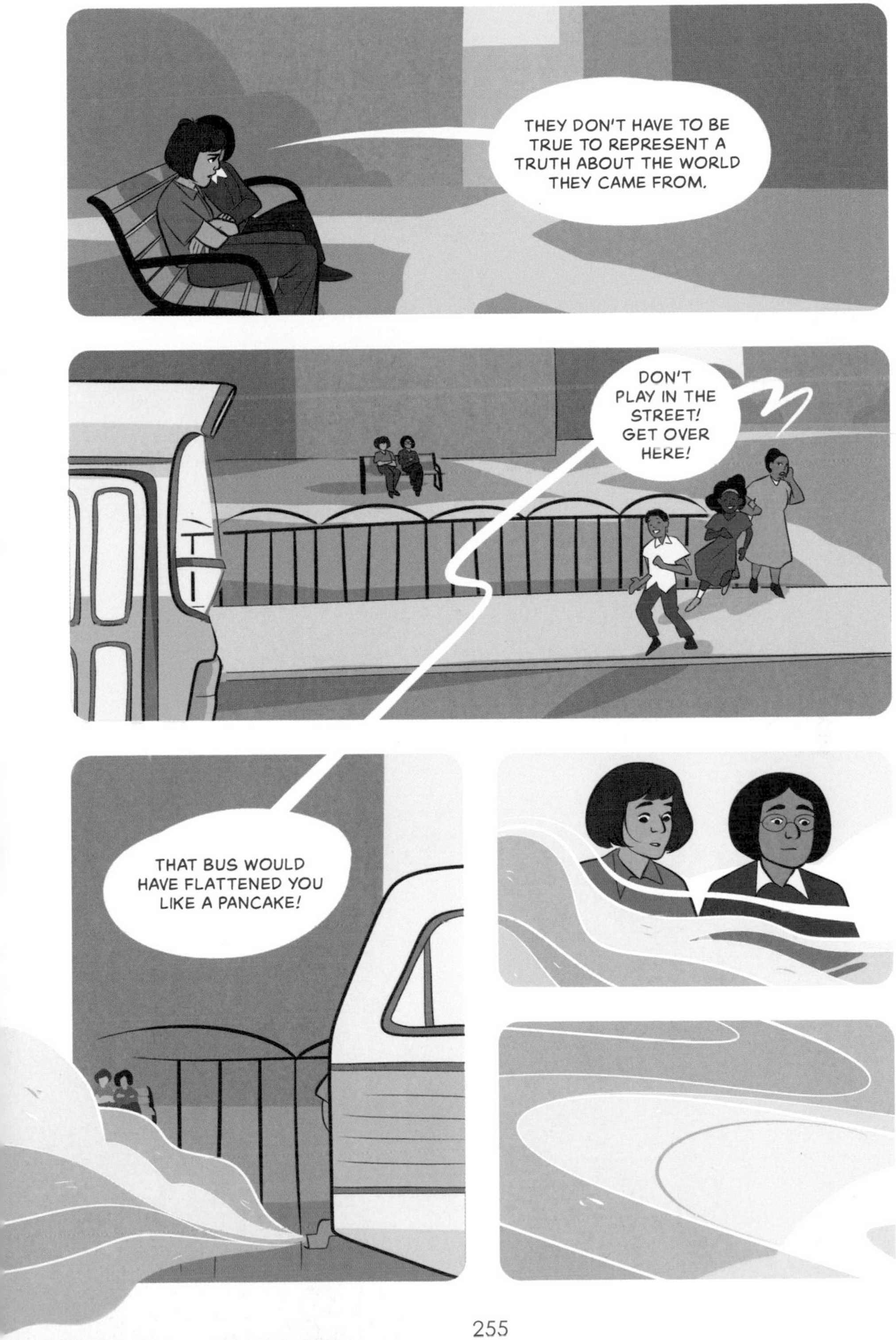
THEY DON'T HAVE TO BE TRUE TO REPRESENT A TRUTH ABOUT THE WORLD THEY CAME FROM.
DON'T PLAY IN THE STREET! GET OVER HERE!
THAT BUS WOULD HAVE FLATTENED YOU LIKE A PANCAKE!

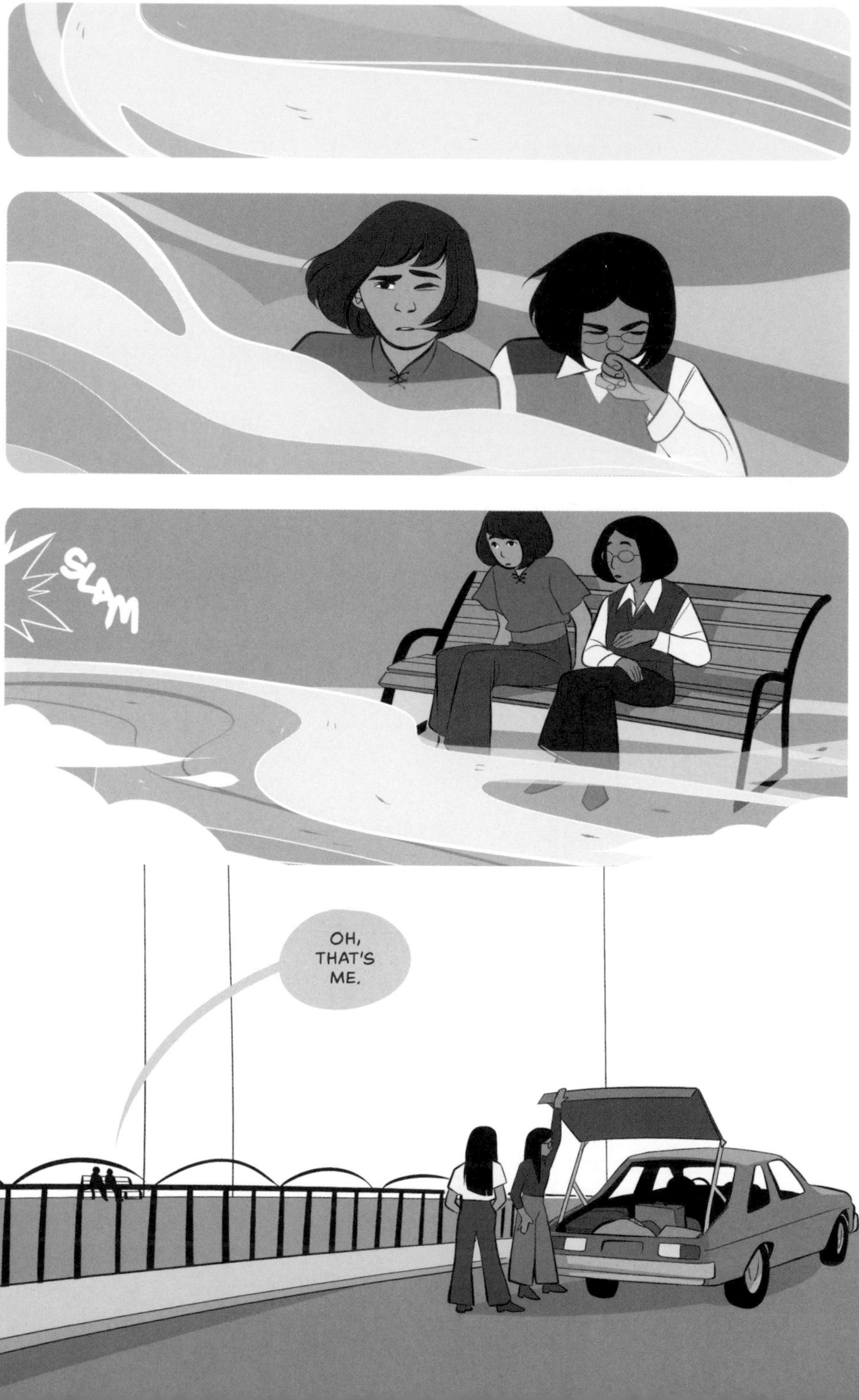
SLAM
OH, THAT'S ME.

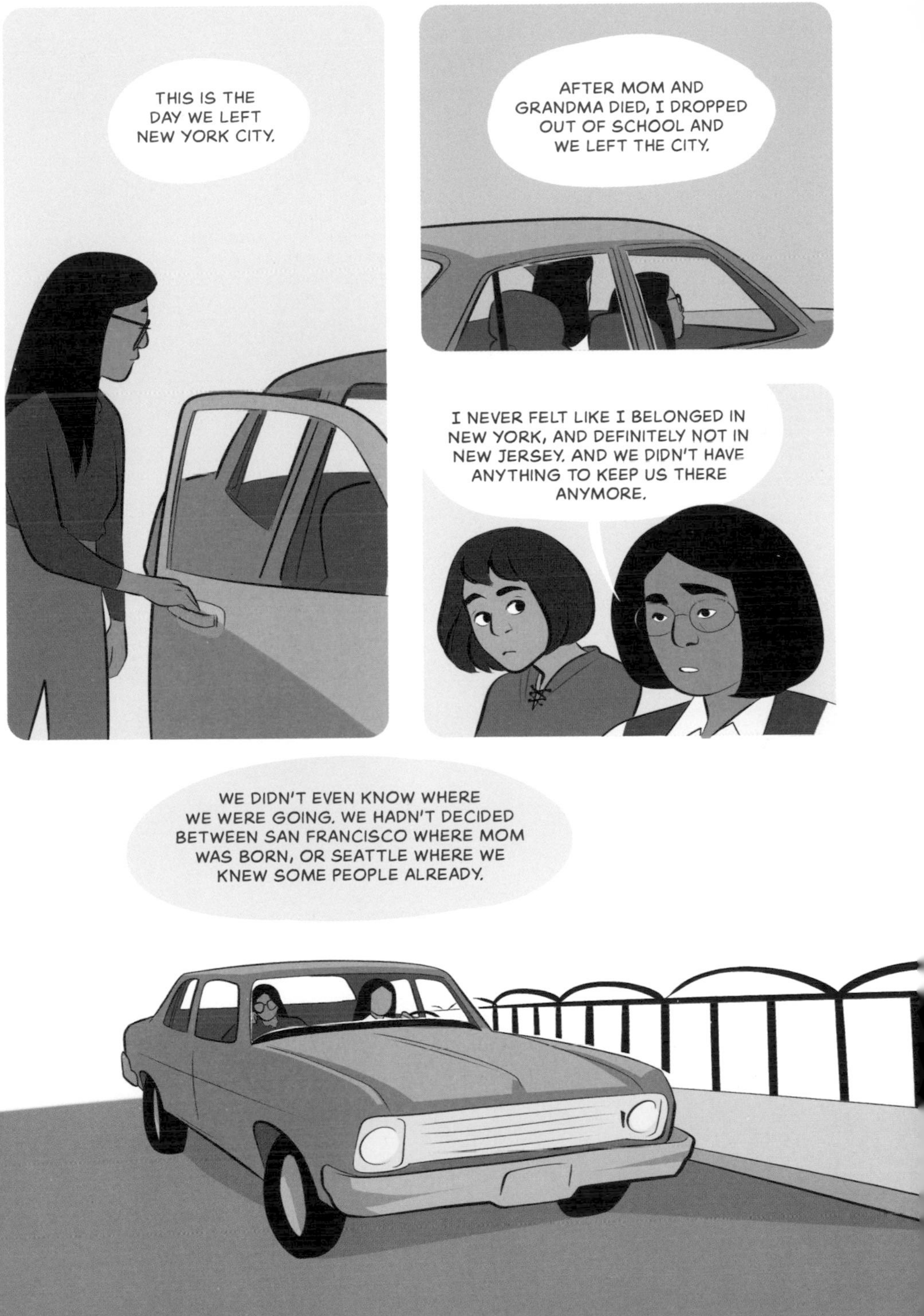
THIS IS THE DAY WE LEFT NEW YORK CITY.
AFTER MOM AND GRANDMA DIED, I DROPPED OUT OF SCHOOL AND WE LEFT THE CITY.
I NEVER FELT LIKE I BELONGED IN NEW YORK, AND DEFINITELY NOT IN NEW JERSEY. AND WE DIDN'T HAVE ANYTHING TO KEEP US THERE ANYMORE.
WE DIDN'T EVEN KNOW WHERE WE WERE GOING. WE HADN'T DECIDED BETWEEN SAN FRANCISCO WHERE MOM WAS BORN, OR SEATTLE WHERE WE KNEW SOME PEOPLE ALREADY.

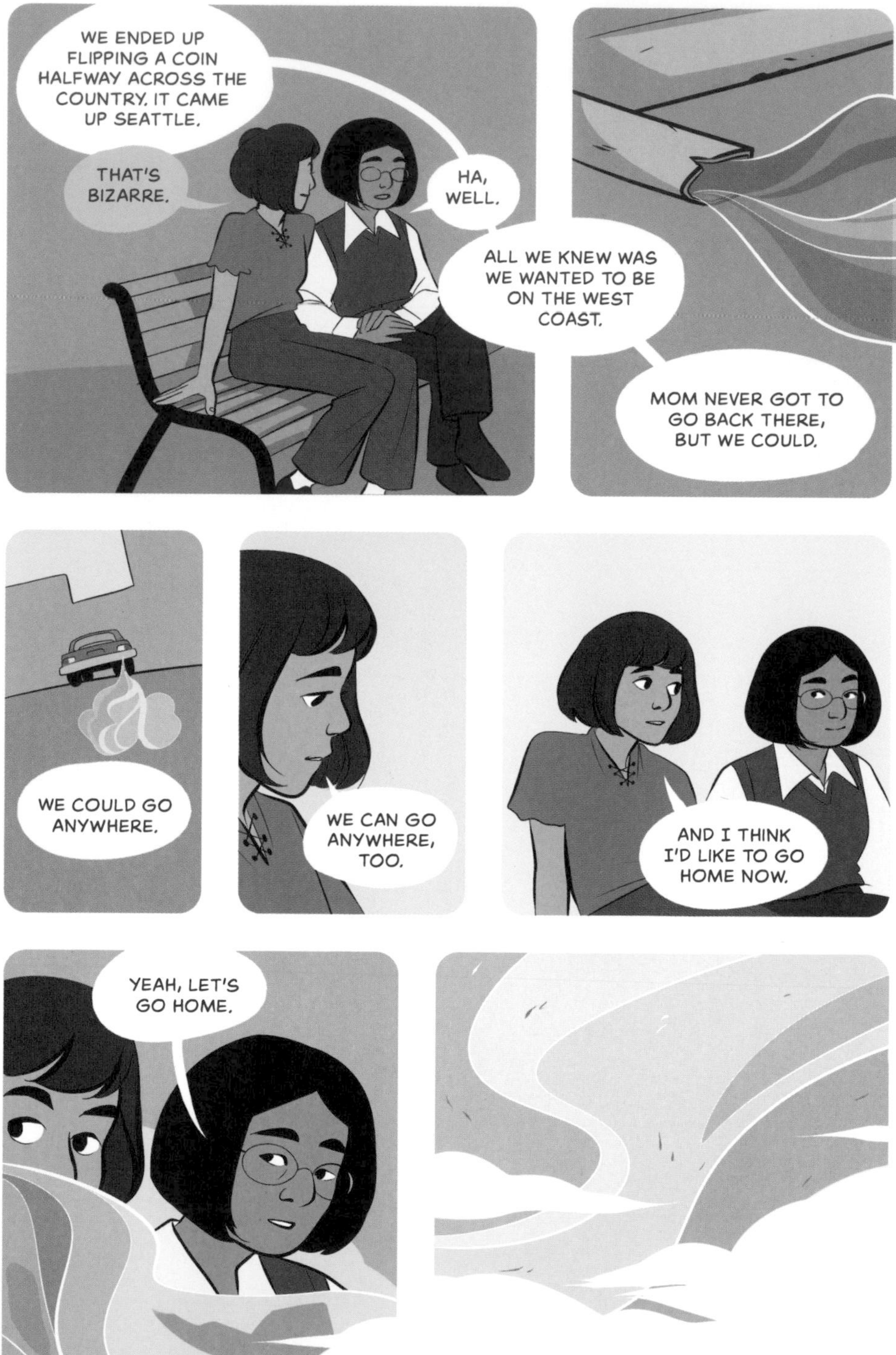
WE ENDED UP FLIPPING A COIN HALFWAY ACROSS THE COUNTRY. IT CAME UP SEATTLE.
THAT'S BIZARRE.
HA, WELL.
ALL WE KNEW WAS WE WANTED TO BE ON THE WEST COAST.
MOM NEVER GOT TO GO BACK THERE, BUT WE COULD.
WE COULD GO ANYWHERE.
WE CAN GO ANYWHERE, TOO.
AND I THINK I'D LIKE TO GO HOME NOW.
YEAH, LET'S GO HOME.

part IV:
home

10

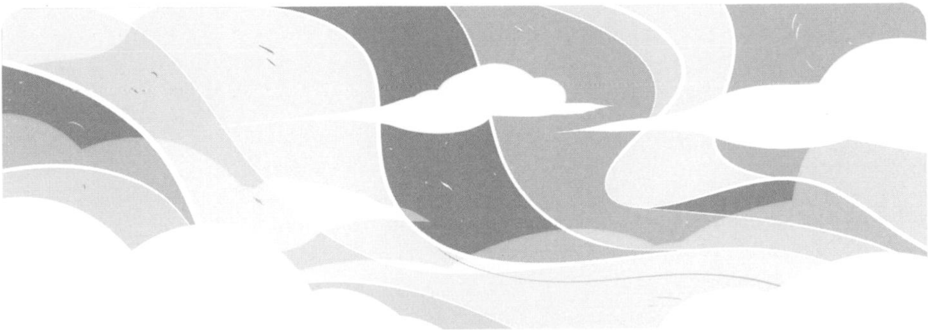

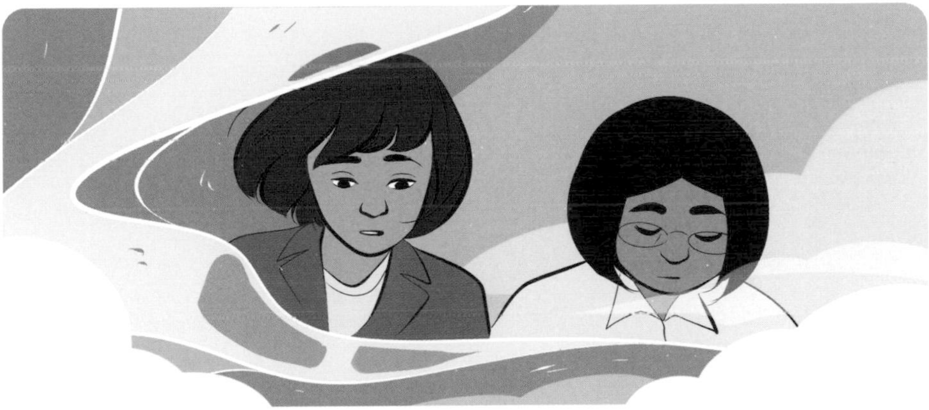

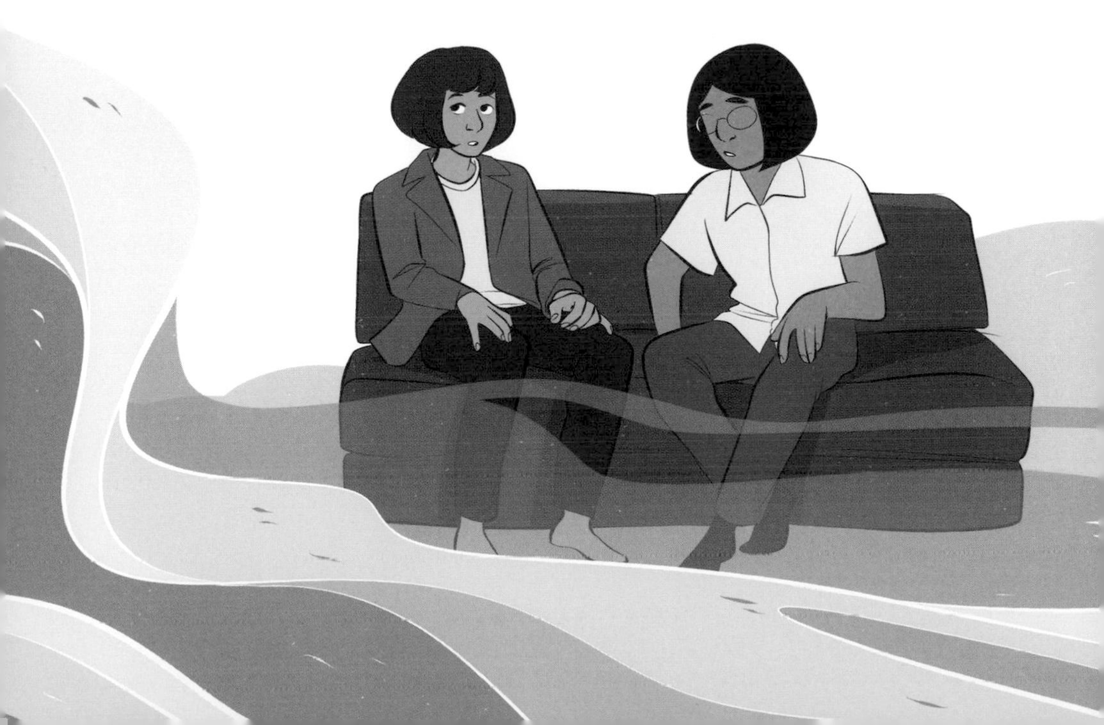

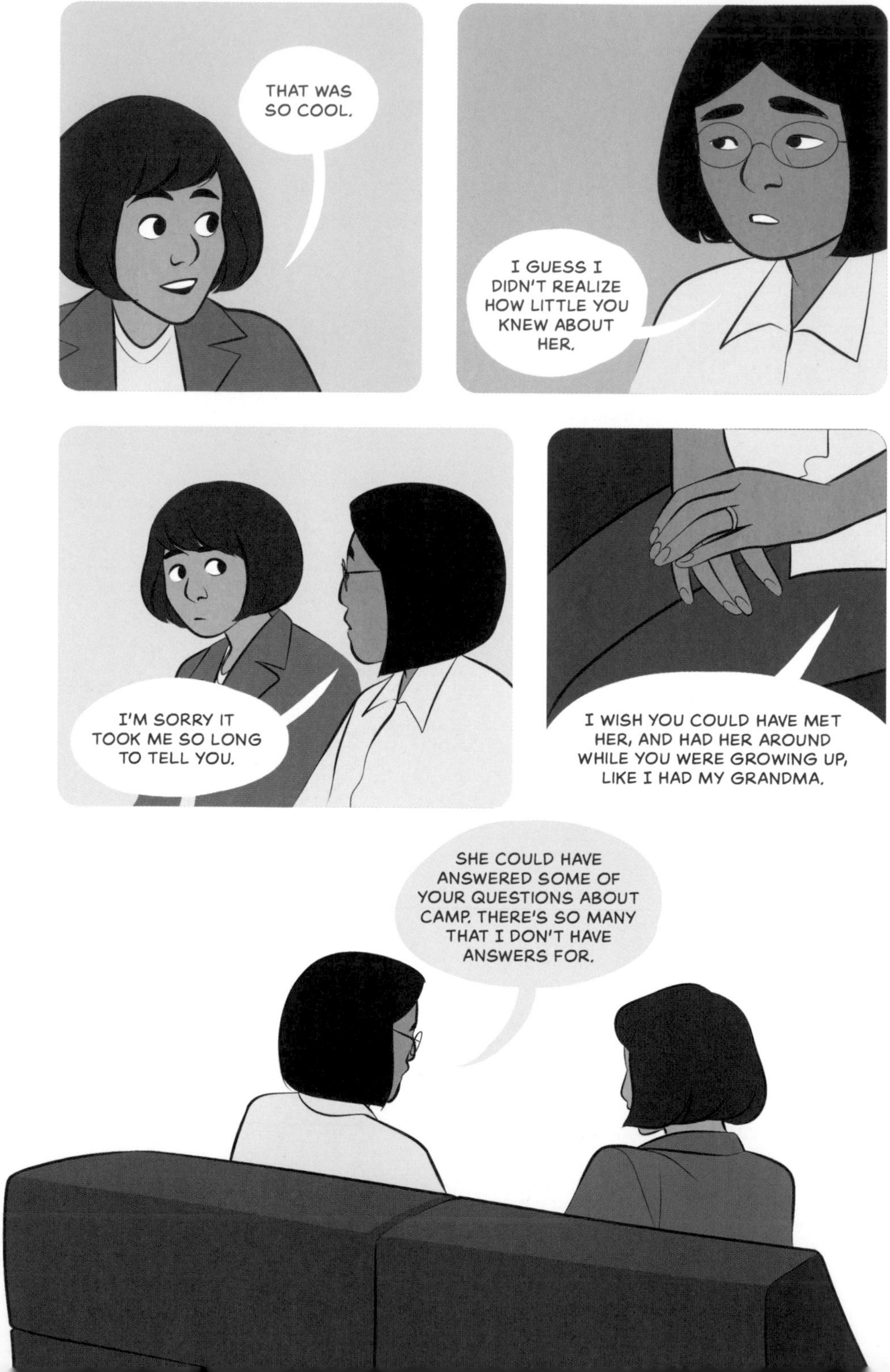
THAT WAS SO COOL.
I GUESS I DIDN'T REALIZE HOW LITTLE YOU KNEW ABOUT HER.
I'M SORRY IT TOOK ME SO LONG TO TELL YOU.
I WISH YOU COULD HAVE MET HER, AND HAD HER AROUND WHILE YOU WERE GROWING UP, LIKE I HAD MY GRANDMA.
SHE COULD HAVE ANSWERED SOME OF YOUR QUESTIONS ABOUT CAMP. THERE'S SO MANY THAT I DON'T HAVE ANSWERS FOR.

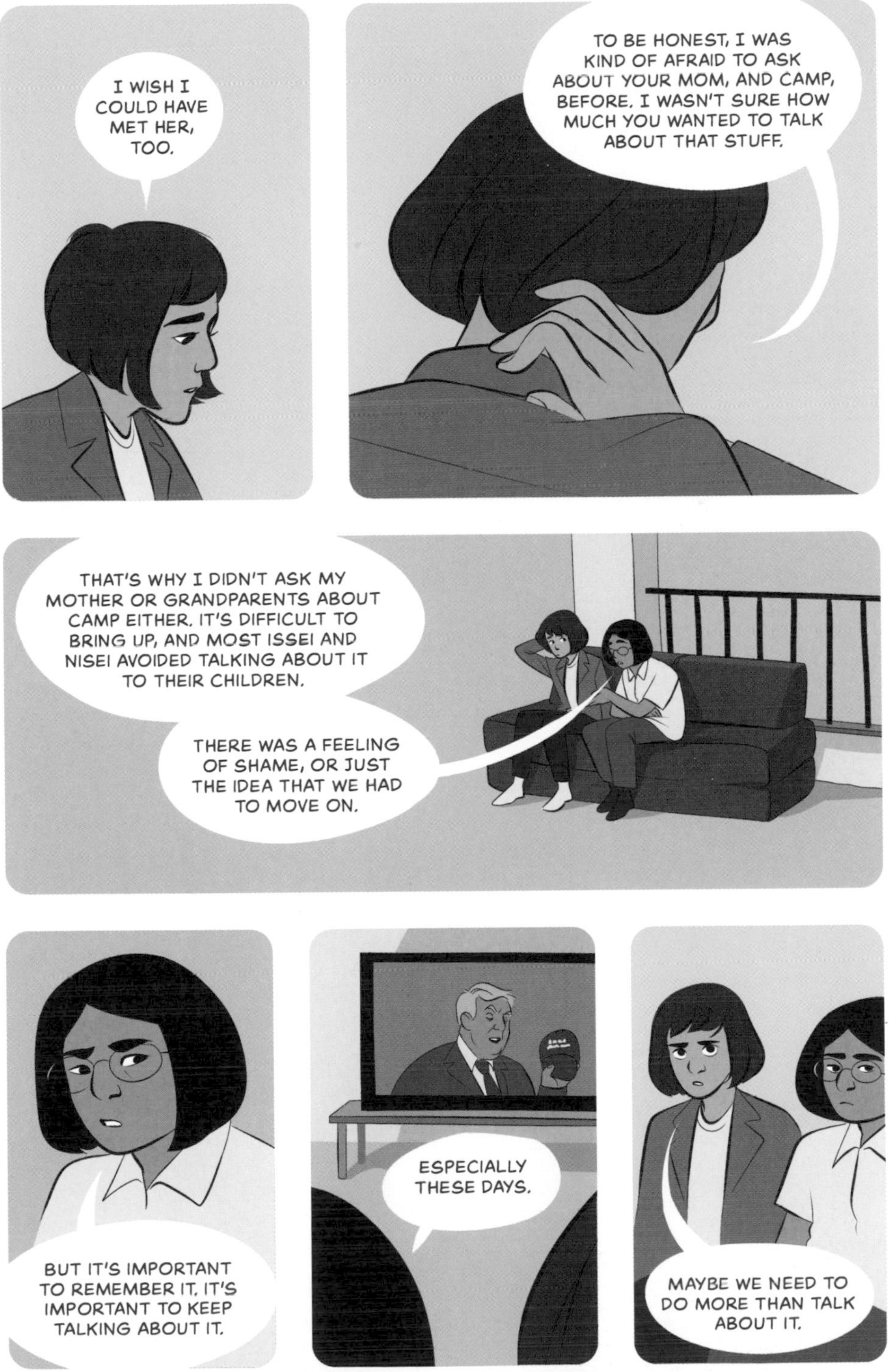
I WISH I COULD HAVE MET HER, TOO.
TO BE HONEST, I WAS KIND OF AFRAID TO ASK ABOUT YOUR MOM, AND CAMP, BEFORE. I WASN'T SURE HOW MUCH YOU WANTED TO TALK ABOUT THAT STUFF.
THAT'S WHY I DIDN'T ASK MY MOTHER OR GRANDPARENTS ABOUT CAMP EITHER. IT'S DIFFICULT TO BRING UP, AND MOST ISSEI AND NISEI AVOIDED TALKING ABOUT IT TO THEIR CHILDREN.
THERE WAS A FEELING OF SHAME, OR JUST THE IDEA THAT WE HAD TO MOVE ON.
BUT IT'S IMPORTANT TO REMEMBER IT. IT'S IMPORTANT TO KEEP TALKING ABOUT IT.
ESPECIALLY THESE DAYS.
MAYBE WE NEED TO DO MORE THAN TALK ABOUT IT.

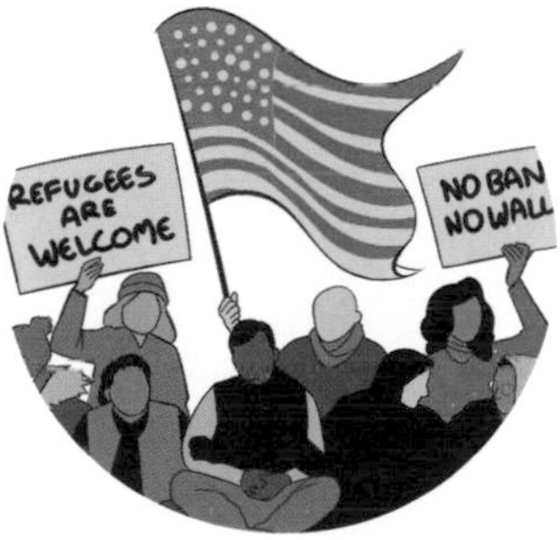
REFUGEES ARE WELCOME
NO BAN NO WALL

11

MOM AND I STARTED DOING OUR OWN RESEARCH ON THE CAMPS. WE WENT TO LIBRARIES, GENEALOGY SITES, NEWSPAPER ARCHIVES.

WE FOUND MY GRANDMA'S YEARBOOK FROM TOPAZ HIGH SCHOOL. WE FOUND GOVERNMENT RECORDS OF WHEN SHE AND HER PARENTS ENTERED AND LEFT CAMP.

MOM BROUGHT OUT OLD FAMILY MEMENTOS THAT MY SISTER, MARIKO, AND I HAD NEVER SEEN. PHOTOS AND KNICKKNACKS.

INCLUDING...

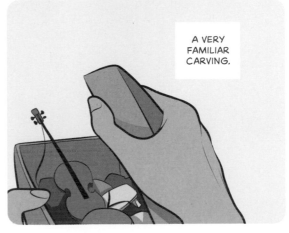

A VERY FAMILIAR CARVING.

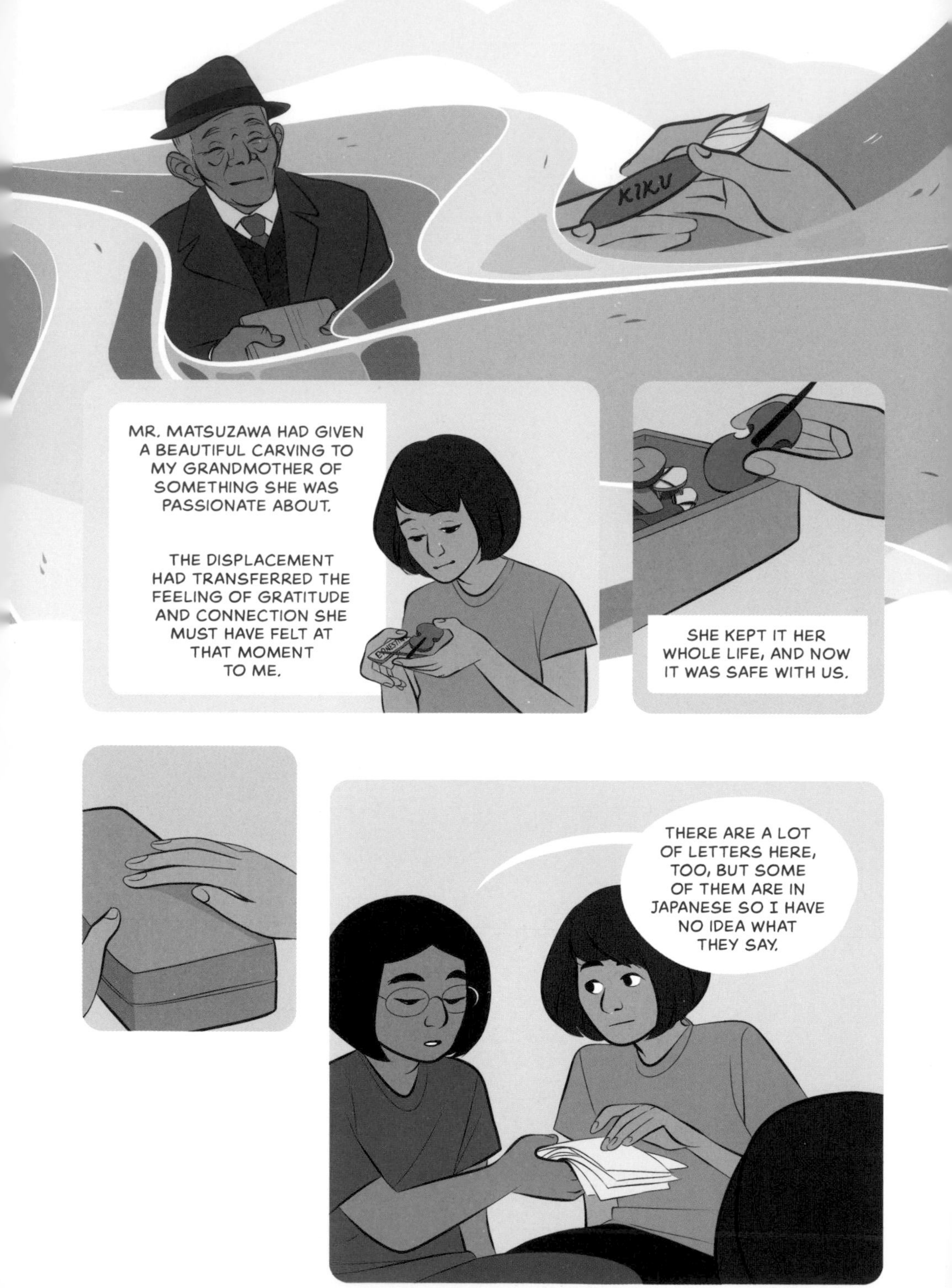
KIKU
MR. MATSUZAWA HAD GIVEN A BEAUTIFUL CARVING TO MY GRANDMOTHER OF SOMETHING SHE WAS PASSIONATE ABOUT.
THE DISPLACEMENT HAD TRANSFERRED THE FEELING OF GRATITUDE AND CONNECTION SHE MUST HAVE FELT AT THAT MOMENT TO ME.
SHE KEPT IT HER WHOLE LIFE, AND NOW IT WAS SAFE WITH US.
THERE ARE A LOT OF LETTERS HERE, TOO, BUT SOME OF THEM ARE IN JAPANESE SO I HAVE NO IDEA WHAT THEY SAY.

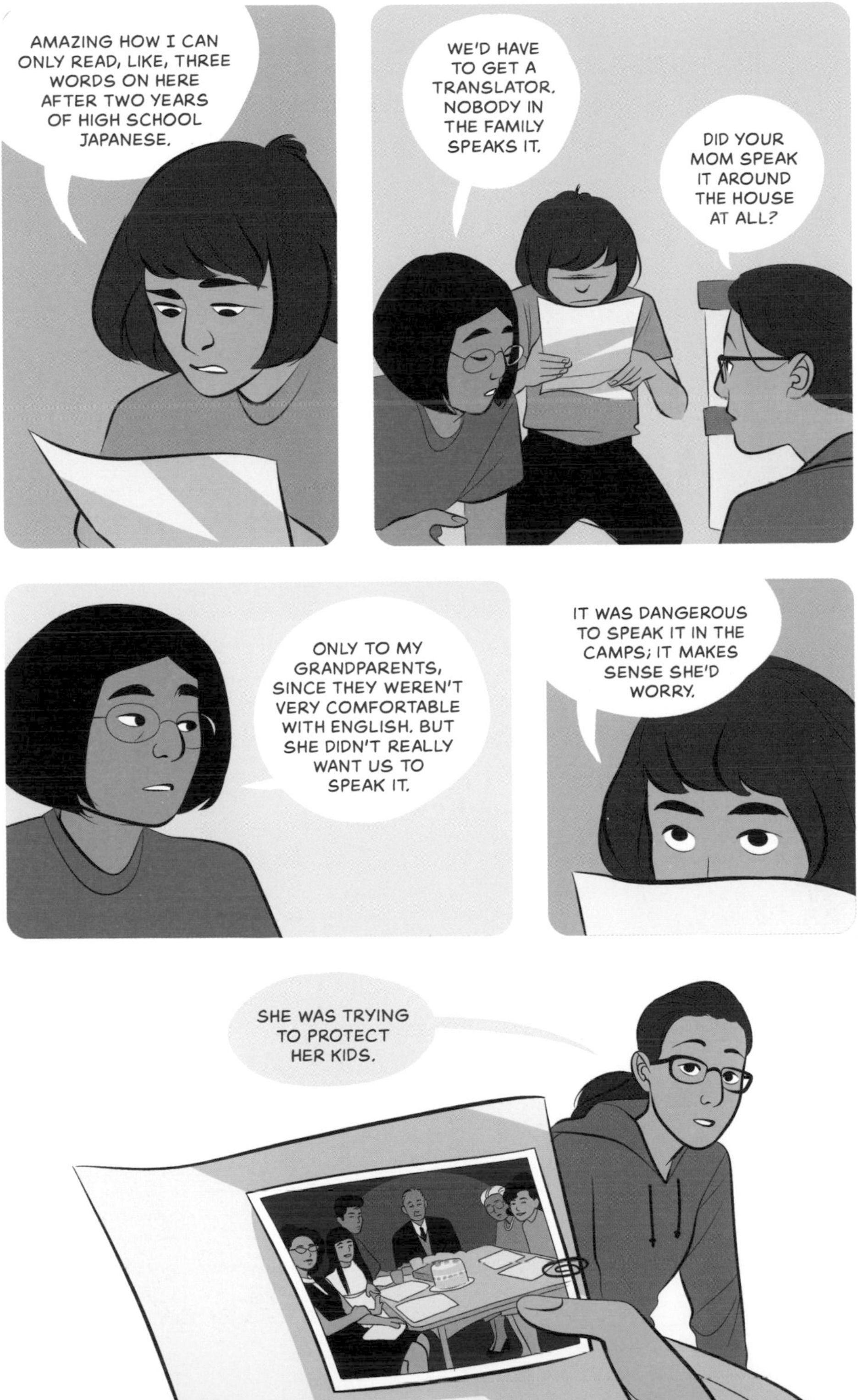
AMAZING HOW I CAN ONLY READ, LIKE, THREE WORDS ON HERE AFTER TWO YEARS OF HIGH SCHOOL JAPANESE.
WE'D HAVE TO GET A TRANSLATOR. NOBODY IN THE FAMILY SPEAKS IT.
DID YOUR MOM SPEAK IT AROUND THE HOUSE AT ALL?
ONLY TO MY GRANDPARENTS, SINCE THEY WEREN'T VERY COMFORTABLE WITH ENGLISH. BUT SHE DIDN'T REALLY WANT US TO SPEAK IT.
IT WAS DANGEROUS TO SPEAK IT IN THE CAMPS; IT MAKES SENSE SHE'D WORRY.
SHE WAS TRYING TO PROTECT HER KIDS.

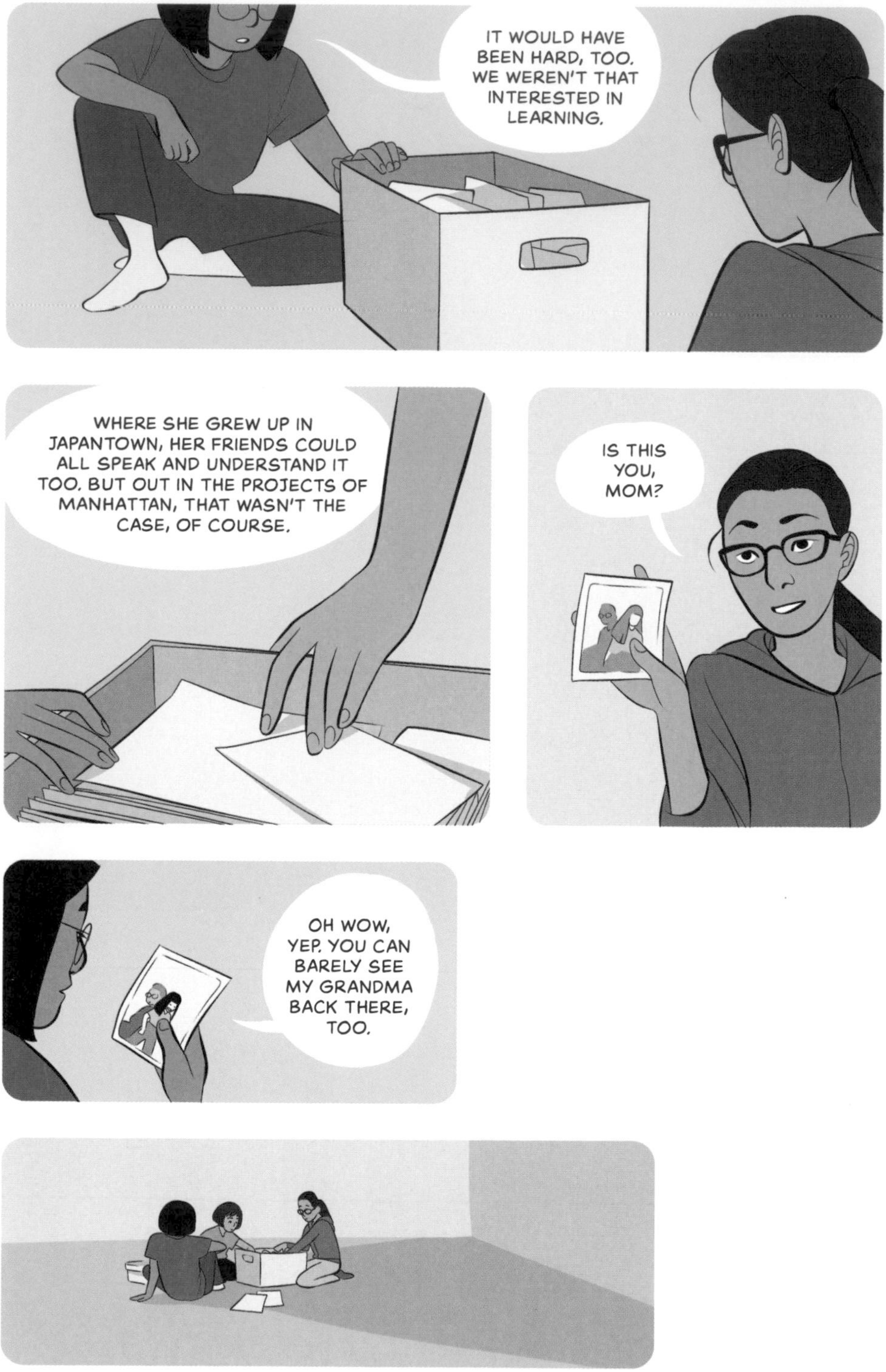
IT WOULD HAVE BEEN HARD, TOO. WE WEREN'T THAT INTERESTED IN LEARNING.
WHERE SHE GREW UP IN JAPANTOWN, HER FRIENDS COULD ALL SPEAK AND UNDERSTAND IT TOO. BUT OUT IN THE PROJECTS OF MANHATTAN, THAT WASN'T THE CASE, OF COURSE.
IS THIS YOU, MOM?
OH WOW, YEP. YOU CAN BARELY SEE MY GRANDMA BACK THERE, TOO.

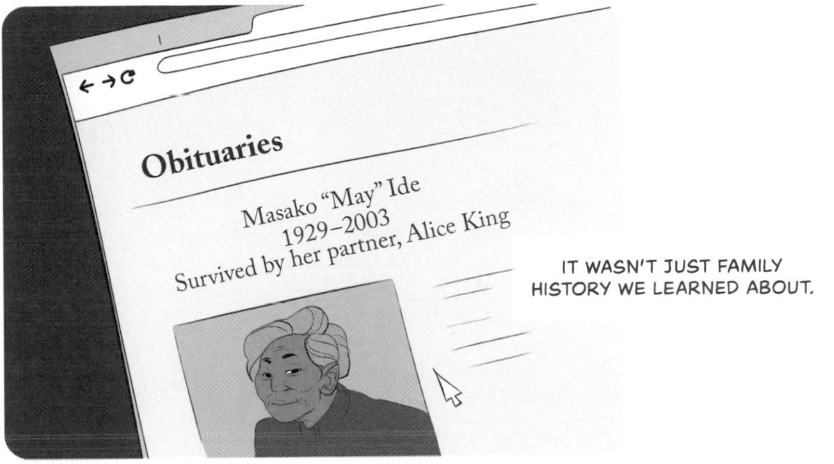
← → C
Obituaries
Masako "May" Ide
1929–2003
Survived by her partner, Alice King
IT WASN'T JUST FAMILY HISTORY WE LEARNED ABOUT.

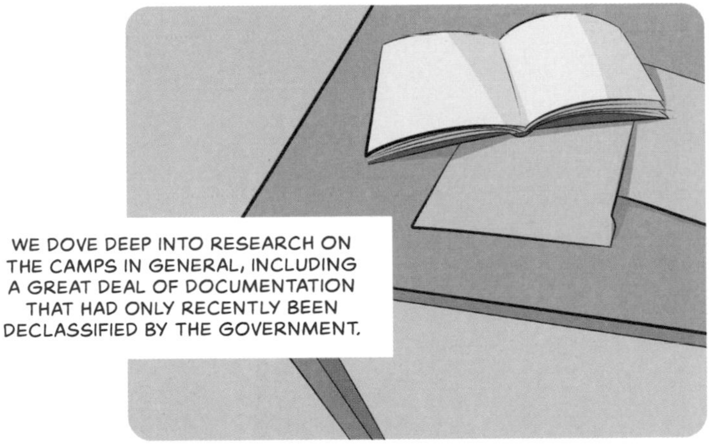
WE DOVE DEEP INTO RESEARCH ON THE CAMPS IN GENERAL, INCLUDING A GREAT DEAL OF DOCUMENTATION THAT HAD ONLY RECENTLY BEEN DECLASSIFIED BY THE GOVERNMENT.

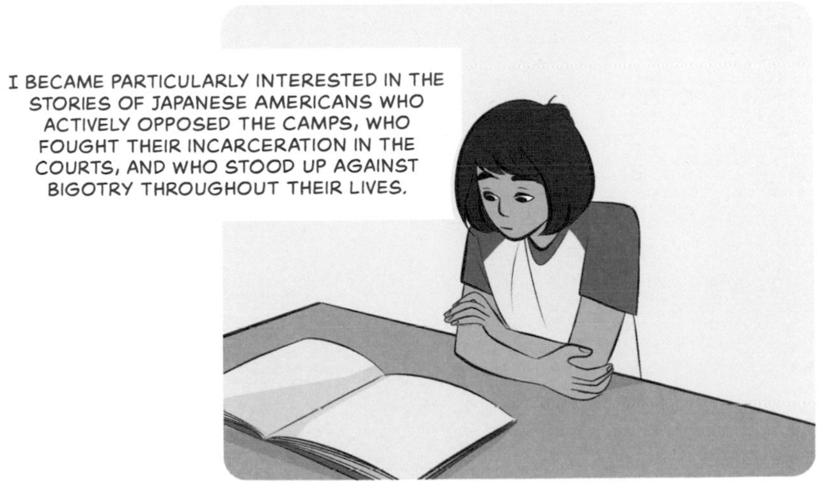
I BECAME PARTICULARLY INTERESTED IN THE STORIES OF JAPANESE AMERICANS WHO ACTIVELY OPPOSED THE CAMPS, WHO FOUGHT THEIR INCARCERATION IN THE COURTS, AND WHO STOOD UP AGAINST BIGOTRY THROUGHOUT THEIR LIVES.

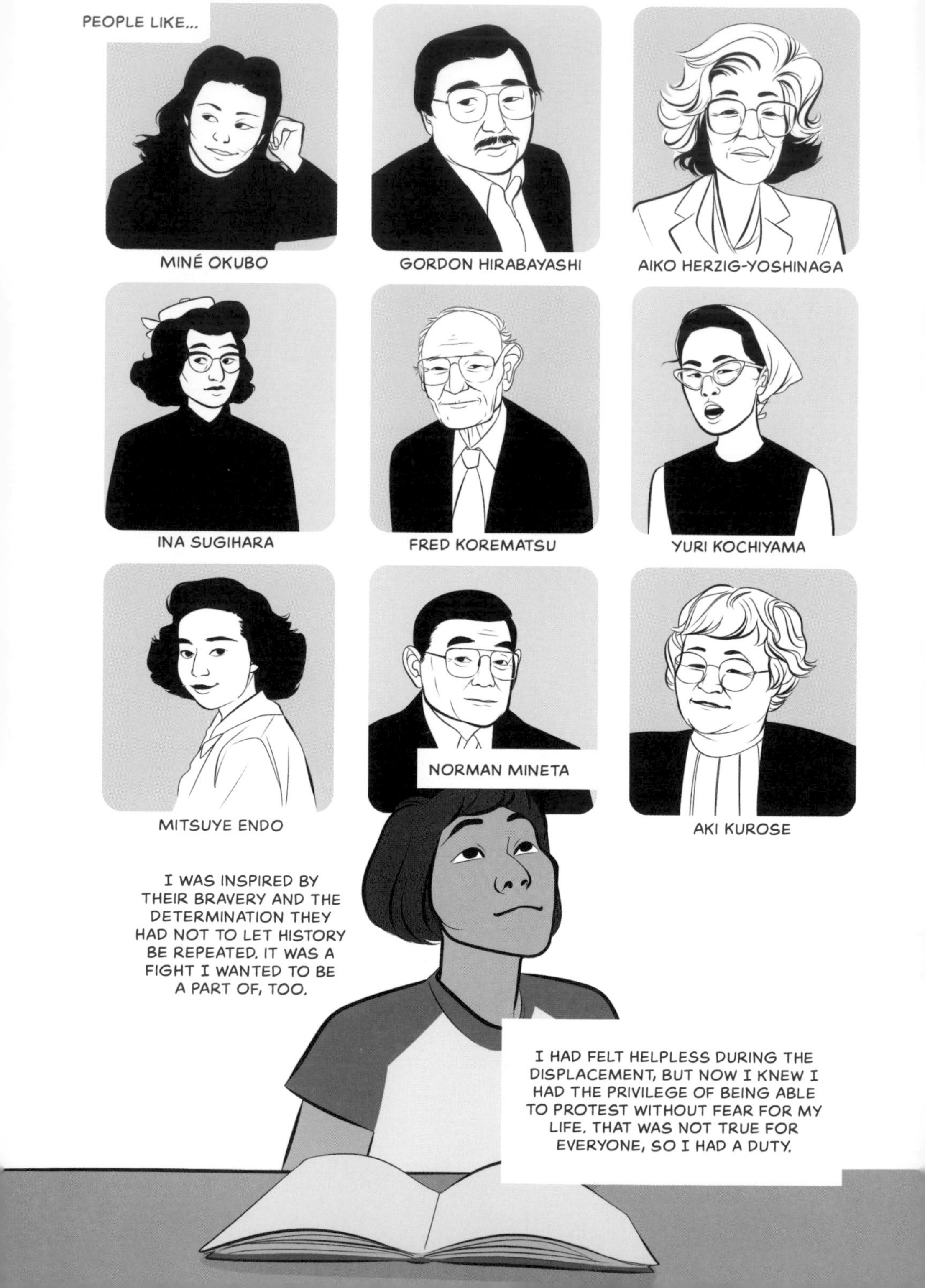

PEOPLE LIKE...
MINÉ OKUBO
GORDON HIRABAYASHI
AIKO HERZIG-YOSHINAGA
INA SUGIHARA
FRED KOREMATSU
YURI KOCHIYAMA
MITSUYE ENDO
NORMAN MINETA
AKI KUROSE
I WAS INSPIRED BY THEIR BRAVERY AND THE DETERMINATION THEY HAD NOT TO LET HISTORY BE REPEATED. IT WAS A FIGHT I WANTED TO BE A PART OF, TOO.
I HAD FELT HELPLESS DURING THE DISPLACEMENT, BUT NOW I KNEW I HAD THE PRIVILEGE OF BEING ABLE TO PROTEST WITHOUT FEAR FOR MY LIFE. THAT WAS NOT TRUE FOR EVERYONE, SO I HAD A DUTY.

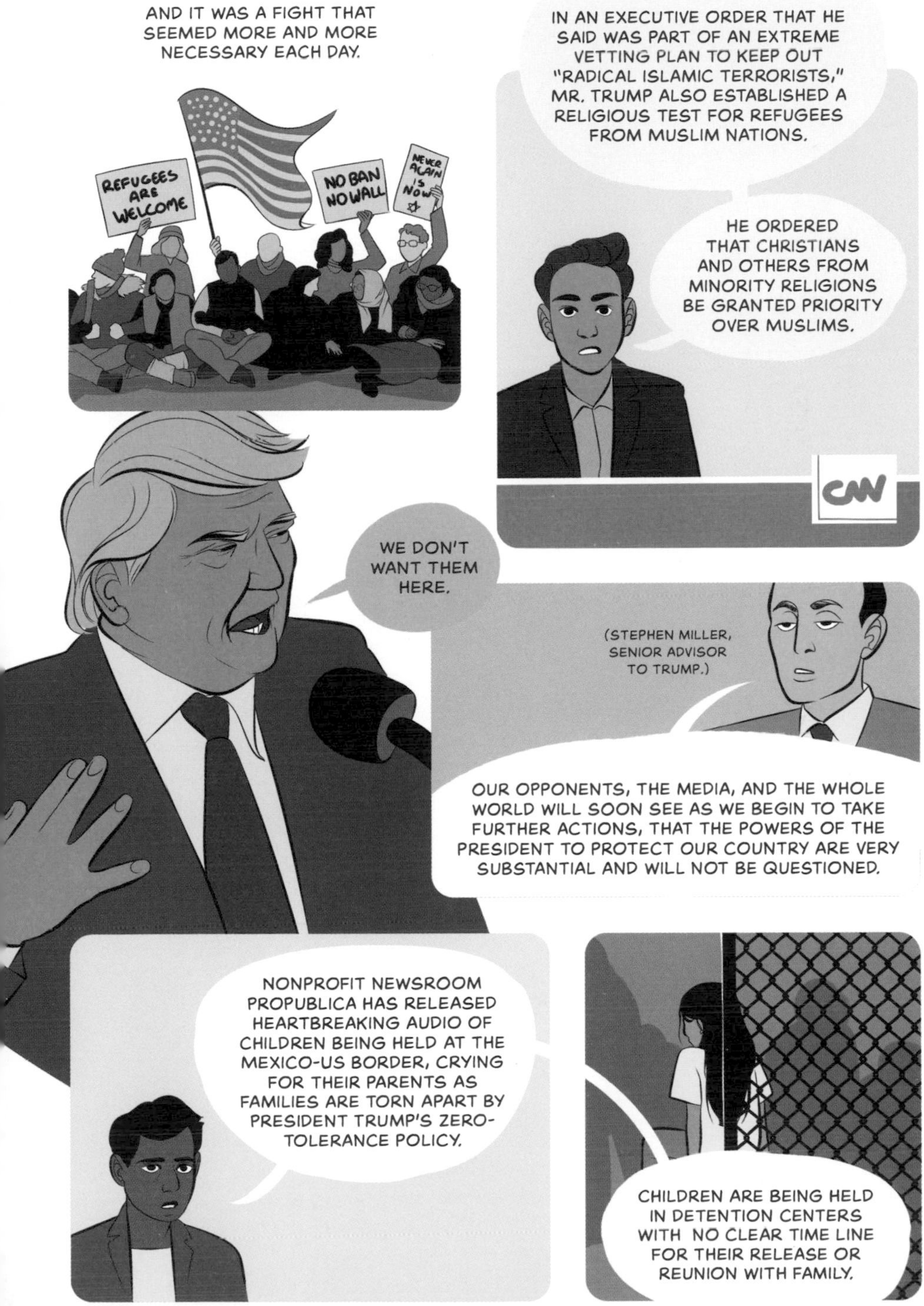
AND IT WAS A FIGHT THAT SEEMED MORE AND MORE NECESSARY EACH DAY.
REFUGEES ARE WELCOME
NO BAN NO WALL
NEVER AGAIN IS NOW
IN AN EXECUTIVE ORDER THAT HE SAID WAS PART OF AN EXTREME VETTING PLAN TO KEEP OUT "RADICAL ISLAMIC TERRORISTS," MR. TRUMP ALSO ESTABLISHED A RELIGIOUS TEST FOR REFUGEES FROM MUSLIM NATIONS.
HE ORDERED THAT CHRISTIANS AND OTHERS FROM MINORITY RELIGIONS BE GRANTED PRIORITY OVER MUSLIMS.
CNN
WE DON'T WANT THEM HERE.
(STEPHEN MILLER, SENIOR ADVISOR TO TRUMP.)
OUR OPPONENTS, THE MEDIA, AND THE WHOLE WORLD WILL SOON SEE AS WE BEGIN TO TAKE FURTHER ACTIONS, THAT THE POWERS OF THE PRESIDENT TO PROTECT OUR COUNTRY ARE VERY SUBSTANTIAL AND WILL NOT BE QUESTIONED.
NONPROFIT NEWSROOM PROPUBLICA HAS RELEASED HEARTBREAKING AUDIO OF CHILDREN BEING HELD AT THE MEXICO-US BORDER, CRYING FOR THEIR PARENTS AS FAMILIES ARE TORN APART BY PRESIDENT TRUMP'S ZERO-TOLERANCE POLICY.
CHILDREN ARE BEING HELD IN DETENTION CENTERS WITH NO CLEAR TIME LINE FOR THEIR RELEASE OR REUNION WITH FAMILY.

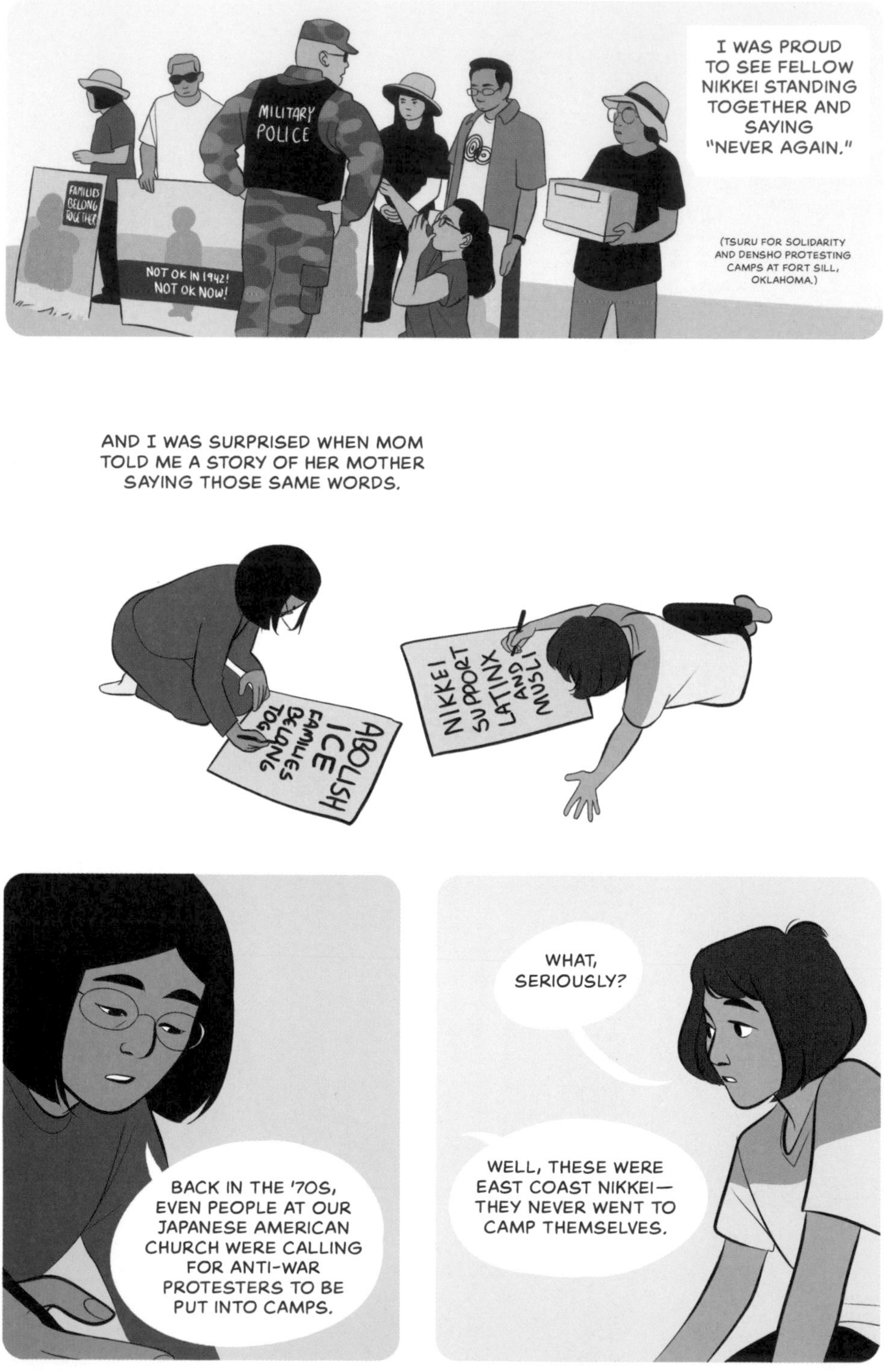
I WAS PROUD TO SEE FELLOW NIKKEI STANDING TOGETHER AND SAYING "NEVER AGAIN."
MILITARY POLICE
FAMILIES BELONG TOGETHER
NOT OK IN 1942! NOT OK NOW!
(TSURU FOR SOLIDARITY AND DENSHO PROTESTING CAMPS AT FORT SILL, OKLAHOMA.)
AND I WAS SURPRISED WHEN MOM TOLD ME A STORY OF HER MOTHER SAYING THOSE SAME WORDS.
ABOLISH ICE FAMILIES BELONG TOG
NIKKEI SUPPORT LATINX AND MUSLI
BACK IN THE '70S, EVEN PEOPLE AT OUR JAPANESE AMERICAN CHURCH WERE CALLING FOR ANTI-WAR PROTESTERS TO BE PUT INTO CAMPS.
WHAT, SERIOUSLY?
WELL, THESE WERE EAST COAST NIKKEI— THEY NEVER WENT TO CAMP THEMSELVES.

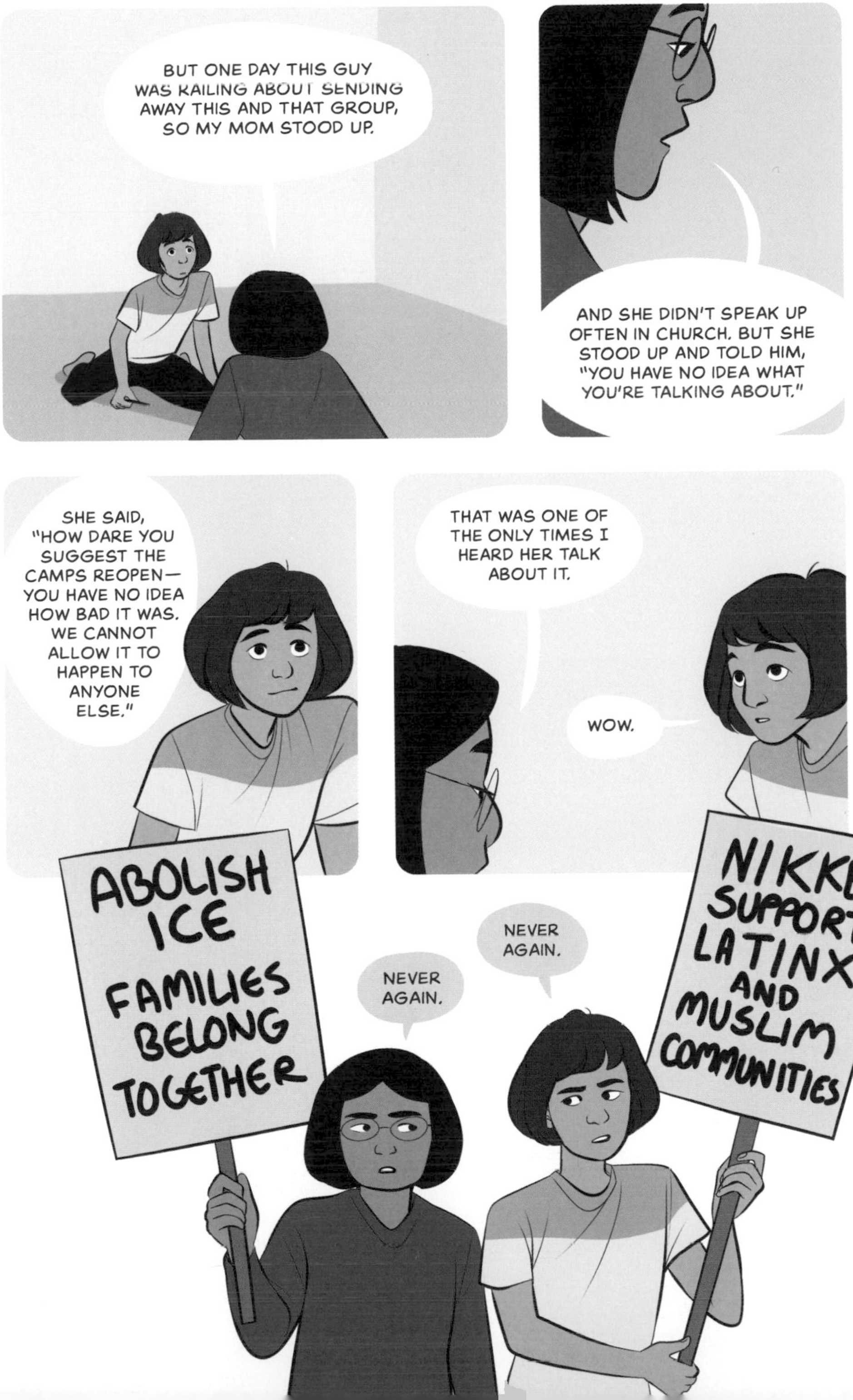
BUT ONE DAY THIS GUY WAS RAILING ABOUT SENDING AWAY THIS AND THAT GROUP, SO MY MOM STOOD UP.
AND SHE DIDN'T SPEAK UP OFTEN IN CHURCH. BUT SHE STOOD UP AND TOLD HIM, "YOU HAVE NO IDEA WHAT YOU'RE TALKING ABOUT."
SHE SAID, "HOW DARE YOU SUGGEST THE CAMPS REOPEN— YOU HAVE NO IDEA HOW BAD IT WAS. WE CANNOT ALLOW IT TO HAPPEN TO ANYONE ELSE."
THAT WAS ONE OF THE ONLY TIMES I HEARD HER TALK ABOUT IT.
WOW.
ABOLISH ICE
FAMILIES BELONG TOGETHER
NIKKEI SUPPORT LATINX AND MUSLIM COMMUNITIES
NEVER AGAIN.
NEVER AGAIN.

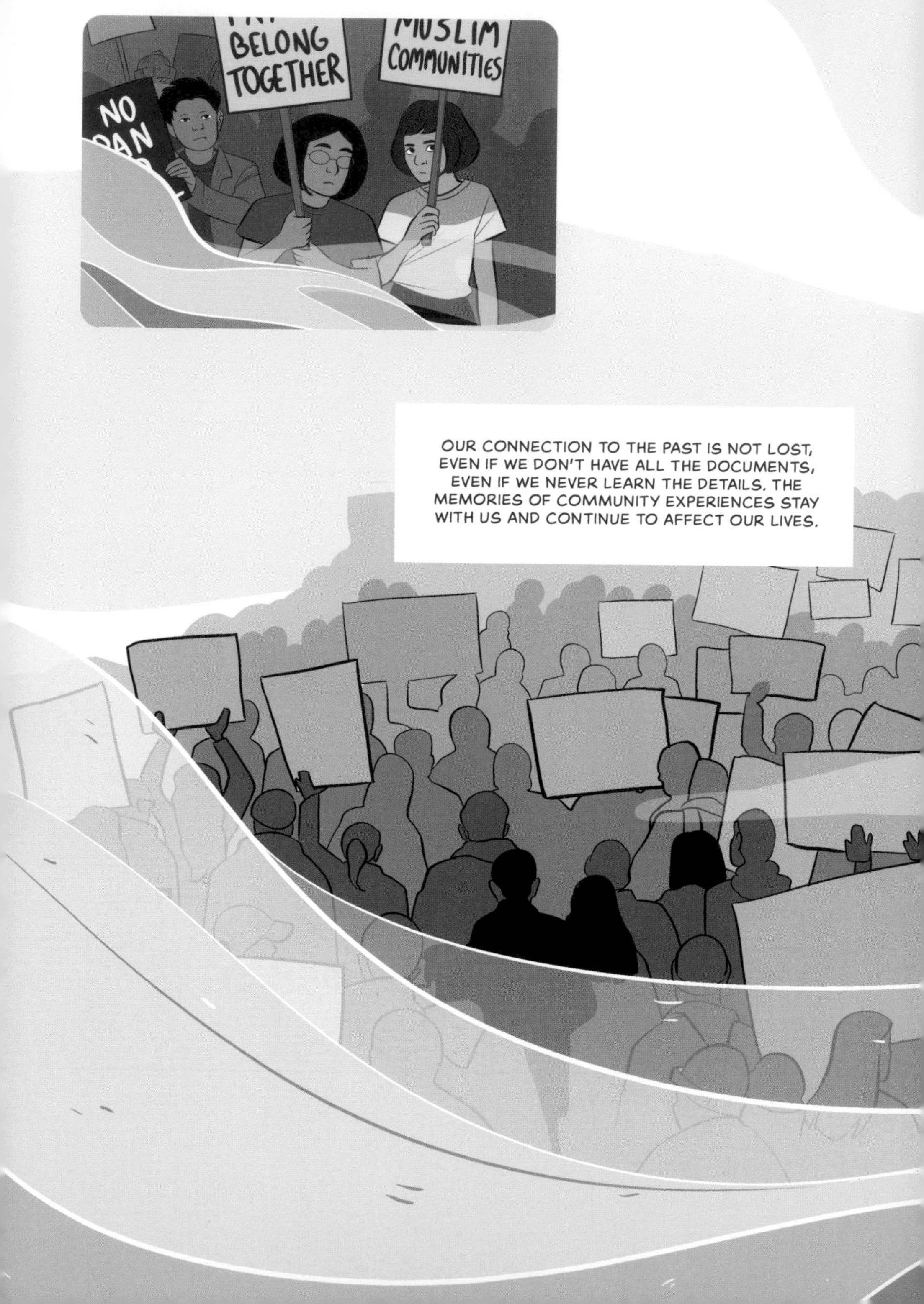
NO
BELONG TOGETHER
COMMUNITIES
OUR CONNECTION TO THE PAST IS NOT LOST, EVEN IF WE DON'T HAVE ALL THE DOCUMENTS, EVEN IF WE NEVER LEARN THE DETAILS. THE MEMORIES OF COMMUNITY EXPERIENCES STAY WITH US AND CONTINUE TO AFFECT OUR LIVES.

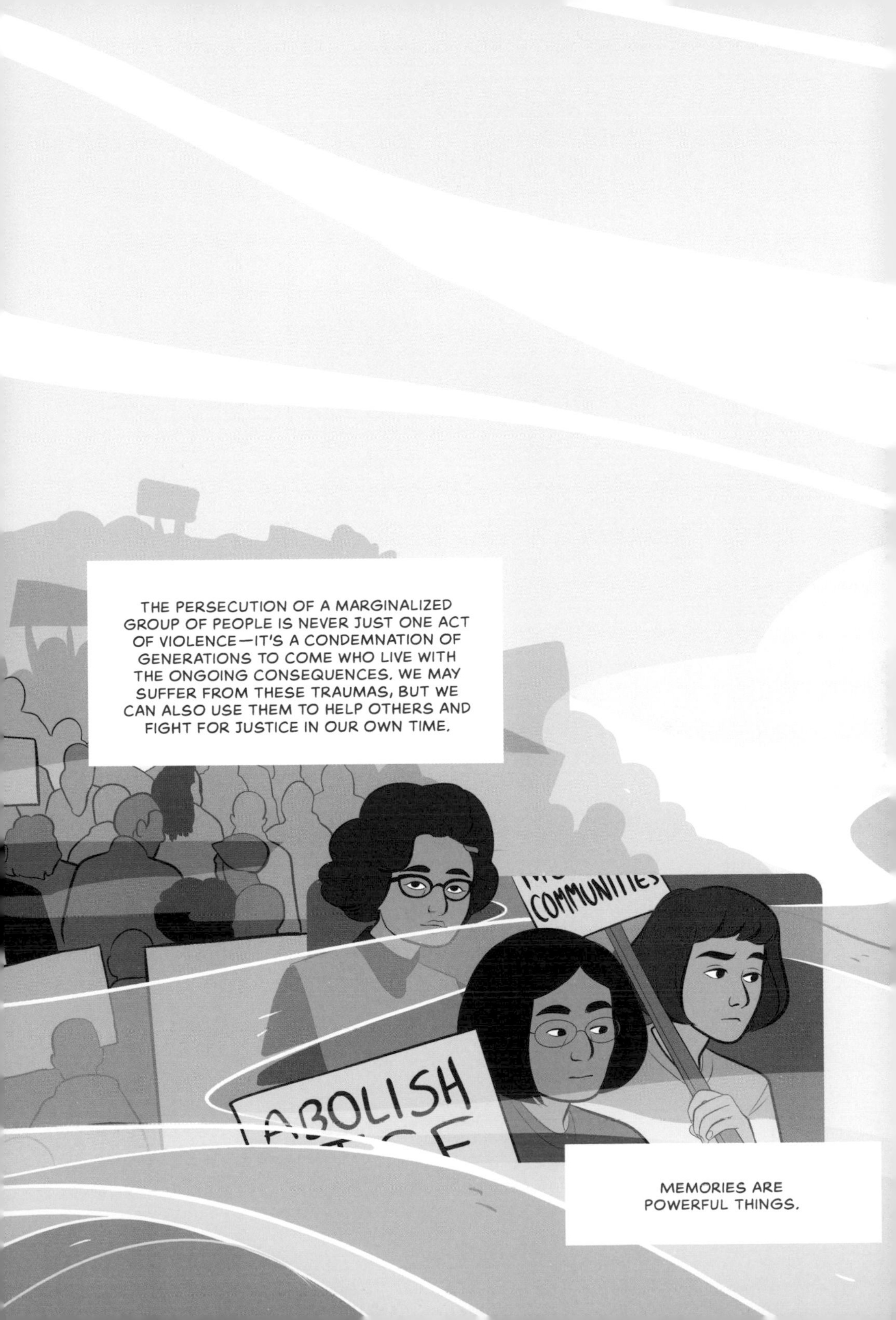
THE PERSECUTION OF A MARGINALIZED GROUP OF PEOPLE IS NEVER JUST ONE ACT OF VIOLENCE—IT'S A CONDEMNATION OF GENERATIONS TO COME WHO LIVE WITH THE ONGOING CONSEQUENCES. WE MAY SUFFER FROM THESE TRAUMAS, BUT WE CAN ALSO USE THEM TO HELP OTHERS AND FIGHT FOR JUSTICE IN OUR OWN TIME.
COMMUNITIES
ABOLISH
MEMORIES ARE POWERFUL THINGS.

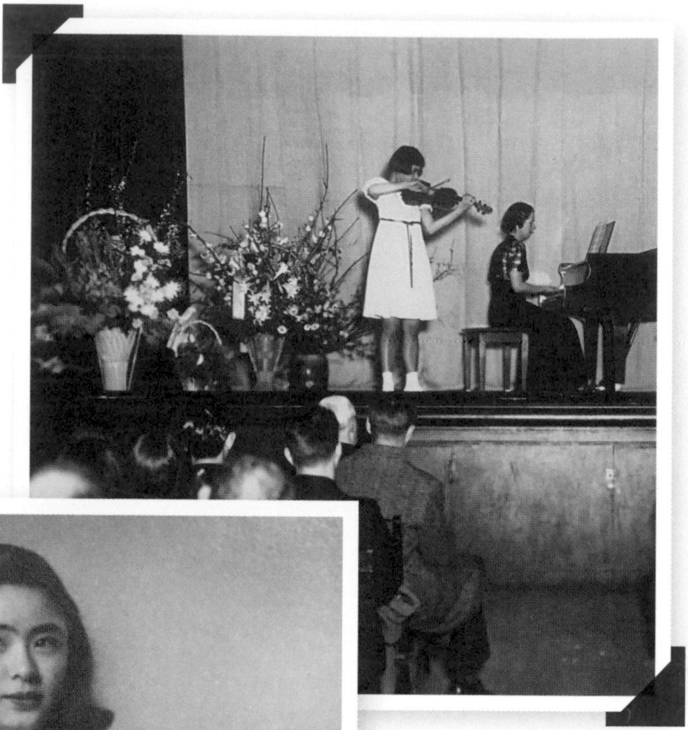
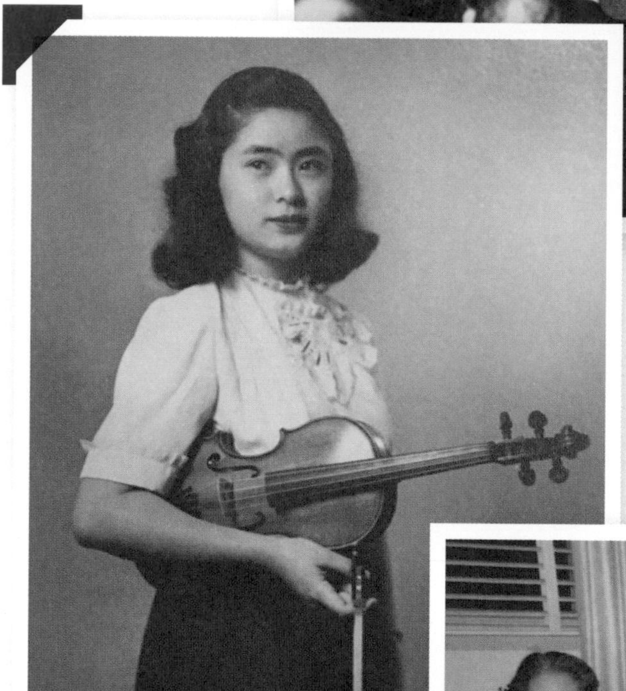
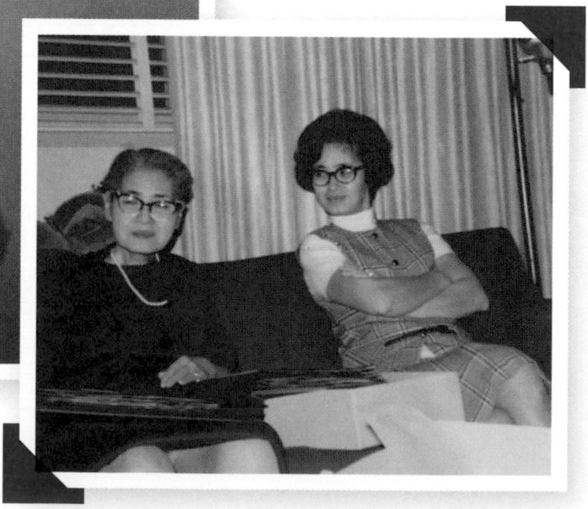

author's note

The events in this book are a mix of fact and fiction, history and memory. I knew early on that I could never tell this story in its entirety—there were too many missing pieces of information. I was never able to meet my grandmother and ask her about her time spent in Topaz, and like many survivors of camp she died having left many parts of her life unspoken. But it wasn't until I began researching in earnest that I realized how much I never knew about the camps. The more I learned, the more I understood that my grandmother's story never ended with her. The camps left scars on our whole community that were passed down through generations. Even seventy-five years later, I felt their effects in ways I hadn't ever examined.

I know now why I grew up with only a handful of Japanese words in my vocabulary and why we rarely participated in traditional events. The camps scattered the Nikkei community and broke up their neighborhoods, and the lingering fear of appearing too Japanese discouraged the passing on of language and culture. This loss left me confused and unsure of my footing in Japanese American spaces, but researching for this book helped me understand and reclaim my place in it. History and memory have tremendous power to heal us and give us the tools we need to know ourselves and navigate the world.

As history repeats itself, as racist hysteria is used to carry out human rights atrocities once again, those tools must be used to help the victims of our own government's actions. These stories are vital, but only if you use them to take action. I hope this one can demonstrate how long-lasting and wide-reaching the damage of community trauma can be, and how vital it is that we fight against those who would inflict it on our most vulnerable neighbors.

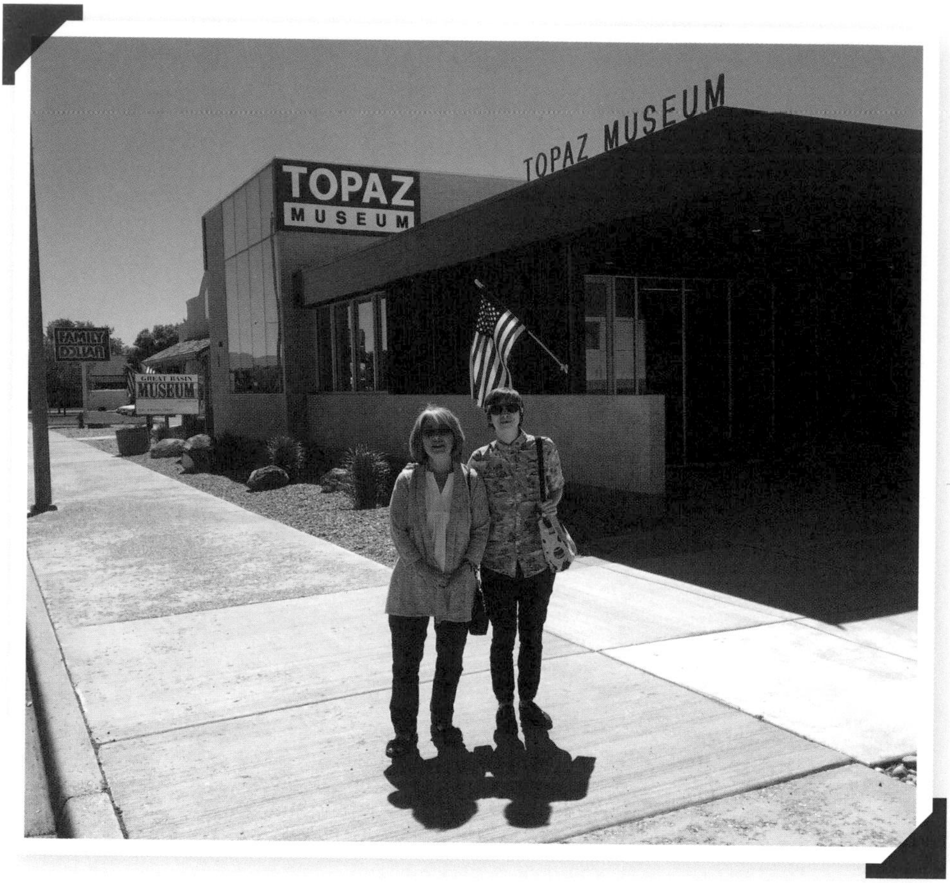
TOPAZ MUSEUM
TOPAZ
MUSEUM
FAMILY
DOLLAR
GREAT BASIN
MUSEUM

acknowledgments

Special thanks to my family for their tireless support—Mom, Dad, Mariko—and to my grandmother Ernestina and great-grandmother Chiyo, strong women without whom I would not be able to tell this story. Thanks to First Second for taking a chance on my first book, and especially to Whit Taylor, editor extraordinaire, and Kiara Valdez and Molly Johanson for their help and encouragement. To all the incredible people at Densho, whose tireless work preserving our history was essential to my research, and who are fighting every day against racist injustice and modern concentration camps. To the Topaz Museum, Wing Luke Museum, and the National Parks Service for aiding my research. To Miya for the translations and emotional support. To all my friends who have cheered me on and helped me through burnout and emotional ruin. To my amazing girlfriend, Cy, who not only supported me throughout this process but used her librarian skills to help me with research. And finally to Octavia Butler, whose work inspired this book and who will always be a hero.

glossary of terms

Incarceration camp: The term you are probably most familiar with in regard to Japanese American history is "internment camp," and while that is still a common way of referring to them, there is debate about its accuracy. The reality is that "internment camp" is used by the government to pacify the real history of the camps. Some people prefer the more accurate term "American concentration camp," but that can draw very inaccurate comparisons to the Nazi death camps in Europe. Therefore "incarceration camp," while not a perfect description, is the term I've used in this book.

Generational terms:

Issei: first generation, people who emigrated from Japan

Nisei: second generation, the first generation born in the USA

Sansei: third generation

Yonsei: fourth generation

Nikkei: a general term for people of the Japanese diaspora

further reading

Okubo, Miné. *Citizen 13660*. University of Washington Press, 1946.

Taylor, Sandra C. *Jewel of the Desert: Japanese American Internment at Topaz*. University of California Press, 1993.

Tunnell, Michael O. *The Children of Topaz: The Story of a Japanese-American Internment Camp Based on a Classroom Diary*. CreateSpace, 2011.

Cahan, Richard and Michael Williams. *Un-American: The Incarceration of Japanese Americans During World War II*. CityFiles Press, 2016.

Inouye, Karen M. *The Long Afterlife of Nikkei Wartime Incarceration*. Stanford University Press, 2016.

"Army Recruiting Team Coming." *Topaz Times*, April 2, 1943. Utah Digital Newspapers, https://newspapers.lib.utah.edu.

Bell, Lorne W. "Administration Statement." *Topaz Times*, April 12, 1943. Utah Digital Newspapers, https://newspapers.lib.utah.edu.

Tani, Henry. "The Tanforan High School." Japanese American Evacuation and Resettlement Records, BANC MSS 67/14 c, the Bancroft Library, University of California, Berkeley.

Najima, Haruo. "The First Month at Tanforan: A Preliminary Report." Japanese American Evacuation and Resettlement Records, BANC MSS 67/14 c, the Bancroft Library, University of California, Berkeley.

First Second

Copyright © 2020 Kiku Hughes

Published by First Second
First Second is an imprint of Roaring Brook Press,
a division of Holtzbrinck Publishing Holdings Limited Partnership
120 Broadway, New York, NY 10271

Don't miss your next favorite book from First Second!
For the latest updates, go to firstsecondnewsletter.com and sign up for our enewsletter.

Library of Congress Control Number: 2019938064

Hardback ISBN: 978-1-250-19354-4
Paperback ISBN: 978-1-250-19353-7

Our books may be purchased in bulk for promotional, educational, or business use.
Please contact your local bookseller or the Macmillan Corporate and Premium Sales Department
at (800) 221-7945 ext. 5442 or by email at MacmillanSpecialMarkets@macmillan.com.

First edition, 2020

Edited by Calista Brill and Whit Taylor
Cover design by Molly Johanson
Interior design by Molly Johanson
Printed in China by 1010 Printing International Limited, North Point, Hong Kong

Paperback: 10 9 8 7 6 5 4 3 2 1
Hardcover: 10 9 8 7 6 5 4 3 2 1